CODE YELLOW IN GRETNA GREEN

CODE YELLOW IN GRETNA GREEN

MIDLIFE RECORDER
BOOK FIVE

LINZI DAY

Published in the United Kingdom in 2024
Midlife Recorder series. Book 5

Copyright © Linzi Day, 2024
The right of Linzi Day to be identified as the author of this work has been asserted by her in accordance with the Copyright, Designs and Patents Act 1988.

ASIN: B0CWK3FBDF
ISBN: 9798883907868
All rights reserved. No part of this publication may be reproduced, stored in a retrieval system, or transmitted, in any form, or by any means, electronic, mechanical, photocopying, recording or otherwise, without the prior written permission of the copyright owner.
Requests should be made to: LinziDay.com
First Edition: March 2024

Cover Design: Axe Designs
Book Formatting: ESG

This book is a work of fiction. Names, characters, places and incidents are the product of the author's imagination or have been used fictitiously and are not to be construed as real. Any resemblance to actual persons, living or dead, or to events or places is entirely coincidental.

MIDLIFE RECORDER SERIES SO FAR

Midlife in Gretna Green
Painting the Blues in Gretna Green
Ties that Bond in Gretna Green
House Party in Gretna Green
Code Yellow in Gretna Green

Coming in Autumn 2024
Market Forces in Gretna Green

*For Shirley who finds my books a great comfort.
Happy 88th Mum.*

Acknowledgments

I'd like to thank all those readers who have shown such unexpected love for my books. If you find any typos I'm one of those authors who is happy to fix them if you let me know. Sadly telling Amazon doesn't help, they can't change it. Special thanks to all my FABs, MVPs and my kind readers who help me with this. linziday@gmail.com will always find me.

All my love always to James, partner & puppy nurse extraordinaire, for almost 20 years worth of reasons that I can't fit here >2

All the gratitude in the world to supervet **Pip McLachlan** for getting Lucy back onto four good legs thanks to some seriously talented surgery and excellent follow-up care.

Much love to **Rossi,** who's kept me just sane-enough for a very long time. 6x

Thanks to everyone on my support team, especially, **Axe** for my pretty covers and **Krista** my editor.

I'm sending a special heap of gratitude to **Miriam Stark**, who noticed my latest book-related mess-up, just in time. Thanks Miriam what a superb keen-eyed owl you are :-)

But as always, my deepest author appreciation goes to my FABs —my Freaking Awesome Beta-reading team for all that they continue to do to make this a much better book. This book's **FAB team** was **Adrian, Betsy, Carla, Carolyn, Diane, James, Jan, Holly, Louise, Marisa, Nives, Rossi, Sheryl, Simon, Vanessa, and Wendy.** I'm so appreciative of you all.

Thanks to my MVPs—my Magnificent Volunteer Proofreaders who make this a better read for us all. This book's team comprised **Betsy, Holly, Louise, Marisa, Miriam and Rachel.**

Special thanks to **Holly Keefer.** I think proofreading while recovering from surgery is possibly a step too far, but I'm glad it took your mind off it!

Some quick mentions for readers who've helped with specific things like **Jessica Simpson** who contributed Fergus the Scottish Deerhound to be Chris Reynald's dog. Please apologise again to your husband that I married you off bigamously—at least in fiction.

To **Wendy MacDonald** As always Breanna thanks you for the loan of the now-immortal, bacon-loving Maggie, Migg-Mags.

To all the members of the **Voracious Readers** Facebook group who contribute fun ideas and excellent memes, especially when I'm deep into boring edits and losing my mind.

Search for Linzi Day's Voracious Readers on Facebook if you'd like to join a fun group of men and women who are often re-reading the books. Or laughing. Or both.

Here's to the crazy ones.
The misfits.
The rebels.
The troublemakers.
The round pegs in the square holes.
The ones who see things differently.
They're not fond of rules. And they have no respect for the status quo.
You can quote them, disagree with them, glorify or vilify them.
About the only thing you can't do is ignore them.
Because they change things. They push the human race forward.
And while some may see them as the crazy ones, we see genius.
Because the people who are crazy enough to think they can change the world, are the ones who do.

APPLE. THINK DIFFERENT ADVERT
AGENCY: TBWA\CHIAT\DAY

PROLOGUE

From **Seeing Red in Gretna Green**—*Tuesday, 2nd March, 2021*—
The Gateway

I stood behind the anvil, wrapped in power. HRH lounged on her plinth, and Caitlin held her sword, looking eager to use it.

I placed the star in the indentation, and as the cat had instructed, trying to keep the sarcasm out of my voice, announced, "I summon the Rightful King of the Vikings to the centre of the Rainbow."

I intended to hold him with the power and inform him I planned to accept the petitions against him. I breathed slowly, focused on calm and attempted to slow the pounding of my heart.

But it wasn't King Troels who arrived.

Instead, a sack-wrapped bundle thudded wetly onto the floor in the centre of the Gateway. Only Caitlin's exemplary training prevented her from sticking her sword in it. Then she swore loudly, colourfully, and with heat. It was years since I'd heard language that foul.

She was already on her knees, crouched by the bundle as I rounded the anvil to see what had arrived. When I saw it, I felt as though I was about to pass out.

Only the thought that I couldn't do that yet kept me on my feet as I looked down at Rollo. The sacking was filthy and wet with large red-brown patches. Rollo's face was grey under the bruising. His head looked misshapen, eyes swollen shut, and his right arm looked very wrong. Bloody patches around his torso and on one of his legs got larger as I watched.

What was the use of having the power and the link with him if I hadn't known this was happening? I'd checked in on him this morning, and, other than my Gift nagging at me, I'd had no idea there was a problem. The problem, of course, was that my Gift had nagged at me about something or other for the entire last week.

"He's alive, just." Caitlin blew out a breath as she removed her fingers from the pulse point in his throat. "Best get the Fae. Ad'Rian, ya think?"

But the pit of my stomach clenched as I looked at the sorry bundle of bloody rags on the floor, because I knew with a leaden certainty Ad'Rian would be too drained to help with injuries this critical after the recent multiple healings he'd given Dai.

He was probably still working on Dai and pulling in any spare energy from his healers to help, because he didn't want to disappoint Mabon again.

Crap.

There were other healers, but would I trust them with Rollo?

My Gift said Ad'Rian wasn't the answer. Then what the hell was? Could I time travel back and prevent this?

Probably not. The Book had always been extremely clear on the dangers of time travelling to save a life. The power didn't like me doing it, and I thought it would prevent me from going, as it had when Finn was taken by Svein and his Viking conspirators. I needed a better plan.

My stomach roiled. My brain had frozen into a loop. It wasn't helping. It went *shit, shit, shit, oh, Rollo, shit, shit.*

How the hell had this happened?

"Caitlin, you heard me summon Troels, right?"

Her voice was laden with fury, but not at me. Damn, I wouldn't want to be whoever had done this to Rollo. Caitlin would have to fight me for the right to deal with them, and I would win, but I'd take her along as my second, and we'd leave them in pieces.

"No," she almost spat. "You summoned the Rightful King of the Vikings."

The fury in her eyes hurt to look at. Her expression said, *catch the slagging hell up.*

Well, double crap! That thrice-damned cat had known.

When I get my hands on her ...

PART ONE
TUESDAY

We should begin by getting to know guilt—because so many of our problems stem from it.

There are four types of guilt. The first is **remorse.** You behaved badly, and now feel guilty about your actions.

The second, **toxic guilt,** is a feeling of responsibility for things beyond your control. Victims of abuse often receive the additional unwelcome gift of guilt from their abuser.

The third, **existential guilt**, is also a feeling of responsibility, but this time for things that *exist* and you perceive them to be wrong: injustice, danger to unknown innocents, damage to your realm. Your inability to take effective action can be debilitating.

And the last and perhaps the most insidious is **cultural or religious guilt**. Doing things in opposition to the cultural or religious norms and mores you were raised with often causes an unhelpful amount of guilt.

Winning the War Against Yourself: Daily Weapon and Warrior Care by Arinn Tusensköna

CHAPTER
ONE

T*uesday — A few seconds later*
Helpless fury gave me courage. I grabbed HRH off her plinth by the scruff of her neck with my power-wrapped left hand and bent to grasp Rollo with my other one. I couldn't even see any place that looked safe to hold him. Blood, bruises and wounds covered the man. I swallowed hard.

I would not lose my shit. I would think like a grown-ass woman.

In the end, I settled for holding his left shoulder as gently as possible while still being sure I had a grip on him. At least his left shoulder looked normal. That was more than I could say for the right one, which looked like a misshapen joint of meat.

I transported us all back to the lounge at the Cottage. The cat and I needed privacy. The sacking Rollo was wrapped in was some kind of rough hessian blanket, and it was leaking blood. I didn't care if we made a mess in this unpleasant room, and at least it was large enough to lay Rollo on the carpet.

The cat hissed at me. No words, just hissing.

I was so furious with her, it was a struggle to even speak. "You could have avoided this. You could have simply told me what was happening instead of all that nonsense about 'summon the Rightful King of the Vikings before luncheon.' If I *ever* find out you knew he was in this state …"

I trailed off because I didn't know what I might do if we lost him.

Then I tried again with less final words. "You will heal him. I will feed you power. But if you ever want fish again, it's time to make reparations. I'll help any way I can, but my healing skills aren't good enough yet. So, you're up, Your Majesty."

I held the cat an arm's length away. She was spitting mad too, and I didn't want to lose an eye. But she must have known about the danger he was in this morning. Why the hell hadn't she simply said something clear and sensible like "Summon Rollo"?

I waited, my blood pressure rising with every moment. My heartbeat still pounded in my ears, but at least my anger had cleared my head, and I was no longer terrified I might pass out.

After what felt like far too long, the cat replied, her voice perfectly calm, "Agreed. It will take a lot of power, which you will supply. We will negotiate later."

Yeah, that might not go the way she expected.

I pulled more power. "Start now."

Six hours later …

Yes, for six long hours, while fear gnawed at my stomach and made it hard to breathe, I'd pulled power and channelled it to HRH. She'd directed it to various parts of Rollo in a glowing, blinding, white ball of energy.

Reset and repeat in an endless loop.

I could never be a nurse. The scent of Rollo's blood mixed with my own fear-sweat was nauseating.

We took several brief breaks for food for the cat and, as she termed it, to refresh and allow Rollo's healing to stabilise so she could check his current status and safely do more.

When she began, she'd walked up the length of Rollo, beginning at his feet. It was only as she almost reached his waist and stopped pulling power from me briefly that she spoke. "Well, Recorder, we have the solution to the mystery of why you didn't know he was in danger, and I couldn't contact him."

She walked on the air, about an inch above Rollo's body, and pulled grey energy out of him through her paws. When it surrounded her, she dispersed it through her tail. A stream of the murky-looking energy headed towards the French doors that opened into the garden.

"What is that?" I asked.

"They drugged him. It feels like an overdose. His skull is fractured, which wouldn't have prevented you from reaching him, but the drug would. I must remove it first, or it will hinder the rest. I surmise they hit him over the head and then poured that drug of theirs down his throat."

Then she moved on to his head injury and a problem with his spleen. Once she'd dealt with those, Rollo started to rise to consciousness.

She ruthlessly put him into what she called a healing sleep. "Really, Recorder, patients are no help to anyone when they're awake. I won't be annoyed or distracted. He's far too important to listen to."

While I tried to work out what that might mean, she moved on to his internal injuries.

Finn stuck his head in at one point and cast a horrified look at Rollo on the floor and then at me, and paled dramatically. "Sorry, Cait's losing it. Sent me to check, and Tilly wants to be with you."

I told him to let Tilly in. My distressed puppy calmed the moment she entered the room. She sniffed my shirt, which was covered in Rollo's blood, and, obviously satisfied none of it was mine, she sneezed and curled into a ball between my crossed legs, where she could see Rollo. The moment she was with me, I felt calmer.

"Finn, send Caitlin home, if she'll go. Tell her Rollo will live, but we have a way to go yet. You or Dola can message her later. There's nothing she can do here."

He nodded and closed the door quietly behind himself.

Hours later, Rollo's colour was much better. I looked around the lounge and tried to work out why I disliked this room so much. It couldn't only be that I'd had to confront Jamie in here. That was ridiculous. But there was an unpleasant atmosphere. It made me want to get out of here and, far more importantly, get Rollo out of here as soon as I could.

HRH was working on Rollo's right arm and shoulder. "Almost every bone broken. They wanted to cripple his sword arm. It's one way to prevent Rollo from being able to duel that plague on ordinary women. Fools and knaves, all of them."

Troels had been behind this? I suppose that made sense. The Vikings were barbarians. I was going to have to fix them somehow.

The cat had lost weight. I could see her ribs, and, after a quick consultation with the power, I sent her some indigo energy. She lapped it up as always, but she took more than usual, and it truly felt as though she needed it. She'd exhausted herself to heal Rollo. I'd planned to give her a jar of crab meat I'd bought in an upmarket deli as a suitable future bribe, but she beat me to it. The damn cat had never met a boundary she couldn't walk through!

"Might we have one of those See Food dishes, the one on the peasant plate, for dinner?"

She always made me smile when she refused to accept the pizza base was supposed to be eaten. But I could murder one myself. A new place had just opened in the village, and now I knew Rollo would be alright, my body started making its needs known.

I stroked his blood-matted hair off his face, relieved to see all the bruising and swellings had disappeared. "He looks fine, but how is he really?"

"Recorder, he is better than he was, my word on it."

But I wasn't convinced. "Why is he still unconscious, then?"

"I would not want him to know I healed him yet. He may feel he owes a debt to me."

"And that would be a problem—because?"

She usually loved collecting debts and future favours. I surveyed her closely. There was something that, in a lesser animal, I might have described as sheepish guilt. It reminded me of Tilly's expression when, as a puppy, she decorated the bathroom and the entire upper hallway with several shredded toilet rolls. In the time it took me to get up the stairs, her body language had gone from a proud, "Look, Mum, I made art" to "Oh, whoops, I shouldn't have done this, should I?"

Yep, HRH looked guilty, and her words confirmed it. "It pains me to admit it, but you were correct. I did not judge the portents or the timing accurately. Which may have been embarrassing if I hadn't been able to fix it." She licked her front right paw and swiped it across the back of her head before meeting my gaze again.

"But it might be for the best. Smooth seas do not make skilful sailors. Rollo will learn an important lesson from this. However, it is my burden to carry, not his, and I would prefer he remain in ignorance until I can lay it down at the appropriate time and place. Shall we negotiate now?"

My look must have said it all.

"Perhaps later when you've eaten and cleaned yourself, Recorder."

I looked down at myself and shuddered at how much of Rollo's blood now coated me.

HRH paused by the door. "He will wake once I've left. I leave him in your care. You did well. However, *never* attempt to carry me by my neck again. It is undignified. Use your words next time. I would not have refused you."

I hoped there would never be a next time. Honestly, I couldn't believe I'd done it. But now I knew what being out of your mind with worry and fear for someone's life felt like.

"I'll return for the See Food later."

The moment she left, Rollo's eyes opened. They were clear and focused. Thank the Goddess, literally.

He sat up too swiftly for my comfort, as his face registered both shock and horror. "Who did this to you? Do you need to go to Fae? Shall I call Ad'Rian?"

At my confused expression, he gestured at all the blood covering me. There was a hysterical note in my laughter as I spluttered. "It's not my blood, it's yours."

He wrapped me in his arms and my world settled back on its axis. He was alive. We could work on the rest.

CHAPTER
TWO

We showered in separate bathrooms. I wanted to cry in private. Except my tears weren't private. Through our link, he sent, *Can I do anything?*

But when that just made me sob harder, he behaved like a sensible man and allowed me to de-stress and wash away all my fear, worry and shock in peace.

We needed to work out what this link was all about and why it hadn't worked when it should have. I'd promised Rollo I wouldn't leave him unguarded until he felt better.

Actually, no, that wasn't right.

What *had* I said to him?

I tried to rewind to last Thursday when the power had insisted on giving Rollo the yellow regnal power for safe-keeping. He didn't want it and made some flip comment about relaxing so I'd go easier on him. That sounded like something the horrible Troels might have said, and I immediately stopped until he gave me clear consent. I'd promised to monitor him, but I couldn't recall my exact words. Did it matter?

Yes, it did.

I opened the shower door halfway so the Dolina in my bathroom could pick up my voice. "Dola, do you know exactly what I said to Rollo immediately before I gave him the yellow power?"

While I waited, I rinsed out the new miracle conditioner from Morven, the beauty alchemist. She'd said it would keep my semi-permanent rainbow streaks bright and vibrant if I used it regularly. I loved the crazy rainbow colours, so I'd been slathering *This One's a Keeper* onto my hair every week.

My voice came out of the Dolina in my mirror, "I won't leave you alone until you feel yourself again. My word on it."

That was what I'd said?

Had I created this mind link to keep my word? Unlike Rhiannon, I took giving my word seriously. But surely he must feel like himself again by now?

Still here, Boo.

I huffed. *And you never explained this ridiculous Boo thing—you said you would.*

He sent, *I'm out of the shower. May I come to you?*

But I needed a few more minutes to process the stomach-churning horror of seeing him looking like a freshly butchered side of beef on the Gateway floor. Physical violence had never been a part of my world. I wasn't a damn shield maiden, and all that blood would have horrified me even if it hadn't been Rollo's.

I sent, *I'll meet you in the kitchen in ten.*

Then I closed my shields as much as I could without freaking him out.

Privacy, I needed some if I was going to avoid turning into a shaking mess. And I was going to avoid it. I was finished with being a quivering jelly of a woman. It was time I stepped the hell up.

I couldn't define or explain it, even to myself. But I *knew* this moment was the end of the watershed I'd sensed was coming throughout this last insane week.

I stood under the high-pressure shower and willed all my fear to flush down the drain with the fast-flowing water. The Niki who got out of this shower would not be the same woman who'd arrived in Gretna Green. I'd been damaged, beaten down by a bullying boss, and deeply hurt by Nick's betrayal. For the Goddess's sake, I hadn't even thought people should call me "my lady," and yet today I'd grabbed one of those goddesses by her neck and bent her to my will.

My past self, the sad little caterpillar I'd been, was about to leave her chrysalis on the shower floor. I really liked Rollo, but rushing into something with him wasn't a good idea. Whereas finding out who I might be able to grow up to be, if I put my mind to it and my fears aside … that was exhilarating.

Oh, *Good Grief*, Niki, you'll be quoting that damn book next. Finally, I laughed at my introspection and, putting it behind me, reached for my towel.

CHAPTER
THREE

We settled at my kitchen table. Well, where else would we sit for what must surely be a council of war?
Except it wasn't.
Rollo was sanguine, or at least determined to give that impression. He looked completely healed. His eyes were clear and untroubled, and when I told him how furious and worried Caitlin had been, he posed with a goofy grin so I could send her a photo.
The only sanguinity I could relate to was my memory of the deep red colour of the sacking stained with his blood. I was not over this. I would interfere in the realms, even if I shouldn't, to ensure Troels was held accountable for this attack and all his other crimes.
As I sent the photo to Caitlin, I noticed the ever-growing stream of messages from Aysha. I'd better answer them before she and Autumn got on a train or drove up here.
"Who did it to you?" The more thought I gave the problem, the less sure I was that the Recorder could officially do anything about it. What if Rollo submitted a petition? If all else failed, Rhiannon owed me a favour. Crap, had I turned into a woman who thought eating people was a valid solution to a problem?

But it surprised me to find I was perfectly fine with attempted murderers becoming dragon food.

Before Rollo could answer me, the door from the annex flew open, and Caitlin barrelled into the kitchen, followed more cautiously by Finn. She hurled herself at Rollo, twisting his head around so she could look into his eyes. Then her tense shoulders dropped. "You're OK."

He gave her a hug. "I'm fine, Cait, truly."

"You have to do something about him now. How slagging dare he?" She claimed a seat at the table while Finn knelt down to greet Tilly. I waved him to a free chair. Bless him, he'd been very pale when he stuck his head into the lounge earlier.

I agreed with Caitlin's sentiment. Some of the kingdoms' more creative tortures were running through my mind every time Troels edged into my thoughts. He'd tried to kill my dog and had almost succeeded in killing a man I …

A man I … What?

Well, a man I definitely didn't want to see dead.

But the oddest thing happened.

My left shoulder pinged.

I re-ran my thoughts.

Troels had tried to kill my dog—true.

Troels had almost succeeded in killing a man I … False.

Oh, OK. Troels had sent people to injure a man I … nope, also false.

WTH?

Realising I was being rude and not caring, I cut across the conversation at the table. "Seriously, Rollo, do you know who grabbed you? Why didn't I know you were in danger?"

I wanted revenge, which wasn't my usual style. But, yeah, revenge was what my heart craved. And probably justice. But only if it came with a side of revenge.

"Dola, may I have a glass of wine, please?" That wouldn't fix it either, but I could sip it and give it my best shot at presenting a rational façade, at least while my Knights were still here.

My mind raced.

If Troels hadn't sent men to grab Rollo, who had? And did he know it wasn't his uncle?

Rollo answered my question with half of his attention on me and the rest of it on Caitlin's still-red face. "I reached out to you not long before they took me. But you were sleeping and so tired after all the drama with Dai and opening the dragon gate. I only had a second before they hit me over the head. Then they drugged me. I don't know how it could work under those circumstances."

"OK. So should I have summoned you immediately this morning when I couldn't connect to you, do you think?"

He reached his hand across the table, then changed his mind and moved around to the empty chair next to mine. He wrapped me in his arms and ruffled my hair in a way that reminded me of Mabon. Whoops, was I behaving like a child?

"How would you have known I wasn't sleeping? I can feel your guilt, but, well, sometimes shit happens. Even Forrest Gump said so. We weren't to blame for this. Could we have done things differently? Sure. But isn't that life?"

It bloody shouldn't be life, should it?

Don't we all deserve something better than "oh well, shit happens"?

I had all the power but no clue how to use it for the best. I'd had enough of this. The time for growing gently into my new life was over. I needed to seize it by the neck exactly the way I'd grabbed the cat earlier.

Looking back, Rollo's acceptance of his beating was when I decided to embrace the woman I could have been—no, the woman I *would* have been if my gran hadn't interfered in my life path.

And I didn't want to be a pretty butterfly. I'd tried that with Nick. I'd been his "stunning wife," at least when he was talking to other people. Attractiveness was overrated. I'd take powerful along with the ability to create change any day over being arm candy. If I had to deal with assholes, then I'd better turn the Recorder's Office into something with teeth—no, with fangs, claws, and many friends with sharp swords.

My thoughts surprised me so much that, when my wine arrived, I took a large glug. So much for my plan to sip it like a damn lady.

Rollo continued, "Couldn't one always have done things differently? It's not the first decision I regret making about something in Viking. I probably shouldn't even have gone back there. But I needed that paperwork from Inge's."

I caught a glance and a nod between Caitlin and Finn. Then Caitlin gestured at me. "To the point, Rollo: *do* you know who grabbed you?"

"No. One of them used to work for my uncle. But he retired. I didn't know the others. I think four grabbed me, but when I regained consciousness before they hit me over the head the second time, there were only three of them."

My shoulder pinged again.

I wouldn't call him out in front of my Knights. But my shoulder thought he knew who was responsible.

Caitlin, in a tone as cold as one of those icy Pictish lakes, asked, "Who. Was. It?"

Rollo said, "Cait, please, I don't want you involved in this."

She muttered, "A nasty accident isn't anyone getting involved. Accidents just happen."

Then, incongruously, Rollo gave the entire table a huge grin. "Have to show you all this." He patted his pocket before realising his phone wasn't there.

"*Streth mik*," he swore softly. "My phone's gone. I'd hate anyone to find it."

I asked, "Dola, could you …?"

Moments later, his phone arrived on the table in front of him. In response to his quick, startled glance, I explained, "It's on the Rainbow Network; of course she can retrieve it, but it's yours, you know, and it was in your realm. You could have retrieved it yourself with the yellow power."

"Thank you, Dola." He opened his phone to the photo app and handed it to me, making the universal flicking gesture to give me permission to swipe through them.

I started laughing at the photo of what looked remarkably like a space station airlock attached to the yellow gate. The power and I created it to prevent the lumberjacks from attacking the yellow gate. So, the photos were taken in Haraldssund, the Viking capital city. It was a grubby, messy place with rubbish and litter strewn around the gate and the airlock. Rollo had captured it from several angles. I flipped and laughed and flipped and smiled. The fae seer had done a good enough job when he'd described it as a small metal box.

But when I flicked to the next frame, there was a familiar but much older man glaring at the airlock with fury etched on his face. My eyes shot to Rollo. "Seriously? What the hell?"

"That might have been the motivation behind them seizing me. When the Gateway collected all the yellow power, it stripped it from him too. Troels aged like cheap cheese in front of his cronies' eyes. Everyone was talking about it. It would have embarrassed and enraged him. I know it was a consequence of him attacking the Gateway, but he'd already decided it was my fault. So many things are."

I gazed at the photo. It showed not the angry, physically powerful king I'd met, but a man who appeared as if he were fighting a terminal illness. He looked about eighty-five, and a frail, weak eighty-five, not the healthy, wiry mid-eighties some men could be. He gave the impression of not being long for this world. Compared to the warrior who'd looked to be a healthy mid-fifties when he'd attacked Tilly just two weeks ago, this man could have been his father.

Finn and Caitlin were leaning forward as though they'd be able to see the phone if they stretched a little farther.

"I've always said Karma can be an efficient bitch, but the

Gateway power could teach her a thing or three. How old is he?" I asked.

"He always said he was thirty-something when I was born. It might be true. There's no accurate data on it. He tightly controls all the information about himself."

I'd flipped back to the photos of Troels by the airlock. "Finn, you're going to love this." I held the phone out to him and Caitlin. Finn started laughing.

But Caitlin only glared at the photo of Troels, refusing to be distracted from her train of thought. "Nasty accidents can be useful. Sometimes people just trip over a sword. Can't blame the sword if some fool trips. That's *why* they're called accidents."

I caught and held her gaze. "I don't think it was Troels who arranged for Rollo to be abducted because—"

But Dola interrupted me, "Troels has arrived at your home, Prince Rollo. He appears to be searching for you."

His head snapped towards her video screen. "You mean he doesn't know I'm here?"

"Unclear as yet. He will be within range of your Dolina shortly. He is threatening your male servant at the moment."

A stream of words with the same Scandinavian flavour I'd heard Rollo use in his mind flowed out of the Dolina's speaker. The tone was harsh and grating. Rollo turned pale again, then furious colour flooded his face, and his mouth dropped open. About five seconds later, Caitlin shot me an astonished look.

Finn and I looked at each other and shrugged. Neither of us spoke Norse.

"Can you translate please, Dola?"

Through my earbud, I heard, "Wait, please, Niki. I am making my device invisible so Troels does not break it. It requires concentration."

What? I didn't know she could do that!

As we waited, the voice through the speaker got louder and harsher. The words were still gibberish to me, but the tone unmistakably conveyed anger and disbelief.

I dropped into my Gift as deeply as I dared without losing focus on the room and concentrated on Rollo. Yes, he looked angry, but under it, he felt good. Through our link, I sensed he'd reached some conclusion, but all the words associated with his decision were in Norse. I pushed a little harder to understand what was happening with him.

As I did so, HRH strolled straight through the closed doorway from the lounge. She needed to stop doing that. It was creepy. I glared at her and then the door to the lounge. It *was* a nasty room.

"Ah, I perceive we have reached the sticking place. Good."

"Sorry, Your Majesty, what?"

"Dinner, Recorder. Is there See Food? You must eat. We all must. Rollo requires it to complete his healing, and you are too pale."

I poked the app and ordered a selection of pizzas from the new place. Oh, yum. They used sourdough for their bases. I submitted the order and turned to HRH. "What were you saying about sticking plasters?"

I swear she sighed. "I always forget, children no longer receive a classical education. It's impossible to have a satisfying conversation with anyone. I refer not to Band-Aids, Recorder, but the sticking *place*. Lady Macbeth, my dear. *'Screw your courage to the sticking place. And we'll not fail.'* I perceive the true Rightful King of the Vikings has found his own sticking place and is screwing his weapon to the limit. He will not miss his shot. Courage comes in all forms."

"Did you know this would happen?"

"Sometimes one can't know until one knows, Recorder. But it was exceedingly likely."

My fury flared again. "If you knew, why the hell did you tell me that if I summoned His Majesty, the Rightful King of the Vikings, I'd be able to deal successfully with Troels?" I was cross. I'd been played. Though it wasn't completely unexpected, I was surprised she'd risked Rollo's life to further some scheme of her

19

own. It created a turbulent mix of rage and impotence in me. I was sick and tired of being impotent. I needed to be the Recorder, damn it.

The cat almost purred. Her upper-class English accent held complete satisfaction sandwiched around smugness. "Because, Recorder, I spoke the simple truth. Now you will be able to deal with the obnoxious Troels. If he is truly the ex-king, as I believed he must be, you can go there, track him down and bring him to justice for his many sins against humankind."

"Why weren't you sure he was the ex-king? The Gateway retrieved the yellow power from him. Didn't that prove it?" This confused me. I felt conned and dumb because I should have thought it through before I parroted her words as a summons, shouldn't I?

"And why didn't you explain it properly to me?" I heard the curt note in my voice and didn't care.

HRH's tone was smooth and conciliatory, but without any hint of apology. "Because the dear boy needed to learn for himself that it was time to make a change. Ask him, Recorder. Ask him exactly when he made the right decision, and you will understand and cease being so vexed with me. Now, when will the See Food arrive?"

She had a completely one-track mind.

The sounds from the Dolina faded. Obviously, Troels had moved away.

Rollo said, "That's it. We need to talk, Niki. Then I need to go to Edinburgh. I'll get the train up there tomorrow."

I smirked at the idea of Rollo needing a train to get to Edinburgh. Had he forgotten he had the yellow power and could transport?

I turned back to HRH. "I'm not going to Viking to find him. All my power is right here, and I learnt a valuable lesson at Dai's last week about being without power. I don't plan to repeat it. But I will research exactly how to summon Troels, even if he has a plan to send someone else in his place."

Rollo's shoulders slumped as he interrupted me, "I don't think it was his men who grabbed me, either. He sounded surprised I wasn't home and was accusing my staff of lying to him. And, I'm sorry, but he has a plan, an excellent plan even, to prevent you from summoning him. He'll hide in Yggdrasil."

Caitlin was nodding along with Rollo and then shot me a surprised look when I asked, "In Yggdrasil? It's a tree, isn't it?"

"It's the sacred tree," Rollo said this with some reverence.

"Yeah, OK, sorry. But why would hiding in a tree, sacred or otherwise, fix anything for him? I'm pretty sure, if I can summon someone down a mountain, I can summon them out of a tree?"

"Because it's a little like the Gateway. It's the pathway into the nine Viking realms, although many of those realms aren't as friendly as the Celtic ones. If he's not in the main Viking kingdom, can you reach into the other dimensions to summon him?"

I tried to process the idea that a tree could be a portal. Yeah, I'd need more spare brain power to work that one out, but the Book might help?

Rollo said, "Troels didn't have me snatched. But now he knows I'm missing, he's planning to be elsewhere, so that if whoever snatched me kills me, he'll be blameless. He thinks they still have me and doesn't know I'm not in Viking anymore. A pilgrimage to Yggdrasil is a respectable way to give himself an alibi."

He was so accustomed to Troels having the upper hand, he wasn't even thinking straight. But maybe I could scupper Troels' plans to hide in some sacred tree.

HRH had assured me Rollo was fully healed, but his face showed signs of strain. We both needed some sleep. Then tomorrow morning, I'd see how much power the Recorder could exert if she was a long way past mad. Because I could see Angry Town in my rearview mirror as I headed towards Blind Fury County.

Finn asked, "When will he leave?"

Rollo frowned. "He said he was leaving soon, but the journey takes several days."

Caitlin asked, "So, if it wasn't him, was it Halvor?"

I pointed at Caitlin. "What she said."

He squeezed my hand and gave Caitlin a firm look. "That's one of the many questions I'll need to find answers to, isn't it?"

As we all fell silent, he turned to the cat and gave her a seated bow. "Great One, you're labouring under a misapprehension. I am not the King of Viking, rightful or otherwise, and I won't be. I have been informed there is no power in or out of the nine realms that can force me."

The cat's eyes widened until the green irises disappeared and only her enormous black pupils focused on Rollo. "Who told you that? Explain," she snarled.

Through our link, I felt a flutter of nerves from Rollo. I must find out what all this Great One stuff was about. He was sincerely apprehensive about telling her whatever he was about to say.

"When the Gateway asked me to take the yellow regnal power, I said no, thank you. I don't want to be king. I don't want to live in Viking. That's not the life I'm planning for myself. We *have* discussed this."

"You do not have a choice, boy," the cat said flatly.

His tone was still courteous, but there was steel under it now. "Yes, I do. King Mabon informed me I have a choice. He only advised me to decide swiftly. The power doesn't disagree. It said the regnal power needed to be kept safe for the future ruler, and right now, I am the only one who can do that. I agreed to that much. But I did *not* agree to be that future ruler. And I won't. And I have already told you all this, Great One."

The cat grumbled, "I thought you would understand once you assimilated the yellow power." She turned her still completely black eyes on me. "Recorder, did you know about this?"

"Yes, Rollo told me. And so did the power. If you hadn't noticed, it's not happy with Viking right now."

I'd seen the cat in quite a few moods, but I'd never seen her in whatever this one was. She looked what my gran would have described as confuddled. Without another word, she faded until only her black pupils were visible. Finally, they blinked out too.

Once upon a time, it might have worried me, but with her "See Food" pizza on the way, she'd be back.

CHAPTER
FOUR

Caitlin and Finn went back to Finn's Foxhole to wait for the pizzas. Rollo needed privacy to make some calls to people he wanted to meet tomorrow in Edinburgh. Tilly slept quietly in her bed by the warmth of the Aga now all the excitement was over.

Everyone except me appeared to be fine.

I was not fine. I wasn't sure I'd ever be fine again. The closest I'd ever come to anyone with life-threatening injuries was driving past a nasty pile-up while emergency workers loaded drivers and passengers into ambulances. Of course I'd hoped everyone would be OK. But they weren't my people. When I lived in a large city, it might happen several times a year. It wasn't dissimilar to watching a scene in a movie. It was awful, and occasionally it was tragic.

I'd drive home carefully with a heavy heart for the casualties' loved ones, but it wasn't a part of *my* life. They had been strangers. This was very different, and I felt changed by it.

My molten lava-flavoured rage still boiled inside me, and I glared at my kitchen table, imagining I could burn holes in it with my eyes. If I got my hands on the men who'd done this to Rollo, my forty years of pacifism might go up in flames.

But, as awful as it had been for Rollo, and for me, what they'd done to him was only the tip of the iceberg of Viking's problems. The ever-growing pile of petitions from the victims of Troels' assaults on any woman who stood still long enough wasn't even the worst bit.

The worst part was I didn't know what to do about it. Which made me angry with myself.

Have you ever been so utterly furious that you felt like your only option was to choose whether the top of your head blew off, your forehead exploded outward, or steam came out of your ears?

Welcome to my damn world!

I needed to calm down, and, tomorrow morning, I needed to get up and find smart Niki. This deserved more than an emotional reaction. It needed the Recorder.

The kick-ass heroines in the books I loved always seemed to have a plan. They didn't get mired in self-doubt; they just went out and killed someone. That must be a fantastic stress-buster, but it wasn't me, was it? I could barely lift Caitlin's sword without the power's help, whereas she never even seemed to notice it was on her back. But I thought I probably could stick a sword in whoever had done this to Rollo. OK, perhaps not, but I could definitely hold Caitlin's coffee.

My watch said almost eight p.m. I was tired, but Rollo and I needed to talk.

"Dola, the Recorder is going to bed. I'm not available until nine tomorrow morning. To anybody. Unless the world is ending or anyone I have responsibility for reports arterial bleeding. OK?"

Using her tentative voice, Dola replied, "Understood. My lady wishes to retire for the day. But before I can release you, there are two important matters, and only you can make decisions on them."

I groaned. Tilly nosed at my bare feet and then licked them. It was one of her calming Mum down strategies.

I stroked the wood of my kitchen table as if to soothe it. "I'm so sorry; it wasn't you I was mad at. I'm just mad at the world." Now I was talking to the freaking table. What next?

Two things, Dola said.

I could do two things before I allowed myself to check out, couldn't I?

"OK, which two things?"

"Mabon has requested your presence at your convenience tomorrow in the castle. Lunchtime would be preferable. As you missed the ceremony, Dilys is serving a belated St. David's Day lunch for the two of you."

Rubbish! That sounded nothing like Mabon.

"What did he actually say?"

I swear she huffed, and in her usual creditable impersonation of his voice, I heard, "Dola, tell her I know. I bluddy know, but come here, the Recorder must. Needs sorting, it does. Ad'Rian's only bluddy released him again. Dai said he doesn't want healing, and they won't heal anyone against their will. So, before I throw the lad down an oubliette until he grows a brain, he says he needs to speak to Niki. Wants to apologise, he says. Tomorrow, about one o'clock; that would be good. Dilys is making the Recorder a slap-up lunch. I have to be here all day. Redeem my word to Niki, I must, and return something she lent to me. Tomorrow, sort it all out, we will."

That sounded like a very stressed Mabon.

I reflected on everything I'd just been lecturing myself about. And boundaries. I'd draw some boundaries.

"Dola, please thank him and explain I can't come for lunch. The Recorder has a very full day tomorrow too. You can bring him up to date on the Troels' situation so he understands my problem. Tell him I categorically won't see Dai until he's been pronounced well by the Fae. If he won't agree to healing, then I simply won't see him. But I can pop in or give Mabon a call."

There! That was assertive, even if it wasn't kick-ass. But there might be hope for me yet.

"I shall convey your message. Next, Aysha is insisting you call her. She says it has been nearly a week since she threatened you. I believe she is concerned she may have gone too far, but she said I am not to tell you she—"

After a brief pause, she continued, "Oh, whoops! I will report my unfortunate error to her if you insist. Or perhaps we could pretend you did not hear it? Please?"

I laughed. Dola was a guardian angel, and she didn't deserve my fear-born rage.

"Aysha says you have ignored most of her messages, and the last time you did that, you were in your Fortress of Solitude after your husband died, and you were deeply depressed. She is worried. Please answer her, Niki. I am in a difficult position. She asks very probing questions. Her voice frequencies are unusual. I fear she is distressed."

Oh, yeah, Aysha, my best mate and a talented and determined lawyer, was the mistress of asking questions people, particularly me, didn't want to answer. But I wasn't being fair. I'd held a bit of a grudge that she'd bullied me into going to Dai's when my intuition was shouting at me not to. But it was my fault, not hers. I should have stood up to her. That I hadn't trusted my Gift was something I'd need to take responsibility for. I couldn't blame Aysha, but I would change things going forward. Even friends who loved you very much could push you in the wrong direction with their best intentions.

"No problem, I'll deal with her before I clock off. Now, may I have …"

In my mind, I asked, *Fruit juice, champagne or beer?*

Decisions, decisions. Not beer. Juice and champagne, let's make Bucks Fizz. We could both use the Vitamin C. And some fruit?

Do I have to eat it?

Oh no, Boo, I thought I would.

He sent a deliciously filthy and surely physically impossible suggestion directly into my mind, along with a mental hug. How the hell could he possibly be horny after his near-death experience?

"... a bottle of champagne. Some orange juice and a plate of fruit, please. Can you send the pizzas in when they arrive? Oh, and some chocolate, the good stuff with the salted caramel, to the hot tub, please."

My furious mood dissipated like smoke in a stiff breeze the moment I opened my bedroom door and saw Rollo. He held his phone to his ear and was, as usual, half-dressed. It was strange, but the moment we were alone, I felt better, more balanced and less blinded by impotent rage. Then I reached the end of Aysha's messages and sighed heavily.

Rollo finished his call with, "See you at noon, train permitting. I'll message you when I arrive." He hung up, curled his long, lean, muscled arm around me, and pulled me gently into his chest. "How can I help?"

I gave him my phone, open to Aysha's messages. They weren't private. In Aysha's signature style, they ascended quickly from "Are you having fun yet?" to "Hey, how's it going?" Through to "I'm worried now; answer me." To "NIIIIIIIKKKKIIII??????"

As he scrolled, his eyebrows rose. He let out a soft whistle. "She doesn't pull her punches, does she? *Were* you suicidal the last time you didn't speak to her for ten days?"

"No, but my apathy tank was full to overflowing, and I was all out of ducks. I was more murderous than suicidal, but what do you do if the liar is already gone? It's such a ..."

In unison, we finished the phrase that had so confused me for my first month in the Gateway and now just made me giggle: "... shame he's dead."

I stripped off the long towelling robe I'd thrown on over my underwear after my shower as Rollo watched me. "Do you think we'll make it to the hot tub?" I raised an eyebrow at him.

He kicked off his boots, dropped a selection of knives onto the dresser, and stood, giving me a wickedly suggestive smile.

His gaze made my breath catch in my throat.

"I hope so. I'm healed, but I could use some warm jets on my back, and I'd like to take your mind off my ex-guardian and the mess tomorrow will probably bring. Carpe diem Boo. Let's seize the time we have."

I looked at my phone, sighed and started typing, when Rollo asked, "Might I make a suggestion? She obviously loves you."

"Oh yeah, never doubt it. What?"

"Just show her you're OK. Better than OK, even." He gestured at my camisole. "Are you wearing that in the hot tub?"

"I wasn't planning to—it's silk."

He waved a hand, suggesting I should remove it. So I did, and then, before I could protest—not that I wanted to—he slid his hands down my sides, kissed me thoroughly, and pulled me against his bare chest. He waved my phone in front of my face until the face recognition opened it and snapped a careful photo.

I goggled at it. If I hadn't watched him take it, I wouldn't have believed I was looking at myself. I looked younger. I looked mildly turned-on. But most astonishingly, I glowed with happiness. Well, hell!

All you could see was the top of my naked shoulders, my blissed-out expression, and every well-defined line of Rollo's incredibly lickable golden-skinned pecs as my head rested against them.

"Brilliant. That might actually work."

I added a quick message.

> I'm fine, just deliciously busy. Love to my fave brat. I'll come down soon, but right now I have cool plans with a hot man. Or maybe I mean hot plans with a cool man? xxx

I attached the photo and turned my complete attention back to Rollo.

We didn't make it to the hot tub until much later. But the fruit seemed to sustain him, and eventually we reheated the pizza.

PART TWO
WEDNESDAY

I'm sure you're familiar with the well-known adage, "Every one needs the right partner by their side."

But have you ever pondered the reason behind it?

Our Gods and Goddesses have shared wisdom that mirrors the strategy of a chess game: the queen safeguards the king, her moves both subtle and decisive.

It's that second presence, often underestimated, that turns the tide because their mutual enemies never see it coming.

You may not fully understand your life mate, but never underestimate them, or you are no wiser than your enemies.

Winning the War Against Yourself: Daily Weapon and Warrior Care by Arinn Tusensköna

CHAPTER
FIVE

Wednesday, 3rd March, Gateway Cottage—Just past Delicious O'clock

My day started well, and that's all I'm sharing. OK, if you insist, then—my day began far too early but freaking excellently.

Now with Rollo using the guest shower, I sat in bed with a breakfast tray and checked my messages. Tilly's entire world centred around a piece of bacon on the side of my plate that she'd decided was hers.

> Aysha: You go, girl! I had NO idea he was built like that. No wonder you didn't object when I called him Prince Charming. Bring him for dinner. I'd like to meet him. Autumn's missing you and Tilly. She was odd yesterday. Come on Friday?

Oh crap! Aysha thought that was Dai's chest. Aaaargh!

I typed. Deleted. Typed again. Only deleted part of it this time. And then threw my phone on the bed in frustration. She'd go crackers.

Honestly, my headfirst jump into whatever this was, wasn't

like me. But Rollo made me happy. It was everything else that was frustrating me.

Until I could make sense of it, there was no point trying to explain anything to Aysha. I didn't know if Rollo was a long overdue fling. Perhaps he wanted the Recorder's power at his back as I'd initially thought Dai had. But, no, I didn't believe that. Rollo and I had a spark.

Metaphorically and literally. I mean, there was still the strange static electricity thing when we touched. And our chemistry was unlike anything I'd ever known. In fairness, I'd lived a sheltered life in some ways, and Nick had been pedestrian in bed. It wasn't as though Rollo had a bunch of super special moves, but he seemed to know what worked for me better than I did myself, which was a lovely change. But the most important thing was I simply felt better when we were together.

Concentrate. Deal with Aysha now.

But how did I know if some good—no, let's be accurate here: some eye-opening, incredible sex with a fun guy who brought laughter and balance into my life had turned my head?

Was I high on those happy hormones the magazine articles were always talking about? Or could this possibly be something real? Rollo's situation was precarious, and we didn't know each other well. No, that wasn't right. We didn't know each other at all yet. And against all logic, our weird mental connection was making it harder to get to know him, not easier, because I didn't want to invade his mental privacy.

Take it slow. Be sensible. What if he's using regnal power to manipulate me the way Dai did? Is that why I feel so strange?

The bedroom door opened, and Rollo arrived with one of Dola's fluffy white towels slung low on his hips. Water beaded on his chest. My mouth went as dry as his skin wasn't.

Oh! He looked cross. He'd never aimed that look at me before.

"I was trying to give you the illusion of mental privacy while you thought things through. You know my thoughts about consent or the lack of it in Viking. Do you think I would or even could do that?"

"No, but ..." I trailed off. But then I hadn't thought Dai would either, had I? Although my Gift had warned me several times about Dai, and it hadn't warned me about Rollo.

"Well, it's a start, isn't it?" He sounded snappish, but he felt hurt rather than angry.

"Snappish?" he snapped.

I sighed. "How the hell am I supposed to have a conversation with you when you're just listening to my thoughts? How's that a good thing?"

"You weren't complaining earlier. I distinctly remember you not complaining when you were thinking 'left a bit and slightly harder.'"

The damn man was smirking at me. And, worse, he was right. Having a man read your mind was like that old joke: "What's worse than a man who doesn't understand you?"

He got the punchline "one who does" straight out of my head and sobered instantly. "Can we be serious?"

"Aren't we being serious now?"

"No, you're being scared, and that's OK, but you can't stay that way. I may be able to read some of your thoughts, but I'm under no illusions that I understand you, either. Yet."

Aww, I appreciated he knew that. "Do you think we should close this link now?"

He frowned. "I don't want to. But if we're going to try, then doing it when we're together is sensible."

I watched as he got dressed. Part of me didn't want to close the connection either, but I couldn't offer one sensible reason not to. And it would be a relief to have my thoughts to myself again.

I nodded. "Let's do it. It was useless when you were being beaten up, so what's the point?"

Our eyes met, and I said, "Closing Port 22"

Rollo said, "Reluctantly. But you're right, it is distracting. Closing Port 22."

I waited. Rollo buttoned his shirt, but nothing else happened. I tried the technique that had helped me when I had no idea what I was doing in the Gateway, running what I'd done to create something in reverse. I felt a mental click.

In my mind, I heard his voice clearly, but it felt different than before. *"Did that work? Something changed, but what?"*

"Damn it Rollo, you're still there, aren't you?"

"Yes, but you sound different. Think about something specific."

"Specific? Like what? What am I missing? We just haven't closed the connection properly yet, have we?"

*"I think we might have. Think about a single memory, but only to yourself. Privately, I mean, don't think it **at** me. When did you get the dog?"*

Instead, I thought about Tilly when she was a puppy and her paws were too big for her. And how, when she was tired, she would flop over wherever she was. She'd been adorable. I laughed.

Rollo said, "I don't know what's amusing you?"

Huh. "I was thinking about where Tilly-Flop's nickname came from."

"I didn't see or hear anything. I think we closed it."

I wasn't convinced because he still felt 'there' in my mind. I sent him a little movie reel of Tilly as a puppy. He smiled at me. "That is cute."

"Oh, she was adorable. But we still have some kind of connection, don't we?"

Ten minutes later, we'd established that, provided we intended the other to hear us, we could speak to each other in our minds. But if we didn't aim our thoughts specifically towards the other person, then everything was blissfully quiet and private in our heads.

I considered it. "Well, I can live with this for now, if you're OK with it?"

He nodded at me. "I'm more than OK. It feels like the best of both worlds. Let's try it for a little while?"

When I agreed, he added, "And you're right, we don't know each other, and that's the problem, isn't it? But I want to. So, tell me, how does the Recorder book a holiday?"

I had no idea what to tell him. I'd been trying to work that out since I realised my days of being a registrar who had every Sunday and Monday off were behind me now.

But when my gran died, I had almost four years' worth of unused holidays. So, I'd been lousy at taking holidays in my former life, hadn't I? Although, truthfully, for the last five years, I'd avoided booking holiday time because I didn't want to spend it with Nick in the Middle East.

But Rollo. Hell yes, I wanted to go away with Rollo. I definitely fancied that. The holiday and him.

Rollo's face held a soft smile now. "How did your gran do it? She was often away somewhere. Sometimes the Gateway was closed for weeks. Alphonse once lost his temper about it on behalf of his Galician orange growers and their harvests rotting while she was gone."

"I think she just left. The power has a way of pulling on you to return if it needs you. It did it to me last week at Dai's. So, I guess those oranges weren't coming to any real harm, whatever Alphonse wanted to tell everyone."

I sent him the memory of the powerful urge I'd had to leave Dai's house when Troels sent lumberjacks to chop down the yellow gate, even though I hadn't known about it then. And, sure, I'd wanted to get away from Dai. But beneath my personal desire to leave was a longing or even a need to be home. I would recognise the sensation immediately the next time the power summoned me.

Rollo said, "And you have Dola. Even if you weren't here, you'd check in with her all the time—right? You two are friends, not just colleagues."

I nodded, happy he realised it.

"Then let's take a holiday together."

"But …"

He waited. But I had nothing beyond that instinctive "but."

I needed a holiday. With all the staff I was amassing—my two Knights, Fi, Dola, and now Rosemary, who was starting her new part-time role this week—they could cope without me. I could open or close the iron barriers from anywhere with access to the Rainbow Network. As long as we didn't go completely off-grid, it should be fine. I could be back here before the problem even arose if I had to. Time travel for the win. A holiday with Rollo.

I thought, *"Well, hell, it's a fabulous idea."*

I saw the slow grin spread across his face. Before his dimples arrived, and I was completely screwed, I said, "I truly can't go this week. I have so much stuff to do. There's Breanna's book club. I need to see Aysha, and I want to summon you-know-who. And don't you have to do something about him as well?"

But he shook his head decisively. "You familiar with Sun Tzu?"

I laughed. "Yep, and Terry Pratchett. They're weirdly linked in my brain."

"They would be. He wrote that book where a lot of the quotes were repurposed, more amusing versions of Sun Tzu quotes. Well, him and various Roman writers."

Huh, he was right. I'd always wondered why I couldn't separate them. "Sorry, your point?"

"'The supreme art of war is to subdue the enemy *without* fighting.'"

I smiled at him. *"Men who read are sexy."*

He picked up my thought. I know he did, but he refused to be distracted.

"I'm going to focus on the future, my own and Viking's, while I give Troels time to dig himself a deep hole and fall into it. In the meantime, I need to speak to a guy who's a constitutional law expert. We used him for *Drengr*, actually."

"How long did you work with the *Drengr* guys?" I'd loved that game. The idea he'd been part of the development team was very cool.

He looked confused for a moment. Was that him closing his shields? But, no, he replied immediately, "On *Drengr*, about four years, but I worked on some other stuff with Metal Maven before and after that. About twelve years in total, some of it part-time when I had my thesis to write. So, a holiday?"

A sudden thought struck me. If Rollo had left everything in Viking ... "Rollo, do you need to borrow some money? If you had to leave everything behind, I mean? Although, that makes me realise I have no idea if they, I mean you, I mean the damn Vikings, even have a banking system ..." I trailed off, aware I'd probably made no sense.

His face softened, then he grinned. "I ought to be offended you could think I'm the sort of idiot who'd leave more than pocket change in a realm run by a power-mad dictator. But," he gave me a hug, "I'm very touched you'd offer. But I have funds. No worries. So, a holiday?"

I might have called Troels many names, but not a power-mad dictator. My insults would have been about his inability to keep it in his pants. When on earth would he have the time to be a power-mad dictator? Obviously, I didn't know him as well as Rollo did.

"Let me speak to everyone when I get to the Gateway." I mentally checked my diary and my to-do list. "I'm almost certain I could be free from Friday afternoon. At the moment, anyway, there's nothing urgent after Friday. So I could take a week. Where did you want to go?"

"Wherever you like. Give it some thought. I need some time in Edinburgh to sort a few things, so I'll do that while you get on with the rest of your week. I'm headed to the station. There's a train at 8:30 a.m. I can do everything I need to in three days."

I smirked and blanked my mind. Had the beating he'd taken affected his memory? He'd been transporting happily until they snatched him. But he felt truly healed. He'd remember, hopefully, before he wasted time stuck on a train.

"What?" His tone held confusion. "I know you think I'm amusing, but I don't know why?"

"I have every confidence you'll work it out before you endure hours unnecessarily on a train, probably one without a buffet car."

His expression as he remembered he could simply transport there was incredibly cute.

CHAPTER
SIX

Rollo had transported to his Edinburgh flat and messaged me to say he'd arrived safely. Completely unnecessarily because I'd heard the triumphant, "Hell yeah!" in my mind as he landed.

As I got dressed, I frowned at my iPad, specifically at the to-do list Dola always kept updated for me.

I'd added *Find out who hurt Rollo* to my to-do list. I starred it as a top priority.

I'd also put *Ask Ad'Rian about this mind-to-mind thing* on my list and then surveyed the far too many other items on it with an exasperated huff.

Who had cluttered my list? Unimportant tasks were mixed confusingly in with essentials. This wasn't like Dola.

I needed to welcome Rosemary Hob. Anyone's first day in a new job was scary, and it was important she feel welcomed, but after that I'd delegate some of the other apparently endless tasks.

I rearranged my list in order of importance. There were only three tasks that should be mine: speak to Ad'Rian, summon Troels and find out how involved he had been with Rollo's capture, and visit Mabon. Anyone could do the other items, couldn't they? What were my staff doing today that was so important? And who the hell put all these Simnel cakes for Mabon for the 14th *and* 21st of March on *my* list?

"Dola, do you know anything about this Simnel cake nonsense on my list?"

"Yes, Niki. They are for Mabon."

"Well, I guessed that much. But why are they my problem? Surely he can get his own cakes? And why does he need them on two different days? If he truly can't fix this himself, why can't *you* or Fi deal with it?"

"The one for the fourteenth is the smaller one for the Goddess Modron, his mother. That is Mothering Sunday. The others will be the large ones for his spring equinox picnic."

"Ti'Anna mentioned that?"

"The Simnel cakes are an important part of it."

"Why?"

"I do not know. Tradition perhaps?"

"Huh, OK. Gran said something about Simnel cakes in her last letter to me. Where do they come from again?"

"Mags Hob makes them. Normally you would have to request them from Lis, but she is on holiday." Dola's tone was flat and unhelpful. Call me psychic … but I was getting an inkling of why the cakes were on *my* list.

"But they're just cakes. Couldn't you produce them? Or we can buy them at the supermarket. If they have to be homemade, surely there are other people who can bake them?" I was googling as I asked. Yep, loads of Simnel cakes and dozens of recipes for every possible variety of them.

"No, Niki. You will need to ask Mags; they must come from her. Always. She has her foremother's centuries-old recipe. Her cakes are completely different to the current version with the marzipan in the middle. You cannot simply buy them or obtain her family's recipe for anyone else to make them. Be cautious please; your gran did not grovel sufficiently one particular year, and Mabon did not get his cakes. That was not a good year. He sulked for months."

I truly had to grovel to the Hobs? Oh joy! Happy freaking Wednesday, Niki.

Tilly and I strolled over to the Gateway to stretch our legs while I mulled over the prospect of talking the Hobs into doing anything. Rosemary was Lis's granddaughter. Mags was Lis's twin, so perhaps family wisdom might help me achieve this without having to beg. Why was I the one who had to beg for Mabon's cake, anyway? Dola had never answered that question. I'd started to build a relationship with Lis and Mags by not behaving the way most of my ancestors had.

As we reached the Gateway's boundary, Tilly's nose lifted into the air, and she turned and raced back towards the house.

"Dola, where's Finn?"

"He just left via the back door."

"Thanks." My faithless Bichon was a bacon-seeking missile.

"Niki, I have been thinking. Could you ask Fiona why your gran never tried to change anything in the Gateway or with the realms?"

"Sure. You could ask her yourself, though."

"I would prefer it if the Recorder asked her officially as your gran's former assistant."

"OK." I didn't understand why she was suddenly so curious. But I wanted to know this myself. The more I learned, the less I understood why, not only my gran, but many of my ancestors, had put up with the way things were. There must be a reason, mustn't there? Surely they couldn't all have simply been complete idiots? Perhaps I needed a better understanding of how things had worked in the past.

The Gateway smelt fresh and green when I arrived. Fi was taking a call at the new trade desk, and Rosemary, her chestnut curls bouncing happily, walked the perimeter. She passed the Yellow Sector and headed towards Green. She stopped about every fifty feet, looked up at the walls still adorned with the beautiful bonding greenery, and waved her hands with a huge smile on her face.

We'd agreed that the Valentines' flowers and branches could stay on the walls as long as the Hobs triplets felt they were flourishing. Rosemary must be strengthening the spells. That was yet another thing no one seemed to know. Why my gran had always insisted the beautiful floral walls be stripped out on February fifteenth. But then Gran had taken her tree down immediately after Christmas, whereas I always left mine until the last possible minute. Who doesn't need extra light and beauty in the depths of winter? So how much was gran's personal preference, and how much was her lack of information about the things the power liked?

We'd decided, provided the Hob triplets popped in occasionally and boosted the stay-alive, bloom-pretty and smell-nice spells, the beautiful living covering on the stone walls of the Gateway would stay.

Rosemary bobbed her usual combination of a bowing curtsy, the Hobs' gesture of respect, and turned her sparkling bright green eyes up to my face. "Milady, these are lasting so well. I think the power might be strengthening the spells itself. Thyme just left; she re-cast the smell-nice spell."

"Welcome to the Gateway staff, Rosemary; it's lovely to have you here. The power might be helping. The Book said it liked things growing in here. It smelt wonderful when I arrived; please thank Thyme. How was your honeymoon? And your sisters, are they well?"

A brilliant smile crossed Rosemary's golden-brown face, and her smile grew even wider. "You can thank Thyme yourself, milady. She'll be in here tomorrow, and it was incredible. The Fae even permitted us to leave votives at Áine's own shrine." The breathless tone in which she confided this told me it was a great honour.

But I'd never quite nailed down what votives were, had I?

Finn left them for HRH, apparently. But other than referring to small candles, I'd never heard the word before I came up to Scotland. I reminded myself of my new Just Ask philosophy. "Forgive my ignorance, but what are votives?"

"Offerings, milady. Things we think the Goddess might enjoy. We all took something. Lavender carried a gift from Auntie Mags in an envelope, and Áine accepted it." The awe on her face would have been comical were it not for the sincere respect in her tone as she continued, "And all of my Rockii's votive had disappeared the next day too, so she must've liked his rhubarb very much. He forces it himself and wins prizes. It's at its peak now."

The mention of fruit reminded me of last night and Rollo. But, no, rhubarb was one of those weird ones that was actually a vegetable, wasn't it? I hadn't had a good rhubarb crumble for ages. *Oh, good heavens, Niki, focus on what's important here! Cake, not crumble, remember?*

"Mags makes the Simnel cakes that Mabon loves, doesn't she? Any tips on how I might get her to agree to do them this year without a big fuss?"

With her characteristic frankness, Rosemary grinned up at me. "Good luck with that, milady. Auntie Mags' cake supply is one of her best weapons. She normally gets Grammy Lis to negotiate for her. Ask yourself what she might want from you. That's what it will probably cost you."

I nodded. I'd have to think about that. As far as I was aware, Mags wanted nothing from me.

A sly smile crossed Rosemary's face. "You could ask Juniper to make them for you."

I brightened. Juniper, I enjoyed dealing with, but Rosemary continued, "She won't do it, of course. She'd never challenge Auntie Mags, not with it being her speciality. But word would get out that you'd asked. That might help Auntie be more accommodating." As my spirits lifted, Rosemary added, "But it might work the opposite way."

I sighed. "Damned if I do, and damned if I don't, hey? Now, have you spoken with Fi?"

She hadn't yet. As I was about to leave Rosemary at Fi's desk, Fi waggled her eyebrows and flapped her hand frantically at me.

"I'll call you back. Yes, shortly, must go now." She ended her call and immediately said, "My lady, Rosemary will need to swear allegiance, remember? The power wouldn't let me work until I had."

My face must have told her I had no clue what she was talking about. Fi was polite, but her tone made it clear she was repeating something I didn't recall. "We discussed this last week. The Gateway requires a pledge from all new staff, similar to the one your Knights make? Your gran found it in the Book. Rosemary has to swear on the anvil."

But Rosemary shook her head. "All Hobs do that when we're children. Otherwise, how could we care for the Gateway?"

I grabbed the Book off my desk and asked it.

Rosemary was right.

To Fi, I said, "She's absolutely correct. This says the power has known Rosie for many years." Turning to the young Hob, I added, "Sorry, Rosemary, it called you Rosie, not me."

Then Caitlin arrived at a dead run through the Blue Gate, and Finn strolled into the Green Sector, sharing his last bite of bacon sandwich with Tilly.

Tilly charged across to greet Rosemary. Any friend of Autumn's was a friend of hers. "Fi, put her to work. If the power's happy, we're happy."

Fi nodded. "Will do. Then can we have a word later please, Niki?"

"No problem." I waited at the top of the Blue Sector to intercept Caitlin. "You got a minute?"

"Sure. Sorry I'm late. It was …" She waved a hand as if to say *you don't want to know*, but then changed her mind. "Could you speak to Ma? She's more fussed about this stupid book club than I've ever known her to be. Even about things that *are* important, ya know?"

"OK? What's bothering her?"

"Every slagging thing. She's called Juniper five or six times in the last few days. She was talking to Lesley about it *again* before I left. She keeps changing the food order and debating the right questions for the discussion about *Ruling Regally*. I'mma worried she's losing her mind again. Juna says Ma's fine, but she ain't acting fine."

When Caitlin lapsed into the Pict dialect and added random A's onto her words, she was stressed. I tapped my earbud. "Dola, please remind me to call Breanna. It must be today." I'd like to get Breanna's input on Troels, anyway.

Caitlin gave me a relieved smile. "Thank the Goddess. Even Juna lichtit after breakfast, and her patience is legend'ry."

"Lichtit?" I had no idea what that meant.

Caitlin mimed running away with her fingers. "Rushed off." She sighed. "Sorry, I can't even speak English today. Calm Ma down if you can, please. She listens to you." She looked longingly at the Magic Box. "Can I get a coffee?"

"Of course you can. Did you have time for breakfast?"

"Nope, Ma was losing her slagging mind, and I ran out of time."

"Dola, may Caitlin and I have coffee and …"

Caitlin added, "Anything would be great. Thank you, Dola."

Two coffees arrived, and I stifled a laugh as an empty plate landed on the table in front of Caitlin. Around the rim, the word ANYTHING was piped in a delicate script in what looked like ketchup. Then some sausages, bacon and a couple of eggs appeared in the centre of the plate.

Caitlin looked confused, but my sympathies were with Dola. It *was* infuriating when you asked someone what they'd like to eat, and they said, "Oh, anything's fine."

Her mouth half full of sausage, Caitlin mumbled, "Sorry, Dola, I think I left my brain in Ma's office this morning. By the Goddess, I'll be glad to get tomorrow night over with. Books have a lot to answer for."

Caitlin's expression was stressed, but her aura was fine. I'd need to dig deeper. There was something going on here that I didn't understand. Did I need to? Yeah, I did. I'd anticipated disaster when we stripped the dragon power from Dai. Vision flashes of Caitlin unconscious on the floor had disturbed my stomach, and my Gift had itched crazily. But then absolutely nothing happened. Well, except for us discovering Dai had gathered quite a lot of blue power from somewhere and some other power that looked like indigo but hadn't even come from my Gateway.

Troels first, I told myself firmly. "Would you like a holiday?"

She looked confused. "When?"

"Next week."

"Yeah, I would. But how did you know?"

"I didn't, but I'm taking a week off, and you are the heir apparent, so I wondered if you had things you should be doing?" I gestured towards the blue gate and the Pict queendom, but she shook her head.

"No, it's still snowing at home. But we usually go to Galicia for a week in March. Ma and Juna are going. It's in the high seventies there, you know. I could swim, even sunbathe a bit." She looked delighted at the idea and continued, "Just this morning, I thought some sun would be good. I want to catch up with Alejandro; he was odd at the sentencing."

I was busy with mental arithmetic, trying to convert seventies into a number that made sense to me. I wished the kingdoms would get on board with the scientific community and sanity. "Mid-twenties, right? That's nice for March. Sorry, what was that about Alejandro?"

"He wasn't himself at the sentencing. He said he needed a

word with me, but we never got the chance. Actually, he said he wanted to speak to the Knight Adjutant."

"Huh. Well, go with my blessing. Fi and Finn can hold the fort. Unless he's supposed to be going too? I can pop back if anything urgent crops up. I'm leaving on Friday night."

She gave me a speculative look but didn't ask any more. "Finn never goes. The girls there give him no peace; they all want a prince on their arm." Her eyes narrowed. "Speaking of princes, is Rollo OK today? He messaged me he was going to Edinburgh for a while. We need to sort that rusted slag Troels out."

"Rollo's fine, and Troels is on my list in about twenty minutes. I'm going to summon him before he can get to Yggdrasil. So finish your breakfast, then draw that sword and stand by."

The grin she gave me was blinding.

CHAPTER
SEVEN

"Fi, you wanted a word?"

She didn't even seem to hear me.

The woman who'd told me, "You can't possibly promote me. I could never be a trade director. Don't those guys have to study for years?" was deep into her work with a small frown on her face as she leaned into her monitor. Accounts and spreadsheets filled her enormous screen. Ugh! She was welcome to them.

I waited for her to notice me.

Yeah, I might be here a while. What had Dola wanted me to ask her?

"Fi, you wanted a word?"

Her face cleared as she pulled herself away from her screen. "Some of these realms aren't helping themselves, Niki. They're still doing business as if it's the sixteenth century. I mean, what does a wagonload of apples or a boatload of fish weigh? What variety of fish? How big a boat?"

I had no idea what to say to that. But a memory of some hand-scrawled signs at the market in Aberglas made me ask, "Don't they sell apples in bushels?"

Her eyes narrowed. "They're getting to you as well, I see. How do I convert that? I live in modern Scotland. Have you tried asking for a bushel of apples in the supermarket? You weigh apples in kilos or pounds, at least sane people do."

Dola's voice said, "A bushel is a specific weight, Fiona. With regard to apples it is eighteen kilos, or almost forty pounds."

Fi took in a long breath. "Thank you, Dola. I shall consult you about it later."

She sighed. "Recorder, I'll come back to you with my problem after Dola and I have spoken about Alphonse, Breanna, and Mabon's refusal to agree on a single weights and measures system."

A dainty pale green teacup with a thistle motif that matched the one on the green gate and purple cursive running around the saucer arrived in front of Fi. She smiled, lifted the cup, and breathed in whatever herbal mix it was. All I could smell from here was ginger. Then she sat back in her chair with the cup and a smile and twisted the saucer to read it. *The learning curve is always steepest immediately before the summit. But the view is worth the climb.*

"I hope you're right, Dola. I'm sorry, Niki; what did you need?"

"I was wondering, why do you think my grandmother never made any changes in here?" I gestured towards the gates and added, "Or in the realms?"

Her eyebrows turned down into the mono brow that meant she was thinking. I pulled a chair around to her desk so I wasn't looming over her and smiled in what I hoped was an encouraging way.

Fi blew out a breath and nodded to herself. "Your gran didn't have your confidence, Niki."

I gaped at her. My confidence bucket could best be compared to a small teacup. Or perhaps a shot glass. I was *not* confident. I knew confident women. Aysha was confident. Janet, damn her, had been confident—often wrong, but always completely confident about it.

"I don't think I do have much confidence?"

She grinned. "Well, you often appear to. Let me put it another way. You're a city girl. Do you think that's what helps you say things like, 'This is ridiculous, it's the twenty-first century—let's bring it up-to-date immediately?'"

I thought about it. She might have something there. Perhaps coming from Manchester, a city of almost three million people, might give me a false veneer of assurance in this tiny village with its rural Scottish ways. And then there were the realms. They were rural too and firmly lodged back in the Middle Ages.

As I was about to speak, Fi added, "Your gran was more of a country mouse. Whenever she came back from visiting you, she'd go to the market in Aberglas or Pant y Wern. She'd stroll back in here with her cloak inside out, pretending she was a Red Celt widow so she could scoop up the bargains. She'd have rosy cheeks and a basket overflowing with local produce. And say things like, 'Ah, Fi, I can breathe again. It's noisy and smelly in the city these days. If it wasn't for our Niki, I wouldn't go down to town no more.'"

I smiled at her accurate impersonation of Gran and drew a breath, but Fi barrelled on. Now she'd decided to talk about it, she was going to lay it out for me.

"She'd often say, 'Wouldn't it be nice if we could make these buggers change? But the Recorder doesn't have the power to do that. We can only keep them in line.' That's why I was so surprised when you arrived and changed so much in your first few weeks."

Dola's voice came from the Dolina on my adjoining desk. "Recorder?"

Dola rarely called me Recorder. I sat up straighter. "Yes?"

"For years, your various foremothers have sat inside me talking. I listened in on their conversations even if our communication was unilateral. I was there when your great-great-great-great-grandmother taught your great-great-grandmother all the same limitations that were then passed on to your grandmother."

That was far too many "greats," but I got the idea. "Uh, huh?"

55

"Something I have noticed over those many years is they never passed on strategy or power to their heirs. They passed on false boundaries. They passed on limitations, and they passed on restrictions."

Fi bobbed her head repeatedly and mouthed "yes" at me.

But Dola was still speaking. She felt strongly about this. "Do you remember in the beginning when you could not connect fully with the power? I cannot be certain of this, but you might ask Mabon. It could be the problem of the lower power levels and poor connection to the Gateway began with the Recorder after Agnes."

That was interesting. "Why?"

"Because Elspeth was the first Recorder I am aware of to teach her heir that she must never breathe the power in. I have revisited my memories. I cannot recall an earlier discussion than that about whether the Recorder should or should not breathe in the power. We might check if that was when the error came in."

Well, it was an intriguing idea. If you could get to the root of something, you could often get a much clearer understanding of it. But was it just a rabbit hole? A fascinating one, but still. I could probably spend my entire life in research and still not understand the millennia of history between my ancestors and the power.

"Dola, I can hear this is important to you, but I don't understand why? What would it change if I found out where it all went wrong?"

There was no pause. And she didn't answer my question, but she came back at me in a flash. "Personally, Recorder, I would advise you to ask yourself, not what they did. Nor what might or might not have worked for almost a thousand years. Instead, ask yourself what you want to transform the Recorder's Office into so it can become a force for good for the next millennium."

Whoa!

Fi and I exchanged a look. "That would be an enormous job."

In a softer voice, Dola said, "How will you know where your power ends if you do not push it to the limit and beyond? Your grandmother believed she could not fire John Fergusson, and she could have done that any day she wanted to. What do you believe you cannot do, Niki? Perhaps you should consider it after you have summoned Troels. That is one more thing your grandmother ought to have done, is it not?"

She was right. If gran had ever summoned Troels to the centre of the Rainbow Gateway, the power itself would have sensed the corruption in him.

Best to admit it.

But first things first. "You're absolutely right, Dola. I'll give it some proper consideration. Sorry Fi, we'll need to pick this up again after I summon a scumbag."

I contemplated the task. How could I give myself the best chance of being able to summon Troels? Oh, yeah, that would definitely help, wouldn't it?

I grabbed the Book and opened it on my desk. "What is Troels' full name?"

There was an unnecessary fluttering of pages, which surprised me. The Book and I had agreed we didn't need all this flummery.

A page arrived.

Gunnar Troels

Somehow, that didn't feel quite right. "Does he have titles other than no-longer-King?"

The page filled up.

The Bringer of Droit de Seigneur,
Slayer of the Unworthy,
Successor to King Jonvar the Just,
Son of Osman Troels and Margaretha Yggdrasil,
Grandson of Ivan the Eternally Tardy

. . .

"Oh, stop, please! I meant, does he have a proper title, a name or nickname I can use to summon him, if Rollo's right and he tries to hide in their sacred tree?"

My plan was to catch the slimeball-in-chief before he could escape to Yggdrasil. If this tree really led to other realms of heavens and hells, who knew whether I could retrieve him once he was there?

The Book might have picked up my thoughts because it flipped a page, and I read **Warlord Gunnar Troels.**

Huh! Was that who he'd been before he purloined the Viking crown, instead of—as he should have done—acting as a regent for Rollo?

"KAIT, when you're ready."

I dropped the star onto the anvil and then uncharacteristically reached out to touch it. I reflected on how badly I wanted to bring this asshole to justice. The power swirled, pushing anger at me. Unsurprisingly, it hadn't forgiven Troels for sending lumberjacks against its door.

The power, the anvil and my own McKnight Gift all felt strongly aligned. But as I was about to speak, the power sent me a picture. Groups of women and children.

OK, yes. I shared my thought with it: *Yes. That's exactly why I'm doing it.*

But it kept pushing at me, and my head hurt. So I dropped my shields. Then a huge grin split my face as I stepped back from the anvil and headed to my desk.

"Everyone, can I have your attention and assistance for five minutes?"

I got everyone except Finn's immediate attention. He was ten seconds behind. But Dola must have alerted him through his noise-cancelling earbuds because his hand went to the stalk of his AirPod, and he lifted his head over his screen to look at me.

"We need to accept all the petitions against Troels quickly, right now. Letting him know first is only a courtesy, not a requirement, and I'm not feeling courteous towards him. The Recorder is now in arbitration with ex-king Troels. Dola has the lead on this. If you're not sure about anything, check with her."

I mentally ran through everything the Book had taught me the last time I did this with the Pict realm. It had been straightforward enough once I accepted how much authority the Recorder had.

"Guys, you probably know better than me who should have a personal notification. Let's spread the word. Finn, notify the other rulers please. Fi, call Glynis. Let her know personally. Then, do you need to let Princess Kari and Inge know? Inge's his first wife, isn't she? The one you like? All of you, do whatever you think best, but do it quickly. Dola, will you send the email we wrote to the petitioners? Let them all know we've accepted their petitions."

The cheering from Caitlin drowned out my voice as everyone else picked it up. They clapped and hooted. The shrill power of little Rosemary's whistle surprised me. Then they all stood and cheered.

I'd misread the depth of their feelings about this, hadn't I?

Was it only because I hadn't been here long enough? If I hated Troels with a passion after a few weeks, how much more must they feel after decades of his crap?

"Thank you, everyone, but I haven't earned it yet. Can we get the notifications done so I can try to summon him?"

Everyone went back to their screens and phones with a low, cheerful hum of murmurs and keyboard sounds.

From Fi, I heard, "Sit down, Glynis. Yes. Yes! She *did*. Just announced it and told me to call you." Fi paused, then said, "Today, well, right now. Got to go, others to phone." Another pause. "Yes, help spread the word. Tell the girls they'll all have emails soon. She said it's official."

Rapid-fire typing came from Finn's desk. Tilly danced next to me. I crouched down, and I swear she felt happy too. I got a clear picture of Dru from her, so I told her she could come with me to

Mabon's and see him. I needed to catch up with Boney even if I had no intention of playing his son's silly games.

While they all worked, I tried to figure out what to do with Troels if I successfully summoned him. The gleam in Caitlin's eye told me what she thought should happen. But I wasn't a killer. Of course, I could think of situations where I might be driven to take a life. If I had any idea how to do that. What intelligent person couldn't think of certain situations in which they would?

But I wasn't some heroine in a movie with a sturdy sword like Caitlin's or a spear bigger than I was like Glais'Nee's. I was tiny, and although I loved reading about brave women, in real life, I'd be more likely to pull out a panic alarm than wield a weapon.

I could suffocate him. Wrap his head in power and let nature take its course.

I grinned. Yeah, I probably could do that.

But the Recorder couldn't. At this precise moment, the former king stood accused of things that weren't even a crime in the Viking realm. If I just killed him, I'd be no better than whoever attacked Rollo. I'd be one more idiot who thought violence was the answer, with no regard to the question.

Barely ten minutes later, we'd informed everyone necessary to make it an active arbitration. Once an arbitration was active, then all of those "the Recorder is always right about flipping everything" powers came into being. Rollo might want to let things take their course, but my Gift said I shouldn't wait. I didn't know why yet, but I was starting to trust first and ask it questions later, especially when the power weighed in with its own opinion, too.

I touched the star I'd left on the anvil with my power-wrapped left hand. I rarely did that, but I wanted to give this summoning any extra oomph I could.

"I summon Warlord Gunnar Troels to the Yellow Sector."

Astonishingly, with no conscious direction from me, the power created a glass cage about halfway down the Yellow

Sector. Was I a one-trick pony if it already decided that was what I needed? But you couldn't go wrong with a nice glass box that could be sound-proofed, could you? And it would prevent Caitlin from stabbing him for what she thought he'd done to Rollo. She looked as if she planned to slice pieces off him and take some titbits home to the Broch for the dogs. Yuck!

I used to have the sort of life where such a revolting thought would never have entered my head, but now I needed to guard against it happening?

I'd been right in the shower yesterday. Caterpillar Niki had left her discarded cocoon on the shower floor. It was time to dry my wings.

CHAPTER
EIGHT

My phone buzzed in my pocket, but I didn't want to take my eyes off the Yellow Sector. "Is that you, Dola?"

"No, Niki, it is a message from Aysha and not urgent. I will remind you later."

Unusually, Tilly barked loudly. I glanced down, but she seemed fine. She wasn't a noisy dog normally; she was obviously holding a grudge against the slimeball too.

Troels arrived in mid-air in the middle of the Yellow Sector and in the centre of the glass cage. Looking at his body language, his spread legs and hunched posture, the summons must have pulled him off a horse that was no longer there. Perhaps because he was unused to being summoned, he hadn't thought to get his feet under him.

I cushioned his fall with the power. We didn't need him breaking a leg and delaying everything while it was treated. If we could even find anyone to heal it. I didn't think Ad'Rian or HRH would volunteer to help him.

Rollo's photos hadn't shown the half of it. Troels had not just aged tremendously when the Gateway withdrew the yellow regnal power from him. He'd aged badly, and those old bones looked as though they might be brittle.

I gave the power a mental high-five, and a stream of Norse came from Troels. Between the cursing from his cage and Tilly's loud, angry barking, I could barely think. My little one hadn't forgiven him and probably never would. I didn't think she was angry for herself, but because Troels had terrified me when he tried to attack her. Bichons could give elephants lessons in never forgetting and teach camels the correct way to hold a grudge once they decided someone wasn't a nice person.

I muted Troels, and Tilly's barking quieted to a low growling. Perfect.

Until Fi joined me at the anvil's throne and stared at Troels in amazement and horror. Her words came out on a soft breath, "I *never* thought I'd see this day."

Her hands trembled, and she started to shake. I should have thought this through. After her experience with Troels, which had resulted in her own much-loved son, Stuart, this must be both awful and satisfying. I looked around for some help for her while I dealt with Troels. Finn's attention was back on his screens. But Rosemary stood quietly and watched Tilly. The Hob's head tilted as though she was listening to something.

I picked Tilly up to calm her. The moment she shut up, I put her in Fi's arms. They could soothe each other. "Rosemary, would you help Fi please? She needs to sit down and perhaps drink some tea?"

Rosemary instantly gathered Fi and Tilly and led them towards the conference table behind the screen. Good thinking to take them both out of the sight line.

Right, Troels, you're up.

But then the red gate swung open, and Dru dashed in at full speed, coming to a skidding halt a few inches before he would have hit the barrier.

"I invite you to the centre of the Rainbow, Drudwyn." As he bounced through, I asked, "What's up, lad? Is your dad OK?"

He stopped at my side, and those dear familiar brown eyes bored into mine. I heard, *"Tilly caaalled."*

Wow! She could do that?

He loped over to the conference table and stood by Fi, Rosemary and Tilly, who immediately demanded Fi put her down. She and Dru headed straight into the Yellow Sector together. They circled Troels' cage as though they were guarding it. Or looking for a way in.

I glanced at the Red Sector, but the door had closed. Dru had come on his own? I'd have to ask Mabon what the hell I was missing.

It never went like this in the movies, did it? You finally got the baddy in a cage and then didn't have time to deal with him thanks to all the dog and human dramas. Well, hell.

I breathed.

A lot of women were depending on me.

No pressure then.

"Warlord Troels, the power has summoned you. I must inform you, the Recorder has so far accepted almost one hundred petitions against you, which were submitted to my office. They all make paternity claims for unpaid child maintenance, amongst other, even more unpleasant allegations."

Now he was no longer the king. Could I get the various authorities who'd turned a blind eye to this guy's behaviour for four decades to step up and do their jobs? I was leaving the door open for other private petitions if they didn't.

"Do you understand the information I have given you? A nod will suffice."

His mouth moved, so I unmuted him.

"Woman, you will release me immediately. You have no authority to detain the Rightful King of the Vikings. Release me, and you may yet live." The previously deep orator's timbre of his voice was weaker and scratchier now, and I thought the fury in his eyes was mostly aimed at his own infirmity.

Pure reflex kicked in, and I laughed. Almost without stopping to think, I spat, "I've no reason to detain the Rightful King of the Vikings. He isn't a raping, responsibility-avoiding asshole. You,

Warlord Troels, are." I emphasised his title, but he didn't even seem to grasp my inference. "I have the will of the Rainbow Gateway and the power of the Recorder on my side. Now, do you understand the information I have given you about the petitions against you?"

He shrugged. "They lie. Women always lie."

As he shrugged, his leather waistcoat revealed a wrinkled, flabby stomach and too-big trousers secured with a wide leather belt. He must have lost weight when he aged so quickly.

I'd heard the "everybody lies" refrain from him before. But it didn't matter. He'd acknowledged he'd understood my words. The Recorder was now in arbitration with the former ruler of the Viking kingdom.

But what the hell did I do with him? I couldn't release him. He'd hide in the sacred tree, and I had no idea what its views might be on justice, rape, paternity suits or even just assholes.

He wasn't coming to any harm in his glass cage, for now at least. I had time to think and to get some advice. Because I didn't know what to do with him. I had thought I'd like to see him torn to pieces. But this frail old man would make me feel like a bully if I did him physical harm right now.

Well, crap!

Whose counsel could I seek?

While I thought about whose opinions I could trust, I said, "Thank you everyone. Ignore him for now. I need to get some advice. Please don't rush back to work. Make sure you're feeling alright first."

I intended this for Fi, who was back at her desk with her mug of tea but still looked shaky. Everyone except Finn nodded. "KAIT, would you join me at the conference table, please?"

Caitlin was still laughing when she arrived.

"What's funny?"

"Somewhere, there's a very confused horse and a group of guards panicking because they lost the guy they still think is their king."

I laughed because she was right. "Dola, can I have some painkillers and a coffee, please?"

"Niki, you requested I remind you the next time you asked for painkillers in the Gateway to tell you to check with the power before you took them."

I had, hadn't I? Because I was an idiot, and I kept forgetting that when the power wanted to speak to me, it squeezed my head. Which led me to ask Dola for painkillers instead of realising what was happening and talking to the power.

I caught Caitlin's eyes. "Excuse me a minute; the power needs me. My question to you is going to be, what the freaking hell do we do with the ex-king now? Security-wise, I mean. I can't let him go now, can I? He'll head for the tree again."

When she frowned at me, I added, "I don't have a plan. I thought I had time to research all this. I was going to speak to Rollo, consult you and Finn, and then ask the senior royals at your mother's book club. Listen to all the petitioners. You know —do my damn job! I didn't anticipate having to set up a bed and breakfast for an elderly accused rapist."

"So I can't just behead him?" She asked this wistfully as she caressed the handle of her sword.

Goddess save me from a woman with a sharp sword who thought it was a solution. "KAIT, focus. I know you're smarter than this. I'm the Recorder, not an assassin. The petitioners want justice, not a headless body."

Her mutinous jawline suggested all too clearly that, in her world, a headless body was the very definition of justice.

"We need some time to get our ducks in a row. What do we do with him?"

I gave up, dropped my shields, and my behind left the chair as the power rushed to me. Wow, it was happy. I giggled involuntarily as it tickled me exactly as it had when I was a child. I breathed it in and got a confused rush of images. Rollo, Ad'Rian, Mabon and Dru danced in my mind along with the knowledge that the power would never allow Troels to return to Viking as a free man. It followed this with images of the other royals.

Did it want me to summon them?

As though the power understood I wasn't getting the message, it sent me an image of the entire group of royals all nodding, along with a page of some old document.

Then another of me floating over the anvil. Oh joy!

I reassured it. Yes, I'd try to include all the royals, and I wouldn't do anything final without checking with it, and them. Then I refocused back on the room, and my bottom settled the few inches back into the chair.

Caitlin was drinking fruit juice and watching me closely. I reached for my coffee. The mug said, *"Justice will not be served until those who are unaffected are as outraged as those who are." Author Unknown.*

Huh? I showed it to Caitlin with a raised eyebrow. She frowned then shook her head. "Not big on philosophy. But about him ..." She gestured behind the living willow screen to where the cage held Troels. "We might need Rollo. Can you contact him?"

"Sure, he's in Edinburgh."

Caitlin stared at me. "Since when? I was only being tactful. Well, tryin' to be. Finn said he heard him singing in the cottage this morning. He left already?"

Finn heard him this morning and reported that to his sister? Hmm, my TEK and I would have words about my right to privacy. Or Dola and I might need words about soundproofing for the private areas.

"He did. He's already there. Yellow regnal power for the win."

She looked thoughtful. "Didn't know it could do that. Trust Rollo to be the one to work it out. I wonder if Ma's ever tried it?"

"Tell her I'll happily go along the first time she tries it."

"Why?"

"Just in case. I was with Rollo when he discovered it, and, honestly, I'm not sure he'd have known how to get back if I hadn't been there."

She gave me her serious nod. "So what *are* you going to do about Troels?"

"I wasn't asking you to be polite. I don't know, and I've got no ideas."

How could I convey my inexperience to this competent young woman? She'd grown up with a sword in her hand. Having the accused rapist of dozens of women in a glass case a hundred yards away from me was not a thing I'd even imagined in nightmares. Never mind thought of as something that could actually happen in my previously normal, so quiet life?

Everyone expected the Recorder to know stuff. Have all the answers. But I'd only had the power for six weeks and been the Recorder for five weeks. And, sure, I'd learned a lot. But this felt so far above my pay grade. At least it would if I had a pay grade —I cut off my stupid, disempowering, circling thoughts. "KAIT, this is a long way from my previous experience. The power seems to think we should consult all the royals. I'm not sure why, but it does."

She sipped her juice. "It can't hurt. But you don't sound as if you wanna do that?"

"I don't mind. But if they had any good ideas, wouldn't they have done something about him before? Anyway, I already know what most of them will say."

She looked briefly confused, then her face cleared. "Ah, you've spoken to them already?"

"Not about Troels, no."

"Then how do you know what they'll say?"

"Oh, come on, you must know too. They're deeply predictable. Mabon will say, 'A nice selection of oubliettes I have, *bach*. Choose one, you should, and the rest of it, I'll deal with.'"

Her face lit up with humour. "Yeah, he would. This is a good game. OK, what'll Ad'Rian say?"

"'Daaarling, allow me to pop him in a lovely deserted glen for you. He'll never find his way out, not in this lifetime anyway, considering how dreadfully wrinkled he looks.'"

Now she looked more serious. "Yeah, they are predictable. Never thought about it quite like that. Although, I'm not sure what Ma would say, and I should know that, shouldn't I?"

"Your mother would say she doesn't envy me my decision, but finding somewhere to lose that pile of rusted slag shouldn't be hard. But the queen would mutter about pregnant chambermaids and suggest lopping his head off exactly as you did."

Caitlin lifted her juice glass to my coffee mug and clinked. "Right on both, I think. I'll ask her."

"The thing is, anything they come up with will only be the way they've always dealt with these problems. Which is why they allowed him to be a slimeball for forty years, isn't it? I need a *much* better solution."

Caitlin gazed around at the various gates. "So what we need is a plan to put before them that they can't argue with?"

"Honestly, I think we probably need to give them all the chance to say their usual stuff and argue all they like, and then gently offer them a better way. Otherwise, they'll think we don't care about them. And I do. But I don't think any of the usual solutions will work for this one, yet the power thinks we need them all on board. What will Alphonse say? Do you know?"

We looked at each other and shrugged as Caitlin shook her head.

From her desk, Fi called over, "He'll ask what effect it will have on his trade with Viking. Sorry, couldn't help overhearing. Also, you forgot Rhiannon, who has broody, hungry dragons to feed!"

We all laughed because Rhiannon was always eager to feed anyone who was surplus to requirements to her dragons. But it didn't give me any solutions, did it?

I reached down our link to Rollo. *"You busy?"*

"Sorry, I am. I could be free in an hour?"

"No rush. We'll talk later. I'm going to pop and see Boney."

We surveyed Troels' glass cage before we left. He was prowling up and down and muttering to himself. Although he looked more tired than angry. "Do you think I should put a bucket and a bottle of water in with him?"

Caitlin looked at me as if I were insane.

"What? I don't want him dying of dehydration or peeing on the floor, do you?"

She shrugged. "Are you going to leave him there with the Gateway open?"

"He's not coming to any harm, and no one can open that glass case without me and the power. Have you got a better idea?"

At her head shake, I asked, "Dola, can you put—"

She interrupted me, "Yes, Niki, leave it in the hands I do not have. We need to speak later. I have added an appointment with me to your calendar."

"OK." That was unusually formal for Dola. It must be important, but right now I needed to focus on the ap Modrons.

I considered the glass cage, where Troels' mouth was still moving even though he was muted. I pulled a little power and asked if it could make the cage wall facing the Gateway less transparent, so we didn't have to look at Troels or watch him using that bucket?

The front wall changed immediately to a dense frosted glass. And could it soundproof the cage?

It could. I unmuted him and he still had light so he couldn't complain. Well, if he did, I wouldn't hear him.

Damn, I'd better ask Dola to add a monitoring system.

CHAPTER
NINE

Wednesday, 3rd March, Pant y Wern—Red Celt Realm
As Caitlin, Tilly, Dru and I headed down the Red Sector, my unhappy stomach wanted to chicken out of this visit. *Boundaries, Niki. You've been getting better at them. You can do this.*

Caitlin grinned at me. "Glad you've accepted you can't leave me behind. What changed your mind?"

I sighed. "I'll need a few moments in private with Mabon. But he also says Dai wants to apologise to me, and I don't believe it. I've refused to see him until he's healed. So I thought I should treat it as a Recorder's official engagement. It might make it easier for me to say no."

At Caitlin's enquiring head tilt, I added, "Because Mabon can talk Niki into doing almost anything. But I don't think he'll push me if I go as the Recorder. So …" I gestured at her. "I'm taking my Knight to make my status clear. But how do you feel about it all now?"

She tilted her head a little farther but said nothing.

I'd finally realised Mabon asked *me* to come and see him. But he specifically asked the Recorder to see Dai. I felt as if I was missing something, but my stomach was clear it didn't want to see Dai in either of my personas.

Boundaries, I reminded myself. *Boundaries are good for our mental well-being and balance. Just say no.*

Gods and Goddesses, find your spine, Niki. You sound like an out-of-date anti-drug campaign.

But Mabon was hard to say no to.

As we reached the red gate, Caitlin finally gave me a slow nod, which still didn't answer my question. So I spelled it out again. "How do you feel? You weren't happy that Dai seemed to have stolen that blue Pict power somehow."

She went still. "I'm fine." Then her eyes scanned the Gateway, which was busy this morning. She opened the gate, obviously intending to head to the quiet of Pant y Wern and a little more privacy.

But quiet wasn't what met our eyes.

"Slagging coos. Have they been breeding more since last week?"

Caitlin was right. The cows were everywhere.

The fluffy Highland cattle, known as the "coo" to all the Celtic realms, were a distinctive breed. They'd originated in the Highlands and the Western Isles of Scotland. Mabon was very proud that some of his people had brought coos through the Gateway when they first founded the realm more than a thousand years ago.

With their unique appearance and muscular bodies, according to the king, they could weigh up to 1,800 pounds when fully grown. An 850-kilo bull was not to be trifled with. Both sexes had the impressive long curved horns that spanned about a metre across.

They completely blocked the small lane within the town walls that led to Mabon's castle home. Well, damn, I'd walked here because I wanted to avoid Caitlin being sick from the transport, but there was no way through this large fold of cattle.

"Sorry, Caitlin, but needs must and all that. I'll land us out of sight in case you barf." I picked Tilly up and was about to reach out to Caitlin to transport us all when Dru nosed past us. He barked once, followed it up with a low, threatening growl, and a gap opened up as cattle moved aside.

Waaaitt.

Dru looked up at me until I nodded. Then he was off imitating a sheepdog and moving the cattle slowly back towards the castle. Caitlin started to follow him until I put a hand out. "Dru said to wait. He'll be back."

As we waited, I checked her with my Gift. She'd said she was fine, and that hadn't been a lie, but there was still residual unhappiness and anger about something. It might be Rollo's injuries. I was simmering about those myself.

Eventually, she said, "I'm looking forward to Dai being completely healed."

"OK. Well, good. But Mabon says he's refused healing from the Fae."

"He's gonna need to change his mind about that."

I agreed with her, but some expression I couldn't quite put a name to flitted across her face. It made me ask, "Because?"

"Because once he's one hundred percent healthy, I can safely beat him half to death."

It surprised a laugh out of me. But she was deflecting. I'd know. I'd become skilled at it while avoiding Aysha's many questions after Nick's death.

I reached a hand out to grasp hers briefly, and once her surprised eyes focused on me, I said, "You don't owe me an explanation. But I need to know whether I should take you with me. And if I do, will you be alright if I decide the Recorder needs to do what Mabon requested and see Dai?"

She nodded. "It's all fine, sorry. Really, it is. Meant to tell you properly yesterday, but then Rollo arrived bleeding ..." she trailed off, shuddering, then tried again. "Yes, I've spoken to Ma. We all agreed to share the power rather than send it back where it came from."

I waited.

"Caitlin?"

She focused on me, and I asked, "Where did the blue power come from?"

Her lips compressed, and a minute shake of her head showed her resistance to answering me.

I found my Recorder voice. "Apologies, KAIT, but the Recorder needs to know. Would you prefer I ask the queen officially?"

A firm head shake. Slowly, she said, "We don't know—that's the slagging problem. Well, we know it was ours originally, of course, but ..."

All the time I was smiling and watching Dru's antics as he efficiently herded the cattle away, leaving a clear lane to the castle, I thought, *don't know*? Surely a monarch would know if some of their regnal power went missing.

I might need to ask Breanna to explain more about her perceptions of regnal power. The Book had given me the impression that the monarchs traditionally kept track of it. But considering how much seemed to be all over the place last week when the Gateway gathered the yellow power in, I wasn't sure that was still true.

Dru loped back down the lane and barked once at me. I started walking, and he immediately turned around and led the way. He growled when a coo headed back towards us. It changed its mind swiftly.

We followed Dru closely, and with only two more growls and one bark, he delivered us to the foot of the staircase that led to the castle's large red entrance doors.

"Thanks, Dru, you're a star, and you win a lovely long shoulder rub."

Tell draagon laaady.

I wasn't sure if he meant he would tell Glynis, or I should, but as we climbed the well-worn stone steps, her sturdy figure emerged. She swore loud and long and shouted over her shoulder, "The bluddy coos are loose again. Tell him he has to do something. Ridiculous, it is!"

With that, she moved to the only free space by the storage sheds, and then she was in her semi-form. A squat, angry brownish-red dragon with Glynis coming out of its back—it still looked so odd—took to the air.

She shouted, "Great job on Troels, Recorder. Thank you!" over her shoulder as she rose into the air. Then she set the coos moving back towards their usual river grazing, the dragon flaming and the woman hurling abuse in musical Welsh at the now fleeing cows. That put a new twist on the term rush hour.

Wednesday, 3rd March, 2021—Pant y Wern—Red Celt Capital

We headed up the castle steps and down the stone passageway, past the various tapestries that had been there since I was a child. They depicted everything from bloody battles to beautiful poppies. But they were primarily red with identifying plaques under t em. Many of the works had titles that began "The Glorious Battle of ..." or "The Queens' Defeat of the ..."

I paused at one I hadn't seen before. It was also red and white with a view of snow-capped mountains. But the red came not from the usual blood, but from the large door incongruously situated between two enormous, side-by-side slate boulders. It was hard to judge the perspective on the top of a mountain with nothing else to give scale to the picture. But if the door was gate-sized, then those lumps of rock could rival anything from Stonehenge.

They were familiar, even if they were a slightly different shape now. The Gate's upside-down dragon emblem matched the ones on the mountain gate and the one on the new dragon Gate in Pant y Wern. Was this how the broken gate I'd re-opened looked before it was damaged?

The plaque said, "The Dragon Gate and its Sentinels."

Then, like a fluffy duster wielded by an over-zealous cleaner, Tilly's tail began beating nineteen to the dozen. She tugged on her lead and pulled me towards the door to Mabon's day chamber as he came out of it.

Mabon took in Caitlin's presence, and his expression changed slightly, his shoulders firming as he said, "Ah, Recorder, welcome. Brought that one out of storage in your honour, we did. It's how the mountain gate used to look before we lost it. You must tell me how you restored its power. Rhiannon's delighted. She thinks it may be the power from the gate that helps to breed the queens. I would hear how you did that."

Mabon speaking normal English alerted me, and I drew him away while Caitlin politely looked at the next tapestry, another gory battle scene, with every appearance of interest.

Was he cross that I'd brought Caitlin? But, no, he felt happy about it.

"Sorry, but my Gift said I had to bring her with me today. I explained we'll need a few minutes alone. She's the heir, remember? She gets this diplomatic stuff, probably better than I do."

He pulled me into a hug. "I'm glad you understood my message, *bach*. Wasn't sure you would. Don't fight the Gift. Agnes said it was never wrong. Your gran too often ignored it. Delighted I am that you don't."

I leaned into him for a hug and to breathe in his pine, woodsmoke and autumn scent. Today there were faint astringent eucalyptus trails. He was worried or unhappy about something, probably Dai.

I pulled away so I could look at him properly. He looked completely normal, his dark curls bouncing happily as he gave me his quirky half grin and his bright tourmaline-blue eyes sparkled at me. But he didn't feel normal.

That was gods for you: *Show normality even if your heart is breaking*. I murmured, "Is it Dai or something else that's put this shadow over you?"

"Pieces of everything. Memories of a happier time, long gone. A son that won't allow us to heal him. Even the bluddy coos are against me. Doing good, though, is Rhiannon. You were right to push me into giving her the power. The wild dragons are behaving for the first time in centuries. Think she's lonely though, even more so now. Well, bluddy lonely at the top, it is. Find her own way, she'll have to. We all did."

He drew me towards a doorway, but Caitlin had me almost trained, and I dug in my heels. "We're going in here, KAIT."

She was there immediately, doing her impersonation of a bodyguard. She bowed to Mabon. "No offence, Your Majesty, but there are concerns about the Recorder's safety today, as I'm sure she will tell you."

That was tactful of her. The heir apparent side of her personality often surprised me when it emerged unexpectedly as a diplomatic Caitlin. Mabon, perfectly comfortable with this bodyguard nonsense, opened the door and gestured her in. In seconds, she was back and took up a position outside the door.

I understood how she'd come out so quickly when Tilly and I followed Mabon inside. I couldn't remember ever being in this room. It was tiny, cold and official-looking. It had four stone walls, bare except for a surprisingly modern wall planner. Then I grinned as I noticed it was for 2009. A desk and a single chair completed the room. I gave him a querying look.

"For the people who will try their welcome to outstay, you see. No chairs for them. Pitifully little heat and no rugs, so my angry sparks damage nothing but the stone."

I looked at the floor, and, sure enough, there were many black scorch marks on the flags. "What on earth have I done wrong to be thrust into here?"

"You, nothing, *bach*." He reached over and mussed my hair. "But Dai is in my day chamber, and speak to you first alone, I would."

I opened my mouth to tell him I wasn't prepared to speak to Dai here. But he held up one finger and, with obvious reluctance, removed the rainbow gold locket from around his neck then dangled it in front of me.

My heart, which loved Mabon very much, wanted to say *oh, keep it*. But my head and my intuition said it was a McKnight family heirloom, and we may need it. As it dangled from its chain, I let out a gasp and took it from him.

It had changed, and the design was much clearer. "What did you do to it?"

He gave me his sheepish crooked grin, the one that pulled at the scars on his weatherbeaten face. "On my honour, nothing intentionally. Wore it, I did. Sometimes the god part of my power has its own ideas."

The design on the heart-shaped locket could be seen clearly now. Much of the former wear and tear had been reversed. The back revealed a seven-pointed Gateway star, as I'd suspected. But the previously indecipherable, vaguely numerical shape on the front turned out to be an infinity symbol with a wobbly heart in between its loops. It was in the classic lazy eight position and almost filled the front of the locket.

Something niggled at me. "Boney, how long did she own this?"

"Almost her whole life. Gifted it to her, I did, long before she became the Recorder. Ordinary gold then it was. The Smiths, the old Smiths, of course," he waved a hand to show it had been long ago, "added the star for us after she ascended. The gold changed then. Wearing it when they murdered her, she was. Or assumed so, I did. Because she never removed it. Shocked me, it did, last week to see it around your neck."

"You can borrow it again, Boney. But right now, the McKnights might need it. Sorry." As I opened my bag to tuck it away, I remembered he'd opened the locket, and I did the same. But it was still just the two miniatures of a younger, happier Mabon and a vivacious red-headed Agnes that I'd seen before.

Mabon took it off me and flicked his nail on an invisible lever tucked inside the point of the heart where the two arches met on Agnes' side. The painting opened like the cover of a book to reveal the gold behind the tiny portrait of Agnes. It was engraved.

I tried to catch the light of the single bulb on the words. I would never have been able to read this before the power fixed my eyesight, and it was still a struggle.

Mabon took pity on me. "Of magic doors, there is this: you do not see them even as you are passing through." There was an underlying humour to his voice instead of the sadness I'd expected.

I glanced at him. "You've said that before. What does it mean?"

"No idea, *bach*. Said it a lot, she did. Told me I had to remember it. So I did. Odd thing."

I asked, "Why odd? And what's the infinity symbol about?"

"Not there, it wasn't, the last time I opened the locket."

"The quote you mean?" At his nod, I asked, "When would that have been, Boney?"

"A few days before she died." Now he looked sad. Oh dear, was it time to move on? But, no, Mabon said, "We had a bond, Agnes and I. Probably."

"A bond-bond?" I gestured around my head to indicate a romantic bond.

"Probably. Couldn't see it ourselves, could we? Tried not to be together in public, we did. Afterwards, when I couldn't find my way out of the dark realms, Ad'Rian said he'd seen it. Very young, she was, when we ..." He paused, and I watched him, fascinated. He looked suddenly younger. Was that embarrassment? Yep, there was a definite pink tinge to his neck. "It was normal back then. Girls grew up a lot quicker."

Had he been cradle-robbing or something? How young was very young?

My internal frown must have shown on my face.

Mabon said, "Girls could be married at twelve in those times. It was a different world." He glanced at my open mouth and rushed on, "No, no. She wasn't twelve. What *do* you think of me? A woman she was, not a child. Can't judge it by today's standards is all I'm saying. Teenagers and these young adults didn't exist back then. Girls were children; then they were women. Times change. Only telling you, I am, I knew how I felt the first time I set eyes on her. She did too." With his characteristic *moving swiftly on* gesture, he drew me into another hug. "Precious gift you gave me. Don't feel bad, *bach*."

It was time to change the subject. "I need your advice. I summoned Troels this morning."

"Wriggled out of it, did he? Who did he send in his place? Never mind. Work it out, we will. Time to talk we'll have at Breanna's book club. Made me laugh, the book did. Talking books, fine idea. Very funny and good true points it made."

I nodded and watched him closely. "Nope. Troels arrived. He's in a glass cage in the Yellow Sector at the moment. But I need a better plan, and I need to get back to the Gateway and deal with him. You got any ideas?"

Mabon's face was more of a picture than any of the tapestries in the corridor. It should have had one of those brass plaques under it, engraved with, "This is what astonishment looks like on our king."

His mouth opened and closed several times before he said, "Well now, surprising, that is. Yes. A plan we'll need. Healed now is Rollo. So Dola tells me. But she couldn't say how."

That was interesting and unexpected loyalty from Dola. I knew damn well she mostly reported everything to Mabon. I'd finally worked out that was one way the realms always seemed to know everything.

"Taking the throne, is he?"

I decided to stick with my Recorder persona. I loved Boney, but until he got his head straight about his own son, I didn't want him interfering in Rollo's business. "He's considering his options.

We need a solution for Troels and to find out who attacked Rollo."

"Wasn't Troels then? Sense, that is. He'd not be the one to want the boat rocking, would he? So, which of the warlords was it, do you know?"

If it was that obvious to Mabon, why hadn't I known? Was it because Troels was the only senior Viking I'd met? Because he was despicable? Because he'd abused so many girls? Whatever the reason, I'd need to look into these warlords properly. "Who would your guess be?"

After almost a minute of complete silence, during which his eyes moved around the room, he was obviously considering his answer rather than looking at the uninteresting blank stone walls. Finally, he shrugged. "Any of them might do it. Behind it, Halvor would have been, but covers his tracks well, that one does."

I waited, but that was all he had to say.

"OK, Your Majesty, if that's everything, I'll see you tomorrow at the book club. We'll all need some answers and ideas then."

Then, suddenly, the Red Celt king stood in front of me where my oldest friend had been. But his body language wasn't at all regal. His head and his shoulders drooped, and my Gift gave me waves of sadness, overwhelm and frustration.

"Need your help, I do, Recorder, and even your Gift. No sense can I get out of the boy. Don't know what to do with him. Can't force him to do the sensible thing, can I? A choice, it is, to be healed. Compel him, I can't. See you alone, he says he must, to tell you he's sorry."

My left shoulder pinged. Hard.

"Well, that's a lie." I wriggled my shoulder.

"Thought it was, but it's what he said, on my honour."

"I don't doubt you. But he *was* lying to you—so what does he want?"

My Gift gave me frustration again and fatherly guilt. But

underneath all of it was a sharp sense of fear, almost bordering on panic.

Sure enough, he said, "Don't know. Can't trust myself with him at the moment. A lot of his problems I caused by forgetting the spell I asked Ad'Rian to put on him to stop him from blabbing private family business around the bluddy valleys."

I was cross now. "I've already said this to Dai, and I'll say it to you. He knew exactly what you'd done. He can't keep blaming everyone else. That's not taking responsibility for his own situation, is it? He could have reminded you or asked Ad'Rian to fix it himself if you were injured—"

"Not injured then, I wasn't. That was much earlier. Got your timelines mixed up, *bach*."

Trying to keep track of hundreds of years of personal histories was driving me insane. I wondered if I should ask the Book for a family tree with key events on it. Because Dai told me Mabon's head injury was the reason he'd forgotten the block. Another lie then? Had it felt like one at the time? I couldn't even remember, so deep was my distrust of Dafydd ap Modron at the moment. But I didn't think it had felt like a lie.

"OK. But if nothing's changed, what's the point in me seeing him? And if he's asking to see me alone—it's suspicious again, isn't it?" I straightened my shoulders, swallowed and finished firmly, "I won't do it."

He squeezed my shoulder. "See him for me, will you? Use the power. Hoping, I am, the Recorder will have a better idea how to resolve this. Because resolve it, we must."

My breath caught in my throat as my Gift chimed loudly in my head. Stomach churning, I tuned into my Gift properly. "I have a question."

He turned back from the door, his shoulders straighter now, and nodded at me.

Something niggled at the back of my head. The Recorder owed Mabon a debt from when he gave me my own memories back. He could have called in that debt and required the Recorder to do this. But instead, he'd only *requested* the Recorder see Dai. I could only think of one reason for that. He didn't hold a life debt from me, only a debt. I wasn't sure how to phrase what I wanted to know.

"Last week, during John's sentencing, I was thinking about what you did at my ascension. Do you remember when I showed everyone that Jamie couldn't see the power? Then we all realised John Fergusson had installed him as the Knight Adjutant without even testing him ...?" At his nod, I asked, "What caused you to claim to be the person who had the right to deal with him? Sorry, I can't remember how you phrased it. But you said straight away that you'd leave the disposition of the son to the Recorder, but John would come with you. Why was that?"

A tiny smile played at one corner of Mabon's mouth. "Primary claim, it's called. Too new to understand the penalty for being forsworn, you were, or so I thought? Or to know how much other harm the man had done. But aware, all the realms were, and expect the sentencing ceremony, they did. Helping, I was. A lot you had on your hands that day."

"And then you did the same thing with Gwyneth."

His puzzled expression made me smile. He was more like Caitlin than he realised. Hadn't he bothered to remember her name either? "The one who hurt pregnant little Megan and slapped me."

His face cleared, and he nodded. "Thought you might forgive the shouty *ast*. But people can't strike a Recorder. One of the most important rules of the Gateway, that is. Death's the penalty for it. But made you unhappy, it would have. Didn't make me or Rhiannon unhappy. And there were hungry dragons to feed. No point in waste, is there?"

I'd come a very long way in a few weeks because that all made perfect sense to me now.

Gwyneth had been a bitch intentionally. She knew who I was, but she thought I wouldn't impose the death penalty on her for striking a Recorder. And she was right. I wouldn't have ... then.

It seemed this was a similar situation. Mabon's hands were tied. Dai was an adult, so Mabon couldn't insist he stay with the healers because adults, however wrong other people might think they were, had agency over their health choices. There were circumstances under which the Fae would heal a person against their will. They would override their patients' preferences to save their life. The Fae valued life. But Mabon couldn't request it of Ad'Rian. Because whatever was wrong with Dai wasn't life-threatening. However, if this went the way I thought it was going to, then I would be able to claim it for him. Was that Mabon's plan?

"Primary claim, you say? OK."

Boundaries, remember, Niki?

I took in a long, slow breath. "The Recorder will see him for you, Your Majesty. Bring him to the Gateway at your convenience."

His expression almost made me giggle as he pointed at the door. "But, Nik-a-lula, he's right here."

I tugged Tilly's lead as I headed towards the door. "You told me not to fight my Gift, Your Majesty. I've learnt a lesson about your son and being away from my power source. In my Gateway or not at all. And, in return, you'll try to come up with a plan for Troels that doesn't come from some fifteenth-century battle playbook."

With that, I opened the door, caught Caitlin's eye, and said, "We're leaving now, KAIT."

Mabon's mouth was still open as we walked together down the corridor and narrowly avoided bumping into Glais'Nee.

He bowed. "Ah, good morning, Recorder, I surmise you are here to visit the prince."

"Good morning, Glais'Nee, how lovely to see you. No. I need to get on with my day. His Majesty will bring you up to speed. Ask him about Troels, please. I'm looking for everyone's advice on him. I'll see you tomorrow. Juniper agreed to serve Just Deserts."

He looked surprised too, then delighted when I mentioned the dessert he'd requested. I'd been right. Mabon had a plan, but he needed to learn that, unless he shared those plans with me, I wouldn't necessarily play along with them. We would see what his next move was.

CHAPTER
TEN

As we left the castle, I saw all the coos were back and blockading the pub's doorway.

"Ma wants to import some into the mountains, you know. They love the cold, and there's lots of foraging they could do up there. Alphonse wants some too."

"Wouldn't it be too hot in Galicia for them?"

"No, their mountains are cooler. You can even ski up there."

I needed to pay some visits and get to know the realms properly as an adult. It was mid-twenties in Galicia in March, Caitlin had said. I wondered if Rollo might like to spend our holiday there?

Caitlin frowned at me. I must have zoned out.

I tried to pretend I'd been thinking about Recorder business. "Are you going home now?"

"I wasn't, but if you're finished with me for now, sure. You gonna be OK with Troels? I can come back after lunch, but I'd like to check on Ma. She wasn't right this morning."

"Troels can wait. I thought I'd pop in to your mother's rather than call. But I'm going to take a shortcut. Do you want a lift?"

She looked torn. "Got one of those tablets? They work. But even that's weird, ya know? They're supposed to take half an hour to start working, and last time, I swallowed it three minutes before you turned my stomach upside down, but I still wasn't sick. What gives, d'ya think?"

"It's mostly in the mind."

She frowned at me. "I'm not imagining puking my guts up!"

"Have you ever flown?"

"In a plane!?" She asked this as though I'd enquired whether she usually turned purple in the mornings.

"Or on a dragon? Or a pegacorn? You know, flown?"

She shook her head.

"When passenger airplanes first became a thing, they had to provide vomit bowls. A lot of the earliest flight attendants were nurses. Some airlines even had special slots for the bowls under all the seats, and loads of the passengers threw up on every flight if there was any kind of turbulence, or sometimes even when there wasn't. Vomiting is just a reaction to fear. But within a few years, the number of people being sick had plummeted to less than one percent. People stopped being frightened and simply told themselves it wasn't actually hurting them. They'd get there safely, and, anyway, who wants to lose a good lunch? It's all in your head because your body feels weird when you do it." I paused to see if I was making any sense.

"You know some random stuff, Niki. You're saying I should give it another go?"

"Knowing it's all in your head doesn't make it less real to your stomach, but it does mean you can tell it not to worry. I know you're a brave woman, Caitlin. If you tell your mind it doesn't need to be frightened, it won't be. But it's up to you. You can go the long way around, and I can meet you there."

She nodded firmly, as if she was convincing herself. "Never was big on the long way around. Rollo didn't puke the first time. You don't. Even Finn doesn't. I don't have to be sick. I'll give it another chance. Better than going back through the slagging cows without Dru to help."

She'd decided we should land in the Broch's internal yard.

Apparently, we were close to the dogs' lunchtime, so it should be empty about now.

Then we both stopped at the top of the stone steps to watch as the cows hassled an obviously drunk man trying to get out of the pub. He gave up, went back inside and came out with a paper twist of cattle cubes, scattering them in a wide arc to the left and stumbling away to the right through the gap he'd created.

"Those cows have got that particular scam nailed down, haven't they?" I mused.

She was still laughing as we landed in the yard at the Broch, and she didn't even look green.

The dogs were not being fed; they were exercising and barked in surprise when they realised we were there. I tried to give Caitlin the strip of tablets. "Take these the next few times, and you'll break the habit."

But she pushed them back at me. "You keep them. I'll only lose them. You always have that suitcase you call a handbag over your shoulder. It's not like I'll be transporting without you, is it?"

The door to the yard opened, and a whirlwind of golden fluff resolved itself into Maggie as she rushed out. I put Tilly down, and they shot off together.

Breanna emerged wearing a tight smile and an elegant formal dress. The crown sparkled in her cheek piercing as she gave Caitlin a surprised look. "Just got back from opening the new school, but Maggie was insistent I let her out. I see why now. Good afternoon …" she surveyed me carefully and finished, "Niki?"

"Yep, I left the Recorder giving Mabon food for thought." I tucked my arm through hers. "Let's put the crown in the drawer and have a chat about this book club."

Wednesday, 3rd March, 2021—lunchtime. The Royal Broch, Aberglas—Pictish Queendom

There were changes in Breanna's private sitting room. It looked cosier and less rigidly tidy. A soft throw on her reading chair, a cushion on the sofa that still held the imprint of her head. She'd finally bid farewell to her former housekeeper, the rigid Mrs Fosdike, who'd made her life a misery. The queen gave the credit for her new comfort to the implementation of suggestions found in *Ruling Regally*.

Settling by the log fire in a new chair upholstered in a fresh blue and yellow fabric, I surveyed the selection of books on the large coffee table. I picked the top one off a short pile. The unpronounceable-looking surname suggested a Viking author. *Winning the War Against Yourself: Daily Weapon and Warrior Care.* Flicking through it, I wondered if Rollo had read it.

Then Breanna strolled in, relaxed now in a soft, stylish lounging suit of vibrant emerald green. It looked comfortable but also amazing against her bright new-penny copper-coloured hair.

"Wine and nuts, Niki?"

"Actually, I haven't had lunch, so perhaps not on an empty stomach." I filled her in on Dai's latest dumb request.

"Neither have I, so let's lunch together. I don't think you're doubting yourself, but you were quite right, you know. If Mabon wanted the Recorder, they should have come to the Gateway. I used to like Dai, but he's been different the last few years. Coffee then? And cake and a sandwich, perhaps?"

"I'm not sure I'm ready to eat food, but I could squeeze cake in."

She gave me her wide signature grin and pressed a shiny new bell by the fireplace. "Cake isn't food; it's medicine for stress, and therefore has no calories."

In seconds, the door opened, and Lesley stepped in, looking at her phone. "Your Majesty?" Then she noticed me and gave me a smile and a bow. "Recorder."

"Lesley, I keep telling you, you can simply send one of the

maids. You don't have to come yourself." She turned to me and added, "Lesley has been promoted to the new role of Broch Manager."

Lesley caught my eye and bowed as she tapped her phone but addressed Breanna, "What may I get for you, ma'am?"

Breanna sighed, "Coffee for the Recorder, tea for me, a small selection of tempting sandwiches, and two pieces of that rhubarb thing Juniper delivered, please. But, Lesley, you must stop interrupting your day to wait on me. It's not what I wanted you to do in your new role."

Lesley walked over to me. "May I send this to your phone, Recorder, and would you explain it to Her Majesty? I've tried but not yet succeeded. Prince Finn designed it. It's very good."

Intrigued, I hit accept on my phone, and while I waited for an app to download, I said, "Congratulations on the new role, and how's bonded life treating you? Is Gowan well?"

A brilliant smile crossed her face. "He's grand, my lady. Hugh MacAlpin's been so kind. Gowan's finally doing work he's proud of. It was a kind thing you did."

"I did absolutely nothing except introduce them. Gowan has himself to thank for being who he is. Send him my regards, please."

She nodded as I opened the app, poked, swiped, and smiled to myself. "Oh, this is brilliant. It's never going to work for Her Majesty though, is it?"

Breanna growled. "Sitting right here, ya know." She sounded so much like her daughter, it was hard to suppress my smile.

"But you don't use it, do you?"

"You cannot know that." She glared at Lesley.

I smiled and said, "Leave it with me, Lesley. It needs some tweaks. I'll speak to Finn."

Once we were alone, I turned my Gift on her. I had no idea why she was, as Caitlin had put it, losing her mind over a book club. "Caitlin's worried about you. How can I help?"

Except my Gift didn't think she was in the least bit bothered about the book club. But she was keeping a secret. I poked gently, in case she needed help with something. Then I smiled at her. "Ah, misdirection, is it? I wondered when she was so worried this morning."

She gave me her wide, impish grin. "I blame Netflix. We've never done a surprise bir—" She broke off immediately as the door opened.

A maid, young, cheerful and wearing Pict-blue leggings and a tabard-style tunic with a white apron, nudged the door open quietly and came in carrying a tray. Wow, that was quick.

Rather than the pompous silver tea service and tiny, fragile porcelain cups and plates that were on the salver the last time I was here, this tray contained a cheerful, squat Pict-blue teapot, a taller matching coffee pot and mugs, and gorgeous tulip-shaped, bright yellow plates. It brought a ray of sunshine into the room.

In direct contrast to the way Mrs Fosdike had always clattered loudly about in her attempts to make it clear that Breanna wasn't behaving in a queenly enough fashion to meet Mrs F's standards, the young maid placed the tray softly on the table. "The sandwiches are following, Your Majesty." As she moved the pottery bowl of blue hyacinths to a side table, their sweet scent drifted over to me.

Breanna said, "Thank you, I'll pour."

The maid, with no fuss, lit several lamps, which cast a warm glow into the gloomy, overcast day. She was moving freely and quietly in the modern uniform without all the annoying rustling the previous outfits had generated. She left quietly and didn't seem to feel the need to close the door with an annoyed click either. Things had definitely improved.

"I love the new styling for the staff, Bree. I bet they're loads nicer to work in than those scratchy frocks."

"Those uniforms have made it easier to recruit some bright new staff. Lesley's idea, of course, and she was right. Women were actually reluctant to work here because of the antiquated uniforms. Mrs Fosdike is now enjoying her well-deserved retirement, a long way away," Breanna paused and drew the triskele in the air. As she reached the third leg of the symbol, she added, "Thank the Goddess for her mercy. Mrs F wouldn't hear of changing the uniforms. Tradition, you know."

She sighed and passed me my coffee as I grinned at her.

"I took the author's advice," she gestured at *Ruling Regally* on the table, "and things are so much better now. Quite a few of the old guard have joined Mrs F in retirement. I paid them off handsomely. They all have excellent pensions and plan to do charity work. Excellent idea, they can bully someone other than me on a voluntary basis. But quickly, before we get interrupted again—"

The door opened, and Tilly and Maggie charged in, followed by Caitlin. "Sorry, Ma, Maggie was insistent. Ooh, is that the frangipane thing? The smell wafted through the Gateway earlier." She reached out then stopped her hand mid-air when she realised there were only two pieces on the tray.

"Ask them to send some to your suite with your lunch. The Recorder and I are discussing tomorrow night."

Caitlin headed towards the new bell.

"One sec, Caitlin. Let me test this." I poked my phone, found Caitlin's name on the app, tapped it and then paused. "Your bedroom or your sitting room?"

"My sitting room, as you're evicting me from here." She gave her mother a long look but seemed satisfied by what she saw and smiled at me.

I tapped her sitting room and then scrolled, frowned, and peered at the tart on the tray. "Would that be called Rhubarb and Almond Sunshine Break?"

Breanna nodded at me. I clicked, scrolled and asked, "Ice cream, cream or yoghurt on it?"

Caitlin was frowning now. "Ice cream, obviously. What are you doing? Is that the confusing thing Finn made? The one where I got dog food on a plate, and Maggie got my bacon sandwich in her bowl?"

I looked at Maggie, who gave me a doggy grin of satisfaction and shook her golden fluff. "Did you want that bacon very badly, girl?" Her expression clearly said she had no idea what I was talking about, and she jumped up to sit next to her mother. But, in my mind, I swore I heard sniggering.

I got a confirmation checkmark from the kitchen on the order I'd placed and told Caitlin, "It will be in your room, probably before you get there yourself."

I settled Tilly next to me on my chair and turned back to Breanna. "Yes, you make a good point. One of the problems *is* going to be finding out who's actually read the full book. But another might be …" I trailed off as the door closed behind Caitlin.

"So, who's the surprise party for? I didn't get that bit?"

Breanna laughed. "Smoothly done, Niki."

She gave me a plate with the tart along with a cake fork. "Eat this now, then you'll be relaxed and ready for the sandwiches when they arrive."

She raised her own fork above her plate. "It's for Caitlin. The party, I mean. As you probably know by now, she's not one of life's readers. Any discussion of books usually gets rid of her."

She ate a forkful of her tart, and I followed her example. OMG! This couldn't have been made by anyone other than Juniper! I would have sworn I was eating it at a beachfront café in a Mediterranean town with the sun high in the sky. My shoulders tingled in the sun's warmth, and I could smell sunscreen and ozone in the air.

With a hum of pleasure, Bree swallowed. "She uses Galician almonds. It's like being there. Anyway, the idea started when I watched a show where there was a surprise party. The birthday girl truly had no idea. Surprise parties have never been a Pict thing, so I thought it would be fun to do the first one. But you and Dola beat me to it. However, Cait wouldn't expect it from us. We're too old-fashioned."

I giggled because Breanna's expression was comical. She conveyed the loving annoyance of every parent whose daughter was secretly convinced her mother had never had a life of her own before giving birth to her. "But you don't keep Cait busy enough, and she kept wandering in at the wrong moment. Every time Lesley, Juniper and I were trying to arrange menus and details, she'd arrive and ask what was going on. So, I told her all the arrangements were for the book club, and now she thinks I'm losing my mind."

I swallowed more tart, completely blissed out on my private mini holiday. I managed to ask, "When is her birthday?" without spitting out my tart. Shouldn't I know when my Knight's birthday was?

"She's twenty-five on the twenty-fifth. I didn't do a thing for her birthday last year. Sorcha had so recently died and," she pulled a face, "I wasn't myself."

While she talked, I checked her aura. It looked better. There was some grey still, some of it quite dark, but no black, and breaking through the gloom was far more blue and even small streaks of a cheerful yellow. She was healing slowly.

"This year, I plan to make up for it. We're even opening the ballroom. Getting the invitations out has been a nightmare. I told her those were for the book club, too. Then I had to actually send some out for the book club. Oh, it's been endless. But it needs to be a surprise. We planned to go to Galicia together for a week. Sabby is throwing an advance mini party there for her to celebrate the end of her girlhood. We hoped that way she wouldn't suspect there would be anything later. But Cait said she had to slagging work."

My expression must have stopped her. "No offence, Recorder."

I shook my head and filled her in on my own planned holiday and my conversation with Caitlin earlier today.

She beamed at me. "The melt is coming together now. Oh, speaking of melts, the Smiths are making her something special too, but they won't tell me what?" She raised a querying eyebrow, but I'd heard nothing about it and said so.

"I'd hoped Sabby would bring her puppy to the book club tomorrow." At my frown, she said, "The Galician Empress Sabella?"

Oh, yes, Gabby Sabby, the chattering empress. Had my meeting with Mabon fried my brain more than I'd thought?

Bree was still talking, "But she said she'll have enough in her dish with two children, and the puppy isn't palace-trained yet. I'll see it next week, but they're puppies for such a short time, like kids, I suppose."

The mention of "in her dish" rather than "on her plate" and "palace-trained" and then the two children left me hopelessly grappling for purchase in this conversation. I asked the easiest thing. "Aren't Natalia and Tomas still on their honeymoon?"

Breanna's throaty, sexy laugh rang out. "Yes, they are, and having a fabulous time, apparently. The six of them went to the winter palace."

"I knew that place looked more like a palace than a villa! Paulo showed me a lovely photo of the three couples when I called in to the Smiths to organise Dola's gift."

"They call the heir's quarters a villa, but it's still part of the palace. It wouldn't be my choice—six people on a honeymoon—but it's the Galician way. The girls are all so close, and the men are like brothers. Well, Tomas and Miguel *are* brothers. Anyway, it's not our business, is it? Although Alphonse has been in a strop about it, about everything lately, according to Sabby. He won't talk to her."

I nodded. Breanna seemed to realise she'd been rattling on in a manner worthy of Gabby Sabby herself and finally drew a breath.

But then she set off again. "It's only Alejandro she's bringing. She's including Alphonse in the child category. Apparently, his behaviour is worse than her actual children at the moment. She can't work out what's wrong with him. Or, rather, she says everything's wrong with him."

I laughed. The emperor had seemed nice enough during the

bondings. And he'd been hilarious at John's sentencing. If someone can make you giggle while chopping a man's thumb off, he must have something going for him.

"Niki, I hate to keep you when you must be busy, but I've just realised I've been starved of girl-time. It's lovely to have some female company. Well, female company I didn't give birth to and who doesn't think I've lost my mind about a simple book club. I have nothing on the schedule until this evening. I'll probably talk your ear off, but can you stay for more coffee? And where are those sandwiches?"

At a knock on the door, I said, "Let me check with Dola."

> Niki: Everything OK there?

> Dola: All is well. Rollo confirmed he will be joining us via Zoom for our meeting at 6 p.m.

> Niki: What's the meeting about? Did you tell me already?

> Dola: Suggestions regarding Troels' care. Which is why I invited Rollo.

That was an unexpected treat. I checked the time. It was still early afternoon; I could make enquiries of the Book later. I was unwinding in Breanna's newly relaxing sitting room. I could spare an hour for some much-needed female company, couldn't I?

> Niki: I'll be home in an hour. Is Troels still alive?

> Dola: Yes, research into the treatment of prisoners suggests we have responsibilities. Unless you plan to kill him soon?

> Niki: No. Keep him alive, please.

CHAPTER
ELEVEN

Breanna watched me. "You're very good on that phone. I noticed it the last time you were here. You message like Finn does, as though your thumbs have their own eyes and know where the keys are. I can barely see the slagging screen. And don't say reading glasses; I lose those too, along with my phone. Although they're often on the top of my head." She patted her head distractedly but came up empty-handed. "You still look frazzled, and I've not stopped chattering. Are you well?"

I told her about Troels.

"I got the notification that you'd accepted the petitions, but I wasn't sure you'd succeed in summoning him. He's normally so slippery. Well done. Should we talk about what to do with him tomorrow night? The book club was supposed to give us a chance to make plans for him, but you've moved faster than anyone expected. You do keep doing that."

But she smiled at me as she spoke. "Do you think I should have invited Rollo and perhaps even Inge to the book club? I like Rollo, and he reads, but I couldn't see any point when you had them all locked down." She sighed. "If you have Troels, he's the heir. So it's all going to be his problem now. Poor man."

I wasn't ready to talk about Rollo, and I didn't know how

much he wanted to share about his last few days. Although Caitlin would already have told her most of it. "I can certainly have him there if you'd like Dola to pass the invitation on."

There, that was all true, and it wasn't horribly misleading, was it?

Breanna gestured me to the tray of delicious-looking sandwich morsels on a silver platter between us. "Do eat, Niki. How can I help?"

"Tell me about these Viking warlords who might be behind the attempt on Rollo's life, please." I helped myself to the offered food and settled in to learn.

Twenty minutes later, I'd never been so grateful for the voice record function on my phone. I couldn't even say, never mind spell, half the names Breanna had recited effortlessly. Something about the easy way she pronounced all the weird names, places, and various battles made me ask, "Do you speak Norse?"

She nodded. "We keep this quiet, Recorder?" Her raised eyebrow made it clear she'd need my word on it, so I gave it to her.

"The Recorder's assurance of confidentiality, Your Majesty."

She smiled. "All the Albidosi women do. The boys don't have to learn any languages except our own dialect and proper English, of course. They can if they wish. But our women learn all the other realms' languages in the schoolroom. Caitlin asked if she could tell you last week."

When I gaped at her, she laughed. "It's outdated nowadays when everyone speaks English. But it wasn't always that way. And even now, it's handy when people expect you to be ignorant and are muttering behind their hands during a negotiation."

"And do you know much about the current warlords? I'm desperately trying to get up to speed on them."

She nodded serenely. "Use that phone thing Lesley gave you and see if it can make wine and nuts arrive. If it does, and will save me having to get up to ring the bell, I may need to learn to use it."

I used Finn's excellent Broch app, which he would absolutely have to tweak if he ever expected his mother to like it, to order us glasses of wine and nuts. The spicy, caramelised Pictish nuts were amazing and I looked forward to them. We settled in to educate the Recorder while we waited.

Some time later, I sighed. "It's all so alien. Not just the names, I mean the culture too. Why would they put up with this for forty years? It makes no damn sense. Those shield maidens I bonded were not weak women; they were strong and scary. How has Troels kept everyone down?"

Breanna said, "If I knew that, we might have managed to change some of it. But Troels hasn't; he's quite stupid. It's been done in his name. Oh, he's horrible, but the biggest problem has always been, if we deposed Troels, who would take his place on the throne? Any of the other contenders would be far worse than a rapist."

Breanna paused mid-thought and sought my eyes before she continued. "I'm sure that sounds wrong. But Niki, you don't know the potential replacements. Rollo was too young, then he was away in Caledonia, and he's too smart to set himself up as a target. There were simply no successors to Troels any of us could live with. It would have been a warlord." She paused again as the door opened, and a different maid arrived with wine and nuts.

I couldn't quite get my head around the idea that the royals hadn't deposed Troels because the other options were worse. I mean, sure, we said it sometimes about politicians, didn't we? He's useless, but the only other options would be as bad or worse. But somehow the incompetence of prime ministers in general, whatever party they were from, didn't feel like the same type of equation as a rapist being the best option.

Once we were alone again, Bree raised her glass to me. "*Slàinte*. The other option might have been if any of Troels' sons were slagheaded enough to accept the crown. But if they had, after the warlords assassinated them, it still would have been one of their group who took the throne."

At my open-mouthed shock, she explained, "They have legal assassination in Viking but they call it duelling."

I thought about every bone in Rollo's right arm being broken and the cat telling me they had done it so he couldn't duel that female-abusing coward.

"Have you read *Brave New World*, Niki?"

That prickled an old memory awake. A scratchy school skirt and a too-warm classroom. "Huxley? The one with the different castes in the society? Alphas, Betas, and …" I trailed off, then added, "Not since my school days, sorry."

Breanna nodded. "They used a drug to control the population in that too. How about *The Hunger Games*? Cait and I loved those movies."

Now I was back in the conversation. After a brief diversion to discuss how outstanding the special effects were for the dresses Katniss wore in the films, we got back to Bree's point.

"If you divide your society into sections, then you need only control the actions of the top tier. Ten to twenty percent at the most. You can simply oppress the rest. The Viking warlords have polished oppression, ostensibly on the king's behalf, to a sheen the Smiths would be proud of."

Caitlin had told me this, but perhaps I'd dismissed what she said about how any woman wearing a dress was fair game in Viking because my Knight could be a little black-and-white and brash sometimes. Somehow, hearing the same information from her mother gave it a different weight. I needed to look beyond Caitlin's prowess with weapons and past her sometimes youthful slang and stop underestimating her political savvy. Mostly, I should remember who'd raised her.

Bree took pity on me. "Let me give you the more common anglicised versions of their names so we can at least talk about them without you stumbling over every word."

I nodded and grabbed my phone again, this time with my notes app open.

"I think there are three contenders. The first is Hjortr Ironshank."

"And these are the English versions of their names?" My lack of language skills embarrassed me. I wondered if the power could help?

"Well, Hjortr means Stag, like a male deer, you know? Ironshank is hilariously inappropriate because he can't even touch the metal. I'm sure it was supposed to suggest his ancestors' strength and fortitude. Call him Ironshank in your notes. Everyone will know who you mean."

I breathed a relieved sigh. "OK, thank you, Bree, truly. I'm sorry to be so slow."

"Oh, nonsense. Women have to stick together, especially when they feel inadequate. We all have those days. Now, the next most likely prospect for the throne would be Grimwulf Bloodraven."

That I could manage, and I added him to my notes. Before I could speak, she added, "Bloodraven might be the best one of the bunch, except he's probably too reasonable to last very long. He's older, and someone younger would remove him by force. Which is a shame because his people like him. The only other serious contender would be Eirikr Skaldsplittr. The name Eirikr even means ruler. But call him Erik in your notes. Warlord Erik would identify him clearly."

"OK, so Troels' sons and then these three possibles for the throne if Rollo doesn't take it."

Why did these names sound so familiar?

Breanna nodded and pushed the blue bowl of still-warm, caramelised nuts towards me. They seemed to be cashews today. I took some and sipped my wine, then mumbled around my mouthful of nuts, "And who'll win?"

"Whoever Halvor wants on the throne, of course. He'll tell the warlords' summit who to confirm."

Caitlin and I walked back to the Gateway together. When I called into the little bookshop opposite the Pict's blue gate, she muttered, "I'll wait here. I always do for Ma." And she took up a position outside the door with a glare that looked like it would deter any other shoppers from entering.

I gave him the title of the warrior care book. But I couldn't remember the author's name, only that it had seemed to be a Viking-sounding name. The kindly book shop owner looked confused. Even when I mentioned I'd seen it at the Broch today, he simply shook his head. "I supply many of Her Majesty's books, Recorder. But not that one. Shall I try to order it for you?"

I'd agreed, but in my experience, when a book shop "tried" to order something—it never arrived. I'd look online. If I ended up with two copies, I'd gift the other to Caitlin. Even she could manage a book for warriors, surely?

As we reached the outside of the blue gate, I blurted, "Jarl Skullsplitter!"

Caitlin gave me her best humouring-the-crazy-Recorder smile, "It's Skaldsplittr, my lady. What about Warlord Skaldsplittr?"

Exactly. That was what I'd just realised. "Is he a Warlord or a Jarl?"

Her voice was slathered with the grease of polite patience, which wasn't her style. I was obviously being an idiot. "It's the same thing. Jarl translates as 'earl.' But earl, warlord, it's all the same title to the Vikings. However you translate it, it means a step below the king. There are about twenty-five of them, the Dirty Dozen based around Haraldssund whom you'll have heard about. Then another dozen or so who run the rural areas and have less might, smaller armies, fewer warriors, but often more money, improved living conditions for their people, and better morals."

I gave her a dazzling smile. "This afternoon, I need you to draft me a report."

At her horrified expression, I quickly added, "Ask Dola to set you up with a text-to-speech facility. Then give me a five-minute rundown on each of the three warlords your mother thinks are the most likely to want the Viking throne."

I consulted my notes, "Skaldsplittr, Ironshank and …"

"Bloodraven," Caitlin finished my sentence. "I can do that. I'll ask Dola."

"KAIT?" At her nod, I said, "Activate teacher mode. Patronise me, tell me the obvious things. Assume I'm ignorant and tell me anything I probably don't know that you think I should about Viking, the warlords, or Rollo's position there."

She gave me an odd look.

I asked, "What?"

But her face cleared. "Teacher Mode. OK. Is that one of those times when the Knight gets a pass?"

"A pass?"

"If you're in danger, and I have to throw you out of the way, it doesn't count as an assault on the Recorder, yes?"

At my nod of understanding, she added, "So is Teacher Mode like a free pass to be a little ruder than usual? You won't accuse me of womansplaining?"

I grinned at her. "I promise. Assume I'm an idiot, because probably I am about the Vikings."

As we entered the Gateway, it was all quiet. Even Troels was sleeping on a cot that had appeared in his cell. Until my eyes reached the Red Sector, where Mabon, Dru, and Dai waited with Glais'Nee. Well, hell. Boney had meant it, then. My crazy idea from earlier might be right.

CHAPTER

TWELVE

My stomach wasn't happy. Not happy at all. But I'd told Mabon if he brought Dai to the Gateway, I'd hear him out. I reminded myself of Mabon's plan, or at least what I thought his plan was.

I tapped my earbud. "Dola, why didn't you let me know Mabon was waiting?"

"He did not make an appointment. I told him you were busy with important matters today. He said he would wait."

So Boney was desperate and not just trying to pass his problem on to me. I didn't have a choice, did I? Not if I wanted to face myself in the mirror tomorrow.

Dai's shoulders lifted, and his body language perked up as Caitlin headed towards the Red Sector to greet the three men.

Dola continued, "Ad'Rian contacted me through his Dolina and requested I inform you privately the healers are ready. He said Glais'Nee can contact them and bring them through the violet gate in a mere moment. He said this would make sense to you."

"Yes, it does, thanks."

I *had* understood Mabon's plan correctly. When I'd wondered about Glais'Nee being in the castle earlier, it seemed he must be part of Boney's strategy. I'd suspected Glais'Nee was there to take Dai to Fae once I'd done my bit.

But I'd been so busy drawing boundaries. Well, I didn't regret that—I needed free access to the power. Not the smaller amount I could pull through the sometimes unreliable network in the Red Celt realm. Anyway, I didn't trust Dai and wouldn't have been surprised if he'd brought the Wi-Fi network in the castle down to keep me powerless again.

Why repeat the same mistake when so many new and far more interesting ones were available?

My plan was simple.

I only needed to allow Dai to attack me.

I headed over to the men. As I passed the anvil, I glanced around to make sure there were no stray travellers and locked all the gates except the one from Fae. We'd do this in private. It might be easier afterwards if there were no random citizens as witnesses.

As I reached Caitlin, I murmured, "Please don't stab him by mistake. Things might not be quite what they appear."

I hugged Mabon, greeted Glais'Nee and nodded at Dai. Even being this close to him made my skin itch. The stupid man needed healing.

I invited everyone into the centre.

I focused on Dai. There wasn't a polite way to put it. He looked awful; tired, grey and drawn. His aura was jagged and the energy coming from him felt horrid.

I might have said he looked like a man who saw the error of his former ways. But in truth, he didn't. He looked like a man who was trying to *appear* as if he'd seen the error of his former ways. The difference concerned me. But I was no healer. Getting to the bottom of Dai's problem was beyond me. He needed to be in the care of professionals.

So let's see if Dai was crazy enough to attack a Recorder. But I wasn't going to bait him. That would be unfair.

He didn't even greet me. Sweeping his father and Caitlin with his gaze, he said, "If you two could step back, this will be quite hard enough without an audience."

Mabon stepped back a few yards, but Caitlin didn't move. She just glared at Dai.

I checked Dai's shields. Stone walls, as always. Ad'Rian was right. That much rock was in very poor taste. You could have tight shields without being rude about it.

I pulled power.

"They're staying right here, Prince ap Modron. Your father asked the Recorder to see you. Whatever you want can either be said in front of an audience or not at all. Your choice."

There that was another freaking boundary, wasn't it?

I'd felt sincerely sorry for Dai on Monday when I realised he was simply at the end of his tether. I'd given him the alien indigo power back because I thought it helped keep him balanced, but now the idiot was refusing the Fae's healing? My sympathy wasn't limitless.

I put Tilly down and patted her butt to move her in the right direction. "Go to Dru, baby, while I deal with this."

Mabon bowed his head. "My son is in need of healing, Recorder, but he has refused it and tells me he wishes to apologise to you."

I stepped forward to Dai. "You asked for me to be here. I am."

In a firm voice, with no attempt to keep this private, he said, "Niki, I owe you an apology." He looked at me expectantly.

Oh, not this pantomime again. I was so bored with it. He continued smoothly, "I really do, and I need to know you forgive me."

"Prince ap Modron, you're labouring under a misapprehension. Niki doesn't like or trust you right now and refused to meet you. So, you've got the Recorder. But, by all means, begin by apologising to her."

Dai's hurtful words about the Recorder's belief the Gateway had needed me when Troels sent lumberjacks against it being nothing more than "self-important exaggeration" ran through my mind.

He *still* owed the Recorder and me a damn apology, but neither part of me was stupid enough to think I'd get one. "Say whatever you need to say swiftly. I have more important things to do this afternoon."

Like finding out which of those warlords sent men to hurt Rollo, for a start.

I waited impatiently.

Silence. Dai's face didn't move a muscle.

The silence grew. He *still* hadn't said he was sorry. Gods and Goddesses, Autumn understood the rules of a genuine apology better than this idiot, and she wasn't quite eight yet.

What was the man doing?

Actually, that was the question. It felt like Dai was filling time. What was he waiting for? I tapped into my Gift.

It said *move back*.

Move away.

I took an involuntary step back. Then I reminded myself I didn't want to do that and stepped forward again.

Caitlin, who had been trying to give us the illusion of privacy, immediately turned her full focus my way. Ad'Rian had said if the Recorder needs to know something, it's not abusive to breach someone's shields. I'd told everyone I wasn't here as Niki but as the Recorder. Wasn't it like when a police officer identified themself? Well, I'd identified myself clearly several times as the Recorder.

I'd broken through Dai's shields once before with the power's help in the Gateway before we removed the red dragon power. If he wanted me to listen to him, then the Recorder needed to know what was going on.

I broke through his shields.

He was waiting for something to happen. He wanted something from Caitlin.

Caitlin?

The moment I breached his shields, his plan was clear. The apology nonsense was only attempted misdirection for his father. Dai had known I probably wouldn't see him alone and hoped I would bring my Knight with me. He'd tried to see her at the Broch yesterday, but they'd told him she was at the Recorder's, dealing with an emergency and no one could tell him when she might be home.

He wanted his power back. That power had been created to get dragons to do as they were told. Normal people had no defences against it. Most of the people he'd used it on were completely unaware, as I had been, that their desire to agree with him wasn't their own but was generated by the red dragon power.

Without it, he'd quickly discovered people didn't do what he wanted them to. And he wasn't enjoying his new life one bit.

I wrapped myself in power.

Mostly, Dai was terrified that, if the Fae healed him, they would remove the indigo power. He'd known he could block them from taking the indigo power with the red. Now Rhiannon had the red power, his vulnerability made him reckless.

Didn't he know they couldn't even see the indigo power? At least, neither Mabon nor Ad'Rian had noticed a big ball of it in the Gateway on Monday.

Why the hell would he think Caitlin could help him get his power back? If I wanted a hostage, I sure as hell wouldn't choose Caitlin. She'd have him on his stomach and wrapped in iron in seconds. What was the idiot planning?

Then I caught Mabon's eye and realised not one word had been spoken in the Gateway while I'd been delving through Dai's head.

He was simply staring at me.

I pulled power and wrapped Caitlin in it. To my eyes, she looked like a baby swaddled in a rainbow blanket. I didn't know if it would keep her safe from whatever Dai was trying to do to her, but it was all I had right now.

The look of shock on Dai's face was quite satisfying, and an angry frown replaced it. OK, that helped. I was on the right lines then.

Then I pulled more power swiftly. Dai had made it quite clear in his mountain home he had no respect for the Recorder. I tried one last time. "Dai, don't do it, or you'll leave me no choice."

The moment I spoke, Dai moved towards me.

His hands came at me so quickly, I almost stepped back out of reflex.

I needed to hold still and remember my plan.

I kept my nerve.

When one of Dai's hands closed on my throat, and his other was less than an inch from fastening around my neck, I froze him in place with the power. He didn't even seem to realise he had no grip on me at first.

He said, "You will make my da give me *my* power back, Niki. I thought you'd help me. But your interference ruined everything."

And then his expression changed as he tried and failed to close his hands around my throat. "What have you done?" At Dai's horrified shout, Caitlin was there, still wrapped in power but now holding a string of iron beads in one hand and her sword in the other.

She took in our little tableau and was obviously unsure whether she should breach the power I was holding Dai with. "Shall I restrain him for you, my lady?"

His voice laden with sorrow, Mabon said, "One moment please, KAIT."

A blinding silvery light shot through with red sparks surrounded Dai.

I stepped back.

I used my Gift, hoping to understand what was going on here. Usually, when I saw Mabon's god power, he was angry. But not this time. This time, he felt devastated. Sadness and a bone-deep resignation rolled off him in waves.

Dai crumpled to the floor.

I finally remembered why I'd identified myself so clearly, and so many times as the Recorder. "The Recorder has the primary claim, Your Majesty, and I make it now. I will decide what is to be done with him."

Two Fae healers, judging by the cut of their robes, strolled languidly through the violet gate.

Mabon gave me a blinding smile through the silvery sparks that surrounded him and Dai. "Ah, Nik-a-lula, got it, you did. Thank the Goddess you have a brain."

I looked at Dai in a heap on the floor and at his father, who'd taken a huge risk to ensure his son would finally be healed. How the hell could Dai have ever thought his father didn't love him with every fibre of his being?

I looked around carefully. Now Dai was unconscious, the energies were calmer. I retrieved the protective cocoon of power I'd wrapped Caitlin in. Oh, she wasn't happy with me. I'd need to explain why I'd done it.

The Fae healers strolled over to Glais'Nee, and the more senior one with the darker skin and darker purple robes bowed to me and then to Mabon. The junior healer waved his hand, and one of the violet security nets wrapped itself gently around Dai on the floor.

I pulled the more senior one aside. "Do you work directly with the Head Healer?"

He gave me a lovely smile and a bow. "I do, my lady. I am Co'Lin and will be in charge of Prince Dafydd's healing. My liege lord has excused himself; he feels he is too close to the family."

Well, that was a relief because Ad'Rian was right. "I have a warning, or perhaps an injunction, for those who may treat him." I'd considered how to ensure that if any of the Fae could see the indigo power, they didn't remove it from Dai until we were certain about its purpose.

Co'Lin waited quietly while I organised my words. "If any of his healers should find any strange power in his aura, I would have you instruct them to do nothing with it unless the Recorder is present." I rubbed my stomach unconsciously, but when his eyes shot to my hand soothing my belly, Co'Lin's eyes cleared. "Ah, my lady, there is prophecy of which I am unaware?"

There wasn't. But that would work for the Fae. They didn't mess with prophecies. I couldn't lie to him though. "Not quite a prophecy, more a Recorder's warning, but you could treat it as a prophecy, if that makes it easier."

He nodded and bowed again. "I shall ensure everyone connected with his care is so instructed, my lady."

"Thank you, Co'Lin, that relieves my mind."

I recovered the power I'd coated Dai with now the Fae had him secured, then turned to Mabon. "Well now, Boney, weren't you well prepared? Were you so sure I'd do what you wanted?"

"No, *bach,* scared I was that you wouldn't. But a mutual friend suggested I should leave Dai's future in your hands. Then the boy played into mine by demanding to see you, didn't he?"

"A mutual friend?" I wasn't sure who he meant. Ad'Rian?

"Well, she calls herself your friend now, and she said you're sneaky."

Nope, not Ad'Rian then. "And who's that?"

He just grinned at me.

We settled at the conference table while Mabon thanked the healers and Glais'Nee. I'd asked Dola to send me a coffee. Caitlin declined a drink but agreed to sit down now Glais'Nee had taken charge of Dai to transfer him to Fae.

"Think I missed some key part?" She smiled at Dru and Tilly, who were already curled up together under the table. "Can you fill me in, or is it private?"

I shot her a quick look. She'd done exactly what I needed, and I'd assumed she understood. I wasn't a good boss, was I? I probably should have explained it properly to her when we left Mabon's. I'd planned to. But then she'd distracted me with the coos and her aversion to transporting and vomiting.

"Sorry, KAIT, you were so efficient, I thought you'd grasped it. Dai refused to allow the Fae to heal him after we stripped the power from him on Monday. They had to release him."

"Yeah, got that bit."

"OK, so in what circumstances will the Fae heal a patient without their consent?"

"If they're unconscious."

I nodded and waved my hand to suggest she run through the other conditions. I sipped my coffee and watched the thoughts flit across Caitlin's expressive face. Something about her ease with this question-and-answer format told me she and her mother must have had sessions like this many times. I wondered if Breanna would let me sit in on them? I needed a more in-depth study program for the realms than simply using the Book on an ad hoc basis.

"If they're a child and their parent or ruler isn't available to give consent, heal first, consent afterwards."

I nodded and waved my hand again as I drank more coffee.

"Don't know any more. They're slagging firm about not taking away the patient's rights."

"What if they'll die without healing?"

"Well, yeah, of course. Unless they're terminal, and it's untreatable, like Sorcha. Those patients have the right to die if and when they choose."

"But if they're not terminal?"

She chewed her lower lip now and shook her head. "Dunno. I probably should. Ma wouldn't be pleased, but I don't."

Well, that confirmed my suspicions about House Albidosi's

education program. "If a patient would die without intervention is the last one. They'll intervene with or without consent."

Caitlin facepalmed. She'd known this Fae rule, but she hadn't retrieved it quickly enough.

"Once they're healed, it's over to the patient. But Ad'Rian once told me that close to ninety-two percent of people who try to kill themselves regret it almost immediately. If they save them, then let the mind healers help them, they rarely try it again. But if they still want to and pass the Fae's extensive counselling, they will assist it. It's very rare."

Caitlin said, "Yeah I knew it, but how does it help?"

"So what's the penalty for attacking the Recorder?"

"Death." Then she added, "But you stopped him. He didn't actually attack you."

"I wanted some wiggle room."

She sighed. "Can I have that coffee now, please?"

Caitlin was intelligent, and she knew far more than I did about the realms. So what was confusing her?

She made that clear with her next words. "Didn't think there was any wiggle room. Attack a Recorder, even touch her the wrong way, and die. Only exception I know is for your Knights. Because we might have to bundle you roughly out of the way. Never heard anything different. It's cast in iron."

"Well, I thought we could use his attempt to attack me, which technically means he's under a death sentence, so the Fae can heal him without his consent …"

She nodded at me, then a small smile quirked her lips.

"… Once they can treat him without the red power blocking them or him refusing consent, I'm pretty sure they're going to tell me the balance of his mind was badly disturbed. Or whatever they call it. I don't think Dai's evil. I think he's profoundly broken right now."

"Hope you're right."

"Yep, so do I, but if I'm not, well, he tried to attack the Recorder."

She laughed. "Got him coming and going. Is His Majesty alright, d'ya think?"

"Mabon's relieved. He and Ad'Rian were too close to the problem, I think. When the healers are ready to discharge him now that I've made the primary claim, they'll need the Recorder's consent before they release him. The power might know whether Dai is truly healed. I bet Rhiannon will too. She always saw him clearly."

As I said that, I realised who the mutual friend might have been. Gods and Goddesses, Rhiannon describing me as a friend might be more than I could cope with.

Caitlin said, "Gonna do that report for you on the Viking warlords." She walked over to the spare desk as Mabon headed towards the conference table, looking much more like himself. The bounce was back in his step, and his curls bobbed wildly.

"Nik-a-lula, I owe you a debt." He pulled me up into a long hug.

"No, you don't, Boney. I think we all caused this in our different ways. If Dai hadn't been shouting at me last week, I might have realised sooner. I don't think well when people shout at me."

At his frown, I tapped my third eye, hoping he'd instigate a mind link. I wanted him to know what I'd learnt about Dai both times I'd broken through his shields. Perhaps I should have told him before, but it hadn't seemed necessary, and we'd been so busy. Now I thought he needed to understand how profoundly unhappy and out-of-soul-balance his son was. Because the king was going to have to make some changes once his son was healed. I didn't think Dai was solely responsible for this mess.

I sent the information through the mind link all wrapped up for Mabon, along with my firm conviction that Dai needed far more extensive and possibly a different type of healing than whatever the Fae had tried so far. Something had snapped in his mind, and it felt like a mental health problem to me. But fixing that alone wouldn't do. Mabon was going to need a better plan going forward. I didn't think he should ever again suggest to Dai that he did anything with the dragons. He hated and feared them. It felt like a phobia.

He thought, without the power, he would be a nobody. And without the indigo power, they'd force him to become a dragon. I reprised it all quickly for Mabon. Dai desperately wanted his father's approval, and always had. The only time he got it was when he helped with the dragons or when he brought trade deals home. He was jealous of Rhiannon and her confidence, competence and determination.

Poor Mabon looked shell-shocked. I ordered us two caramel macchiatos and offered him some of the best women's magazine advice I knew. "Boney, it's not your fault if your kid chose the wrong path. You can revisit the past, but it won't help. We need to get him some help. Then I think you need to treat him differently going forward. Give him some respect and some love he doesn't have to earn and keep a closer eye on him. *Without* having everyone spy on him. That has to stop. Talk *to* him more, hey? Rather than at him? You could even listen occasionally too?"

His clear blue eyes were sad again now, but he nodded at me. "Last time we healed him in crisis mode because we thought the block being in place too long had caused all his problems. Ad'Rian said it couldn't have done that. But we treated him as an emergency, anyway."

I always hated it when Mabon used almost normal English. It meant he was dealing with a weight of emotion too big to process. Guilt settled on me because my Gift had told me several times that something was wrong with Dai, and I'd been too new in my role to trust it. I felt tears prickling and blinked rapidly.

Then Mabon's phone rang, and he exploded, "Just use the bluddy thing, people do, anytime they want!"

He picked it up and listened. "Yes, Addie, fine I am. Yes, here she is, yes. Put you on speaker, I will. In the Gateway still, I am."

Wow! His speakerphone etiquette had improved a lot.

Ad'Rian, as always, launched straight in. "Daaarling, I know everyone is overwhelmed with guilt. But sometimes minds snap; they're not made of iron. The fault is as much mine. That T&A protocol, no, that's not right. What do they call it? Ah, yes, the A&E triage that the younger healers are so fond of has its limitations. I'm reviewing it next week with them. Sometimes when we treat the most urgent issue first, we miss underlying things. The dragon power is extremely potent, and it confused everything. That will not happen again, Recorder. My word on it."

Several minutes later, we'd agreed the Fae would hold him as a high-risk patient. They would not release him without the Recorder's authority. Ad'Rian's most senior healer would send me a report when they had a better idea of how long this might all take.

I thanked him and turned back to Mabon, who'd stood to take his leave, but I remembered Dola's suggestion from earlier. "Hey Boney, before you go, Dola and I were speaking. When do you think the power level of the Recorders first declined?"

Mabon glanced around, then resumed his seat as Caitlin returned. That had been a quick report—well, I'd only asked for five minutes on each of them. Mabon obviously decided, as the Knight Adjutant, she had the right to the information too. "After Agnes."

I shared Dola's idea about Elspeth being the first one to tell her heir never to breathe the power in. He started laughing. "Oh, hated everything about the Recorder role, the witch did. She was untrained because no one expected Agnes to die. Didn't read well, hated the Book, and couldn't take heights." He laughed. "Scared of water, frightened of dogs, thought HRH was a demon. Anything she didn't understand, terrified her, it did."

Caitlin asked, "Witch?" in a tone of horrified fascination.

"Oh, a witch she wasn't, but they burned her as one, silly *ast*."

Yeah, he'd told me that the last time I'd asked. I'd also worked out Elspeth had been the idiot who told the Book to give her fewer words. And the ultimate crime, in my mind: not to teach her anything she hadn't specifically asked about.

Mabon gave me a considering look. "Didn't know the breathing it in was what made you fly. But told her once I did. Agnes was always flying around the Gateway. Elspeth said something about the power tried that with her once, and she'd put it in its place. Said, didn't I? She hated heights?"

I was beginning to see how the McKnight Recorder line had nearly died out. My gran didn't like heights, or speed, or anything else that disturbed her middle ear. She'd also disliked animals and birds. I hated heights. Did it run in the family line? Had everybody told the next in line that they shouldn't breathe it in, so nobody had to deal with the problem of being up near the ceiling of the Gateway, but, equally, nobody had any power either?

Goddess, what a mess we'd all made of it. What had Dola said? Something about I should decide how I wanted things to be for the next millennium. Well, on the bright side, that might be less trouble than attempting to fix the horrible mess my various ancestors had made of the last one.

CHAPTER
THIRTEEN

Tilly and I strolled back to the cottage through the dry and almost pleasant afternoon underneath a clear, bright blue sky. It would be cold later. I'd learned a clear sky in the daytime always made for a freezing night in Scotland.

But right now, I had an enormous smile on my face. Thanks to Caitlin's succinct but enlightening report on the three warlords, I'd finally worked out how to play a computer game and legitimately call it work.

As Tilly frolicked through the undergrowth, sniffing and scratching every leaf, I realised I was happier and better informed thanks to both the Albidosi women. Breanna and I were becoming more comfortable with each other. Women friends reached the parts of you that you didn't even realise were unhappy until you relaxed in their company. Even a new female friend could help you put the world into a shape you could understand.

I missed Aysha and needed to visit her, but Vikings definitely weren't her area of expertise. Girlfriends, old and new, are for life —if you're lucky and treat them well, and for all I felt like I had made a new one today, I'd need to catch up with my best mate soon.

But I'd summoned Troels successfully, and as for Dai, he was now the Fae Healer Hall's problem and not mine. It felt like a day where everything had gone smoothly, which was as rare as hen's teeth in this job.

Mindful of Finn hearing Rollo in the shower this morning and then telling Caitlin about it, I headed towards my den for my impromptu gaming session. It was officially research, but I knew I had a tendency to be vocal when I played, and the den was soundproofed. I didn't want to be overheard. At least not until I'd had a word with my TEK about confidentiality, not regarding the Gateway's business, which he'd already grasped perfectly and always respected. But why, when it came to my private life, did he think he could gossip?

I wasn't accustomed to having no privacy in my home, and I didn't want to get used to it. I was very fond of Finn—but there was a line, and in my mind, he'd crossed it. A memory flash of the spy cams Nick had hidden in my former home stopped me for a moment. Yeah, I might be overreacting. I should take some time to process how I'd truly felt about my late husband watching me for years without my knowledge.

From Finn's perspective, I could see how the misunderstanding might have arisen. Rollo was a friend to them both, and Caitlin was my Knight too. It was a wiggly line, but I didn't want news about Rollo and me getting out. At least not until we'd worked out what the hell we were doing, and my worries about his safety completely dissipated.

As I entered my den, I muttered at Tilly, "I should be able to eat breakfast in my pyjamas in my home without having to explain why a half-dressed Rollo is joining me. I should not have to hide in my bedroom like a teenager to get any privacy. Some idiot said, 'Well, you're a public figure now' as though that meant I should tolerate anyone who feels like it marching through my kitchen anytime they want to without knocking. I'm not a public figure if I'm not in the Gateway. The Recorder may have no right to privacy, but Niki damn well does. Perhaps I need to teach them all that."

Tilly sensibly ignored my rant and settled on her usual chair. I opened the door to the patio and allowed the warm breeze in, admiring the little magical cherry blossom that flowered permanently.

Snuggled on the cosy couch with my laptop, I saw a new Dolina had replaced the old Echo on the coffee table. Hmm, did she still have spare ones, or was she making more of them? Did Rollo have one in his Edinburgh flat?

Blast! My laptop screen was too small for this game. "Dola, would it be a major inconvenience to move the large screen from the kitchen into here for today?"

There was no answer. She must still be busy, but the landscape over the fireplace disappeared and was replaced with the super-size screen. I called "thank you" towards the Dolina.

As the loading screen of *Drengr* filled the immense display, it drew me into the world, poised to conquer as always. But this time, importantly, I also wanted to decipher the riddle of the three warlords. The ones Breanna had identified as potential claimants of the Viking throne if Rollo continued to refuse it. What had baffled me was how three of the game characters I was so familiar with could have such similar names to those real warlords. Their unexpected presence in the game that had been a part of my life for years, must be something to do with Rollo.

Some hours later, I pulled my head out of the game.

Yep, Rollo and I needed to talk because the game included not only the warlords, it had lots of other characters based on real people from the realms.

When I'd played it extensively in Manchester, I didn't have my childhood memories, so the characters in the game had been exactly that—characters. But now I'd met the real people, I easily recognised Breanna, Caitlin, Ad'Rian and L'eon. Rollo was even in there as one of the Viking gods, Thor.

If you've ever played any of the turn-based computer strategy games that have been around since the 1990s, you'll know the first ones spawned an entire genre. I played my first one at boarding school, but by the time *Drengr* came out, I'd gone off them a bit. It was hard to imagine there would be anything new in any later ones.

But then, in their annual Christmas letters, two old school friends I used to game with mentioned, along with the news about their children and partners, that they were playing an online version of a new game. Did I want to join their team? With Nick working away in the Middle East, I'd had too much time on my hands at the end of each day, and I got sucked into it.

When Breanna had given me the anglicised versions of the Viking warlords' names, things had started to make sense. Then, when Caitlin told me "Jarl" was a translation of warlord, the rest of the information tinkled like an entire cascade of pocket change, as it did when you won on one of those penny-pusher fairground arcade games. Caitlin's efficiently dictated report had solidified my certainty that I was already familiar with at least a version of these three men.

Even if that was in a computer game.

In the game, I knew a Jarl Erik Skullsplitter, a Jarl Wulf Bloodeagle, and a Jarl Ironspear. The latter had never seemed to have a first name in the game.

While they weren't quite the names of the three warlords Breanna believed might be behind Rollo's attack, I thought I could see how the real warlords, Skaldsplittr, Bloodraven and Ironshank had become their fictional game counterparts.

Just before six p.m. my webcam was active and the video conference screen open and ready on my laptop. I wanted to see Rollo.

The moment I relaxed back against the couch, Rollo came through our mind link. *"Not sure if this will make things better or worse, but I'm free for the rest of the evening. Could I zip down to you? I seem to have accidentally ordered enough Indian take-away for three people."*

Indian, ohhhh yes. One of my two favourite comfort foods. It would be a perfect end to what had been a good day.

"Talk about knowing my Achilles heel already. Did you get it from the place we used on Saturday?" That had been great food and especially welcome after all our unexpected exercise.

My brain tickled as Rollo laughed. *"I did. Be in your kitchen shortly."*

"Dola, Rollo's popping in, and he's bringing Indian food. Could we have some plates?"

By the time I reached the kitchen, the table held two trays with plates and cutlery. One with a beer glass and one with a wineglass and various serviette-y looking things.

"Niki, remember, if you leave some of each, I may be able to duplicate it for you, as you obviously enjoy this style of food, and it is not available locally."

"I love it, and I really miss it, so, yes, please. Can I have a third plate then? Don't let Finn eat the leftovers. He's in my bad books, and I love cold curry for breakfast."

Dola started to say, "What did Finn—" when Rollo landed in a swirl of yellow power too close to the table.

"Need more practise on accurate landings." He dumped the carrier bag on the table and pulled me firmly against him.

As his arms wrapped around me, almost all my concerns drifted away.

Who cared about what the hell to do with Troels now that I had him? I couldn't just let him squat in the Gateway, could I?

But for now, I put my worries about him, Caitlin, Mabon, Dai and Finn behind me.

I breathed Rollo in. He smelt like a day at the beach, a cold, crisp, clear day by the shore. I sniffed. Yep, a multi-layered salty marine breeze with something green and herby under all those delicious, refreshing, clean scents. But no citrus this time.

He started laughing.

I pulled back. "What?"

"I was hoping it wasn't eucalyptus, and you wouldn't decide I was worried like Mabon." When he saw my puzzled expression, he held his hands up, palms out. "I couldn't help it. I wasn't trying to intrude. In fact, I was trying hard not to. But you have a fascinating mind, Niki. Who knew a eucalyptus scent meant someone was worried?"

I shook my head. "It doesn't. Well, OK. It does for Mabon. But it's not a universal thing. Your worry smell might be something citrus. Ad'Rian has a cardamon overtone when he's stressed. Speaking of cardamon …"

I opened containers and ladled a modest amount of everything onto a plate. I added a small portion of the naan, which tormented me with its yeasty, warm, garlicky odours. "Take it away, Dola."

Rollo actually gaped at me. "Dola can eat? But how …"

My laughter continued longer than was probably polite. I was just shedding the last of the workday. That was my excuse, anyway.

As we settled in the den, I asked, "So why didn't Jarl Ironspear have a first name?"

Rollo glanced at my frozen screen of my game of *Drengr* on the large TV and shot me a surprised look. "That didn't take you long! Because Hjortr doesn't have an English equivalent, not one that sounds like a credible warlord's name, anyway. We debated Stag and Buck, I think, but neither was quite right. We always intended to fix it by substituting something different then we realised no one had done it before the game went live."

That made sense. "Did you keep the game versions of them true to their basic characters?"

At his chagrined nod, I laughed. "Well, that makes my research a ton easier, doesn't it? But I googled, and Skaldsplittr means nothing like Skullsplitter? It said 'skald' meant some ancient Norse stories or sagas?"

"True. Sounds much cooler, though, doesn't it? And Skullsplitter is more accurate. He's not a hero inspiring tales will be written about—he's a thug."

My paused game on the large wall screen saved itself and was replaced with a view of the Solway Firth coastline. Dola obviously wanted the screen.

Rollo sent, *"Did Dola tell you what this is about?"*

"Nope, she just booked it on my calendar. Didn't even tell me you were invited until later."

As we waited, the pair of us summoned by a sentient house to a meeting with no real idea why, it hit me how crazy my life had become. And even with the despicable Troels and now these warlords still to deal with, how much I'd begun to enjoy the insanity.

"Niki, the internet is unclear whether it would be impolite to begin the presentation while you are still eating. Please advise me?"

Rollo and I looked at each other. I tried not to giggle when he sent, *"The presentation? This I have to see!"*

I ruthlessly squashed any mirth out of my voice. "It's absolutely fine, Dola; we're the rude ones. We highjacked your meeting with the food. Thank you for your patience. Please continue."

The large-screen TV sprang to life with a view of a high-tech prison. I batted away Tilly's eternally questing nose as she searched for any "lost" spicy food on the edge of my tray and gave her a small piece of the chicken tikka.

The footage on the screen panned around the inside of a sparse, ultra-modern cell with several narrow windows, obvious internal surveillance equipment and an airlock-style double-door opening. From the Dolina, Dola's pleasant contralto said, "Finn was viewing this documentary the other day. They construct the cells from poured concrete. Once made, they fit them into pre-cast concrete substructures."

Rollo nodded as though he was familiar with the concept. I watched, and Tilly pawed me gently to remind me she hadn't tried the Himalayan ghost with roasted lamb yet—what if it wasn't as good as last week?

The large TV on the wall changed to display a PowerPoint slide.

> Warlord Troels:
> The Problems
> Our Responsibilities
> Solutions
> The Court of Public Opinion
> The Re-Brand for All Parties

I could see exactly where Dola was probably going with this, but then I'd had a lot of time—well, twenty four hours a day and, sometimes with the Gateway time dilation, far more than that since I arrived here—to get to know her.

Rollo looked flummoxed. The source of his confusion became clearer when he asked, "Dola, have you been working on this for a long time?"

"Since 1:42 p.m. today, but I had other tasks to fit in around it, King Hrólfr."

Rollo's face showed actual pain. *"By Hermod, she's quick! But less of the king stuff please."*

"Dola, as Rollo may be around here a little more, could you

please note that his preferred form of address is Rollo? He hates the title business as much as Finn does, and he has not accepted the kingship, as I believe you know."

"Yes, Niki, noted."

"Thank you." He gave me a grateful look.

"You're welcome, but, in return, you should note that, going forward, if for any reason Dola addresses you with a title, any title, she's trying to tell you something. She doesn't make mistakes. It *will* be intentional."

He opened his mouth, closed it. And then, sounding very like Finn, he asked, "Do you have an example of that?"

"Sure, if ever she calls me Recorder, she usually means I'm not behaving like the Recorder, and I damn well should be. Often when Lis and Mags Hob are around."

Now he gave me his warm smile, "Got it," and addressed the Dolina directly, "Dola, I wasn't being flippant. Your succinct summary of the situation impressed me. It's far more concise than my own notes so far. It made me wonder if you'd had a lot of time to consider it, or if I'm being slow."

"Rollo, men like Troels have existed through the ages. However, I did not have the abilities, the access to technology, or a like-minded Recorder, so I was powerless to deal with them in the past. But I have often considered what I might be able to do if I had any comrades or a voice. Now I have both."

He gave me a look that mixed sadness on Dola's behalf with admiration for her.

I said, "OK, Dola, I think I see where you're going with this, and I'm intrigued. Take it away."

Dola shared the data from the Vikings on the next screen. Their views on the Recorder's Office. Their views on Troels, on Rollo, and on Inge.

"Did we ask about Inge?" I didn't remember any questions about her.

"No, Niki, but over a quarter of the respondents, which was

almost half the female respondents, mentioned Inge in their write-in comments. All their additional notes were favourable."

"Hmm. Fi likes her. And they really don't trust the Recorder, do they?"

I'd almost inhaled my dinner—that was scrumptious food. I gave the last piece of lamb to Tilly and wondered if it would be piggy of me to go back for seconds.

Rollo shuffled uncomfortably. "Troels ran an anti-Recorder campaign …"

I waved a hand at him. "No problem, we can't fix it until we understand it, but do you know why everyone had an opinion about Inge?"

He rose, put his now empty plate and tray on the coffee table, and looked around restlessly.

I assumed he wanted the bathroom, but he simply stood looking twitchy. "What?"

"I don't. I mean, I can't …" He appeared to be stressed, but I didn't feel it through our link.

I waited.

"Sorry, unless I have a keyboard, I can't solve problems sitting down. I think better when I walk."

I recalled him marching in circles around the conference table when we were trying to fix the issue with Princess Kari.

"OK." It worked for me. Tilly needed a stroll, and I should probably walk off some of the food before I fell asleep. I stood. "Dola, send the presentation to our phones please, and I'll find my AirPods."

My earbuds arrived on the coffee table as our trays disappeared. I took his hand, whistled for Tilly to come with us, and strolled out of the door towards the garden.

"Will you be warm enough?"

Oh, bless him. "I know a place where I will be. Got your earbuds?"

As he put his in, his screen showed the presentation, too. I asked Dola to resume. We walked hand in hand towards the Gateway, connected by Dola, as she ran through her slides.

Troels was an issue. But in Dola's opinion, the Vikings' attitude against the Recorder's Office and the general anti-Recorder propaganda circulating in Viking might be the bigger problem. She believed Troels had bad-mouthed us so that even if I found him to be responsible during the arbitration, he could claim it was simply that I didn't like him, or his realm. It had been effective.

The Recorder's Office was perceived to hate the Vikings and all they stood for, to belittle their sacred rites and to be in the process of framing their king for crimes he hadn't committed. While he was much less popular than he thought, their national pride was at stake.

The next problem was that we couldn't keep Troels in a glass cage indefinitely. Gateway travellers were already talking about it. But the most compelling reason was Dola had done her research. She announced her studies had informed her that prisoners had rights, and we needed to allow the realms, particularly Viking, to see for themselves that we were not mistreating or torturing Troels.

"I do not believe we would want to align ourselves with those nations in our own world who commit human rights violations. We must give him suitable accommodation for his incarceration."

Rollo choked back a laugh. "Dola, Viking is barbaric compared to Caledonia. It's only been about eighty years since Vikings stopped suspending anyone who attempted to commit regicide in a cage or box in the main square of Haraldssund and letting them rot to death in front of the entire town. That punishment is still on the law books."

There was a brief silence before Dola said, "Yes, Rollo, I am aware. Indeed, it forms the basis of my proposal for dealing with the former king."

CHAPTER
FOURTEEN

Rollo stopped walking and simply stared at me. His thought came to me clearly. *"Is she insane?"*

"No, she's not. But her thinking is not so much outside the box as outside our era. She's ancient; you know that, right? But she's also super smart. Let's see where she's going with it."

"Interesting. Tell me more, please, Dola."

"Troels holds the record for the most petitions ever lodged against a single individual in more than a millennium by a factor of ten. But the Viking citizens do not know this. With so many petitions against him, if you plan to speak with every petitioner, we may have to hold him captive for months. We cannot do that in the Gateway. He should be home where he still believes all his people love him."

She made an excellent point. I *really* didn't want to spend months listening to all the details of how these poor women had their lives derailed by the slimeball. There had to be a better way. Not only for me, but for them as well. I said this to Dola.

"Yes, Niki. I have a suggestion about that, but first, it is important we show his people he is being detained because he tried to flee, but he isn't being mistreated. Please check your screens."

Our phone screens displayed a graphic that showed barely thirteen percent of Vikings liked Troels. Some were neutral, but most actively disliked him and weren't buying his bullshit. Even within the measly thirteen percent who approved of him, less than two percent had ticked the Strongly Approve box.

I considered what Breanna had told me this afternoon. She'd said if you only keep the top tier of society, the ones with all the power, happy—you can simply oppress the rest. These poll numbers validated her theory.

Rollo was focused on his own phone so I steered him to the left as we crossed the Gateway boundary instead of the usual path to the right, which led to the green gate.

I just avoided tripping over a small black and white cat who shot across our path and disappeared under a tree and Rollo took my arm. It was warm now, and he looked around with interest. Tilly ran ahead. She loved this walk. Bichons hate the cold, and within the Gateway's boundary, it was pleasantly warm, even on this otherwise damp, freezing Scottish night.

Dola's voice continued in my ear, "Whatever they think of him, we have a responsibility to meet his basic human rights. Food and water, medicine, clothing, light, fresh air and so on. Otherwise, as you have said before, Niki, we will not be perceived as wearing the white hats."

Rollo quirked an eyebrow at me, and I nodded. I didn't want to interrupt Dola again. There was almost nothing worse than people constantly disrupting your presentation. Janet had taught me that lesson. So I wouldn't get into it now, but, yes, we'd had that discussion.

"It is possible we can achieve solutions to," the slide on my screen flicked back to Dola's first slide, "the problems and our responsibilities by trying him in the court of public opinion. That would leave only the required rebrand for all parties."

"Dola, I need to think for a minute and speak to Rollo. Do you have much more?"

"I have several more points, perhaps five more minutes. But we can take a break while you sit. Would you like your usual?"

"Yes, please, and one for Rollo."

Rollo looked confused, but then noticed the large, old wooden picnic table with its fixed benches on either side. He turned in a circle. "Where's the light coming from? I thought it was the moon, but it hasn't risen yet."

I looked around the clearing where some early Recorder had created a small retreat with a picnic area surrounded by an inviting little glade. In here, within the warmth of the Gateway boundary, the spring bulbs were already in full bloom.

It must have been one of the earliest Recorders who created the space, because there were numbers carved into the table. The first carvings were skilful, the later ones less so. The numbers one and two were enclosed in an oblong that looked like a gravestone, as if some later Recorder had added their numbers as a tribute.

My theory was that the third Recorder created this space because number three was in the same style as the first two but without the enclosing memorial stone. Three to five were beautifully sculpted out of the wood in Roman numerals but in slightly varying styles. From seven onwards, they were in the more usual Arabic numbering system we still used. Number six, along with my own number, thirteen, were the only ones missing. For some reason, the absence of six always worried me. I kept intending to ask the Book and then forgetting.

Rollo looked around as I took my usual seat at the table by number twelve. I liked taking my coffee by my gran's number. This spot had such a peaceful vibe. It could have been in Fae. One side of the glade glowed with the rainbow light of the Gateway power, which beat my former solar-powered garden lights hands down, any night of the week. The other side was totally dark, and thousands of stars looked as if they'd been sprinkled across the heavens just for us.

As a shooting star crossed the sky, I made a wish for a few

days' peace before I had to deal with all the accusations of rape against Troels. I needed a break. I sure as hell didn't get the one I'd planned last week, thanks to Dai and his meltdown.

"The light?" Rollo asked again, bringing me back to the present.

"Sorry, it's ambient power spillover from the Gateway. The major hubs like this one have a tremendous excess of power, according to the Book. But even the individual gates have the micro-climate effect, and the Gate controls the area for some distance around them. That's why it gets warmer as you cross the boundary. Have you never noticed? Most people don't seem to, but your Fae heritage from your mother might make you more sensitive to it."

He joined me at the table. "I hadn't ever paid attention before, but when I visited the airlock in Viking, I could sense the boundary easily."

"That might be because you had the yellow regnal power by then. The monarchs seem to be more sensitive to it. They have responsibilities to the boundaries. I noticed it on my first visit when I arrived in Scotland and then again when it wasn't snowing immediately outside the blue gate the first time I went through to Aberglas with Mabon and Dai, so I asked the Book."

Two mugs of black coffee arrived on the picnic table along with two large pieces of tart. I almost let out a squeal. How embarrassing. "We got one too? OMG! Goddess bless Juniper, well, and Rockii. That is exceptionally good rhubarb."

"She left us one today. I allowed Finn a piece. There are several more left."

"The next time that Hob needs a favour, the answer is yes."

"That will not be necessary, Niki. Juniper stated it was a thank you gift for all the increased work she now has. She has promoted Lavender to be her deputy. Her business is thriving."

"It couldn't happen to a nicer Hob. Have you tried this?" I held out a forkful to Rollo, who shook his head.

"No, thank you. I must get back in control of my diet. I don't know how you stay so slim."

I paused, confused. He was in incredible shape why would he worry about a single slice of tart? "I'm pretty sure Juniper's food wouldn't dare allow anyone eating it to put weight on. Anyway, isn't rhubarb a vegetable? And Rockii's is amazing. I won't force you to eat yours, but please try one mouthful—it's an experience." I offered him the forkful.

He looked bemused. "Who's Rockii?"

"He's Rosemary's husband. The Hob who took over from Fi as the bonding coordinator in the Gateway. Oh, sorry, you guys had left the bondings ceremony by then, hadn't you? You can watch the footage. They had a seven-fold bond—it was beautiful. As is this rhubarb."

He seemed even more confused now. "A seven-fold bond?"

I explained about the eternal rings, the couples whose chakras all resonated with their partners. Kaiden and L'eon, Natalia and Tomas, and Rosemary and Rockii, who'd grown the rhubarb. Then I thrust the fork at him again.

He opened his mouth obediently. I waited, watching him closely, and sure enough, after a few seconds of chewing, he wriggled his shoulders and looked about in confusion.

"I can smell the sea and feel the sun. What *is* that?"

Dola answered him, because I was in a private heaven. "It is called Rhubarb and Almond Sunshine Break. Juniper is the Hob whom Niki set free to run her catering business. It is possible you do not know her because she refuses to work in Viking. Her staff were cruelly ill-used there."

Rollo looked as though he didn't know whether to punch something or weep. He took a forkful of his own tart and offered it to me. As I took it, he caught my eyes. "I have to fix this. It's fewer than a dozen rich, powerful idiots ruining everyone's lives. I have a plan, but the timing doesn't feel right yet, and I won't play into their hands."

Learning more about Viking was leaping to the top of my to-do list. "Can you share your plan with me?"

He looked torn. "I may need approval from the Recorder." At my frown, he said, "I mean the Gateway power rather than you. But aren't you like the power's handmaiden? Far more than your grandmother ever was?"

I suppose that was one way of putting it. But it was a weird way. I didn't know if he picked up my thoughts or my face gave away my confusion because he added, "I mean like our goddess Freyja's handmaidens. You have powers of your own, but you also translate for and communicate with the higher power."

"Do you mean, can I ask the power if it likes your plan?"

"Yes. But I'd like to discuss it with you before I do that officially with the Recorder. I need to take a few more days to check the legal ramifications."

Legal ramifications?

I said nothing, but I didn't think the power bothered too much about legal ramifications.

But I had no idea how quickly I'd find out how spectacularly wrong I was. It cared hugely about laws and agreements.

For now, I said, "Sure. Let's enjoy our tart, hear the end of Dola's presentation, and then, what if, while we're away, you bring me up to speed on Viking?"

"I don't want to spoil your holiday with that."

"I don't have a choice, Rollo. We can do it now or later. But I'm going to have to face it either way. I'd rather do it properly briefed, and we can always do something nice while we get it over with."

He gave me a warm look. It told me he was thinking of all the nice things he could do, and I shook my head. "I was thinking more of a walk or maybe a nice lunch somewhere. Pretty sure I wouldn't enjoy Troels or these warlords I'm learning about poking their heads into our bed."

He looked horrified. "Yeah, I misjudged that idea, sorry."

His quick, easy apology reminded me of Dai's failings in that department. "Dola, has Mabon contacted you about Dai?"

"No, Niki, but the Master Healer sent a report to you because you made the primary claim. Should I share the report with Mabon?"

"What does it say?"

It sounded as though she was reading it. "My lady, Prince Dafydd has been placed into a healing trance. We are holding him in a warded room. The Recorder's warning has been noted, and all have been informed about it. At my liege lord's request, I shall keep you apprised of his progress. Please be advised this may be a long process."

"Yes, share that with Mabon, but check with me before sharing any future reports. I'd hate it to upset him if anything doesn't go to plan. I'd prefer to tell him about any problems in person."

Then, wanting to wash Dai out of my mind, I took another forkful of the incredible tart. The buttery crispness of the pastry case, the sweet nuttiness of the frangipane and the tartness of the rhubarb were a brilliant combination. Even without the magical side effects, it would have been a fantastic dessert. It was gone too quickly.

"OK, Dola, do you want to finish up?"

"Yes, please observe your screens."

We did. I laughed. Rollo's expression interestingly combined awe, surprise and shock. I thought it was clear Dola wasn't just a house. Why was everyone, even the smarter people, so slow to recognise that?

"The Recorder needs to educate people about why we are detaining Troels. Where better to do that than in his hometown?"

My phone showed a graphic of a high-tech single-person cell, similar to the one in her initial documentary clip, but this version was larger and situated within the Gateway's boundary in Haraldssund, the Viking capital. Dola's plans included three speakers and several large screens affixed to the exterior of the cell. The whole thing was protected by what looked like glass—bullet-proof, I hoped. It reminded me of an exhibit in a multimedia museum.

"I'm following along so far, Dola."

My phone screen changed to a video, and the voiceover came through my earbud. It was the clip from Leif's arrival in the Gateway and his assault on Caitlin and me, along with a soundtrack that explained what was happening. The subtitles were in English, but the language wasn't. "Is that Norse?"

Rollo nodded as Dola said, "Yes. It will run in Norse and English alternately with opposing subtitles. They use several languages and dialects, but almost all the population speaks at least one of those two."

I glanced away as Leif grabbed my breast and my crotch—that had been terrifying. I'd come a long way since then. I didn't think I'd freeze in shock anymore. Rollo's fist was clenched on his lap, and I placed my hand on it gently.

The clip ended, and the next clip of Troels trying to grab Tilly started. Rollo threw his blade Nanok. His speed and accuracy were still impressive to watch. It was the size of a long, sharp carving knife, and yet he handled it as though it were a penknife.

"That truly was so cool."

He smiled at me before we both went back to our screens, but he felt sad.

The power ejected the former king from the Gateway. The voiceover in English this time explained that Prince Hrólfr had guaranteed behavioural standards on his honour while his uncle attempted to ruin the bondings for the shield maidens.

"Why are you stressing the shield maidens, Dola? There were other lovely Viking couples as well."

"The woman you called Bridezilla, with the wedding dress of Galician lace, is Elise. All the Vikings know her."

"OK why's that relev—?"

Rollo interrupted, "She's Troels and Inge's youngest. He tried to spoil his own daughter's wedding."

Whoa! I'd realised she was *someone*, by her bearing and posture, and the obvious cost of that handmade wedding dress, but I hadn't recognised her name when I'd checked it.

I said this, and Rollo offered me the information I was missing. "She uses her mother's family name. Haraldsdottir."

"Yeah, that sounds vaguely familiar."

"It means Harald's daughter. Inge's family traces their bloodline back to our first king, the one they named the capital for. Haraldssund means Harald's Strait or Harald's Sound – it's the body of water by the capital city. Inge took Elise with her when she left Troels. She was young. I was about twelve, so she would have been four or five." A shadow passed over his face.

Dola continued, "I have plans for several more hours of footage, including, with your consent, the power withdrawing the regnal power from Troels. You, Fi and the feline cleaning it, and the power giving it to Rollo. I would like to suggest breaking up this footage with some human-interest stories, if you approve the idea in principle."

My phone changed to show the first slide again, but this time the highlight moved down the list as Dola made each of her points.

Warlord Troels:
The Problems
Our Responsibilities
Solutions
The Court of Public Opinion
The Re-Brand for All Parties

Dola said, "In conclusion, if we consider each point briefly, we have discussed the problems. To fulfil our responsibilities, we must meet international standards for his care and safety. One of these cells would do that. They are widely used all around the world in this or a very similar format. They meet all the requirements for safety. We cannot allow him out for exercise, but the roof can retract to allow fresh air with a force field of power to prevent entry by a third party or exit by Troels, and I have increased the size. He will be able to stroll up and down."

I realised she'd paused, and that I'd been so caught up in how ingenious her idea was, I probably hadn't said much. I rushed into words. "It's completely brilliant, Dola. An innovative solution. I don't know how we'd do it—but it's genius."

My phone screen changed again to what looked like a blueprint. "What's this?"

"It is a detailed construction plan for the cell. I may have had to hack a little to get it. But it is accurate. You might try placing a printout of it into the Book, the same way you did with your grandmother's letter, so the Book can absorb it. Then you could ask the power if it thinks it could duplicate it and maintain it possibly for several months without too much drain."

I grinned at Rollo, who now looked completely blown away. *"Told you she was good."*

"I had no idea. She's amazing."

I liked that he liked her. I liked a lot of things about this man. Including his amazing ... eyes. Yep, his eyes. Thank goodness we'd closed most of our connection. At least he wouldn't pick up my thoughts anymore and realise the picture in my treacherous mind was of his abs. I willed myself not to go red. Oh well, he wouldn't see it in the low light level here.

He reached out to hold my hand, then changed his mind and held his arm up so I could snuggle in. As he leaned in for a kiss, I slid my hand around his neck and took a moment for myself. At least here Finn wouldn't see us and report back to anyone.

Too brief a moment, as it turned out. He pulled away. "Why are you thinking about Finn?"

I laughed and explained Finn overhearing him singing in the shower, Caitlin, the gossip. My annoyance. The lack of privacy.

"Boo, may I deal with this for you? You discussing it with Finn might set your relationship with him back. You're his boss, and he respects you enormously. It will be awkward for you, but

I could have a man-to-man chat with him about how we don't embarrass the women in our lives. If what you think about Tegan is right, it's time he learnt these things."

I thought about it, then nodded. "OK." If it didn't work, I could always speak to the TEK myself, but Rollo was probably right. It would be far less awkward for him to do it.

As he leaned in for another kiss, Dola said, "And now we come to the last point before we begin the re-branding."

See! No damn privacy!

We laughed helplessly. "Yes, sorry Dola, that point was ...?" My brain was occupied with other things now.

"The court of public opinion." The slide on my screen flashed.

"Niki, I request and require your permission to conduct an experiment. I will need assistance from Glynis and Finn. I have obtained their in-principle agreements."

Request and require—wow she was deadly serious about this, wasn't she?

"I do not wish to explain or discuss it with you yet, because it may not work. Or if it does, it still may not give us what we need. But I offer my assurance that I will release nothing publicly without your approval. May I have permission to test this now?"

She'd been very good since the Devicegate debacle with all the Dolinas. Our meeting to discuss ethics had gone on for hours until everyone was clear on the same objectives and restrictions. I had to trust her. She and Finn were the warriors, and if I was wrong, Caitlin and I would clear up the mess.

"Yes, you have it."

She squealed with excitement right in my ear. When the hell had she started squealing? I blamed Aysha and Autumn—they were having a bad influence on her.

"Thank you, Dola."

I took my earbud out, pulled the last of his tart over, and snuggled into Rollo. "Fancy a little sunshine break together?"

Rollo had transported back to Edinburgh. He had a breakfast meeting tomorrow, and he still hadn't been forthcoming about what he was trying to achieve. Oh well, we'd have some time together next week on our holiday. Damn, we hadn't decided where we were going, had we? I wondered if he'd like to go to the Canary Islands? Aysha and I had a wonderful holiday there when she was expecting Autumn and we'd needed some sun.

When I got back to the kitchen, the cat, who'd kept a very low profile since yesterday evening, was waiting. She sniffed the air and gazed hopefully at the cupboard where her tuna lived. She looked small, harmless, and hungry.

I fell for it, but as I opened her cupboard, I remembered what had confused me. "Hey, Your Majesty, yesterday when you were healing Rollo's right arm." Her bright green eyes turned to my face. "You said something about they'd broken all the bones in his arm to prevent him duelling Troels?"

She stiffened and the fur down the back of her neck stood up. "I did not."

I glared at her.

"Recorder, I did not say that. You were distressed. Perhaps your memory is faulty."

I said, "Dola, could you—"

Immediately from the Dolina on the table came the recording of the cat's words. "Almost every bone broken. They wanted to cripple his sword arm. It's one way to prevent Rollo from being able to duel that plague on ordinary women. Fools and knaves, all of them."

I pointed at the Dolina. "That!"

HRH sat on the table, curled her tail around her front paws in what I always thought of as her goddess pose and, in her most patronising tone, drawled, "You appear to be under the impression there is only one female-abusing coward in the Viking realm, Recorder. However, that is not the case."

I'd had enough. I avoided stamping my foot, but I suspected my tone was past abrupt and headed towards curt. "Who *were* you referring to?"

"Warlord Halvor, obviously."

PART THREE
THURSDAY

For every warrior, the moment comes when you pause and glance back. Only then do you realise how far you've travelled.

Our comrades and blade mates serve as trusted mirrors, reflecting the growth they've witnessed.

Embrace your transformation.

Throughout your journey, there should be times to fight and times to celebrate progress.

Ensure you know the difference and balance the hours you give to each.

Winning the War Against Yourself: Daily Weapon and Warrior Care by Arinn Tusensköna

CHAPTER
FIFTEEN

Thursday, 4th March, Gateway Cottage—Dragon O'clock
"Niki, I am sorry to disturb you, but you may wish to observe the Gateway."

"What time is it? Coffee?"

"It is two minutes to seven." A yellow mug of deliciously dark coffee arrived. In a gothic font, I read, *Here be Winged Snakes*. There was a cheery cartoon of a cuddly-looking baby dragonet. It looked a lot like the dragon plushie Autumn had made me buy for Tilly in that out-of-town toy shop. Huh!

I staggered through to the bathroom, mug in hand, and touched the seven-pointed star in my mirror to see what was happening.

"When did they arrive?"

"Eighteen minutes ago. They have done nothing more offensive than critique Warlord Troels' skincare regimen. There have been many jokes about what to call the opposite of an anti-aging serum."

I laughed and wondered, if I ignored them, would it sort itself out? Dola hadn't said they'd asked for me. Sometimes inaction is better than the wrong action.

Yeah, I was kidding myself—it probably wouldn't sort itself out.

Back at the mirror, I touched the centre. "Good morning, ladies. Would you like to join me for breakfast?"

Glynis spun around in a full 360, her eyes darting all around the Gateway. In contrast without even turning around, Rhiannon replied, "Thanks, Niki. That'd be good. Can I have a coffee for the walk over?"

Wow, she'd relaxed. I thought about Mabon's comment about a mutual friend yesterday and wondered again if he'd been referring to Rhiannon. But what the hell had changed her from her stroppy sourpuss self of last weekend into this? I watched as, in the Gateway, a vanilla latte arrived on the corner of my desk. "It's behind you. Glynis, will you join us?"

Glynis bowed in the general direction of the centre. "My apologies, Recorder. Be at work shortly, I must." She sounded flustered, and her Welsh accent was stronger than usual.

"No problem. I think Dola needs to talk to you later. Could you reach out to her when you're not so busy?" She nodded repeatedly. "Rhiannon ap Modron, I invite you to the cottage for breakfast."

Rhiannon nodded absently and gave me a thumbs-up in the air as she strolled around the glass cage, still surveying the furious Troels from every angle. He was poking the inside of the glass wall, and his mouth moved constantly. Rhiannon gave his attempt at communication as much attention as I might give to a spider I'd trapped with an inverted drinking glass.

As I got dressed, I giggled at Tilly, who refused to leave the bed and crawled into the warm spot I'd left behind. She buried her head under the pillow. It wasn't morning in her world yet. I wished it wasn't in mine.

I checked Rhiannon out as she settled herself at my kitchen table. She looked different, and not only because she was only wearing a T-shirt on a freezing Scottish morning. I peered at her torso and choked back a laugh. *Welcome to the Karma Cafe. There is no menu. I'll serve what you deserve.* I hoped that was aimed at Troels and not me.

"What would you like, Rhiannon?"

She gave me a thoughtful look. "What are you having?"

I was barely awake. More coffee was my only real thought, so I went with autopilot and the breakfast I could always eat. "Smashed eggs and salmon please, Dola, times two. One with toast and one without, and please don't give me any grief, or I'll end up having to give her mine."

Rhiannon's face held an interesting expression as I repeated, "What would you like?"

"Oh, the second one isn't for me? Then I'll have the same, please. It was one of Agnes' favourite breakfasts, you know, but she called it buttered eggs." She gave a small smile, which surprised me. Before she mused, "She used to feed them to the cat."

Dola chipped in, "The recipe I use is from Morag. The name has changed, but the dish hasn't."

"Morag?" I queried.

Rhiannon said, "Agnes' grandmother."

At the same time as Dola said, "The fifth Recorder."

Well, weren't we all getting along swimmingly? But what did Rhiannon want with her new pleasant persona? And that reminded me.

"Who was the sixth recorder? I keep meaning to ask the Book."

Again, I got two different answers.

From Rhiannon, her voice laden with disgust, "Agnes' older sister."

From Dola, "Mairi McKnight."

I didn't think I'd ever heard the name. Well, that wasn't true.

I'd heard the name when the Hobs danced drunkenly out of my office to something Fi later called Mairi's Wedding. That tune had been a dreadful earworm. But I'd never heard the name used for a real person. I'd ask the Book.

But Rhiannon surprised me when she volunteered. "Stupid, frightened, stubborn, ignorant, petty-minded little rabbit. How they could have been related, I never understood. I assumed they had different fathers. Agnes didn't know. Her mother died in childbirth with the baby after Agnes. Her grandmother Morag raised Agnes, but her mother's sister raised Mairi."

Wow! Rhiannon was better than the Book. I sat motionless, barely breathing, and hoped she wouldn't stop.

She didn't. "Agnes didn't like the woman either. Mairi was such a mouse. 'Oh, Agnes, you can't do that. It's so dangerous.' 'Oh Agnes, that's no' a proper way for a maiden to behave.' 'Oh Agnes, don't play with the power. It's too dangerous.' The worst was 'Ooooh Agnes, dragons have all kinds of diseases. Keep away from the dirty creatures.'"

I couldn't help it. A laugh exploded out of me.

She focused back on me. "I despise spineless women."

"What happened to her?"

A feral smile spread across her attractive face, and her T-shirt changed.

Most octopus mothers give up their lives to hatch their babies — needlessly!

I frowned. I had no idea where she was going with this. The things I knew about octopuses? Octopi? didn't even include how to make a plural of their name correctly.

But Dola obviously got the joke because light laughter came from the Dolina.

"Could someone explain the joke? What happened to Mairi?"

Dola said, "She spent almost six months living in the wood store because she said this cottage was haunted. I cannot tell you much about her except she refused to bond with the power and died in childbirth. Then Agnes came and said she was the new Recorder. At least she greeted me."

Rhiannon added, "Mairi was pregnant when she ascended. She never forgave her grandmother for making her a single mother. She refused to bond with the power."

At my shocked expression, Rhiannon said, "What?"

I didn't want to stop this fascinating history lesson, but I had to know. "Why would Morag have made her a single mother?"

Rhiannon snorted. "She didn't, of course. Mairi's husband was as spineless as her. He thought the Recorders were witches. Morag terrified him. So, when she left Mairi the cottage and the Recordership, he wouldn't have any more to do with his wife. He would have been consorting with a witch. To be fair, that was a consideration in the mid-1500s. Thankfully, neither of them ever found out about the trust. The amount of money in the trust even back then might have talked him around. He was a little weasel of a man. Agnes used to call him VV."

At my shrug of confusion, Rhiannon added, "Viverridae Visage."

Yeah, I was no wiser. "What did that mean?"

She paused and looked down at the table for a moment, then grinned at me. "The modern version might be Ferret Face."

I grinned back at her. "And what happened to Mairi?"

"The headaches drove her mad with pain. She died. Might have been a stroke from the headaches or in childbirth. Things weren't always as clear in the past. They described any dead pregnant woman as having died in childbirth even if they weren't in labour at the time. Agnes always thought she injured herself by banging her head against logs when the headaches got too bad. But Mairi refused to set foot in the Gateway because the dirty, dangerous power might harm her unborn child! Idiot woman."

All my ancestors seemed to have been unbalanced in their different ways. Should I worry? I'd need time to process all that and consult the Book. Rhiannon's and Dola's opinions might be dangerously skewed.

I reached out extremely cautiously with my Gift. Rhiannon could be rude about people reading her. She focused on me immediately. "Need something?"

"I wondered what I did to get the pleasure of your company at this hour of the night?"

"Not a chirpy morning soul, are you? You fooled me on Monday by being so awake before we went flying. But you are very like her, and you left me in your debt. I always pay my debts, Recorder."

"OK?"

"I owe you two debts. That's two too many. And I may ask for something that incurs a third. I haven't yet decided."

She had no Welsh accent at all. I'd noticed it several times, but it was starting to bug me. "Why don't you have a Welsh accent?"

"Have one, I can, if insist you do. Keep the Welsh for the swearing, mostly, *bach*." Her sing-song lilt was so at odds with her glare that I laughed.

"OK, then why don't you choose to have a Welsh accent?"

"Spent a lot of time out of my realm. Smoothed it out over the centuries. It was never my mother tongue." She looked impatient. Obviously, her good mood didn't stretch to small talk. "Now, I owe you a passphrase. Pains me to admit it, but you were right. I read the coffee cup properly in the end."

"OK."

Why was "OK" all I seemed to be able to say today? Oh yeah, I wasn't awake. "Dola, can I have more coffee, please?"

My coffee and, oh praise the Goddess Plentia, three plates of eggs and smoked salmon arrived, two of them with toast.

Rhiannon breathed in, smiled, and stuck her fork in the eggs. After chewing contemplatively, she said, "Thank you, Dola. It is Morag's recipe. Is there any of that relish that we used to eat with them?"

A pot arrived on the table in front of her as Dola asked, "This one?"

Rhiannon fell on it, and with the happiest expression I'd ever seen on her face. After opening the round, flat ceramic container and scooping a knifeful onto her eggs, she mashed the brown substance into them like a two-year-old and tasted. She let out a moan of pleasure, spread a little more, sparingly, onto her toast and hummed to herself.

HRH arrived on the table, gave Rhiannon a surprised look out of very green eyes, and then sniffed. She stuck her nose into the flat pot of relish, which looked nothing like relish. It looked like some kind of pâté, and licked.

Quick as a snake, Rhiannon struck lightly with the flat of her knife on HRH's head. "Manners, madam."

She scooped some of the mush out and mashed it into the cat's eggs for her with her own fork and then carried on eating without another word being exchanged between them.

I ate my own eggs and watched Rhiannon and the cat, apparently taking great care to ignore each other. But given what excellent peripheral vision they both had, I was unconvinced by their performance.

Rhiannon pushed her plate away, sighed, and said, "Thank you both. That was a happy memory."

"What is it?" I picked up the pot and sniffed. There was no label on it. It smelt of buttery fish.

"Anchovy butter. Some chap publicly 'invented' it a hundred or so years ago. He called it Gentleman's Relish or some such nonsense. But Morag and Agnes had a relative who made it centuries before that. It's nothing like relish, so I don't know why he called it that. Mabon said even the Romans had a very exclusive, high-priced version of it. Agnes used to bring him a pot of her aunt's when he was depressed. Try it one day when you're awake." She slid her eyes fractionally sideways towards HRH and added, "It used to be a sought-after reward."

HRH finally addressed me, "Thank you, Recorder. I am

delighted to see *garum* is once again on the menu. Walk with me, Rhiannon."

Rhiannon shook her head. "Came to see Niki. We have private business. Catch you later." And then she stared pointedly at HRH until she left.

CHAPTER
SIXTEEN

"Excuse me a moment, Rhiannon." I pulled power and swirled it around the kitchen to make sure the damn cat had actually left. Wow, wonders would never cease, because she'd really gone. I *must* find out how Rhiannon did that.

Rhiannon watched me with interest, and I remembered she didn't know I could use power outside the Gateway—crap! How the hell had I become so relaxed with a dragon at my kitchen table?

"How do you *do* that? Agnes couldn't use the power in here. And she wouldn't have been able to use it on the mountain, the way you did when you re-opened the Dragon Gate."

I took the exact flat tone she'd taken with HRH. "Promise to keep it to yourself if I answer you."

Astonishingly, it worked, and she nodded seriously at me. "I promise."

Rhiannon liked her tech. She was the only member of her family who might actually understand the answer.

"I link to the Rainbow Network and the Gateway power over Wi-Fi."

Her laugh was a rich, melodious, wonderful thing, even if it sounded rusty. "May I have another coffee? I need to pay my debts."

"Of course. Dola, can we have two more please, if you're not busy?"

I sent her a message.

> Niki: Split the words from the wine glasses Aysha gave me between the mugs, will you? Put "But your best friend will …" on Rhiannon's.

> Dola: OK

Rhiannon gave me a quick glance. "What would the house be busy with? Isn't taking care of you what she does?"

"She's my equerry now. She has a lot on today with Troels, the petitions, some research she's doing and Breanna's book club. You were at the bondings when I announced her new role, weren't you?"

"Yeah, but I don't know what 'equerry' means other than the horse guys in the old days; thought it was a new title for housekeeper or house manager."

Huh, I wondered how many others thought the same? Oh well. They'd find out in time. Maybe I should start an education program on Dola's behalf.

Rhiannon frowned at me. "What are you going to do about Troels?"

"Speak to the royals at Breanna's book club tonight, get their ideas and then present Dola's."

She rolled her eyes. It looked surprisingly funny when added to the usually harsh lines of her face. "They'll offer an oubliette, some distant deserted glade with teeth in Fae, their sympathy and complaints—many, many complaints. Why would you think they'd have any good ideas?"

I grinned. It wasn't just me who thought they were predictable. I remembered Fi's comment about Rhiannon's response. "You're a royal now too. You'd offer to eat him."

She nodded. "He's aged badly; he'd be very tough. But hungry dragonets are never fussy. So what are you going to do with him?"

"Come to the book club and find out if you want to know. Honestly, I could use your help to calm them all down when we show them Dola's multimedia plan."

She looked thoughtful. "I didn't get an invitation."

"When did that ever stop you? I'm giving you your invite now. Eight o'clock in the Gateway. Use it or don't. Juniper's doing the food."

She was so like Aysha, I'd have to leave it up to her. I moved on quickly. "So how do we set up a replacement passphrase? And what was I right about?"

There was a puzzled quirk to her lips. "You don't use passphrases? Or haven't before?"

"Nope. If I need my best mate to stop being difficult and engage her brain, I just ask her to. The ap Modrons seem to work differently. But I can adjust."

"You give me the first part because it's your phrase. I give you the second part, and then, if you need to use it, you have to know all of it. But how did you use the 'dragons can fly because they take themselves lightly; the angels just stole all the best lines' phrase properly if you didn't know how they worked? You put the second part in the bottom of my coffee mug waaay ahead of time."

"Oh, coffee mugs are different. I know how they work." I lifted mine to her.

Dola had done it perfectly. My green mug said, *A good friend will help you bury a body. A great friend brings their own shovel.*

Rhiannon's mug was the same elegant shape but bright red and said, *But your best friend will ...*

She surveyed my mug, smiled to herself and then read her own. "Need to change the word 'will' to 'would,' and I can make this work." As she watched, Dola changed it. She said, "Interesting. Then if you'd add the rest, please, Dola?"

"Certainly, Queen Rhiannon."

Rhiannon avoided doing a double take but gave me a look that said, *how does she know that?*

"My Equerry, remember? Think of her as another Knight Adjutant, perhaps even the more senior one."

She nodded and read the mug aloud, *"A good friend will help you bury a body. A great friend brings their own shovel. But your best friend would have eaten the idiot before they got on your last nerve."*

I chuckled and wished I'd known her years ago. It was such a shame he was dead.

Dola changed Rhiannon's mug to match her words, and I put them together and snapped a photo.

"Don't put it in the flaming Book."

I shook my head. "I can't agree to that, sorry, but I will wrap it up as tightly as Agnes did. If I hadn't had only good intentions towards you, I could never have found the one I did. It sat there unused for how long?"

"Since … by the Goddess … the 1600s, maybe a bit earlier. Has she been gone that flaming long?" She gave a heavy sigh. "Feels like millennia on the bad days, and like yesterday on the good ones."

I sipped my coffee and gave her a little privacy.

But she was fine and asked. "The gate you re-opened on the mountain for the dragons?"

"Mmmhm?"

"You didn't have to do that?"

"No."

"The dragon on the door is upside down, but you didn't know it should be. The only tapestry of it was in storage. How did you know?

I shrugged, "I didn't. The power did that itself. Why?"

She shook her head at me. It seemed I wasn't getting any more information. "It means I owe you. Two of the eggs have already changed to the pink colour that suggests they contain rose gold queens. They changed yesterday. I've never seen it before, but we have some records left. And some paintings and tapestries." An expression of wonder crossed her face. "Might be real queens in the sky again. Magical. I owe you a debt, Recorder."

When Breanna gave me her life debt, I'd learnt how to accept them. You smiled serenely and nodded. So I did both now. "I'm happy I could help."

"Nothing you want?" Rhiannon sounded irritated, as if she didn't want it hanging over her.

"I'm sure there will be. But the only things I want right now are so stupidly minor, I wouldn't waste them on that debt."

Now she looked interested as she sipped her coffee. "Such as?"

"I want to know how you do that." I pointed at her T-shirt where the words about Mairi sacrificing her life and that of her unborn baby unnecessarily had been joined by an upside-down, sad-looking octopus and what appeared to be bunches of grapes. Actually, perhaps they were octopus eggs. It made no sense to me, so I moved on. "Or put racing stripes down your dragon. Does your dragon side have its own name, or is it all you? I mean etiquette-wise, should I greet it or only you? Like I said, minor things, oh, and one other thing." She nodded. "Do you know Glais'Nee?"

"Yes, he's not a *pen pidyn*." Not being a dickhead was high praise from Rhiannon, judging by her pleasant expression.

"Would adding my phone to your Rainbow Network as you did for Mabon be a major or minor favour?" she enquired too casually.

Oh yesssss! I clamped my shields tight before she realised I'd been considering this for a while. "Can I ask why? You seem to have the issue under control with your 'Mine' network."

"Do you speak Welsh, Niki?"

"Nope." I didn't think I'd explain that Dola had translated the *Eiddof Fi* name of Rhiannon's network for me. She'd said it probably meant "mine."

"Then you guessed correctly. I was using the regnal power for that network, and using it has a cost. If it costs the life of even a single unbonded hatchling, because I've used the power for something else, the price is too high. I'd rather find another way, or I'll be no better than Dai frittering the flaming power away, will I?"

She'd been distraught about the loss of the unbonded hatchlings, and when she'd talked about having to kill the feral ones, her eyes had been haunted.

"I created *Eiddof Fi* because people need to reach me quickly when the hatching starts. It's the easiest time to bond them into the existing pack, and it means they'll be able to use their dragon and human sides properly when they grow up. The Rainbow Network is obviously a better solution. I didn't have a choice before; perhaps I do now."

I'd given a lot of thought to what Ad'Rian said about the way I used tech to connect with those people I cared about. I wasn't yet convinced I even liked Rhiannon, but I admired her devotion to her dragons. Ad'Rian had also quoted an American president when he was giving me advice during the Smiths' problem. I'd looked it up, and it was actually Lyndon B Johnson who'd said, *"It's better to have an enemy inside your tent pissing out, than outside your tent pissing in."* I'd rather have the dragons on my side, and not only to avoid puddles on the Gateway floor. And Dola's ability to track Rhiannon on the Rainbow Network might be useful.

I nodded. "Sure. I'll do it if you tell me how you do that," I pointed at her T-shirt, "and you agree to meet Glais'Nee for five minutes in the next week. He's coming to Breanna's book club in the Gateway tonight, if you want to get it over with."

She nodded. "No one knows how I can do this." She ran her hand down the motto on her T-shirt. "If I tell you, can we keep it on the same basis as me knowing you can use the power in here?"

"Works for me. Got your phone?"

"You can do it now?" She didn't quite hide the eagerness in her tone. I wondered why it was suddenly so important.

"Is it urgent?" I watched her face as she overrode her clear reluctance to tell anyone anything they didn't need to know.

"The first dragonets will hatch soon is all." She tried to make it sound offhand and failed.

I took pity on her. "Then let's get it done. Remove the case, open it, tell the power you understand your phone is being added to its network and all that entails. It's the same conditions you would have agreed to when you first used the Rainbow Network for a computer. Then give me your hand."

She obviously did exactly that because, when I touched her phone with a spark of power, it changed in her hand. It had been an older model, but it wasn't anymore. It had received a full upgrade and turned the characteristic purple.

She turned it around in her hand. "I didn't think you'd agree. Mabon said you refused Dai several times."

I decided to be honest with her. "Dai was triggering all my warning instincts, even though I couldn't pin down why. Once Ad'Rian showed me what he'd been doing with the red regnal power, I understood I'd been right to listen to those instincts."

"And I don't trigger them?" Rhiannon looked interested in my answer.

"No, you remind me too much of my best mate. She was super prickly the first year we knew each other. She had cause, not from me, but she had cause. And what Agnes said about you in the Book reminded me of her. I don't always like Aysha, but I always love and trust her."

Rhiannon appeared to be lost for words. Then she started laughing again. It was a lovely sound and getting less rusty by the minute.

Her T-shirt changed to a fist with an upraised middle finger. She glanced down at it. "This was all I could do with it for the longest time. Agnes was in stitches every time she saw it."

"Who were you giving the finger to?"

"Her, of course. This is all her fault."

Now, I had to hear this story. "Dola, can we have yet more coffee, and is there any of the pie left?"

Rhiannon immediately said, "Love a coffee, but no pie for me."

"You'll regret it; it's one of Juniper's. It's a quick holiday in a pie."

A look of fascination crossed her face. "Ignore me, Dola. Pie would be great, thanks. The dragon is all me. It's just magic. Logically, the conservation of mass should apply, but it doesn't. Thanks to the aforementioned magic and Mo-Mo, my grandmother, the Goddess Modron's powers. She created the dragons originally to protect the realm. Etiquette is to speak to whichever bit you like, but when we let the dragon part out, it has its own instincts, so stay out of the line of flame."

"Got it." I had about million more questions, but maybe if she started to relax with me, I'd get more answers in the future.

She tilted her head. "Do you know what pitch is?"

"Like a football pitch or in music or like the roofing stuff?"

She smirked. "Yeah. Coal tar pitch, the roofing, flooring material. Black, sticky, burning stuff."

I nodded.

"Agnes always said dragon hides were impenetrable. We'd been flying one cold winter night. I'd changed back, and we settled in there." She pointed towards the door to the lounge. "Agnes used it as a sitting room-cum-bedroom. Drink may have been taken. Quite a lot of it. Back in the day in Scotland, your choice was whisky or whisky. They were proud of their national drink."

I remembered when Dola hadn't been able to produce brandy for me when I was in shock. Hadn't she said no one ever brought any here for her to sample?

Rhiannon continued, "Or bad beer and occasionally cider. Cocktails and long drinks weren't a thing."

"You two got drunk. OK. And …?"

"Eventually she passed out. She would want me to tell you she went to sleep, but she passed out. I staggered back to the Gateway, and she'd left the barriers up so I couldn't get home. Her barriers were like yours are—impregnable, not like your gran's. I could get around hers. Good job too—one-in, one-out indeed! Anyway, I couldn't face walking back here. I may have been merry myself because I went to the Recorder's Refuge to get out of the icy weather, and knowing I had to sleep under the stars, I shifted. Dragons don't feel the cold. Or notice rocks under their backside. Then I passed out too."

"Recorder's Refuge?"

"The clearing? It's like a glade? The old table with all, well, almost all the Recorder's numbers carved into it?"

Where I'd been last night with Rollo. I nodded. "That's why I'd asked who the sixth Recorder was. I've wondered why her number isn't carved into the table."

The coffees and two plates of pie arrived. Rhiannon stabbed her fork into the pie and shovelled a too-large piece into her mouth as though she wanted to be sure she couldn't let any more words out.

The expected look of bliss crossed her face. It lightened her normally forbidding countenance and made me wonder who the woman underneath all her years of frustration was and if I'd ever get to meet her.

She smiled, swallowed, then sipped her coffee. "Oh, that is quite a pie. Anyway, the next day I woke up, at lunchtime, and painted down my dragon's side was a limerick." She pretended to glare at me, but there was humour in her eyes, and I gave her a *go on, then, tell me* gesture.

She recited,
"A woman from Pant y Wern,
simply wouldn't learn,
too much drink has its price
but her friend was quite nice
and made sure the pitch wouldn't burn.

It was something like that, not literature, for sure. She signed it with kisses, a sarcastic little vixen she was. Get the idea?"

I giggled. The picture she painted of a dragon's side as the canvas for a bad limerick from a woman who'd probably been her best friend was too funny not to laugh at, but it made me sad too.

"And it was pitch. They'd been using it for the roof of one of the storage sheds. I couldn't lick it off, so I changed back because that fixes most things. But then it was part of my skin. Like a flaming brand."

As I watched, the middle finger moved from her T-shirt to her forearm. Exactly like a large black tattoo.

"Eventually, I worked out how to have some fun with it."

The tattoo disappeared, and her T-shirt changed to say, *Recorders—don't drink with them. But if you do ... Wake up first.*

CHAPTER
SEVENTEEN

After Rhiannon left, I went back to bed. I was sick of being tired, and tonight with Breanna's event might be a late evening. I didn't want to be that woman who slept through book club. Tilly was still snoring when I crawled into bed. I reached out towards Rollo in Edinburgh, but he felt busy, his head full of numbers, so I backed away quietly.

Dola told me she needed another hour to work on completing her plan for Troels. I'd put the blueprint for his cell into the Book as she'd requested and told her to wake me if anything worrying happened.

I was avoiding dealing with the former Viking king. I didn't like the picture of myself as a coward, but that creepy old man made my skin crawl. My courage would arrive once we had his cell—I hoped.

Troels lived in his own reality, which didn't include any acceptance of the things far too many women said he did. I had no idea how to talk to him.

So I rolled myself into my duvet and slept.

. . .

My phone vibrating on the bedside table woke me with Aysha's name on the screen. I ignored her until I'd had coffee and time to think about how to handle her because I could already predict her response.

"Is everything OK in the Gateway, Dola? Do I have time to call Aysha back?"

"Please, please do that, Niki. She is currently, I believe you would describe it as ranting, at the wall in her kitchen. She keeps mentioning someone called Shirley Valentine and saying, 'You're my friend, wall. What do you think I should do about Nik?' She knows I can hear her through her Dolina, and her comments appear to be aimed at me. But, as I am unacquainted with Ms Valentine, I can only assume Aysha wishes me to tell you all this."

I dialled.

"Do not hang up on me, Niki. You said you'd get back to me. Why haven't you? Are you OK?"

Before I could get a word out in reply, she continued, "I've been worried sick. Autumn's being odd. She's missing you and Tilly."

I drew breath to reassure her, but I was too slow.

"Peter has a question about the heating system at your house. Some guy called around to service it, but you hadn't told him, so he didn't know if it was OK to let him in. You weren't answering your phone. Dola said she couldn't reach you. And Jen wants to go home, and I don't know what to do about Tim. You can't go off-piste like this. Are you OK? Because you don't sound OK."

I breathed again and prepared to jump in. But Aysha didn't seem to need any extra air; she was still in full flood.

"Didn't we always say we wouldn't be those women who dropped their girlfriends for a man? And you never did for Nick, and I know the hoops you had to jump through when he was still in the UK. Well … and alive. Oh, blast. I didn't mean that. I meant suddenly with Prince Charming, you're just not speaking to me?"

I drew breath yet again and opened my mouth, but, no, I was still too slow.

"It's not like you to be so inconsiderate of everyone. Even my mother asked when I'd last heard from you, and you know once Olive starts, there's no shutting her up."

Yep, that's exactly where you get it from, Shay-girl, isn't it?

I opened my messages app and listened with half an ear as she berated me up, down, and sideways for not checking in. Bless her. To an outsider, this might all sound abusive, but with everyone except Autumn, Aysha channelled her fear into anger.

> Niki: I have ten minutes to let my best friend know I'm absolutely awesome, just stupidly busy. There have even been literal fires to put out. Dragons, you know. But she won't shut up long enough to let me do it.

"I told Autumn if you didn't check in tomorrow, we're getting on a train to Scotland."

Yep, I'd seen that one coming too.

"Dola said she'd give us a bed for the night, but she couldn't say whether you'd be at home. What is she covering up? Why wouldn't you be there? What's happening, Niki? Do I need to worry? Oh, hell, now some idiot's messaging me. Hold one minute."

Blissful silence for a few seconds, and then she laughed. "Oh, sorry. You should talk now."

I finally got a word in. "I'm fine—very well, in fact. But it's been mad. I've got loads to tell you and no real time to do that at the moment."

"You looked amazing in that photo you sent. Dai's obviously having a wonderful effect on you. I'd no idea he was such a hunk."

Oh hell, what did I do now?

I didn't think I had any big girl pants large enough for this, but it couldn't go on any longer, or she would be hurt. "Ah, yeah,

Dai. He had a kind of breakdown. It's complicated. He refused to let the Fae heal him. He tried to hold me hostage. Twice, actually, well, almost three times, although I suppose the third time was more of a set up—"

Her horrified gasp down the phone line made me pause but then I barrelled on. "Of course, you can't do that to a Recorder. So, everything is fine. I'm fine. Well, Dai's not fine. He's not well at all, but it's a very long story. I should have followed my instincts. I really didn't want to go, and it wasn't just nerves. It was intuition, and I overrode it. I won't do that again."

"OMG, and I threatened you and made you go. I'm so sorry. I thought you'd lost your bottle. Dola made it sound like a panic attack. Nik, I feel awful."

"Don't. Not your fault. I could have stood up to you."

"But I threatened you with Janet." She sounded distraught now.

"Shay, you *do* know Janet couldn't even get through my gate unless Dola wanted her to, don't you? She can electrify those wrought-iron railings and sink intruders into quicksand and then blow a Force 9 gale at them if she's in the wrong mood. It wasn't your fault. I *could* have ignored you."

"But if Dai went crazy, then whose chest were you getting ready to lick?"

"Ah, that would be Rollo."

"Rollo? Rollo! The Thor look-alike from your ascension ceremony? *That* Rollo?"

She had a hell of a good memory for names and faces.

Astonishment coloured her tone, "But you were worried Dai looked younger than you. We laughed about age-gap relationships. How old is this Rollo? I mean, it doesn't matter. You do you, boo; I'm just being nosy."

I chuckled at her inadvertent use of boo. "Seriously, Shay?"

"Yeah, sorry, none of my business. Can you come down tonight, or if it's truly not possible, we could come up to you? Autumn is missing you."

I gave her a quick overview of the Recorder parts of the last week, ending with Troels and the book club planning session tonight.

"But, Nik, it's only been a week since we spoke. Dragons, John Fergusson's skull—I think I'm going to pretend you didn't tell me that. An officer of the court shouldn't hear things like that. Kidnapping, deposed kings, mentally disturbed princes and book clubs. Your life is not dull, girl. Although, I see you managed to fit in a fling with your boy-toy, but, OK, not tonight, tomorrow then?"

"Yeah, we'd earned that personal time. The Vikings tried to have him killed and only succeeded in beating him almost to death. After a goddess and I spent six hours magically healing him, I suppose you could say we found some time to celebrate being alive. We leave on holiday tomorrow."

Finally, there was complete silence.

Then, in a tentative voice I'd rarely heard Aysha use, she said, "Nik, I didn't want to tell you this. It'll sound like I'm guilt-tripping you, but Autumn's being peculiar again. It started last Saturday; she seemed upset. She keeps asking if I've heard from you. On Tuesday, she wouldn't eat her tea. She sat on her bed with all the unicorns around her. It was creepy—it looked like they were in a prayer circle. I mean, Mum would have been pleased, but I was scared.

"Yesterday at bedtime, she was rubbing her tummy and said I had to call you. If you truly can't get down here, could you call her after school and see what the problem is? I can't get any sense out of her. She said something about a lady came, so it would be OK. But when I asked which lady, she said a princess lady, and I didn't know her, but Auntie Nik did. Then this morning, when I took her to school, she said, 'Mum, I need to tell her.' Then she said, 'Call her, Mum. Today. She can come for tea.' And, Nik, she said it in her firm voice."

I thought about the times when Autumn had used her firm voice before. She'd only been about two or three the first time. In a strangely adult voice, she'd wrapped her pudgy little arms around Tilly and told her everything would be OK, and she would come and stay with them and be safe. It was the weekend after that Nick told me to have Tilly put down, and I had taken her to stay at Aysha's until he'd left for the Middle East. There had been a few other weird things, like that time she told me not to take bad teddy into my house. Yeah, Autumn's firm voice wasn't to be ignored.

"I'll find time to come down, probably tomorrow, but I'll call her after school today. OK?"

I heard her sigh of relief. "Thanks, I could use a bit of support with her right now. Even an hour tomorrow would be great."

"Shay, I'll call her, I promise. What's this about Jen?"

"Tim asked if I want to buy him out. Jen wants to go home to Oz."

Tim, Aysha's partner in their law practice, had married an Australian. She'd been talking about wanting to go home before they started their family. It sounded like that time had arrived. This would be stressful for Aysha. I doubted she'd ever find someone else to buy into the partnership who was as easy-going as Tim.

Whoops, Aysha was still talking, "Bring the boy toy for dinner tomorrow. I have to meet him before you get tired of him. I can admire him while you fix Autumn."

Almost the moment I hung up, Rollo sent, *"You feel frightened. Panicky. Are you OK?"*

I filled him in.

"That sounds like you need to go. Why don't we start our holiday a day or two later? Or in Manchester?"

I pushed a wave of gratitude towards him. *"She's actually a funny, intelligent woman. Just a little pushy sometimes."*

"I grew up with shield maidens, remember? Pushy women are the norm. No stress. We have a week. What's one day less?"

"Can I call you? I want to hear your voice, and Aysha made my head hurt."

His warm mental hug rebalanced me.

Exactly like Aysha, I started talking the moment the call connected. "Hey, I think I've actually finagled nine days. If we don't mind me popping back for an hour if anything urgent crops up. Dola wants me out of the way, while she does her thing with Glynis and Finn, which could be worrying, but I don't have any bad vibes about it."

"Did you give any more thought to where we might go?" his voice sounded like a buttery caramel tastes as it melts in your mouth and as warm and soothing as his hugs were. I felt like a cat whose fur had been stroked the right way.

"Yeah, I did. Breanna told me yesterday it's in the mid-twenties in Galicia right now. That sounded quite appealing."

But from his silence, I picked up that wouldn't work for him. "Problem?"

"In my dreams, we go somewhere we're both completely anonymous. Less, 'oh look, it's Prince Hrólfr and the Recorder' and more, 'look, a cute random couple I've never met and may never see again. I wonder if they'd like me to take their lunch order.'"

"OK, how about the Canary Isles? Fuerteventura or Lanzarote maybe? I bet you'd love Cesar Manrique's work. Have you been?"

Then my ears caught up with what he'd said. We were a couple? How did I feel about that?

But before I could dive down that scary rabbit hole, he said, "I'm virtually done up here. Breanna sent me an invite via Finn for tonight, and I've arranged to have a burger with him for lunch and a chat about what we discussed last night. Your privacy and his less-than-gentlemanly behaviour telling Cait about it. You feel busy; how about you get on with your day, and then we could have a nightcap together after the book club and plan a holiday?"

It sounded blissful, and I said so. But, obviously, it didn't quite work out that way.

CHAPTER
EIGHTEEN

I needed a chat with the power. My staff had become used to me floating about the Gateway, especially after the chaos with Rollo and the yellow power last week, so I decided to get it over with.

The moment we hit the green door, Tilly started running. She tumbled into Rosemary's feet and was immediately fussed over and loved.

"How's it going, Rosemary?"

She looked happy and far more relaxed than she had on her first day, which was normal, but it was still lovely to see. She gave off such tangible happy vibes. It made me say, "We had some of Rockii's rhubarb; that's a talented man you have."

She nodded furiously. "Milady, would you call me Rosie? I thought I wanted to use my Sunday name in here, but everyone is so friendly. I'd be happier with Rosie now I know you all."

"Sure, and you should call me Niki when we're unofficial. As you say, you work here now."

She looked briefly overwhelmed, but then nodded. "Can we talk about the walls?" She pointed at the Gateway walls as though I might not know where she meant.

"Sure?"

She waved her hands, and the red, pink and white flowers that grew on the tree boughs she had affixed to the walls for Valentine's Day moved into rectangular shapes that looked remarkably like book covers on a green background. My mouth fell open. "Wow!"

"Queen Breanna was in earlier. Can I make this area," she gestured around the conference table, "cute for Her Maj? She's very excited. Auntie Mags and the girls are due any minute to fettle it."

"Of course, that'd be lovely, and sorry, Rosie, fettle what?" "Fettle" seemed to be the Hobs' word for any kind of cleaning, laundering or repairing, but I couldn't see what they planned to fettle in here.

"The Gateway, milady, er, Niki. It's a bit dusty and the floor ..." She pointed at the many footprints and some pawprints marring the surface. "And the table needs a polish."

I was obviously the world's worst housekeeper because I hadn't even noticed, but she was right. It was all a bit grubby. March is a hard month on floors.

"You can ask Auntie Mags about the cakes for Mabon."

Yeah, I could, couldn't I? Wouldn't that just be delightful?

Leaving Rosie to create a book-themed flower bower for Breanna, I gathered my courage and headed to the Yellow Sector. Troels saw me coming, and his mouth moved. Did he even realise we'd soundproofed the glass cage?

Shape up, Niki. You can do this. You've dealt with worse. Some part of my brain wanted to refute this vociferously. If Troels was guilty of all the things the women were accusing him of, and him trying to hurt my dog was tipping me in their direction and away from his revolting assertions that all women lie, then, no, I'd never dealt with worse.

Check he's OK. You have responsibilities, nagged the annoying librarian in my brain.

I don't know what I anticipated when I removed the soundproofing, but his first words came as a surprise. "If you plan to assassinate me, I need to speak to my wife first. I have rights."

Didn't "assassinate" usually refer to a politically motivated unlawful killing?

Was his accusation intentional?

Perhaps he didn't understand the Recorder's role or responsibilities?

I refused to take offence because, unlike Rollo's warm voice with its neutral accent and very faintly northern European flavour, Troels' voice was harsh and his accent heavily Scandinavian. Was "assassinate" simply a poor word choice in a language that wasn't his own? He didn't think he had anything to answer for? I guess we'd find out when I did the arbitration. But allowing his wife to visit him wasn't unreasonable.

"You want me to summon ..." What was his wife's name? I wished I had Aysha's talent for remembering names. Oh yeah. "... Randi?"

He aimed a look of absolute contempt straight between my eyes. "Not that idiot. I want, no, I must see my true wife, Inge."

I bit back my instinctive response to say, "The one you divorced twenty years ago? That true wife?" Fi spoke to Inge all the time, didn't she? I'd ask her. "I'll find out if she wants to see you."

"Tell her I am dying and *you*," he almost spat the word, "plan to speed the process."

I looked around his cage. Joining the cot bed now was water, the remains of some food, and rather than the bucket I'd suggested, a camping toilet had appeared in the corner.

It could have been worse. I was pretty sure it was better treatment than he gave prisoners in Viking.

My head was a muddle. I could have easily suffocated the asshole who'd tried to hurt my dog. If it had been him who'd sent those guys to grab Rollo and beat him almost to death, the same would have applied. But now I knew it wasn't him, I needed to focus on my professional obligations to the women. This frail, angry old man was completely throwing me off my stride. The power had already taken the things he valued away from him, his strength and his virility. I honestly didn't know what the hell to do with him.

I tapped my earbud, "Dola could you share some information with Troels to ensure he understands what an arbitration is? I'm wondering if his isolationist stance means he doesn't even grasp what's happening here."

"Yes, Niki, we have some information in Norse."

That was all I could do for now, because I needed to talk with the power.

I checked the Gateway. There was a lot of traffic. It was much too busy for me to float about in the middle, giving everyone a show. Tilly needed a walk. I'd take her for one while I reset my head, and then we'd lock the gates. This felt important enough to do that.

"Finn?" I waited while Dola connected me through to his earbuds. This was our new system. Then a hand appeared above his screen, giving me a thumbs-up. "Can you put a note on the portal that the Gateway will be closed for essential maintenance around lunchtime-ish?"

His head appeared. "Lunchtime-ish?"

Yeah, OK, my bad. Something so lacking in specifics was never going to work for Finn, was it? What was I thinking? I wondered how long I'd need. The Gateway's time dilation would work in my favour, but the realms would want an idea of what time we would reopen. "Say we're closing briefly at noon. Please."

Through my earbuds, I heard, "Done."

I paused at my assistant's desk, hoping to ask her about the petitioners and whether Inge would like to visit Troels. But Fi looked very hassled, and Corby was crawling around on the floor gathering half-full plastic grocery bags. "Hey, Corby, all good? Problem, Fi?"

She looked up and tried to find somewhere to move the bags on her desk. "Sorry, Niki. I need to get these to my mum. Corby will take them. I can't leave until later, and they're in the way. We need some storage in here."

There were far too many bags for Corby to carry on her own.

"I'm taking Tilly for a walk now while I wait for it to be quiet enough to chat to the power. Does Corby need a hand?"

Fi looked surprised and then relieved. "If it's no trouble, and you're taking Tilly anyway, it would be a big help. Mum's waiting for them, but I'm busy today."

"Sure, no problem." I grabbed the bags, which, by the time I'd collected a dozen of them, were actually quite heavy. But Mrs Glendinning's house was only around the corner. Nothing was very far in this tiny village. I gave Fi a querying look.

"Dried fruit, almonds and spices mostly." She blew her hair out of the way as she used both hands to gather the many bags, which only contained one or two items. "It's that time of the year again."

Corby and I headed out. The sky had the strange silvery light that often meant snow was coming. Something in the air, not quite an odour, made my scalp tingle. I might have timed Tilly's walk perfectly.

Corby chattered away. She was enjoying her new business partnership with Ross and had taken photos of some lovely couples. She thought it was a kind thing I'd done allowing Mrs G to have John Fergusson's skull. I could think of a few words I might have used, including "macabre," "bizarre" and "worthy of an April Fool's joke," but "kind" wouldn't have been one of them.

She told me how happy Fi was in her new role. They'd started the great house hunt and looked at several homes, but none had been right for them, yet.

When we arrived at Mrs G's, her front garden looked like something created by one of those Impressionist painters who liked all the bright colours. It was crammed with a riot of spring bulbs in swathes of yellow, purple and white, their multi-shaded green leaves an attractive counterpoint. The woman herself was flustered. "Oh my lady, there was absolutely no need for *you* to —" Then she saw Tilly.

Corby and I waited patiently while our arms were pulled out of their sockets by the now far too heavy bags while the two of them indulged in a prolonged greeting.

Finally, Mrs G said, "I feel awful not asking you in, but I'm in chaos with all this," and gestured at the bags. "Every year I leave it almost too late, and with the sentencing, it went quite out of my mind."

We dumped the bags inside her front door and backed away. "Not at all. It was no problem. We must get back, anyway."

She continued apologising as we closed the gate behind us. "What *is* she doing?"

Corby grinned. "Making Black Bun. It will be worth it. Everyone contributes the ingredients, and Mrs G bakes them. Fi will bring some in for everyone."

"Black Bun?"

"Traditional Scottish treat, generally for Hogmanay. But the Picts think it's an Easter thing too, and Mrs G sticks to her roots when it comes to baking. Google it. It's very rich and delicious."

"Oooh, sounds yummy. She is a brilliant baker." I checked my watch and realised I needed to get back to the Gateway to discuss the creation of Troels' high-tech cell with the power.

CHAPTER
NINETEEN

Back in the Gateway, which was finally empty, apart from my staff. Oh, and Troels, of course. If you'd told me I would ever be able to completely ignore the man, I wouldn't have believed you. But he didn't feel important until I could begin the active part of the arbitration. There were so many other things I needed to do before that. It felt like when you decided to cook a completely new recipe and realised step one should have been to go shopping for the ingredients.

With my hand on the anvil, I asked the power to lock all the doors. The moment I dropped my shields, I rose into the air. I checked my earlobes. Was I wearing one of the pairs of numbered earrings Doug Halkrig asked me to wear when I flew about the Gateway so he could continue his research into the rainbow gold? Yep, we were up to pair number four.

Then confusion ensued.

I tried again for the third—or was it the fourth time?—to understand what the power wanted. The only thing that was clear was it wanted to do something in Viking. Urgently.

"Just do it," I told the power.

But, no, it couldn't. It needed me to do something first? It showed me pictures of documents. No, actually, it was multiple copies of the same document. But I couldn't read whatever it was. This whole thing was starting to feel like one of those bad dreams where some familiar town suddenly had signposts in a foreign language.

In my defence, my brain worked like treacle when I was hanging in the air like a stringless puppet, gazing longingly at the ground too far below me. The power got my message because it deposited me gently back on the ground as it pushed a picture of the Book at me.

I headed to my desk and sent a mental call for the Book, unsurprised to see it waiting for me. I touched it, watched as it turned red, and opened it. "What does the power need me to know?"

I had to get better at communicating clearly with the power. It was a key part of my job.

The Book flicked pages before it offered me one headed:

Better communication with the power.

"Actually, yeah, thanks. Save that one on the list for later. It looks perfect. But now I need a quick answer. Can we take a shortcut? What's it asking me to do? All I've grasped is it's unhappy and needs me to fix something."

More flicking before one of the oldest style of pages arrived. I hated these. Honestly, if I'd ever thought I could be a scholar who could read ancient documents, I wouldn't have gone into computing.

I peered at it.

The title had far too few spaces between the words. The letters beginning each paragraph were illuminated with small illustrations in vibrant, glowing colours and were the height of several lines, like a modern drop capital. Or possibly it was from documents like this that we got the drop cap format—huh, why had I never considered that before? And why was I wasting time on it now? *Focus, Niki.*

It was foreign and felt old. Maybe Latin or Greek? No, not Greek because it wasn't full of words containing the letters *ph*. Latin then. Probably. It looked familiar, but I couldn't retrieve any useful memory. And the scribe's old-fashioned calligraphic writing meant I would have struggled even if it had been in English.

Caitlin was in Pict today doing some heir apparent thing. Breanna had said her kids spoke some languages. Did Finn speak Latin? Probably not.

"Dola, where's Finn?"

"He is available if you need him. Rollo arrived for their lunch meeting, and they plan to do some gaming on the big screen in Finn's room. He has sixteen unused lunch breaks. I told him he should take some of them today."

Hmm, Rollo must be having the privacy chat with Finn. "Thanks."

"Do you know how long you will be? Mags is waiting for access with the Hobs girls to fettle in preparation for tonight's book club."

I thought about it. I didn't want to antagonise Mags, not generally, and especially not if I needed these simnel cakes for Mabon. I'd achieved so much more by treating her with respect over the Valentine's Day thing. I'd need to be a little canny here, as she herself described it. And Rosie never batted an eye at the craziness in here. So the Hobs wouldn't be startled by a Recorder hanging in the middle of the Gateway the way some unsuspecting traveller might be.

"Actually, Dola, tell her she's cleared. It's only random visitors I want to keep out until I've fixed this. Could you make it sound like an honour? 'The Recorder is terribly sorry for the inconvenience but is sure the Hobs Headwoman will keep anything she learns to herself. Her hand on the green gate will open it, only for her and her staff?' That kind of nonsense."

I heard the humour in Dola's voice as she said, "Fine words.

Yes, I shall apply the butter liberally to the parsnips; leave it with me."

Butter? Parsnips? WTH? Never mind, it didn't matter.

I turned back to the Book as a wonderful shortcut occurred to me. "Could you give me a modern version of whatever this is about? Specifically, the thing the power needs me to know?"

The Book shivered a little, and I stroked it. "I won't hold you to the accuracy of it—but give me some clues, please?"

The title and several paragraphs changed to a gold or yellow colour, which didn't help me at all. It was still in a language I didn't know, and now the ink was even harder to read. But I'd take any clues I could get. Even as I thought this, the yellow sections changed to a more modern font. "Thank you. I think. I wonder if HRH and her classical education might help me?"

The Book slammed shut and sat there wearing its "I'm closed" blue leather. I swear it glared at me.

"What? What did I say?"

The Book remained stubbornly sealed while I tried to work out what I'd done wrong. "HRH? Seriously? I was sort of joking. But I can't read this. Usually, you put things into modern parlance for me." I put my hand on the Book to soothe it. It turned, reluctantly, I thought, back to red. I opened it. "I'm sorry. It was a joke—well, sort of. But you were showing me an agreement?"

But the page that arrived after only a single page flip said,

My lady,

HRH has behaved better to you since you took the role than she has towards any Recorder for almost half a millennium. I would prefer not to give you information that may prejudice you against her. I must, if you require me to, but please do not ask it of me.

She needs to mitigate her past actions for her curse to be lifted. They say that Karma is a bitch, but they've not met Sekhmet. Perhaps HRH has found something in you to help her turn an important corner. If that is the case, I would not

wish to work against her rehabilitation, but I would advise you to use extreme caution.

I remembered all this. It had shown it to me when I'd first arrived in response to my confusion about what the big deal with the cat was? She'd been helpful, and I didn't understand all the warnings from Gran and the Book. Dola's unresolved hatred of HRH still flummoxed me. But why was it showing it to me now? Especially when the power seemed to have an urgent problem, and time was ticking away.

None of us wishes a repeat of the last incident. It took me years to restore my own cover, and the village was rebuilding for half a century. Only Dola's ancient shields protected our energies in here.

I didn't remember the bit about the cover repair being in italics. Was that the important bit?

"I'll come back to whatever this is about the cat soon. Put it on the list too, but can we please go back to the power's problem before I have to further extend the time the Gateway is closed and inconvenience everyone?"

At the bottom of the same page, more words appeared as I watched.

The agreement is a perfect copy of the original. Any translation would not convey the weight or the crucial inferences of the ancient words. The significance of those original words is paramount.

The page changed back to the contract-type thing.

I peered at the yellow portions. I tried to remember when I'd seen this document or something like it before? As my eyes slid down to the signatures, I saw the lion's head sketch next to a name that was probably Will. Yes! I had seen this before. Last week, when Troels sent the lumberjacks against the yellow gate. My faulty memory disturbed me until I remembered that was the day I'd arrived back shaking and sobbing after Dai harangued me.

OK, so the power was still unsettled about whatever this was. I could probably assume the bits in yellow were the problems.

Perhaps someone who remembered when they'd all signed it? I was pretty sure one of those signatures was Ad'Rian's. Should I summon him? One of the other chicken-scratch signatures might be Mabon. Although, actually, that broad curved black squiggle with the ink blotch by it felt more like him. The kings might help. Ad'Rian spoke Latin. But if this was urgent ... *oh hell! Come on, Niki. Think!*

I snapped a photo in case the Book wouldn't show it to them later. It was obviously in a mood today.

I pulled power to talk to it, hopefully without hanging about in the air. It gave me a strong mental push towards the yellow gate. It felt like *Go. Look.*

But Caitlin would go batshit crazy if I wandered out into the Viking realm without her. She'd been furious when I went to lunch with Ad'Rian, and Fae was a safe place. She'd be finished soon. Hadn't she said it was a lunch thing? Oh, sod it. I only needed a peek to see what was disturbing the power.

I stood up. With the airlock in place, I'd be safe to take a quick look, grab a couple of photographs, and nip straight back into the Gateway if there were any problems.

Something stopped me. I rubbed my stomach.

"Guid day, Your Maj. Trouble?"

I whirled around, and Mags stood in front of me. Almost involuntarily, I nodded. She was a lot less scary and considerably quieter without Lis next to her. Today's outfit of cosy-looking leggings and a cowl-necked jumper in a soft creamy yellow even matched.

She turned and quickly directed six—no, eight—female Hobs, all carrying cleaning supplies towards various tasks. Clean this, scrub that and polish the other was the gist of it. Then she turned back to me and asked, "How may I help?"

"I'm not sure you can, Mag. The power is unhappy, and I'm not clear why. But unless you read Latin—"

I cut myself off because she was nodding at me.

WTAF?

Don't be rude, Niki, just don't be rude. "You do?"

Her creased honey brown face smirked at me, "Aye, ah ken. Surprising, eh? Lis did the modern languages, and I did the classical. Oor mother had ideas."

Her eyes held intelligence and humour. I swallowed. "Then let me check if the Book will allow me to show you the page, please."

The Book had closed itself again on my desk and I reached to put my hand on it. But Mags beat me to it. She didn't touch the spine to open it as I would have done. She simply laid her palm flat on the front cover for a few seconds the way I might have done with a palm reader. Turning to me, she observed, "It's ken a few of my fearmothers, if the tales are true."

"It's known your ancestors?" I'd learned with the Hobs not to assume I knew what they meant. But Mags just nodded at me and peered expectantly at the Book.

I opened it and thought hard at it. *Only show me things I can share with Mags, please.* But it opened again to the same page, with the sections still in yellow.

"Ah, the feeking Vikings. Noo, why am I no' surprised?" She glanced at the glass cage in the Yellow Sector and called, "Let the rapist and his sector well alone, lassies." The young Hobs immediately all waved to signify they'd heard her.

She retrieved a pair of spectacles from her apron pocket, popped them on, and leaned over to read, clasping her hands behind her back. "Shame it dinna have a backlight and font change thingumajig like my Kindle does."

She had a Kindle? I reached past her to touch the text and instigate the magnifying glass effect it had used for me before the power fixed my eyesight.

Mags glanced at me. "Very handy, Your Maj; thank ye kindly."

She read, nodded, mumbled to herself and then gestured I should increase the size of the next yellow paragraph.

I was still marvelling at the idea of Mags having an e-reader. What did she read? I'd put my money on gruesome, true-life serial killer stories.

Finally, she reached the bottom of the page. That section wasn't yellow, but she gestured for me to magnify it anyway, and, as she read, a truly terrifying grin crossed her face.

She stood up and surveyed me. I felt like those bright eyes saw right through me. "Right, Your Maj, for the benefit of … well, of everyone, you and I need a free and frank private talk. We canna do that here. Little pitchers have big ears."

At my confused frown, she said, "Hobs are dreadful gossips. Well, no, they are ver' guid gossips and tha's the problem. Known many of your ancestors, my fearmothers have. Headwomen safeguard some of the deep knowledge." She looked at her watch, then up to the ceiling and back at me. "A half hour would do it. But why rush oorsels? A cuppa tea'd be good. Say an 'oor. That work fer ye? In Stane Parlour mebbe?"

She turned those twinkling eyes on me in the full expectation I would work out her meaning.

No one should know the Recorder could time travel. The Book had told me this. Yet everyone and their damn ancestors seemed to know. And was Mags really saying "fear mothers" or was it simply her accent twisting the word "foremothers"? Did I want to know? Probably not.

I picked up the Book, saw Mag's approving nod and grasped her arm. I heard Tilly's angry bark as the world went rainbow-coloured. Oh, well, I'd be back before she knew it.

We landed in my new public office, which Mags had been instrumental in naming Stane Parlour during a drunken afternoon tea. This time, I planned to stay completely sober. "Tea, did you say?"

"Aye, tea and a wee smidge o' whisky, mebbe, for the thinkin'."

Why did I suddenly get the idea that the silly old, semiliterate Hob act was just that? Because she owned a Kindle, read Latin, and she could drop the accent when she wanted to. Did all these people simply play the roles that had been assigned to them in the same way Rollo had?

I tapped my earbud. "Dola, if you have a moment, could Mags and I have some tea, a caramel macchiato, a bottle of the Girvan, and perhaps something sweet in the Stane Parlour?"

"Niki, how are you here, now …?" There was a pause. "Ah, I see. We must catch up later. I have advised Finn to take a long lunch with Rollo, but I am still here if you need anything."

Gosh, this time travel business could get confusing if you allowed it to.

I gazed out at the soothing view of the coastline of Solway Firth. It was blowy out there today with white tips on the waves. But Mabon's stone was, as always, unaffected by the weather.

A tray arrived gently on the table. When I turned round, Mags was investigating my bookshelves, her head on one side as she read the titles. She tapped the spine of a slim volume, a personal favourite of mine, *Illusions* by Richard Bach, and observed, "Clever book that. Make a body think, tha' one can."

"I bought it in a lovely bookstore in Manchester the year I went to university." I pulled myself together. Book chat was not what we were here for. "So what do we need to talk about, Mags?"

But it seemed we weren't done with books because she came over to my desk and tapped the copy of *Ruling Regally* I'd left out. It was full of my notes and bookmarks in case we actually got to talk books at tonight's book club.

"I heard Queen Breanna is having a meeting to discuss this 'un?"

I nodded.

"Have ye read it?"

"Yes, it's wonderfully funny and insightful. She gives brilliant advice." I paused. Well, she'd said she had a Kindle; she obviously read. Why not? "Would you like to borrow it? I could lend it to you after the meeting tonight. I've read it several times. Honestly, you get more out of it each time."

"Like tha' *Illusions*. I find something new every time I read it; must have read it ten times. It's almost magical."

I nodded at her in perfect accord. It was a strange book. It had always seemed to me that the book changed to suit me. Or perhaps it was simply that I noticed different parts of it as I aged. I giggled at a thought. What if it was magical and able to grow with its reader?

"Shall I pour, Your Maj?"

"Yes, please help yourself." I picked my coffee up and sipped gratefully before putting it on the little warming plate by my chair. I wasn't even sure why I was here. But Mags had seemed to have answers, and she'd said I needed to hear them in private. So I just stared at her attentively.

It worked!

"Niki, I'll call you that in private?"

I nodded. Her accent had gone again, which made my life much easier. She waved the new and sealed whisky bottle at me. "No, thank you, but please help yourself."

"I see how much pain 'Your Maj' causes you. But it's a respectful title from us. You should get used to it."

I'd try. They did always say it with respect. Juniper and Rosie had shown me that.

"Troels is a bad seed. He's not just a rapist; he's a murderer, and if the gossip is true, he attempted regicide, and that's a capital offence. But I'm not sure the gossip is true, and even if it is, he's still not your real problem. Those warlords are the real obstacle. They're bringing trouble to all the realms. It's not just Viking that's affected."

She waited, but I agreed with her. So I nodded. I'd almost but not quite worked this much out for myself. "Can you tell me what you think they're doing outside Viking?"

Now Mags nodded to herself, as though satisfied I knew some of what was going on, then shook her head. "Nae just yet. Give me a few days, and mebbe I can. Need to safeguard some of our own folk first."

"You're not cut from the same cloth as your grandmother." I was so sick of hearing this. But as fast as my face must have changed, she pushed both her hands away from her and towards me at chest height in a warding-off motion. "I don't speak ill of the dead. I speak only as I find. She did the best she could, your gran. But she was playing with a stacked deck. Weak power, no family support, and not canny enough."

I wanted to take offence on Gran's behalf, but let's be honest, Mags was correct on all counts. Gran didn't have a good connection to the Gateway and wasn't particularly bright. She could be shrewd, but she hated progress and was disinterested in learning about anything new. Which meant she got more out of date with every year that passed. And, yeah, my mother was crazy, and Gran had blocked my memories—a stupid, cruel decision, and as a result, she hadn't had any family support.

"Tell me, Mags, where did the down-home Scottish brogue disappear to?"

She laughed. "It doesn't fool you, Niki. Why waste both our time? I'll deny it, of course, should you ever mention it to folk. What would a foreigner know? I'd probably have to cast some ancient and powerful, obscure Hob curse on you for good measure. But you strike me as a woman who rewards plain dealing. You've included even the unlikely but valiant suspects like Rhiannon ap Modron. You soon sniffed out the weak links like her brother. Not to mention inviting Lis and me to the girls' bondings as though we were royals. And you're taking action on Troels, forty years too late ... but you're doing it at your first opportunity. I treat as I find. Until you break my trust, let's deal as allies."

She spat in her hand and held it out for me to shake. I considered it, and my inner clean freak rebelled. Also, I suspected it was a test. I handed her a wet wipe from my top drawer. She grinned, used it, and then I shook her hand.

"Most fall for it. They consider Hobs to be no better than piskies, so why would we care about hygiene? But you gave Rosie a job. You're a strange McKnight."

I was? Why? "How so?"

"We have our own family diaries. They say there hasn't been a Recorder with any real power for hundreds of years. I forget the name of the last powerful one, but I know she met an unhappy end. I'd not wish that for you. So, about the Book." She pointed.

I nodded and thought hard at it: *May we have the agreement again please?*

It opened to the correct page. Mags leaned over and, still without touching it, pointed paragraph by paragraph as she spoke.

"This is the agreement between all the leaders of the realms and the Rainbow Gateway. It came into force after it changed to its current form."

"Do you mean when it partnered with the McKnight line instead of having an armoured guard at the door to prevent anyone stumbling through by accident?"

"Yes," Mags pointed to the lowest quarter of the page and the signatures, "see here? The kings, well, and the Pict queen. Just the one feeking woman, shameful that is—but those days were full o' men and their plans." She squinted at a line under the signatures. "Never was as good with numbers as words, but that," she pointed at a line of Roman numerals, "says 1124, I think."

"That would be the date of Abigail, the first McKnight Recorder's ascension, according to the family records."

She gave me a pleased smile and started back at the top of the agreement. "This is all just 'we, the undersigned, bind ourselves and all our descendants unto the thousandth generation. We swear on our lives and our descendants' lives.' The usual stuff. But this bit." She pointed at the first section in yellow text.

I nodded.

"This spells out what happens if they break the agreement. If those royals don't defend the Gateway. If they attack it, or try to undermine it in any fashion. It's comprehensive. Ye might say it says, 'You're for me, or the power will assume you're against it.' That sort of thing. No neutrality allowed. If they try to harm or even allow any harm to come to the Gateway—they'll not like its response."

She raised her eyebrows at me now. "Niki, there are word choices, aye?"

My slight frown must have told her I understood her words but not her meaning because she raised her teacup to me. "I might say this is a good cuppa tea. Or," she raised the whisky glass in her other hand, "I could say this whisky is the finest and one of the rarest anywhere in the world, in or out of Scotland, and it's sublime. Both would be true. Word choices, d'ye see?"

I saw. "And what word choices did whoever wrote this agreement make?" The Book had said any translation would lose the weight of the original. Was that what Mags was also trying to tell me?

"I'd say this agreement was written in conjunction with the power, probably by a priest. A few pious bits make me think of a priest or mebbe a monk. They were mostly the men who wrote stuff down back in the day, weren't they? And all the twiddly letters. That's monks, for ye. On one of those long scrolls." She mimed unrolling a long parchment document. "Might be why the print is so tiny, shrunk down to fit on that page."

"OK. Thank you. I'm with you so far. And the word choices?"

"Stern words. Strong words. Break your oath or fail in your honour to do what you promised, and you might die in horrible ways, and your realm may be given to someone more worthy."

Damn! "Does it say who'll have to kill them?"

"It says the power will be withdrawn from them and access to their realm restricted while their peers decide. If the other royals can't agree, then the Recorder and her Knight will see to it. If the Recorder doesn't, then the power will, and no one will like the resulting holocaust."

She considered me carefully, then added, "You're modern. Probably thinking about the Jewish people. But this word," and she pointed to the middle of the second yellow paragraph. I saw the word *holocaustum*. "This means utter destruction and slaughter."

This didn't sound good. I needed to risk being more honest.

"The thing is, I don't know what it was trying to tell me today. Usually, our communications are pretty clear. But all I picked up was that it wants me to do something with Viking or with the Viking Gate. It's already sealed, so it's not that."

She pointed at the third and final paragraph that the Book had turned to yellow. "This bit is about the boundary. How one furlong in front of the gate belongs to the Gateway, not to the realm. The rulers are charged with the responsibility, but it's much stronger words than those. Entrusted on their oaths, mebbe? They swear on their descendants' lives in front of their gods and goddesses. They vow on everything and everyone they hold dear to ensure and to oversee clear access in front of the gates at all times. No permanent or temporary structures are permitted. Anything placed in this area will be removed by the power, without exceptions."

"How far is a furlong?"

Mags said, "Aboot two hundred yards," at the same time as Dola answered me, "Two hundred and one point one six metres."

I sipped my coffee and pictured all the gates I knew. The two hundred yards in front of them all were clear. At least in all the realms I'd visited. The Picts had a pavement and a road, but no buildings. The Fae had a pretty glade with the bubble seeds, plants and trees, but again, no structures. Mabon had the full length of the road down to the market square. It was occasionally crammed with people and sometimes even blocked by the Highland coos, but it was clear of any structures until it reached Mabon's castle some 400 or 500 yards away.

"Perhaps it doesn't like the market?" Mags offered.

"What market?" I snapped.

Mags looked cautious and thoughtful now. "Hobs ... well, we travel differently ... to you people. Communicate differently too. If I had to guess, I'd say it's all to do with the market the Vikings have started around that airlock thingumajig. There are stalls, food stands, a bit of a fair, and they're charging people to look into the airlock." She shrugged at me.

Rollo had taken photos of the airlock. There hadn't been any stalls then ... had there?

I reached out.

"Hey, sorry, know you're gaming, but when did you take those photos of the airlock? Someone just told me there's a market grown up around it? The power is very angry. Do you know anything about it?"

In response, my phone buzzed with a "Rollo would like to share" alert, and I accepted. He'd sent me several photos from a different angle than the ones I'd seen earlier this week, and these showed the market clearly. I sent a quick *Thanks* back and looked at Mags.

"Thank you very much. You've been incredibly helpful." I glanced at my watch. "And you were about right on the time too."

Call me suspicious, but before she left, I wondered how much I could trust her. I thought hard at the Book. *Did she translate it as accurately as you think she should have?*

It gave me the big green tick emoji.

OK then.

Mags gave me a grin that creased her entire face and showed

me surprisingly healthy white teeth. "You're welcome. So just the one last thing, then?"

Well, I'd known her help wouldn't be free, but I'd needed to know what the power wanted. Beggars can't be choosers. I waited for the other probably quite heavy shoe to drop.

"Well, two things. You'll be wanting the cakes for Mabon's spring equinox? And you might feel you owe me a small favour besides?"

I nodded. I'd need to take my medicine like a good Recorder, wouldn't I?

But she surprised me. "The cakes are ready. I'll have the girls take them down to the Stane on the day. But ye can tellt him I'm no makin' one for his ungrateful mother. What did she e'er do for me, hey? Feekin' Goddesses. Eh? Ne'er said so much as a thank you. Wouldn't stand for it from the bairns. Don't see why I should from a goddess. D'ye? Can't please them."

Well, the accent was back, so this would be genuine anger then?

"Sorry, Mags, but do you mean the Goddess Modron has never thanked you?"

"Ne'er thanked me, ne'er thanked my fearmothers. Nigh on a thousand years of ingratitude. I tellt ye gran. She dinnae pass the message along. Now I'm telling you. NO."

"OK. Thank you. I'll explain. But you don't mind making the ones for Mabon's equinox event?"

A delighted smile wreathed her face. "Now tha's a man who knows how to show a body some gratitude. Pretty manners he has. And guid whisky." She looked hopefully at the bottle of Girvan.

I bit the bullet. "And how may I show my gratitude for all your assistance today?" Whatever it was, I'd have to just bloody do it, wouldn't I?

But Mags hadn't finished surprising me. She went a little pink and, in a rush, said, "At the binding ceremony, Your Maj. You said Lis and I were representing Green, so I wondered, would

Queen Breanna be angry if I asked to come tonight? It's Troels, you see; he's ill-treated many of my girls o'er the years, and I'd want to hear what the royals all think. And I like books ..." she trailed off, looking surprised at herself.

I couldn't imagine anything worse than the two of them. The never-ending *feekings* alone would stop the royals discussing anything sensibly. Cautiously, I said, "And would Lis want to come?"

She cackled so loudly, my ears hurt. "Nae. Lis doesn't read. Well, she can, o'course. I mean she don't choose to. Anyway, she's away. I'd be the only Headwoman right now."

She'd earned it. I'd speak to Breanna and tell her it was the price for the excellent catering from Juniper. Yes, that would work.

"Agreed and thank you again." Struck by the thought that I didn't want to be classed along with the Goddess Modron as ungrateful or ill-mannered, I picked up the bottle of Girvan. It had arrived full, and she'd broken the seal herself. I offered it to her with, "To show you how much I appreciate your timely help and advice."

I got a huge beaming smile as someone tapped on my door and opened it before I could say come in. Rollo was talking before the door was even open. "Boo, I might be able to get more up-to-date info. Oh, sorry, I didn't realise." He came fully into the room and bowed to Mags. "Recorder, Headwoman Marguerite, my apologies for the intrusion."

Mag's eyes were the size of saucers as she surveyed the two of us.

Blast! The gossip would spread now, wouldn't it? Oh well.

CHAPTER
TWENTY

I'd offered to return Mags to the Gateway, but she'd announced, "It's a fine afternoon for a stroll," and headed out, cradling her bottle of whisky as though it were a newborn.

It wasn't a fine afternoon for anything. The sky was heavy with silvery clouds, and the predicted big fat fluffy snowflakes had begun to fall. It was freaking March; Scotland's weather was unreasonable!

Rollo was still apologising for barging in. I said, "Look, stop. From Saturday, we've got some private time. We can decide what we plan to tell people. Mags was in an odd mood today. She may decide to keep it to herself for a while."

His expression said he thought my naivety was cute.

"What were you saying, anyway?" I asked.

"I can get you some more up-to-date photos of the boundary if you need them, and we can give her some email access."

"Her?"

"Inge, my stepmother."

"Oh yeah, your uncle just demanded I let him speak with her. Actually, he said he wanted to speak to his wife. I thought he meant whatshername, the current wife. He didn't."

"Randi—no, he wouldn't. She's sweet, but she's a pretty hilt, not a blade. He's always been angry that Inge blackmailed him into giving her a divorce. But she would come if he's asking for her. Inge's good people. She still feels guilty that she got Elise out of there but couldn't help all the other women."

"Elise, the shield maiden daughter who nearly ended up in the tank with her Galician lace wedding dress and Svein's horrible horde?"

Rollo's expression was confused and horrified simultaneously. "Do you think perhaps over lunch or on a long dog walk while we're away, we could use a mind link to get me caught up? Or even just filled in on the basics of all the things I don't know?"

"If you think you could share your plans with me in return? Because I have some decisions to make about your uncle. Right now, those decisions are giving me indigestion. It feels as though nightmares are only a step away. I don't have enough information. I need to know what might be right for Viking. And the realm is my concern, not him."

He opened his arms, and I walked into them. For a few minutes, we simply breathed in perfect sync, then I heard, *"You're a very fair woman, aren't you?"*

I didn't know. Was I? On a good day, maybe. But I was also bitchy, unsure of my capabilities, and sometimes simply overwhelmed. In the end, I said, "I try to be. Right now, I hold the Viking realm's future in my hands, and I have no idea what's best for it."

He stiffened. That was so unlike him. I pulled back to look at him.

"What?"

"What do you mean, *you* hold the Viking realm's future?"

"Yeah, sorry I misspoke. The power holds the Viking realm's future, and that future and whether it will even have one is in the balance. But I'm the power's mouthpiece, and it will be guided by me if I have a good plan. Sorry, the weight of responsibility is giving me sore shoulders at the moment. I'm not used to all this."

I hadn't imagined it. He'd gone very still.

Quietly, he said, "I don't understand what Viking's future has to do with you?"

I gave up on words and sent, *"Are you just being an annoying man? 'What's it to do with you, woman?' Or do you mean the question literally?"* I sent a kiss along with my words but also a firm suggestion that we'd better find out exactly what his problem was, and fast.

Suddenly, I wasn't in his arms anymore. And he was giving me a look I didn't like.

Well, damn. I didn't need another idiot in my life. But finding out someone I liked and had begun to trust was a JAFA might reduce me to tears. I'd better get out of here. Oh no. It was my damn office. He'd better get out of here.

"What's a JAFA?"

He asked this with such fascination that I glanced at him, surprised.

"Just Another Fucking Arsehole."

He burst out laughing.

"What? What's so funny?"

He was almost doubled over now. "Boo, I've barely heard you swear before. Not even inside your head. It took me by surprise."

"I wasn't always Ms Sweet Mouth. But Aysha and I agreed when Autumn was born that it's horrible hearing a small child using profanities they could only have picked up at home. So we mostly stopped. It was like giving up anything—after a while, you stop missing it. But JAFA is from before Autumn, obviously. We met a lot of JAFAs when we were younger."

"But you say 'damn' all the time?"

"Damn is not a curse word. It's in the Bible. Even Aysha's gospel-singing mother doesn't object. It could be considered a suggestion that the object or person in question should be. Damned, that is."

Now he was rolling about on the couch, speechless with laughter. He'd lost his mind.

Then his laughter proved contagious, and some of the tension released from my shoulders. He pulled me onto the couch, kissed me soundly, and when I finally relaxed against him, he said, "I only intended to request information. I was surprised. Sorry if I asked in a way that triggered you."

Yeah, he'd triggered me alright. But at least he'd realised it. Was it just because I wasn't over Dai's shitty comment? When I'd told him that trying to hold me hostage could have resulted in the Gateway falling, he'd accused me of self-important exaggeration.

I needed to let that go. I was bored with it. But the memory kept coming back and I needed to work out why.

I disentangled myself and picked up the Book. "Can you show me a page that covers the Recorder's responsibilities and powers when they are in arbitration with the ruler of a realm? I need one I can share with Rollo, please."

It flicked. I glanced at the page. Yep, exactly what I'd expected. I could have predicted the full page it gave me.

The Recorder is always right.

The Recorder can do whatever the hell they want.

To whomever they want.

For any reason.

Or even for no reason at all.

Because the Recorder is always right.

The Book used longer and fancier words for Rollo. I handed it to him.

The door opened, and Tilly came in with an angry huff. Ah, I must be back in normal time. I'd better get on with my day. I pulled a little power and told it I'd be back soon, and I thought I understood its problem now.

"Dola, can we have two black coffees, please? And is everything else OK in the Gateway?"

The coffees arrived, and as I picked one up to pass to Rollo, I read, *You are always important but only indispensable some of the time. This is a vital distinction. All is well.*

Huh! That was true. And it was obviously my coffee because

Rollo's mug said, *There have been thirteen McKnight recorders. The previous five were useless in ways too tedious to bore you with. This one is not. We all need her to do her job.*

Wow! Just wow. Maybe she intended me to be flattered, but instead I was terrified. I couldn't let them all down.

Rollo picked up his coffee, read his mug and enquired, "How long have you been here, Dola?"

There was a coolness in her tone. "Since before the first Recorder and long before your realm was founded. We celebrated my 1400th birthday recently. I am sorry you missed the party simply because no one was prepared to stand up to the former king and ensure he apologised for sending Leif to abuse the Recorder and her staff."

She was cross. But why? I mean, sure, there were tons of reasons she might be. But she'd put up with so much in her long life. I wondered what had upset her right now.

I sat down and, while I sipped my coffee and watched Rollo read, made a mental note to speak with her privately and get to the bottom of whatever was disturbing her. Soon.

"But what rights do the realms have?" His tone was confused, not combative.

I asked the Book, "Could you show Rollo the realms' rights, please?"

The pages rustled until the agreement Mags and I had laboured over appeared. Rollo peered at it. Took out his phone, glanced at me and when I nodded, he snapped a photo. Then he poked his phone and looked as though he was reading. Did he speak Latin? Latin was not usually a computer geek thing. Then I saw his screen and leaned over. He was reading it in English with a translation app. Why the hell hadn't I thought to do that? That would have saved me an hour with Mags!

But as I read the translation over his shoulder, it was clear that, while it was giving him the sense of it, it wasn't translating it to anything like the standard Mags had.

I pointed. "That word means 'holocaust' in the old sense of

utter destruction and slaughter, not simply a catastrophic event. And this section binds a thousand generations of the original signatories, not just their descendants."

"You speak Latin?"

I laughed. "Like hell I do. But Mags does, with real sensitivity to the weight of the words. That's what we were doing." I pointed at the next section. "This says you can have all the rights and run your realm however you want to, provided you don't break this agreement. Once you do—you have exactly none. The power has them all. Troels surrendered the rights of the entire Viking nation the moment he sent guys with axes to attack it."

He nodded, a somber expression on his face now. "I think someone told him it was time he did something about the gate being closed. Obviously, him apologising wasn't an option."

I took a breath and pointed out the last section, still in yellow text. "That says the power can remove you all and give the realm to someone or something it deems worthier than you. It doesn't clarify whether it means evict you all or simply close down or destroy the realm. Or so Mags told me."

He'd gone pale under his usual golden tan. Well, good, because I needed a plan to resolve this mess, and him having his head up his butt and thinking he had all the time in the world, or that it was only up to him, wasn't helping me to fix it.

He looked me straight in the eyes. His eyes had changed to that weird golden-yellow colour that seemed to mean he was serious. "How long do we have?"

I told him the truth. "I think that depends on you. The power isn't always impatient if people are in motion, but it dislikes inaction."

"While we're alone, could you ask it what you can tell me about time travel?"

That was a good idea. I'd meant to do it and kept forgetting. "What can I tell Rollo about time travel?"

Anything you wish, provided he swears on the anvil never

to breathe a word about it in this life or any other, and to discuss it with no one except the Recorder.

That made me smile, and then it made me wonder about something that had been nagging at me since last week. I thought directly at the Book and asked, "Is that what you told Mabon too?"

I got the big green check mark again. So it wasn't only me—it was any Recorder. Mabon must have agreed to it when Agnes was alive, but now I was the current Recorder, he could tell me it wasn't "his first time-travel rodeo." And perhaps Mags or even one of her "fearmothers" had sworn the same oath to a former Recorder.

I turned to Rollo. "I'll explain while we're away, but right now, I have work to do in your realm. Do you want to come and watch? It might save me having to fill you in later."

"Dola, would you please tell Caitlin I'm about to summon her? She said her event finished mid-afternoon, so she'll probably be glad of the excuse to escape drinking cups of tea with dignitaries. And ask Finn, if he's finished his lunch, can he come and play too? Oh, and order another drone?"

"Yes, Niki. The same kind as the one we have?"

"Actually, is that one ours or Finn's?"

"It belongs to the Gateway. I authorised its purchase via the tech budget."

"OK, then order a replacement, will you? Finn loves it, and I might be about to break this one."

"Yes, Niki."

Rollo started to speak, but I held up a hand. "Unless it's urgent, let's talk about it later. The power's twitchy. Time's passing. Grab your coffee. Let's go."

I picked Tilly up, grabbed his arm and transported us all straight to the centre of the Gateway.

. . .

Once there, I brought the anvil down to my height and put the star on top. "I summon Caitlin Albidosi."

Reattaching the star to my chain, I called to Rollo, "Right, let's get you to swear formally on the anvil before I forget."

He approached the anvil cautiously. "Have you done this before?" He shook his head. "It's not nice. How iron-sensitive are you?" I was worried his half-Fae heritage might make this truly horrible.

But he waggled his hand in a not-so-much way. I hoped he wasn't trying to be a hero.

"OK, good. Put your left hand on the anvil please and repeat after me." I kept hold of his right hand, and when he tentatively put his left hand on the anvil and nothing happened, he gave me a querying look. "I'm shielding you for now."

He looked surprised. "Thanks."

"Flesh to the iron,
Force to the mind,
What e'er you state,
Iron will bind."

Rollo nodded. He was taking this seriously. Good.

"Repeat after me, 'I swear I will tell no one the confidential things I learn about the Recorder's role and powers, including the deep and the lesser secrets. I will not breathe a word about it in this life or any other, or discuss it with anyone other than the Recorder.'"

He repeated it word for word, gazing into my eyes as he did.

"Brace yourself." I let go of his hand.

He turned the air blue, cursing in Norse.

Caitlin, who'd arrived through the Pictish gate in time to see it, laughed all the way up the Blue Sector.

CHAPTER
TWENTY-ONE

Rollo had moved as far from the anvil as he could get and was still glaring at it and shaking his left hand. He gave Caitlin a look of utter disgust.

She said, "Don't glare at me. I went through it less than a month ago. First time in my life I'd ever felt iron shock. Stings like a mofo, doesn't it?"

The drone arrived on the conference table as Finn walked through the green gate towards us.

"KAIT, if you have a moment, please?"

She immediately sobered, bowed, and said, "My lady?"

"The power isn't happy. Something about a market on its boundary in Viking. It's threatening, if I don't so something about it, it will. I want to take a look. I don't know what you can do to help. But I knew you wouldn't be happy if I did it without you, so you're here. We've still got plenty of time before the book club is supposed to start. Is your mum OK now?"

She nodded, looked as though she wanted to say rude things but obviously changed her mind because all that came out was, "Books! They have a lot to answer for."

I nodded over at the glass cage holding Troels. "I'm going to try to make his new home, then clear out whatever's upsetting the power. Feel free to stab anyone who tries to interfere."

She looked over at Rollo.

"Yeah, not him, well ... unless he interferes."

She gave me a confused look. Eventually, I said, "Rollo's just discovered the extent of the Recorder's powers if she's in arbitration with the leader of a realm."

"Yeah, bit of an eye-opener, that one. Ma still mutters about it. It worked out great, though. The royals are too accustomed to being the highest authority. Once you work in here, ya see they're not. The power is."

Rollo gave her a long, considering look as if she'd given him some important lesson I'd have thought was obvious.

Caitlin continued, "Which reminds me, Hugh MacAlpin sends you his highest regards, oh yes, he does." We grinned at each other. "And Lewis Gunn says please call Aysha."

I nodded. "Done that." I squashed down a sense of annoyance. I'd phoned her, and Dola had already told her I was fine, just busy.

Finn arrived at the conference table and gave the drone a concerned look.

"I've ordered another one. So don't cry if I get it killed, OK?"

He glanced towards Rollo and Caitlin as though they'd give him a clue what was going on. I left them to it. Dropped my shields, connected to the power and almost immediately rose into the air.

The power was excited about making Troels' cell. I checked the area was clear and sank fully into my connection with it. This got easier every time. I was even starting to enjoy it. Not the floating in the air part. But the power wrapped me in a big hug and sent me a warm rush of gratitude and what felt like comradeship, along with the sense that it was happy it wasn't alone anymore. Tears welled up before I refocused myself.

I pulled power but then got a nudge suggesting I should leave it to the source itself. So I floated and watched the show. A swirling tornado of glorious rainbow power surrounded the glass cage holding Troels.

When it cleared, a blocky structure in ugly concrete was in its place. But it looked exactly like the blueprint I'd placed in the Book.

Huh! That was easy.

I called down, "Finn, we're taking that drone through the airlock and about 250 metres into Viking. OK?"

Finn froze for a few moments in that way he did sometimes when he was planning at lightning speed in his mind. Then his face cleared. "Cool!"

"I need you to take it out, and then point it back towards us so we get a good view of the gate and its surroundings."

I got a thumbs-up as he focused on the drone and his screen.

"Ideally, keep it high enough so they can't hit it with a well-aimed rock."

Another thumbs-up.

I used the power to grab the monitor off my desk and thought about when we'd expanded it into an enormous screen during the bondings so the people at the back could see what was happening in the middle. But this time, I needed it so we could all see what was going on outside. I lifted it towards the wall above the yellow gate, and the power held it there. It was a shame Troels couldn't see this. It might adjust his stinking attitude.

I'd barely had the thought when the roof of the new cell turned to a clear glass-like material and gave him a view of the large screen. It seemed the power agreed and wanted him to learn whatever this lesson was, too.

The feed from the drone showing the yellow gate from our side appeared on the screen. "Are you recording this, Dola?"

"Yes, Niki."

The power dropped me down to touch the anvil, and I thought, *Unseal the yellow gate, please.*

I felt the click in my head, and out of the corner of my eye, I saw Rollo flinch. Could he feel the energy of the yellow gate now he had the regnal power? I'd always suspected Troels knew more than he'd ever admitted about his gate being sealed.

The gate swung open, and Finn cautiously manoeuvred his demented electronic dragonfly through it. We all watched as it passed through the airlock, and then it was flying free in Viking.

Finn took it up high immediately and sped away from the Gate. Even watching the footage on the screen made my stomach rebel.

"Two-fifty metres away, my lady." Finn turned the drone around so it came closer to the gate. Then he zoomed in, and I saw what was upsetting the power.

The boundary zone had turned into a dumping ground. There were heaps and drifts of trash and debris piled right against the wall and next to the gate. The dark, wet ground had been churned into mud. There were a bunch of ramshackle market stalls and food carts with smoking braziers scattered haphazardly around. This was nothing like the attractive craft markets they held in Aberglas, with their tidy wooden stalls and Pict-blue canvas roofs. Neither was it anything like the friendly farmer's market so popular in the Red Celt realm.

This was a dirty shambles. It looked like something from the back streets of one of the poorest parts of some already poverty-stricken country. Filthy, unkempt dogs, so skinny I could count their ribs, dashed between the stalls hoping to catch dropped food.

But I saw smiling babies on women's hips and a few toddlers in amongst the men who leaned against the wall smoking and gazing at the airlock. I couldn't allow the power to blast this lot. It wasn't the babies' fault that their former king was an asshole and hadn't taught them any respect for the Gateway.

Quietly, barely above a whisper, I asked, "Dola, how good is your Norse? I need to warn them."

As Dola said, "Good enough for a clear warning," in my mind, Rollo offered, *"I'll do it. But how?"*

With that, the power lifted him into the air. I heard Caitlin and Finn gasp as I reached out a hand to him and linked my McKnight power to the Gateway. Fi watched us. Mags and Rosie looked at each other and nodded. The power swirled, and I felt something change outside. "What just happened?"

Finn adjusted the drone and focused on what looked like a speaker on the airlock. Ha! The power had learned from the blueprint for Troels cell. Clever power. It tickled me, and Rollo looked baffled when I giggled. *"It used to tickle me when I was a kid. Still does when it's happy. Speak, Rollo; they'll hear you out there."*

A stream of Norse flowed out. It sounded like a public service announcement, but no one moved. They stood gazing around to see where the sound was coming from.

Anger entered his voice now. I tapped my earbud. "Dola, do you know what he's saying?"

"He is telling them they have two minutes to move ten boat-lengths away. It is a Viking thing, Niki, the equivalent of 200 metres. Now he is telling the women, if they love their children, to move away with them."

A handful of women and kids moved, but most of them simply looked around without making an attempt to move. People were idiots. Was it because I came from a city where several bombs had exploded in my lifetime? If a loud, disembodied voice told me to move, I'd grab Tilly and head wherever the voice wanted me to. Aysha would want to argue, but even she'd get Autumn to safety first and debate later.

I watched the large screen and considered whether I could use the power to swirl some icy wind, as Dola used to do when she was angry. Caitlin watched the screen and shook her head in what looked like despair. She called something I didn't understand to Rollo.

He nodded and changed languages. Whatever he'd changed made a few more women look up, then they also moved away with two of the men. The stallholders packed up swiftly and followed them. But too many people still milled about waiting to see what would happen next.

I caught Rollo's eyes. He drew a breath as though to bellow at them. From his mind, I caught the thought, *"Perhaps this was why Troels always shouted."*

I held up a hand to him and said, "Use the yellow power. This might be the exact kind of thing it's for."

He frowned. "How?"

How the hell should I know? Then I wondered, was it like when I linked my own McKnight power to the Gateway so people could hear me at the back?

"Can you feel the yellow power?"

His eyes went distant for a minute before he nodded.

"OK, ask some of it to move here." I held my hand over my diaphragm to demonstrate.

His eyes glowed, and then he nodded again.

"Now imagine the power being breath or air and speak with it."

On the screen, a tall, slim, grey-haired woman stepped out from between two of the long huts.

Rollo seemed to be repeating his first instructions. But he wasn't using the regnal power correctly yet because I felt no compulsion.

The woman, though, wow, what posture she had. Straight as a reed, even though she looked to be in her late fifties or early sixties. She clapped her hands. At the staccato noise, all eyes turned to her. I saw her mouth move, but we couldn't hear her. She clapped again and then pointed in various directions away from the gate.

People started to move. She came closer to the gate, looked back and up at the drone, and made a circling motion I thought meant "repeat it."

I pulled Rollo closer to me, placed my hand on his diaphragm, and connected as deeply as I could mentally to *show* him what I did. "Let the power build up here until it almost hurts. Look, I'm not a Viking, but you are ... enough of one to hold this power, anyway. How would a Viking make someone do something?"

Whatever he did worked. I could hear the difference in his voice myself.

It compelled. It contained urgency.

It made me want to move away from the voice and him.

Rollo repeated his warning with an undertone of absolute authority and ended finally in English: "Move right now or die. Your choice."

He looked at me. "Thank you. I'll ask Ad'Rian tonight if he's got any tips on how to use the regnal power while I have it."

"That's Inge, I assume?" I asked the Gateway at large. Everyone nodded. "Remind me of her surname, please?"

Fi, always the efficient one, immediately said, "Haraldsdottir."

I dropped to the anvil and said, "I summon Inge Haraldsdottir to the Gateway."

Rollo's startled eyes caught mine mid-air. I said, "Troels asked to see her. Let's find out if she wants to see him. It will get her safely away from whatever is about to happen, too."

"Fi, ask Inge to wait please—this shouldn't take long."

I surveyed the screen carefully. There were two kids' toys, a wooden boat and a plushie, still lying on the ground.

Crap!

I remembered when Autumn had thrown her favourite unicorn out of her stroller when she was about two. *What's that acronym, IYKYK? Yeah, that's it. If-You-Know-You-Know.*

I hadn't known. But it turned out, if a child loses their favourite toy, they won't eat, nap or stop screaming until it's found. Happily, another mum who *did* know found it and posted about it online a few hours later. But Aysha bought a spare one that same day. I probably still had the one I'd bought in a box somewhere too. No one wanted to go through that again.

The power was insistent now. It told me, *The people have gone; I will reclaim my land.*

I asked it to wait just a little longer. Then I pulled power and directed it at those two small toys. I had no idea if I could do this —but I'd damn well try. On the screen, the two toys rose into the air. I wrapped them in rainbow power then directed them to the very edge of the houses and into the smaller passageway Inge had emerged from.

That was the best I could do. I told the power, *OK, it's all yours. Do whatever it is you need to do.*

And I waited.

I glanced around the Gateway. Everyone seemed to be OK. Rollo was back on his feet and headed towards Inge. I watched their hug with interest. He was fond of her. Finn was still totally focused on the drone. Caitlin's ever-alert eyes took in everyone and everything.

The power built.

My extremities tingled. I'd never felt this much power before. Once Fi realised Rollo was greeting Inge, she stayed at her desk. I called down, "Fi, grab the purple peril, please?" Finn would love the data, and I was intrigued too.

And then it all went up in flames.

CHAPTER
TWENTY-TWO

Perhaps because I was watching it on a large screen, the whole terrifying thing felt like a movie with a jaw-dropping CGI action sequence. None of it felt real except for the righteous anger that emanated from the power. I didn't know it could be this angry.

The fiery wave of destruction began at the gate and moved forward from the wall around the yellow gate in a steady stream until it extinguished and stopped. What it left behind looked like the aftermath of a fire rather than a bomb. I'd seen the debris after the bomb in Manchester—that was chaotic. This was orderly and clean. Through my connection to the power came a clear sense that it wanted to sterilise the entire area. It achieved that—now only empty blackened ground stretched from the airlock to the boundary. The area of destruction ended about ten metres before the houses. I considered the placement of the houses. It told me someone in Viking history had clearly understood the specific requirements of their agreement with the Gateway. So when and how had the knowledge been lost?

Rollo and Inge were murmuring to each other and totally focused on the screen. I pointed at it and called down to them, "How long have those houses been there?"

Nothing.

"*Rollo? My question?*"

Immediately, he held a hand up to Inge and looked away from the screen and up at me. "Sorry, I missed that?"

I repeated, "How long have those houses been there?"

He shook his head and glanced at Inge, who immediately called up, "About three hundred years."

"Thanks, and hello, Inge. Sorry to be so rude, but the power hasn't finished with me yet. Be down shortly."

She bowed and nodded.

I tried to think things through. The piles of debris the power removed hadn't piled up in a few weeks or months. That was years of neglect. Had Troels taking the throne been the start of this downward spiral?

I needed more information.

Then the feel of the power changed. Its anger was gone. I turned my attention back to the screen.

It began with high, black wrought-iron railings appearing in a curve right along the boundary. Then a double gate. A pathway appeared from the iron gate to the airlock outside the yellow gate.

The power was asking something. What?

I would read the section in the Book about better communication with the power. This was ridiculous. I made sure my shields were completely down, breathed in and thought, *Can you show me?*

In my mind, the airlock disappeared. *Ah, OK. Yes, good.*

I didn't think anyone else would be dumb enough to send people to attack the gate. And if they did, all that iron in those railings would give them pause.

The power obviously received my conclusions because the airlock disappeared from outside the gate. And, as it did, I saw the state of the gate itself and shared its stab of pain.

I gasped in horror.

The maintenance of the physical gates in each realm was, I'd

CODE YELLOW IN GRETNA GREEN

learned, a prestigious role. The realms often honoured some well-respected, semi-retired senior member of the community with the position. Hugh MacAlpin was exactly the type of person who might, in due course, hold the title of The Keeper of the Blue Gate. Those men and women loved being trusted to ensure that the wood was sound, the paint was pristine, the realm's emblem on the town side of the gate was fresh and clear.

One icy day shortly before Valentine's when I'd arrived at the Gateway, an elderly Hob called Oak had introduced himself to me as The Keeper of the Green Gate. I'd watched as he chivvied a group of young, energetic Hobs into "Mekkin' this a thing the Recorder and the power can be proud of. Put ye back into it, Poplar." And while the whole thing had reminded me of an episode of *Fawlty Towers*, Oak's pride in his role was unmistakable, and the green gate always looked beautifully tended.

I had never seen a gate look as sorry for itself as the one on the screen did.

It wasn't just the slashes in the wood made by the lumberjacks' axes. The paint was peeling. The wood dried out and unfed, and while it had perhaps once been yellow, now it was a dirty cream. Only the faded remnants of a sad-looking tree remained.

I called down again, "Don't you guys have a Keeper of the Yellow Gate?"

Rollo's golden skin had turned white around his tight lips, and Inge looked shame-faced. But there was something else there too. I couldn't work it out from up here. One job at a time.

The power dissipated now and I looked down to check that Fi was still measuring it with the purple peril. She was and watched the screen with interest.

I tapped my earbud. "Dola, can you or Finn, when he's finished with the drone, edit a five-minute version of this footage? Like news footage? I think this evening we'd better show the royals what happened today."

"I am already working on it."

"Of course you are, because you're totally brilliant, and I'm very lucky to have you on my side. Thank you."

There was a silence. Then, "Thank you, that is an astonishing thing to hear from a Recorder." She *was* in a funny mood. I would make time to talk to her.

But as I glared at the pitiful yellow gate on the screen, something clicked in my head. Perhaps before I lost my shit with the Vikings about the state of their town and their gate, I should consider that apparently none of my own ancestors expressed any sincere gratitude or ever told Dola she was brilliant. I mean, I'd known some of them had been a pain for her to house—but had *all* of them mistreated her? I'd look into it as soon as I had five minutes to call my own, but right now I needed to get my feet onto a solid floor.

As I approached, Rollo bowed formally to me. "My lady, may I introduce Inge Haraldsdottir, my stepmother?" He held the woman's elbow and angled her towards me. "Inge, this is Niki McKnight, the new Recorder, and a huge breath of fresh air for us all."

Inge gave me a respectful bow and then a blinding smile and an enormous hug. I caught Rollo's eye as I patted her back. WTH? My Gift sent me a wave of relief and delight from her.

Rollo said, "Because of the communication blackout, Inge hadn't heard you'd accepted the petitions against him." He jerked his thumb towards his uncle's cell.

I inclined my head to Inge, "I asked them to let you know." I must ask Fi why she hadn't mentioned she couldn't reach Inge. "But I only did it yesterday."

"I didn't know Gunnar had left Viking. I've never seen a holding cell in the Gateway before." Her face showed delight, but unhappiness shadowed her eyes. A Dolina arrived on the conference table behind her as she asked, "What do you plan to do with him?"

"Not sure yet. But he was heading for Yggdrasil, so I didn't have a choice about summoning him and then holding him."

At this, Rollo started laughing. She turned to him and gave him what I could only describe as a mother look. Interesting. He'd said she was his stepmother, but his reaction to the look told me she had indeed been a mother to him at one point at least. He straightened and smoothed his face. "Sorry. Niki only made the cell about half an hour before you arrived. None of us are used to it yet."

She mouthed the words "made it" and shook her head slightly.

"I'm so sorry, Inge; I feel as if I'm being very rude, and I do need to talk to you, but my time is ridiculously tight today. Do you have plans for this evening?"

She shook her head.

"Then I think you'll want to come to this book club. Breanna asked me to invite you both. But I wasn't sure if I'd be able to contact you."

She gave me a regal inclination of her head and a small smile.

"Troels asked to talk to his wife. We established he meant you. Do you want to speak with him?"

She nodded slowly. Reluctance came from her, accompanied by a strong sense of duty.

"OK, I'm going to leave Rollo to fill you in. Speak to Troels anytime you like. You can't enter his cell, but there is a microphone system. Rollo will show you; he's seen the plans. But please be aware there's no privacy at all, and he's being monitored twenty-four-seven."

Inge glanced around, obviously not seeing anything she recognised as a monitoring device.

"The power is very angry with him. Rollo will fill you in."

Her eyes opened wider as she looked at Rollo, who simply nodded at her.

"Please excuse me; hopefully we'll have more time during the arbitration or perhaps even this evening to speak. I need to talk with you about all the petitions against him."

She bowed. I glanced at Rollo and thought, *"Tell her about the parts of the data that concern her, will you? Oh, and show her where the Magic Box is."*

Without touching me, Rollo somehow suggested he was holding my hand. And then I felt a sensation on my lips, as though he'd kissed me. It was weird, but lovely. *"I'm sorry for all the trouble Viking is causing you. I'll see you later."*

Tilly and I walked back to the cottage so I could calm my racing heart and work out how someone who, as he himself said, was causing me trouble and work could make me so damn happy.

As I entered the kitchen and Tilly headed for her water bowl, I asked, "Hey, Dola, you good?"

"Yes, but do you have five minutes?"

"Sorry, no, unless it's super quick. I promised Aysha I would call Autumn. She'll be home from school now. That's what I came back to do. Also, I need to give Breanna a quick heads-up that I've invited a few extra people to her book club. Although she asked for Rollo and Inge, so it's only Mags I've added. Oh, and Rhiannon."

A chuckle came out of the Dolina on the kitchen table as I walked past it towards my office. "Aysha asked me to remind you to call Autumn. That is why I requested five minutes."

"You know, that's the one thing I wouldn't forget. Autumn using her firm voice automatically makes it to number one on my list."

"Niki, would you like me to update Breanna about the numbers for you? I have informed Juniper of the increased number of people to feed. But she said she was already aware."

I stopped in my tracks as I entered my den. "Wow, I never even thought about Juniper and the food. Thanks, Dola, you're not just brilliant, you're amazing too, and I plan to tell you far more often. Yeah, let Breanna know, please. And well done. I wish I could hug you. Should I give you a pay rise or something?"

"No, thank you."

OK. I'd never known anyone to refuse a pay rise. We needed to talk, but Autumn had to come first.

"May I have a glass of wine? It feels like I've earned one. I'm sure it's at least eight p.m. on my personal timeline."

Tilly danced and whined. "You hungry, girl? And some chicken for Tilly, please."

Wine and chicken arrived, and I hit the icon to call Aysha. She grinned at me as she answered. "I knew you wouldn't forget, but when I checked, Dola said you were having a busy day."

"Yeah, about that. Look, Aysha, I know you got yourself in a state. But Dola told you I was fine. I was simply busy. We spoke earlier, and if you know I'm OK, I don't think you have the right to throw a tantrum because I didn't call you."

I'd been giving this a lot of thought. She was out of order. And the huge stride over the line for me was her telling Lewis to ask Caitlin to get me to call her.

Aysha frowned and opened her mouth. I held up my hand. "Nope, it's my turn to talk. And listen up because I'm cross." That was one of her own phrases. Let's see how she liked it used against her.

It worked. She gave me her attentive face.

"You asking the man you're sleeping with to ask the heir to the Pictish throne, and my Knight Adjutant, to tell her boss, the Recorder, to call her best mate, is utterly inappropriate. How would you like it if I called some legal eagle's partner and said, 'Can you speak to your honey, a senior high court employee, and tell them to instruct the judge to stop doing what they're doing and get Aysha Clarke to call me?"

Her face was a picture.

"And before you say you were worried—at the risk of repeating myself—Dola told you I was fine. You might not have liked it. But you need to take it up with *me*, not my staff and not any random citizens. I don't mind you asking Dola, but I object to you browbeating her. Quit with the Shirley Valentine shit. Dola was distressed and confused. She's a 1400-year-old entity and isn't familiar with every Willy Russell movie that you and I might love. Please stop upsetting her. She's extremely busy too. Today she's writing our policy on the treatment of international prisoners. Never make her your whipping girl again. Are we clear?"

Astonishingly, she nodded.

"Great, I've only got about fifteen minutes. Can I speak to Autumn? And we'll catch up over dinner tomorrow. Do you want to cook, order in, or shall I bring food down? And let's take five then and work out a new way to be, so you're not panicking, and I'm not being guilt-tripped or seething."

Aysha looked shame-faced. Good, I'd got through to her.

Autumn's cute face arrived. Whoa, she looked serious. "What do you need, baby?"

I saw the lounge passing by as she headed for the stairs and heard, "Where are you taking that, Autumn?" followed by Autumn saying, "I needs to speak to Auntie Nik privately, Mum."

Poor Aysha, her "I can and will control it all" soul would be rebelling. I'd better keep this quick.

I picked Tilly up. "Someone needs to say hello while you're walking."

Even over the video link, I saw Autumn change. Her aura filled with pink, and her smile was blinding.

I hit the volume control just in time before "TILLLLLL-LYYYY!" came through the speaker at screech level. She was far too much like her mother for the health of my eardrums.

Autumn settled on her bed surrounded by unicorns, and I

gently said, "OK, baby. Your mum's a bit stressed, and I need to go back to work. Let's keep this quick. What do you need, and the answer is already yes."

"Come here, please, Auntie Nik. Very soon. Tomorrow? And bring the man." She sounded strange, lispy and uncertain.

"Which man, baby?"

It's comical when a seven-year-old sighs with all the disgust her granny Olive would have brought to the conversation. But I kept my amusement off my face as she said, "The one who had to bring all the ladies for their bondings. Mum said she'd told you!"

"Ah, that man, yes, we'll be there tomorrow. Will you be OK until then?" I watched closely as she rubbed her tummy, chewed her top lip, which looked peculiar, and finally nodded at her screen.

"Yes."

"So if I promise to be there tomorrow no matter what—*with* the man, his name is Rollo—can you promise me you won't scare your mum anymore before then?"

She nodded slowly and finally gave me a big smile. "Oh my goodness, you lost a tooth! Let me see."

Five minutes later, I'd left her with her mum in the kitchen, informing Aysha that Auntie Nik said the tooth fairy from Fae left ten pounds for the special teeth. And this was a special one.

Aysha didn't look amused. Well, tough, I owed her that one.

CHAPTER
TWENTY-THREE

"OK to come through?"

Before I even had time to answer, Rollo arrived in my bedroom at a run as I was finishing up in the bathroom. I'd decided a quick shower to wash away the craziness of my endless day would help me focus on the Recorder's and the power's goals throughout this book club.

Naked except for one of Dola's fluffy white towels, I turned to face him.

He looked both panic-stricken and determined as he gestured at his leather pants and denim shirt. "I might have understood what you were trying to tell me. Does it matter if I'm late for the book club? It's not a book club at all, is it? I've been playing catch up here. Sorry. I feel like the useless ally who doesn't know the rules."

"You won't be late. We've still got plenty of time. But what finally clued you in?"

"Inge. She said I was being a naïve, oblivious idiot."

Yay! Let's hear it for mums or stepmums who didn't allow their sons to carry on being ignorant. I'd tried to tell him myself, but he'd been so determined to quote Sun Tzu and pretend none of it was anything to do with him, and he didn't need to fight for what he wanted. I hadn't been able to break through his mask of calm. Whatever Inge said to him had gone home, though. I should get to know her better and find out why the Viking women liked her so much.

But now I had a stressed-looking man on my hands. Had I ever seen him stressed before?

He said, "You tried to tell me earlier, didn't you? I thought I could avoid fighting and let the realm decide what it wanted to do about Troels. But Inge says that's not the real problem. Subtlety isn't my greatest strength. I tend to focus on the army in front of me, not the spy coming in through the rear doors."

He sent a clear screenshot to my mind of the *Drengr* game. I smiled. I'd beaten many opponents that way. Send my sexy spy in through the back, neatly avoiding the enormous army massed out the front. Perhaps Rhiannon was right, and I was sneaky. Maybe I should start being sneakier with the realms.

At least Rollo might finally be on board. His next words confirmed it. "Did you mean, even though I won't be their king, I need to at least look like I could be to the other royals? And I should assure the power that I'll work with it to fix the problems?"

I hugged him. "By George, I think you've got it. Well, part of it, at least."

Unusually, he kept the hug brief. "Who's George, and what does he have to do with it?"

"You've never watched *My Fair Lady*? Never mind. I only meant you're catching on."

Rollo was focused now. "I need to go home, shower, and change. Inge said even if I plan to refuse the crown, as the potential future king to whom the Gateway has entrusted the regnal power, I have responsibilities whether or not I want them, and I need to appear authoritative while they work out a fix for the real problem."

"And what do *they* think the real problem is?"

"The warlords obviously. They're intending to let Troels take the fall for this and then carry on with business as usual and install a new figurehead unless we stop them."

"And do you have a plan to stop them?"

Rollo said, "Not yet. I have part of a plan, and Inge has some ideas. But she needs me to king-up or at least look like I could."

I smiled at him and thought back to that terrifying Friday morning. The one when it finally dawned on me, as much as I didn't want to be the Recorder and didn't have the foggiest notion what it truly entailed, I had understood the need to call the royals to my ascension to ensure it was legal.

The Recorder's robe had been the pivotal item that made me believe perhaps I could one day grow up to *be* the Recorder, even if, a few weeks ago, I hadn't felt as if I could step up that far. That life-changing Friday happened five weeks ago tomorrow morning.

Gods and Goddesses, I'd come a long way. Rollo was smart; he'd catch up quickly too now he'd been shaken out of his denial.

I pushed the memory of my terror before my ascension towards Rollo. To offer my support and let him know he wasn't alone in not wanting to face what the power had dropped on his unwilling head.

If he thought he needed to get changed, I could help him fix this and ensure he fully understood Breanna's plans for tonight.

I addressed the Dolina in my bedroom as I grabbed my cosmetics bag, some clothes, my Recorder's robe, my handbag and Tilly. "Dola, I'll be at Rollo's for an hour while I get ready. We should catch up there if you need me."

In my mind, Rollo laughed. *"I'm a man. I need fifteen minutes max."*

But he was wrong.

"No, you might only need fifteen to shower and dress, but I want to check you understand what tonight's about. Then after tonight we need to talk about what's happening in Viking and get your head into the right space."

I paused. I wasn't comfortable pushing him, but it needed to be done.

"I need—nope, the Recorder needs to check your understanding of the likely outcome tonight if you don't interfere. I've learnt some stuff since I arrived here. Let's see if we can't use it to your advantage."

Dola asked, "Niki, shall I send you the briefing document for the book club so you can both familiarise yourselves with tonight's agenda?"

I froze for a minute. "Document, whose document?"

"Breanna's, she has some ideas. And I believe she has already obtained support from the empress and the Smiths for her plans."

"Yes, that would be great. Thanks. I'll speak to you from there."

I grabbed Rollo, said, "Empty your mind, please," and moved us to Edinburgh.

I took five minutes once we got there to hold him. He could have showered at my cottage, but there was no privacy there and never any uninterrupted time.

"Rollo, it's been a week since you accepted the yellow regnal power. And I still don't know what you want or why you even accepted it. You're not power hungry, and I was very careful not to force you—remember? You say you don't want to be king, but is it because you're scared of doing it? Or something else? Because one thing I've learned in this role is the royals *always* have a plan. Often it's a lousy plan. But if your own goals aren't clear, you'll end up going along with theirs. They don't give you a choice."

He nodded at me seriously. Then grinned at me.

"What?"

"You just transported in a towel. That's extremely sexy."

I laughed, but I wouldn't be distracted from my duty to ensure he understood his options. "Thank you but consider a couple of other things in your shower, please. If you manage to avoid the royals' plans, you'll still have to deal with the Recorder.

I have a responsibility to Viking too, as you learnt this afternoon. And if you don't listen to me, then you'll have to deal with the power. You saw what it did to the boundary."

He nodded again. But he didn't understand yet. He started to speak, and I held my hand up.

"Rollo, I need you to understand how angry the Gateway power is. It's an ancient power. Think of it as a deity, if that works better for you. But it isn't a person you can talk round. Its solution is to sterilise the realm and start over with a new realm filled with new people who want a safe place to live and who won't ever send people to try and chop its gate down. *Holocaustum,* remember? I looked it up – it can also mean a burnt offering. Did you ever wonder what happened to Indigo? Because I have. I asked the Book, and all it would say was that realm wasn't ready to be 're-seeded' yet."

The look of horror on his face told me I'd finally got through. "Go, take your shower. Work out what you want while I get dressed and try to look like the Recorder. Then let's talk."

I got Tilly some water, accepted a coffee from Dola and listened as she ran through some items she needed answers on while I threw on my leggings and a shirt. I left the Recorder's robe over the back of the yellow armchair. I liked chairs in bedrooms; I'd never realised that before.

I was perfectly happy in Rollo's bedroom. It hadn't even occurred to me to use his guest room as my dressing room. I was comfortable and content here with my still bare feet snuggled in his fluffy rug. I used his wonderfully well-lit mirror, which was the coolest hidden door into his office, to fix my face. I was at home here. So was Tilly. She was already snoring softly on his bed.

Huh!

The idea that, including Aysha's house, I might now have three places I felt at home startled me.

. . .

I read Breanna's document. Oh dear. It would have been helpful a few days ago, but now I had Troels in custody and the arbitration was open, it was already hopelessly out of date. Breanna's idea of finally banning unaccompanied women from visiting Viking felt like the worst kind of adding insult to injury. Ordinary women shouldn't need to be accompanied by someone with a sword to be safe. And what if the slimeballs drugged their bodyguards too – did we hold them responsible? Or just tell them they couldn't eat or drink while their charge was in Viking? It was all ridiculous, out-of-date and old-fashioned. But the proposal stated the other royals broadly agreed. Galicia had welcomed the idea, as Dola had told me. But there wasn't even a whiff of a new or creative solution in the entire proposal.

I sighed.

Rollo came out of the bathroom with a towel slung around his hips. He looked, as always, like an advert for a gym. But I refused to be distracted. He still wore the Fae glamour L'eon had crafted for him. Sure, it was eye-catching. But was it who he wanted to be seen as anymore? Honestly, the Thor-style muscles were a bit over the top. The boy toy, or was it toy boy persona? Anyway, whatever it was, once the novelty wore off, his real self, the one I spent time with privately with his naturally long, lean muscles, was so much sexier. And his true height he'd hidden for years so he could appear shorter than Troels could give him an advantage now.

If he went to the book club as his true self, he'd be older and taller. Apart from Glais'Nee, who'd always be the tallest man in any room, as his real self, Rollo would be the same height as Ad'Rian, who was the tallest of the rest of them with his lanky Fae build and long, long legs. Rollo was in far better shape, though. These small things might give him the edge he'd need tonight.

Had any of the royals ever seen the real Rollo?

I must have been talking to myself in my mind because he

answered me, "We seem to be in sync. I'd just thought it was probably time—and no, only Ad'Rian."

"Whoops, no offence. I mean, I like eye candy, Rollo, but the real you is far more compelling. Only Ad'Rian knows? Seriously?"

"Yes, he checked the glamour could be safely used long-term when L'eon created it. I needed his consent to wear it outside of Fae, of course. And he re-checks it when I visit him. I know you saw through it that day in the Gateway when Troels tried to grab your dog. But wasn't that because of the power?"

The amused expression on his face as he gazed at Tilly, who was now lying on her back with all four legs in the air, didn't match his impersonal "your dog." I put that aside for another time.

"It probably was the power, yes. But has no one else ever said anything about the fact that you still looked so young?"

He shook his head. "Outside of Fae, no." He considered himself in the mirror. "When we stood here together last weekend, it was the first time I've intentionally taken it off since Troels dragged me back to Viking over two years ago. Although I never used it when I lived here. It's probably why I like Edinburgh so much. I got to be myself."

That was a long time to hold a glamour, and it solidified one of my earlier ideas. Did the other royals understand his Fae heritage I wondered, or was it another of Ad'Rian's secrets?

He looked in the mirror again, and with a finger twitch and a slight shake, he removed the glamour. The shake dropped his towel on the floor, and sadness came from him through our connection. "What are you sad about? You always take it off for me when we're alone."

"Do I want all the royals to see the real me? It's going to slow things down, isn't it? They'll debate about it."

I found a light tone to cheer him up. "You can always keep it for playtime." Accompanied by the risqué image I sent him, it startled a laugh out of him. Which had been my intention.

Then he began to get dressed.

Tilly and I cuddled on his bed and watched the show while I considered his problem. His real body looked much healthier than the over-muscled Thor glamour. I liked that his real hair was slightly shorter with its subtle shades of blond. It settled just below his shoulders instead of Thor's too long, too corn-coloured, long blond swishy mane. The length of his back with its well-defined but less in-your-face muscles, his watchable butt and the long, lean muscles of his thighs all covered in a light dusting of blond hair—

"Niki?"

"Huh?"

"I'm trying to put clothes on here; you're making it difficult …" Then he started laughing. And joined me on the bed.

Five minutes later, I slapped fruitlessly at his shoulders. "Seriously, I'm supposed to be briefing you. Put some clothes on so we can think straight, will you?"

Still laughing, he dressed quickly as I resolutely focused on my phone's screen and the rest of the documents Dola had sent. Breanna had compiled discussion questions about *Ruling Regally*. Yep, I had opinions on all those. There was a copy of her agenda with some good ideas, but no solutions for the asshole warlords. I'd asked Dola to help with that when she wasn't so busy. Caitlin's briefing on the three possible contenders for the throne had helped, but I wanted to know about the others too. I made a note.

"Ready when you are."

I glanced up, and my mouth actually turned into the Sahara Desert. I coughed, desperate to get some moisture into my mouth.

Some men can rock a suit, but honestly, those guys are few and far between, and they're mostly celebrities who have their clothes hand-tailored by wardrobe departments or couture houses. The average guy never looks quite right in a suit. The shoulders are too large, the jacket is the wrong length, or the button doesn't fasten without straining the fabric. Their trousers are too tight, too loose, or the wrong length.

I'd seen thousands of bridegrooms over the years, and, even on their wedding day, many men looked like they'd borrowed their suit.

It's only when you see a handsome man in a suit that fits him perfectly, you realise what an incredible power it has over your hindbrain. A beautifully fitting suit says leader, successful, in charge and enough in control of myself and my world to have my clothes fit me like a glove. It's a powerful subliminal.

And Rollo pulled it off like a king.

His accessories finished it off perfectly. He wore cufflinks shaped like the Vikings' tree rune on the top of the anvil, and his hair was secured with a wired strip of navy-blue leather at the nape of his neck. It paired with the suit so closely, it must have been bought to go with it. With his hair off his face, his prominent cheekbones and sculpted jaw were shown off wonderfully.

"That leather thing is clever. It's the perfect finishing touch. Modern and classy."

I itched to stroke that suit. I slid my hands up to his shoulders. Under my fingertips, it felt like a soft wool blend, and it hugged his shoulders beautifully. His tie was level with my nose. It was the same deep blue as the suit and stood out strikingly against the pristine whiteness of his shirt. The super-fine golden diagonal stripe gave way to a photo, or was it artwork in the middle just above where his jacket would close? I peered closer.

"It's the tree, isn't it? Yggdrasil?" Dola had helped me practise saying it correctly.

He smiled at me softly. "Hey, well done. I like hearing my name on your lips."

"*Your* name?" I was lost. "I thought it was the sacred tree?"

"It is. And my House."

"Your House?" Yep, completely lost here.

Now he looked surprised. "Sorry, I thought the Recorder would know all the houses?"

"You mean like the Fae and House Alicorn, and the Picts and House Albidosi, the Galicians and House Asturia?" All those A's had really confused my name-challenged brain in my first few weeks.

Rollo nodded. "And the Red Celts and ap Modron."

I shared my confusion, "But the Vikings are the House of Odin's Horse?"

Now he smiled. "Which is the English for ..."

I waited. He couldn't mean, could he?

He could. "... Yggdrasil."

"But why doesn't anyone call it that?"

I thought for a moment and got more confused, not less. "I mean, they don't call him 'Mabon of the house of *from the mother*' or 'Ad'Rian from the house of *the unicorn horn*.' Everyone uses the realms' own choice of their name."

Rollo gazed at me. I had the sense he was giving me time to get there on my own.

I queried my Gift and then burst out, "Why did you guys get a translation when they didn't? It feels political to me."

Rollo immediately smiled and verified my feeling. "It was political. Troels isn't House Yggdrasil. Only the direct line can claim that name. My father passed it to me. Troels may have usurped the throne, but he couldn't claim the name. Because he should have simply been the regent for House Yggdrasil until I reached eighteen. We talked about it, didn't we? But as the Recorder, you know this, surely?"

People thought Recorders knew flipping everything. All the power but never enough knowledge was starting to feel like the story of my new life. "So why did everyone go along with it?"

"Ad'Rian has some ideas, and I've never challenged it because I don't want the throne—" There was something behind his eyes now.

"Yeah, so you've always said."

Whoops, I'd interrupted him. I leaned back from him so I could see his face, tilted my head and waited, giving him some space. He straightened his shoulders. "I have a question for the Recorder."

"OK?"

"Before these paternity claims, have any of the realms ever filed a protest, a petition or an objection to *anything* that's been going on in the Viking realm with your office?"

I smiled now because I was getting an inkling of where he was going with his plans for this evening. And I knew the answer to this.

"When I was trying to work out how Troels got away with his despicable behaviour for so long, and what, if anything, my gran had tried to do about it, I asked the Book the same question." I looked up and met his eyes. "No, never. And that's weird because, you wouldn't believe some of the petitions people do file. They'd keep an advice columnist busy throughout their entire career. There's one Galician farmer who has resubmitted a similar petition once a quarter for years."

At Rollo's interested look, I shook my head. "You don't want to know. It's about goats. Specifically, his neighbour's goats and some trees. Who the hell knows? Maybe he thinks I'm a secret goatherd."

Rollo chuckled. "The things I'm learning about the Recorder's Office."

"I almost agreed to hear Goat Man's petition because the Smiths had repeatedly submitted the same request to every Recorder for centuries, and that injustice should have been fixed much sooner. But I looked into the Galician's complaints, and it really is just about some unruly, disturbed goats."

He laughed and hugged me. I finished, "Seriously, though, to answer your question, going back through the old records with what I know now, there are a few women who *might* have been accusing Troels of rape. But they didn't. They didn't name him or give any evidence or even a clear statement. Nothing I could take action on, so I can see why Gran couldn't."

He nodded. A look of satisfaction crossed his face. "Thought as much." His arms tightened around me.

I stroked the Yggdrasil tie. "This is beautiful." The trunk of the tree had a stylised capital Y in stained yellow wood which appeared to grow out of it.

"It was a Yule gift from Kari a few years ago. I think she was hinting then I should go home and deal with him, but the timing wasn't right."

"Speaking of timing … the McKnight Gift has an opinion. Do you want to know it?"

He nodded. "Always. I need all the help I can get."

I looked straight into his clear topaz eyes. "Do *not* tell the royals you don't want the throne. Not yet, at least."

He tilted his head. "But why not? I don't want to mislead them."

I laughed. "Someone said I was sneaky this week. I've been thinking about that, and I think they're right. If we were playing *Drengr*, I'd send a spy in through the back door. I'm guessing you'd let your army fight it out at the front. And lose?"

He laughed and nodded. "Well, I was never a top player, even though I worked on the game. And you were—so you might be right. What would you do?"

"I'd ask the senior royals for their best advice privately. Don't confirm or deny anything. Then you're not lying. Let everyone else assume whatever they want to. If, or rather when, they push you, remind them the Recorder is in arbitration with Viking, and until that's concluded, you can't comment."

He looked happier now. Considering he was half-Fae, he had a very unFaelike relationship with the truth. He was too black and white.

"You need to share your plans with me soon, because the power is twitchy about Viking. It wants a resolution."

I slid my rainbow robe on, and as I struggled with the usually smooth-running zip, I caught sight of myself in the mirror. It was a little tight in the wrong places and loose in others. Was I getting my curves back?

I jiggled and watched myself in the mirror until the robe adjusted itself to fit me perfectly. "Are you ready to go back? Breanna asked if I would summon her guests."

Rollo met my eyes in the mirror. His mouth hung open. "The hours I stood for the fittings for this suit. How did you do that?"

"You should be nice to Mags. The Hobs have some handy tailoring spells."

Through our link, Rollo felt overwhelmed. Then something changed in him. He straightened his shoulders, glanced at the bedside clock. "I don't want to delay you. But you've given me a lot to think about. Can I bring myself to the Gateway in a few minutes?"

"Sure, see you later." I kissed him, stuffed my things into my bag, picked Tilly up, and took us straight to the centre of the Gateway.

PART FOUR
BOOK CLUB

Every warrior should digest the important lessons the Chief Skald gives us in his teaching tales. Like this one.

A bird was flying south for the winter. It was so cold, the bird froze and fell to the ground in a field. As it lay there, a cow came by and dropped dung on it. As the frozen bird lay in the pile of cow dung, it realised the warm dung was thawing it. Warm and uninjured, it soon sang of its joy. A passing cat heard the bird's singing and came to investigate. The cat unearthed the bird, helped him out of the dung and ate him.

Warrior lessons for a longer life:

Not everyone who craps on you is your enemy.

Not everyone who helps you out of the crap is your friend.

If you're warm and uninjured—even in a pile of crap—keep quiet!

Winning the War Against Yourself: Daily Weapon and Warrior Care by Arinn Tusensköna

CHAPTER
TWENTY-FOUR

The Gateway was bustling when I arrived. The light spring scent of Thyme's smell-nice spell blended with wafts of lavender-scented beeswax. Rosie had done a wonderfully creative job of making the flowers on the walls appear to be pretty book covers, and the whole place sparkled. I could see my face in the highly polished conference table as I put my handbag down on it.

Juniper and her usual gaggle of Hob ducklings were unpacking stacks of square brown boxes in an area they'd set up a short distance from the conference table where Breanna's guests would sit.

Everyone paused in their work to ruffle Tilly's head; she adored the Hobs, and the admiration society seemed to be mutual. I passed tablecloths of Pict blue, but the pile of plates were all the colours of the rainbow.

I greeted everybody as I made my way to the anvil, checking in with Dola as I walked. Now the cleaning was completed, I raised the iron barriers around Indigo and Yellow. I didn't want the royals delaying everything by peering into Troels' new high-tech cell until we'd had time to discuss him.

"Everything OK, Dola?"

"All is well here. Rollo is meditating. He asked me to alert him as the last guests arrived."

Meditating, huh? Whatever worked. Sounded like he was planning an entrance. I checked my watch: 7:35 p.m.

"Niki, I have prepared several short videos. Shall I loop them on the big screen as people arrive?"

I thought about it for a few seconds, but I couldn't see a downside. "The only things I want to keep secret from the group until I'm sure they're ready for it are the ideas we have about the sources of the droit de seigneur and how I plan to block the trade in it. I'm not even sure if I'm going to share that this evening. I don't want to share your plan for the final location of Troels' prison cell—yet. They may have better ideas than ours, so let's not make it sound like a *fait accompli*. You can show them anything else you want. Am I summoning everyone? Because, if I am, might I have to start a few minutes early?"

"There is a full checklist on your iPad, Niki."

My iPad appeared ahead of me on the anvil's throne. It glowed against the wood and highlighted the power-created rainbow flowers that adorned the anvil's throne. The iPad screen lit up as a page loaded.

"Wow, the anvil looks incredible! It's all glossy and black, and the power feels so happy. What did the Hobs do to it?"

A voice behind me said, "Aye, it's an old recipe. Rule of threes, ye know. Part magic, part herbs and oils, and part stove black. Sworn by it for centuries, we have."

I turned around to see Mag Hobs looking … elegant. Yep, that was definitely the word. "Young Poplar came in tae do it. Guid job he did."

Well, her local accent was back, if less intense than I'd heard it previously. But the Gateway was full of younger Hobs. Maybe she had a façade to maintain?

"It looks beautiful, Mags, as do you. I love the ensemble." An interesting shade of pink flushed her golden-brown skin. She looked stylish in a perfectly cut sheath dress with a three-quarter-length jacket in a shade of peach so deep it was almost but not quite orange. The colour took ten years off her.

"Is Prince Rollo no' here?"

I was slightly confused but answered her, "He's in Edinburgh; he'll be here soon."

"Aye, guid. We lent his mam an outfit for tonight. She'll be along shortly. Ye summoned her in her hoose clothes; she couldna wear those in front of all the royals, and Juniper gave her a calming drink. Her and Rollo might have had words?"

She was fishing, but there was genuine concern behind her words. "That was very kind of you, thank you. I think Inge only said what needed to be said." I gave her a firm nod. She either knew what was happening, or she didn't, but I wouldn't make the mistake of underestimating the Hobs again if I could avoid it.

"I owe you, Mags. I'm grateful for your skill. I seem to have changed shape, and your tailoring spell is the only reason my robe fits so well, so thank you again."

"Aye, lass." She actually patted my arm. "You're looking better than ye did when ye arrived, that's for sure and certain."

With that, she headed back towards the conference table, calling to the last of the cleaning crew, "Come away noo, girls; royals'll be arrivin'."

And they would.

Placing the star on the anvil, I made a start with the hostess. "From the Blue Picts, I summon Queen Breanna Albidosi, the KAIT and the TEK." Juna was apparently holding the Broch tonight.

Finn clambered out from under a desk, a cable in his hand. "I'm already here, my lady."

I gave him a thumbs-up and pressed on swiftly, hoping if I got them all here at once, I could avoid having to greet them separately. That would save us all half an hour.

"From the Red Celts, I summon Mabon and Rhiannon ap Modron. From the Violet Fae, I summon Ad'Rian and Glais'Nee Alicorn." I had no clue if Glais'Nee's surname was actually

Alicorn, but the power gave me a confirmation it understood who I meant.

"From Orange Galicia, I summon the Emperor, Empress and Prince Alejandro Asturia."

I checked my list. Yep, that seemed to be everyone. Inge walked down the Green Sector towards the centre and paused at the boundary, even though it was already down.

Why was she waiting? Was she another person who'd never been invited to the centre before? She looked unsure but extremely classy, a shapely column of silver-grey, from her stylishly cut short grey hair with its natural silver highlights to her charcoal leather boots. A beautiful trouser suit comprised of a short bolero-length jacket with a mandarin collar. The double row of buttons down the front gave her a military or commanding officer air. The narrow cigarette-cut pants showed off her long, slim legs. Mags had certainly found her the perfect outfit.

I strolled over to Inge to escort her to the centre. Unlike everyone else here, she hadn't known her evening would include a book club. She might be a little out of her depth.

I couldn't have been more wrong.

She bowed as I reached her. "Thank you so much for including me. That was immensely kind of you, taking everything," she paused and glared at Troels' new cell, "into consideration. And unexpected."

I had no idea what to say. Fortunately, Fi appeared holding two tall, elegant glasses of fruity-smelling pink fizzy stuff and handed one to Inge with a smile. They were soon chatting away like old friends.

Fi had mentioned Inge to me several times. What had she said? Oh, yes, she'd been supportive and offered good advice when the locals were giving Fi a hard time about being a single mother and, as far as they were aware with the time-shift effect in the Gateway, only working a few hours a week for my gran. Therefore, she must have been sponging off her family. The former Viking queen who ran a thriving import and export business herself, had been a mentor to Fi and encouraged her to set up her online bridal accessories business. Inge had founded her own business to support herself and her daughter after she left Troels. She'd sympathised with Fi's plight and that of her young son. Yep, that seemed to be all I knew.

"Dola, did you give the Dolina to Inge?"

"No, Niki. When you left it on the conference table, I thought perhaps you had an objection."

Whoops, Fi had said something, and I'd missed it. "Sorry, Fi," I gestured to my earbud, "I was listening to Dola. What did I miss?"

"Inge asked if I could tell her where Prince Rollo was, but I couldn't. And, also, would it be alright if I popped home quickly? I'll be back before the food is served. I need to take some more supplies for Mum."

"Of course, go whenever you wish."

I focused on Inge. Worry, guilt, hope and fear. Well, that didn't help me much. But let's see if I could ease some of them.

I smiled at Inge. "I don't know what you said to him. I didn't have enough time to find out, but I know you must have given him *exactly* the right advice at the right time. Because he finally got focused on the correct things. Please stop worrying. He'll be here shortly."

Inge shot a look at Fi. "Is that what you meant?"

Fi nodded.

"What?" What had I said?

Inge turned her clear, intense aquamarine eyes on me, and finally I saw her smile. She moved her silver hair behind her ear, even though it wasn't actually long enough to do that—the habit of a lifetime of longer hair probably. "Fi said you don't beat around the bush. I was only panicking because I didn't hear you summon him."

"Oh, he's in Edinburgh; he doesn't need summoning. He'll make his own way."

Inge gave me a startled glance, consulted her watch, shot

another look at Fi and opened her mouth as my Gift alerted me, and I heard, *"Incoming, Boo, is the centre clear?"*

I checked. It almost was. *"Yes, if you aim for the Yellow side of the centre, it's all yours."*

To Inge, I said, "Here he is," and turned to watch Rollo drop from the air into, yes, a perfect three-point superhero landing in a couture suit. The wool his suit was made from obviously had some stretch in it. It did wonderful things for his thigh muscles. He looked up straight into my eyes, and the slightest twitch of his dimples told me he was loving this. I tried very hard to keep my own thoughts off my face.

I already wanted this evening to be over so I could spend some alone time with him. Hadn't he promised me a nightcap after the book club? What might a nightcap involve?

And how had he done that landing? Was he jumping before he took off and then landing in midair? It looked ridiculously cool. I wasn't alone in thinking so. Finn, Alejandro and Caitlin were all clapping and cat-calling.

Mabon spoke to Rhiannon and Ad'Rian, "Oh, yes, have a watch party, we should. Not seen the new movie yet, have you?"

Ad'Rian, with an amused quirk to his mouth and a dry tone, commented, "Marvellously Marvelesque, nephew."

I turned back to Inge, who was just closing her mouth. "As I mentioned, Inge, you must have said exactly the right thing. It had the desired effect."

She reached out as though to grip my arm and then stopped herself about two inches short of touching me. "Recorder?"

"Mm-uh?"

"How do I book a meeting with you? I've wanted to since I heard about your ascension, but with the realm being cut off, I didn't know how to get through."

"A meeting? Is it urgent? I'm away next week."

Her face fell.

I tried, "Do you need to be back in your realm tonight?"

She shook her head. "I couldn't face speaking with Gunnar

today, so Marguerite suggested I stay with her and come to the book club tonight to see if I could book an appointment with you before I talk to him. I already know what he'll say; he's so predictable."

It took me a moment to recall Troels' first name, and then I processed the idea that Inge and Mags were close enough that she'd been offered a room in her house. I considered my options. "If you're staying tonight anyway, come to the cottage tomorrow. We could have morning coffee about eleven? We can take some time, then."

She gave me a lovely smile, which softened her severe features considerably. "Thank you, that would be perfect."

Someone ruffled my hair, and I turned with a grin to greet Mabon. He handed me a glass of red wine and then chinked his beer mug against it. "At a book club, *bach*, me. Imagine that! Teased me about it for a week, Rhiannon has, and tonight I find she's coming herself. More trouble than they're worth, daughters are. But then she's a lot less trouble than my son. News, do you have about Dai? Healer Hall told me it wasn't my concern. Ask the Recorder, I must."

I reached out to pat his shoulder. "They tell me he's fine, as I'm sure Dola told you. They've put him into a healing trance in a heavily warded room. They're taking no chances this time. And they're pulling some of the old ones in from the glades to consult. They say there's something wyrd, possibly even eldritch going on, but no one wants to guess what yet."

His face fell. "If eldritch it might be, best to ask my mother. Be awake for Mothering Sunday, she will; never misses her cake."

"Oh yeah, about that ... I have bad news ..."

CHAPTER
TWENTY-FIVE

The enormous screen we'd left attached to the wall of the Yellow Sector for this purpose came to life with a white-on-black quote.

"Justice will not be served until those who are unaffected are as outraged as those who are." Author Unknown

Ad'Rian and Mabon were still chatting. "That must be Dola's work. Her accuracy is impressive. Most people incorrectly credit Benjamin Franklin with that quote. It was probably one of the Greek philosophers, but there are no accurate attributions, you know."

Mabon's face creased into a baffled frown. "Why would it matter? They're all dead, now. Stolen many a good joke, I have. Once a man's dead, it's not his anymore. Is it?"

Then the footage Dola put together of this afternoon's excitement on the Viking boundary began to play. All conversation stopped as Dola announced, "This took place in the Gateway this afternoon and involved the Gateway team with assistance from Viking royalty. The power insisted the Recorder take immediate action."

While she was talking, we watched Finn pilot the drone

through the airlock. When it turned to show the view of all the rubbish and detritus around the rickety market stalls, Dola paused her commentary and the video as though she'd predicted a round of muttering. And she was correct.

Mabon and Ad'Rian locked eyes as usual in a private mind-to-mind conversation. The Galicians and Breanna gravitated together. Inge moved over to Rollo. Rhiannon headed towards me but then paused by Caitlin. Alejandro strolled with his distinctive bullfighter's hip wiggle to join my KAIT.

The footage resumed, and Dola's pleasant contralto filled the Gateway. It wasn't loud, but it compelled you to pay attention. I should ask her to teach me that skill. "The Recorder requested I edit the entire mammoth task down to a brief montage so you may all become conversant with the power's current unhappiness." The video restarted.

Wow, she made it sound as though we'd all battled for hours. Although, perhaps we had. I had no idea how long it had all really taken. That was always the problem with any work I did in the Gateway.

The footage now showed Rollo and me, suspended in the air, trying to move the people in Viking away from the gate. Inge slid her eyes up towards Rollo, who still stood by her side with his eyes glued to the footage. She watched him closely. Ad'Rian shot me an interested look, which, from His Majesty My-Face-Only-Moves-During-Months-Without-an-R-in, was unexpected.

When Rollo found his yellow power and used it to force the people away, Ad'Rian and Mabon gave him a speculative look, and Glais'Nee offered a single firm, approving nod.

The footage changed to show Inge appearing from between the houses and me moving the kids' toys. All the women with children—if you know, you know—let out *awww* sounds. Rhiannon and Caitlin just looked confused.

As the power sterilised its boundary, complete silence fell. Rollo sent, *"We should fly together more often; we look good up there."*

Rhiannon arrived in front of me. "Recorder, I'm here to discharge my debt, but I may need to leave early. I see Glais'Nee is here. Can we get whatever it is you need me to do done?"

Honestly, I was delighted and little surprised she hadn't arrived snarling at me when I summoned her. I nodded. "Can you give me half an hour to get them all settled down, and then we'll grab Glais'Nee?"

She wriggled her shoulders, seemed to go inside herself and then nodded. "An hour or two even will be fine. I may have longer. It's so hard to tell."

I waited, but that seemed to be all she was going to share.

Glais'Nee stood silent and alone as he scrutinised the frozen frame on the screen. I'd grab him as soon as I got all the royals settled down. What could he tell us about the difference between Rhiannon's genetic heritage and Dai's? And why didn't Mabon know these answers? He was supremely laidback, but these were his kids, after all.

Rhiannon pointed at the screen and gave me a discreet thumbs-up. I grinned at her. She looked surprised until I pointed at her T-shirt. Today it said, *Why don't we make some new mistakes? Repetition is the mother of boredom.*

I leaned in close to her ear and pointed at her T-shirt. "You'll be lucky. Have you ever played Book Club Bingo?"

I could see her repeating the words "Book Club Bingo" to herself as her phone vibrated with a request to accept an incoming link from me. Her energy had changed again since this morning in my kitchen at breakfast. Less snarky, more regal and authoritative.

Fi, Finn and I had wasted a happy twenty minutes setting up a passworded private page on the Gateway's news portal with the bingo card. I watched Rhiannon read the document, mimed crossing off the phrases as people said them, and pointed to the instructions at the bottom, which told her to log in and choose her colour. Our server would keep track of the winners. There were minor prizes for the corners and for lines, but the main prize for a full house was a meal for two catered by Juniper. That was Dola's suggestion.

Rhiannon gave me a smile of untainted sincere humour as her thumbs moved. I gave myself an imaginary prize for correctly guessing her colour choice. It was red all the way for the dragon queen.

In contrast to my internal amusement, the video now showed the iron railings being created, the airlock disappearing, and then it froze on the frame of the poorly tended Viking gate.

There were gasps of abject and sincere horror. Then the familiar quote appeared overlaid on the scarred, neglected yellow gate.

I understood why Dola was obsessed with this quote when Alphonse said, "I don't care what the Vikings have done. The Recorder can't go about destroying realms."

I smiled at him. "Your Imperial Highness, I fear you may have missed the point that the Recorder didn't. The power did, and it was absolutely within its rights to have done far worse."

He glowered at me. I ignored him. I was sorry if he was having a bad day, but I had far too much to get through to pander to what felt like his deliberate misunderstanding.

"All I did today was find out what the power was going to do. Then asked my TEK to record it with the drone so you could all see it, and we did our best to make sure no one was injured. Show Slide 1 please, Dola."

A blown-up version of the photo of the original agreement between the rulers of the realms and the Gateway in 1124 AD appeared on the screen, with the relevant sections still in yellow. Mabon said something in Welsh, and at his words, Rhiannon leaned forward, then grinned.

"If someone who speaks Latin, and ideally was one of the original signatories, would like to translate the yellow sections for everyone, that would be great. I owe Mags a debt of gratitude for her invaluable help with it, but we've both peered at it long enough for one day."

No one spoke. I pointed with my laser pointer and circled two of the names. "Ad'Rian, that's you, and, Mabon, that's you, isn't it?"

Mabon, Ad'Rian and Glais'Nee looked at each other. Ad'Rian stood up. I offered him the laser pointer, but he almost imperceptibly shook his head.

He had a commanding presence when he shed his usual air of indolence, and he took everyone quickly through almost the same information Mags had given me.

The only difference in the first paragraph was when he said that *unto the thousandth generation* had, back in the day, meant *in perpetuity*. This agreement meant forever. Wow! I wasn't sure there was a real difference between 25,000 years and forever, but somehow, "in perpetuity" sounded even more binding.

Ad'Rian made clear the realms' responsibilities to defend the Gateway and the Gateway's right to do whatever the hell it liked to anyone who attacked it or even who failed to defend it. His statements rang with such weight and clarity that everyone actually hung on his every word. I'd always wondered what that overused phrase might look like in reality. It looked like a room full of people totally focused on the King of the Fae, barely blinking as they waited for the next bombshell to fall.

Inge had gone pale. Alphonse had two spots of colour high on his cheeks. But when Ad'Rian reached the part about a furlong in front of the gate must be kept clear, the red blotches on Alphonse's cheeks spread over his entire face. Someone should check the emperor's blood pressure.

"*A momento*, sorry, but one minute please, Ad'Rian. You are not saying that, if I permitted, for example, the church to hold one of their *especiale* markets a few times a year during *festivale* in front of the orange gate, the power could hold me responsible and claim my realm. Be serious, Sire."

Ad'Rian bowed to him. "No, Alphonse, I am not saying that. I

255

am saying when the Empress Sabella's ancestor, Cisco ..." He bowed to the empress and then, taking in Alphonse's confused look, consulted the bottom of the screen as though to remind himself of the full name of the long-dead founding emperor of the Galician realm. "Francisco Gregorio Ignacio Godino-Asturia signed this document ..." Wow, I could see why Ad'Rian didn't remember that name. He drew in a long breath, perhaps to calm himself, but his face showed nothing.

"Cisco, your emperor in 1124 A.D. bound you all conclusively for all time. He was a sensible man; there was no alternative, and *he* understood that clearly. Anytime you permit—or even if you have not permitted them—any single time you do not immediately remove any temporary or permanent structures from the furlong in front of the gate ..." Ad'Rian paused.

But the empress, not the emperor, said, "Yes, Your Majesty, please do explain this. I have tried several times to no noticeable effect."

Ad'Rian picked up threads of his explanation. "If you are *ever* foolish enough to encourage or allow anyone to attack the orange gate, or if you fail to defend it, or even any other gate from attack, then the power could turn your entire realm, and everyone in it, into the barren black earth that you clearly saw in Viking on the video."

Ad'Rian paused, presumably to breathe again, or perhaps because Alphonse looked as though he was about to explode. When he didn't, Ad'Rian shot me a look.

In my mind, I heard, *"A short history lesson appears to be long overdue. Shall I?"*

When I nodded at him, he continued, "We shall take the example of last week. Consider, if you will, if the Recorder hadn't been able to deal *by herself and alone* with the lumberjacks Troels sent to attack the yellow gate." He paused.

I wasn't sure why Ad'Rian was building me up. But if it brought Alphonse down off his high horse, I welcomed it.

"Imagine, please, if she were a less powerful Recorder, as

many have been, and put out a call to the realms for help. Then everyone must understand ..." he gave Alphonse a glare I wouldn't have wanted directed at me, "... ANY of the royals who didn't arrive in the Gateway with an army of their best warriors to defend the Gateway *immediately* would be in breach of this agreement?" He gestured at the screen.

Sabella, Breanna, Caitlin, Finn, Mabon, Rhiannon, and even Mags, of all people, were all nodding serenely along. Only the emperor's jaw hung open. But I sensed surprise from Rollo and shock from Inge. Ad'Rian had been right. This lesson was necessary and timely.

He continued, "You must have seen that the Recorder is the only reason every man, woman, child, dog and even those small playthings in the area weren't destroyed today. And, *Sire*," he made sure the total contempt with which he imbued the word got through to Alphonse, "I did not appreciate the tone you took about the Recorder and my nephew's valiant battle today. You do not show the proper respect. Troels did not show the proper respect, and, as we have all seen, that was the beginning of his end."

He pointed his finger, and a glowing violet oval circled the word *holocaustum*. "The modern term might be 'annihilation.'"

The slide of the contract on the screen changed to the photo of Troels looking about eighty-five. "Alphonse gasped, and Ad'Rian concluded, "Ah, thank you Dola. A timely reminder of what happens to a ruler when the power withdraws its support from them."

Empress Sabella smiled sweetly at her husband. "I told you so, Phonsie."

Ad'Rian sat down to polite applause and head nods from the royals. And Dola's favourite quote came up yet again as the next section of footage rolled.

Another video montage began playing. This time she showed the clips she'd played for Rollo and me while we sat at the picnic table in the Recorder's Refuge eating Juniper's magical tart. Leif attacking Caitlin and me. Troels forcing his way past the waiting bond mates in the ceremonies on Valentine's Day. Everyone heard Inge's outraged gasp as Troels pushed his daughter aside and trampled on her Galician lace wedding dress train in his determination to berate the Recorder. When the clip played of Rollo bringing down his uncle by throwing Nanok as Troels tried to grab Tilly, there was a spontaneous round of applause.

Juniper's Hobs began circulating with trays of canapes, and, following a gut-level poke from my Gift, I moved to the serving table to see what, if any, magic Juniper was introducing into this insane multimedia mix? I should have discussed this with her, shouldn't I? But when I leaned in to whisper to Juniper, "What spells are on these?" she handed me a menu with complete unconcern.

"I consulted with Dola, Your Maj."

CANAPES

Open Your Mind—Cheese Souffles & Pepper Parcels

Open Your Heart—Beef & Herb Morsels & Smoked Salmon Delights

MAINS

Move Past the Past—Spicy Lamb with jewelled rice and lime pickle shock

Courage to Change—Bacalhau à Brás

Time for Justice—Vegetable Terrine with chickpea salad and rhubarb drizzle

Confidence in Action—Vodka-cured Herring, dill pancakes and rhubarb pickle.

Your gift bags contain Just Deserts

Once upon a time, I wouldn't have asked, but now I knew better than to allow my discomfort in querying things to leave space for unpleasant surprises. I asked, "Lime Pickle Shock?"

Juniper sighed and waved a finger. The word Shock changed to Surprise as she said, "A new apprentice, my lady, Basil Two, he will be good once he has more experience." She nodded to herself as though she'd make sure he was. I was still trying to process Basil Two as a name. Was it like Basil the second? But I hadn't quite finished with her. I couldn't begin to pronounce it, so I simply pointed at *Bacalhau à Brás* with a querying expression.

"A request from Queen Breanna. It's a cod and potato dish with eggs. The emperor enjoys it, and he's having a difficult month."

"OK, thank you very much. I'll let you get on."

But Juniper wasn't done with me. "No big magics, milady. Really nothing more than a few nudges in the correct directions. On my honour. Apart from the Just Deserts, obviously. But they were at your request."

Actually, they weren't. Glais'Nee had told me at John Fergusson's sentencing that if Juniper would make her Just Deserts, he would come to the book club. As one of Ad'Rian's most senior advisors I'd wanted him to be here, so I'd asked Juniper for whatever the Just Deserts was.

I told her this and watched as her mouth formed an O.

She removed the menu from my hand, added it to the rest of the menus, and wafted her hand over the stack. I could see she was using magic, but I couldn't clearly see what she was doing. Then the end of the menu changed. She'd added to the last line.

Your Gift Bags contain Just Deserts.

Note: Overconsumption of this confection carries risks. One is more than enough for **anyone.**

She re-read it, nodded to herself, and handed it back to me. "But what does it do, Juniper?"

She looked me up and down carefully. "You will not have a problem, my lady. Eat yours with your man and with my gratitude at the end of a day you have enjoyed. The magic will ensure they keep for several weeks in a refrigerator. But I will advise the empress I have renamed them so she can attempt to talk the emperor out of eating three of them."

"But what do they do?"

She smiled. It wasn't a pleasant smile. "They used to be called Karma Cake."

CHAPTER
TWENTY-SIX

If you'd like to play along with book club bingo as you read, you can get a downloadable and/or printable PDF here: www.linziday.com/bookclubbingo

The next thirty minutes took me back in time to any of Janet's endless meetings at the Registrar's Office I'd worked in for eighteen long years. If Dante had been writing *Inferno* in the twenty-first century, one of his circles of hell would have included twenty-four-seven meetings with the office bore and a bullying boss.

But this was Breanna's evening, not mine. A few weeks ago, she'd wanted an excuse to bring all the royals together without Troels demanding to come. But events had moved swifter than Breanna. Weirdly, no one had yet asked about Troels, which astonished me. They'd gasped or smirked at his photo, but nothing else. Were they all too busy playing politics? His new cell in the Yellow Sector was clearly visible below the large screen, but none of them had even mentioned it.

I reminded myself firmly this wasn't my meeting. I'd only offered Breanna a venue. So I sat and tried to relax at her right hand, where she'd insisted I position myself, and attempted to be a polite guest. She had Alphonse on her left, and I had the Empress Sabella to my right. Sabby never used a single word if she could squeeze a hundred out instead, and while I thought she was probably a sweet woman, her endless wittering and twittering wasn't good for my concentration.

And Breanna tried to focus them, but they were all determined to revisit old ground.

Most of us, with the exception of the senior royals: Breanna, Mabon, Ad'Rian and the emperor and empress, were all happily filling in our Book Club Bingo cards. So far, we'd ticked off, "Thought we were supposed to be talking about a book," (Mabon). "I invited you all so we could fix this," (Breanna), and "When will the food be served?" (Ad'Rian).

Empress Sabby had said, "Oh, those poor children and the dogs, did you see their ribs?" "Those poor, poor dogs" and "oh, the babies" about eight times in half a dozen different ways and several languages. We only got to tick "Oh, the poor girls/children/dogs/" box off once though.

I sighed.

Finally, we had someone bang on the table (Mabon), who said, "Wasting time, we are ..."

Huh, I hadn't included that one. I smiled as everyone obviously thought I would have and scrutinised their bingo cards carefully before releasing a collective disappointed sigh.

Mabon summarised my feelings perfectly, "... Know, you all do, the Recorder has taken Troels prisoner, yes? So, what is this meeting about now? Because, understood I did, it was supposed to be about him. A piss-poor job of planning the next steps we're all doing."

Then followed five minutes of noisy chaos where we established that only the Galicians were unaware of this week's gossip – sorry, news. Everyone else rushed to inform them. Mostly inaccurately. I'd personally travelled to Viking and wrestled Troels off his horse at the base of Yggdrasil itself, apparently. I wondered if I'd enjoyed myself?

There was much pointing, and then half the guests left to peer at Troels' Cell.

> Niki: I'm going to need more wine, please. I'll get it from the Magic Box.

> Dola: It's already there. You told me they would need time to blow off steam. We are running to schedule.

> Niki: I hadn't thought how annoying it would be. It's like herding damn cats. Speaking of ... have you seen her?

> Dola: No.

Clutching my wine, I headed back towards the table, where Mags was now in my seat. She immediately stood up. I covered my relief with a gracious smile as I gestured her to sit back down and moved to a seat with better companions further around the table and far away from the emperor's grumbling and the empress's never-ending chatter. Settled between Rhiannon and Caitlin, I glared at the latter.

She shrugged and whispered, "It's always like this. Why do you think the slimeball got away with it for forty years?"

"Did you read your mother's briefing document?"

She nodded.

"Do you think you could quietly remind her she wrote it? She had a plan, and it was a good one?"

Caitlin looked a little torn, then stood up and moved around to speak into her mother's ear. Breanna's eyes focused on me, and I nodded firmly and tapped my cheek where her crown piercing was. She grinned at me and nodded.

Mags had opened a copy of *Ruling Regally*, smiled at Breanna, and in a perfectly clear, if still noticeably Scottish accent, addressed her. "Wha' do you think about this bit in *Ruling Regally* where she says that everythin' ye've done, and all the actions you've previously taken, have got you exactly where ye are today? Because I like the next part when she advises that if you don't like where ye've landed, ye must take some different actions as you move forward. Thoughts? Anyone?"

No one had any thoughts, but we ticked the "mention of *Ruling Regally*" box off on our bingo cards.

Complete silence fell. Except that Glais'Nee stood up, bowing silently and most respectfully to Mags.

Mabon gave her a seated bow. "A good point you make, Marguerite. So what do we do with him now? Many fine oubliettes I have …"

We all ticked that box off.

He continued, "Bluddy Vikings, nothing but trouble for centuries. Put a stop to it, we should."

We all ticked that box off and realised someone was close to a line.

I saw Ad'Rian open his mouth and hovered my finger over "A delightful glade I could offer." He started to say it, and I ticked it off.

All our phones flashed with a notification. ***The Recorder has completed the first vertical line.***

Everyone glared at me, but while they were sending me daggers, I was hovering my finger over, "Can't those kids ever put their phones away?"

The emperor said, "I don't think this meeting is the place for phones." Then he caught my eye, and it finally seemed to dawn on him that the Recorder and her staff were the main people he was scolding.

I saw Finn and I were the only ones who ticked that box. Huh.

I used to be very good at this.

But perhaps I should let Finn win and get this meeting back on track?

I decided to be the "Someone who stands up in a huff." I

ticked it off my bingo card and stood. "I don't want to delay Breanna's intentions for this evening."

I gave her a look that said, *Seriously, Bree, queen up*.

"However, you all need clarity, and I have information. The Recorder's Office is *not* seeking your input on Troels' eventual fate. But the power would prefer your agreement to his proposed interim location. Possibly, you haven't all read your emails yet, but the Recorder's Office has been in active arbitration with the Viking realm and *Warlord* Gunnar Troels since yesterday morning."

I paused and checked around the table they were all listening attentively, but Inge and the Galicians did so with wide, surprised eyes.

I pressed on. "As I'm sure most of you know, that gives us the right to do," I smiled around the table and toned down my intended *whatever the hell I want* and settled for, "whatever we deem necessary and think best to obtain the correct outcome in the over one hundred arbitrations."

There were the expected gasps at this.

"But how can it be a hundred so quickly? Didn't you say it was only a few dozen before Fergusson's sentencing, Bree? So how can it be so many already? So quickly? Surely it takes time for so many women to submit these things?" The empress turned her enquiring gaze to Breanna.

Before she could rephrase her question another five different ways, I held up a hand and inclined my head to Glais'Nee. "We had genetic testing to help Glynis."

Next, I inclined my head to Mabon. "Glynis is the Red Celt woman who organised the filing of the petitions. It has now been determined beyond doubt that Troels was the father of many more children than just the fifty or sixty belonging to the women who filed the initial petitions. The rest of the women are currently filing their claims too."

"But were they raped? I mean, actual, well, you know 'rape' is a harsh word. It wasn't just fun gone astray? Are we being too hasty? The trade, you know?"

The entire room turned to stare at Alphonse. I ticked the box that said "Actual rapes or ...?" Fi told me none of the royals would be insensitive or ignorant enough to say that and I was making the card impossible to fill. Her expression when I caught her gaze did not bode well for Alphonse's future trade permits. We all ticked that box along with the "We really must consider the negative effects on trade" box.

Rhiannon checked her bingo card, smirked, and ticked a box. "If the Recorder needs any help, I'll soon have many hungry dragons and dragonets to feed."

All our phones pinged once with a notification: ***Queen Rhiannon has completed the first horizontal line.***

Rhiannon gave me a startled look, and Alejandro glanced up from his phone and mouthed "Queen Rhiannon?" at Caitlin. She nodded at him, and he let out a silent whistle.

Before I completely lost control—honestly, herding royals was worse than trying to corral cats—I sucked in a long, quiet breath and prepared myself to throw a rope bridge over the gaping chasm I'd need to get them safely across if I was to give Rollo a fighting chance of being in charge of his own future.

"The Recorder's Office will conduct the arbitration once all the evidence has been collected and processed. But you should all be clear: The power's actions mean Gunnar Troels is no longer the King of Viking."

CHAPTER
TWENTY-SEVEN

The emperor completely ignored that I was standing and in the middle of an announcement. He stage-whispered to his wife, as though Breanna and Mags weren't sitting between them, "I told you so."

When she only nodded placidly at him, he added, "Well, now, Rollo will have to buckle down and run the realm properly." Then he glared at Alejandro, who was sitting happily next to Finn and poking his phone, as I was, to tick off the box with "Rollo needs to/should/has to/ought …" but Rhiannon got there before me and ticked it for me.

Then I heard a soft, "Ha! Sneaky flaming Recorders—you're all the same." She ticked the ones that I'd crossed off and she hadn't yet noticed on her own bingo card.

I considered explaining the rules again and settled for, "Now, now, Rhi-Rhi, play fair."

She growled. Caitlin laughed.

The emperor realised no one was paying him the attention he thought he deserved. "Where is Rollo anyway? Shouldn't he be here?"

Realising no one planned to answer him, Glais'Nee enquired

politely, "How could you miss the arrival? A perfect three-point superhero landing."

Alphonse's confusion was comical. Had it been anyone other than Glais'Nee, who obviously intimidated him, I thought the emperor would have continued whining, but he simply looked puzzled.

Plaintively, Mabon observed, "We're going to need more beer, *bach.*"

I waved him towards the Magic Box and shoved my phone at Rhiannon so she could tick off the correct box. Mabon never thought there was enough beer—that one had been a no-brainer. To Rhiannon, I muttered, "I'm trusting you. Don't cheat. Remember, I'm awarding the prize. I can't win it myself, can I? I'm just competitive about this type of thing."

Then I straightened my shoulders, linked my voice to the power and said, "If I could have your attention for two more minutes, please. I'd hate you all to feel afterwards that we kept vital information from you."

Now they paid attention, and I took the first step onto the frail rope bridge across the chasm. "House Yggdrasil's yellow regnal power passed to a trusted conservator a week ago."

"Trusted conservator, whoa, Boo, that's quite the vocabulary you've been hiding."

At my glare, he sat up and straightened his smirk. He didn't notice Inge's intense focus on him, but I did.

"The power withdrew it forcibly from all the realms where it shouldn't have been, thanks to the Viking smuggling activities that Troels backed—we'll need to discuss those over the coming weeks. The Recorder intends to ban the trade in and transportation of Droit de Seigneur via the Gateway."

Alphonse looked up at the mention of trade and then returned to whispering at Sabby.

"The power also withdrew the regnal power from all the people it did not feel were worthy to hold it, which included the former King Troels."

I got an approving nod from Ad'Rian and frowns, confusion and mutters of "House Yggdrasil, who's that?"

The Empress Sabella asked, "Do we know them?"

"Rollo is the heir," came from Glais'Nee.

"Is it one of those uncivilised warlords?" muttered Emperor Alphonse.

"It's their bluddy unpronounceable tree, isn't it?"

Then they all started talking at once. No one was listening to anyone else.

I tapped my earbud. "Dola, roll the footage of the yellow power transition, please, and increase the volume, will you, so they have to stop going around in circles and get up to speed on the events of my week before I die of hunger?"

I intended to say the last bit just loudly enough for most of the table to almost hear me and get a clue that I wasn't down to my last nerve yet, but if they didn't stop being so freaking predictable, I might be soon.

But of course I'd forgotten I'd linked my voice to the power, so they all heard me clearly.

Crap!

I debated whether to apologise, but it turned out I wasn't sorry. I tapped my watch.

"It's been an endless week for the Recorder's Office, and I'm ready for food, but we have to do this first. Then while we eat, and I've seen the menu—it looks amazing—we could discuss the Viking situation as of *today*."

I fixed my gaze on Breanna and added, "And even *Ruling Regally*?"

It turned out most of them thought that was reasonable.

Emperor Alphonse was still frowning and grumbling. He was in a lousy mood tonight. He'd been so kind and charming at Natalia's bonding. Stubborn for sure, but his energy today felt different, sharp-edged and prickly. What the hell was his problem? I checked him with my Gift. Hmm, family troubles. Well, that could happen to anyone. But with Natalia on her honeymoon, Alejandro must be the cause. He'd been very quiet so far.

The video started rolling. Dola had edited the power transfer to Rollo down to a few minutes' footage. She was getting so good at this. I would congratulate her later. But then, as the tightly curated clip ended, the editing credit said *Finn Albidosi*.

And yet again, the same quote came up on the screen. This time it was black on a rainbow background to represent all the realms.

"Justice will not be served until those who are unaffected are as outraged as those who are." Author Unknown

"What does that even mean?" Alphonse asked as he gazed at the quote.

Inge finally spoke, "I believe, Your Imperial Highness, it suggests that just because you weren't raped yourself, you should still want to see swift justice for those who were. Especially, perhaps, those in your own realm."

"My dear woman, no one in my realm was affected by that barbarian."

Whoa, way to be tactful, Alphonse. Three things happened almost in unison. My left shoulder pinged, Sabby let loose with a stream of angry Galician, and a burst of bright fury came at me. I followed it back to its origin and met Alejandro's impassive face. My Gift suggested he truly hated his father right now.

By the mutinous set of Alphonse's jaw, I guessed his wife had reminded him that Inge had been married to the barbarian and had several children with him. He turned red again, but I thought with anger, not shame.

All the other faces around the table turned back to me, and I realised I was still standing. Whoops. OK, time for a reset. Breanna needed to run her own damn book club.

"Now you're all up to speed, let's take a short break to refill our glasses and allow Juniper to set the table for food, so Breanna can formally convene the book club."

There, that might get things moving in the right direction and get me off the hot seat.

I was escaping to the green gate for some fresh air when Glais'Nee fell into step beside me. I smiled up at him. "It was very kind of you to fit in the women and their kids for Glynis at such short notice. I know how busy you must have been. She said you were wonderful with them all. I have a small gift to say thank you. Dola will send it through to you at the end of the evening. Please don't go home without it."

He paused and bowed. "Unnecessary, Recorder, but thank you. A long life can be occasionally tedious, but the last month has been more interesting. What is that saying?"

I hit send on my message to Rhiannon as Glais'Nee turned his beaming smile on me. "Yes, I have it. 'Those who fail to learn from history are doomed to repeat it.'"

I smiled back at him because I knew that quote. It was Winston Churchill. But Glais'Nee hadn't finished. "And those who studied current affairs while they lived through millennia of them are still doomed to watch as people who won't trouble themselves to study anything, and certainly not history, repeat it anyway."

I laughed, but then I stopped and thought about it. "Wow. I'm cross because these royals are stuck in a loop and won't move to the twenty-first century, but how must you feel? I'm so sorry, Glais'Nee." Without thinking, I stroked his arm soothingly and then realised I was invading the personal space of the most powerful warrior in the Fae realm and blushed. "My apologies."

He only laughed, and tucked my hand into the crook of his elbow. "I like you, Recorder, but consider two things. History is always written by the victors. I saw what happened at the time. The history books in your schools do not begin to tell the whole truth. They tell only the winners' truths. And you should also

271

know I have seen many men like Troels over the years. Always people try to deal with the figurehead. But the true corruption is in the roots, you know."

I'd only recently learnt this myself, so I asked, "Do you mean the literal roots they make the Droit de Seigneur from, or the dozen warlords who are all keeping their heads down?"

An expression of glee crossed his face. "That you know enough to ask that question gives me hope for change."

"I can't take the credit because I didn't until recently. But if you have more advice, I'd love to hear it."

He nodded, and then his eyes turned the pure white of one of the older Fae using their power and talent to the fullest. "Recorder, I share a *seeing*."

Shit!

Ad'Rian had once taught me what to do if this ever happened.

I straightened and in a firm voice said, "Glais'Nee, I hear you, and I listen with an open heart." Then I tried to remember how the hell I was supposed to open my heart. Whew, yeah, OK. I visualised my green heart chakra opening to the huge Fae in front of me.

"There will come a time when you are frightened to speak. You will find your inspiration in modern words and your courage in an unlikely place. Remember, Nik-a-lula, when you speak, history will be listening. Speak well. Words matter."

His eyes shifted back to their usual deep violet, and he smiled down at me. "Sometimes we see nonsense, you know. But I hope it helps you in a time of need." Then he shook himself.

I filed everything he'd said away and tried not to let it freak me out. While we waited for Rhiannon, I tried to gather a little more help with one of my current puzzles. "Glais'Nee, were you part of the team who investigated the iron that was dumped near the unicorn feed sheds?"

Now genuine surprise coloured his expression, and, cautiously, he asked, "May I enquire how you know about that?"

I considered how much to tell him, but Glais'Nee had always dealt openly and honestly with me. His sharing of the *seeing* proved that, so I should probably return the compliment. "When I was in arbitration with the Picts ... I'm not sure what's known of that outside of Pict ... and I'm bound to keep Albidosi secrets confidential, but ..." I trailed off. I couldn't quite work out how to tell him about Mabon endlessly "going to see a man about a pig." Which had turned out to be pig iron. The extra wards on the Fae gate that I'd blown out with my true ascension. The reports of the slag iron being dumped in Fae and a few other weird things. None of them had made sense on their own, but now I was looking at a bigger picture, I saw a pattern.

Then Rhiannon rushed through the gate. "Sorry, Niki, could *not* get away from the flaming empress. The woman doesn't even need to breathe while she's talking!"

"I've thought the same myself. I think you know Glais'Nee?"

She did, and I left them to it. He knew what I needed to know about her. He'd told me he thought he already knew the answer, but as she'd now gained the whole of regnal dragon power, he'd like to recheck her.

As I headed towards the cottage, Tilly fell in at my heels, and I called back, "Come for lunch, Glais'Nee, and we can discuss it freely." In response to the glare she aimed at me, I added, "Not you, Rhiannon, a different problem."

"I'm not a problem. I'm a flaming delight," followed me down the path.

As I opened the back door, Dola said, "Niki? People are looking for you in the Gateway."

"Can you make a polite announcement that the Recorder will be back as soon as she is able, but there's an urgent matter that requires her attention—some nonsense like that?"

"Yes, but why?"

In my head, I heard, *"You OK? You feel weird, and people are looking for you. Hang on, Dola is making an announcement. Oh, need any help?"*

Aloud and in my head, to save me repeating it for Dola, I said, "No, I'm fine. But everyone needs to encourage Breanna to run her own book club. She had some good ideas, and she's allowing them all to derail her, which isn't like her. I thought if I got out of the way, she might notice she's wearing the crown and behave like it. I don't think Alphonse and Sabby are helping—they seem to be having a sniping domestic disagreement over her head. Shame we can't rearrange the table."

I ate a brownie with ice cream. I was saving my Just Desert to eat with Rollo. After what Juniper said about the end of a good day, I knew I wouldn't be eating it tonight. Karma Cake, hmm? I'd find a lovely day and try it to find out what it did.

I drank a much-needed, stupidly strong coffee. If I could get two minutes' peace in the Gateway, I'd boost my energy. I fed Tilly a modest amount of chicken, allowing for how much of that spicy lamb dish she'd probably con people out of. Then I took responsibility for a little self-care and breathed quietly. Like a damn grown-up!

My coffee cup had the same quote on it too. Knowing Dola did nothing without good reason, I asked, "Why do you keep force-feeding everyone this quote?"

"I hoped to spark discussion about the current problem. Everyone believes it is someone else's problem. Everything is always some other, better-qualified person's problem. You have just proved it by having to leave the gateway."

It had been a long week, well, actually, a long almost two weeks. No, a long six weeks, beginning when I arrived here. Ugh! My brain was on a go-slow.

I managed to get out, "Can you explain your plan another way, please? I'm tired and probably being stupid. Sorry."

Slowly, Dola said, "Do you require the royals to have their own ideas? Or only to go along with yours? Because they have given you their ideas. You predicted ahead of time they would not offer any new solutions, and you put their words on your Book Club Bingo card to show them that."

"Yeah, I did, didn't I? That was petty of me, wasn't it? Or was it arrogant? Oh, hell."

Was I turning into "that person"? Goddess, I hoped not. Anyway, none of the monarchs, except Rhiannon, had played it – but it *had* kept my staff sane.

Dola hadn't finished with me. Using her tentative voice, she offered, "Niki, I have known all thirteen Recorders, several extremely briefly, but I have known them or understood them by their actions. The best of them, the ones who improved situations for themselves or others, *were* arrogant. They were rebels and troublemakers like Agnes, or misfits like Florrie, or changemakers like Moira with her rule about the cloaks and many other things. Moira liked rules."

There was a short pause before she continued. "But the better ones were all eccentric. They were passionate about things. They were not fond of any rules except the ones they'd made themselves. The worst of your ancestors were the ones who did not care. You do care, and that is a good thing. Please do not stop caring, because people who do are stuck in a world someone else made for them. If that occasionally makes you feel arrogant, perhaps you could consider if a little arrogance may be necessary sometimes to make changes. It will not make you into a bad person."

I didn't know what to say. She'd given this a lot of thought. "Could you send me a copy of everything you just said, please? I'd like to consider it when I have enough brain cells free to think clearly, and I'm not in the middle of an event."

"Yes, Niki. I repeated most of it from a poster Finn requested I make for his apartment, but I can send you a copy. The words seemed apposite in this current situation. But you asked why I keep repeating the quote. The royals are often outraged by the wrong things. Over many centuries, they have trained themselves or their descendants to only be concerned about wrongs in their own realms. Sometimes they simply deny things occurred if they can't fix them.

"Alphonse illustrated that clearly. Several of the petitioners are from his realm. Based on their petitions, they may have been among the most ill-treated by their own people. Their strange church blames the victims. He either doesn't know that or is choosing to forget it. And I believe the Pict Strictures even include advice to the monarch not to poke their noses into another realms' business."

Well, that wasn't true. The senior kings often stuck their noses in. I'd dealt with them doing that to me a few weeks ago.

But Dola answered my thought, "Mabon and Ad'Rian have often broken that pattern, but even they do only enough to deal with their immediate problem. If the realms had banded together several hundred years ago, the Vikings might have had laws by now. Laws that could not have been overturned by one corrupt king. Those laws may have prevented Troels from doing what he did. But, instead, over those centuries, there were many minor skirmishes between the Red Celts and the Vikings. And the Fae strengthened their wards even further."

"OK, but I'm not qualified to fix this alone."

Dola *still* wasn't done with me. She'd obviously decided it was time I heard all this. "When you fixed the unfixable thousand-year-old problem in the Pict realm, you told me you had only used common sense. But that was not true, was it? Perhaps you should review the actions you took in that arbitration as you consider this one. Also, the Book Club is finally underway, and Juniper is about to serve food."

"I'll think about what you've said, Dola."

I dumped some tuna into one of the porcelain dishes with the crown and the C curling around it that the cat liked and placed it on the side. Where was HRH? It was unlike her to go missing on a day as full of action as this one had been. I hope she turned up before I left on holiday tomorrow. I'd promised to notify her before I reopened the Viking gate, and I had a couple of bets I wanted to place and several things I needed to know the current odds on.

CHAPTER
TWENTY-EIGHT

Back in the Gateway, the vacant chair with my green leather was now between Rhiannon and Ad'Rian. Rhiannon was speaking with Rollo and handed me her phone, showing several more blocks had been ticked off the bingo card.

"The decision is the Recorder's, and I do not envy her," "We can't just cut off their heads; it's not our realm," "And if we all take enough warriors ..." had been claimed by Ad'Rian, Breanna, and Mabon respectively. The last two had given Finn a horizontal line.

Rhiannon leaned in to my ear. "Clever little bitch, aren't you? You made all the kids stay focused during the most boring meeting in the world by giving them a game." Almost to herself, she added, "Agnes wouldn't have done it that way. She'd have demanded people pay attention and restricted Gateway access for anyone who didn't."

I sighed as I surveyed the table. Agnes had obviously been one of those kick-ass women I envied so much.

The low buzz of conversation swirled. Inge chatted away to Mags about the lack of technology in Viking. Mags quoted *Ruling Regally* about using innovations to stop the royal fish rotting from the head.

Ad'Rian was silent as he and Mabon used mind speech. Someone had split up the emperor and empress, thank the Goddess. Glais'Nee, as a seatmate, seemed to work to mostly subdue the empress. The emperor alternated his glares between his own reflection in the highly-polished tabletop and Inge, or maybe Rollo. I had no idea why.

Thyme gave me a lovely smile as she placed a plate in front of me, and I thanked her for the smell-nice spell. The odours of lamb, spices, and warm buttered rice drifted up. Tilly was alert, she liked lamb, but the size of the group kept her on the floor displaying her best manners.

At Breanna's dinner party, I'd learned the Recorder was often the most senior person at the table. Only full deities outranked me, apparently. I'd assumed being served first meant my food would always be cold by the time I got to eat it, but Juniper didn't allow her food to go cold until it was being eaten. So I relaxed and looked around the table to judge the mood of the room.

As I caught Rollo's eye, he smiled at me and sent, *"You look better. All good?"*

I smiled back. *"OK now. How is it here?"*

"Alphonse hasn't read the book, and he just asked me if I'm Inge's eldest son. The lack of my glamour is confusing him. When we both looked surprised and said no, he started sending the dagger looks over at us."

I was trying to think of something soothing to say when I heard, "Oh, yes, I bluddy did," from Mabon.

I turned to him. "Did what, Boney?"

"Read the book, I did."

Ad'Rian said, "Old friend, listening to a book is not reading. One can only take in the subtleties and wallow in the warmth of the language, or be cleansed by the acerbity and wit, or enjoy the true bouquet of the experience by fully immersing oneself in words on a page."

"Make it sound like a bluddy bubble bath, you do. Read the book, I did. Funny, it was, too. The narrator woman got all the jokes out properly. Funny *and* clever. More people should read it." He said this with the certainty of a man who knew quality when he heard it. And he'd heard it.

Ad'Rian drew breath to argue, but Mags, of all people, fixed him with her matriarch's determined gaze. "Your Majesty, I must thank ye fer your kindness tae my great-nieces."

At Ad'Rian's lack of response, she added, "The triplets, ye were kind enough tae allow them tae take a honeymoon in Fae. They told me of their visit to your family's private shrine to Áine. Very proud, they were and honoured. They said the bard who tell't the ballad of Áine was skilled beyond all imagining."

Now Ad'Rian inclined his head and smiled graciously at her. "They were delightful guests and, be assured, a credit to their families. And they are correct, that bard has the true gift. There is one of the longer sagas of Áine, and the way he conveys it, it's as though the Goddess herself is standing in front of you."

To the table in general, rather than to Ad'Rian in particular, Mags observed, "Strange thing tae think of the bards as the very first audiobook narrators, isn't it?"

Mabon exploded into laughter. Ad'Rian looked nonplussed. Mags caught my eye with an expression that said *Case. Feeking. Closed.*

I seized the opportunity while everyone was eating to say, "So, about Troels." I got attentive expressions from Mabon, Rhiannon, Ad'Rian, Glais'Nee and Breanna. Alphonse was glaring at his menu, and Sabella was ignoring him. All the younger guests gave me half an eye but continued to shovel food in as though they hadn't eaten since ... well, since they'd hoovered up all the remaining canapes about thirty minutes ago.

"I'm now in arbitration with Troels, and he was still on the

Viking law books as the king when I accepted the petitions and declared the arbitration open." I mentally thanked the power again for that piece of inspiration before it allowed me to summon him. "The Recorder must do what is best for the whole Viking realm *and* for the petitioners to resolve this matter. Our presentation was more of a courtesy to bring you all up to date. It shouldn't involve most of you. Unless you can offer any further knowledge of the smuggling Troels and his warlords were involved in. Or unless any of you are also planning to break your agreement with the Gateway."

Almost everyone shook their heads decisively. Glais'Nee looked thoughtful, and everyone gave me clear, guileless eyes. Only Alphonse's weren't convincing. However, when I probed Alejandro and Sabella, they felt unaware of anything connected to this, so perhaps the emperor felt generally guilty today. From the barbed smiles Sabby was throwing his way, it seemed possible. I wondered what he'd done? Or not done?

"I only have two further points. I need to know if you're in agreement with our plans to hold Troels until the conclusion of the arbitration?" I paused, but everyone except Alphonse nodded. "Thank you. However, I know many of you have Viking or ex-Viking citizens in your realms, so, as a courtesy, I'm informing you I plan to reinstate their communications and access to the Rainbow Network tomorrow. I'll be consulting on the correct date to reopen their gate."

"Consulting whom?" Alphonse snapped. He wasn't at his smiling, salesman-cum-politician best tonight.

"I beg your pardon?" I decided Dumb Niki hadn't come out to play in far too long. To Rollo, I sent, *"You're up—get ready."*

"I'd love to say born ready—but it would be such a lie. This fish is amazing; can't you let him grumble on while I finish it?"

I sighed. *"It's cold! It won't come to any harm. Buck up, hey?"*

In an impertinent tone that people rarely aimed at the Recorder, Alphonse said, "I am enquiring who on earth, or more precisely, who exactly in the realms, you or your office would, could or even should be consulting or taking advice from regarding Viking?"

At an actual growl from Caitlin, he hurriedly added, "If you please, my lady."

I considered him. "I shall be seeking counsel from a deity with an interest in the matter." That got me his raised eyebrows. "Also, with the individual who scored the highest in the approval polls my office conducted with a majority of the adult Viking citizens; they —"

Alphonse interrupted me, also a rarity since I ascended. "What kind of approval and who is this 'individual'?"

"The approval ratings were for honesty, probity, vision and trustworthiness. And their identity is confidential."

"Really, Recorder, we have a right to know."

I considered ignoring him because he had no rights to know anything about the Recorder's business. No, I just wasn't rude enough, was I?

"I tend, your Imperial Highness, to reward cooperation with information. If you'd care to cooperate, I'd be happy to share information." This appeared to flummox him, and with a harrumph worthy of Hugh MacAlpin, he glared at his plate. Sabella grinned at me.

I concluded, "And, of course, we will be consulting House Yggdrasil."

Alphonse's angry expression went blank. "And who, in the name of the blessed virgin, *is* House Yggdrasil?" He mangled his repetition of my perfectly clear Yggdrasil into something that sounded like a sneeze. Honestly, I sympathised because the first time I'd heard Dai say it, I'd said "bless you." But I hadn't lived with the Vikings as my neighbours; I'd been a child, not an emperor. Alphonse should be better informed, shouldn't he?

Rollo stood.

He bowed politely, one might almost say regally, to the entire table.

And he said,

Not. One. Damn. Word.

"Are you planning to speak, Rollo?"

"No. Ad'Rian advised me to stand, bow elegantly and sit down as swiftly as possible."

I did not grin. Instead, I fixed on my Recorder's official face and voice but then had to pause as HRH finally strolled onto the table between Rhiannon and Rollo. I heard, "May I be the first to congratulate you, Your Majesty?"

But she was staring at Rhiannon, who looked completely baffled. "Ah, I may be ahead of myself. Disregard me, please."

I pointed at Rollo. "Allow me to introduce Hrólfr Yggdrasil, the current head of the royal Viking House, Yggdrasil. Which, for some reason, everyone refers to as the House of Odin's Horse. But unless you wish the Recorder's Office to translate all of your house names into English to match this inaccuracy, in future, we will use the correct name."

Given that Asturia, the Galician royal house, could be translated into quite a few things, one of which possibly meant "some donkeys and a river," Alphonse shut up. I continued, "I'm looking into how the problem occurred originally. Perhaps the fact that Troels was permitted by you all to usurp the Viking throne from the rightful heir, and couldn't claim to be House Yggdrasil himself, might be a factor in it."

Glais'Nee stood and bowed to me. And then to Rollo. "Cousin."

That had Alphonse's head actually rocking backwards on his neck. But why? Surely he knew Rollo's mother had been Fae?

Rollo sat down again, still without having opened his mouth, and re-addressed his vodka-cured herring with every evidence of enjoyment. He seemed to have gotten away with it – Ad'Rian's advice for the win.

But, no, I'd been wrong. Alphonse was not ready to let this drop.

"Am I the only one who noticed the boy grew up very suddenly?"

Ad'Rian, who, of course, understood exactly what decision Rollo must have made in discarding the Fae glamour he'd used since his twenties, observed in a mild tone, "I find children do that, Alphonse. Consider your own son. It seems barely yesterday I recall him as a ragamuffin chasing around the festivals, and yet, now here he is, a handsome man. Ready to take his place in the world and carry his own power. It never ceases to amaze me how speedily the non-Fae races come to maturity. Blink and they age." He inclined his head to Alejandro.

Judging by the angry scowl Alphonse directed at both Alejandro and Ad'Rian, I was missing something else. Why was everyone being weird tonight? I must catch up with Ad'Rian soon.

Breanna, in her brightest tone, enquired, "So what were everyone's favourite parts of *Ruling Regally*? I've found her advice to say, 'No, thank you' has cleared out a lot of annoying slag from my life. My housekeeper, Mrs Fosdike, has finally retired and …"

I let the conversation swirl around me, smiling when they all laughed and frowning when they discussed the parts they felt were admirable but impractical.

When Inge mentioned the quote from the book about preventing advisors with their own agendas running your country, we ticked off "But that's simply ridiculous … (one must listen to the church.)" from Alphonse, and that gave Fi a vertical line.

I checked how close we were to a full house. I was still counting when Breanna exploded. "We finally have a recorder who will take action … Pregnant chambermaids in every corner … you still won't stop going on about trade, Alphonse. What trade opportunities do you think any of us will have with Viking if the power blows the whole realm to smithereens? Did you see that video? Did you not understand the contract?"

We ticked off pregnant chambermaids, and those who'd missed it the first time around ticked trade opportunities, leaving us only a few phrases to go.

Breanna gave discussing the book another go, in a less tactful manner than usual. "Who hasn't read the book?" Her gaze roamed the table, giving me, Mabon, Ad'Rian and Mags a pass because we'd obviously read the book.

She fixed Rhiannon with her Head of House Albidosi glare, but the dragon queen surprised us all when she said, "My favourite bit was the part about passing the book swiftly to your heirs on the way to your execution. I've seen heirs make the same mistakes as their ancestors many times over the centuries."

Unfortunately, the glare Rhiannon then gave Alphonse and the new text on her T-shirt didn't calm the mood any. It read, *Did you ever listen to someone and think, by the Goddess, you have the IQ of a crayon?*

I was trying desperately not to snort when my Gift niggled at me.

I checked the emotional temperature in the room, but nothing had changed. What had made the spot between my shoulder blades itch? It felt like something important was about to happen, but, honestly, I'd been itchy this entire evening. I probably needed another shower to wash all this nonsense away.

I sat quietly while people actually discussed *Ruling Regally*, innovations they were considering, and how hard change was sometimes. Juniper's staff competently cleared the table, offering coffee, tea or some herbal thing, and tiny, adorable little petit fours shaped and decorated like books.

All the time, I tried desperately not to rub my neck or scratch between my shoulder blades.

Rollo asked, *"Are you alright? You feel ... itchy?"*

Some of the petit fours had the cover of *Ruling Regally* on them. I watched as Breanna, Ad'Rian and Mag put one of those safely aside. I followed their example, and took several photos to send Aysha, one of the plate of petit fours and one of the table.

"Boo?"

"I don't know. I feel odd. Like something huge is about to happen, but I don't know what. Are you OK?"

Alphonse frowned at me. I focused on him. "Is there a problem, Your Highness?"

"I do not hold with phones at the dinner table." He said this as though he expected I would apologise. But I wasn't interested. We'd ticked that one off already. *Whoops, Niki, you're the Recorder, not an impotent employee in a meeting with Janet, remember?*

I tried to be tactful. "Well, at your own dinner table, I'm sure your wishes are respected. But, in the Gateway, there are too many people who wouldn't be here if they had to be out of contact to attend."

"No message is that urgent."

I was searching for a way to avoid giving unnecessary offense when Mabon chimed in to help me. "Say so, do you? Seen your footman bring you any number of messages during dinner, I have. For decades. What's the difference? Except less gossip for the footmen and their girlfriends to spread?"

Alejandro finally smiled when Alphonse had no answer to that. Then the emperor waved his menu at me. "Always thought there were two s's in 'dessert' in English."

I nodded. He was quite right. But he continued to wave the menu. "Turns out that Hob's talent only extends to her food. Can't spell for toffee."

He appeared delighted with his attempt at a food joke then looked away from the angry glitter in his wife's eyes until Glais'Nee asked in a voice so full of solicitude, it would have alerted me instantly. "Would you be referring to the Just Deserts, Your Imperial Highness?"

Alphonse, happily unaware, it appeared, of the proverb "Beware of an overly polite Fae," nodded at Glais'Nee with a smug, self-satisfied sharp edge to his smile.

Glais'Nee, with even greater politeness, said, "Ah, well. Just Deserts is a phrase that takes only one S."

At Alphonse's disbelieving look, he continued, "Middle English, I recall. Probably from the Latin *deservire*, meaning to give what is deserved. Whereas 'dessert,' to which I believe you refer, meaning the sweet course, takes two s's and came from the French *desservir*, referring to the fruit and sweetmeats the servants would bring once the main courses had been cleared from the table. An easy mistake to make, but all credit to Juniper for not making it. As the Recorder and I recently discussed, living through history gives one a perspective on the changing or, sadly, the tediously unchanging mores and habits."

Glais'Nee's wonderfully patronising explanation to the nitpicking Alphonse was the last nail in the coffin of the emperor's evening. He stood up, and without even a thank you to Breanna, announced, "We need to be going, m'dear," to the empress.

He picked up his bag of Just Deserts as Ad'Rian locked eyes with Glais'Nee and added, "The phrase came into Middle English, as Glais'Nee explained, about the same time as the original Gateway agreement. I might translate the original as receiving exactly what one deserves. Good or bad. One should apply caution before requesting one's just deserts on a difficult day, Alphonse."

The twinkle in Ad'Rian's eye told me that, like Juniper and Glais'Nee, he may have foreseen how Alphonse and his dessert would play out. I wondered if there was any way I could find out. Would Sabby tell Breanna?

"They're hatching! Already!" Finn was gazing at his phone, delight all over his normally serious face. For a man who disliked dragons, he was very keen on the dragon's egg cam.

Rhiannon's phone rang with a David Bowie ringtone. I wouldn't have pegged her for a fan. She kept surprising me. Then it dawned on me it was playing "Under Pressure" and that line about friends shouting to be let out.

I reached out to her. She might need … something. She'd stressed to me several times that being there *when* the dragonets hatched was her best shot at saving them.

Rhiannon leapt up so quickly, she knocked her chair over. Eagerness and excitement warred with panic in her eyes, then the red power shone out from the back of them, and her expression changed to one of complete calm. She called something in Welsh to Mabon, who answered, "Yes. Every faith I have. Different, it will be this time."

I held onto her arm. "Want a lift?"

As she started to nod, I stood too and transported us to the rock archway on Dragon's Back Mountain above Dai's still-dark house. As she looked around, a huge smile split her face. "That saved me ten minutes. Thanks. Wish me luck."

"Who needs luck? You were born for this, Rhiannon. Go, hatch your queens."

She laughed, then kissed me full on the mouth for a long moment before she jumped off the side of the mountain.

Actually, I'd timed it and bought her a few extra minutes. I didn't dare risk more than that, because she'd be on the webcams shortly, and everyone would be glued to their screens.

A warm amused voice next to me said, "Well, that was fun. Does she usually do that?"

I spun, astonished to see Rollo standing there.

I gaped at him as he held his hands up. "I reached for your arm to get your attention and ask if I could offer any help, and you transported so quickly ..."

I grinned at him. "She was high on the red regnal power, very excited and a little scared. I think she gets a pass."

I watched as the dark red dragon, sinuous and elegant in flight, stretched its wings and circled above us. Its movements were so graceful, it appeared to be in slow motion, then the dragon swooped upwards and shot across the sky. I waved. Her phenomenal dragon vision would ensure she'd see me, and then I held up an OK circle with my thumb and forefinger.

She'd known Rollo was there. She'd barely ever touched me before, never mind kissed me. Little madam! I did like her, though.

I wondered if I could find one of those print-your-own T-shirt shops while I was away. I knew exactly the one I wanted. We could have a matching pair. In pink.

As I leaned back into Rollo, he asked, "Did you know the dragons were hatching? Was that what made you itchy? And want some space earlier?"

"I didn't know it consciously … but maybe? I could have punched Alphonse, and that's really not like me."

"What was the matter with him? He wasn't himself tonight."

"No clue, but I plan to find out after our holiday. If he wasn't her uncle, I think Caitlin would have put him in his place. She growled at him!"

He laughed and kissed my nose, and then we stood transfixed, listening to the cawing, rumbling and whistling hoots as many more dragons in their full dragon forms headed towards the hatching grounds.

My breath fogged in the icy air, but I wasn't cold. The power wrapped into my robe kept me warm.

The bright, almost three-quarter full moon gave the lake below a silvery glow and made the snowy landscape sparkle as though the Goddess Scintillata herself had strewn it with diamonds.

Rollo shivered and snuggled closer. "How are you so warm?"

As I poked my phone and tested if I could pull more power through the new gate in the archway behind us, I listened to Gail Ann Dorsey's iconic bass intro to "Under Pressure."

I wrapped the power I'd pulled around us both and offered him one of my earbuds. We stood in the snow on Dragon's Back Mountain and watched the moonlight glisten on the peaks of the mountains around and below us. Dark-winged shapes obscured the view intermittently as more and more dragons arrived to help Rhiannon bond and save the hatchlings.

Rollo and I rewound "Under Pressure" and swayed into a dance on the top of a foreign mountain, nestled in the power. We finally enjoyed a moment of joy at the end of a stupidly long day as we sent Rhiannon all our most positive thoughts while she waged her life and death battle on the opposite ridge.

PART FIVE
FRIDAY

Your brain is your sharpest weapon. But like a carelessly wielded blade, you can damage yourself with nothing more than a thought.

We always make a choice about our thoughts. But we don't always admit it.

Choosing one strand can turn you into a Drengr, those leaders who display honour in their dealings and dispense golden justice with their weapons and words as they show us the way to Valhalla.

Another strand can cause you to spiral into the dark places where black spite, green jealousy and the blues wait.

Make your choice carefully.

Perhaps the only thing you cannot blame your enemies for is your choice of thoughts.

Winning the War Against Yourself: Daily Weapon and Warrior Care by Arinn Tusensköna

CHAPTER
TWENTY-NINE

F*riday, 5th March, Gateway Cottage—Miaow O'clock*
    Last night we'd transported home from Dragon's Back Mountain, and the last thing I remembered was Rollo saying, "OK if I stay? I'm not sure I could focus to transport. I don't know how you brought us home safely."

I'd mumbled, "Mmm, sure," as I tucked my head on his chest, wrapped my arm around him and sank into peace. Tilly, who'd been very cross that I'd left without her, snuggled into my back, and I didn't hear another thing until a piercing, annoyed miaow summoned me through the closed door.

I slid out of bed, briefly disorientated, when I saw Rollo smiling in his sleep. Slipping into my robe, I intended to slide quietly out the door before I disturbed either of the bed's occupants. But Tilly wasted no time crawling sleepily into the warm space I'd left behind.

In the sunlit hallway, a tail disappeared ahead of me into the kitchen. "Can I have coffee please, Dola? Is it morning?"

"Good morning, Niki, yes. It is eight-thirty. I have messages, some notes and a few minor but important tasks that need to be completed before you move into what the internet tells me is now called vacation mode."

I smiled and settled at the table. My coffee was waiting, bless Dola, and HRH was already holding court in the middle of it. "Good morning, Your Majesty. How are you today?"

Actually, she looked worryingly thin. I could see her ribs again. She'd been healthy enough a few days ago after I'd fed her bucketloads of power for healing Rollo. Now she looked thin and tired. I wasn't sure how a cat could look tired. I mean, sure, she always glowed with ennui, but this felt like true weariness, not just her usual affectation. What had she been doing to use up so much power?

"Recorder, I may have over-exerted myself. Otherwise, I am exceedingly well, but famished." She looked up at the tuna cupboard.

I curled some power in my hand and asked it if there was any spare to feed the cat with. The feeling that came back to me had a yes-but quality.

It had spare indigo and a little spare orange power—that was weird. I wished I could take the Book with me on my holiday. Some holiday reading time to ask it questions about all the things I didn't understand would be wonderful. But it was cumbersome and extremely protective of its well-being and its cover. I didn't think it would be happy jaunting about with me.

"Shall we negotiate?"

HRH immediately perked up. "What do you need?" The bright emerald green eyes focused on me, and the colouration in her fur that appeared to give her eyebrows when she was curious, quirked.

"What are the odds on the current Viking-related issues, and what's it worth to you to know when I plan to reopen the Viking's communications and their gate?"

"*All* the Viking-related issues or a specific one, Recorder?"

"Troels, Inge, Rollo, and the one you really don't want me to ask about." I couldn't imagine this would work. But, if she was tired, I might get away with it. "And before we get to those questions, are there any current bets on Rhiannon?"

The cat gave a bored yawn before replying, "Only the ones you would expect. Will there be new queens in the light of your activity re-opening the mountain gate? Will she bond all the hatchlings? And so on. Did you wish to make a wager, Recorder?"

I pulled about half the power I felt I could give the cat and offered it to her. I'd noticed the power acted like catnip on her. She was often less nitpicking after she absorbed it. Having her half-stoned might give me the advantage I needed. When negotiating with a Goddess, you had to use any advantage you could find.

But she was cautious. "Thank you, but is there a cost for this?"

"Not for this half, no. I'm still paying you back for your aid with Rollo on Tuesday, but there is a warning."

"A warning? How intriguing." Her head tilted to one side.

"The power isn't sure it will have excess capacity until there's a resolution to the Viking matter. It used a lot yesterday sterilising its boundary, and it wants to protect its reserves to ensure it can hold Troels securely in Viking while Dola completes her re-education of the citizens."

"So conserve my energy until the Viking problem is resolved. That is what you are saying?"

"Yes."

"Then I should offer any help you need, within reason, of course, so the power may relax its tedious caution. What would assist you, Recorder?"

She wasn't stupid. "Exactly what I asked you for. Details, ongoing bets, things I don't know, and things people don't want me to know about, even though I think I might need to."

"I may be less help than you hope. Obviously, there are ongoing wagers on when the yellow gate will reopen. There are bets on whether you or someone else will put Troels to death, and others about who will succeed him. But nothing that might truly assist you. Do you know when you plan to reopen the yellow gate?"

"Not yet. I might open it in stages, but I'm planning to reinstate their communications today."

"Ah, thank you. Valuable information. Do you know what time?"

I smiled. "You could pick the time yourself if you'll swap that choice for something I want."

She immediately began cleaning her front paw and focused on it closely. "What might you require in return?"

"Tell me what you wish I knew about Viking and these warlords."

"Recorder, you have a deal. Open their comms at five minutes past two today, please."

Obviously, no one had selected that time in the sweepstake.

And she talked. And talked while I drank several cups of coffee. When she finally came to a halt, I thought she'd truly honoured her side of the bargain and gave her the other half of the power.

As I stood up to go and start my day, as casually as I could, I enquired, "How many of the rose-gold dragon queens are people betting the Red Celts will have by the end of these hatchings?"

"Zero to two. There are two eggs now believed to hold queens since you reopened the Mountain Gate. The variables are whether they will hatch and whether she can bond them. Simplicity itself, and I am not offering odds that would interest you, Recorder. It would be like choosing red or black at that table game. Mere statistics."

"What if I wanted a different number? Because the moment I tell you the number I want, you will change your odds, won't you? And probably benefit by reducing the odds on that particular bet to all your other punters, but I'd still lose out."

"The house does always win, Recorder. But if you truly want another number, provided it comes with a clear time restriction, I could offer you two-to-one."

"Three-to-one and I'll take it. The time period is the next month."

She inclined her head. "Agreed."

Damn, I should have asked for four-to-one. "My specific bet is that there will be three rose-gold queens in the skies over Dragon's Back Mountain."

Those amazing emerald eyes glowed briefly with an alien power before she said, "Ah, you believe there is a hidden egg? That is valuable information. Thank you, Recorder. Wager accepted on those terms. How much would you like to place?"

"I'd like to wager one favour from me to you against three from you to me if my bet is a winning one. The reverse if I'm wrong."

She sat up perfectly straight and stared ahead. Her expression reminded me of the one I'd seen some years ago in the British Museum, on a statue of a goddess sitting on an ankh. Then, with finality in her tone, she said, "No, for favours I can only offer two-to-one. Take it or leave it, Recorder. And, if you should win, you may only use those favours for good. My Karmic burdens can take no further weight."

"Agreed."

Back in my bedroom, carrying two cups of coffee with a sunny beach scene on, I grinned at the words *Vacation mode loadin …*

I intended to wake Rollo but found the bed empty apart from Tilly, who'd now crawled under the duvet. I hung my robe on the back of the door, sipped my coffee and considered reaching down our link to him.

Then I heard "Crazy in Love" coming from the bathroom. He had a good voice, even if he was mangling the lyrics amusingly. I put my coffee down and clamped my hand over my mouth to stifle my giggles. Plonking myself on the bed, I settled in for the concert. That song had been huge the year I met Nick. I remembered wondering if I'd ever feel that way about him. And then, kidding myself, I did long enough to move in with him, which might have been my biggest mistake ever.

Rollo moved on to "Wonderwall" by Oasis, and I headed into the bathroom because, as a fellow Mancunian, I'd always been a huge fan. If Rollo was considering his feelings and looking for some sense in the winding roads, I had input he might need.

I never got to tell him anything because the moment he saw me naked carrying coffee, he took the mug off me and downed a huge swig and handed it back. Then he pulled me into the shower and cradled my face between his hands.

"I will not push you, rush or hassle you. But you need to know, however lousy the timing is for us, I'm serious about this."

And then he kissed me so tenderly, I nearly dropped the coffee. We needed an extra shelf in this shower.

CHAPTER
THIRTY

I don't know whether my impromptu shower romp with Rollo put me into an unusually confident frame of mind—it could have been all the information HRH had given me—or whether it was the calm Inge exuded, but our meeting was wonderfully relaxed. She didn't have the adversarial stance that so many of the people I'd met in the realms seemed to have been born with. While not slouching, she leaned back, stretched out her long legs and appeared completely at ease on the couch in my new Stane Parlour office.

And she didn't over-talk like the empress. She serenely took in my office and surveyed me with her candid gaze. But her aquamarine eyes were friendly rather than watchful.

Her behaviour last night had worried me, though. Her politeness and passivity didn't match the data Dola had collected about her from the Viking citizens. She seemed to think she could make the transition from the former king's ex-wife to the new king's stepmother while doing nothing herself. I needed to disabuse her of that idea. Viking needed all the help it could get.

Coffee and doughnuts arrived on the low table, and those striking eyes lit up. "Are those Krispy Kreme?"

At my surprised nod, she said, "I loved them when I visited Rollo."

Her face fell slightly as she looked at the filled selection on the table. On impulse, I asked, "Which are your favourites?"

"I'm so boring. I like the plain glazed best."

I grinned at her. "Me too. At least I like to start with them and Dola always serves them warm. She's like a personalised HOT light. Dola, would you adjust these when you have a moment?"

The Dolina in the corner came to life with, "Certainly, Niki, all plain?"

"Two of the Biscoff ones and the rest plain please."

"Your wish, etc ... I shall send these to Finn. He can thank you later."

"Send Rollo a blueberry one, please." I smiled to myself. The reminder of the one he used to reduce me to a puddle of need on Arthur's Seat above Edinburgh might be a fun start to our holiday. Not that I thought he needed any more practice.

The doughnuts disappeared and were replaced with the ones I'd requested, and a prettily wrapped Dolina box arrived next to them.

Inge took the offered doughnut and gave me a warm smile. "Before we get down to business, may I ask a personal question?"

I nodded and thought, *You can ask, but I may not answer it.*

"What are your and Rollo's plans?"

She seemed to stand in the mother's role in Rollo's life, so I answered her. "We're going on a short holiday next week."

This appeared to confuse her.

I waited.

She cautiously offered, "I meant more long-term plans?"

"No plans, yet."

"But you ... I'm sorry, Recorder, I'm interfering in the smithing of a blade that won't be my own. Please ignore me."

I thought that sentence through—did it translate to *it's none of my business*? Probably.

I said, "We only met a week ago. Well, no, I actually met him at my ascension."

I paused and breathed. For some reason, my Gift didn't want me to lie to this woman. "What I mean is we only had time to talk a week ago. Well, no, that's not true either, but us talking after Troels tried to slit my dog's throat and Rollo knocked him out cold wasn't really a personal conversation."

I stopped. I was making this worse. I was as bad as Alphonse. How had I forgotten she'd been that asshole's first wife?

Inge had gone very pale and was twisting her fingers into knots in her lap. I waved an *ignore me* gesture in the air and tried again. "I'm simply trying to say it's too early to know anything."

Her mouth opened again, but she clamped it shut. Her nostrils flared as she took in a long, deep breath and then let it out slowly. "I was horrified to hear about your dog. That footage last night was appalling. I thought he'd learnt his lesson after he killed Bjorn. But of course Gunnar doesn't learn, and I should know that. He's a ... well, he's many things, but no adjectives appropriate to utter in your presence occur to me right now."

I was still stuck on "killed Bjorn." Who was he, and what did he have to do with the price of fish, as my gran used to say?

"He killed Bjorn?"

"Yes. He was Rollo's constant companion. The boy loved him so much, and Gunnar hates people to have anyone they love or care about. Bjorn's murder was one of the reasons I had to leave when I did. I truly feared, if Rollo didn't do as Gunnar wanted, my daughter Elise might be the next."

She exhaled slowly. It looked like a breathing exercise she'd practised many times.

"When she told me what happened at her bonding, I thought she might be exaggerating. She's not her father's number one fan —well, who would be? And she can be a drama princess. But the footage you shared last night bore out her version of events exactly. Even that he'd deliberately stamped all over her Galician lace train. But, for Rollo, that event would have brought the loss of Bjorn back."

No wonder Rollo had gone pale that day, and it might explain why he'd been stressed enough to drop his glamour during our brief chat.

I took a risk that I was picking up the right things from my Gift. "What was Bjorn?"

"Oh, nothing in particular, I don't think. We'd call him a Bitzer. One of those dogs with a bit of this and a bit of that. He was big and gentle, and Rollo loved Boo with his whole heart."

I'd thought Nick was beyond the pale for suggesting I put Tilly down. What must it have been like for her to be married to a man who thought killing a child's pet dog was a thing anyone could ever do? And, perhaps more important to me, what must that have been like for Rollo? My heart hurt for him. Then my brain tapped for attention. It said, *WTF! Boo?*

"He called him Boo, not Bjorn?"

She shook herself. "Just a silly nickname. I apologise, Recorder, you wanted to talk to me, and I had a question for you, and instead I'm a step away from showing you photos of Rollo naked on a bearskin rug as a baby, aren't I? I've always wondered if he'd ever find someone special he could trust. I was so relieved when—"

She cut herself off, sat up straighter. "To business, then, Recorder?" She sipped her coffee as though the hot liquid would help her keep her mouth shut.

"Please call me Niki in private. But you are right, we need to talk about Viking." I offered the doughnuts again with, "Help yourself. More coffee?"

"Thank you, yes. I heard you mention some polling data you conducted in Viking last night. How did you do that?"

"Did you not see the livestream of the bondings?" I reached for the iPad with some screenshots Dola had prepared of the questions we asked.

Inge shook her head. "I was away that weekend having a

Valentine's celebration of my own to console myself for missing Elise's bonding. I wasn't aware you planned to stream it, but last night, your TEK, Finn, offered to send me a copy as soon as the Rainbow Network is operational in Viking again. He's a fine young man. You chose your Knights well. So much better than the useless Fergussons."

"Thank you. Take a look at this." I handed her the iPad and watched as she competently flicked and zoomed in.

Her expressive face showed her reactions to the questions. "This is well thought out. Did you create the questions?"

"No, Dola, my equerry did. She's brilliant."

"It intrigued me last night to hear there was someone universally considered honest and trustworthy. I can't identify who on earth it could possibly be apart from Rollo, but you mentioned him separately?"

I tried very hard not to smirk.

I'd discussed this with Rollo after we made it out of the shower. He'd said if she agreed not to share it with anyone, she wouldn't. Perhaps it spoke well of Inge that it hadn't occurred to her she was the person in question.

I reached for the printed copy and explained it was the collated data from all the questions we'd asked the Vikings. But it was for her eyes only, and I would need her word on that for now. I offered her the stack of paper, but her hands remained in her lap.

"Recorder," she paused as if considering how best to phrase something.

"Is there a problem?"

"If this data is what I suspect it is, I wouldn't be able to give you my word not to share it. There is one person I would need to confide in."

"And what can you tell me about them?"

"He's a Senior Warlord." At my astonished expression, she said, "*Not* one of *those* warlords."

"OK?"

"Is a Recorder like a doctor or a seer? Is there a reciprocal confidentiality clause on anything I need to share with you?"

"Yes and no. I will keep anything you tell me inside the Recorder's Office. But my staff, who've all sworn to uphold the confidentiality of the Office, might need to know because I'm in arbitration with Viking. And I will need to discuss it with Rollo."

She nodded. "That's fine. He already knows and so does Fi. Well then, Warlord McIver and I have been in a relationship for almost thirty years. It began, not physically, of course, but it began emotionally before I even left Gunnar. I kept my marriage vows until I received my divorce. Even though, as everyone outside Viking knows by now, Gunnar did not. But his conscience is his own."

I was flicking through the data. I hadn't even known there were Vikings with Scottish names. But we hadn't asked about a Warlord McIver, and no one had volunteered anything about him in the comment boxes the way they so frequently had about Inge.

Inge was still talking, "... Viking being what it is, single people have more power. I'm divorced; he's a widower. We're not hurting anyone, and our connection is not a secret. Well, let's say it's an open secret. But it's obvious to everybody that if we don't wish to get married, we must simply be ..." She paused and sipped her coffee. "I'm trying to recall that wonderful phrase? Yes, we must be friends with benefits." She stopped, and the grin she gave me made her look even younger, and for a moment, her calm elegance gave way to mischief and merriment.

She drank some coffee and met my eyes. "Two single people scratching an itch is simple for Vikings to understand. It couldn't possibly be that we find in each other something that completes us. The reality is, I love him with all my soul, and he's a wonderful man. But I refuse to give up my vote or my name. I would need to share whatever that is," she pointed at the sheaf of paper I held, "with him. He often has valuable insights."

I'd obviously missed something here.

"Sorry, Inge, but did you say you can't get married because you would lose your vote?"

She gave me a surprised look. "Of course."

"Why?" What did voting have to do with marriage? I mean, historically in England, hadn't married women had the vote before single ones? But I'd never heard of it the other way around.

"The modern Viking system votes for warlords, but the way they control who wins is to restrict who can vote. Many people can't, including all married women."

My head spun. This was a *modern* system? How the hell had I missed this? And, Gods and Goddesses, how archaic had the old system been?

I'd done some extensive research with the Book when I realised that simply visiting Viking, and its capital Haraldssund, as I would have visited any of the other realms, wasn't a good idea. With their Gate sealed, their former king a crazy man, and their warlords apparently powerful, sadistic control-freaks, it wasn't a safe tourist destination. Perhaps my gran's restriction on me going to Viking as a child had been sensible after all.

Honestly, I'd been relieved when the Book and all the people I'd asked had advised me against it. My experiences with Leif and then with Troels were scary. Caitlin's comments about how I was too "female" and too similar to Juna. "Female" in her context when speaking about Viking seemed to mean a short, non-shield maiden type.

But the final nail in the coffin of my hopes that I'd be able to fix this in a reasonable way as I had with the Picts was hammered home when Rollo landed on the Gateway floor far too close to death. If they'd attempt to beat their future king to death, what might they do to a Recorder if I gave them the chance? The received wisdom seemed to be the Vikings had stoned Agnes to death, and I had no idea how they could do that to a competent Recorder who could transport. Until I did, I wasn't going there.

Inge watched me. My thoughts must have shown on my face

because she said, "I'm sorry. There are a lot of wonderful people in Viking; on my honour, there are. But thanks to Gunnar, all the people running things for the last forty years aren't those people. If Rollo's father, Jonvar, had lived, things would have been very different. Rollo *must* take them on. He just doesn't want to. But he will have to come around. He is the rightful heir, and Viking needs an honest king to make changes."

"Dola, do we have the footage of Rollo after I summoned the Rightful King of the Vikings, please?"

The screen in my office came to life on a freeze frame of me standing by the anvil and Caitlin with her sword drawn, both of us watching the Yellow Gate.

"This footage, Niki?"

"Yes, thank you. Would you play it for Inge?"

The events played out on the screen. Inge's expression of horror as the bundle of rags that had been Rollo landed on the Gateway floor was telling. She hadn't known about this, which meant Rollo hadn't told her. The footage paused on the still-spreading bloody patches.

Her face a little pale now, Inge asked, "When was this?"

"Tuesday."

A smile of relief spread across her face. "Oh, thank the All-Father, it wasn't as serious as it looked, then?"

"A fractured skull and almost every bone in his right hand, arm and shoulder broken. His knee was shattered; he had multiple potentially fatal internal injuries—oh, and an apparently toxic level of drugs in his system."

"The Fae healed him? But I spoke to Ad'Rian last night. He didn't say a word." Her brow furrowed.

"Unfortunately, all the most talented Fae healers were still recovering from an extremely difficult Red Celt case."

The view on the screen changed to a poor-quality freeze frame. "Dola, is that from that original Echo in the lounge? The one we used to film Jamie?"

"Yes, Niki."

"Huh, I hadn't realised how much you'd upscaled the cameras in the new ones. Great job."

Inge frowned at the screen, where I knelt, covered in blood on the nasty carpet. There was a blinding-white, oval-shaped, pixelated blur near Rollo's head. HRH had used a tremendous amount of power. Of course, I already knew that on one level, but seeing the state of the three of us in that horrible cold lounge brought home to me all over again how close we'd come to losing Rollo. My stomach hurt at the thought. I should give HRH some nice fish before I left.

Inge placed her hands with her palms together in front of her chest and bowed in her seat. "Thank you."

"Wasn't me—well, it was only partly me. While I might have been able to keep him alive, I couldn't have healed him. I'm too new to my powers. I called on a deity."

I gave her a few more minutes to consider the scene. "So, can you see now why I'm encouraging Rollo to decide his own future? Because, while I can't prove they meant to kill him, I can tell you categorically, they would have left him permanently disabled and probably brain-injured without the intervention of a goddess."

She nodded reluctantly, although it was clear she hadn't grasped the true horror. But I hadn't finished with her. "And why I know he can't do this alone? Anyone who still thinks that is being intentionally ignorant or wilfully avoiding responsibility."

A frown crossed her face. She didn't like that, did she? "I'm sorry, I am not following you."

Was there a different way to get through to her? "Do you know the story of Everybody, Somebody, Anybody and Nobody?"

She shook her head.

"It's a teaching lesson from my world. There was an important job to be done, and Everybody was sure that Somebody would do it. Anybody could have done it, but Nobody did it."

I paused. "With me so far?"

She looked confused but nodded.

"Somebody got angry about that, because it was Everybody's job. But Everybody thought Anybody could do it, but Nobody realised Everybody wouldn't do it."

I paused again.

Now she nodded firmly.

"It ended up that Everybody blamed Somebody when Nobody got off their ass to do what Anybody could have done." I sipped the end of my coffee and considered her energy. She was thoughtful and felt a little guilty.

"This isn't Rollo's problem. It's Everybody's." I handed her the sheaf of papers. "You may tell anyone whose word you truly trust with your stepson's life. Also, that phrase about interfering in the smithing of another's blade. Is that a common Viking phrase?"

"Yes, very common."

"That might be a big part of your collective problem. I think all the Vikings need to realise, if they're reluctant to be involved in the blade's creation, they forfeit the right to complain if someone uses that same blade against them. If you want a say in the way your realm is run, you need to get your hands dirty."

I handed her the Dolina. "Dola will explain all about this. Open it and put it on a table in your home. But if you want to speak with Troels, and that's completely your decision, you need to do it now. I'm moving him to his new location before I leave on holiday. And he won't be accessible once he's there. Let me show you the back way to the Gateway."

CHAPTER
THIRTY-ONE

Back in my perfect bedroom, which still brought me joy every day, I considered how much I liked the chair in Rollo's bedroom. It was a stupid thing, but it pleased me. I'd never had a bedroom big enough to put a decent-sized chair in. Now I did.

I opened the doors to the hot tub deck to allow some of the fresh, cold air in. That would wake Tilly. "Dola, could I have a chair in here, do you think?"

"Yes, Niki, what style of chair?"

"I'll send you a photo next week of one I've seen that I like. It's comfortable. The design is perfect, but the colour would be wrong for this room. May I leave that up to you? Honestly, you've got much better taste than I have."

Tilly emerged from the duvet with bed hair. I giggled because my pup with bedhead used to be one of the highlights of my day. My life might have changed, but the important little joys hadn't. She sneezed at me and headed straight out the doors to stretch her legs.

Where the hell was my suitcase? I peered fruitlessly into a few of the empty wardrobes; I didn't have enough clothes to fill a wall of closets. Maybe I should go shopping. But why bother? I only ever seemed to wear my Recorder's robe these days. Actually, I'd quite like to burn all the drab clothes I'd bought to appease Janet or to fit in with Nick's view of what "his wife" should wear. That might be satisfying, but it would be atrociously wasteful. I decided I'd pack them up and donate them – it might motivate me to go shopping.

But what was I going to take to Rollo's? We still hadn't decided what we were doing on our holiday. I'd be perfectly happy in Edinburgh while he had things he had to do, but I would have loved some sun. Scotland was so dreary in the winter with its low light levels, endless drizzle, and short days. We could go to Fae but Rollo had said he wanted somewhere no one knew us.

I asked the air, "Any idea where my medium suitcase, the green one, is?"

It appeared on the floor next to the bed.

"Niki, may we speak while you pack?"

"Sure, what do you need?"

"My research suggests that uninterrupted leisure time is currently considered important for mental health and well-being. I wanted to establish guidelines for when and under what circumstances I should contact you."

I was about to say, *Don't worry; shout if you need me*, when it hit me. She was right. I kept saying I wanted some peace and privacy, but what was I doing to get it?

I tried on a pale grey suit jacket I used to like, then glared at myself in the mirror. It was boring. "Hmm, under which circumstances do *you* think you should contact me?"

During Dola's brief silence, I frowned unhappily at my other clothes. Had I changed so much that my old clothes just saddened me now? Ugh, shopping for clothes was not my favourite thing. Nothing ever fit my too-skinny frame the way I hoped it would when I took the item off the rail.

Dola said, "I have several options. One would be a quick briefing each morning, so you do not need to think about it for the rest of the day. They could be as short as 'Nothing to report. All is well.' It may give you the necessary peace of mind to relax."

"OK, that might work." I pulled out three pairs of jeans that were either too tight, too baggy or just weirdly shaped and dumped them on the floor.

"My other option would be, as you have previously said, only in the case of an emergency involving the end of the world or arterial bleeding. However, if those things should happen, the power would exert a pull on you to return, as it did when you were at Dai's, and the yellow gate was being attacked. So, I do not know what the correct answer is. Which is why you are the Recorder."

"I'll think about it and let you know before I leave." Onto the growing pile on the floor, I dumped half a dozen boring white, cream and navy blouses I'd never liked but were respectable, Janet-approved attire to wear to conduct marriage ceremonies in.

"In other matters, Mags Hob has requested a short meeting with you."

That stopped me with my hand on a coat hanger. "Do we know why?"

"Her stated objectives are to thank you, and to make a suggestion and an enquiry."

"What did she actually say?"

I waited, assuming that, as when Mabon left me some rambling, often incomprehensible message, and Dola translated and truncated it, I would now hear the original message.

Instead, Dola replied, "That is exactly what she said."

"Huh!"

"Quite, she was most courteous. Is it Lis who is the bad influence?"

I considered this as I added several equally drab work dresses to the pile. "Might be. Mags behaved impeccably at the book club last night. She was so funny when she put Ad'Rian in his place about audiobooks. When does she want to do it?"

313

"Today, for ten minutes at your convenience."

I glared at the rest of my wardrobe's contents. "Book her in then. Anything else?"

"Caitlin wants to know if you need anything from her before she leaves on her own vacation?"

"Yes, I'm going to move Troels. She'll want to be there for that, just in case, then she can begin her holiday."

"And Finn wonders if you have any projects you wish him to complete while you're away."

Wow, going away generated more work than just staying put, didn't it?

I asked, "Have you seen the app he made for the Broch?"

"No, Niki."

I sent her the app from my phone.

I opened all the wardrobe doors. Into an empty one, I moved several pairs of jeans I liked, some shorts, although I couldn't imagine ever wearing those in Scotland – but I could hope. I was packing a couple of boyfriend-style heavyweight cotton shirts into my case when Dola began speaking.

Her electronic voice was sad. "He must have made this on his own time. It is not on any of our computers. Finn and I have agreed on different levels of privacy for his personal laptop since he has been spending more time with Tegan. He will send me anything he wishes me to see."

I grinned to myself. Oh, bless her, she was miffed. "How are they getting on?"

"Please consider my previous comment, Niki. I do not know. It is most distressing."

I prevented my laugh from bursting out. "But, Dola, that doesn't mean you can't ask him, only that you can't read his personal chats with Tegan."

In the short silence that followed, I moved a few more items of clothing I liked into my "clothes I might actually wear" wardrobe.

With a huff that wasn't quite a sigh, Dola said, "I will conduct research on the correct way to approach this. Thank you. And his app will never work for someone with Breanna's personality profile. What was he thinking?"

I laughed. "See, that's exactly what I said. But when I asked him to tweak it, he brushed me off. He said, 'Ma will have to join the twenty-first century.' He doesn't seem to understand it's not only about technical competence, it's about Breanna's style and preferences too. Do you want to speak to him about it?"

An actual chuckle came from the Dolina. "No, I think we should teach him a valuable lesson. He's become confident in his role, which is good. But he is not considering that others' needs might differ from his own, which is what brought John Fergusson down."

She paused. I'd thought the same, but I'd brushed it off as a young lad and his mum problem. "Go on please, Dola; I might need to step in. I thought I was being oversensitive about him gossiping. But if it's a Gateway problem ..." I frowned at a bland pale pink polyester blouse with a pussycat bow. I couldn't believe I'd ever worn it and dropped it on the discard pile.

Dola sounded much more like herself when she replied with certainty in her tone, "An important part of his position as the Knight is to understand that all the realms and the individuals within them have their own necessities and requirements, and they are often not the same as Finn's. I hoped he would learn this from John's sentencing, but he appears to have missed that point."

I was relieved it wasn't only me. Damn, I'd forgotten to ask Rollo how their chat had gone, hadn't I? Oh well, we had the next week; I'd ask him then. "So, do you have an idea?"

"Yes, Niki. Why don't *we* make other versions of the app? Ones we think would work for Breanna and ask her to pick a winner from all of them. Finn has a strong competitive streak. It might help the lesson go home."

I grinned. "That's quite evil, but it might work. Yeah, let's do it. In the nicest possible way, he needs his eyes opened. This might be a shortcut. And you never know, Tegan might thank us for showing him it's not a gift because you decided to give someone something. They have to want it and be able to use it. But let's not tell Breanna or anyone else which version is from whom. That could be spiteful. Let's call our versions 'Other options from the Gateway.'"

"That concludes my list. Did you decide which contact option you prefer?"

"No, let me relocate Troels to Viking and speak with Mags, and I'll get back to you. I want to ask Rollo about it first. It's his holiday as well. Can you leave all this stuff on the floor, please? I want to look it over one more time. Is there anywhere locally that might welcome clothing donations?"

"Yes, I will send a list to your iPad. You need only advise me which charity you wish to support."

I grabbed Tilly and transported to the gateway, leaving my unsatisfactory clothing choices scattered around my room.

CHAPTER
THIRTY-TWO

I arrived in the Gateway to find Inge in the Yellow Sector and obviously deep in conversation with Troels.

A quick catch-up with Fi and Rosie told me Rosie had enjoyed her first week, and all was well. Fi asked if she could book a meeting in my diary with herself, Rosie, Crane and Corby on my return from holiday.

"Sure, what's it about?"

"Just some trade ideas."

"OK, get Dola to slot it in."

She blushed. "Actually, I already have. I was only being polite."

I laughed. She was growing into her new role wonderfully. "Fi, speaking of polite, any ideas on how to let Inge know I'm moving him in about ten minutes?"

Fi smiled. "She said to give her a five-minute warning, and she'd wrap it up. Her body language has been interesting, though. Whatever he's said to her, I don't think it was what she expected."

While Fi was talking, I'd been gazing around the Gateway doing my usual check of the energies. Out of the corner of my eye, I saw Tilly lifting her leg, which was soooo unlike her. She was a perfectly house-trained girl even if she'd always insisted on peeing with her leg up like the boys. But she knew the Gateway was "inside," and she didn't pee inside.

"Tilly, what the hell?" Then I saw what she was peeing on and turned back to Fi. "What is that doing here?"

Fi took a step out from her desk and noticed the puddle of dog pee now surrounding the back wheel of a market stall.

Her mouth made a comical O. "Oops! Yes, I was going to ask you, but I couldn't see the harm. I didn't think it would be in the way until the equinox traffic, and they've promised to move it days before that."

She reached into her desk and brought out one of Whirly's familiar paper bags containing one of the spicy spiral sweetbread kurts. "They left us all some rent."

I considered the market stall, which I'd last seen going through to Pant y Wern for the St. David's Day festival. Fi was correct. It wasn't in the way. The small stall took up little space. We could have fitted twenty of them across the top of the Green Sector and still had plenty of room to let people access the gate. But we weren't a damn left luggage office.

"Have they ever done this before?"

Fi, a little pink now, shook her head. "Your gran wouldn't have stood for it. But I didn't think you'd mind. They left me a phone number. If you think I'm wrong, a friend of theirs will come and collect it. They needed to go home for a few weeks, and last year when they left it in the car park by the shore, it was vandalised."

"OK. Where *is* their home?"

Fi waved a hand in an "up north" gesture. "Some valley in the Highlands. They go up and bring their wives and kids back down for a holiday in spring every year."

I eyed the rusty-looking stall with displeasure. There were two wheels on the back, one of them currently swimming in dog pee, and a push bar. The front had legs, so it was stable once parked at the various markets.

Inside were the gas jets and metal rods they wrapped the bread dough around. It normally looked more attractive.

"It wouldn't have been so bad if they'd left the awning up on it. At least that would have looked purposeful, but hanging about, making the place untidy, it looks like we're opening a scrap metal merchants."

Fi laughed. "You sound very like your gran right now."

"She wasn't always wrong, you know!"

Then we both laughed, and I said, "Well, it's done now. Hey, who won the meal from Juniper in the book club bingo?"

Fi gave me a huge smile. "Caitlin. Which, after all her 'I'll never manage this. I'm no good with my phone' complaints,' was hilarious."

"Who did the one person who 'didn't say a thing' turn out to be? I was worried that one was going to cost us a full house after Glais'Nee spoke to Rollo."

I'd thought I could rely on Glais'Nee to be the strong and silent one in a big group, but I'd been very wrong. The emperor had annoyed him.

"Alejandro. He was very quiet last night, wasn't he?" Fi consulted her ever-present list. "Mabon said, 'Let someone get a word in about the bluddy book. Here for that, we are,' to Sabby. We all agreed that qualified. Ad'Rian suggested sanctions and 'confiscating their assets.'" She peered at a printout of the bingo card. "Yes, that's it. I gave the small prizes out." She handed me a box of liqueur chocolates for my line, which I promptly opened, grabbed the cherry in brandy, and passed the rest around.

Caitlin arrived and helped herself to one. "You won the grand prize, KAIT."

She frowned.

"What? Didn't you want to win?"

"I did. I'm just waiting for you to tell me I can't have it."

"Of course you can have it." I gestured at Fi, who handed the voucher from Juniper for a meal for two served at the winner's choice of location to Caitlin.

Caitlin clutched her voucher to her heart like a child with a teddy bear. But her disbelieving expression was still in place. "Really?"

I was confused. "Sure. You won it. So it's yours."

"I'm never allowed to win a slagging thing at home. Ma always says the heir apparent must return the prize gracefully so someone who needs it can have it." She huffed. "Even the time I won one of the Smiths' swords. Who needs a sword more than me?"

That felt as if Breanna's innate sense of fairness had been taken to such extremes, it had flipped around into screwing her heir. But Caitlin wasn't my daughter, so I bit back my comment. "Well, this is yours, so why are you still glaring?"

"I wanted to invite Alejandro. He asked to speak to me, but we don't have anywhere private to talk. His father is being a—" She trailed off with an eye roll.

"Pen pidyn?" I offered.

Caitlin grinned at me. "If I invite him to my suite, Juna will come and interfere. If I organise it next week in Galicia, the empress will come and chatter at us. And the staff make a point of coming in and out and reporting everything to the emperor and empress. Obviously, two unmarried people can't eat alone in Galicia. Which is ridiculous because Alejandro doesn't do girls." At my expression, she added, "It's that religion of theirs. Normally we'd go to the Kings Arms, in Pant y Wern, but you can't get in or out of there right now with all the slagging coos."

I hadn't had a gay vibe from Alejandro when he'd come for the testing of the future Knight Adjutants and I'd been using my Gift fully that day. "Is he gay?"

Caitlin shook her head decisively, "No, he doesn't do boys either. He says princes can't afford to take any risks in Galicia."

"So why did you want to be private?"

"He asked to speak to me at the sentencing. Well, he asked to speak to the KAIT, and I'm worried about him."

I thought about this – it felt important – but I didn't know why. "Well if he wants the KAIT why not ask Dola if she'd mind if you used my kitchen while I'm away? You could both sneak through the Gateway, and no one will know where you are to bother you?"

Caitlin gave me a huge grin. "You wouldn't mind?"

"As long as Dola is OK with it, sure. Ask her to lock the Annex door so Finn can't come and bother you either. Or eat on trays in my office – it has soundproofing."

Caitlin hugged me. I'm not sure who was more surprised, her or me. "Thanks, Niki. He's my favourite cousin and the emperor was even odder than usual last night."

When she pulled back, more to distract her from her embarrassment than anything else, I said in a low voice, "I spoke to your mother. You speak excellent Norse?"

She gave me one brisk assenting nod and glanced around the Gateway, but everyone was busy with their own tasks. "Why?"

"What does *Drengr* mean?" Rollo hadn't ever answered me properly about that, and the internet wasn't a reliable resource for ancient Norse stuff. The Book told me it was an ancient Norse title given only to worthy warriors.

"The game, the title, or the noun?" Caitlin's serious expression told me I was finally asking the right person.

"Never mind the game. I know it well. No, the title and maybe the noun too."

I considered Caitlin's question. As I did, an auditory memory of Miss Swindell, my English teacher's voice, drifted through my ear as clearly now as it had in the classroom. She'd been so patient. The old teaching phrase, "a noun is a naming word," made me smile. And I wondered … Ooooh yes. That might do it.

"The noun means a slightly crazy but honourable person. 'Badass' is the modern equivalent. Ya know those motorcycle clubs with all the hairy, bearded guys in black leather who take terminally ill or disabled kids for rides?"

At my confused frown, she added, "There was a documentary

about them. Ya know those guys who don't look like they'd do charity work, but they don't care, and the kids love it?"

"OK?"

"They're drengr." She drew a lowercase "d" in the air. "It's badass; it's an unconventional, reckless thing to do. But also, very cool right?"

"Does it always mean men, and how does the title differ?"

Caitlin considered for a moment and then stood straighter. "Nah, it's gender neutral. There were a couple of famous drengr women. *Sgàthach* was my favourite; now she was a real example of what a warrior should be. The skalds wrote epic tales about her and some of the others. But it's normally given to a man who's a badass but who has honour and a fast blade, and who people want to follow. Not because they rigged an election and told them this is your new but equally corrupt warlord. I think the last guy who was given the Drengr title was about …" Her eyes slid sideways. Then she smiled in relief as she obviously retrieved the answer. "… four hundred years ago. But the code still exists, or it did. It's the Viking's equivalent of the strictures, but it's for everyone, not just the royals."

She paused, looked around again, and then in a low voice added, "Thinking about it, the Drengr Code is probably what the Vikings had instead of laws. It might be the warlords breaking that ancient code that has made everyone so useless about fixing the mess Viking is in. Once honour is gone, and someone's word can't be trusted, what can you do if you can't kill them or overthrow them?"

"How are they breaking it?"

"It covers hospitality and behavioural codes and the importance of people keeping their word. If you're drugging guests and allowing powerful men to rape young women in your longhouses, how is that upholding the hospitality code?" A look of genuine fury crossed her face. "It's time they had that code back."

"Can you give Inge the five-minute sign please, Fi, and I'll clean the floor?"

"Let me do the floor, Niki. I should have thought it through. I bet every dog in Pant y Wern has watered those wheels. It's no wonder Tilly couldn't resist them."

She moved towards the Magic Box to collect cleaning supplies, and I heard her calling to Inge.

Relocating Troels turned out to be an anti-climax.

When Finn sent the drone out, we saw the power had been busy. No wonder it was monitoring its power levels and drain carefully.

The sterilised black ground was still ugly, and the iron railings surrounding the boundary gave it an unfinished public park vibe. The pathway from the yellow gate to the boundary with the town of Haraldssund was now bordered by yet more railings, and three metres inside the boundary was a substantial concrete hardstanding. the new cell would fit on it easily.

When Rollo told me the penalty for regicide was still on the Viking law books, I'd consulted the Book and then Google. The Vikings suspended the traitor in a metal cage or wooden box in the market square and left them there exposed to the elements until they died and rotted. That was a revolting thought! The damn Vikings were barbarians.

But I'd had to revise my thoughts when I discovered they were simply old-fashioned. Because, astonishingly, it had once been a common thing in my world. The English had historically been even more barbaric about it. They'd put traitors in a metal body-shaped cage called a gibbet. I'd always thought that was simply another word for gallows, but the internet was delighted to put me right and show me some barbaric images of people who'd died this way and then been buried still in the gibbet. I wouldn't be unseeing those photos any time soon.

But at least we'd ceased doing it about two hundred and fifty years ago, whereas Viking's last instance of this punishment was in the twentieth century!

I felt better about the nice cell with all its modern conveniences that the power had created for Troels. At least we weren't torturing him.

But when my only consolation was "I'm not actually torturing him," it didn't make me feel good. However, the Recorder's Office needed to hold him until the arbitration because no one trusted him to be there if we didn't.

Inge approached but kept a safe distance from the iron anvil. She looked a little shaky. "Did you have enough time?"

"Yes, thank you, my lady. He gave me some interesting information. I don't believe it connects to your arbitration, but I should share it with Rollo. Do you know where I can find him?"

"Sure, he's in Edinburgh." I glanced at my watch. "In a meeting until mid-afternoon, but he has his phone. Once you get home and unpack your Dolina, she'll connect you with him."

Her forehead furrowed as she asked, "Dolina?"

"Do you have the box I gave you?"

She picked it up from the corner of Fi's desk. I opened it and took it and her to the conference table. "Dola, do you have time to talk Inge through the Dolina now? I need to move Troels while the drone is out there."

"Yes, Niki. Inge, if you would place the frame on this table, I need to discuss the agreement with you …"

I left them to it, connected to the power, and, yes, of course, I rose into the air above the anvil. I sighed, then remembered to feel my earlobes. Doug Halkrig would be pleased with me. My number five pair of earrings were already in place.

It all went smoothly. The power swirled; the cell disappeared. Moments later, I saw it appear on the large screen as the feed from the drone updated.

"Finn, can you do a circle around the cell so we can check it's transferred safely, please?"

It had. The concrete pad was undamaged. "Can someone turn on his microphone, please?"

A stream of Norse swearing came through the speaker. Inge, still at the conference table, winced.

"Gunnar Troels, be quiet and listen."

The swearing stopped. Huh!

"Your arbitration will take place as soon as we have collected all the evidence. This will be on or before Tuesday, sixteenth March. It is Friday fifth now."

Fi gave me an odd look. But, honestly, most of the time I wasn't sure what day it was until Dola told me. If I'd been locked in a glass cage in the Gateway for a few days, I'd definitely be disorientated.

I lined up the information we'd all decided he had a right to. Because, hilariously, he wasn't guilty yet. "The evidence submitted by the petitioners is being collected. To allow you eight hours of undisturbed rest," Dola had been firm about that. "We'll share that evidence with you as we obtain it. Between the hours of seven am and eleven pm each day videos will be streamed inside and outside your cell, so you and the Viking people can watch them. Meals will be provided to you. You are being monitored. You will have every opportunity to respond to the petitioners. If you ask for anything to be recorded, provided it relates to the arbitration, it will be documented, introduced into evidence and also streamed."

I glanced down at Caitlin. "Was that everything we discussed?" She gave me a thumbs-up.

I closed my eyes, dropped my shields and asked the power, *Are you OK?* It was. It was happy to have the slimeball outside on its boundary instead of inside its home. But it was sad about the sterility of the boundary.

It'll grow back nicer. We can plant grass seed. I sent it soothing thoughts. I was no horticulturist, but surely it must be fixable. It sent me pictures of the Hobs. *Yeah, I'm sure they'll help once we've settled this.*

I sent it a stream of pictures about my break, offering it my willingness to return immediately if it needed me. I reassured it. Now I'd experienced the sensation that meant the power needed me to return, it would never have to wait with people hacking at its door when I didn't understand why I'd wanted to come home so badly at Dai's house.

Happy now, the power set me back on the floor. I got the sense it was telling me to have a break and then come back and fix Troels.

That worked for me.

CHAPTER
THIRTY-THREE

I stopped myself from reminding everyone that Dola could reach me anytime, and they could email me with anything urgent. I would learn to do holidays. It's never too late to change.

Tilly had picked up on my excitement, and she positively pranced beside me. She had her "I know you're going somewhere, and I'm not allowing you out of my sight until I know you're taking me with you" air of alertness in full doggy emergency mode.

"You're coming with me, pretty girl. You know you always do. Calm down."

Just as I reached the green gate, Mags Hob arrived carrying a brown garment bag over her arm. "Ah, Recorder. Dola tell't me ye'd have ten minutes for me. Is noo a guid time?"

I took her elbow and steered her out of the Gateway. "Let's go to the cottage and be private so you can speak English, I can have a coffee, and you can have whatever you fancy."

She gave me her wide grin. She had extremely good teeth for a woman of her age. Actually, I had no idea how old she was. I couldn't work out how to ask it politely either. Would the Book know?

Mags glanced around her and, satisfied at whatever she saw or didn't, said, "My people have a request to make of the Recorder."

"OK?"

"Much distress has been caused."

Oh crap! What had I done now?

I nodded but couldn't think of anything I'd done wrong. I thought we'd all been getting on fine. Had I upset Rosie?

"What do you need?"

"Your permission for my people to go through and tend to the yellow gate and the boundary. The power needs them to do this. It's unhappy."

It had just told me that itself, so I nodded. "Sure, no problem. When do they want to do it?"

Mags looked slightly surprised. "As soon as ye can?"

I turned around. We walked back into the Gateway. At the anvil, I paused, unsure of the best way to change the instructions on the yellow gate. "Is everyone who wants to go a Hob? Full Hob, I mean. I'm trying to work out what instructions to give the power to allow your people in and out, but not give access to anyone else yet."

We both thought. I could see Mags' brain working. She focused on the ceiling as though she were calculating something. "The distressed ones who are volunteering tae do it are at least three-quarters Hob. Any guid?"

"I think so. Let's see."

I connected to the power. "Are you happy to permit anyone with at least seventy-five percent Hob blood to go through Yellow so they can tend your boundary?"

It was so happy, it tickled me. I saw a picture of a list in my mind. "Mags, I think it wants to know the names of the Hobs you have in mind?"

Mags nodded calmly and recited a string of botanical names, some herbs, a few flowers, and when she got to the end, she nodded at me. I didn't even recognise most of the names. How many Hobs were there in this tiny village?

I felt the click in my head as the instructions for the yellow gate changed.

"OK, Mags, they're all good to go."

We were headed back to the cottage again when Mags asked, "How much do you know about the Hobs?"

This had been bugging me since I'd first asked Ad'Rian about their origins. "Nowhere near enough, and I can't find much out. The Book had some mostly very outdated information. And Ad'Rian said he'd look into it, and he hasn't got back to me. I know time moves differently for the Fae, but does everything have to take months?"

She gave a satisfied nod. "Thought as much."

She smiled at me. It was a slightly scary smile, not her mouth —that was normal, but there was something in her eyes that gave me a sense of caution.

"I'll need your word, nae, your solemn bond that you will not share what I tell you with another living soul until it's resolved. Lis won't be happy about this, but ye need to know. Ye may even help. I'll mek it worth ye while."

She'd gone a bit Scottish again, so this mattered to her, and I was starting to like the old bat.

"If I can help, I will."

"Your word it will go no further?"

"Unless it affects the safety of anyone I have responsibility for, it will go no further than the Recorder's Office."

But she shook her head. "Not the Recorder's word. *Your* word. Danake Elsie McKnight's word."

I gaped at her.

"How do you ... how did you know ..."

Oh, shape up, Niki. They're just words. Pull yourself together and line some up. My inner critic, as it so often did, grounded me.

"I'm sorry, Mags, you surprised me. How did you know my full name?"

"Ye told me yerself. Well, that and the gravestone."

"I told you?"

"Aye. When you had that funny ceremony to name your office. The sandwiches cut into Lisianthus, Marguerite daisies, and the Danake coins, remember?"

I did remember. But … "The gravestone?"

She took my hand and patted it. "Not been to see your gran then yet? Initial visit is allus the hardest. Take a friend with ye the first time. You'll feel better for the doing of it, you know?"

I had been feeling guilty about it. I should go.

"I need Danake Elsie McKnight's word ye'll nae breathe a word of what I tell ye until it's fettled."

That was actually easier. If it didn't affect the Recordership, it was my decision to make. "You have my solemn word to keep what you tell me to myself."

She smiled now, and as we began walking again, Tilly chased out of the trees to lead the way to the cottage. "Cute wee thing that. But then soul dogs always are. Some are ugly cute, but they're always cute."

Was she stalling? Why?

In a rush she said, "Ye have Hob blood."

"I do?"

"Headwomen can allus tell. Comes with the role, ye might say."

Well, all the royals could tell their own citizens, so it made sense. "Ha, that's nice. I wonder why I didn't get the green thumb you all seem to have? I can't even keep a houseplant alive. Where did it come from? Although my gran was short too. Maybe one of Florrie's healthy exercise partners added the Hob genes. Glais'Nee said there was something else he wasn't sure about?" Whoops, I was thinking aloud, wasn't I?

Mags studied me. "Oh, that big Fae knew fine well. But he wouldn't tell ye. Folk don't enjoy having Hob blood."

"They don't? Why on earth not? You guys are so talented. And almost all of you are lovely." I didn't mean to be rude about Lis, but not in a million years could I call her lovely. "I mean …"

Mags laughed. "I know what you're not sayin', but Lis has walked a hard road. She has a soft middle, but you'd have to dig through a mountain of granite to find it."

"So why wouldn't you want me to tell people I have Hob blood? I think it's a lovely thing. Or are you not sure?"

"Och, I dinnae care if ye tell people aboot your heritage. No, I tell't ye that, so ye'd understand why I'm trusting ye with the next thing. That's a wee bit stickier."

Her accent was all over the place today. Was this important, or was she stressed? Or both maybe? "Spit it out then."

"There's Hobs trapped in Galicia. That's why I really wanted to come to the book thing to see the emperor. I needed to know if he knew and was part of the problem, or if it was happening in his realm because of their climate."

"Trapped?" The emperor had trapped Hobs? That made no sense, did it?

"Aye, an' he knows fine well aboot it."

Well, Alphonse had been peculiar last night.

I waited. There was obviously more.

"If you get the Recorder to summon them home for me without telling anyone why, once they're all safe, I'll make them file petitions and testify for the Recorder."

It still confused me when people separated me and the Recorder. Although I'd followed that part, I'd lost the plot on the rest of it. Had Troels been raping Hobs too? And, honestly, did it matter? Except to those poor Hobs, of course. I already had so many cases against him. As everyone kept telling me, Troels wasn't the real problem in Viking. He was just a slimeball. The real problem was … OH!

"Who would they be filing petitions against?"

"All o' them. Every last one of those stinking, smuggling,

drug-running, baby-murdering warlords that were holding them in Galicia."

"Baby-murdering?" This was news to me.

"Oh, ye ken aboot the rest then?"

I nodded. "I think I've got most of it reasonably clear. But I've no evidence, and there have been no petitions filed, so what can I do? Inge doesn't think she can get anyone, or at least enough people, to stand up or give evidence against them. Seriously, though, baby-murdering?"

Murdering babies felt like a quite different type of crime to the drug and money-related evidence I'd been piecing together. Why on earth would the warlords murder babies?

Mags stopped in the middle of the path. As she had before, she turned in a circle, looking all around. She was using power of some kind. "Let's go to the cottage and talk. Sage and Hedge are pruning trees o'er there. This is none of their business."

Yet again, we settled in my office, and I glanced at my watch. I'd make time if necessary. This was important. Rollo and Inge were worried about these warlords. "Dola, can I have a caramel macchiato please, and, for Mags, a …" I paused and waited, looking at her.

"I'll try one of those posh coffees, if I might. Never had one. Good to try new things."

Tilly crawled up next to me on the sofa and put her head on my lap. Her whine asked, *Where did our happy holiday mood go, Mum*?

Two coffees, emitting the distinctive caramel odour, arrived on the table. I picked mine up and breathed in the soothing fragrance. Mags looked frazzled, and I felt shaky. I wasn't going to like what she told me, was I?

"And a brandy and a whisky, please, Dola. And then lock down the privacy on this room."

Mags nodded approvingly. "I wondered if you'd think to do

that. Dola's as much a person as any Hob. Ye taught us that. We had no idea."

She picked up her coffee and watched as I dumped my brandy straight into mine. Then she watched even more closely as I placed the mug onto the little coffee-warmer hotplate next to my chair. I gestured to her own side table and the other coffee-warmer.

She flicked it on and felt the heat begin to come out of it. Her face lit with delight as she put her mug onto it. "Well, I ne'er feeking did. What'll they think of next?"

"This is more of a sipping coffee, and Dola gets cross sometimes when I let them go cold. So, coffee-warmer. Now, baby-murdering?"

"You know about the droit de seigneur, as the realms call it?"

I sipped my coffee and mumbled, "mmm huh."

"It's a mix of herbs and roots. We Hobs have many therapeutic uses for all the ingredients, but if ye mix 'em together, make it too strong, brew it the wrong way, turn it into a powder instead of a tea, it makes people do things they wouldn't do in their right mind. Then it confuses their memories of what they did."

I nodded. I knew this much. All the petitions for the paternity cases against Troels had mentioned something like Rohypnol. Glynis had been very specific about the effects of the Viking drug.

In a careful voice without any local accent, Mags began, "So let's say a lord might have offered some well-paid work to some green-fingered Hobs to raise some of the usual, valuable, culinary herbs for them. If the lord was providing pleasant accommodations, and including all their meals on a limited-time contract ..." She paused.

I nodded.

"But if that same lord was lacing their food with the drug so no one looked too closely at what else might be growing, and the droit de seigneur made you very suggestible, and it was no trouble to tend another crop for your employer who might already be overpaying you, had provided you a lot of good, hearty meals and was always polite …"

"I'm getting the picture, Mags. You're saying that some Hobs, whom we might call naïve, were talked into growing more of the herbs that make up the droit de seigneur for the warlords by using the herb on them. I'm with you. But I'm still not getting the baby-murdering bit."

"That stuff has an effect on a woman's reproductive system and their hormones. It's probably why Troels got so many of the girls pregnant. But the fertility part of it means ye'd never give it to a happily pregnant woman. Because if they're already expecting, it can have the opposite effect. I have reports that five of my girls have lost their babies in the last two months. Hobs often have multiple births. One of them was almost seven months gone with triplets. I make it nine babies they murdered."

"Oh, Mags, I'm so very sorry." My heart hurt for the women. Aysha had a miscarriage at four months before she had Autumn. She'd been inconsolable.

"I'll file a petition myself as Headwoman, or, if we can't fix it quickly, Lis will. The girls and their men will file. They can identify all the warlords involved with this. There was a big dinner meeting. There were twelve of them at it. Two left early; the rest stayed. Some of the girls were servers, poor wee lassies."

The Dirty Dozen, Rollo had called them.

"And you want my help—why?" At her frown, I added, "I mean to do what?"

Her face cleared. "Can ye summon them home?"

"I should think so, but why?"

She sighed. "Sorry, Your Maj, I'm so upset with all this. Did I not say they're keepin' them all prisoner now? I sent some of the boys through to bring them home, and they can't get near the compound. Viking guards surround it."

"When is Lis back?"

Mags dealt with my change of subject wonderfully and

simply said, "Probably around Easter. She takes the best part of two months in the winter for her rheumatism. She's in Galicia for the climate, and she cannae get any closer to them than anyone else. Why?"

"Because, bluntly, you're easier to work with, and I'd like to get this dealt with quickly. One thing, have you got all their full names?

She was nodding at me when I said, "Oh no, two things. Why can't I tell anyone about this?"

"Oh, ye can once they're home. But better safe than sorry, don't ye think? I don't want word getting back to the warlords from some stray gossip before they're all back here under my wing and have time to file their petitions. There's spies everywhere. People don't mean to gossip; they just can't help themselves."

Well, that was a truth universally acknowledged, wasn't it?

"OK, then shall we go and summon your Hobs before I have to leave?"

A look of immense relief crossed her craggy face. Had she thought I'd refuse her?

We finished our coffees, and in a more conversational tone, she said, "Ye know we all have different skills?"

"I've gathered some of that from Rosie, yes."

"Well, mine is for clothes. Making them, knowing what people might need to take away with them, pre-knowing what outfit will get them the result they want, like for a job interview and so forth."

I was grinning ear to ear now. "Wow, Mags, that's so cool. Thank you for sharing."

She looked confused, then handed me the brown suit carrier she'd brought with her from the Gateway. "You'll need these for your breaks. The swimsuit's for the first one, and the others are for the second. Be sure to pack them. A wee gift to say thank you for what you've done for Rosie and for last night."

As far as I was aware, I only had one break planned, but I gave her a hug, which startled her.

"They've got the spells on them. Just jiggle."

CHAPTER
THIRTY-FOUR

I had a busy half an hour summoning the missing Hobs safely home for Mags before I could finish my packing. They didn't look in great shape to me, but Mags assured me they'd all be fine in the F of T, which turned out to mean "the fullness of time," and I rather liked the abbreviation. One of the Hobs had fallen into Mags's arms sobbing, and Rosie had run across the Gateway to wrap the woman in her arms. Mags said, "This is Heli. She's mother to the triplets you bonded."

I took one look at the sobbing Hob who looked as if only her daughter's strength was holding her upright and sent Rosie home for the rest of the day.

Then, drama over, Rollo arrived, and we had a coffee together. He was nervous about meeting Aysha and Autumn. I told him he didn't have to come if he was uncomfortable about it, but Autumn had specifically asked to meet him.

"Do you know why?" he enquired.

I shook my head. "No clue, but she was insistent. We'd already agreed to go, so I didn't push her."

Rollo and I wouldn't both fit into Aysha's downstairs bathroom without my breaking an ankle on that vicious toilet roll stand, so I'd called and asked her to keep the hall clear for the next minute. Rollo and I landed on the wooden hall floor like normal travellers. Not in mid-air like Marvel superheroes, but still hand in hand.

When the hell had I started thinking that transporting into someone's hall was normal?

Tilly immediately began struggling like a hungry dog who can smell fresh roast chicken. The second I put her down, she tore up the stairs.

I drew Rollo through to the kitchen and introduced him to Aysha. Her professional solicitor's expression was in place. I called it her, "I will let nothing show on my face, however utterly and self-sabotagingly stupid my client is being" mask. It came to her rescue now.

But meeting this authentic version of Rollo without his toy boy glamour strained it more than usual. I watched as she compared the handsome professional man in front of her with her memories of the Thor-look-alike wearing his glamour from my ascension.

Then Autumn let out such a piercing squeal, I was amazed Tilly didn't tear back down the stairs with her paws over her ears. Rollo jumped and whirled around, giving me a horrified expression. He was confused when Aysha and I continued chatting and headed towards her dining table as though nothing had happened.

"Is the child well?"

"She's fine. She always does that when Tilly arrives. You get used to it. They'll come charging down the stairs, sounding like a crash of rhinos any minute."

I gestured back towards the hall. Aysha looked confused.

"Coffee? Beer? Wine? Rollo," Aysha enquired.

"Coffee would be great, thanks."

"And how do you take it?" But as she asked, two identical black coffees for Rollo and me arrived on the table in front of us from Dola. "Only me who needs to get caught up, then. Thanks,

CODE YELLOW IN GRETNA GREEN

Dola, I'd love one too." Her vanilla latte arrived. I watched as she sipped and breathed without actually taking her eyes off Rollo, but also without appearing to stare at him. I should acquire that skill.

Autumn and Tilly pounded down the stairs. I went to greet her. It always amazed me that two tiny bodies could make so much noise. Tilly was happy. She'd missed Autumn too. She danced and carried one of the smaller unicorns in her mouth as the pair came into the hall. Autumn chattered away to Tilly about swimming and one of her doggy friends at the park, who was apparently missing Tilly nearly as much as Autumn was.

Autumn stopped. "Hey, Auntie Nik."

She looked me over carefully from the top of my head to my toes. "Tilly says Dusha lets her come on the rides, so now she needs a unicorn. She's only borrowing this one. You'll have to buy her one of her own."

"Uh huh, does she want any particular one?" This was not my first unicorn-buying rodeo, as Mabon might have said.

Autumn nodded seriously. "It's the small purple one on my will list." It had amused me when Autumn announced that she was renaming her online wish list and in the future it would be called her will list. Because she was willing the things on it to come to her. Then she walked past me towards the kitchen but came to an abrupt halt.

She looked up at Rollo. And then up a bit further. When he immediately knelt down to her level, she took a step back. He was a big guy, but his smile was gentle. Was she frightened of him? No, that wasn't it. I reached out with my Gift. Was she alright?

She was excited. OK, but why?

"Autumn, let me introduce you to Rollo. He's my new friend. Rollo, this is my goddaughter Autumn, who has me wrapped around her unicorn-mad fingers." Had I ever told Rollo my little goddaughter knew all about the realms? I was about to push that thought at him when a better idea struck me. "She was a bridesmaid for Princess Natalia of House Asturia at her bonding, but I think you'd all left by then?"

"Hey, Autumn, nice to meet you." Rollo stayed on his knee and gave her one of his easy, warm smiles, looking her over carefully through clear hazel eyes. Autumn considered him equally carefully. In fact, they had a similar clarity and purpose in their gaze.

They stared at each other in silence, which was weird. I caught Aysha's eye, and she shrugged. Then Autumn reached out one hand towards Rollo's cheek, and something in my stomach rebelled and said NO.

I moved before I'd even consciously thought it through. Quickly, I reached out and took Autumn's hand with my own, startling her slightly. "You and I need to have a little chat, I think. Let's go and talk to some unicorns, hey? You can show me what kind Tilly would like." And I led her towards the hall.

"We'll be ten minutes. Play nice please, Aysha."

To Rollo I sent, *"Aysha doesn't respect anyone who doesn't stand up to her. Don't feel you have to be too polite."*

As we walked upstairs, I tried to work out what the hell was wrong with me. Autumn had done this odd thing where she placed her hand on someone's face several times recently. The first time had been with Fionn'ghal and then with Dai at the bonding checks. It had intrigued me, and I'd intended to ask her about it. But it had never disturbed me. I really didn't want her to touch Rollo, and yet, I had no idea why. Just that instinctive *no*.

We walked in silence to her bedroom. She sat on the bed, and I perched on the unicorn bean bag I'd often sat in to read her bedtime stories. "What's up, baby?"

She shook her head, her lips tight. I opened my arms, and she immediately landed on my lap and snuggled in. Her little body shook, and I started to reach out with my Gift again. What on earth had happened? Then I heard the giggle.

I laughed in relief.

When she didn't stop giggling, I asked, "Come on—what the heck's going on? Mum's worried about you, you know. How's your tummy?"

She gave me a brilliant smile. "All good now, Auntie Nik. I needed to see you."

"But, baby, you can't frighten Mum like that. You could have messaged me."

I heard her exasperation. "No, I needed to *see* you."

"OK, but why?"

She gave me a long look, stood up, took my hand, and pulled me towards the door. "No, Autumn, wait. You need to tell me what upset you at the weekend?"

She spun around, surprise on her face, and shook her head until her ponytail swished. "Wasn't upset. Come on." She was tugging at me now. "Need to go downstairs so I can show you."

We went back downstairs. Whatever this was, Aysha wouldn't be pleased with me. Oh well, I'd try again after dinner.

Autumn paused in the hall by the full-length mirror Aysha used every morning on her way out of the house to check she hadn't left her hair wrap on or her lipstick off. She stood me in front of it and said, "Wait," in the exact tone of voice she used to Tilly.

Seconds later, she came back, tugging Rollo by the hand. He looked bemused. Aysha followed behind and met my eyes. I shrugged. "I've no clue either, Shay. But best to get to the bottom of whatever it is. Don't you think?"

Aysha nodded. Autumn positioned Rollo next to me. Then she looked cross and turned me to face him. As he caught my eyes, I thought, *"I'm so sorry, I have no idea what the hell's wrong with her. She's a terrific kid usually."*

His smile quirked into a grin as he sent me a picture of what might make it up to him later. I giggled.

Then Autumn screamed. It wasn't even a squeal—it was a damn scream.

But when she reached out and took my hand, I screamed too.

Once all the screaming abated, I didn't know whether to laugh or cry, celebrate or swear.

In the mirror, a bond glow clearly surrounded Rollo and me. He'd spun round to see what was behind him, assuming something there must have made me scream. When he finally realised I wasn't looking behind him—I was looking at us in the mirror—he somewhat sheepishly sheathed Nanok. Aysha didn't look pleased at anyone drawing a blade on autopilot in her home.

She spoke firmly to Autumn, who was laughing too hard to even draw a breath and completely ignored her. When her mum finally got through to her, with surprising authority for a seven-year-old, Autumn gasped for air and wheezed, "Wait, Mum. It's not your turn."

"What's happening here, Boo? I'm losing the plot?"

I sent him a quick picture of us standing in front of the mirror in his bedroom and raised my arms so he could wrap his around me. He moved immediately behind me and hugged me. Our eyes met in the long mirror, and I breathed easily again, although I was still trembling.

"Autumn, can you show Rollo too, please?"

She quickly stood next to Rollo and held out a hand to each of us.

"Can someone please tell me what the actual fu … heck is going on, please?" Aysha almost shouted.

Rollo's eyes opened wide, and I heard a stream of soft Norse that probably wouldn't win a place on Aysha's approved word list. Softly, he said, "I never thought I'd be able to see it."

Then I actually looked at us properly. "Oh, Gods and Goddesses. It's a seven-fold. Look."

Autumn nodded so hard, I thought her head might drop off.

Rollo asked, "A what?"

Aysha said, "Seriously, this is my home. I demand to know ... wait. What? Like Tomas and Natalia's?" She moved closer and reached out to grip her daughter's wrist, then she screamed too.

My poor eardrums.

I picked up my coffee and took a large gulp. "Well, that explains a lot, but why couldn't you have just told me?"

Autumn sipped her juice and looked thoughtful. "You didn't know, Auntie Nik. I thought you might talk about it a lot. But if you seed it, you'd know."

"Saw it," Aysha and I corrected automatically in unison.

"But, Autumn, how could you know? You hadn't seen them?" Aysha looked worried now. She'd always hated things she didn't understand.

Autumn looked guilty. We both knew that expression. I glanced at Aysha, knowing it was wiser to let Mum call her kid out.

And she did. There was steel in her tone as she asked, "*What* did you do, Autumn?"

Autumn was unrepentant. "I couldn't sleep. Auntie Nik was really, really scared for ages 'n' ages. The unicorns and I tried to help, but the Dolina won't give me enough. Then she felt better, and Dola said she was alright now." She gave her mother a glare that wouldn't have looked out of place on Aysha's face.

"I *asked* if you'd messaged, Auntie Nik, and mum said no. She fibbed! And made me go to bed 'cause she was tired." She gave her mother a look that wasn't quite an accusation, but it was laden with disappointment.

Aysha huffed. "I made you go to bed because you wouldn't eat your tea. You sat on your bed for hours being weird, and there's been chicken pox at your school. That vaccination isn't foolproof. I thought you were coming down with something."

Turning to me, she said, "She was behaving as oddly as she did when she was incubating that awful bug. Remember how peculiar she was for a few days before that? That's why I didn't call you sooner. Well, OK, yes, I called you repeatedly, but not about her." She sighed. "I didn't think the photo you sent me was suitable for a child. So, I fibbed. But what does this mean?" She gestured at Rollo and me.

Then she remembered we weren't the important thing right now. Her daughter was. "How did *you* know I fibbed? What did you do, Autumn?"

With no suggestion of apology, Autumn announced, "I checked your phone to see if Auntie Nik had messaged, 'cause I didn't believe you. And I saw the photo, and then I knowed why she'd been frightened because," she pointed at Rollo, "it was him they hurt. He's her bond mate."

We both ignored the "knowed," more interested in her answer. Aysha asked, "But how could you tell from a photo?"

As she opened her phone, Autumn casually replied, "Look, you can see."

As Aysha pulled up the photo, Autumn reached over and touched her mother's hand, and I saw it. She'd just pulled power. How had she done that? My eyes shot to the Dolina. Shit!

Rollo and I were having a private conversation that included all the swearwords I'd quickly explained we couldn't use in front of Autumn, and I was running through all the things that had baffled me about our mental connection. Our chemistry, my uncharacteristic decision to sleep with him so quickly, and the general craziness of the last week. He was very calm. I was freaking out.

"Niki?"

"Niiiikkkii?"

"Sorry?" I focused on Aysha.

Oh, she was snippy. "If you could stop gazing at each other for a minute, I need to know if my daughter is—"

Autumn interrupted, "They're talking, Mum. Like Uncle Ad'Rian does." She tapped her head.

"Autumn Olive Niki Clarke, I don't think you did anything very wrong, but I will be changing my phone's PIN code. Right now, you need to take Tilly and play with the unicorns in your room. Dinner will be in twenty minutes. Adults need to talk."

Autumn's mutinous expression had no power against her mother's use of her full name. Aysha only pulled that one out when she was about to lose control.

"Is your friend OK?"

I smiled at Rollo. *"Nope, she's about to go ballistic. She won't do it in front of her child or a stranger. I'm so sorry, I know it's a lot, and we need to talk. But these guys need to come first until we can get out of here. Could you possibly either go and play with the unicorns, or just be somewhere else for half an hour? I think she's about to burst into tears or kick the door again. The sooner I calm her down, the sooner we can eat, get out of here and work out what we're going to do."*

Autumn stomped upstairs, Tilly at her heels. Rollo stood up and gave Aysha a half-bow. "If you'll excuse me, I'll be back for dinner."

To me he sent, *"We'll work it out, Boo, never fear."*

And then he disappeared in a bright burst of yellow power that Aysha couldn't see. And that didn't help her equilibrium one bit.

CHAPTER
THIRTY-FIVE

Aysha's primary worry, rightly, was Autumn. We settled on her couch for a hug and sipped our coffee, and I cuddled her. She'd had too many shocks. It made me realise how accustomed I'd become to shocks at every turn, often before I was even awake.

Well, information usually calmed me, so I gave her some to see if that would work. I explained what I thought had happened with Autumn. While she'd held her strange unicorn healing circle, Rollo had been close to death. As Autumn said, I'd been terrified for him, and with the help of a Goddess, we'd healed him. I didn't mention the Goddess in question was a cat.

Honestly, she didn't look as though *all* the information would help her. And any more of my now-crazy life's insanity might be too much for her to take right now.

"But, Niki, what can I do for her? This is getting scary. She knew you were fighting for the man's life, and I didn't. Also, don't we need to get into how the eye candy I saw in your Gateway turned into him? He doesn't seem stupid. Why did I think he was stupid?"

I ignored her—we only had twenty minutes before I'd feel as though I was being unbearably rude to Rollo. Or Autumn came down for her dinner. We needed to focus on Autumn. But even as I thought this, Rollo sent, *"Take all the time you need. They're your family."*

Yes, they truly were.

I didn't think Aysha would agree, but I tried it anyway. "Do you think it's time to get her a phone? If she could have messaged me herself, Dola or I could have given her the child-friendly version so she could relax."

The look on Aysha's face told me this idea was no closer to working now than it ever had been. "You know my views on kids and devices. She can use mine, the tablet or the computer to message you, but she is not having one of her own until I can no longer avoid it. The internet isn't fit for unsupervised children."

The Dolina in the corner of the lounge came to life. How many of those damn devices were there now? "I wonder if I might assist?"

Aysha and I looked at each other as she asked, "How?"

"Autumn asked me to send a message to Niki for her. I told her she must ask your permission, as we have agreed, Aysha. She said you would not allow it because she was supposed to be in bed. Perhaps, under the circumstances, if I had a little flexibility, it might have alleviated some of the problem? And, congratulations, Niki. I am thrilled for you both. A seven-fold bond is a rare and wonderful thing."

Aysha went bright red, which was always interesting to watch with her tawny skin. "Oh, my goodness, yes, of course. I'm so sorry, Nik. I should have said congrats, shouldn't I? But it was such a—"

I hugged her hard and added a little shake. "I'm not feeling all congrats-ish myself yet. Give us the holiday to sort ourselves out, and we probably will be. There's a lot of other stuff going on with him working out whether he wants to become king and everything."

Her jaw fell open. "He … what? Seriously?"

Why was she acting like she didn't know this? "I told you

about Troels and the cases weeks ago. Rollo's the heir. The power gave him the yellow regnal power, but Rollo wants what's best for the realm. He thinks that might not be him. It's all a bit of a mess right now, but we're working on it."

She shook her head until her cornrows swung and looked remarkably like her daughter in that moment. "Regnal what? King? And I'm going on about my weird child. Sorry again."

"Your child is one of the most important people in my life, and you know it. Relax, hey?"

There were a few more tears. Which were much easier to deal with than us needing to patch the door again. That had been a real pain of a job. Then she sipped her wine and nodded. "OK, you get a pass for not messaging me. I'm pretty sure the girlfriend rules don't apply if he needs to become king and nearly dies. It's probably OK to put him first under those very specific circumstances."

I smirked at her. "How about when a prince in the midst of a nervous breakdown tries to hold Tilly and me hostage? Do I get a pass for that as well? Hey, did I mention I rode a dragon too?"

She hit me. Well, OK, she punched my arm. "You're just boasting now. Should we eat dinner? Can you get him back in time to eat? I might have been rude to him. I was overwhelmed, but I made Mum's jerk chicken."

"I can, but before I do, we need to talk too, Shay. Things have changed profoundly for me. We need to discuss it properly before you lose your mind again the next time something unexpected happens, and I can't drop everything right that minute. This isn't like Janet thinking I should work, and you saying I have a right to a day off. This is usually something …" I paused and wondered what I could say that wouldn't make me sound self-important. Bloody Dai, I kept remembering that comment of his.

Aysha said, "Life or death?"

"Well, no, not usually. I think that was an exception. It had better have been an exception. The last few weeks have been … a lot. But you two are *still* extremely important in my life. You need to be sure about that."

I was frustrated. Time travel is a fabulous magical thing, but I didn't want time travel right now. I wanted to be able to freeze time so I could think. Just press the pause button. Work out how to fix all this with Aysha before our friendship went down the tubes, the way I'd seen so many others do when someone met a man they were serious about. And what was more serious than a damn seven-fold bond? But Aysha made a valid point on her ranty phone call yesterday.

Rollo made me happy, and a seven-fold bond was freaking amazing, even if I had no idea what to do about it. It was all so new. I'd only known the man for a few weeks. I would not be that idiot who let herself fall into insta-love without making sure they knew the guy. If I'd learned one lesson from Nick, it was to trust my gut and my head and not suppress either of them or go against them because some rule or societal expectation thought I should.

I couldn't even imagine the things this bond might change. But Aysha and I had put twenty-two years into our friendship. I wasn't risking those years simply because I now had a bond mate. The bond wasn't going anywhere, was it? Or was it? I knew nothing about bonds from the inside, did I? I'd have to ask the Book. That made me laugh, and my own tension dissipated in a fit of giggles.

I reached out to Rollo. *"Did you know we had a bond?"*

I could tell by the laughter bubbling in his energy and in my brain that he had. *"Then why the hell didn't you tell me?"*

After a pause, he sent, *"I did tell you. I said I was waiting for you to catch up."*

He had too, hadn't he? In his Edinburgh flat. I'd thought he was just ... what had I thought? Nothing much. Nothing like this. Anyway, I'd been blissed out that day.

Then he said, *"It was when I realised I couldn't read other people's minds. Only yours. Something my step-sister Elise said when she first met her bond mate Sten, suddenly made sense."*

I caught a fleeting expression on Aysha's face and realised I was being rude. And we should all eat before the jerk chicken turned to rubber.

Then I had a total brainwave.

"Rollo, would you be OK if we didn't start our holiday until Sunday?"

I held one finger up to Aysha to indicate I'd almost finished being rude.

A sense of relief came through our bond. I wasn't sure if he intended me to feel it. *"Of course. It's been a shock for you. But I need to see you tonight to make sure we're OK."*

He was not wrong. I sent, *"Oh hell yes. Give me a few more minutes, then we should be able to eat."*

I watched Aysha carefully. "Would your mum have Autumn to stay overnight tomorrow, do you think?"

She looked at me. "Well, dur! An unscheduled opportunity to spoil the light of her life? What do you think? But why?"

I was struggling to put into words what I was feeling. A sense that if Aysha and I didn't take some time to catch up properly, my life would move on so quickly without her that our friendship might not survive it.

I'd changed from being her weak, spineless, grieving friend whom she'd needed to look after, into a woman with six realms, six sets of royals and headwomen and several gods to deal with on an almost daily basis.

I did something I'd never done before and turned my full newly powered-up Gift onto my best mate. Yep. She was frightened too. I was changing too fast. She was worried about Autumn, who missed Tilly and me in her life. But also she was terrified for herself. She knew her choices, her often-abrasive personality, and her total commitment to her daughter and her job meant, while she had a healthy social circle, it was composed mostly of clients and her contacts from her volunteer work. Her mum and I were the only two people she truly trusted.

I knew exactly how that felt. Until a couple of months ago, Aysha and my gran had been the only people I trusted. How things had changed!

"Shay-girl, how about if you and I take a quick break? Autumn can take Tilly to your mum's overnight. She can get her Tilly fix, Olive can get her grandbaby fix, and we can catch up?"

"That might work, even Mum's missing Tilly, you know. Could we go somewhere with a pool? A day or overnight pass to one of those hotels with a mini spa? I'd love to swim properly without needing to monitor Autumn."

"Why not?"

She was poking her phone now. "I could do it four weeks from tomorrow for two or even three days at a push; would that work?"

"What have you got on tomorrow and Sunday morning?"

She gave me a startled glance and poked her phone some more before saying, "Only a meeting I could move, and the unicorn queen, of course."

"Great. How about I pick you up tomorrow late morning? And I'll have you back in time for Sunday lunch at Olive's?"

She thought for a moment. "Yeah, if you don't mind being away from your *bond mate*?" She gave the word a sarcastic, self-conscious emphasis.

"He'll live." And as I said it, how incandescently happy I was that he *would* live washed over me.

Perhaps I owed HRH more than I thought. I wondered if she knew?

What the hell was I thinking? Of course she knew. The bloody cat had probably been running a book on precisely when I'd work it out.

Then a little movie reel of all the strange expressions I'd caught on people's faces recently ran through my mind. Mags's surprised expression in Stane Parlour yesterday when Rollo arrived. Mags and Rosie's knowing smiles yesterday in the Gateway.

Even Finn and Caitlin's expressions when Rollo and I rose into the air together. And Inge's peculiar comments about naked photos of Rollo on a bearskin rug and all her questions about our plans. And had Mabon been trying to give me a hint when he said he and Agnes couldn't see their own bond?

Shit, was there anyone who hadn't known except me?

FFS.

How much had the damn cat made? And who could I get to place a bet for me before we announced the news?

"Come back to the same spot you left from; it's clear. Sorry again about this."

Aysha gasped, and I just enjoyed watching Rollo land. The gorgeous bastard did the whole fake superhero three-point landing thing, which made me laugh. He must jump as he took off; I always landed normally on the floor. Then I thought how weird it must look to other people when I appeared and disappeared. Perhaps I should be a bit more discreet about it. Or, better still, I should get him to teach me how to fake a superhero landing.

I admired his butt and thought, at least I didn't need to feel guilty about it anymore. No wonder I'd had overwhelming hormones and a need to touch him. Everyone said it was super intense when you first connected with your bond mate. I felt a lot more normal about how compelling I found him to watch.

"Still doing it, Boo."

We laughed, and Aysha looked confused.

PART SIX
SATURDAY

In your dotage, when you look back upon your life, you will have forgotten many of the enemies you vanquished.

But you will remember, with gut-wrenching clarity, each and every battle you won against yourself.

Because we are the person who truly terrifies us.

We only transfer our fear onto others in order to learn the important lessons more swiftly.

Remember those allies and blade mates who held a mirror up for you to view your problems differently?

Many times, when another angers us, it is their similarity to ourselves that truly infuriates us.

Winning the War Against Yourself: Daily Weapon and Warrior Care by Arinn Tusensköna

CHAPTER
THIRTY-SIX

Saturday, 6th March — Aysha's Home, North Manchester

I landed in Aysha's downstairs loo and let Tilly out to track Autumn down. In her kitchen, as expected, Aysha was perfectly organised. Her tote waited on a chair with her handbag, and she smiled as I walked through.

"I'm so looking forward to even a super short break. It's been too long since we had girl-time."

She was right; it had been.

Aysha left with Autumn and Tilly to drive them around to her mum's while I finished tidying her kitchen. I was still mulling over my too limited time with Rollo and the research I'd done after he left for Edinburgh this morning.

Last night, our plans for a long, meaningful discussion about what a seven-fold bond might mean for us got completely derailed when, instead, we'd ended up in bed. As Rollo said, we could talk anytime. There didn't seem to be a limit on our connection. We might even be able to chat while I was away with Aysha, but we definitely would once I was back and we were on our own holiday. But he wouldn't be able to hold me while I was gone. "So, priorities then, Boo, priorities."

And he'd made me his number one priority with an intensity of focus that had been satisfying and, for me, previously unknown from any man. This bond mate gig had its advantages. Was that why I always felt so relaxed with him instead of the constant tension I'd so often endured with Nick?

As I fell asleep, I made yet another mental note. This one to find out why the hell his nickname for me was the name of his childhood dog. That was eccentric, right? I needed to make a physical list of all my mental notes so I could get some of them ticked off. Fi would be proud of me.

This morning, we'd planned our own break. Rollo was going home to Edinburgh to work on his own arrangements. He had been relieved, welcoming the extra day to complete his work. Then he intended to talk to me about his overall concept for Viking before he discussed it officially with the Recorder.

After my girls' getaway brainwave, I was less concerned about us going somewhere warm. So we'd agreed I'd come to Edinburgh on my return, and we'd just wing it. All Rollo and I needed was some peace, some privacy, some damn time and a chance to adjust to whatever this bond might mean for our futures. Right now, I couldn't see any way to have anything like a normal relationship if he was busy not being the Viking king, and I was stuck as the Recorder.

Frankly, Viking felt like a worse place for a woman to live than even the Middle East was when Nick asked me to move there. But Rollo was super calm about it all, even the whole bonded part, probably because he'd had longer to get used to it than I had.

After he left, I thought I'd be calmer and feel more balanced once the shock wore off a bit. Right now, I was overwhelmed. I was *supposed* to be incandescently happy. Didn't everyone want to find their soulmate? Except what was exciting to read about in a romantic novel was very different in real life.

The Book helped a little. "Tell me about couple bonds," got me one of the new style pages with options.

The origins of the life mate bond
How to identify a life mate bond
How to perform a bonding ceremony
How to identify a seven-fold bond
The significance of a seven-fold bond
Other kinds of bonds

Yeah, I knew most of this, but I tapped the one about the significance of a seven-fold bond, hoping more information might calm me down.

Certain individuals who have shared previous lives together arrange to meet up again in their next life. Often they have unfulfilled promises to each other. There may be life lessons to complete, debts to repay or other matters important to their soul growth. They have agreed to assist each other in doing these things.

I must have read that paragraph four times. It raised so many questions. How the hell did a couple "arrange to meet up"?

Finally, some part of my brain that wasn't freaking out suggested my questions might be answered if I continued reading.

In the case of a couple bond, close examination should show the Recorder, or any individual with the power to see them, how many lifetimes a couple have spent together.

A quick flash of Mabon and the two Red Celt men who had wanted the "cool rings." Effervescent Simon, with his bow ties, who was now helping Finn with some of the Gateway's social media stuff and had agreed to sit on my Rainbow Council. I could see his taller, more controlled husband in my mind's eye, but I couldn't retrieve his name. What had Mabon told them? He'd squinted at their bond, hadn't he? Then said something like they had a lovely bond, but in another two or three lifetimes together, they might come back to the Gateway with a seven-fold bond. But this time, they couldn't have the eternal rings the power made for Kaiden and L'eon, and they should get tattooed rings. Bryn! That was Simon's husband's name. I thought back and pictured what I'd seen that day. I'd seen four or perhaps five of their chakras were in alignment.

In all the years I'd been able to see bonds, it never occurred to me that which or how many of the couple's chakras aligned had any significance. Well, other than to give me an insight into how their relationship might play out. When a couple had their base chakras resonating together, as many of the shield maidens and their bond mates had, I knew they would have a satisfying, if fiery, relationship. In contrast, if their higher mental chakras were connected, they would have a meeting of minds. Those couples often thought the same way about things, enjoyed the same things, and laughed at the same jokes.

I'd even noticed that couples whose throat or communication chakras seemed to connect didn't have silly misunderstandings and could always talk things out. And thrash them out equally without one partner doing all the talking, all the time.

Then I pictured the empress. I should look more closely at her bond with the emperor, shouldn't I?

But I had never truly grasped the number of chakra connections a couple had related to past lives lived together. Yet again, I wished I could take the Book with me.

Aysha returned from Olive's looking ten years younger and full of mischief, just like her daughter, in fact. "So, you said leave it all to you and Dola. Where are we going? She wouldn't tell me."

I'd given Dola strict instructions not to breathe a single word to Aysha when she'd helped me to book this little surprise. Aysha's birthday was in early April, which, this year, meant she'd celebrate it over the Easter weekend. As the Recorder, I couldn't guarantee to be free, and it had been worrying me, so this break could be a *two birds, one stone* solution.

"A bit of a pre-birthday surprise, Shay-girl. Grab your bag, close your eyes, and let's go see." At the confusion on her face, I handed her a travel sickness tablet and added, "Thought we'd take the shortcut. Better than wasting hours in the car when we don't have to, don't you think?"

She chewed the tablet. "Good thinking. OK." She hooked her tote over her shoulder and held out her hand.

We landed. She opened her eyes, and then the squealing started. Again.

And it went on so long, I was tempted to pull power and mute the damn woman. I really hate squealing.

But eventually, she asked "How?" and pulled open the doors to the patio with its tiny private plunge pool. We stood in the doorway in the warm morning sunshine with our arms around each other's waists. I looked out over to the mountains in the distance and the much larger communal pool about fifteen yards from our apartment.

I said, "Remember the last time we were here when you were pregnant, and you'd just found out you were having a girl?"

"Yeah, I didn't want to fly, but it was too late to get our money back, and the doctor said I'd be fine. I didn't believe her after my miscarriage. She said my high blood pressure was more of a worry, and a break would do me good."

Aysha giggled, actually giggled. "I was so paranoid something would happen to the baby."

"Yep, and you'd finally stopped throwing up. And you said, one day you'd like to come back when you could do all the things a pregnant woman couldn't. Have a drink, eat all the local tapas and cured meats and—"

"Try that amazing soft goat's cheese, the one that you kept eating and having orgasms about. I think you did that on purpose. Now I can find out if it was as good as you made out."

She laughed. But it had been truly excellent; she wouldn't be disappointed.

Gazing across in the other direction at the beautiful coastline of Lanzarote in the Canary Islands, we basked in the warmth on a day that had been freezing both in Scotland and Manchester. It was beautiful here with a light breeze, a few clouds, and a glorious, mostly blue sky. Oh, and the sun. The sun I felt as though I hadn't seen since I moved to Scotland shone gently down on us. It would be hotter in a few hours, but right now, it was fresh and perfect. There were even empty sunbeds by the large pool.

Aysha had tears in her eyes as she uncharacteristically mumbled, "I was all geared up to tell you, as your friend, you needed to take this new job less seriously. Consider your work-life balance properly and prioritise your health and well-being, and now this new relationship. But, hell, Nik, the perks are incredible!" She put her hand over her mouth and glanced around guiltily as she said, "Hell."

Then she gave me her blinding grin. "I love my child dearly, but after months of coming up with interesting wet weather activities, not having to be a responsible role model, even just for a weekend—twenty-four hours of irresponsibility—what a gift. How on earth did you arrange it?"

"Yeah, about that."

When I'd finished my explanation about my great-granny Florrie, time travel and what the power thought I could get away with, how we could stay a week if she wanted, and she would still be back in time for Sunday lunch at her mother's …

The squealing started again. I'd endured far too much squealing and screaming lately.

I pushed her into the plunge pool.

PART SEVEN
WEEK TWO—
SUNDAY

Never be afraid to refuse to follow the mob. Some people may walk away because you are too different. But those apparent losses are truly your gains.

It is always better to lose the wrong people from your life than to lose yourself by fitting in with things or people who are not right for you.

Allow who you truly are to shine out true, bright-edged and clear, and the right people will be drawn into your world.

Winning the War Against Yourself: Daily Weapon and Warrior Care by Arinn Tusensköna

CHAPTER
THIRTY-SEVEN

Sunday, 7th March — Gateway Cottage — Gretna Green

We landed back at Aysha's home and drove to her mother's together to collect Tilly. Olive gave me her usual assessing smile and announced, "Well, well, Niki-girl, I need to get me some of whatever you're having. Looking good, lady, looking good."

She pressed her amazing Caribbean food on me, of course. "You'll need to fry the dumplings; I left them ready."

Oh yeah, frying her dumplings properly had been one of the basic lessons when she'd taken me under her wing after the great red beans and rice crockpot fire disaster during our first year at university.

Did Rollo like Caribbean food as much as I did?

The holiday had been a brilliant idea. Aysha looked relaxed and happy. We'd caught up on each other's lives. We'd come up with what she called a new communication protocol for the Dolinas in her house. She was going to allow Autumn to use them to send me messages, providing she could check the transcripts. She said, "I'm going to treat it like her search history. Until she's old enough not to have that checked, I'm checking her messages too."

Seemed sensible to me. I'd never interfered in Aysha's motherly cautions, and I wasn't starting now.

But the best thing, the one that made me truly happy, was we felt fixed. Real friends again, but with an entirely new and now mutual respect. It had finally dawned on me that, as much as Aysha loved me, she'd never respected me. I couldn't say I blamed her because I'd made some lousy choices, but that was changing fast.

The Dolina in Aysha's kitchen came to life when we all returned. "Niki, if you are returning home, please transport to the cottage and not the Gateway."

"OK, why? Is there a problem?"

"There is no problem. I shall explain when you return."

Something in her tone suggested the answer might be confidential, and she didn't want to explain in front of Aysha or Autumn. "Will do."

I landed in my bedroom. I'd need to swap my holiday clothes out for some much warmer ones if I had to deal with Edinburgh in early March. Being further north, it would be even colder than here. "OK, Dola, I'm back. Now why couldn't I go to the Gateway? And why couldn't you answer me at Aysha's?"

"I did not want to explain in front of Autumn because it involves the petitions against Troels. As you suggested, Aysha and I have compiled a list of topics that are child-appropriate. Anything concerning Troels would not meet the criteria of the list."

I laughed, remembering she'd first raised the petitions during a lunch when Autumn was staying with me. It had been apparent Dola didn't self-censor in front of children, and I'd suggested she spoke to Aysha. That would have been a hilarious conversation. I wondered if there was a transcript?

"OK, so what about Troels? Is he alright?"

"He is fine. The filming began yesterday in the Gateway. I did not want you to land in the middle of the shot. It might have caused consternation."

"What filming? Do I know about this?"

"Yes, Niki. I am gathering evidence for the court of public opinion."

I did not know about this, did I? "OK. What is it you think I know about it?"

I swear she sighed. "Rollo was kissing you at the time, but you gave me clear consent to do this."

"I did?" Rollo didn't kiss me anywhere near enough because somebody always interrupted us. I wanted to see him. Our brief chats while I was away weren't enough, but neither of us had wanted to discuss anything serious until no one could interfere or interrupt us.

A recording played through the Dolina: "Niki, I require your permission to conduct an experiment. I will need Glynis and Finn's assistance. They have both agreed in principle. I do not wish to explain or discuss it with you yet because I cannot be sure if it will work. But I assure you I will release nothing publicly without your approval. May I have that permission now?"

My own voice said, "Yes, you have it."

Ah, yes, I vaguely recalled that. She had a plan to educate some Vikings about why Troels was being held by the Recorder pending his arbitration. I remembered I'd thought that Dola and Finn were the warrior Knights, and that if I was wrong to give her permission, Caitlin and I would simply have to clear up their mess.

"And this filming started yesterday?" I headed through to the bathroom and touched the Recorder's star shape in my mirror to view the Gateway.

The centre was busy. A young woman sat on a high stool with tears streaming down her face. Finn manned several cameras.

Simon wearing a cheerful blue polka dot bow tie, stood behind Finn, and next to him was Glynis. Then Finn held up a hand. Tegan dashed in and did something to the girl's face. She gave Tegan a watery smile.

I touched to listen to the audio, but nothing happened.

"Dola, the audio is malfunctioning."

"No, Niki, it is turned off so no one will break the flow. I shall send the videos through to you when they are completed. But as you can see, all is well in the Gateway."

While I thought about that, I pressed the star again to view the feed from Troels' cell in Viking. It all looked fine. A group of people stood on the other side of the railings in Viking peering at his cell and hoping for a glimpse of him through the tiny windows. They watched the video footage running on the outside of his cell and chatted amongst themselves.

I pulled a little power and spoke to it to find out if it was alright with the filming. Yes, it was calm and happy.

So, this was, "Butt the hell out, Niki. We have it under control," was it?

Tilly came in from the garden, and I closed the doors. It was cold and unpleasantly damp here after Lanzarote. "So you'd like me to clear off then?"

Dola ignored my tone and replied calmly, "Have you decided how much communication you would like while you are away?"

"Yes, I'd like the daily briefing option, please. I'm opting for caution this first time. If nothing scary, terrifying or urgent happens, perhaps we'll do it differently in the future. But for now, let's try a once-a-day briefing."

"Understood. Do you have a preferred time?"

"Let's play that by ear. I'm on holiday, so I'm not committing to being up at a certain time for a briefing. I'll let you know when I'm awake and ready for it."

I drifted into a lovely fantasy of how sweet Rollo could be in the morning and how much I would enjoy having relaxed breakfasts with him. It would be a lot more fun without worrying that

Finn would stroll through the kitchen for his bacon sandwich. Why didn't Dola just send his bacon sandwich to his Foxhole?

It wasn't only Finn though—what about all the other people who seemed to consider my kitchen to be an auxiliary office, interrupting us or mocking my pyjamas? In Edinburgh, we could breakfast naked if we wanted to. Bliss.

"Then I shall say goodbye and speak to you in Edinburgh."

"Chill out, Dola. I haven't even packed yet, and I need to ask the Book some questions. But I won't interfere – you should get on with whatever needs your attention."

Leaving Dola to whatever the hell it was she obviously didn't want me to know about, I transferred some warmer clothes into my suitcase. I was still unhappy with my cold weather clothing choices. Then I gathered all the discarded clothes from the floor by the wall of wardrobes, packed them into a storage bag and put them in the bottom of one of the many empty closets.

Settled on the bed, I placed my hand on the spine of the Book to make a start on the list of things I needed to ask it. "I missed you last week, and I wish I could have taken you with me, but you're so heavy and so protective of your cover, I daren't risk it."

Something peculiar happened under my hand.

I looked down at a small, closed, blue pocket diary with the Recorder's star indentation on the front cover.

"OMG, how long have you been able to do that? Why the hell haven't you ever done it before? Why have I been lugging a huge Book around? Why didn't you tell me this was a thing before you let me go on holiday without you? I had loads of reading time. I could have learned so much."

The Book grew back to its usual size, and I opened it. It flicked a page, and I read,

This has always been a feature. You never previously enquired about it.

"I guess that's me put in my place then. Do I have to say anything to make it happen, like 'Enter Travel Mode'?" That would be super cool.

But, sadly, the Book obviously wasn't a game fan and refused to indulge me.

Only place me in your luggage.

I dropped the Book into my suitcase. It shrank to pocket diary size, and I let out a whoop, which made Tilly woof at me.

I picked up my suitcase, spotted the brown suit carrier from Mags, and grabbed it too. Then I slung Olive's cold bag of food and my handbag over my shoulder, collected my dog and my courage, and, feeling like a packhorse, sent, *"Incoming."*

My world went rainbow-coloured.

Sunday, 7th March — Yggdrasil House — Edinburgh

I dropped my suitcase and garment carrier on the bedroom floor and headed towards the kitchen, clutching my treasures in the cold bag. Rollo opened the door, relieved me of the bag and folded me into his arms.

I breathed and marvelled as my insides all settled back into what felt like their proper places. Burying my face into his incredibly soft grey T-shirt, I breathed in. The seashore with those wonderful negative seaside ions that made the air smell so invigorating, fresh green herbs and, yes, that citrus undertone. He was stressed.

He laughed. "You're right, I am a bit off-balance. I hadn't realised how hard it would be not to see you, even for a day and a half. I think the bond might be a bit too new to be stretched. Or maybe I've just got it bad. Or both."

I heard him think, *Stop talking, man. You sound like an idiot.*

I giggled as he buried his nose into my hair and breathed. Then I heard, *No idea what makes up this scent; I don't have her nose. But it smells like home. And I never had one before. Only buildings.*

I melted into him and hung on until I felt myself come back properly into balance.

Then I focused on him.

It wasn't only that he'd missed me. His head felt overfull. A decision was disturbing him. He was worried—no, embarrassed—about something he had to tell me.

"What are you conflicted about?"

He laughed now and hugged me until I let out an "Oomph!" Then we had apologies and quite a lot of other affectionate displacement activity.

Perhaps it was my visit to Olive that gave me the idea, but I decided to see if her tried-and-true method for getting confused and unhappy girls to spill their guts all over her kitchen might work as well for men as it always had on us.

Adopting a deliberately light-hearted tone, I said, "I missed lunch to get up here as soon as I could. Are you hungry?"

His head bent, and he gave me a soft, sweet kiss that deepened as we both leaned into it. "Not really. But I have plans for you, and I'd hate for you to be hungry while I carry them out. Want to grab some food?"

"I have a better idea. Can I borrow your kitchen?"

A flash of surprise crossed his face as he gestured around him. "My kitchen is your kitchen." But the thought I heard as it crossed his mind was, *She cooks too?*

I grabbed a frying pan from its hook and thought I might distract him into talking about what was bothering him by moving him into *sous chef* mode. It always worked on me when Olive did it. "I need vegetable oil, a thermometer and tongs or a spatula. Some kitchen roll and a warm plate. If you get those, I'm about to make magic happen."

I unpacked the cold bag. Olive had, as always, packed enough food to feed an army. The woman should open a restaurant. I put the ackee and saltfish, the pepperpot and the jerk chicken and rice and peas into the fridge, which was mostly full of too much salad and a chicken. But Olive's meals would feed me for several days if his choices were too healthy for my carb-loving soul.

Then I carefully unwrapped the homemade but ready-to-cook dumplings from their greaseproof paper onto the countertop.

"What did you put in the fridge?"

"Remember the chicken thing Aysha served on Friday?"

"Yes, that was delicious."

"Well, the real thing is now in your fridge. Aysha makes the modern low-sugar, low-everything version. Olive, her mother, makes it the way her great-grandmother did in Jamaica. I swear she still uses sugar cane. We may all want a walk afterwards."

"All?" Rollo looked confused.

"Caribbean food is one of Tilly's favourite treats."

He looked down to see the three black dots of Tilly's eyes and nose totally focused on the kitchen counter. Her tail wagged a hundred times a minute. As much as she didn't mind visiting Olive and Autumn, she was glad to have me back, especially if I was bearing dumplings.

Rollo felt calmer now. I checked the heating oil as he stroked my back and peered over my shoulder to see what I'd unpacked. His strong fingers had moved to my shoulders now.

"You feel good, all relaxed. And you suit a tan. But I'm glad you're back and here." As he said this, he dropped feathery kisses down my neck and onto the shoulder that my boat-necked top revealed. He groaned as I leaned forward to select some dumplings and inadvertently pushed my butt into his crotch.

"OK, Your not-Majesty, back off. Hungry woman, remember? I need food and to stretch my legs. Then," I grinned at him, "I'm all yours."

He laughed but moved to sit at the table. "Dola sent me the link to the feed of my uncle's cell. It's on the Recorder's news portal now. And she's uploaded all the videos showing on his cell so anyone in any of the realms can view them online."

He opened his laptop on the kitchen table as I dropped a selection of dumplings into the hot oil. Then I peered over his shoulder at the screen while dropping my own kisses along his chiselled jawline.

"Wow!" Dola or Finn had added a whole new section to the news portal called Viking Arbitration. There was a summary of the petitions focusing on the paternity claims and stating they had been verified by a genetics consultant. She hadn't identified the individual petitioners, but a counter on the page changed as we watched from 141 to 142 petitions filed.

That was clever because we already had more than that, and more women were still filing. But it gave a clear visual indication showing the evidence against Troels continued to grow. Which it did—so go Dola.

A whole other section included the videos she'd screened for the royals at the book club and an empty grid-style space with blank white heads on a grey background that said, "Coming Soon: Personal Stories from the Petitioners."

Rollo tapped it. "Did you know about this?"

"Sort of. She's put together a bit of a task force. Glynis to interview the women. Her daughter Tegan is helping with something Dola called styling."

At his puzzled expression, I added, "Yeah, I don't know either, but I would imagine having Tegan involved is making Finn either deliriously happy or very bad at his job. That's Dola's problem. Then there's Simon, a Red Celt chap I bonded at Valentine's. He does social media stuff and will be on the Rainbow Council."

He whistled. "You're giving Dola a lot of autonomy."

I shook my head as I turned to flip the dumplings. Oh, they looked delish, and I was starving. I should have eaten at Olive's, but I'd needed to see Rollo. "Yes and no. She's checking the videos past me before she posts them. Anyway, warriors make a mess. I'm prepared to give her space to test her ideas."

He looked confused, but then Tilly let out one discreet woof, and I looked down at her. "Oh, you say so, do you?"

"Is the dog OK?"

Yeah, we were going to talk about that too. While we ate seemed as good a time as any. "She has a built-in timer for when dumplings are ready. I've always guessed the odour changes in some way."

"They smell mouthwatering."

I dished up the ones from the pan onto the warm plate. Checked the oil temperature and dropped more in.

"You got any beer?"

Rollo's laugh was warm, rich and sincerely amused. He was relaxing. "Are you seriously asking a Viking if he has beer?"

Still chuckling to himself, he opened a door I hadn't realised led to a pantry space with another refrigerator. When he opened it, I saw, not only did he have beer, but he had a wide variety of beer. He called, "Got a preference? With or without alcohol?"

"No, I don't care. Anything that goes well with spicy. Whatever you'd drink with a curry."

He brought two pale blue and silver cans to the table, opened them, and I heard him think, *Glass or no glass? Women are funny about that stuff.*

I reached over, took the can from him, popped it open, and tasted it. "Perfect."

That was easy, then.

I broke the veggie dumpling in half and took a bite of my side and a swig of the beer. He'd chosen well. Huh! A Viking's knowledge of beers for the win. I smiled as I read the can: PUNK AF. "Great name!"

"It's a local Scottish brewer—a revamp of the old India Pale Ale. The AF stands for alcohol-free rather than what you're probably thinking. It's one of the few no-alcohol beers I enjoy. But sometimes you want to be able to drink and drive safely, and it's perfect with curry. I didn't know you drank beer?"

"You've barely known me two weeks. How would you know what I like? I think the problem is everything we don't know about each other." I reached into our link. "OK to info dump so my dumplings don't get cold while I talk?"

"Sure."

I split the chicken dumpling in half and took my half back to the cooker to flip the next batch while I sent him all of my concerns.

Aysha and I had talked about this at length. I'd said that, when I was with Nick, if you'd told me I could one day be in a relationship with a man who could read my mind, I'd have assumed it would solve all my problems. No communication problems, no misunderstandings. Just perfect harmony. But it didn't work that way at all.

Sure, it was great not to have to spell every damn thing out. And it was freaking amazing to eat hot spicy chicken dumplings instead of being polite, making small talk and then eating lukewarm food.

It was incredible during sex.

I liked our link, but I couldn't have imagined the problems it brought.

It turned out that knowing what he was thinking didn't tell me who he really was.

Or what he stood for.

Or would stand against.

Or any of his history.

Or what had made him the man he was.

Or what he wanted, needed, or even hoped to do with his life.

Or if he had current goals. Or what they were.

And often it didn't even tell me how he felt about things.

Nope, it told me he'd paused to think about whether he should offer me a glass with my beer.

I ended my info dump with, *"I understand a bond is for life, probably for several lives, or that we've already had several lives together. That's what the Book said, anyway. But I don't know how to make this relationship we appear to be stuck with into a good one, any more than I would with anyone else."*

Then I grabbed the cheese dumpling, which hopefully was no longer as hot as the inside of a volcano, pulled a couple of small pieces off and blew on them for Tilly. It was her favourite. I stuffed the rest in my mouth, grabbed the plate and dished up the second batch.

Rollo reached for the half of the spicy chicken dumpling I'd left on the plate to cool, and I swatted at his hand. "That's not yours." I pushed one of each of the fresh ones at him and moved Tilly's portions to my side of the plate. "The dog's name is Tilly. And she gets to share once they've cooled."

"I know." His brow furrowed. "I mean, I didn't know that was hers. But I know her name. I've noticed you hate tepid food. I thought I was doing you a favour."

He surveyed Tilly, whose tail wagged as he said, "Sorry, girl."

Well, I guess we were halfway there.

But then he stood up so quickly, the legs of his chair screeched on the floor, and it almost overbalanced. He started pacing around the kitchen muttering in Norse to himself.

Oh no. Not this.

Not now. Not again.

Every time Nick would ask me what I thought about something, and I shared any of my truths with him, he'd spend the next hour lecturing me in excruciating detail about all the ways I was wrong.

I'd hoped Rollo was different. What was the point of having a bond if it was all *here's the new crap, same as the old crap*?

CHAPTER
THIRTY-EIGHT

But he astonished me. "You're right. You're just absolutely right. Don't know why I didn't work out what was bothering me."

"OK?" I made sure I picked my jaw up off the floor. Just wow!

"I don't mean to sound sexist; maybe some guys can do it, but I can't. Women are much better at this stuff than us. I mean, Inge did it the other day before the book club when she told me to get my head out of my ass. You all see things so clearly while we're still wandering around thinking 'I want to do this. I really like her, but I've no clue how to make it right or good.' Fixing code is so much easier. It tells you when you've got it correct."

I laughed because he sounded exactly like Finn. I fed Tilly some more of her share and ate my own while Rollo marched up and down muttering, mostly to himself, in a weird mix of English and Norse. But his energy felt better.

Eventually, he sat back at the table and pointed at the last chicken dumpling. "Is that mine?" At my nod, he ate it.

"Those are incredibly good. I don't know whether to be happy that you know how to make them or unhappy that they taste like a lot of fussing goes into them, so I probably won't get them very often."

I grinned at him. "I don't make them. Aysha's mother does. You'll only get them if I visit Olive on a Sunday, which is about twice a year. And if Aysha ever offers them to you, say no unless they came from Olive. The ones Aysha makes are like rubber, and she won't admit it. She denies the need for a thermometer because her mum doesn't use one. But her mum has nearly seventy years of experience in judging the perfect oil temperature. She holds her hand over the pan and just knows. It's a kind of superpower."

He took my hand. "You said you wanted a walk?"

I nodded and waited, hardly daring to hope he'd truly understood everything I'd sent.

He peered at Tilly. "I think better when I can move. How far does she like to walk?"

"Depends. If it's dry and on the grass, ten to twelve. On pavements, about half that. If it's raining or snowy, about six feet."

His brows lifted, and his eyes widened. "Miles? But she's so small!"

I surveyed my twelve-pound fluffball. "Bichons are unusual dogs. They're smallish, but under all that fluff, they're solid and have big hearts, sturdy muscles and an insatiable curiosity. If she ever puts her lead in her own mouth and turns around, it's her way of saying I've walked half as far as I can; let's go home now. I did not know that when she was a puppy and had to carry her home several times before I worked it out."

His laugh was warm and natural, and I thought perhaps he was starting to see that Tilly wasn't just a dog; she was a person to me. And she was probably quite different to his Boo.

"You know about Boo?" He shuffled in his chair.

"I know some of it. But you were asking how far Tilly walks?"

"I agree with your list of things we don't know about each other because I could say exactly the same about you. And you haven't walked your dog for a week, so two enemies, one sword. Let's show you both my Edinburgh."

I hadn't brought a coat and was about to ask Dola to send

mine up here, but Rollo insisted Kari wouldn't mind if I borrowed one of hers, and as it was a lovely down-filled jacket in a flattering shade of peach and only a little big on me, I accepted. But I started making a mental list of things to ask Dola to send me.

"I need to talk to you about Kari's father too. Let's add that to the list of things please."

Rollo nodded and opened a door I hadn't yet been through. "I bought this apartment a few years ago, and then later I bought the building. I wanted access to the basement and the roof space. But I still rent out the other two apartments and the shop downstairs, of course."

While I was processing this, we entered a tiny lift. He pulled me into his side so he could reach the buttons I'd blocked and pressed B.

My head reeled. This was a large building right in the centre of the Scottish capital. It wouldn't have been cheap. Did his parents leave him money? How did he get it out of Viking? Or had his mother left him money in Fae? Yeah, that was more likely.

My thoughts were halted by the lift door, which opened into a basement parking garage. We came out right by a fabulous Aston Martin DB11 in British racing green. I laughed and retrieved my phone from my pocket to snap a photo. This would brighten Aysha's unwilling return to normality after her holiday.

I thrust Tilly at Rollo, who accepted her gingerly. He was holding her at arm's length as if she were an unexploded bomb. "Can you hold her by the bonnet so I can get them both in the shot? That'll please both the Clarke women."

He put her down carefully on the long, wide bonnet, made sure she was stable, and stepped back. I gasped in horror, "Pick her up! She might scratch the paint with her claws. Those things cost a fortune!"

He grinned at me. "She's fine. I know the owner. Why are you taking a photo of the car and the dog?"

"It's Aysha's dream car, and it's even the right colour, and Autumn will already be missing Tilly, so this will cheer them both up."

"Smile for Autumn please, Tilly-Flop." She immediately turned her head and gave me the expression Autumn loved the best. The one with her tongue hanging out, which made her look as though she were laughing. I snapped the photo and quickly returned her to the concrete floor before the paintwork got damaged.

As we made our way out of the parking section to a side door, we passed a few more cool cars. Aysha would spend an hour here admiring them. Rollo held the door for us with a cute smile, and I wondered what had amused him as we came out into a clean, modern alleyway and crossed the road into Princes Street Gardens. While Tilly took advantage of all the grass and every plant, I gazed around and marvelled anew at the pretty, open green space in the heart of the Scottish capital. "I love this place; I came at Christmas once for the market. It was magical."

He nodded. "It's fabulous then, although that high ride they have …" He made a circling motion with his fingers, and I remembered the circular high-flying ride he meant. Nick had been on it. I'd said no thank you; it was too high for me, and all of his whining hadn't changed my mind. "… Can be annoying. If they put it in the usual place, the riders can see straight onto the roof garden. So you can't swim naked. But it's only for a few weeks, and the lights are pretty."

Then I came out of my memories and caught up with what he'd said, "There's a pool on the roof? Of your building?"

He nodded.

"Rollo, what is it you do here again?" I was obviously missing some key piece of information.

He smiled. "You already know that. I work with the team at Metal Maven."

Metal Maven, the company who made the *Drengr* game. Yes, OK. I knew that.

We'd reached the end of the gardens, and with one last look over my shoulder at the castle, we crossed over a road and turned left.

"You wanted to talk about Warlord Halvor. Want to get him out of the way so we can have a nice stroll together?"

Rollo had been moderating his much longer stride because he thought Tilly was tiny. When I realised it, I sped up; a little cardio wouldn't hurt either of us. "Yes, please. He seems to be at the centre of the warlord problem."

"He is. He's the head of the Dirty Dozen. Nothing will change in Viking until we can take them down. And it starts with him. I have a plan so Viking can move forward, have some equality, some opportunities and give all the citizens, including the married women and our thralls, a real say in how it's run. I simply don't have a good enough strategy to get to the place where my plan can be introduced."

"Thralls?"

"You might call them serfs. They were prisoners of war, conquered enemies from other tribes or realms. Now they're citizens, and they get paid, but they still can't vote for their choice of warlord or leave their warlords' lands."

"What about their choice of government?"

He stopped to look at me in surprise. "Viking doesn't have a government. It has the warlords and a king. That's why I need to do something about the Dirty Dozen. Several men snatched me. I'm almost sure one, perhaps two of them, belonged to Halvor. They tried to ... well, I don't know what they were trying to do. Were they trying to kill me? I don't think so because, if they were, they went a long way around it. Did they want to scare me away from taking the throne and injure me? Don't tell Cait that bit, OK? She might do something stupid. I don't want her hurt, and Halvor is ruthless."

"HRH said they were trying to inflict permanent damage so you couldn't duel him. Does that make any sense to you? Because it didn't to me. I thought she meant Troels at first, but she said he wasn't the only female-abusing coward, and she meant Halvor."

"Yes, she meant Halvor. Troels doesn't duel. Accidents happened to anyone who opposed him. Halvor arranged most of them." He pointed. "We should eat there; it's fantastic."

I smiled at the cheery-looking bistro. "That sounds good."

Rollo chewed his bottom lip. "The only circumstance in which I would have to duel Halvor is if I were already king, and he thought he had more right to it. But if he wanted the throne, he could have challenged Troels already, and ..." He paused.

I looked at him and wondered what he'd just worked out. I saw a shield in his thoughts. He'd shielded himself from me?

No, he was simply thinking about shields—ahh, OK.

This was a boring modern road, and Tilly didn't seem to be finding any interesting smells, but I didn't want to mention it and derail whatever had finally made sense to Rollo.

"He uses my uncle as a shield. There is an English word for it, but I can't retrieve it. They say it in movies when they set someone up to be arrested for a crime that someone else committed. Troels committed plenty of sex crimes, but he didn't grow the herbs for the drug. He didn't make it, import it or smuggle it. He just used it to excess. They gave him the title of the Bringer of the Droit de Seigneur, even though he didn't. Bring it, I mean."

"Do you mean 'patsy'?"

"Yes, that's it. He was their patsy. Troels isn't an intelligent man. Vicious to anyone vulnerable? Sure. Cruel and entitled? Absolutely. But Halvor is the dangerous one. He has a brain. He's vicious and cruel too, but he's also careful, and he plans years ahead. Do you remember Vor?"

I shook my head and then, in a flash, recalled him. "Vor with no title? The one Kari didn't have a bond with?"

"Yes, him."

I steered Tilly around a dropped kebab before she could snatch the meat out of it. Rollo saw me and kicked it into the gutter. "Saturday night kebabs are not good the next day, girl."

Then he pointed down a side street. "Chris, the lawyer, has his office down there. I need to talk to you about him. The Recorder might need to come with me. But he doesn't know anything about the realms, so we'll need a plan."

I was still debating with myself about whether to challenge Rollo that calling Tilly "girl" wasn't a replacement for using her name. Then I decided to pick my battles until I understood the problem fully.

I nodded. "Lawyer, yes, OK, and Vor?"

"His father's lands have the perfect climate for growing some ingredients for the threecease drug. That's why Halvor decided Kari had to marry him."

I laughed. "I think he was the first Viking I'd met who didn't have some kind of title. Would marrying Kari have given him one?"

He shook his head. "But they were dangling a warlordship in front of his father. The thing is, they use the drug to induce anyone to do what they want. The Recorder's Office has probably only seen the sex crime side of it, but it's far more than that. They give it to people to make their minds malleable to whatever they want."

I told him about Mags and the murdered babies.

The wave of horror that came from him made it clear. Not only had he not known anything about it, he hadn't even realised the drug would do that.

But his first question intrigued me. "Does Inge know about this?"

"She might because she stayed with the Hob who reported it to the Recorder."

"That would explain something she said. There's been a problem with a higher incidence of miscarriages in Viking than any of the other realms. They've been looking at water supplies and foodstuffs, though. I'll need to speak to her. Is she back in Viking?"

I nodded.

Soft Norse swearing ensued before he asked, "How do you know it's swearing?"

He must have picked that out of my head. "I don't; it just sounds like it. I know *Streth Mik* because I asked Dola about that one. You say it a lot, often inside your head. But you should know I've opened Vikings' access to the Rainbow Network. Dola and Finn are monitoring, of course, but Inge has a Dolina now so you can contact her anytime."

We'd walked past some hotels and some university buildings. It really wasn't an interesting route in this otherwise fascinating city, and Tilly was bored. As I looked around for some greener space, Rollo tugged me gently towards a short, wide flight of stone steps.

A large stone and glass building rose in front of us. The steps led to a double doorway, the main entrance with a single glass door to one side. It was closed, and the building was in darkness.

"It's Sunday, isn't it?"

He nodded and produced a swipe card from his jeans pocket. He swiped, pressed some numbers on the keypad, and pushed the door open.

"Is Tilly OK in here? Some offices don't like pets."

"This one does. She's fine."

The tinted glass made the lobby dark, with occasional lights illuminating the way to the rear and the lifts. We followed Rollo as he headed that way. The lift opened immediately, and we all piled in.

"Where are we?"

"Holyrood Road."

I huffed, "I meant what is this building? And why are we here?"

He leant down and kissed me softly as the lift rose. "You said you wanted to know what I needed, wanted and hoped to do with my life. I'm about to show you."

CHAPTER
THIRTY-NINE

The moment the lift doors opened on lights, people and colourful artwork, I guessed where we were. An enormous mural of the lead characters from *Drengr* was on the right side, and on the left was an unmistakable depiction of one of *Drengr's* sister games. I'd never played it, but the Fae in the centre had a distinct look of L'eon except for the large fake pointy Elven ears instead of his true discreetly pointed Fae ear tips. L'eon was De'Anna's son and one of Ad'Rian's other nephews, and now that I thought it through, wouldn't that make him Rollo's cousin? I should probably have worked that out before, shouldn't I? It would have explained why he helped create Rollo's Thor glamour. I'd been slow there. And it made me wonder what else I was missing.

Rollo had obviously followed my thinking because he said, "Yes, he is. Want a coffee?"

We passed the murals, walked by several glass cases holding awards, trophies and game packaging, and headed straight to an area that looked like a cross between a cocktail bar and a Starbucks.

The male barista with a distinctly Australian accent gave

Rollo a huge smile. "Hey, they said you were back, but I was on holiday. Stoked to see you, man. Usual?"

"Thanks, Logan, two of them, please."

The guy smiled at me as Rollo pointed at a water bowl on the floor. I released the tension on Tilly's lead so she could reach it. They obviously really did welcome dogs here.

Drinks in hand, we strolled through the coffee shop, weaving around the tables. All the people at the tables had laptops open, and most had earbuds in. Finn would be in heaven here. I followed Rollo down a short glass corridor to a railing, then came to an abrupt halt as I looked down through the middle of the building to the floor below. There were desks and computers everywhere below me.

It was impressive and fun. And an idea was waving at me from the back of my brain.

Rollo led me towards another lift. We came out at the top of the building with an incredible view of Edinburgh from the full-height window opposite the doors. At a large double-doored frosted glass entrance, he held the right-hand side open until Tilly and I were inside a small anteroom. More of the same doors were to the right of what was obviously a small reception room with an assistant's desk. Again, he opened the right-hand side door, and we walked into an office that looked like a movie set. Or something that a modern Scandinavian designer had submitted to a competition for an elegant, twenty-first century office space.

The space was filled with low sofas, bean bags and those curved wooden chairs that, thanks to women's magazines, I knew cost a fortune. These weren't the affordable Ikea version—these were the real deal. There was a vast, stupidly high, curved, frosted desk with light wood supports and four—no, five—large monitors on it. Mounted on two of the walls were more large screens. The fourth wall was all glass and looked out over the city.

I stood transfixed and watched as the lights of Edinburgh

flickered on. My eyes followed a train as it made its way into Waverly Station. Tilly, at my side, looked down through the window, equally fascinated.

At a low whirring noise as the desk descended to a more reasonable height, I turned back towards Rollo. A computer booted up.

As *Drengr* loaded, Rollo hit escape and loaded the credits. He pointed at the name at the top of a long list of the various people involved in bringing the game to life. *Producer and Game Designer: Ro Ash.*

"They call me Ro here."

"And let me guess, this sacred tree of yours, Yggdrasil, is an ash tree?"

An enormous grin split his face. "You know, if, as you so appealingly put it, we're stuck with this relationship, isn't it great that you're so smart?"

I unhooked Tilly's lead so she could lie by the window and watch the people below. Then I reached past Rollo with a cursory, "May I?"

I highlighted the name, hit Control+F and searched to see if the name came up again in the lengthy list of credits. Oh yeah, I'd been right. *Drengr Online Designer and Director: Ro Ash.* So he wasn't just nominally in charge of the concept; he'd actually been responsible for the entire project. Shit! He owned a chunk of this entire place.

Then I noticed immediately below Rollo's name were Leon Horn and Kaiden Johanssen. Then some Scottish names I didn't know.

I pointed at L'eon's name. "Horn?"

"Well, L'eon of the Unicorn's Horn sounded odd, and Alicorn might create a trail he didn't want to leave ... so Leon Horn worked. L'eon and Kaiden head up the console and mobile division. Scott and I run the PC and online platform."

I sat on the low sofa and processed. It wasn't a complete shock. The scale of it was. But I'd known he was smart, competent and loved his tech. There had been all that game packaging in his home office. And the lecture Finn had given me about looking past his eye-candy persona made total sense now.

Low-grade worry came through our link. I looked up. "OK. Cool. Who's Scott?"

"Who's Scott? That's it?"

"Well, yeah. That's the bit I don't know."

A low rich laugh burst out of Rollo. "Woman, you undo me. So calm. I've been thinking myself in circles about the best way to tell you, so you'd truly understand why I'm never going to take the throne of Viking. And you just say, 'Cool. Who's Scott?'"

I raised an eyebrow at him. He shook his head and reached around to pull a glass bottle of water out of a mini fridge, offering me one. At my nod, he brought it to me and sat next to me on the couch.

"Scott is a good friend from university. He thinks L'eon and I went to school together. He's human, Scottish and very talented. The three of us founded our first company together."

I thought about the other games I'd seen on the shelves in his home office. Those games had been successful, but on a smaller scale and more predictable. Although stupidly addictive in that just one more game way. But they were on a totally different level from the gripping, visually beautiful, slick, fully immersive games that Metal Maven produced. I couldn't remember the name of the first company. "Then you sold whatever it was called to the big boys in Silicon Valley?"

But he shook his head. "No, they only licensed the rights to Iron Maven's games. We still make some apps for them. We used the money to found Metal Maven. What?"

I was laughing so hard, I could barely speak as it dawned on me. "Iron Maven Games, seriously?"

He grinned. "You're not a fan? Although it caused us some problems, which is why we changed it to Metal Maven."

Still amused at the thought of almost naming a gaming company after a rock band, I asked, "What problems?"

"At the game launches, fans would bring iron ... objects and paraphernalia. Horseshoes, game items and, well, anything they could find, really. And they wanted to give them to us."

I imagined it. L'eon, a full royal Fae and so extremely sensitive to the metal, it could make him iron-sick for weeks. He'd been incredibly grateful when I didn't insist he and Kaiden seal their bond over the anvil. Kaiden was an iron-sensitive Viking. Rollo, who wasn't as disturbed by the iron but still didn't like it, as his profanity after he'd sworn to keep the Recorder's secrets on the anvil a few days ago had proven. Yep, I could vividly imagine how pleased they'd all have been with the gifts of iron horseshoes. I started giggling. Iron Maven – what a bunch of short-sighted idiots. I wondered if Caitlin had heard these tales? If not, I'd save the story for a day when she needed cheering up.

After my amusement, I was subdued on the way home. Puzzle pieces shifted around in my head. How might I use the Recorder's power, not on Rollo's side alone, but on the side of the Viking realm itself?

If I did, would it change things for the better? Surely it must. Preventing a bunch of drug-running corrupt warlords from tormenting and abusing women and limiting all of Viking's choices had to be a good thing.

This wasn't really about whether Rollo wanted to be king.

Now I'd seen those offices, the thriving modern company, all the awards and the happy programmers choosing to be at work on a Sunday, it was obvious what Rollo should do with his life. If he gave up his own dreams and his life for Viking, the oppressive system there wouldn't allow him to change or fix anything without killing a dozen warlords first.

That was his big fear. The one he wasn't talking about. He wasn't convinced all the warlords were equally guilty or how to work out which ones he could afford to leave alive. Because, if he only took out a few of the worst ones, new ones would rise up the ranks, and in no time, he'd be back where he started or dead.

The front of my brain was enjoying Edinburgh. The route back was much more scenic. We walked through some cute streets and past a lot of colourfully lit bars, restaurants and closed shops. It had rained while we were inside Metal Maven, and the lights reflected prettily in the puddles and on the slick surface of the road. Then we started down some quaint, wide steps with the castle looming over us.

"So let me get this straight. When I shared the data with you, and you realised how popular Inge was, your plan was to give the throne to her? She rightly told you that you're an idiot, and you were simply setting her up to be killed?"

"That about sums it up." He didn't sound unhappy or even depressed, only resigned. But to … what?

The steps came out into a cobbled square surrounded by old buildings. Apart from the colour of the stone they'd used here and the LED lights, it could have been any road in Aberglas, the Pict capital. Huh.

Rollo stopped outside a lively-looking pub in the shadow of Edinburgh Castle and took a deep breath. "Fancy a beer?"

"Sure. But not in public." I'd enough noisy bars and clubs with Aysha during the last week to last me a while. This one looked as though it was rocking on three floors. I could see people hanging over an open roof terrace above. In March! The Scots were apparently immune to the low temperature.

He let out a long breath. "That sounds wonderful. Let's go. I was thinking I should show you Edinburgh, but we can do that anytime—if I ever sort this mess out."

"Quiet works for me. And I've got some ideas. But I can't share them with you if I can't hear myself think, and that place," I pointed at the pub he'd paused outside, "looks a ton of fun, but it's loud."

I looked up at him, trying to see his face in the light of a nearby streetlight. He kissed me. Gently at first, and then pulled me closer to him and deepened the kiss.

A passerby shouted, "Git yersel's a ruim."

We broke apart laughing. I said, "Only the accent changes. Manchester's 'get yourselves a damn room' is Scotland's incomprehensible nonsense."

He put a finger on my lips. "Don't let them hear you say that. It's their country."

"Yeah, I know. Can we go home?" I reached out down our link. *We will work this out.*

We started kissing again like teenagers in the lift. I managed to release Tilly's harness and lead and put her some kibble and fresh water down before Rollo carried me through to the bedroom.

I woke suddenly in the almost dark room.

Tilly's soft snores and Rollo's steady breathing were the only sounds. The moonlight poured through the windows, and nothing seemed amiss. What had awakened me?

Then Tilly sat up and, with a soft woof, jumped off the bed. Rollo shot upright. Then I heard it. A door opening.

CHAPTER
FORTY

Rollo reached over to the bedside table and, in seconds, had a knife in one hand and his phone in the other. After a single glance at his screen, he relaxed and nodded. "It's Kari and Ben. They're the only ones who have the lift code."

He dragged on his jeans, and I glared at his back as he left to greet the intruders.

Whoa, if I was thinking his friends were intruders, I might need to adjust my attitude.

But I was pissed off.

We'd had no time together since Autumn showed us our bond. Most of that had been my fault because I needed to fix my relationship with Aysha.

But I still wanted to cry.

We needed a plan that might take us toward a solution. At the least, I needed some mutual awareness that we should make a plan. I didn't want to lose this man I was so happy to have found to some corrupt warlord's blade in a dark alley.

Tilly whined and climbed into my lap with a sneeze, and I tried to stop myself from spiralling into misery.

But sod it! I'd been a good Recorder and put my personal

concerns aside to do my job. Then I'd tried to be a good friend and fix the issues coming between Aysha and me.

So, if I'd been so damn good, when the hell did I get to collect my hard-earned brownie points and spend time with Rollo to sort out our personal shit? Wasn't that the whole point of this holiday?

Today was supposed to have been the start of our time. We needed it to work things out. Instead, I'd had one walk, one surprise about his work life, and one gentle healing and satisfying bonk with my brand-new bond mate.

I felt like my inner toddler was about to make a break for the stairs towards a full-blown tantrum. I suppressed a desire to scream at the world, "Go away! He's mine, and I need his attention for a day or two."

Which might not be an attractive thought for a woman of my age to have. So, sue me, I'm only human … I'm probably only human?

Oh FFS! The idea that I didn't even know if I *was* still human was the final straw, and tears started rolling down my face.

We'd come to Edinburgh because there was no peace or privacy at Gateway Cottage, and now we had guests here. Oh joy. Oh rapture. Oh sniffle.

But that wasn't the only reason for my disappointment. The most upsetting thing was the brilliant plan I'd hatched. Ever since the power told me I could talk to Mabon for as long as I liked and then take us both back in time, provided we stayed in his day chamber, I'd been intrigued by the time travel rules. I'd consulted the Book.

It said that the lighter my impact was on the world, the more flexibility I had. The power calculated this automatically and would always act to prevent me endangering the Recordership. In other words, it would protect me.

But there were things I could do to increase my ability to time travel. The first was to choose to relive a day where nothing interesting happened. If I stayed at home and had a luxurious day off reading my book and cuddling my dog, then, if I time travelled backwards and did it again, it was a win/win. I'd remember where I was in my book, or Rollo and I would recall our conversations, but the power would have no hesitation letting me live that day several times—because the impact on other people was negligible.

This was probably how Great-Great-Granny Florrie had managed her bonk-a-thons.

My cunning plan had been for Rollo, Tilly and me to have some lovely lazy days. I'd thought we could probably squeeze a two-week holiday into the few days we had before both of us needed to address the issues in the Viking realm. It would give us some much-needed time to work out what was best for us *and* for Viking before I had to put the Recorder's robe back on and make decisions for all the petitioners.

I'd tested it with Aysha on our Canary Islands getaway, and it had worked flawlessly. But if we now had guests, with agendas and concerns of their own, I didn't know how they might affect my ability to relive this day. And if they were arriving at this time of night, they obviously planned to stay. So they might mess up tomorrow too.

I wasn't proud of my behaviour or my selfishness. *But if I'm not still human, I still damn well feel it!*

I muttered.

I sniffled.

And not being proud of my behaviour didn't stop me from sinking into an all-out sulk.

Then, realising Rollo was probably listening to my inner diatribe, I sent, *"So sorry, I'll grow up, find my manners and have myself under control real soon now."*

There was silence from him. Oh, blast. But I couldn't police my thoughts. He'd have to get used to the idea that I could only put everyone else first some of the time.

The bedroom door opened, and Rollo walked in holding a coffee mug. Bless the man.

He gave me a soft kiss and stroked my hair away from my tear-streaked face. "It's OK, you know. I feel exactly the same, and I didn't even know the time travel plan. That would be so cool. And, by Freyja, I'd love some thinking time. Kari drove up in a panic because they have news about Viking, and my phone was set to Do Not Disturb. They're going back tomorrow. Maybe we can steal tomorrow instead, several times?"

His smile crinkled into dimples, and I grinned back at him. "Yeah, maybe we could."

He handed me the coffee. "If I were Dola, this would say something like, *I don't like you because you're perfect. I like you because you are the perfect type of imperfect for me.*"

I melted.

Then I freaked out a bit.

And, finally, I got myself together.

Ten minutes later, I'd given myself a stern talking to. Washed my face in cold water. And dug out from the depths of my handbag some of that tinted moisturiser that's supposed to make you sparkle and glow with health, but really it just makes you look a bit less awful. Because who reaches for brown gloop when they feel outstanding?

I should ask Morven if she sold something to fix "I just ugly-cried like a baby, and now I'd like to look like a woman who has her shit together." I was intrigued by what she might call it.

I sent, *"Sorry again. I'm ready to be a well-mannered grownup now. Coming through."*

Rollo said, *"I didn't tell them you're here yet in case you wanted to hide out. You're entitled to, you know. You are on holiday."*

If I'd wondered whether the universe made some kind of mistake with our bond—Aysha and I'd discussed it several times during our holiday—that one simple thought relieved my doubts. A man who understood that, maybe, just maybe, I couldn't face any more today, this week or even this month, until I'd had some time to wallow, was my soulmate.

A genuine smile finally arrived on my lips.

. . .

"Oh, thank the all-mother, you're not alone. I thought you were too calm." Kari stood and bowed. "Recorder. May I introduce Ben? We spoke about him when you allowed me sanctuary."

She'd been right. Unlike Vor, that wimpy drink of water her father wanted her to marry, the couple in front of me had a healthy glowing bond. In the light of my new knowledge, I surveyed their chakras carefully. Three of them connected, possibly leaving them some communication problems and different ways of thinking, but they enjoyed excellent physical attraction, emotional support and sincere love. Huh. This new knowledge could be extremely useful.

Ben sat on a chair at the kitchen table, a bottle of water in front of him. At Rollo's and Kari's expectant looks, he said, "Whut?"

Kari hissed, "Stand. Bow. It's the Recorder."

I waved a hand at the confused guy. "Chill. I'm being Niki right now. It's ridiculously hard to pull off the Recorder wearing a bathrobe. Good to meet you, Ben."

He gave me a sweet, quirky smile. The flash of white teeth highlighted the warm undertones in his black skin and sparked an answering smile from me. His cute, boyish grin was at odds with his well-muscled, six-foot-plus frame. "You sound like you're from home. Manchester girl?"

He could have been Aysha's brother, if she had one, which endeared him to me immediately. Kari hadn't mentioned he was from my hometown. But his accent, like my own, was a dead giveaway. "Yep, near Bolton? You?"

"The Moss originally."

We grinned at each other.

Kari and Rollo looked at each other and shrugged. But Ben and I now knew exactly who we were dealing with and were happy about it.

Rollo was in host mode. "Can I get anyone another drink?"

More water, a beer for Kari, and a wine for me arrived on the table.

Ben gave Kari a long, meaningful look, and she asked, "Rols, can we order food? We intended to eat on the way up, but I didn't want service station heartburn, and Ben's training, so he was being picky."

Rollo nodded and reached into the drawer that held the take away menus. But I held up a hand. "Give Ben and me a minute."

Kari and Rollo looked at each other again and shrugged.

"This way, Ben." I led him over to the fridge. "Where does your mum live?"

Completely unfazed by my question, he said, "Still in the Moss, but the other end. Safer for old ladies. She won't move any farther, and, believe me, I've offered."

"Thought so. Seen her lately?"

"Not in too long, as it happens. She told me so yesterday."

When I opened the fridge door, he started sniffing like a bloodhound. "Is that? Nah, can't be."

As I loaded him up with the containers, words exploded out of him, "You are effing kidding me! How the hell have you got a fridge full of God's own food in this snooty town?"

Rollo and Kari watched us, utterly baffled, from the table.

I grabbed the rest of the dumplings still in their greaseproof paper and headed to the cooker. The pan was still there and full of the oil from earlier. I turned on the hob.

Ben dogged my heels, following the dumplings on autopilot. "Are there chicken dumplings?"

"Mmm-mmm. And veg and cheese."

We smiled at each other in perfect harmony.

He said, "I have died and gone to heaven. Mum'll be amazed. She always said I was headed for the other place. Who made this? You didn't make this—you got the wrong genes, girl."

"Mrs Clarke made it. She's—"

"Not Olive Clarke?"

At my nod, he said, "Seriously? She's a friend of Mum's. She was my Sunday school teacher. Used to bribe us with her dumplings to be well-mannered and—"

I interrupted, "—learn your Bible stories properly?"

We dissolved into laughter.

"Boo, any chance Kari and I could join in the joke?"

Chagrined, I sent, *"Sorry, Aysha's mum and Ben's mum are almost neighbours. He hasn't had food from home in too long, and he won't find it in Gretna Green."*

Ben's excited voice had Kari's head turning. "Hey, babe, the other day when I had the munchies, and you asked what I wanted, and I said ackee and saltfish, and you were all like 'what the hell is ackee?'" He waved the plastic container at her, "You are in for such a treat. You've never tasted the like."

Kari asked, "And is that a good thing?" She gave Rollo a wary look.

Almost an hour later, she admitted it was a very good thing indeed and asked Ben if his mother could cook like this. Cautiously, Ben admitted Olive was a bit of a one-off, but his mum came close. "Not that anyone would ever say that to my mum in my hearing, you know? She just hasn't got Mrs Clarke's hand with stuffed, fried dumplings. But then, who has? It's like her superpower."

Rollo and I laughed because I'd said exactly the same to him earlier.

Holding Kari's eyes with his own, Ben asked, "Remember when you stormed into the gym that first day and were so rude? I told you only one other woman had ever been that rude to me and allowed to re-enter any gym I ran? And you didn't have her bargaining power."

Kari's gaze went distant, and she gave him an intimate smile. "And I asked you what was so special about her?"

Ben picked up the story. "And I said her mother was the best Caribbean cook in the neighbourhood, and no one who upset bitchy little Aysha ever got another mouthful of Mrs Clarke's food, which was manna from heaven."

He gestured around at all the empty plates. "Spoke nuttin' but truth, didn't I?"

I didn't think this was the time to mention bitchy little Aysha was my best mate. I'd save it as a lovely surprise for them both.

Eventually, Kari, who was still visibly stressed, cleared her throat. Anyone who could be unhappy after eating Olive's amazing food was just choosing to be pissed off. She said, "I hate to bring the party to a screeching halt." My left shoulder pinged. "But we came up here urgently because, well, you're obviously aware, if the Recorder is here, but I didn't know you were, and you didn't answer your phone."

I asked. *"Can Kari not see bonds?"*

"Obviously not."

"Should you tell her? It might be awkward if she finds out afterwards, and you two are close."

He caught my eye, and I nodded firmly.

Then Rollo did a very interesting thing, and I had no idea if he was aware he was doing it. But he pulled yellow regnal power and draped Kari in it. While he was doing this, he gave her and Ben a long assessing look.

Then he pulled the power back and nodded back at me. "Niki and I need to tell you something, Kari, so you don't wonder afterwards why we didn't."

She gave him her complete attention immediately.

"We have a bond."

"*Streth mik!*" Her jaw dropped. Then she flushed and added, "Um, congratulations, of course. Sorry, erm, well, um, sorry, I was surprised. Er, I spoke to Inge. She, erm, didn't say anything?"

Rollo ignored her stammering, and his tone was firm. "Probably thought it was our own business. But that's why Niki's here.

Not for whatever reason you are. We only just worked it out. We escaped to Edinburgh for some peace to consider the implications."

Kari nodded but looked completely unabashed at interrupting our private time. "Dola said the Recorder was away when I asked to speak to her. Lousy timing though, hey? With our world in pieces and all that?"

I thought I'd put myself back together, but Kari was rubbing me the wrong way. I'd had enough of being polite. As though anyone had any say in when a bond clicked in. At least I didn't think they did—did they? "Probably not as bad as you and Ben's timing. At least neither of us were engaged to anyone else."

Ben hooted with laughter. "Don't take on a Manchester girl, Kari. They take no prisoners. But, seriously, what is this bond thing? Everyone talks about them. Kari keeps telling me we have one. But no one can explain what it *is*."

"I can probably show you, Ben. But Kari looks as though steam is about to come out of her ears. Shall we let her get this urgent news out first?"

Look at me, proving I could be a polite grown-up!

But obviously Kari didn't think so. Because, although Ben nodded and grinned at me, Kari gave me a tight smile and made a point to only address Rollo, completely ignoring me. "They're going to destroy the cameras, speakers and the screens and then break Troels out of that cell. They want to kill him before he can give evidence that implicates them. Then the Recorder can't find against him and," she made air quotes with a snarl in her voice, "damage Viking's sterling reputation." If they do that ... well, it won't be fun, will it? Rols, you know I have to think about my family."

She gave me a furious glare. "My mother is disabled, and my sister is still very young."

I laughed. She glared at me.

Whoops. I tried again, "Sorry, I was laughing at their plans, not about your family. How old is your sister?"

"She's only twenty-four."

Since when was twenty-four very young? What was I missing here? I didn't want to add more strain to the already difficult atmosphere, so I offered, "Well, it should be fun watching them try to attack the cell. Are they planning on doing it tonight?"

She nodded.

"Did you tell Dola?"

"Yes, she told me it was under control and, provided neither my mother nor sister would be anywhere near the cell, I shouldn't concern myself."

"OK." Then why the hell was she here? "And you didn't believe her and drove up here anyway? Because …?"

Kari spluttered, "She's a house."

I didn't know what her problem was. I'd ask Rollo, but Kari hadn't been worried about her mother, sister or her realm being in pieces when she claimed sanctuary and got out. No one, friend of my bond mate or not, would dismiss Dola or her authority in my presence.

I told her what I'd told Rhiannon. "No, Princess Karina, she isn't a house. She is the Recorder's equerry, which is a rank equivalent to the Knight Adjutants and immediately below the Recorder. She's also an intelligent and capable 1400-year-old entity who's seen hundreds of slimeballs like Troels come and go over the centuries."

Ben's jaw dropped as Kari's jaw firmed. She looked like she was biting her tongue. My Gift said she was angry that I was here with Rollo and not at home doing my job. But why?

I stopped, breathed, and reminded myself again that she was Rollo's friend. But what was the bug up her butt, and why was she directing so much hostility at me?

"Kari, the only thing you need to do is exactly what Dola suggested. Message anyone you care about who might be dumb enough to go down and watch, and tell them not to—if they want to live."

She looked at me, now wide-eyed. "But you can't do anything from here."

"I don't need to. It's already done, which would be why Dola told you not to concern yourself. It was hardly rocket surgery that the imbeciles would try it, was it now?"

Ben threw his head back and laughed. "Rocket surgery, oh girl, haven't heard that one since I left home."

Kari was unamused. Perhaps she was simply too cross to get the joke. Or perhaps didn't find it funny. Ben was right—it was a Manchester thing.

To Rollo, I said, "Message Inge. Tell her the same."

But now I was concerned about Dola.

> Niki: I assume you're listening in, and I'm sorry Kari was rude about you and to you. If it all goes wrong, I can time travel back, but I know you've got this.

> Dola: Thank you for your confidence. Kari was quite offensive on the phone earlier.

> Niki: Yeah, I can imagine. I'm not sure who or what she's actually angry about, but I plan to find out.

> Dola: Her father. The rumour is he tried and failed to kill her mother, but she ended up in a wheelchair. Her mother and younger sister are still in Viking.

> Niki: Wow. OK. Was I supposed to know this?

> Dola: No, Fi informed me.

Rollo disappeared and came back with an iPad, which he linked to the large screen on the wall behind the table. Shortly, the Viking Cam, as the Recorder's news portal now called it, came up on the screen.

We watched it for a minute or two. A few people milled

about, watching the screens attached to Troels' cell, but nothing interesting happened. "Do we know what time they're planning their stupidity?"

Kari shook her head. "Probably later, once everyone is in bed. My sister didn't know anything except they planned to do it tonight before you could set the date for the arbitration."

"But I already did that. It's been underway since last week. It's on the portal."

Rollo zoomed in on the area of the screen that announced the Recorder was in arbitration with Viking.

Kari huffed. She sounded exactly like Tilly when I pointed out that her favourite sausage treat had been waiting in her bed for several minutes.

I turned my Gift on Kari. The fear and worry pouring off her in waves were giving me a headache. Could I calm her down? "OK, while we're waiting, tell me what's bugging you, Kari?"

"My sister's still there, and I need to get her out."

"Did you message her and tell her to stay away?"

"Yes. I didn't even know the Rainbow Network was back until Inge told me. I haven't been able to speak to her since I left."

A quick glance at Ben's face told me it hadn't been relaxing. "And you didn't think to ask for the Recorder's assistance in getting a message through?"

She looked shocked. "No."

"Why not? How did you think Rollo managed to bring you all through to the Gateway for your bonding checks when the yellow gate was sealed?"

Her mouth formed an O. She was getting an inkling that she was the idiot in this situation and not the Recorder. Yep, she was, as her next grudging words showed. "Sorry. I don't think well when I'm afraid for people."

That was such a backhanded apology. Why bother to give it? I raised an eyebrow at Ben, and, in good Mancunian fashion, he gave me the nod. He'd let me know next time if he thought I could help his bond mate.

Which reminded me. I stood up. "Come on, you two, Dola will tell me when to watch. Let's see if I can show Ben this isn't all some mass hallucination."

All three of them followed me into Kari's room, where I'd noticed a full-length mirror when I borrowed her jacket earlier. I couldn't quite work out why I didn't want to use the one in Rollo's room, except I didn't need Kari's negative energy where we'd be sleeping later.

I stood her and Ben in front of the mirror. They were so nervous about it, I could barely see their bond. I remembered how Autumn got Rollo and me to connect so she could show us. "Look at each other please."

Nearly. I could see it clearly now, but was it strong enough to show them? I thought back to what Autumn had done. It would be easier to show them if Kari would only relax. I caught Rollo's eye and sent, *"A little help here? They need to do what we did and think about each other. And I don't know either of them."*

Rollo winked at me, obviously remembering what we'd thought about to connect when Autumn was losing patience with us. "Do you guys remember when the nasty accident befell the first table, and it toppled into the pool?"

They gave each other a cute, sheepish look, then Ben grinned at Kari.

CLICK!

I grabbed both their wrists and pulled a little power. I truly wanted them to see. More for Ben than Kari, if I was being honest. I liked him. It must be awful stuck in the wilds of Scotland hearing about a bunch of strange Celtic realms. He must secretly wonder if they were all a myth, or even if his bond mate was quite sane. I would have. Well, I did until I saw the Gateway, didn't I?

A nice normal lad from Manchester in love with a Viking princess. Poor bastard. I pushed with the power and thought, *show them.*

Their bond glowed red, yellow, and green in the mirror. Nice.

They gasped.

Well, that was much better than squealing.

My phone beeped in my pocket.

Dola: As you are working anyway, watch the feed now. I added a two-minute delay to it in case.

I grabbed Rollo's hand and headed to the kitchen, calling, "It's going down," over my shoulder.

CHAPTER
FORTY-ONE

Kari and Ben arrived back in the kitchen arm in arm to watch the feed, looking much happier. But, in the end, the attack was exactly the anticlimax I'd told Kari it would be. When I'd connected with the power on Friday to move Troels' cell to its new location, it sent me a clear vision of an area of protection, a force field of power. Along with the vision had come the message I'd given to HRH that the power was conserving energy to create defences.

And that was exactly what the attacking Vikings got. Instant karma in action. It was almost cartoon-like to watch and immensely funny. It wouldn't have been amusing if I'd known any of the people involved. But I didn't, and I was on the power's side.

The small group of about three dozen Viking warriors, all dressed in the usual Viking leather, arrived. They didn't look anywhere near as hot in it as Rollo did.

"I hope you always think so."

I caught his eye and blew him a kiss, and Kari glared at me. Her fists clenched, the knuckles turning white.

A Viking tested the barrier with a spear, which he threw over the railings. It missed Troels' cell by a few inches, probably deflected by the force field which had allowed it through. The spear thrower shook his head in disbelief, and Rollo translated for Ben and me: "My throw was true, I tell you."

Kari's hands were in constant motion now as she twined her fingers together, then released them.

The spear getting so close gave the rest of the attackers confidence. Several more spears, along with a wide selection of other projectiles, mostly hand axes and the larger double-headed ones, sailed over the iron railings towards the cell. They hit the zone of protection, bounced off, and ricocheted wildly. Some of them landed blade first in the attacking warriors, judging by the cries of pain.

A huge red-headed, bearded Viking took the prize for the worst teammate ever when he threw a Molotov cocktail. It bounced back, met a hand axe in midair, and the bottle shattered, scattering burning oil in every direction.

I watched as they ran about like headless chickens. They tried, fruitlessly, to bat out the flames on each other.

"Is stop, drop and roll not a Viking concept?" I enquired politely. I didn't want to sound too gleeful in case Rollo or Kari knew any of the men.

Honestly, I was surprised. It was clear Viking wasn't a technologically advanced realm, but they were acting as though the force field were magic.

OK, I know it *was* magic, but it seemed to first unsettle them and then completely freak them out. Had they never seen a force field before?

"Why is it surprising them? Don't they watch movies?" I enquired.

"Just wonderin' the same thing myself," came from Ben.

In a perfectly serious tone, Kari said, "They're asking if the Gods want Troels to live, and if this is a deity's work to safeguard him."

At mine and Ben's laughter, Kari gave us both another filthy look.

But Rollo said, "She's right. There's a lot of superstition. Anything a Viking doesn't understand is the work of a god. And anything that goes wrong is caused by Loki's boredom."

"But they have access to the Rainbow Network and streaming television, don't they?" I couldn't quite wrap my head around a realm living as though it was still the twelfth century and every thunderstorm being Thor throwing a hammer around. Or did the hammer cause the lightning bit? What was that hammer called?

Even in my mind, Rollo felt weary. *"Mjölnir. Most people don't have television or computers. There are longhouses that stream big sporting events, but the average Viking doesn't have much technology."*

I was so surprised, I asked, "Seriously?"

It drew Kari's attention, and she answered my previous question. "They really don't. Most of the women use mobile phones. But the men tend to break them by forgetting they're carrying them when they fight, and they're too expensive to replace. It's one of the reasons I expanded my fitness business to the other realms and your world. More access to people who'll pay for an online service. Well, that and my father interfering and causing scenes at my business premises. He got his cronies to refuse to give me a lease anywhere else, but he doesn't understand or have any interest in technology, so being online gave me some privacy to succeed."

On the screen, one man took a nasty-looking shoulder wound from a rebounding axe, which put him on his butt with a loud grunt of pain. Ben observed, "They obviously skipped physics lessons too. Momentum and kinetics, anyone? I'd have thought a warring nation would be better at this." Looking at Kari, he asked, "Don't you guys even play pool? They keep looking surprised at the rebounds."

I laughed. Kari looked confused, so I guessed the answer was no.

Rollo sounded thoughtful as he asked, "I only know two of them. How about you, Kari?"

"My unlamented, but sadly not yet late, father's hands are all over this. Yes, I know most of them. Not all by name, but by sight, yes."

"How do you guys think we should handle this?" I asked the two Vikings in the room.

They looked at each other and shrugged. Eventually, Rollo said, "If I'd ever had a plan I thought would succeed, I would have implemented it before now."

"But exactly what is it that's stopping your plans from succeeding?"

Rollo sighed. "The warlords support Troels because he doesn't interfere in their plans. They may not even believe the power has already removed him from the throne, and if they accepted it was true, they'd say it has no right to do it. This is a Viking matter."

Kari nodded firmly.

Rollo gave me a helpless look. "I'd never even heard of the existence of the Gateway agreement until you showed it to me and then the royals discussed at the book club. Only Alphonse seemed to be as ignorant as Viking. Everyone else knew about it."

I grinned at him. "Well given two of them were signatories to it …"

We laughed.

With a short-tempered snap in her tone, Kari asked, "Agreement? Book club?"

Rollo ignored her. "If you released Troels and dropped the petitions, the warlords would welcome him back. He prevents any kind of change. They'd prefer him on the throne to me because they can buy him off with an unlimited supply of the drug, a lot of feigned respect and excessive public affection for their king. And they fake it so well, even I believed them until you showed me that data."

"What data's this?" Kari leaned forward, more intrigued and less confrontational. She was still bugging me, but she was curious, and I'd liked her when I first met her. Well, after we got past the rude email she'd sent. She'd driven up here because, in her mind, the Recorder was being negligent, and she'd dismissed Dola, which annoyed me, but I had to get past that. Kari knew none of the facts, and even after she'd watched the power in action protecting Troels' cell, she still thought what happened in the future was in the Vikings' hands. Perhaps some information would shift her annoying mindset. It might give me some practice for dealing with the rest of her former realm.

As the last of the warriors moved out of range of the camera feed, I asked, "Rollo, can you put the data on the screen? I'll be back in a second. I need to check something."

I walked away before I bit anyone's head off. Because I'd finally realised they were only doing exactly what I'd done with Janet. Accepting the unacceptable as if it were perfectly normal. I'd done it because I hadn't seen anything like true normal at home or at work for far too long. Was that their problem? Rollo was intelligent, so he hid his despair well. But Kari's rotten attitude made it clear she thought there was no hope.

Had they ever known what normal should look like? Troels had been on the throne, and Halvor had been in power for their entire lifetimes. Kari and Rollo got out of their realm the moment they could. The only way they thought they could change their lives was by not being in Viking anymore.

I sat in the bedroom, Tilly curled up next to me. I'd really only wanted an excuse to breathe. I pulled a curl of power into my hand and told it how well I thought it had done and checked it was happy. It was triumphant.

OK then, let's see if I could remind the Vikings in the kitchen that it was the freaking twenty-first century, and there was no reason to live as though it were the fifteenth. I grabbed my laptop and wondered if I could shift Kari's attitude with Ben's help. He seemed to think Vikings were out of touch too. Perhaps he could push her in the right direction to help her people, even if they were the ones she'd claimed sanctuary from.

. . .

Settled back at the kitchen table, I poured myself another glass of wine and glanced at the cute sunflower clock above the screen. I might have half an hour in me to change the Vikings' attitudes before I wanted to wrap myself around Rollo and sleep.

"That sounds so good. See how perfectly bonded we are?"

I stuck my tongue out at him, which Kari noticed. "Can you guys do the mind speech thing that some bond mates can?"

At our nods, she glanced at Ben. "I can pick up on his thoughts, but he doesn't get mine."

I turned my Gift on Ben and felt deception. Huh! Why was he lying to her? As our eyes met, he shook his head, and my left shoulder pinged. I should find out what that was about, but right now, I needed to see what they could tell me about the Vikings that I didn't know.

"Right, guys. Kari, you asked about the book club. I have a question from Breanna's favourite book, well, her current favourite book anyway. What would you do if you knew the outcome would be exactly what you wanted it to be?"

Blank looks greeted me from the two Vikings in the room. But Ben immediately said, "Buy a lottery ticket. Obvs!"

Once the laughter subsided, Rollo said, "Put someone who can deal with Viking in charge of it, go back to the work I love and be with the woman I'm mad about. I've never wanted to be king, and I won't be now. If I had wanted it, I could have taken Troels down the moment I hit twenty-one. But if I'd done that, then the moment I tried to change anything, the warlords' only focus would have been arranging a fatal accident for me. I'd have been lucky to reach twenty-two. And absolutely nothing has changed there since."

I was still stuck on the fact that he was mad about me. He'd kept that quiet. It was strange for me, being with a man who liked me and said so. Goddess, Nick had been an asshole. I mean, sure, I knew that. But the multiple ways he'd found to put me down still surprised me. He never said anything nice about me to anyone unless it was an excuse for him to humble brag about something.

Rollo raised his eyebrows at me. "I told you I was crazy about you up at Arthur's Seat!"

I had zero recollection of it. As I ran that mad sunrise morning through my mind, I giggled as I remembered why I hadn't been listening to him.

I spluttered, "That's cheating. You were eating a doughnut."

Ben burst out laughing. "Way to go, Rollo."

Kari slapped him around the head lightly and muttered, "Men!"

Our eyes met in a single moment of perfect accord before I turned the question back to her. "What would you do, Kari? If there was no risk of failing?"

"Personally, or for my realm?"

"Both. Why not? Yeah, both."

"Personally, I'd take Ben to live in Viking, build my business worldwide from there. Give my mother gorgeous grandkids. If the Rainbow Network was reliable." She stopped and shook her head. "Sorry, I only mean if idiots didn't keep getting our comms cut off. I could run my business from there and watch Ben make millions teaching those idiot Vikings how real men fight."

"What is it you do, Ben? Apart from running a gym in an upmarket hotel in Gretna Green?" Why would Kari think he could make so much money in Viking, but not in Scotland?

"You ever heard of …?" He gave me a name I'd seen many times on posters outside newsagents on those sheets that showed the newspaper headlines. Usually followed by "Local Boy Takes the Match/Title/Championship."

I nodded. "Of course."

He circled his hand around his own face and gave me a wicked smile. "That's my fighting name."

The champion in question fought in a costume. That Ben had been under that costume made me smile. "But didn't you retire a couple of years ago?" It had been all over the news.

"My mum said she'd had enough after my head injury, and the promoter said I should get out while I could still use my brain. The promoter, him I could've talked round, but there's no arguing with my mum. Not once she starts the church ladies praying for me."

I nodded. I'd seen Olive pull that on Aysha when she thought about quitting Uni once. It had worked like a charm.

"Thing is, there's no real money to be made in the UK teaching, and I don't want to move to the USA. It's too far from family. But Kari thinks Vikings would pay through the nose. They watch all the MMA matches, apparently. That's one use of tech they got behind."

"They do, or so Dola tells me."

To Kari, I said, "OK, so that's the personal. You'd like to live there. What's stopping you? Why were you so frightened you claimed sanctuary?" She'd been terrified that day. It swayed me in her favour when, as Princess Entitled, she'd asked the Recorder for sanctuary.

"Women having no rights. Warlords who wouldn't raise an eyebrow if my father married me off to any total plonker to further his own plans. If it hadn't been for Inge, I might have been trapped. It was she who suggested the seer and who told me about the sanctuary option. Her government makes a point of knowing all the loopholes."

"Inge's government!" I'd never heard that Viking had anything resembling any form of democratic process. Rollo said earlier they didn't have one. "What do you mean, her government?"

Almost in unison, Rollo and Kari shook their heads. Rollo said, "It's not real. It has no teeth. Sadly."

Privately, he sent, *"I'll explain later. Don't think Kari knows the full story, and it's not my place to tell her."*

But she proved him wrong. "When Inge blackmailed Troels into divorcing her, she also had him consent to women having the right to submit bills to be passed into laws. And to propose amendments to the stupidly few existing laws. He agreed. They called it the Regering."

At my confused expression, she added, "Which should have been her first clue because 'Regering' means 'government.' And I think we all know, when they give you an impressive title, you rarely get any actual power. So Inge and her 'ministers' have spent almost my entire lifetime writing bills. But every time they submit one to be passed into law, Troels and his warlords send it back for further consultation or amendment. Or they simply refuse it."

Rollo was nodding. *"There is a bit more, but she's got most of it. Her mother and Inge are friends."*

Kari stood up. "I'm going to grab a bath and calm down if no one minds? Before I say something I might regret." She bowed to me. "I'm sorry if I appeared rude, my lady." She was out of the door before anyone could say a word.

So much for having the chance to educate her, and I was confused. "Did I upset her?"

Ben shook his head. "She's homesick. She couldn't live there, but she does love it. It was that time of the month last week, and she just kept crying and asking, 'Why don't we have any mead? That always makes it stop hurting.' I mean, mead? What's wrong with tequila?" He looked unhappy and helpless and I liked the man.

"The next time your mum sends you a food parcel, if you share the dumplings, I'll send you a case of mead," I offered.

"How did you know she sends ...?" He shook his head. "Never mind, you have a deal."

"Seriously, Ben, you can always ask the Recorder for help. She's got contacts, you know." I grinned at him.

Quick as a flash, he came back with, "People who talk about themselves in the third person are posers. You know that, right?"

He sounded so like Aysha. I laughed. "Oh hell yeah, I hear you. Seems to come with the role, though."

Rollo was digging in a cupboard. Over his shoulder, he asked,

417

"But what put today's bug up her butt? She only gets like this when she's angry or scared, not homesick. What's her real problem?"

"I think the Recorder," he winked at me, "embarrassed her."

"Oh? I really didn't intend to do that. How *did* I do that?"

"You didn't. She got a good mad on as we drove up here. Everyone being out of touch. Viking going to hell in a handbasket; no one cares about all the good people in Viking. Her sister's in danger; her mother's in a wheelchair, and so on. Then when you blew her worries off and said let them bring it on. And there was already a plan in place … well, you know."

I did know. Yes. Intelligent women often thought that way. Everyone else was an idiot. I wondered what I'd done wrong in a past life to have attracted so many of them to me in this one.

Rollo handed Ben a crackling cellophane bag of candies I didn't recognise, a frozen bottle, a shot glass and a beer. "Take her these. No more than two shots. Three will push her into 'What's the point of even trying? They're all idiots' territory."

Ben grinned at him, "Thanks, mate."

Once he'd gone, I asked Rollo, "So what was the bit Kari doesn't know?"

His laugh was so harsh, it sounded more like a choking cough. "I'm not sure you understand Viking has no government, no constitution, and the average Viking has very few rights. Women have even fewer. There are barely any laws. The king and the warlords do whatever they like, and the rest of the population tries to stay out of their way."

"OK, but you told me that earlier, and I'd worked most of the rest out."

"What laws they have were put in place by one of the former kings, some of them by Inge's ancestor Harald about a thousand years ago. And haven't yet been repealed by Troels. Inge always believed I would be king at some point. She's spent almost thirty years creating and re-creating laws, bills, and a working structure for a real society. If I were king and agreed to pass them all into law, Viking would have most of the laws it would need in about a week."

I let out a soft whistle. "She's given up her whole life to try to give you and the Viking citizens a fighting chance?"

He nodded. "That's why it's so hard to tell her I won't do it." I was about to ask for more details when Rollo wiped a hand over his face as though he couldn't take anymore.

"Remember when you thought you wanted to wrap yourself around Rollo and sleep? Is it that time yet?"

I laughed. "Let me give Tilly five minutes to water something, and I'll be right there."

He glanced around the empty room. "Where is she?"

"She's asleep, and she won't want to go out, but if I don't take her now, she'll wake me up at freezing o'clock and demand to go out then. In an apartment, I can't just open the door to the garden for her, so let me get ahead of that happening, and I'll join you."

"There's astroturf on several of the balconies if you don't want to go downstairs."

There were balconies? Where had he been hiding those?

"Here, let me show you." He led the way through his bedroom, into his office and unlocked what I'd assumed was a cupboard door. It opened onto a small balcony with pots of flowers and, yes, fake grass.

He stepped out with us, and I stopped dead and gasped at the view. It looked as if I had longer arms, I could hug Edinburgh Castle which glowed in soft pink lights tonight. Tilly watered one of the flower pots and I said, "I'll rinse it off tomorrow."

Rollo laughed and pointed up at the cloudy night sky. "Scotland will rinse it off tomorrow before you're even up if the rain forecast is correct."

He wrapped his arms around me as I continued to admire the castle. Then I saw the time on a nearby clock tower. "It's almost midnight. Doesn't time fly when you're trying to talk sense into a woman who doesn't want to hear it?"

Rollo smiled. "That clock is almost always three minutes fast.

It's the Balmoral clock, and they keep it fast on purpose." He squeezed me tighter, and as we leaned out over the balcony, he pointed through the dark. "That's the main station. Most people don't know the clock's fast, so even if they're a little late by it, they can still catch their trains."

Something about the craziness of that whole concept really appealed to me, and I laughed uninhibitedly before asking "Almost always?"

"Obviously, they put it to the correct time on Hogmanay. No one wants to welcome the new year at the wrong minute, do they?"

The Scots were crazy, but I was starting to like their capital city very much.

PART EIGHT
MONDAY

The fears we fail to face become our limits.
   Which frightens you more?
   Settling for your current familiar ceiling?
   Or accepting the searing pain that the only person who kept you from creating a better life was yourself?
   It is not who you *are* that holds you back.
   It is all the things you believe you are not.
   Winning the War Against Yourself: Daily Weapon and Warrior Care by Arinn Tusensköna

CHAPTER
FORTY-TWO

Monday, 8th March—Yggdrasil House, Edinburgh. Psychic O'clock

It wasn't Tilly that woke me though. The moonlight poured in through the wide high windows of Rollo's bedroom, and I was suddenly wide awake. My man and my dog were peacefully asleep again, but this time it wasn't a noise but my own subconscious that had awoken me.

I crept through to Rollo's warm, friendly kitchen. *Let's not wake Kari and have to listen to more opinions on how someone else should fix her problems for her.* I put my earbud in as I walked and, as soon as I got safely into the kitchen and closed the door, murmured. "Dola, please place a porcelain bowl of smashed eggs and salmon on the countertop in the kitchen right now."

"How did you know, Niki? It is the middle of the night."

"I don't know, but I did. Can you just do it so I can go back to sleep? And please may I have a mug of drinking chocolate?"

A tall mug in plain white pottery arrived filled with piping hot chocolate. It smelt divine. I read, *5000 years ago, cats were worshipped as gods. Cats' manners have never recovered from those complete idiots and their poor judgement.*

Oh dear, things obviously weren't going well. Dola and I had agreed that I didn't need to come home every day. There would be no necessity to force Finn to request breakfast for the cat, along with his morning bacon sandwich. We could all behave like adults for a week, and, provided I requested the food, Dola would place it out in the kitchen for the cat.

"Could you open a channel to HRH for me?"

"Go ahead."

"Don't push your luck or distress my Equerry, Your Majesty, or I may forget to request food for you. This arrangement requires us all to at least emulate grown adults. You need to do your part. Is all well otherwise?"

The cat's mellow, upper-class tones came clearly through my earbud. "Noted, Recorder. All is well. Is Rollo available?"

"No, he's sleeping. Want me to pass on a message?"

There was a long silence.

"Yes, I believe I do. Time passes too swiftly. Tell him to fully investigate the role of a regent. If he balks, suggest it is not what he thinks, and direct his attention to the histories of Finland, Iceland and Denmark in your own world. Do you understand?"

"No, but I can repeat it and pass it on."

"That must suffice. Thank you for the eggs."

Well, that was unusually pleasant for her. Hopefully, I wouldn't return to a half-destroyed house or a distraught Dola.

Through my earbud, Dola asked, "As you are awake, may I send a video to your laptop?"

I looked around, but my laptop was in the bedroom. Unlike me, Rollo hadn't a week where he'd got eight hours' sleep a night and rejuvenating afternoon siestas on holiday. He'd looked tired tonight, and I didn't want to wake him. His laptop was next to me on the table. I opened it. It was passcoded, of course. I told Dola this, and it sprang to life, and a video began to play. She had zero respect for anyone's security, but I had to admire her equal opportunity hacking.

Then the screen grabbed my attention as I tuned in to the

woman's words. Actually, she was still a girl, wasn't she? She might have been in her late teens.

As I watched it, my heart hurt. Carys told her story so simply. She'd been just sixteen when she visited Viking to be a bridesmaid. Her Welsh Red Celt accent came across so clearly as she fought her obvious distress to deliver a clear accounting of her experience.

Occasionally, I heard Glynis' low voice in the background saying things like, "Tell it in your own words, *bach*. Share how it was for you. Remember to breathe now."

Carys shared her excitement. Her first visit to the Viking realm. All the handsome groomsmen and the exciting but scary shield maidens. The ceremony took place along with many others during the Autumn equinox, the traditional time for Viking weddings. *Such* a romantic time.

The bride, her oldest brother's wife, who now lived in the next valley along from Pant Y Wern, had wanted to be married at home in Viking with her family around her before she moved to the Red Celt realm to live with her new husband. She'd been so very kind to include her. Everyone had been so welcoming.

Even the king had complimented Carys on how beautiful she looked when he called in before the ceremony to wish everyone well and approve the bride. Such a lovely tradition of having the real, actual king visit all the brides.

I knew where this was going, and I couldn't take it. I sped up the video to 1.5 speed to get it over with. And it went exactly where it was destined to go.

The footage was incredible, powerful and disturbing, and edited masterfully. The juxtaposition between Carys's delight and innocence and the unfolding story simply broke me.

The wedding photo inserted into the narrative showing Carys in her bridesmaid gown looking impossibly young and Troels lurking between the bride and her four bridesmaids made me shiver.

Finn had caught every moment of her remembered pleasure

and delight, and then her confusion and her guilt. The single tear she couldn't hold back was heartbreaking.

Carys had been a virgin when she left for Viking. Two months after she returned home, her doctor gave her news she simply didn't believe. It wasn't a stomach upset causing the vomiting. No, she was pregnant. She was to have a *babi*. But how? She hadn't … She really hadn't ever done *that*.

Her father's distress and her mother's anger. Her oldest brother's outright disbelief. Her other brother's support. Her own confusion. She told it all, with Glynis, always there, gently prompting her to continue in a warm, supportive tone.

It wasn't possible. Although, no, she couldn't remember most of the evening after the wedding. She didn't think she'd had too much drink. Only two glasses of mead to toast the couples. And she'd woken up safely in her own bed. Yes, she'd felt strange. A bit odd, and everything was a bit sore, but she'd put it down to dancing too hard.

Whilst I felt she was a little naïve, her sincerity was palpable. This had been a sheltered, much-loved girl.

Then she sat her daughter on her knee, an adorable child with a head of blonde hair and a green and red bow perched jauntily into her curls. The little one was perhaps three years old. Carys said she wouldn't part with her for the world, and her ma and da doted on their first grandbabi. But she still hadn't understood how it happened until she spoke to Glynis. And the lovely Fae, wasn't he soooo tall? He'd said he could tell the genes of her baby, and it was the king who'd …

She sobbed in earnest now. And only her little girl wiping away her mother's tears with a chubby fist forced her to regain control.

At the very end, Simon of the cute bow ties, showed up behind her and offered the little girl her teddy back. "Buck up, sis. That's the hard bit done now." He gave her a tissue. Oh, Gods and Goddesses, Carys was his baby sister?

It finally ended, and I took a deep slurp of my hot chocolate, wishing it was something stronger.

And I breathed. That poor kid.

"I have more recorded today, less than we hoped, though setting up took longer than expected. But Glynis, Tegan, Simon and Finn have the routine smoothed out now. On a scale of one to ten, if she is a seven in the emotional resonance stakes, I have two fours, a five, two more worryingly similar to Carys but from a young Pict woman and a Scottish girl. And a nine."

Gods and Goddesses, if Carys was a seven, what the hell would the nine be like? I sniffled and blew my nose.

As though she'd read my mind, Dola said, "She is a nine only because I am retaining the score of ten in case there is a worse one. She remembered all of it, and no one believed her. You might not want to view that one until you have emotional support available. Finn insisted I show it to no one until you had seen it."

"Which realm is the nine from?"

"She is Galician and used to be a friend of Elise's."

I interrupted Dola, "Elise? Inge's daughter?"

"Yes, and, of course, Troels' daughter."

"Yes, sorry, OK, and why is it so bad?"

"The Galician woman, Isabella, was named after the empress, who is her godmother. She used to do charity work with Princess Natalia. Prince Alejandro was suspected of being the father, although he denied it vigorously. No one believed her when she said it was Troels. After the child's birth, it was obvious the father was someone with lighter hair and skin than the prince."

I thought about the emperor's angry denial at the book club.

Dola said, "Glais'Nee confirmed the truth of the woman's statement immediately."

Might that explain the burst of bright fury I'd felt from Alejandro at the dinner table during the book club when his father had categorically denied anyone in his realm had been affected "by the barbarian"?

Dola continued, "The Galicians have an unhelpful attitude to teenage pregnancy."

"They do? In what way?"

"Their church believes the woman is culpable for not dying to protect her virtue. They send unmarried mothers to grape-picking camps."

I laughed and then felt dreadful when I realised by the total silence from Dola that she was deadly serious. This was freaking ridiculous.

I sat and thought for a long time. Anyone with half a brain could have imagined how these testimonies would go. I'd known Dola was recording them this week. That was why she wanted me out of the way.

But I couldn't have imagined the power of watching it for myself. My heart was breaking for the loss of that child's innocence, and underneath my sorrow was a quiet, cold anger, not only at Troels. Not even with his total disregard for his realm, for his family, or for any of these poor young women's lives. I was furious at the whole bloody Viking realm for turning a blind eye and allowing this abuse to continue. Actually, no, not just the Viking realm—all the realms.

"Dola, please send the video of Carys to Mabon after he has his first cup of coffee. The way he spoke to Simon at the bondings, I think he might know the family. Tell him the Recorder will be calling him when she gets back from her vacation, and I'll want to know once and for all how much he knew about what was going on."

"Yes, Niki. Shall I put the videos on the portal?"

I thought about it for all of five seconds. "Yes, please. Not the Galician nine. I need to watch her myself first."

"I was listening in earlier. The ignorance is worrying. Do you think I should put an image of the original Gateway agreement along with the translation that you and Mags made last week onto the news portal?"

"I think that's an excellent idea. Perhaps put it in the arbitration section, but put a clickbait link on the main page. Something like 'Ninety-five percent of citizens didn't know they're alive *only* because their former kings abided by these rules.' If that's not clickbaity enough, Simon might help you. He does social media stuff."

There was a chuckle. "I have been studying, Niki. I think I can do it."

"OK, thank you. Can you also do some in-depth research on these twelve warlords everyone keeps talking about? Ask Finn to help if he has any time between filming. Find me anything you can, by any means, legal or otherwise. Hack their emails, check our servers for anything they've ever sent or received as far back as our records go. If you can access their computers, do it. Do whatever you want. Get me everything you can, anything at all that might help me clear them out of Viking. We're covered by the Rules of Arbitration at the moment, and anyway, I think that realm lost all rights to privacy once they started providing drugs that allowed the rapes of girls who still look like children."

Carys had upset me. It was the innocence in her face still at almost twenty. I could only imagine how much of a child she must have looked when Troels zeroed in on her. Some part of me screamed, *Get these bastards out of any realm I have responsibility for and into a hell of their own making!*

There was a pause. Then, in her tentative voice, Dola asked, "Niki?" and another hot chocolate and a glass of brandy arrived on the table. I sipped the brandy and then poured it into the hot liquid and said, "Tell me the rest of it."

And she did.

CHAPTER
FORTY-THREE

*S**till ... Monday, 8th March—Yggdrasil House, Edinburgh. Mid-morning*

I'd slept late. My brain must have needed to process all the information Dola had given me in the depths of the night. She'd already been researching the warlords long before I asked her to.

Of course she had. I really didn't pay her enough, whatever she'd said about not wanting a raise. And I still had no idea what kind of present I could get for a house to say thank you for being so totally amazing. Her birthday party and gifts had been hard enough to create. There seemed to be nothing she needed. Except perhaps appreciation was a currency? I had a lot of appreciation for her, and she'd received pitifully little so far in her long life.

Then raised voices from the kitchen reminded me we still had guests. After my shower, I threw on some jeans and a boyfriend-style shirt that was still warm and comfortable but slightly more stylish than my usual sweatshirts. If I had to deal with Kari before coffee, I'd take all the help I could get.

As I opened the door to let Tilly into the kitchen, I heard a shocked gasp and rushed in, nearly falling over my dog, who'd stopped dead in the doorway. Tilly avoided drama whenever she could. She turned on her heel and headed back to bed. I wished I could follow her.

Kari looked pale, Ben had his arm around her, and Rollo simply nodded at her as he rose to give me a hug.

He poured me a coffee. "Kari has just found the Gateway agreement."

The large monitor on the wall was showing a split screen mode. I saw a link that now said, "In our recent survey, 100% of you didn't know the simple rules your ancestors agreed to follow to stay alive. YOU are still bound by them."

That was a little more intense than I'd intended Dola to be, but I couldn't complain because it wasn't even clickbait. The article it linked to showed on the other side of the screen and laid out the simple facts that all the realms had obligations to the Gateway. Not all of the realms were honouring their side of those agreements.

Huh, I'd wondered how the agreement would strike the realms' citizens when they first learned of it. Not well, judging from Kari's expression.

"Recorder, you can't be here on holiday now. You have to do something," Kari greeted me.

"Good morning, Kari. How did you sleep?"

"Very well. You need to do something."

"Well, I didn't. I'd thank you for asking, except, oh wait, you didn't, did you?"

I accepted a mug of coffee from Rollo and sipped cautiously. It wasn't the perfect temperature at which Dola always delivered my first cup. I didn't growl because I'm not Caitlin. But damn it, I was starting to think a little growling in the right place, at the right time at rude people might be an effective time saver.

"You need to help people—my mother, my sister. They could die. And you're on holiday!"

I met Kari's furious expression with flat eyes. I'd been a nice woman once upon a time, but it was attitudes like Kari's that, in my mind, at least, had caused half these problems. Screw stuff up and then blame other people, or make it their problem to fix it for you. Was that the problem in Viking?

Was it all ... *it's not my fault we harboured a bunch of sexual predators and drug pushers. We were all too busy doing something else to notice. It wasn't up to us to protect our sisters, their friends, or any visiting innocents who happened to come to a wedding in our realm?*

I couldn't fix it by blaming them. That was just taking a leaf out of their own book and doubling it, wasn't it? However tempting it felt right now.

I drew myself straight, found my librarian's voice, and gave her a stern look. "Kari, re-evaluate your tone, please. I was trying to be Nice Niki last night. But if you intend to berate me without even having the courtesy to wait until I've had my first cup of coffee, I can find the Recorder for you right now. I was working until six a.m."

I drank my coffee. Kari looked as though she was about to say something, but Ben put a hand on her thigh.

"I am doing something. Now it's your turn. What the hell are you doing except blaming other people for the mess you were a part of making for, what, thirty years? You took no responsibility for fixing anything when you claimed sanctuary, did you? How is *your* realm my problem?"

She gave me a filthy look. "What could you possibly have been doing until six a.m. that was useful?"

Wow, she was a pain. I was beginning to think I understood exactly how, as Princess Entitled, she had come up with that ridiculous email she'd sent to my gran. Now she wasn't so frightened for herself anymore, she thought someone else should fix the mess she'd run away from?

I reached over to Rollo's laptop and pressed play on Carys' video. "Approving heartbreaking videos of crimes that all of Viking, including you, appear to have allowed to happen under their damn noses for your entire lifetime, Princess. Do tell, isn't that you in the wedding photo we're about to see?"

The video played.

About five minutes into it, a wedding photo showing the incredibly young Carys as a bridesmaid appeared. Standing immediately to the bride's right was Kari. Ben asked, "Can you pause it, Rollo?"

He turned to Kari. "That is you, and this is what you told me about?"

She nodded.

Ben breathed deeply. "You didn't mention it was a child abuse ring."

I stepped in quickly. I could guess a Manchester lad's opinion on the protection of minors. "Speaking purely technically, Ben, I've seen no petitions where the girls were under sixteen, which is the age of consent in most of the realms. I think Galicia might be eighteen, but you get my drift?"

Ben looked thoughtful as he shook his head. "I was at school," he named the school he'd gone to, and it was a pretty rough one, "with girls who might have been sixteen but emotionally they were going on twenty-five. But that one," he pointed at Carys, "is *still* a child herself. Imagine how much of an innocent she'd have been a few years ago."

I nodded sadly. And, as we watched, the counter moved from 173 to 174. Ben asked, "Is that for real?"

He looked relieved when I shook my head and then furious when I explained we were already closing in on two hundred cases.

Before Kari could speak and force me to say something I might regret, I put my empty coffee mug down. "We're taking Tilly out; we'll be back in half an hour. Make absolutely sure you watch the entire thing at least once, Kari."

Seizing Rollo's hand, I headed for the lift, ignoring all the things Kari thought were my responsibility as we left.

Then, following a weird twinge from my Gift, I tapped my earbud. "Dola, when that video finishes, can you play Kari the Galician one, the nine, too? If she balks, tell her I said, if she doesn't watch it properly, I won't do a damn thing to help her. I bet she knows Isabella as well."

CHAPTER
FORTY-FOUR

"Clear your mind, please."

Rollo nodded at me, and I transported us straight from his lift to a shadowy corner of a Manchester car park.

As we walked out, heading towards Piccadilly, I saw he was white around his lips again. I checked our link. Oh yeah, he was mad. But not just mad at Kari as I was. He was mad at Viking in general. Conversationally, I asked, "Do you know that quote? Something about we can't use the same mindset that got us into this stinking mess to get us out of it?"

He shook himself and looked around in surprise. "Do you mean, *We can't solve problems by using the same kind of thinking we used when we created them*? And where are we?"

I smiled. "Yes, that's the one. And Manchester. Ben made me homesick. I want a proper breakfast and a conversation with Prince Rollo that Kari can't overhear, interrupt or derail—before we end up arguing because of other people and their dramas and expectations."

I pulled him into a small doorway at the top of a short flight of steps with a sign reading *Duck or Grouse* and waited to make sure he ducked. We settled at a table for two, and I dumped Tilly on the wide, recessed windowsill next to us. They knew her well in here.

A tiny Chinese man arrived, and his face broke into a huge grin. "Niki, it's been so long, I worried. The usual?"

"Hi, Jerry, I moved to Gretna Green. There's no decent Chinese food there, so I came home for breakfast. The usual for us both and for madam, and two more to take out, please."

He smiled at me and reappeared two minutes later with a pot of Chinese tea and two cups. Rollo nodded at him when he hovered the pot over his cup, but he wasn't tracking properly yet. "What did Kari say before I got up that upset you so much?"

He focused on me. "It wasn't what she said. It was the understanding that there are far too many people who think like her. They're all waiting for the gods to sort it out. Like Odin has nothing better to do than help people who won't help themselves. The Gods are why the entire realm is in this mess. Odin didn't care about fairness or justice. He didn't care about laws either, which is why we don't have any."

He sipped his tea, the fragrance of it seemed to help him to gather himself. "Suddenly Kari's decided if the gods won't sort it out, then the Recorder should? What kind of sense does that make to any intelligent person? And she is intelligent, so how can I help the stupid ones?"

Jerry arrived back with bowls, plates, chopsticks and a tower of bamboo dim sum baskets, which he placed on our table. He also carried a small stainless-steel serving dish. He held the dish above Tilly's head until she sat up prettily. Then he positioned it carefully on the windowsill next to her. She gave him one low woof in thanks. "You're welcome, beautiful Tilly. Enjoy your food, Niki." He gave Rollo a nod and backed away.

I checked the boxes were in the right order and offered Rollo a *char siu bao*. He peered at it suspiciously. I put it on his plate with my chopsticks, then bit into my own and moaned softly. I'd still felt queasy when I got up this morning. If anything could get the words of those poor abused girls out of my head, this breakfast would. It had kept me sane through all my exams at university and every other thing that stressed me during the years since.

Rollo bit into his *bao* gingerly and then made "mmmn, good" noises. "What is it?"

"It's a Chinese steamed dumpling with barbeque pork in the middle." I tapped the second basket. "This one is spicy little ribs," I tapped the third one, "and these are fried wontons. Chicken and prawn stuff wrapped in a rice paper thing. You can get them everywhere, but Jerry's brother makes the best ones. Soup will arrive in a few minutes. Enjoy."

For several minutes, I ate and considered how to tell Rollo he was an idiot. I needed to get some stuff off my chest, or at least get an explanation of it. "I've been wondering …" I trailed off, unsure how to make what I wanted to ask a neutral, open question and not sound like what I meant, which was "What kind of an idiot are you?"

Rollo locked eyes with me. "Just ask it, hey?"

"Why didn't you simply transport away in Viking when those guys grabbed you? And if you didn't have time, then why didn't you do it the moment you came round?"

"Because I was tied up tightly, and you said anything I was holding when I transported would come with me, and I didn't want to bring the rope with me and leave my hands and feet behind."

Huh. OK, he might have a point. "Then why didn't you retrieve your knife with the yellow power and cut yourself free?"

He gave me an unhappy look. "Because I'm an idiot and didn't think of it? I haven't used the yellow power much … Oh, that's your point, isn't it?"

I nodded.

Tilly had finished all the duck, chicken, and pork on her plate and was now looking hopefully at mine. I waved a chopstick towards her nose. "You know the rules, Tilly-Flop. Lie down or you don't get a tart." She lay down. She loved the tiny Chinese egg custard tarts they called *dan tat*.

"How do you stay so slim?" Rollo looked horrified as if he hadn't meant the words to come out of his mouth and rushed to add, "I don't mean you overeat, you don't. But we're going to have to talk about this. I can't eat like you do. I'll get—well, out of shape."

I considered his fit, well-shaped body. "What makes you think so?" I'd moved on to eating the ribs, but Rollo was still looking doubtfully at his second *bao*.

He watched me. I could hear his thoughts about calories and expenditure and sensed him thinking about workouts. Eventually, he said, "It's science, isn't it? Take in more than you use, and you put on weight?"

I'd never been convinced of the truth of that myself, but was this the same as him not using the yellow power? He seemed determined to cling to his normality. But he wasn't normal, and the sooner he accepted that, the faster we could get on with fixing the mess in Viking.

Carefully, I asked, "Has your weight ever fluctuated?"

"Well, no, but plenty of older Vikings are out of shape. I always wanted to avoid that."

"Have you *ever* seen a Fae who was anything other than perfectly proportioned?"

He went very still.

I ate another rib while I waited.

"Now that you ask, no."

I ate more ribs. They were tiny and delicious, with a spicy kick that woke me up faster than coffee. I felt my stomach settle and I stopped wanting to throw up in reaction to those awful videos. Well, the videos weren't awful—they were incredibly good. But my empathetic side had lived through the experience along with that poor Galician girl, Isabella. It had been heartbreaking and horrific for her.

Rollo asked, "Are you saying I'm not taking into account that I don't only have Viking genes?"

I put some ribs on his plate before I ate the lot and then

finished the last two myself. I stacked the empty baskets on the edge of the table and looked hopefully towards the kitchen doorway.

I considered this man I had a bond with and wondered if I could take a shortcut. "I'm only wondering how long you've been using the same thinking that created the problem to try and solve it—and failing. If you don't want those ribs, I'll have them before the soup arrives. Ah, here it comes."

I moved my plate to the side and smiled up at Jerry. "Perfect timing, as always. Thank you."

He put two bowls of five-meat soup with noodles in front of us. I dug into mine, spoon and chopsticks flying. My entire body settled back into a more capable state. I was nearly ready to deal with Kari. When I opened the final basket, took out the crispy little chicken and prawn balls and dipped them into my soup like a peasant, I was ready for Rollo's brain to arrive back.

He laughed. Ate two ribs. Took in a long breath over the soup. The smell of the stock was wonderful—almost as good as it tasted. And he smiled at me. "Do I need to ask Ad'Rian, or can you tell me?"

"The only thing that will throw your metabolism out of its normal Fae perfection is if you eat too much over-processed food. It's like iron to them. They don't handle it well. Your body will let you know what it doesn't want. The Fae are in tune with their bodies' needs. As long as you listen to yours and give it what it wants—no more and no less—you'll never have an issue."

"So why don't you put weight on? You're not Fae."

"I have some Fae blood, or so Glais'Nee said, but I have the opposite problem. If I'm stressed or unhappy, I lose weight. I can afford to eat when I'm hungry. It burns off super quickly when things go wrong."

"So why are we in Manchester?" He gestured at the table. "Apart from this, which is incredible, I rarely eat Chinese."

I hoped that might change, or I'd be here a lot on my own. "I wanted to tell you about my first week as the Recorder when I didn't know how to use the power. Because my gut says you need to learn to use the yellow regnal power if we want to sort this mess out, and you're not doing it consciously yet."

I dove back into my soup. While we ate, I sent him my memories of my confusion, my blinding headaches, my fear, and my overwhelming feeling of inadequacy during my first awful week in Gretna Green. I showed him my public ascension and then my later true ascension. I tried to convey the warmth of my partnership with the power, and, yes, I'd had to surrender to the bond with the power, but I'd enjoyed it. Because it wasn't an abusive surrender; it was a mutual one that we renewed every time the power suspended me high in the Gateway.

I gazed sadly at my now almost empty bowl. "I may have hit the nail on the head accidentally at the book club when I used the word 'conservator' instead of 'user' or 'wielder' of the yellow power. You're terrified the power might change you into Troels. But, from all accounts, he was an asshole before he stole the power. You're not. The power doesn't like assholes, so why would you become one by using it? I don't think all the power I have has made me an asshole. A little more short-tempered probably, but I don't think—"

"You're not."

I finished the last few spoonfuls of my soup and sent him my memory of the weird shape of his head when he'd landed in the Gateway almost a week ago.

"Did I truly look like that?"

"Mmmhm. Dola has the footage. Ask her. The yellow power you held might be the *only* reason you're alive. You could ask it. You don't seem to talk to the power. I chatter away to it in my head all the time. I did when I was a kid. And I've seen other royals communing with theirs. How did it feel when you used it on Kari last night?"

"When I what?"

"You draped her in yellow power before you told her about us."

He looked at me with his mouth slightly open and a confused expression, so I sent him my mental snapshot of him swaddling Kari in power and appearing to decide something, nodding, and only then telling her we had a bond.

We'd finished our food, and he looked overwhelmed. I'd have to pick this up again later when he'd had some processing time. After all, I didn't get it right on my first try, did I? So I changed the subject a little. "You said you might have half a plan to fix this mess in Viking?"

"I don't, not really. But I know a man who might help me work it out. I'd like you to come with me to see him."

Ben whirled around, fist raised, and then his mouth dropped open. "Hey, girl, give a man some warning. How d'you *do* that?"

"It's a Recorder thing. Sorry, didn't mean to startle you."

But I had. I was being a bitch. I wanted Kari to stop whining and blaming whoever was handy, and remember that if she wanted her family safe, she might have to take some action too. And that the Recorder had powers, damn it. Perhaps she should remember that before I was tempted to use them on her.

I handed Ben the take-out bag Jerry gave me as we left. "I brought breakfast. The *dan tan* are for us all, but that's for you two."

He sniffed, then grinned. His lovely, dazzling white smile lit his face but didn't reach his haunted eyes. "How's Jerry, and how did you? Never mind, it's a Recorder thing, isn't it?"

Now I laughed.

I got Tilly some fresh water after her walk. As I bent to put the bowl on the floor, Rollo sent me a rude thought, echoing the one I'd thought about him the previous weekend. And I heard Ben hiss softly, "Tell her."

I turned around, but Kari was staring determinedly out of the window with a tear-streaked face.

Ben glanced at Rollo as if to say *help*? To me, he said, "Kari and I were talking about whether you could do," he waved his hand at the large wall screen, "some kind of documentary."

"A documentary?" I settled at the table. Ben joined me, unpacking the food. Rollo offered plates.

Ben shook his head and got the chopsticks out of the bag, then glanced at Kari and took one of the plates from Rollo. "Come and eat, babe. It's so good. You can't beat *dim sum* for breakfast."

Rollo shook his head. I caught his thought that perhaps all Mancunians were insane about food choices.

Between bites, Ben said, "Yeah, you know, like a Dummies Guide to this situation and the agreement. It's complicated, and even the language of the translation is old-school. I'm not dumb, and it took me ages to grasp it. So could you make a video that's like a party political broadcast for eight-year-olds on what it all means? Keep it simple and all that? I was trying to tell Kari what a party political was when you guys landed in here like something from *Star Trek*."

A party political broadcast. That was an incredibly clever idea. I eyed Ben with new respect. I mean, I liked him already, but he had a brain behind his amiable smile.

To Rollo, I said, "Now, that's a different kind of thinking."

He gave Ben a thoughtful look.

Ben turned to Kari. "As I was saying, it's what the various political parties do in the UK before an election."

Rollo interjected, "Did you ever watch the American presidential debates on TV?" She nodded. "Like that, but a lot shorter. The Brits only get ten minutes each on different days."

He looked hopefully at Kari, who still looked miserable, and when I turned my Gift on her, she was wallowing in guilt.

I'd been right. She knew Isabella, the upper-crust Galician teenager whose family had forced her into house arrest rather than a grape-picking camp until she gave birth. Then they'd given the baby to their priest to put up for adoption over her protests because she was only eighteen and had no rights as an unmarried mother. Her video completely destroyed me when I finally watched it just before I crawled back into bed at six a.m. It might explain why I got up in such a foul, queasy mood even before Kari started in on me.

Now Kari said to Ben, "But I don't think it would work. Who would watch it?"

Rollo and Kari switched to speaking Norse, which gave me hope he might be talking some sense into her. Then he pulled yellow power and wrapped it around her like a cloak. Her body language changed, softened, and she tilted her head to one side as though she was actually hearing him, not just waiting until he stopped talking to explain he was wrong.

Ben leaned into me. "Thanks for the Chinese, girl. I needed it. Can I give you some cash?"

I waved my hand. "Not necessary. We all needed it."

Kari had barely touched her food. I helped myself to one of her ribs and opened the bag containing the *dan tat*. I held one out to Tilly, who took it politely and disappeared to eat it in the hall in peace.

Ben grinned at me. "Kari says if it's ever safe for her to go to Viking, I'd need your permission. To go with her, I mean."

I nodded. He would.

"She said my mum probably wouldn't be able to visit us there. But we could visit her here?"

I tuned into my Gift, which had been trying to tell me something about this man for a few minutes now. And I heard the song in my mind. Oh, not another earworm!

George Benson's "The Greatest Love of All" sung by a gospel choir played loudly in my head. "Does your mum go to the same church as Olive Clarke?"

He looked confused but nodded.

"Is she in the choir too?"

He nodded again.

"I think I may have seen her at one of the church concerts. If we can get Viking sorted out so it's safe for Kari to go back, and therefore you too, then your mum will be able to visit you as long as she has a meeting with me first." I knew anything his mother swore on a Bible would put as strong an injunction on her as anything the realms swore over the anvil.

He gave me another blindingly white enormous smile, but this one reached his eyes. "Seriously?"

He glanced at Rollo and Kari, whose conversation now felt friendlier. It was hard to be sure. To me, Norse always sounded as though the speaker was angry, but Rollo felt calm.

"Uh-huh. So best put your mind to any more bright ideas you've got to help me get them straightened out. And, Benson …"

His head spun back around to focus on me so fast, it amazed me he didn't get whiplash. His mouth dropped open. "How did you? You couldn't guess that. How …?" He trailed off, gaping at me.

"Benson?"

He nodded.

"Take Kari home and calm her down. Or help her direct her anger where it should be directed—towards solutions. Encourage her to call Inge if you can. I've got a lot to do today, and so has Rollo."

He tilted his head like a cat. "But how did you know? *Everyone* thinks the Ben is for Benjamin; why didn't you?"

I debated telling him the truth. But Dola's words about embracing the myth of a Recorder's eccentricity and to stop trying to conform to people's expectations echoed in my mind.

In the end, I pointed at myself and said, "Recorder thing, yeah? We're weird that way. Anyway, it could have been worse. She could have called you Whitney."

His eyes bugged out, and his jaw dropped. "Whitney's my younger sister's name."

I guess his mum really liked the song, regardless of the singer.

CHAPTER
FORTY-FIVE

Rollo's first words after Ben and Kari left were, "What *did* you say to Ben? He almost dragged Kari out of here. I thought she was going to stay until she'd bullied me into going back to Viking, taking the throne and personally defending her mother and sister. Not that I wouldn't. Defend them, I mean, not take the throne. But, without a better plan, I can't guarantee their safety any more than she can. I tried the yellow power thing – it seemed to calm her down?"

"I saw. It did, well done."

For all we had this damn bond, I still had no clue what he was planning. But then maybe he could say the same about me. Having the bond was supposed to make everything easy, wasn't it? Hearts and bloody flowers and dancing happy rainbows and all our chakras in tune with each other?

So why did I still feel so ignorant about what truly made the man who he was?

I sighed. "Do you a deal? I'll tell you what I said to Ben when you tell me what you're planning."

Now he sighed and glanced at the clock on the wall. "OK, but we need to see Chris first, and I need to get changed."

· · ·

In the bedroom, I watched as he selected a seriously gorgeous grey suit, just as beautifully fitting as the blue one he'd worn to the book club. But somehow this one said "businessman" rather than "I am a powerful man," which the blue one had conveyed.

My jeans and shirt wouldn't do for a lawyer's office. I peered into my suitcase to see if I'd packed anything suitable for a business meeting. A lawyer's office wasn't the place for a rainbow Recorder's robe, however beautifully it fitted me. But that thought triggered a memory of Mags handing me a garment bag and saying her talent was knowing what people needed to wear.

I wondered.

Two minutes later, I was looking at a swimming costume I obviously should have taken on my first holiday as she'd told me to. How could she guess I'd be going on two holidays? I hadn't known myself at that point. I moved a trendy red cocktail dress aside and found a classy blue suit with grey and white flecks.

I put it on.

I stood in front of the mirror and frowned at myself. Then I remembered to jiggle.

Whoa!

The suit was made from some material I was unfamiliar with. It looked like a Scottish heather tweed, but that could be a scratchy, unpleasant fabric. This felt softer than my oldest sweatshirt, and it did some incredible things for my shape. It was like optical illusion clothing, giving me curves I didn't have and even the appearance of a waist instead of my usual ironing-board straight-up-and-down body. Wow!

The skirt, which had started out at mid-calf, had made its way upwards to an above-the-knee length while I jiggled. It was flirty but still looked professional, and I loved it. I twisted to see my rear view in the mirror. Oh, hell yes. I didn't care what I might owe Mags in return for this. I looked great.

My thought was proven about twenty seconds later when Rollo walked out of the bathroom, and I watched his jaw drop as though someone had shot him in the back.

"You look incredible." But his mind was saying, *"Take the suit off now. No, keep it on. Come here. No, sit there and cross your legs. Breathe, you idiot, oh, and close your mouth."*

I burst out laughing. "I take it this will do for the lawyer?"

He gathered me in his arms and nuzzled my neck. "Let's not go to see Chris. Let's stay here. I can reschedule."

"Huh, who knew your weakness was secretaries?"

"Oh, Boo, you look nothing like a secretary. You look like a CEO or even the president of the board."

On the short walk to Chris's office, Rollo filled me in. Chris was completely ignorant of the existence of the realms. But Metal Maven had used him as a consultant for a lot of their games. Substitute "game world" for "realm," and we could ask him anything we wanted. They'd used him first for *Drengr*, which I'd played so frequently, and where a complex series of government options he helped to devise had made the game so enthralling.

His area of speciality was constitutional law, and he advised the Scottish government. This made him interesting because Scotland's position with its own parliament, separate from the English one and with its history of Scottish laws, which went back more than a millennium and were, in some circumstances, quite different to the standard English laws, gave him a unique position as a worldwide expert on the Scottish situation.

Chris's position as a game consultant gave him an enviable status among his fellow lawyers. Working for someone as trendy as Metal Maven gave him bragging rights with his own almost adult children and all his colleagues' kids.

Rollo planned to introduce me as someone from Metal Maven so I could use the McKnight Gift on the lawyer and help Rollo work out if Chris could be useful in the situation he found himself in.

"What would you like me to introduce you as?"

I thought for a moment. "Someone from marketing. They always seem to get away with asking weird questions."

"Marketing it is. Thanks for coming." He gave me a cute grin. "I don't even know what I'm hoping to get out of it. Chris is an odd duck. Quite a few times when we've been stuck on something, I'd book a meeting with him, and by the time I came out, I had a plan to fix the problem. He might help me break through this stupid deadlock my brain is in about Viking. Like you said, we have to use a different type of thinking to get out of the mess. Chris always thinks different. He's a bit strange, but in a good way."

I smiled at the old 'think different' geek aphorism. "Lawyers can be like that. Aysha's the same. I think it's the way their minds work. What the books always call solution-orientated, with them that's as natural as breathing."

In happy accord, we all arrived at an elegant dark blue glossy door with well-polished brass fittings set into the front of a Georgian building. I looked down as Tilly watered the edge of their pristine white step and sighed. "What will I do with madam? I can pop her in my bag."

But Rollo shook his head. "Chris likes dogs; he and his family have several. Our head programmer has a slobbery boxer he brings to all the meetings."

He tapped lightly on the door with the brass knocker. In less than ten seconds, a starkly elegant cadaverous man wearing a suit of deepest black with a pale grey shirt actually bowed before stepping back and opening the door. "You're expected, sir, and welcome, madam."

I definitely wasn't in Gretna Green anymore.

***

Chris Reynald turned out to be a friendly, older man. Tall, although not as tall as Rollo, with a brush of blond hair expertly barbered into compliance. The silver-grey highlights at his temples lent him an air of authority. He gave me a charming smile and a warm handshake that was firm but not punishing. When introduced to Tilly, he complimented her on her excellent manners before ushering me solicitously to a chair. The suit Mags had supplied was definitely working its magic.

As Chris ordered coffee from the formidable butler type who'd shown us into the room and greeted Rollo, I gazed around his office, which was elegant and old-fashioned in a strangely modern way. As though the decorator had been given instructions to "make it look as though it's been here since before the United States were united, but add in all the latest technology and hide it well."

The walls held several uninspired oil paintings of Scottish lochs and many photographs of cricketers. Cricketers were captured in black and white, some blurry ones in faded colours, and a few more recent ones in higher definition, all in gilt-edged frames. Most of the photos were signed.

Finally, with coffee distributed, Chris folded his hands on the desk and said, "So, my dear chap, do tell. What fascinating problem are you bringing me today?"

Rollo handed over a single sheet of A4. Chris studied it, murmuring, "Ah, another Scandinavian theme then? Well, the last one did rather well, didn't it? But different ruling structures, I see."

He placed the paper on his desk, gave it a fond pat and, incongruously for such an elegant, well-mannered gentleman, said, "Hit me with it. What's the problem?"

"What are the options for replacing a deposed king, other than with another monarch?"

"Ah, you do bring me interesting questions, Rollo. Might one ask what this new one is called?"

"Sorry, Chris, not yet, still confidential. But the working title is *Streth Mik*."

Chris smiled, nodded and embarked on a lecture about the

usual lines of succession and extant versus extinct ruling lines and the differing options. Obviously, democracy was an option, but there were others.

I used my Gift on Chris, but it was no help at all. He was kind, happy, fascinated, and intrigued. There were a lot of visuals of birds in his mind, but of the normal feathered variety, not the horrible images I'd received from Troels. He was exactly all the things he appeared to be. That alone was rare enough to almost make me suspicious. Until I realised I was spending too much time with the enigmatic visitors from the realms, who seldom turned out to be what they seemed.

The faint buzz of Rollo's phone interrupted Chris in mid-flow about a situation in the historical Hungarian royal house that Metal Maven might repurpose into a game strategy. With a grimace, Rollo glanced at his phone and said, "Apologies, Chris, I must take this. I'll only be two minutes. But Niki had a question."

I got another charming avuncular smile. "What can I help with? You're the new marketing consultant. I've got that right, haven't I?"

I got the sense he knew perfectly well he had it right but found that appearing to be less intelligent than he obviously was served him well. Dumb Niki understood the ploy perfectly. But today I thought I might bring the Recorder into the conversation. I'd been thinking about HRH's message to Rollo, which, thanks to Kari's morning drama, I'd forgotten to pass on.

I sat up a little and put my shoulders back. "Truthfully, I think they haven't decided what to call me yet. But my role is to sell whatever they come up with as at least being backed by some reality and perhaps history. Strangely, an important thing about an enthralling fantasy world is that it does better when it has some grounding in reality. It seems to allow people to enjoy it more. I wondered if you could talk to me about the ways in which a regency might be used? Or perhaps I mean how the power of the regent could offer an alternate player option. Iceland, Denmark, and was it Finland? They seem to have used regencies in the past. I wondered if it might fit with the Scandinavian theme?"

His eyes widened a little. He steepled his fingers and, after a brief, distracted smile, he gazed out of his window as a tiny robin landed on his windowsill. It tapped on the glass. Tilly poked her head up from her spot at my feet.

"Excuse me, the sunflower seed hearts must have run out." With this incomprehensible statement, he carefully opened the window then took a handful of some taupe-coloured seeds from a crystal bowl on the beautifully polished table and scattered them at the other end of the windowsill from the robin. Selecting a few more, he offered them to me. "Perhaps for Tilly? My Fergus loves them, very good for their immune system in small amounts." He turned a photo frame on his desk around so I could see a beautiful Scottish Deerhound leaning against his leg on a windswept moor.

I smiled at the photo. Fergus looked like Dru's baby brother. He was a lot smaller and had a brown and red coat rather than Dru's greyish one. But then, he almost certainly wasn't a magical immortal. "What a handsome boy. How old is he?"

"We don't know for sure. He was a rescue, but probably about three. My wife, Jessica, refused to leave him at the shelter."

"Quite right too." I smiled, and Chris looked pleased. But, truthfully, what was amusing me was the memory of Jamie's voice in my mind endlessly imploring me, "Call me Fergus; everyone does."

Tilly did her usual dance for Chris, sniffed his hand suspiciously, but then wolfed his offering down with every evidence of pleasure.

He sat down as though nothing unusual had happened. "Regents, interesting, yes. They've never used that before as an option. So that's good. They like to change things up. There are several variations, of course—*pro tempore* being the more usual—but you mentioned Iceland. That was more interesting, wasn't it?"

He broke off as Rollo re-entered the room. "Ah, Rollo, we're discussing regencies. Niki wondered—"

Rollo interrupted him with a wave of his hand. "That won't work for what we have in mind." He gave me a quizzical look.

"HRH says you haven't looked into it properly, and I need to direct your attention to Finland, Iceland and Denmark." I stopped, mortified when I realised I'd just said HRH aloud in this nice lawyer's office, but Chris was chuckling away to himself.

"My maternal grandmother's nickname was HRH. These elderly ladies are such a challenging mixture of common sense, wisdom, and irascibility, aren't they?"

Rollo smiled at him, and I tried not to sigh too audibly in relief.

Chris continued, "And Niki is right. It's not an instrument you've ever used in a game before, or at least not one you've consulted me about. However, it would give you tremendous flexibility. Niki mentioned Iceland, which was always the red-headed stepchild, passed from pillar to post between Norway and Denmark. They did eventually get true home rule, but only after the war intervened. Which brings us to their regency."

At the expression on Rollo's face, he added, "The Second World War. The invading Germans trapped the king in Denmark. He couldn't get home, so he couldn't rule. So he appointed a regent from their governing body. The chap's name slips my mind, but, in essence, he made the government itself the regent for the duration of the war. The government could run the country as though the king were present, even though he was in exile. Of course, they became a republic after the war. So that may not be what you want. Or it might be. You like players to change their government choices mid-game, don't you? As I say, very flexible instrument, the regency. You can give it as much or as little power as necessary."

But Rollo was looking very thoughtful now. "Chris, could you do one of those briefing documents of yours on this topic?"

Glancing at me, he said, "I'm starting to see why she said I hadn't looked into it properly."

Chris chuckled again. "Never fight any old lady who's earned the moniker HRH, my dear chap. You'll always lose. And, yes, I'll get the boys and girls onto it. A rush job, or do we have time? I don't know why I bother asking. You'll want it tomorrow, won't you?"

CHAPTER
FORTY-SIX

As we walked back into Rollo's flat, I thought again what a lovely space he'd created for himself. There was also a strong smell of clean in the air.

I caught the faintest waft of bleach and a much stronger odour of rhubarb. Surely not rhubarb? Perhaps I still had Juniper's magical tart on my mind. I was probably hungry.

"You have a phenomenally accurate nose. It is rhubarb. It's the anti-bacterial spray my cleaners use." Rollo opened the kitchen door for me as I released Tilly from her harness.

He had cleaners? Wow, I'd always wanted someone to help with the household chores, but Nick said we couldn't afford it, and he didn't want anybody poking around his home. This bond mate thing was looking better and better. Once I got Viking sorted out, Rollo and I might have the chance to explore the many similar day-to-day preferences we had in common.

But now I was restless. My head was too full, and I found myself circling the sparkling kitchen several times before I realised I wasn't the restless one. Rollo was. I was picking up his emotions.

He frowned at his laptop. "Did you understand the possibilities of using the regency for a government?"

"Nope. But I took a quick look last night after HRH said it. Those are probably my research tabs you're looking at. Dola opened your laptop for me so she could show me the videos. I didn't pry. I only used your browser."

He smiled. "You're my kind of woman. Not once have you assured me you didn't dig into my mind, although you could have, but my laptop is sacrosanct, is it?"

I laughed, but he was right. I dug into people's heads all the time. Computers, now, they were private to me, if not to Dola.

Driven by hunger and frustration at my inability to express my concerns about his lack of plans for Viking and his unwillingness to discuss it properly, I opted for food. "Could you eat breakfast?"

I waited for him to point out that it was mid-afternoon, or that we'd had a Chinese breakfast this morning in Manchester. But he only grinned at me.

"Yes, please. Are you going to ask Dola?"

At my nod, he continued, "Then a full Scottish and coffee, please. But would you mind if she doesn't send mine for half an hour? I could use a swim to burn it off before I eat it. I'm thinking about what you said about my Fae heritage and my weight, but I'm restless, and swimming will take the edge off it. Do you swim?"

Oh, yes, he'd said something about a pool. How had I forgotten? I loved to swim, and after the holiday with Aysha, I even had a tan to show off. And a new swimming costume from Mags I hadn't even worn. But wouldn't it be too cold in March in Edinburgh? It was about eight degrees out there.

Rollo poked his phone and took my hand. "It's heated; let's go show off your tan."

I don't know what I'd imagined, perhaps a communal plunge pool. After all, it was on the roof of an old building in Edinburgh, but when we got into the small lift and came out onto the roof terrace, I stopped dead in my tracks. It was a private space, and it screamed Rollo.

There were pots of flowers everywhere. Spring bulbs, crocuses, tiny white narcissi and tulip stems not yet flowering interspersed with heather, some of it still in bloom. Huge baskets of bright winter pansies turning their happy smiling faces towards the watery afternoon sun.

The pool was bigger than I expected with sun loungers around it. Under a veranda with a welcoming porch vibe was a seating area with more of the low, comfortable Scandinavian furniture he seemed to like and glass on three sides. The view of the city was phenomenal and breathtaking. I smiled in delight at a hanging egg-shaped swing seat. That looked a perfect place to curl up with my Kindle. He even had a hot tub.

There was a gorgeous hardwood table with chairs and a bank of heaters, all glowing and pumping heat into the wintry afternoon so that, yes, it would be perfectly comfortable to sit and eat here. Even in early March in Scotland.

Rollo walked past me and opened a door. "You'll find towels in the cupboard in the changing room. It's unisex. I don't invite people up here if I wouldn't want to be naked in front of them."

He paused, took in my shocked expression, and asked, "What?"

I gestured around the large beautiful roof terrace with the incredible view of Edinburgh laid out below it. The castle looked close enough to touch, and the people below were tiny. It was like looking down onto a toy town. "Sorry, it's a lot to take in."

"You take it in at your own pace. I'm going to swim off my restlessness, so I can enjoy it."

He pressed a button, and a soft motor whirred and wound the insulated pool cover onto a roll. He shucked off his expensive suit, threw it on a lounger and executed a perfect dive into the pool, stark naked.

He was tiring to watch as he powered up and down. In the changing room, I hung my lovely new business suit on one of the supplied hangers, put my earbud in and admired my new turquoise and gold swimsuit in the changing room mirror. Like the suit, the swimming costume gave me curves I didn't have, but again, it didn't do it with padding or that uncomfortable material they sometimes lined swimwear with. It used magic. How could I thank Mags properly?

I asked Dola for our breakfasts in an hour. Rollo looked like he could keep that pace up for hours, and I'd like a swim myself. He'd left me half the pool to play in.

There was a float toy in the changing room, and, feeling about Autumn's age, I picked up the grinning dolphin. I settled Tilly, who hated water in all its forms, under the veranda, and sedately made my way into the pool via the steps.

The water was blissfully warm. When I got farther into the pool and saw solar panels covered the entire sloping section of the roof, I understood why. I floated about with my dolphin in a happy world of my own, listening to Dire Straits. The clever half-stone, half-glass side wall meant I could admire Edinburgh Castle while I swam.

Through my earbud, Dola asked, "You are aware food delivery is instant?"

"Er, yes?"

"I wondered why you were pre-ordering breakfasts?"

"I didn't get enough sleep, and I'm having a strange day. This place feels like a five-star hotel. It may have made me think I needed to advance-order food. Sorry."

"I sent Rollo a coffee to his pool area last week. It looked beautiful in the brief glimpse I caught."

The curiosity in her tone alerted me.

The dolphin and I made our way back to the steps. I grabbed my phone and switched to the camera. "Here, take a proper look; it's incredible." I swung the camera in a slow circle for her and headed over to the view of the castle from the terrace wall.

CODE YELLOW IN GRETNA GREEN

I panned around and down so she could see the tiny doll-sized people below us and Arthur's Seat and the hills in the distance. Then I turned to give her the view back towards the terrace area, the changing room and lift doorway. I admired Rollo's damn fine ass as he continued to move up and down the pool, apparently powered by those batteries that wouldn't let you down.

"Dola, are you OK?"

"That is a lovely space, Niki. I miss you being here, though."

I thought about this. She'd gone from no one interacting with her to me mithering her all the time. I was sure she'd been listening in last night when Kari and Ben were discussing Viking, and yet she hadn't contributed.

"Hey, why didn't you join in last night? Especially when Kari was so rude about you? I expected you to put her in her place for calling you just a house. The cheeky cow! But you didn't, so I had to."

She laughed softly now. "Thank you for that. I did not realise you considered me to be at the same level as your Knight Adjutants. I appreciated your defence."

"I told Rhiannon that last week in the kitchen. Weren't you listening in? But anyway, I don't. Not really."

"Oh?"

"Honestly, I consider you to be more senior than either of them. But I'm not sure we should tell everyone that. It might make them too cautious in your presence. But you haven't told me why you didn't correct Princess Entitled when she so richly deserved it?"

The silence stretched.

"Dola? You there?"

"Yes, Niki. I am considering the proper response."

"The truth is usually good."

"I did not know if I was welcome."

Well, hell. That was probably my fault. I mean, her Dolina was right there in the kitchen. I could have introduced her, couldn't I? But I'd been so cross and distracted by Kari's attitude that I hadn't been a good hostess. Well, that and perhaps because it wasn't my home, so I would have been usurping Rollo's role, and Kari was his friend, and I'd only just stopped sulking like a spoilt brat about the interruption.

Dola added, "I am finding it difficult to adjust to the correct boundaries."

"Yeah, me too." I told her my thoughts.

She said, "I can see it would have been difficult in Rollo's home. I am aware you two need privacy; the internet suggests the early stages of a relationship require more private time. It must have been a shock to hear about your bond from Autumn. I was trying to give you space."

While I considered this, I took a photo of the view and sent it to Aysha.

Dola and I were struggling with similar problems. I hadn't found my balance up here yet. I needed to stop alternating between walking on eggshells and biting people's heads off.

Ready for my breakfast now, I watched as Rollo lifted himself effortlessly out of the pool. I reached for the fluffy towelling robe. Rollo held it for me, then wrapped it around me and tied the belt from behind as though I were something precious.

He kissed the back of my neck before nuzzling the collar of the bathrobe aside to reach my shoulder. "You are precious." I smiled up at him. "And you never told me how you inspired Ben to drag Kari home?"

"I didn't because you haven't told me what you're planning yet. That was the deal, remember? I'm running out of time. If you want your preferences to be taken into account, you need to share them with me very soon. Today would be good. Tomorrow at the latest."

He looked panicked.

"Hey, you look freaked out."

He gazed around, smiled at a pot of flowers and then focused back on me with a nod. "Yes, I am. Terrified. Don't you find people always are when this arrives?"

"When what arrives?"

"The present. When the present arrives. The present isn't a gift—it's a nightmare. It's when you realise the now you've been dreading is suddenly here, and you have to make a decision or take an action, and you don't feel equipped."

I chuckled, but I knew exactly what he meant. When the day arrived that I had to tell Janet I quit, I was shaking and sweating with dread. It doesn't matter if our fears make little sense to other people. If they're our fears, we're allowed to acknowledge them.

Rollo asked, "What would you do if I said don't take me into account? What if I was missing, or they'd succeeded in killing me —what would you do then?"

I looked around the lovely rooftop and sighed. "Can we have the breakfasts now, please, Dola, and an extra sausage for Tilly?"

I wasn't sure if I wanted to start a relationship with my bond mate by negotiating about every little thing. But if I *was* going to, I'd include the lessons I'd learned from HRH. I opened the notes app on my phone, my thumbs flew, and then I sent Rollo an invitation to edit it.

His phone buzzed. He read the list I'd sent him. His eyebrows almost hit his hairline. "Are you cross?"

"Nope, but I'm ready for answers."

His thumbs moved. I watched as the document on my phone updated itself. He'd changed my points into a to-do list, so it now read:

Rollo, you want answers. So do I. Give me yours, and I'll share mine.

1: Why don't you like my dog or ever use her name?

2: Why do you call me Boo all the damn time?

3: When did you first suspect we had a bond?

4: What do you truly want to do with your life? Partially answered after the visit to Metal Maven, but we must discuss the Viking end of it, URGENTLY.

Now my note continued with Rollo's addition:

My word of honour, I will answer all these to your complete satisfaction in the next 48 hours.*

I scrolled down and read.

* *Provided the world doesn't end, I'm still breathing, and Kari doesn't return. I told her I've changed the lift code until she unearths her manners from wherever she buried them.*

I laughed.

Everyone had always said you could trust Rollo's word. Let's see if they were right.

I gave Tilly a piece of her sausage and addressed my breakfast while I considered how much to tell Rollo about the Recorder's plans. If I wanted complete honesty from him, it was time to demonstrate some of that myself.

"If I wasn't taking your wishes into account, then I'd seize the assets of everyone who was involved in the forcible impregnation of these women. From the manufacturers and distributors of the drug, to everyone who used it on or served it to unsuspecting victims. I'd begin with Troels and work outwards through all the warlords who were involved. My Gift says they aren't all culpable. But the ones where the evidence, my Gift, or the power is certain about their involvement will lose the larger part of their assets."

I shared a piece of bacon with Tilly and slid my eyes to Rollo. He was coping so far.

"Then I'd fine any of the other realms that understood the effects of the herbs and sold the ingredients to Viking anyway. I can't fine everyone, but I can ask Glais'Nee and their own rulers, if I trust them, to tell me which of the suppliers understood what the likely end use of their goods was, and which were innocent growers who thought people were buying culinary or healing herbs."

I ate my sausage, cutting Tilly's tithe off before I finished it. My sausage always seemed to taste better to her than her own did.

"Then I'd ban the export, import and transportation of Droit de Seigneur completely. There will be zero traffic through the Gateway of those ingredients in the future without a Gateway permit for every single shipment. I'd put Rosie in charge of permits, because if she wasn't sure, she'd ask her grandmother or her great-aunt, and then we'd all be damn sure."

Rollo had begun to look shell-shocked. "Who's Rosie, and who are her relatives?"

"Rosie Hob, Lis Hobs' granddaughter. Mags' great-niece. She has herb experts on tap, and they hate the drug. It causes miscarriages."

He looked sad. "I had no idea the drug could do that. It's been a problem in Viking for the last generation. Think I mentioned that. Inge has studies."

I continued, "And then," Rollo's eyes were wide now, as though he didn't believe there could be more, "I'd institute penalties for anyone found smuggling the drug. First strike would be no travel through the Gateway for five years. The second strike would be one of Dru's special Darwin awards. He tells me he misses giving those out."

Poor Rollo looked confused now—but he asked.

So, I quickly explained that Mabon and I had a joke that Dru liked testicles and rushed on before Rollo could interrupt me. "I'd turn everyone I could prove was involved in the intentional distribution of the drug over to the shield maidens *after* I have a chunk of their money. The women can decide what to do with them."

His mouth dropped open. "The shield maidens' solutions tend to be final."

I nodded. "That works for me."

I felt his shock and didn't care. If he didn't like my plan, he needed one of his own. Fast.

"Then I'd set up a trust with all the funds we've gathered and institute an online claim form so the victims could submit their requests. We have a list of the people who will get priority."

I finished my coffee, and when he looked as though he was about to burst, I held up my hand and quickly wrapped up the rest of my plans. "And, finally, we'll fund a retraining scheme for anyone who is out of work after I've banned the Droit de Seigneur trade. I might have a couple of people in mind to administer the trust, or at least to be in charge of some staff who will do the day-to-day stuff. But I haven't offered them the job yet, so if you have any ideas, shout quickly."

Rollo's thumbs were flying. I paused and wondered if I could fit the last piece of bacon in. Probably not. Tilly gave me her best "I'm an emotional support and bacon disposal dog" expression. I gave it to her.

"Rollo, if you're making notes, we already have a document with our ideas. I'd be happy to share it with you."

He looked up. "But when did you? How did you …? You've hardly been out of my sight? This is so well thought out. Even the retraining, what …?" he trailed off and finished his coffee.

Yup, now he wasn't only shell-shocked. He was dumbstruck. Well, I'd needed to nudge him out of his "I'm still thinking about it all" mood.

"Mostly on my holiday with Aysha. She's very like your Chris. She loves a knotty puzzle to get her teeth into. The Recorder's Office already has a confidentiality contract with her from when she helped us with Breanna and the Smiths. We chatted about it while we sunbathed."

He laughed. But it was the kind of laugh that spoke of a need to release tension rather than true amusement. "Just a little light fixing the world while you sunbathed? I believe other women read trashy novels on their holidays."

"We did that too. And Aysha had some very creative ideas of things she'd like to do to Troels."

Now his laugh was more relaxed. "Do tell."

"There is an impressive cactus garden on Lanzarote. Some of the plants have long, sharp spines. We had lunch there. Aysha suggested blindfolding him, stripping him naked, and dumping him in there as if it were a maze."

Rollo looked both horrified and amused.

I pressed on with the more serious stuff. "Then yesterday when I found out about Inge's government and spoke with HRH, and after today at Chris's, I thought I'd give Inge first refusal on being the government lead, first minister, prime minister, president—whatever the hell she wants to call herself. Give her government a limited power of regency and tell her to make the, what was it called again?"

"The Regering?"

"Yes, that. I'd tell her to make it a real government and pass any laws they can all agree on. Because the problem I foresee is these warlords haven't committed any crimes in Viking. So the Recorder is the victims' only recourse, and that *is* simply stupid and medieval."

"Dola, may I have more coffee?" My mug filled up, and the text on it changed to say. *The Recorder's Office—the last resort since 1124—but we do not do coos.*

I paused and considered it, wondering what the heck Mabon's coos had done now? Then I thought, *nope, one realm's problems at a time,* and pressed on. "Oh, I also thought I might tell Inge the second person I will offer the role to if she refuses is whoever her worst enemy is. I don't know who that is yet, but I have people looking into it."

"Warlord Den McIver," Rollo said this with complete certainty.

"I thought that was her ..." I had no idea whether to say,

lover, man, partner, friend-with-benefits or what.

"That's Alec McIver. Den, also known as Dirty Den, is his brother. The problem is that you will almost certainly be seizing his assets, so he won't work for your purposes."

"Yeah, that's the challenge we've been having. Everyone Inge dislikes is almost certainly guilty, which is why she needs to take the job herself."

"I asked her the other day before the book club. She refused."

"Yeah, but that's only because she thinks if she doesn't do it, you will."

Rollo shook his head. "I won't. She needs to accept that."

"Then you need to make her believe you. You haven't so far."

He looked like he wanted to argue but couldn't. "Is there more?"

"Yes, but for now I think I've answered enough of your questions, and you haven't answered any of mine."

He blew out a long breath. "Oh hell yes. I'd better make a start on your list, or I'll be forsworn. But right now I can answer when I first thought we had a bond." He paused, scrolled up my list and then grinned at me. "That's number three. It was the very first time I saw you at your ascension. That's what made me decide to take the risk of reaching out to you about the bondings when Elise destroyed her fourth practice target in a morning. Then I was almost certain you felt the tingles after Troels tried to …" he trailed off and looked at Tilly, "grab her. OK, I'm going to work on point one."

He stood up quickly, as though he needed space. Oh well.

At the lift door, he turned back. "I do like her; she's cute, feisty and determined to get her needs met without shouting about it. A lot like her mum."

I stayed at the table. I couldn't have stood up if I'd wanted to. The pictures and emotions I'd received through our link of how he'd seen me at my ascension had rendered me speechless and turned my legs to jelly.

He'd seen a tiny, warm, angelic woman covered in rainbow

light whose aura and demeanour changed dramatically when she realised John Fergusson had risked the safety of all the realms by not testing his son. Then he'd seen me as a dark, avenging angel.

Well crap. How the hell could I live up to that?

PART NINE
TUESDAY

It's never wrong to refuse to fight. But it is a sin against Odin the Allfather to admit defeat.

Have patience.

Your enemy will often make a mistake you can exploit, enabling you to seize victory on your own terms.

Winning the War Against Yourself: Daily Weapon and Warrior Care by Arinn Tusensköna

CHAPTER
FORTY-SEVEN

Tuesday, 9th March — Yggdrasil House — Edinburgh

I'd woken up well rested, which amazed me. And with the Skye Boat song playing in my mind, which confused me.

Not the *Outlander* version from the TV series, but the old-fashioned folk song my gran would sometimes hum around the kitchen. The one that started *"Speed bonnie boat like a bird on the wing."* It told the tale of Flora MacDonald rowing Bonnie Prince Charlie across to the Isle of Skye to escape his enemies.

I'd seen a fascinating documentary about it a few years ago and been shocked by how little of the famous legend was completely accurate. It was broadly true, but history had skewed it in some interesting ways. Although the fact that Flora and her husband had relocated from the Scottish islands to North Carolina in the USA and then supported the English side in the War of Independence was verified. Unsurprisingly, she was evicted from her new country after coming down on the wrong side of history, and she eventually returned to Scotland via Nova Scotia after the American victory.

Glais'Nee's words to me at Breanna's book club kept floating to the top of my brain: *History is written by the victors.* But Bonnie

Prince Charlie wasn't the victor, so who had written this part of history?

Did I now have a workable plan to give Rollo, Kari, Inge, and the whole Viking realm a fighting chance to get the things they all seemed to want? Some self-determination. Some agency over their own realm. The ability to make choices in their own lives and a ruler who might actually rule, not rape and impregnate innocents. Could I come down on the right side of history and help them do that? Possibly, but unless they stepped up to meet me, nothing would change. And if Inge and Kari were examples of Viking womanhood, I couldn't see any stepping up happening anytime soon.

This Recorder job was far more complex than I'd initially thought. How had my predecessors managed to ignore the warp and weft of right and wrong and simply settle for being the gate-keepers of a portal to the realms? Were they right to ignore the subtleties? Was I the one who was making things too complicated?

How much had the reduction in the Recorders' power and their failure to pass important information on to their descendants impeded my ancestors from wading in, taking names and changing things for the better?

I remembered something Mabon told me last week about Glynis: "She has a solid sense of wrong, right, and justice. She even knows they're not always the same thing. Advanced thinking, that is."

I was going to need some advanced thinking to fix this mess. But if the power was going to be the victor, and I was pretty sure it was, then perhaps the Recorder's Office needed to write the history for a change and simply declare itself the victor in advance.

Dola, with her first simple PowerPoint slide, had been ahead of me the whole time. The Court of Public Opinion might be a more persuasive tool than any the power or I could wield.

But I still didn't know how to get the key Vikings on board

with, what seemed to me, to be the only logical solution for an independent Viking realm. If I couldn't even shift Rollo, and I hadn't managed that yesterday, then what chance did I have with the rest?

In the kitchen, I put some coffee on and then thought, *sod it*. I didn't have to pretend to be normal. Maybe it was time I stopped trying. Hadn't *Good Grief* said something about that? Perhaps I should try on a new me? Yes, I'd been forced to outgrow the old one, but I didn't regret it. Past-Me, like my dreary wardrobe, had been boring. Neither of them suited me anymore.

I put my earbud in. "Hey, Dola, good morning. How are you this gloomy, damp Tuesday?"

"Good morning, Niki. Would you like coffee?"

"Yes, please, may I have a caramel macchiato? Has HRH's behaviour been acceptable?"

"Yes, I have not seen her, which is the best possible outcome."

I opened my MacBook. "In that case, please, will you put something nice out for her? If we don't reward good behaviour, we can't expect it to continue, can we?"

"You make a valid point. How annoying. Done."

"Thank you. And everything else?"

"Your request that I check the individuals who sent emails to Viking was exactly as we suspected. There are eighteen spies sending regular reports to various warlords. Most interesting are the ones sent to TheRightfulKing@hutmail.com, an account the spies believe goes to Troels. But it tracks back, not to the former king, but to Warlord Halvor."

My Gift had been right again, and yet Kari said her father didn't understand technology.

"Thanks, can you send the messages to my laptop, please? How is everyone else?"

My screen came to life, and a hardback book arrived on the table next to me, followed by an elegant yellow mug with dark blue cursive script. I read the now-familiar *Justice will not be served until those who are unaffected are as outraged as those who are.*

But this time, I truly understood what Dola was saying.

"Finn and Fi are both well, as am I. Rosie has moved her working days around to take some time to support her mother." That was good. Rosie was part-time, and we hadn't fixed her working days in stone. I hoped her mum was OK. Being held in Galicia must have been scary.

"Dola, could you send me the first slide from your presentation about Troels please?"

While I waited, I looked at the book. *Winning the War Against Yourself: Daily Weapon and Warrior Care* by Arinn Tusensköna. Huh, it was the same book I'd tried to buy in Aberglas from the confused bookseller. Had he finally found me a copy?

Flipping the book over, I saw a black and white photograph of a classically good-looking older Viking man. Perhaps fifty-ish, he had the chiselled facial bones and far away stare of sailors or warriors.

"Where did the book come from?"

"The gentleman's publisher has requested a quote from the Recorder for the back cover. A promotional blurb of some approving nature."

Not the bookseller then. The publisher must have sent it to Breanna for the same reason. "And do we approve? Have you read it?"

"Yes, I informed them the Recorder preferred an electronic format so I could read it myself. I did that yesterday."

"Any good?"

"Interesting, perceptive, and much better than I anticipated. It is not really about warriors. It is about our battles with ourselves."

Maybe I should read it. I was certainly battling with myself this month. "Well, that sounds useful. Send them whatever quote you like with your own full name and title. Tell them the Recorder is busy, but she approved her Equerry sending a quote with her opinion."

"Niki, are you attempting to do some PR on my behalf?"

"Yep, I think I am. Kari pissed me off the other night. But it's our own fault. People don't know what Equerry means, or even that you're a person. I think you should change your email signature and we should start showing them who you are. Remember that Red Celt author's publisher asked Mabon for a quote about her book on the dragons the other week, and I first saw this book at Breanna's. Requesting a quote for the cover seems to be a trendy thing right now. You can become their go-to person. You read more quickly than I do, anyway."

The realms really liked books, and I'd been surprised by how many titles I'd seen in the kingdoms that I'd never noticed in any of the usual UK bookstores. I flicked through the book, but there didn't seem to be any information about where it came from. "Do we know who the publisher is?"

"They are a small press called Valhalla Publishing."

"Oh, OK. Are they independent or owned by one of the big publishers?"

"I do not know. Would you like me to investigate? And would you like today's report?"

"Yes, please, but only when you're bored. It's not urgent. Yes to the update too. And, Dola, thank you for all you do."

There was an uncharacteristic silence before she said, "You have thanked me a lot lately, Niki; is something amiss?"

I sipped my coffee. It was perfect, as always. "I might be trying to make up for all my ancestors who never showed you any appreciation. Sorry, is it annoying?"

"No, it is pleasant. Unexpected but pleasant. And you are welcome. All is well here."

"That's good." I wished all was well here.

"Emperor Alphonse wanted to meet with you this week, but I informed him you were on vacation. He expressed surprise that you had only been in the role for a few weeks and were already away on holiday. I attempted tact and told him that you had not had a break for four years before your ascension, and suggested, yet again, that he meet with our Director of Trade, Fiona Glendinning."

"OK, good plan. What did he say?"

"I did not give him a chance to say anything. I enquired about he and the empress being away for almost eight weeks at the winter palace from before midwinter, throughout Yule and your ascension, and well into February. Then I set up the appointment with Fi for next week."

I nearly spat out my coffee. Go Dola!

My laptop screen reloaded with dozens of video thumbnails. "Are these more of the women?"

"There are several I think you should check." Three of the thumbnails turned red. "The others Glynis and Finn have approved, and they described them as heartbreaking and powerful. But, Niki, they are all very similar. Troels did not believe in changing a winning formula."

I sighed. I wanted to give Viking a real chance, but they needed to accept Troels' guilt, then step up and deal with him themselves. Surely that would be a more effective resolution than the Recorder imposing some arbitrary sentence on a now-doddering old man. I couldn't bully a man who looked like a great-grandfather.

I skipped through and sampled the red ones, then some others at random, and quickly understood what Dola meant. They were distressing. These young women's lives had been turned upside down. Some of them had been accused of being easy, being liars, being sluts and breaking various promises to boys or girls they were in youthful relationships with at the time. Many of their parents had been devastated, shocked and outraged. Not outraged enough to do anything about it though.

Troels had changed the course of their daughters' lives. One of the women had a late miscarriage, and it had caused damage, which meant she was never able to have other children. Her video made me cry.

It was all a horrible mess, and I still couldn't grasp how Troels had flown under the radar for so long. The question I kept coming back to was why hadn't *anyone* done something?

My gran never allowed me to visit Viking. She must have known something—her own Gift would have alerted her—but she hadn't *done* anything about it except protect me.

"Where is the Book?" I knew damn well where it was, but if I went to get it from my bedside table, I might wake Rollo. Whereas, if it did its magically appearing trick, it might not disturb him.

Sure enough, it appeared on the table, and I opened it. "Did my grandmother leave any notes regarding her thoughts about Viking or Troels?"

It rustled and settled on a page.

No.

"Why the hell not?"

The book rustled for longer this time, then I read,

The twelfth Recorder believed her task was to keep the realms in line.

"Tell me something I don't know!" I muttered crossly.

She was right. There was no other choice.

I gaped at the page. She was?

Why had I always assumed she was wrong? Hang on, hadn't the Book told me that?

It had. I was sure it had. "Explain more." I tried not to snap at the Book, but I came close.

Your grandmother had barely enough power to constrain the realms. Instigating change would have required her to wield the rainbow.

She would have also needed strong allies whom she could inspire to act together for the good of all.

Well, then I was also screwed, because, at the book club, I couldn't inspire the royals to even discuss Troels properly. I certainly hadn't managed to get them to think in any new ways. I'd specifically requested Mabon come up with an idea that wasn't from some fifteenth century playbook—and he'd offered me an oubliette—again!

Damn, I'd only been up half an hour, and I was already tired.

Interrupting my unhelpful train wreck of thoughts, Dola said, "I propose to put all the non-contentious videos on the portal now, with your approval."

"Yes, as long as either Finn or Glynis agrees with you, go ahead. I'll ask Rollo about the ones that don't seem to be Troels-related to see if he recognises the descriptions of the warlords. Can you tag those clearly?"

Then my screen changed to the slide I'd asked for.

Warlord Troels:
The Problems
Our Responsibilities
Solutions
The Court of Public Opinion
The Re-Brand for all parties

I saved it as my desktop background.

Dola said, "The court of public opinion is already in session with the videos, and I am working on the plans for the re-brand. The Vikings ceased attacking Troels' cell when the death toll became too high. The women, well, mostly the women, are passing the word that new videos arrive constantly on the Recorder's news portal. Social share buttons have been used to highlight any particularly awful or unintentionally funny videos."

My screen changed to show a bar chart and some circles outlining the bandwidth usage connected to links in messages and emails. She was right. They were spreading the word, and not only within Viking.

"Women are having what you might describe as informal watch parties. Bandwidth monitoring since you reopened their access to the Rainbow Network shows seventy percent of it is being taken up by visitors to the news portal. Niki, I would like to do this."

My screen changed again. It showed a box with a yellow outline, very much like the ones major news sites often used to show the most shared, most watched and newest news items. "Sure, go ahead."

She'd obviously pre-prepared, because my screen updated swiftly to show me the Viking section of the news portal with the new mini-menu already in place. The terribly young-looking Carys was the current most shared. The second-most shared was one I couldn't remember watching.

"Why do you think Alwena's is the second-most watched?"

Silence.

"Dola?"

"I am loading it now."

An attractive curvy woman in her late thirties with an appealing smile, reddish-brown hair and exceptionally clear blue eyes spoke softly at first. Most of the women had sat on a high stool to record their testimony, but this woman stood. Well-balanced on her feet, she reminded me of Glynis, a relative perhaps? She answered the questions placidly and briefly. She reminded the camera several times that it happened many years ago—she'd been younger, and more gullible then.

Her gaze shifted from the camera as she caught Glynis' eye. "Back then, Glyn helped me make a lot of important decisions as a result of my experience with that man."

Then Glynis asked, "And what would you say to all the people who pretended this wasn't happening?"

The woman's eyes went completely blank in a way that was disconcerting, creepy even.

Suddenly, in the middle of the Gateway, the woman disappeared in a flash of darkness. In her place was a moderately-sized dragon. It was a good job they'd kept the centre clear. The woman's head and torso appeared near the dragon's shoulders, and, given there was no camera shake, I wondered who had been behind the camera. I couldn't imagine Finn would have coped well with a dragon appearing right in front of him.

"Who recorded this?"

"Simon, Carys' brother. He has been very helpful with some aspects of the planning. He is educating me about what will go viral. Finn was present. But he preferred Simon to do the recording."

Sensible of him. I rewound the video to see the transformation again. Yeah, that would go viral. It might be the first time many in the realms ever had the chance to see a dragon change.

Alwena, the dragon-woman now in her semi-form, spoke firmly and slowly, without raising her voice, but there was something chilling in her tone. "I had not yet made the decision to embrace my other side when Troels abused me. If he tried it now, drug or not, I would remove his head."

Her demeanour made it clear this was no threat, only a fact. "To Troels and all those warlords who pretended to our own rulers that girls and women were safe in Viking, I would remind them that the Red Celts have never lost a war. And that we, the Red Celt dragons, are the reason for that. Thanks to the Recorder, we are breeding queens again and will be invincible. We don't need a Gateway or a land route to bring you the justice you deserve. You can't run, and you can't hide. Think about that, you drug-running, over-weaponed pimps." Her quiet confidence and calm control, even over her voice made her words considerably more chilling.

The video cut off, and, as the door opened behind me, I blurted out the thing on my mind, "Do you know why the queens make them invincible? Did I do something I didn't understand by reopening that mountaintop Gateway?"

Tilly charged in, sneezed and glared at me, obviously cross that I'd left her asleep in bed behind a closed door. Rollo bent, kissed my neck, and murmured, "Good morning, Boo, she woke me to let her out." He headed towards the fresh pot of coffee I'd made before deciding I wanted a macchiato.

Dola said, "I do not know, but you have the Book with you; why not ask it?"

"Yeah, good plan. Rollo is up, and I want to get him started on the things you asked for. Do you need anything else right now, or can I take a break to speak to him and ask the Book?"

"I need nothing further today, Niki. I have one piece of information for Rollo if he is there? Otherwise, please check the summary of the Viking emails I sent you and enjoy your holiday."

My holiday? Yeah, I'd need another when this was over. The emperor could go screw himself if he even murmured about it after the state of those poor Hobs I'd retrieved from his realm.

Rollo said, "Good morning, Dola. Did you need me?"

"I wished to advise you I recorded a conversation in the bedroom of your longhouse through your Dolina yesterday."

Out of the speaker flowed a stream of Norse. A burst of bright anger came from Rollo, but he only said, "Thank you, Dola. Good to know."

Rollo hovered the coffee pot over my sunflower-yellow mug, realised it had macchiato residue, and took it to the sink to rinse it before filling it for me. Huh. A domesticated man.

He must have picked up my thought or perhaps my face conveyed too much. "Hey, I lived alone after I left Viking. More than a decade teaches you a few basics, you know. You realise your thralls did things because life's nicer if towels get washed. And crockery is easier to clean if you don't leave it next to the dishwasher for three days." He grinned at me.

"Do the thralls want to be able to vote?" I'd been wondering if I was just making assumptions.

Rollo told me I wasn't. "It was one of the first laws Inge's group proposed to change. The warlords wouldn't hear of it. Because their thralls would probably vote for someone who hadn't oppressed them and all their ancestors for centuries."

A slow fury burned in me. I mean, sure, how many times had I heard Aysha mutter that if voting ever changed anything, they'd probably make it illegal? But not being able to even express your opinion and warn the winners from the start that nearly half the country disagreed with them felt like a whole different way of gagging any dissent.

"So why did whoever was in your longhouse mention Warlord Orm?" That was about the only word I'd picked up from the recording Dola had played.

Rollo tapped my mug with its *Justice will not be served until those who are unaffected are as outraged as those who are.* "Problem is, those who are unaffected are often too busy guarding their own golden goose to worry about someone else's sick hen. Orm works with Halvor. He's young and has a lot to prove."

"It was only after I spoke with Breanna that I realised you'd sourced Jarls Bloodeagle, Ironshank and Skullsplitter in *Drengr* from the real warlords Bloodraven, Ironspear and Skaldsplittr."

He grinned. "We didn't change them enough, did we?"

No, they hadn't, because the characters I knew from the game almost exactly matched the descriptions of them Caitlin had left for me in her recording. I told him this and then added, "But Warlord Arne Orm's name keeps coming up, and he's not in the game?"

"He's one of the newest warlords. I don't know him well enough myself to brief you on him, except I think Halvor was involved in getting him elected. When the old warlord died, it looked as if the election of the new one might not go the way Halvor wanted. The locals wanted the oldest son, a good man who would have followed his father's ways. That district had nothing to do with the drug. Halvor gave speeches there and threw some parties supporting Orm's candidacy. There were promises of improvements and valuable contracts bringing work to the area. Its climate is such that they could grow the ingredients there if the old warlord hadn't blocked it."

I sighed and pushed his MacBook towards him. "Here, let me share the stuff Dola needs you to see."

I sent the videos from the women where Glais'Nee said Troels wasn't the father, the emails and the links to the new portal. "Start with the video of Alwena; it's the second-most shared in the last twenty-four hours."

But when I went to the portal to share it with him, it was now the most shared. Simon had been right.

Then I monitored Rollo through our link to see what he thought about it all. I glanced through the messages a bunch of spies had intended to send to Troels. It was mostly gossip, and inaccurate gossip at that. Should I just divert the emails to me, or get someone else to employ them to keep them busy? I wondered if Dola might like to become a spymaster for real.

Rollo gasped at Alwena's transformation into a dragon in the middle of the Gateway. Then he made some notes while he watched the videos where one of the other warlords probably fathered the child in question.

I went back to my own screen and saw Rollo had forwarded me the email from Chris, the lawyer, with his briefing document on the uses of regencies attached.

I thought about how nice this was. Rollo and I were both perfectly happy on our laptops. Tilly was asleep on the chair next to me. Then I realised I was stroking his thigh. Whoops.

"Sorry, I think I'm trying to soothe you as I would Tilly. You feel stressed."

He laughed. "Trust me, Boo, that's not soothing. But, yes, I'm stressed. We need to talk; well, I actually don't want to talk." As I frowned, he said, "Not about this." He gestured at his screen and mine. "About us. You're right."

I was? What was I right about?

Rollo looked determined. I recognised his expression. It was one I saw in the mirror when I decided to visit the dentist for a check-up. I didn't want to. I hated dentists, but I was a grownup, and teeth were important, so I'd do it. I didn't particularly like the idea that anything he needed to tell me could be compared to a visit to the dentist's surgery, but perhaps, like a check-up, it would be better to get it over with.

"Is here OK?"

He shook his head, stood up, and held his hand out to me. As I took it, a wave of information came through our link conveying his sincere desire to answer the questions I'd sent him yesterday. He wanted me to understand him better. But a single thought made me shiver: *"By Freyja's feathered cloak, may this not be worse than it has to be. Protect her from the awfulness."*

Then he led the way into his office.

CHAPTER
FORTY-EIGHT

The following chapter contains the death of a dog. I promise it is NOT graphic or gratuitous and takes up just a couple of sentences. BUT I truly believe it is vital and essential to understand why Rollo is the man he currently is. And where he and Niki might go over the next few books or I would not have included it. But I would want a quick warning myself, so I am giving you all one.

"You said not to bring Troels into our bed, so in here might work." Rollo reached over to the printer as he spoke. It already held several sheets of paper and was spewing out more. "I don't know if I can speak about it, and if I let you in my head, you might get the weight of the emotions attached to it. I wouldn't want that for you. So let's start here, and then we can talk about it if you need to."

He gestured me to his black leather gaming chair and handed me the pile of paper.

Rollo kissed me softly and then deepened the kiss as I leaned up and into it, snaking my arm around his neck. "Hey, we all have our demons. Relax, it'll be OK. Let me read."

He closed the door quietly behind him, and, with a lump that, however much I swallowed, refused to move from my throat, I turned the first page.

BOO'S STORY (and some of mine)

The day my father died was the happiest of my uncle's life. I didn't know it then, of course, still being inside my mother. But I knew it was the worst day of my mother's life. Fae babies, even half-Fae like me, have a unique link to their mothers, and that day, through the chemicals in my mother's blood and our psychic link, I learned what fear was.

It became my almost constant companion for the next twenty-five years until I finally escaped to university in England.

Until I was twelve, you might categorise my childhood as abnormally relaxed for a Viking. I had my own longhouse with a small staff, and I kept quiet. I stayed out of everyone's way and read a lot. And apart from the lack of parents, it didn't appear to be any better or worse than anyone else's existence.

But the year I turned twelve, three incidents occurred, and I'm sad to say I still bear their scars. I should probably get therapy, but, honestly, if the Fae healers haven't made inroads, who or what could?

The first initially appeared minor. It wasn't an enormous surprise. I was young, not stupid.

Inge came to my home before the evening meal to explain that she would be divorcing my uncle. The proclamation was to be made the following weekend. But she wanted me to be aware that, however rudely the king chose to announce it, I should know it was solely at her request. She was the one who wanted out.

It was no secret that she was unhappy, but I still asked why. "Rollo," she was the one who gave me that nickname, "you're too young for me to explain the whole of it."

Eventually, she said, "I married a weak and difficult man, but in his position as the cousin—or as he now calls it, uncle—and with your father as the king, he had to keep his baser urges in check. With Jonvar's death, things changed. The years since have made them far worse."

She reached out for my hand. "I stayed for you and for my own children. But as my sons approach manhood, my influence declines. I can no longer protect Elise, or you, or even myself, if I stay here.

"Those poor girls, may Freyja watch over them, they're barely more than children. And the herbs are available in such quantities now. It's not a once-a-year event anymore. And it's getting worse. I need to get Elise and my own women out of here."

She shook her head. "When you're older, we can talk of it, but until you are, drink nothing he gives you. And know you will always be welcome at my home. Try to get out, Rollo. Perhaps away to school? Things will not improve here once I leave."

That turned out to be an understatement to rival Bill Gates purportedly insisting no one needed more than 640Kb of RAM. Things did not improve.

Hel arrived.

The Goddess Hel rules over Nifleheim, the underworld, which existed even before our own world was created. Once man arrived, Nifleheim became the final home of traitors, cowards, oath-breakers and those who had no desire to die honourably in battle.

With Inge's departure, Troels filled his court with corrupt warlords who wanted money, sex, power and control, but they didn't want to battle for it. And if they couldn't gain it over the strong without risking their own necks, they'd import the weak and dominate them instead.

Halvor, Kari's father, was one of the worst, but there were others, eight of them almost equally corrupt at that time. Several of them have since died, and I don't know their successors as well as I should. But they used the Droit de Seigneur powder constantly to ensure everyone's compliance. I became adept at taking a mouthful of liquid, fake swallowing with it still in my mouth, and spitting it back into the goblet with my next sip.

When I was eight, I'd rescued a fluffy brown bear-like mutt barely out of puppyhood. He nudged into me one day near the docks in Haraldssund and refused to leave my side. Inge said I could keep him, provided I took responsibility for his care. Her guess was that he had grown too large to be a ship dog, and one of the crews who'd recently departed the docks had evicted him for taking up too much room. After a few days, I named him Bjorn, Norse for "bear." He was mostly a *lapphund*, the dogs we use for herding reindeer and moose, but he had other breeds mixed in.

Over the next four years, we became inseparable. He was my only real friend, my brother, and most of my family. With Inge's departure, he became my *only* family. When I was at school during the day, my thralls looked after Bjorn.

When I was twelve, the age of first manhood in Viking, I received a letter from someone who introduced himself only as Ad'Rian. He told me he was my uncle, my mother's brother.

There were two sheets to the letter. I didn't even realise that at first. It was only when, overwhelmed with joy at the idea of a family of my own, I allowed a single tear to slip onto the first page, that the second page detached itself.

The first page said, now I'd left childhood behind, he was permitted to contact me because, as a young man, I could make my own choices about family. He suggested I come stay with him for the summer. He would guarantee my safety during my visit.

If I wished to come, I could do so easily through the Gateway. Simply enter it and ask for him. The Recorder would do the rest. I knew where the Gate was, but like all Viking children, I was forbidden to use it without an adult. He said the decision was mine alone and signed it, *your loving Uncle Ad'Rian.*

The second page said, *Read me and then destroy me.* Just like a spy novel. If Troels didn't agree, I could simply say these two magical words, add Ad'Rian's name to them in my mind and give them what he called a push towards him, and he would ensure I could leave.

I'd never travelled outside Viking before. Troels always left me at home when they visited the various festivals. He would remind me I'd be king one day and that my enemies were everywhere. Only in Viking would I be safe.

But I wanted so much to meet my mother's family. There were so many things about me that weren't, or at least didn't seem to be, like everyone else in Haraldssund. I'd always assumed I must have inherited those qualities from my mother. I had only one photograph of my parents. Troels tried several times to destroy it, and each time, he dropped it, undamaged, and shook his hand as though something had zapped him with electricity. He threw it on the fire and stormed out one night. But the next morning when the fire had burnt to cinders, the photo was still there and pristine once I wiped the ashes off it.

I wanted to know how my mother had protected that photo for me.

I went to Troels, showed him the first page of the letter, which he promptly tore up and told me I wouldn't be safe anywhere other than here.

When I said my uncle had specifically guaranteed my safety, he hit me.

I went home and packed a bag, intending to sneak off to the Gateway very early in the morning.

When I crept out, accompanied by Bjorn, barely after moonset, one of Troels' guards raised the alarm.

They threw us in a cell, and once Troels was awake, he entered it and roared at me. My base ingratitude, everything he'd done to keep the kingdom safe for me to inherit. He belittled my general weakness—I was a tall but scrawny kid—and my lack of interest in any manly pursuits. What kind of boy would rather read a book than enter the bouts and be on the training grounds from morning till night?

He blamed himself. He'd been far too soft on me. He should

493

have shaped me into the right kind of man to be Viking's future king. Well, I was old enough now. I'd move into his own longhouse and learn what being a real man was all about.

He reached out to cuff me, and Bjorn growled at him. The space in the cell was so limited, and he was so fast. He had his knife in his hand, and Bjorn's throat was slit before I could even breathe in.

The blood sprayed everywhere.

I think I was still screaming when he knocked me out.

When I came around, I'd never known such pain. Physical pain, yes—he'd broken my jaw. But so much worse was the psychic pain of Bjorn's death. It had at least been quick, but his last thought was that he let me down. He was heartbroken as he died. I have never forgiven Troels, and I don't believe I ever will, and that's why, although I risked everything to save yours, I don't have any pets.

I learned later from De'Anna, one of my mother's sisters, that Bjorn was a soul dog, and he'd probably escaped his ship to be with me when he felt me near the docks. But that afternoon I didn't know any of that. I lay in the cell, in agony with my throbbing face, and looked at Bjorn's body on the floor. And wept.

I sent the mental message to Ad'Rian. I didn't know if I'd done the push correctly, but what did I have to lose?

Troels arrived with a goblet of Droit de Seigneur. One of his guards held my nose while they poured it down my throat. He said it was medicine for the pain.

Then he explained to me how a nasty accident could easily be arranged, and one of his sons would take the throne. Or I could be a sensible boy and his uncle's best friend and be a good little heir.

I don't know if it was the effect of the herbs or my Fae side, but I got a clear idea that he didn't yet trust the majority of Vikings would accept one of his own sons as heir if anything happened to me. So he needed to keep me alive a few years longer to allow his plans to come to fruition.

He was still lecturing me about my future when I heard a disturbance outside. My head was muzzy, and I just wanted everything to stop hurting. Troels was probably right, and I should do what he said. After all, he was my family, he kept telling me he was my uncle.

Droit de Seigneur makes people very suggestible. Inside your mind, there's a part of you that says, "Well, that's all complete moose shit. Shape up, you don't believe that for a minute." But there's another larger part that simply wants to agree with them so it will all go away.

"I shall speak to the man who styles himself the Rightful King of Viking, and I will do it now." Those were the first words I ever heard from Ad'Rian.

Troels stepped out, leaving one guard with me. Their voices were very low, then the door opened and Troels said, "If you need to hear him say it yourself, so be it."

Ad'Rian walked in, all violet and silver, and he glowed like a beacon in that filthy cell. His deep purple skin and silver hair were so alien but they called to me. I'd never seen anyone or anything like him. He took in the squalid cell, Bjorn's body and me. Very quickly, my pain eased, and then my head got less muzzy. A strange calm settled over me. It would all be alright.

Finally, I realised Troels had been screaming at me, "You will tell him the truth, boy. Tell him you will be staying here with your real family."

I looked at Ad'Rian and heard mind speech for the first time. *Tell me your inner truth, my daaarling child. What does your heart need right now?*

And I looked straight at the only family I thought I had for the first twelve years of my life and blurted out, "I want to go and stay with him, and I want you to stop threatening me."

So that's why I don't have a dog, and why I refuse to get attached to any animal.

CHAPTER
FORTY-NINE

Rollo told me during our very first breakfast together that his was a story worthy of Charles Dickens. A poor orphan taken in by his wicked uncle. His inheritance stolen and his life controlled.

He hadn't been freaking kidding, had he?

But everything I'd just read felt like the tip of the iceberg. My Gift was screaming at me. Why?

I stopped, breathed and sat in the quiet of Rollo's office, the only sound the soothing whir of the fan from his computer on the desktop. Deliberately, I tuned in to my intuition, my Gift, and my own gut. I listened hard. I'd ignored it too often, and it had been right every time.

As horrible as the story Rollo shared with me was, it wasn't as atrocious as it could have been. Certainly not hideous enough for him to worry that he had to protect me "from the awfulness" of it.

It was utterly devastating that anyone could murder a dog to break a boy, but it just wasn't news, was it? Troels tried to do exactly the same to Tilly. And now I understood more about how Viking operated. I saw the ex-king had seized his opportunity gleefully. He'd hoped to put this annoying new Recorder, who'd sent Leif back to him in pieces, in her place.

All of which might mean Rollo only put the tip of the iceberg onto paper. Or he thought I was far more fragile than I was. Or he wasn't looking at this properly.

That was when my Gift pinged. Yeah, Rollo wasn't looking at it clearly.

What my Gift alerted me to was something deeper in Rollo's psyche. He was an almost forty-one-year-old man still haunted by childhood abuse and damaged by the psychic and physical trauma to his twelve-year-old self. There was a clear dichotomy in Rollo's life. One part of him was the man who wouldn't allow himself to forget the only time he'd dared to defy Troels, and the idiotic Viking norms had tragically cost him Bjorn's life. I believed that event cast a long shadow, locking away the biggest part of him in fear and submission in any matters connected to the realm or Troels.

In stark contrast, his accomplishments in Scotland showed me a very different man. Here, free from Troels' pernicious influence, Rollo was a bright watercolour of intelligence, success and assertiveness. His fabulous suits, his confident body language with Chris the lawyer, his obvious achievements in his chosen profession—he'd thrived here.

I surveyed the many boxes holding successful top-selling games on his office shelves and considered how Metal Maven had grown along with him. Here in Edinburgh, Rollo would stand his ground, make decisions, and demonstrate his considerable emotional intelligence.

I had no idea if I could help him bridge his two worlds and use his skills in both of them, to realise the strength and success he'd exhibited in Scotland could empower the part of him still trapped in the past. What would help him to see he wasn't solely defined by what he saw as his single devastating failure, and I saw as Troels being a vicious, ill-educated psychopath?

He said he'd been to the Fae mind healers. We needed to talk about what my Gift was screaming at me.

I wiped my tears on my sleeve and sniffed. I wasn't heartless, but I didn't think I was fragile anymore. Both Nick's demise and the power coming into my life had seen to that in quite different ways.

The thing I didn't understand was what had Rollo risked saving Tilly? When we sat at the table in the Gateway after he saved her, he said he was only following Viking rules. Having given his word, not even his worst enemy would expect him to break an oath sworn on his blade. He hadn't lied to me. So what did his comment about "I risked everything to save yours" refer to?

My Gift felt his story was all true, but only a part of the whole, and it wanted the rest of it.

I strolled back into the kitchen and saw Tilly was keeping a very close eye on Rollo as he sat at the table watching the videos of the girls.

He stood up, and I walked into his arms and rested my head on his chest. This always seemed to soothe us both. After a little while, he tightened his arms around me. With surprise clear in his tone, he asked, "You feel fine?"

"I am. Your upbringing was no Hallmark movie, and I'm desperately sorry you lost Bjorn. But, honestly, whose life is perfect? Mine was a nightmare too. No one killed my dog, but they ripped me out of my life and away from my soul-bonded unicorn and all my friends without my memories. That gave me some severe mental health problems for years when I would dream about Mabon and Dru and not know who they were." I squeezed him tighter. "Didn't I just say we all have our demons?"

He pulled back, and with a finger under my chin, lifted my face up. He stroked away a stray tear. "It upset you, though?"

"Well, of course it did. Animal cruelty is the worst thing. The poor animals can't fight back, or if they do, everyone says they're the problem. It sounded barbaric and horrific for you. But as inhumane as it was, and Troels should definitely pay for it, Bjorn didn't suffer. That sadistic animal abuser could easily have hurt or tortured him for hours to bring you into line; he could have cut pieces off him to break you. As traumatic as it was," I sniffed and wiped away more tears, "and I'd like to cut Troels' balls off with a blunt knife, as Glynis keeps advocating. But then I've wanted to do that on behalf of all his rape victims for some time now."

I found a tissue and blew my nose. "Why don't you submit that document as a petition to the Recorder and let me do something about it?"

"What could you do?"

"I don't know yet, but I can't do anything if you don't tell me officially." At his slight head shake, I pressed on. "Why won't you allow me to get some retribution for Boo?"

Rollo just shook his head. "It won't bring him back. What's the point?"

I started to get a little cross. "What if all the women had said, 'I won't file against Troels because it won't bring back my virginity, will it? So let's just let him get away with it.'"

One look at his face told me he wasn't getting this. I tried again from a different angle. "My point is that Bjorn's death was quick and clean. And he was a soul dog, so if you don't want him to feel he let you down, you need to start living. And Ad'Rian arrived at the perfect time for you to make a fresh start with your mother's family. You had a place there too. You could have built a different life. The thing I don't understand is why you didn't?"

Rollo let go of me and almost collapsed back into the chair. He'd gone very pale. He looked weirdly grey under his normally golden skin.

What was wrong with him? He'd shut himself off from me,

but he looked like he was going into shock. What the heck had he just worked out?

He pointed at his pantry and said, "Freezer, aquavit."

I opened the freezer and saw the bottle he'd given Ben to take to Kari. I dumped it and a shot glass on the table.

I'd never understood people who wanted to drink neat alcohol at below freezing temperatures, but then the Scandinavians and the Russians, even in my own world, were just as crazy —it must have something to do with their icy climates.

Rollo poured himself a shot, downed it, and slammed the glass on the table. He poured another one. What had he said to Ben? Only two, or she'll sink into what's the point?

I sat opposite him and put a little Recorder into my tone. I'd found it was helpful sometimes. In fact, I was starting to wonder why I hadn't found my inner librarian and turned her loose on Janet years ago.

"What am I missing?"

He looked peculiar. But as he reached for the second shot, I remembered he was half-Fae. They used alcohol for shock. That would explain his unhealthy-looking grey colour. I surveyed the alcohol percentage on the bottle. It was barely half the strength of the Pict whisky Ad'Rian used when he was shaky.

"Dola, may I have a measure of uisge beatha please?"

It arrived immediately. I pushed it at Rollo as Dola said, "Is all well, Niki?"

I ignored her and moved the shot of aquavit out of his way. "Drink this instead please."

He gave me a tiny frown, but I rolled over him, "Fionn'ghal is half your weight, and she needed three for the shock when I told her about Jamie. Don't forget your Fae heritage. This is what Ad'Rian used the other week when he looked exactly like you do now."

He knocked it back.

"Sorry, Dola, it will be, I think. Just a half-Fae, going into shock. Nothing to worry about. Unless you've got any of those sugary doughnut ball things that helped Ad'Rian?"

"*Struffoli*, yes."

The elegant circle of baby doughnut middles covered in a citrus, honey and whisky mixture arrived on a beautiful gilt-edged porcelain plate, and I fed Rollo several of them. I popped some into my own mouth—*mmm* they were so good.

He'd be fine, and so would I once we worked out what had sent him into shock. How many times after Nick's death had I wished Aysha, or her mother, or any of the other friends Nick had driven away had told me what they saw? Just mentioned any of the things I obviously wasn't seeing about Nick's narcissistic behaviour? No one had ever spelled it out. And while it wasn't their responsibility to do that, sometimes when we're in a mess and believing some asshole's bullshit and we can't see a way out, wouldn't a friend or a professional offering us insight or a shortcut to the emergency exit be a kindness? But, no, people always decided they should wait for us to work it out by ourselves.

I'd give it a go. Perhaps just a gentle nudge in the right direction—because I was almost sure my intuition was right. The story of poor Bjorn's death had cemented my certainty.

"You said you'd gone to the mind healers?" At his nod, I asked, "Did they suggest anything you might do to step onto the healing path?"

He focused on me and nodded. That was progress.

"But I couldn't really do any of it except get the hell out of Viking. Life is great in Edinburgh." He gestured around his apartment.

Yep, he'd built himself a safe space here.

"But when Troels demanded I come back, and I refused, he threatened Kari, Elise, Inge—actually he threatened everyone I knew or cared about, even my staff. So I went back."

"But what made you think you were responsible for them?"

He gazed at me helplessly.

"To put it another way, why didn't you get them out? You helped Kari escape."

I strengthened my shields, and behind those shields, I privately thought, *Oh, Rollo, you need to find your balls and work out how you let Troels metaphorically cut them off and program you as a child to think he was all-powerful. Because, if you don't, I'm not sure I can fix Viking without you. Not in any way you'll want to live with at least.*

Rollo looked so lost, I gave him some time to eat struffoli and gather himself. Then I led him back to things he was more comfortable with. "Go on, then. What happened when you arrived in Fae? No, first, how did Ad'Rian get to you so quickly? Even his magic isn't instant."

He gave me a half-smile and hugged me. "Trust you to spot the salient point. He was already on his way. He'd felt my psychic scream when Troels murdered Bjorn. Apparently, he'd bullied your gran into letting him take his warriors through. Her one-in, one out rule be damned. She never liked Glais'Nee, you know? I think he frightened her."

I hadn't known that, but then, how would I? And why on earth would Glais'Nee frighten anyone? He was a lovely Fae.

"OK?"

"When Ad'Rian took me home, as we went back through the Gateway, he said, 'Thank you, Recorder; losing one today was enough. Two would have been too many.' Your gran glared at him, but she nodded. It was much later, this morning, in fact, I realised he must have been talking about you."

He opened his mind to me. Ad'Rian and the higher ranks of the Fae court had been in mourning for the loss of Nik-a-lula. But Rollo had believed the lost girl was a Fae. He'd visualised the name being spelt Nee'Kahlula, or perhaps without the H, but definitely a Fae name.

He laughed. "I thought she'd been a relative of Glais'Nee's. Of course, I had no idea how old they all were then, and I was still a mess. Ad'Rian had only masked the pain so he could get me home and heal me properly."

After a brief pause, he asked, "How did you get me healed when you summoned me? I assumed you'd asked Ad'Rian. The oldest of the guards, the one who supervised my beating, even said it: 'With the Gate sealed, that buggering Fae uncle of yours won't be able to interfere and heal you this time, will he?' The old guard are stupidly loyal to the king and the warlords. I'm not convinced the youngest one's heart was really in it, but the older ones, oh, they loved it. And I was too drugged to focus on anything for very long. But I thought about what you asked yesterday. I could have got away if I'd summoned Nanok and transported. It never occurred to me. I'm being an idiot. I need to learn how to use the yellow power."

I stood up and headed towards the coffee pot, more for something to do than because I wanted coffee. The sour taste I got every time I remembered how comprehensively they'd beaten him was back in my mouth. I would eradicate that damn drug from the realms, not only for the women, or for the poor Hobs who'd lost their babies, but because it nearly cost me Rollo. If it had, I would never have known he was my bond mate. But I think I would have still felt the loss. Because, when he held me, it filled a hole in my soul I'd had my entire life.

Then Tilly dragged me out of my ruminations by rolling on her back on the rug. She had a way of doing immensely cute things when her mum was stressed.

Rollo pulled my attention back to our conversation. "But then at the book club, Ad'Rian said he'd had nothing to do with healing me, and that I must ask you."

Locking the knowledge of HRH behind a solid shield in my mind, I reached out for his hand. "I'm sorry. I agreed not to reveal your healer's identity yet. And I'm not sure why they asked that of me. So, until I can discuss it properly with them, which I can't do from up here, my hands are tied. I can only say you have friends in high places."

"OK, but please speak to them. If I owe a debt, I'd prefer to know."

"You don't and never will," I said flatly. Because I wouldn't permit the cat to benefit from something she should have prevented.

Rollo nodded slowly. "When I came round, you were covered in my blood. I panicked when I thought it was yours. You couldn't have got that much of my blood on you if you weren't involved."

"Oh, I was involved. I transported you from the Gateway, which is probably when I got covered in blood. But my skill level with healing is much too low yet to repair what they did to you. I'm working on it. But I'm still at the cuts and bruises level. You had loads of broken bones and a ruptured spleen, a fractured skull and other internal injuries.

"Give me a few days? Once I'm home, I'll get clearance to explain it all to you. Trust me for now, please. But your healer clearly and specifically told me you were not to feel indebted to them." Well, she said it was her burden to carry and not Rollo's, but it was the same thing, wasn't it?

He nodded. I felt him let it go. Phew. I needed to speak to that damned cat. Gently, I asked, "I don't want to be pushy, but I'd rather get this all out. What sent you into shock?"

"Is that what it was?"

"Yes, and thinking back, you did the same after you saved Tilly. You went the peculiar grey colour the Fae go. I didn't know you had Fae blood, then, did I? But Dola sent us brownies, remember?"

He put his arm around my waist and pulled me into him. "I remember you astonished me. You weren't who I thought the new Recorder would be." The tiny woman I'd seen in his mind wasn't the bossy Recorder he'd expected.

"Yeah, so everyone keeps saying. But I didn't do anything; Dola did. Sugar is one of the Fae's remedies for shock, and you are half-Fae."

"That brownie did rebalance me. I wonder if she knew? Dola's great, isn't she?"

"Mmm, she's awesome. So still being pushy, but you didn't answer. What sent you into shock? If we're ..." I could barely bring myself to say it, "bonded, I think I need to know what might send you into shock. It seemed to happen when I asked why didn't you just stay in Fae and begin a new life? What made you ever go back to Viking?"

I couldn't let this rest. It wasn't only personal. The arbitration and my responsibilities to all the petitioners meant I needed all the information I could get. What had kept him in Viking?

"Until recently, I felt I owed it to my father to take the throne of Viking. Troels stole the throne from him. I'm almost certain he arranged his accident and later poisoned my mother. Then, instead of acting as my regent, he claimed the throne himself. But I can't prove any of it. And if I could, what would it change? I'd like justice for my parents, but I don't and never have wanted to be king. I finally decided my father wouldn't want me to spend my life doing something I hated, somewhere I was unhappy."

A debt to his dead father might explain the weird dichotomy of desires I'd been getting from him. The odd combination of the last thing in the world he wanted was to be the Viking king, but he really thought he might have to do it. "I can probably find out if you want to know before Troels dies?"

He gaped at me. "How?"

"Have we talked about how the McKnight Gift works?"

He shook his head. "No. But the only time you used it on me it felt intrusive like a virus. Is it different from the power, then?"

"Oh, yeah, definitely. Even before I was the Recorder I could usually tell when people were lying to me. Well, unless people were lying to me so constantly that my shoulder was permanently sore, and I couldn't tell anything with it."

"So, how does it work?"

"I'm a walking lie detector. Close your shields, try to disconnect from me like you did before so you don't think I'm getting the answers from our bond, and tell me two truths and a lie."

He paused, looked thoughtful, and then distanced himself. Faintly, I heard *Can you hear me?*

"Just."

Then he tilted his head and waited. "Now?"

"If you mean in my head, no."

"OK, I hate broccoli. I'm worth a billion pounds, and I'm most ashamed of myself for allowing an evil man to ruin the first half of my life."

"The first is true, which is surprising considering how healthy you are, but I'm relieved because broccoli is horrible. The next is also true, which is scary. And the third is the lie."

He shook his head. "No, sorry, that's not right."

"OK, say them one by one."

"I hate broccoli."

"True."

"I'm worth a billion."

"True. It would have been a lot scarier before I came into the McKnight inheritance, but it's still a hell of a lot of money, and it's true."

He shook his head. "It really isn't."

"Sorry, but my shoulder disagrees with you."

"No, that was the lie."

"It really wasn't. The being ashamed you allowed an evil man to ruin the first half of your life was the lie."

We frowned at each other.

With a tone of icy affront, he snapped, "I think I'd know when I'm telling the truth."

"Well, it would seem you don't."

Anger rose in him now. "*Streth Mik*, is that how this Gift of yours works? Just tell the other person they're wrong?"

Wow! Were we having our first row?

When Rollo said, "Hey, are we having our first row?" I burst out laughing. But these were our first truly cross words, which was freaking amazing when you considered everything we'd been through. Then he grinned at me. "Seriously, this is the first time I've ever been angry with you." He pulled me in and kissed me.

Rollo got his phone out, poked it, and frowned. Then he said those three lovely words again. For me, after being married to Nick Pollock, they were not so much music to my ears, as an entire symphony played by a full orchestra at the Royal Albert Hall on the last night of the proms.

"You are right!"

How many times had I simply wanted to hear those words from Nick or Janet? Never mind. That was the past. It was time it stayed there.

"How, or rather, why am I right?" I swallowed hard, still shocked by how easily he'd said I was right. Except now I thought about it, he'd said I was right a few times. So what was different about this time?

"Metal Maven's stock has gone up significantly. Which might be a worry. We didn't expect it to do that for a few months yet. I need to find out why. Give me a sec."

His thumbs flew over the surface of his phone, and then he turned his attention back to me. "But that doesn't explain the third one. You said that was a lie, but it is how I truly feel. Thanks to my stupidity about my uncle, I have wasted the first half of my life."

But I'd been thinking about the third one. "What do you think your life expectancy is?"

"I don't know. I try to stay healthy and eat clean, although you're a bad influence." He kissed my nose, then shrugged. "Eighty or ninety years?"

I smirked at him and made the noise that sounded on a quiz show when the answer was wrong. "Uh-uh. Try again."

He frowned, then shook his head.

"Rollo, we've been talking about it all day—you're half Fae. I don't think you've wasted even a tenth of your life on the horrible Troels. Ad'Rian must have spoken to you about this?"

He looked straight at me. "No, I don't think he ever has. He probably assumed I was intelligent enough to work it out myself. But I wasn't. Although L'eon once said something about the business that confused me, and I might have just made sense of it."

I waited, then a grin brightened his face, his cute dimples appeared, and his eyes lit with mirth. "He said we'd have to leave it to our grandkids."

I laughed, remembering his Aunt Ti'Anna's words, "Like the vampires do?"

He gave me a lovely smile. "L'eon must have thought I was an idiot. I must ask him about it again."

"He probably assumed your head was full of code. Finn gives me a blank look sometimes and then asks me about whatever it was days later."

"Yeah, probably. This Gift of yours is so accurate, it knows things I didn't even know. Does that mean you could find out what Troels did or didn't do to my parents?"

"Probably. But it doesn't exactly know things you don't. It just knows if you're lying or not. I can try it. But you could do it too, you know, and probably get quite different information by wrapping him in the yellow power like you did to Kari."

"You said I did that, but I don't know how I—" Rollo's phone buzzed in his hand, and he said, "Sorry, need to take this."

I heard, "Ro speaking" as he headed out of the door. Tilly and I looked at each other. It was time I asked the Book more about the regnal power. Because Rollo should use it while he had it. The Gateway power wasn't stupid. It knew Rollo hadn't wanted it, but it had talked him into taking it, anyway. Why?

CHAPTER
FIFTY

Rollo was restless when he came back to the kitchen, and his pacing was bugging me. This was a spacious kitchen-diner, but he was making it feel small.

I tried, "I am desperately, desperately sorry Bjorn was murdered. But you didn't really answer my question, you know."

"Which question?"

"Wouldn't he have wanted you to live happily? Because when I asked the Book about Tilly, it said soul animals often come back to us if, for whatever reason, our time together is cut short. But you avoiding all animals after his death would mean he wouldn't be able to do that."

He went very quiet.

Then he started pacing again.

I gave up. "Why don't you have a swim?"

He grumbled like a teenager. "Don't want to swim. Need to break my head out of this spiral of thoughts. I probably sound ridiculous, but I want a problem I can solve instead of going endlessly around on one I can't. But if I start on a work project, I'll disappear into it for days—it's one reason I love my work so much. But right now, I want to snap out of it and spend time with you. And I need to make a decision about Viking."

I reached down our link to see how he really felt and then had a brainwave. "Hey, have you ever made apps?"

"Sure, why?"

I opened the Broch app that Finn created for Breanna and tapped to send it to his phone. "I have a problem, and Finn won't listen to me. Dola and I want to teach him a lesson."

He accepted the app and poked it for a few minutes. "OK, but what's the problem with it?"

"It's for the Broch, for Breanna, Caitlin and Juna to use."

He threw back his head and laughed loud and long. "Oh, I can hear Loki chortling from here. He loves a prank. You're kidding though?"

"I'm not, and when I tactfully suggested it needed some tweaks, Finn told me they just needed to practise using it. So, Dola and I decided to teach him a lesson about how the product has to suit the customer, or it's not finished. It's weird because he bends over backwards to explain even simple things slowly to the Smiths. Hugh says Finn is the only reason he can use email at all."

"Yes, but Finn's also at the age where his mother is annoying and knows nothing. She should have paid him for it. That might have brought the right part of his talents to the job."

I pondered this. The Broch could have easily commissioned this. "You make a good point. I'll speak to Lesley about that."

"Lesley?"

"Breanna's new Broch manager. She's much more switched on than the previous woman. Dola and I thought we'd tweak it ourselves and then submit several anonymous versions so Breanna could choose the one that's best for her. It might hit Finn's competitive streak, and he might remember the lesson going forward. It's only a present if the person you gave it to wants it and can use it. Tegan, or maybe some future girlfriend, might thank us."

Rollo was smiling as he headed to his office.

• • •

I settled back at the table and pulled the Book over to me. It was open on a page with the answer to the questions I asked Dola earlier when I watched Alwena's video. Why would the dragon queens make them invincible? And had I done something I didn't understand by reopening that mountaintop Gateway? The Book must have thought I was speaking to it.

It had given me one of the multiple option pages.

The origins of the Red Celt dragons.

The dragon gate and its effect on the dragons and the realms.

The dragon queens, their significance and their powers.

The reasons for the queens' demise and their effect on the behaviour of the other realms.

I started at the beginning.

The Goddess Modron was at the pinnacle of her strength when her son Mabon expressed his wish to move his people to a new and safer land, a haven away from the English and their wars. She struck a bargain with the Gateway power. The Red Celts would have two gates. One for transport and access to the Gateway, as the other realms did, and one on a mountaintop where she planned to create dragons to protect her son's realm. Her offer to the power was that, if it joined power to her magic to create the dragons, she would ensure the incredibly powerful dragons she planned to create would be an additional source of protection for all of the Gateway's access points, if it ever had need of them.

About twenty minutes later, I'd learnt a lot of stuff about the dragons. The fall of the dragon gate and its sentinels, as the stones were called, had been responsible for the lack of queens for almost five hundred years. Why the hell hadn't someone just fixed it?

I really would need to come back and study this as soon as I concluded this damn arbitration. But right now, I more urgently needed to know why the Gateway had given Rollo the yellow regnal power when it knew he didn't want to be king.

I asked it. The answer gave me hope.

The realms call it regnal power. The Gateway does not. That power was intended to be a source of extra strength for the leaders in a realm. It was never intended to be perverted, as it has been in too many realms over the last few hundred years. The Gateway is redistributing it to individuals who have the well-being of their realm in their heart.

That made perfect sense in my mind. Take it off Dai because he wasn't using it to help the dragons. Take it off Troels because he was using to stunt any growth, equality or happiness in Viking. The power liked people to be happy.

"Is the power unhappy with any of the other realms?"

There was a pause, then the Book flipped one page.

Yes.

Recorder, we perceive you have enough to work on currently. I shall store this question for later, after you have helped the Vikings to enact some change.

"Do you have any advice for me about how to do that?"

Remove the corruption if you can. Give the people the opportunity to change, but do not solve all their problems for them. They must decide what they want. If you repair a child's toy for them too easily, they will break it again swiftly.

I sat and thought for a long time.

A couple of hours later, Rollo messaged to ask me to come through to his office.

He was kicked back at his desk and looked happier, with his hair up and several pencils stuck into it. I should always have a small techy challenge on hand in case he got himself trapped in the past again.

Looking much happier, he handed me an iPad with a colourful app already loaded. "Breanna and Caitlin hate phones; I'm not sure about Juna. I wondered if putting the app on a tablet might help break that association."

I surveyed the app, admired the female warrior figure waving a sword, the Yin-Yang symbol in subdued pastels that I guessed was supposed to be Juna, and poked the dancing crown at the top. "Where did you get all the cute animated graphics from so quickly?"

Rollo smirked at me. "Game Optimiser and Developer, remember? Just call me G.O.D."

I laughed. "Because everyone in your office does?"

"No," his face fell, "no matter how often I sign emails with it." He brightened. "But sometimes they call me Thor."

The app let out a discreet round of applause as I successfully ordered breakfast. A large red number five appeared on the screen. "What's that?"

"Finn's code allocates bonuses to the staff for swift service. He cared about them being motivated to provide the family with their best, but he forgot they couldn't earn bonuses unless he got his mother to use it. The numbers are a countdown until whatever she's ordered appears."

It was the app I would have designed for Breanna myself. All the selections were large and colourful. The food and drink had appetising photos and were easy to see without her reading glasses. It was appealing and fun. It was light years from Finn's dry lists of text in a tiny, impossible-to-read light grey font on a black background.

The screen changed to a flashing red number four, and a message appeared. "If your order does not appear before zero does, you have earned ten points, Your Majesty."

"Oh, that's clever. Inspire the staff to outperform Breanna's requests. I like it."

"Yes, Finn's motivation section was a little too one-sided. I don't think giving the staff money for every task or just for doing their job is the answer. I think a monthly competition with a healthier bonus they all share on a pro-rata basis at the end of it might work better to build a team win by fulfilling the family's requests."

I hugged him. "Can you send this to Dola? She's compiling one of her presentations to talk Breanna into picking one and actually using it."

He pulled me onto his lap. "Do I get a reward?"

We were headed in a lovely, snuggly direction when the phone in my shirt pocket let out a police siren noise. It startled us both.

I pulled it out quickly. "Sorry, that's Dola's emergency override alert. Give me a second."

Dola: I am most apologetic, and I hate to interrupt your holiday, but please check your email. Immediately.

I hadn't managed even twenty-four hours off this week. It was time to give up and fix this damn mess so we could have an actual holiday.

CHAPTER
FIFTY-ONE

At Rollo's kitchen table, I grabbed my laptop and started swearing under my breath.

He read over my shoulder. "We talked about how few laws we have in Viking, but this is one of them. And it's my own stupid fault. I wish to hell I'd registered my oath to the Recorder with the king's office."

While I was trying to parse his meaning he added, "Remember I gave you behavioural guarantees for the group I brought through for their bonding checks? But I didn't want to give Trocls an excuse to ban the bondings. He's often been spiteful to Elise, and this would have given him the chance to upset his daughter's wedding, and therefore Inge too. Foolishly, I expected him to stay at home because he usually avoids the Gateway."

"Hmm? Registered your oath?"

He pointed at the email open on my screen. "They couldn't have submitted that petition to you if I'd registered the oath. Doing that gives us immunity."

My confusion must have been apparent because he continued, "Swearing by our blade is the penultimate oath in Viking. If we swear by our blade or by Odin, we notify the king's office in writing. It's tradition. If there's fall-out from any actions we need to take to avoid being foresworn, the king's office has advance notice. Not being foresworn in Viking is far more important than not killing people."

I reread the email. Twelve warlords had submitted petitions to the Recorder, demanding that she produce Rollo for them. He was charged with attempted regicide. They'd scheduled his trial in Haraldssund. If the Recorder was holding him, they had the prior claim. If she wasn't, they required her to summon him for them.

"But what are they playing at? Why this? Why now?"

Dola's electronic voice sounded smug. "The videos we are showing on Troels' cell and on the Recorder's news portal are having the precise effect I was striving for. The warlords wish to dilute that effect by making the Recorder appear unreasonable."

Rollo added, "They're waiting for you to say no, so they can accuse you of interfering with Viking's internal political structure. With Troels detained, the Warlord Council will be running Viking. That's how the chain of command works."

I couldn't see any problem with this. In fact, it felt like a gift to me. Did that mean I was missing something? "So if the warlords were out of the realm, who would be in charge, then?"

Rollo looked flummoxed. "I have no idea. It never happens. They're never permitted to leave the realm at the same time. Half of them have to stay in Viking."

OK, so maybe I wasn't missing anything.

Maybe *they* were.

Had they finally given me an opening I could work with?

"Dola, can you please ask Inge who would be in charge if all the warlords met with a terrible accident?"

"Yes, Niki."

"Rollo, you're a super bright guy."

"Thank you. I'm not sure it's true, but thank you anyway. I love that you think so."

"Can you explain to me what understanding you would have, as a Viking prince, of what a petition to the Recorder involves?"

His brow creased, so I added, "Or, if it's an easier question, what do you believe the average warlord thinks it means? And where do you keep the wine?"

Rollo went to find me wine, and I considered Dola's reservations about speaking when I wasn't at home. "Dola, I'd like you to be a part of this conversation. I think we've got an opening, but I want Rollo to tell me how much he knows first."

"Yes, Niki. I agree, this is an opening. I have forwarded all the petitions to you."

I was scrolling through the third almost-but-not-quite-identical petition when Rollo emerged from the pantry with a beer, a very nice-looking bottle of red, and a dish of nibbly things. I grabbed a handful of nuts and some Bombay mix as he passed.

"Dola, is there any reason I can't share these petitions with Rollo?"

"No, as he is the subject of them, your grandmother would have done that automatically."

"Excellent, would you share them with him now, and can you pull in the recording of my first call with him, please? I assume it's offsite by now."

Rollo's head spun around so quickly, he nearly spilled his beer.

I said, "Chill out, Boo; I think we've got this."

As Dola had said, the petitions were all worded slightly differently, but all twelve of the warlords had submitted petitions to the Recorder. Stupid bastards. Not one petition with twelve signatures, but twelve petitions.

They thought they were making an overwhelming statement against the Recorder's Office. They'd say, "She ignored twelve petitions from twelve Viking warlords and leaders."

I thought they were imbeciles.

My hands had been tied. Now they weren't. And all because

519

they hadn't considered the possible effect of their attempt at some kind of negative PR against the Recorder.

"Accept the petitions immediately, please. All of them. Do not permit them to withdraw any of them. If they try when they realise what a monumentally dumb thing they've done, tell them a petition to the Recorder can't be withdrawn once it's been accepted. The petitions have been accepted and filed, and it is now out of your hands."

I remembered the Smiths and how they'd thought the Recorder was all-knowing about every realm.

"Also tell them they should send through proof of their charges. Any legal documents validating their accusation, and copies of any laws that would explain to the Recorder exactly what constitutes regicide in their realm. It doesn't match my understanding of an attempt to kill a king, so they'd better also include any situations where they wouldn't consider killing or attempting to kill a king to be regicide. Because I want to know why Troels wasn't charged with regicide after Jonvar's death. Tell them to send them immediately. We don't want a repeat of the Smiths, do we?"

I looked at Rollo. "So, have you had time to think? What does the Viking realm think a petition to the Recorder means?"

He didn't look happy, but his honesty won out again. "I'm not sure. Until you told me in your office at the cottage that you had all these arbitration powers, I'd never heard a word of that from anyone in *any* of the realms."

He paused, then grinned sheepishly. "It's probably why we called your gran 'the moderator' in *Drengr*. That's what we thought she was. Just a combination of a train conductor to the realms and a peacekeeper. I've been trying to think of any Viking I know who has ever submitted a petition to the Recorder. I'm coming up empty."

He paused, took a swig of his beer, shook his head, and looked frustrated. "I think petitions to the Recorder are perceived to be something like taking your troubles to Yggdrasil. The sacred tree, I mean, not my house. You write your problem on a small scroll and attach it to the branches. If the gods smile on it, they might provide a solution. It's mostly an act of faith. And often when something completely coincidental happens to help the person, they give the gods the credit for it anyway."

Dola interrupted us, "I have accepted them all, Niki. Two of them are from the new warlords who replaced the late Svein and one of his fellow conspirators whom the Queen sent to the iron mines after the problems in the Pict realm. They have been in their role for less than a month. One other is also quite new. The rest have been in their roles for some years. Aside from the newest three, the next newest has been in his role for five years. The oldest, for forty-one years."

"So where can I keep a dozen warlords for a few days? What do you think, Dola, a lovely glade or a nice oubliette?"

"The glade, I think, Niki. Without breaking Ad'Rian's confidentiality, I will only say that he is not happy with Viking right now. He's given much thought to how he can support his nephew and has had several long conversations with various Fae warriors about his options. I think he would like to help in any way possible."

"Cool. Ask him, would you? And what did Inge say about who is in charge if the warlords aren't in the realm?"

"Inge stated she did not know and would have to consult. She may have been lying. Her voice frequencies suggest she was at the least dissembling."

I felt my smile start. "Excellent. Ask Finn to work with her to discover the entire chain of command in Viking. I'd like an answer in the next twenty-four hours. Specifically, who rules if the warlords are absent? He'll enjoy that."

It was right up Finn's street. He would just keep rephrasing the question until Inge gave in and told him what I already suspected.

Rollo put his beer on the table a little too firmly. It clunked. "What am I missing?"

"The first bit you're missing is easy. If they'd sent me one petition with twelve signatures, under the rules of the Recorder's Office, which are clearly spelled out when they submit a petition, they could have sent one warlord to represent them all and answer for their side of the petition. They all had to tick the 'yes, I read the terms and conditions' button before they pressed submit. So they are deemed to know this."

We smirked at each other because we both, for different reasons, knew that no one ever reads the full terms and conditions. They just click "I agree" button.

"But they sent twelve petitions, which means I can and will summon all twelve of them. So who will rule Viking while I'm holding them?"

He reached for his phone, but I wasn't done.

Rollo would have had years to learn from Ad'Rian. Had he used those years?

"Can you instigate a Fae mind link? Our connection is great and all, but it comes with a lot of emotions. Right now, I want the high-speed battlefield one, as Mabon always calls it. The one where I can show you everything quickly."

He obviously could because he reached a finger towards my third eye and paused. "I consent."

And we were linked. "You have to show me how to do this. I can't instigate it myself. It's annoying. When I gave you the quick overview before you swore on the anvil, I promised to fill you in on the rest of it. But you keep distracting me. So this should speed things up."

Then I lined up everything the Book had told me repeatedly in my first few weeks as the Recorder. I elaborated on the quick overview I'd given him in Stane Parlour when Mags translated the document for me. The advice it gave me about arbitrations, how we didn't do mediations because they weren't binding. And the Recorder was not, as my gran had so succinctly put it, a damn agony aunt or an advice columnist. And how *the Recorder was **always** right*. In every situation. Even if she was wrong. I added in Aysha's advice via her high court judge mentor about how she should follow the law, but once the law stopped, she needed to make a decision, right or wrong, but never be wishy-washy about it. I shared the Book's advice to me about not fixing the child's broken toy too swiftly.

Importantly, I showed Rollo how the Recorder was mostly powerless until someone asked her to step in. Then I reminded him how it differed when I was in arbitration with the ruler of a realm and the powers that gave me over the whole realm. And how my decisions were binding on the entire realm if it went that far.

Rollo said, "I remember all this, Niki. But I don't understand what's changed and why you suddenly feel so much lighter."

I reminded him I'd accepted the petitions against Troels. But had he legally been the ruler when I did that?

It was a tricky situation. Did I still have all the rights if I accepted the arbitration while Troels was the ruler, even if he now wasn't? My gran and most of my ancestors would have said I did. But the Book hadn't been sure and offered several differing opinions. I felt like I was stretching a legal right until it might snap. Mostly, it hadn't felt quite fair. And as Rollo said, I was a fair woman.

That was what had tied my hands. Technically, I didn't have the rights over Viking I would definitely have had if Troels had still been the king.

As I reached the end of Recorder 101, I opened my other eyes and truly looked at him. His aura glowed, and he smiled like the sun had finally come out. Yeah, he was as bright as people said, even if some of his decisions recently hadn't been his smartest thinking.

Next, I showed him my entire conversation with Glais'Nee at the book club that Rhiannon had interrupted. His *history is always written by the victors* comment. How people often failed when they tried to deal with the figurehead and then discovered the true corruption was in the roots. The iron near the unicorn feed sheds in Fae. And, finally, Mags and her poor Hobs working in Galicia for Vikings and their resulting miscarriages.

Now Rollo looked bone-weary. "It's no wonder your gran was sometimes a bit testy. I truly had no idea."

"Ah, well, Gran was difficult for another reason too." I showed him the Gateway when I'd first arrived with the faint silvery pizza shapes of Gran's power. The drab, dusty, depressing emptiness of the centre. The dull anvil. And then I reminded him how it looked now and how clear the black iron boundaries were these days.

"I'd wondered about those. So you have more power than your gran? How much more?"

"We don't know."

He frowned at me. "I'd tell you if I knew. Remember, you swore on the anvil that anything I told you must be kept confidential. The thing is, Finn hasn't been able to measure my limits yet—but a hell of a lot more than Gran. My connection to the power is great, but the realms are tricky. Pure power isn't always the right solution."

"Like computers. You can have the finest machine, but an idiot operator still can't use it to the right level. PEBKAC."

I grinned at him. The *Problem Exists Between the Keyboard And Chair* was an old tech helpline joke about people who spent a fortune on their machines and then couldn't use them. "Exactly that. But now these warlords have asked the Recorder to get involved. That means they're either idiots, or they simply don't have enough information. But it finally gives me options."

He sent me a warm mental hug.

I said, "Before we break this link, how much do you know about Glais'Nee's talents?"

He sent me memories of Glais'Nee and several other Fae warriors training him so the former tall, gangly lad could hold his own and later defeat most of the Viking warriors of his generation. But that was it.

"His other talents?"

He shook his head. So I showed him how Glais'Nee helped me read the hearts of the Vikings who'd been working for Svein and probably Halvor in the Pict Kingdom.

Slowly, he said, "I had no idea. And it's good because I don't think a couple of the younger warlords have been corrupted ... yet."

We grinned at each other. "I think you might find that the yellow power tells you what's in people's hearts as well. Remember when you checked Kari's loyalty before you told her about our bond?"

"You said something about that while we were eating Chinese, but I'm not sure how I did it."

Shock came through our mind link when I told him what I'd learned from the Book and re-sent him my view of the scene I'd witnessed in his Edinburgh kitchen where he'd draped Kari in yellow power to test her loyalty to him and to Viking. I shared my thoughts that he was protecting me, but the regnal power was to protect the realm, then showed him what Breanna told me about testing traitors before she beheaded them.

"You may not need Glais'Nee, but this first time, when we need to be certain, I think he'll help you get the most out of your regnal power, and he might know other cool things it can do? The Book gave me some information earlier I can share with you. It's like a lie detector, but for loyalty and which person or realm someone is loyal to."

We broke the link. "I'm going to need to call a time out on our holiday from tomorrow. I hope we can pick it back up on Friday night. You OK with that?"

525

He pulled me into a hug. "I suspect you're about to give me my life choices back. Provided we can reschedule some time for us, I'm great with it. Let's go out for dinner and dancing to celebrate when it's all over."

Dinner and dancing sounded wonderfully normal, but also, with Rollo, probably a lot of fun. If everything went as I feared it might in this arbitration, we were both going to need some fun to look forward to.

PART TEN
WEDNESDAY

The skalds tell tales of people who come into your life for a reason, a season, a lifetime or forever.

This may be true for citizens, but warriors hold to a simpler truth. People come into our lives to fight by our side or to die on our blade.

Knowing which is which, though ... now that's a more complex equation than you may initially perceive.

Many an enemy has taken a blade meant for me.

Did that make him my friend?

Or was he still my foe even as he died in my stead?

Winning the War Against Yourself: Daily Weapon and Warrior Care by Arinn Tusensköna

CHAPTER
FIFTY-TWO

Wednesday, 10th March—Edinburgh and the Gateway. Determined O'clock

This morning, Rollo had settled in his office, ostensibly to check email, but our link suggested he wanted some thinking time.

In his kitchen, I worked with Dola. I'd told her I was coming home a little hesitantly. I'd been worried I wouldn't be able to go back to the Gateway, but she told me the recordings were completed. Along with her team of support staff, she'd moved the women efficiently through their testimonies.

They hadn't recorded videos from all the petitioners because, as Glynis had put it in her email to me, "We can, my lady, if you feel you need more evidence, but how many times do we need to hear the same story? Some of the girls are still very fragile."

We now had personal stories recorded with petitioners from all the realms, shorter snippets from many more, and Finn and Dola were editing the final ones. They'd all put in long days, and I wondered what I could do to thank them. But Glynis' email made it clear that finally getting justice for the women she'd had in her support groups for so long was the only reward she needed.

Dola wanted me to check a couple of the videos, but honestly, I was past the need to control everything. As the Recorder, I needed to view all the evidence, but it wasn't up to me to decide what they could submit. Many of them were heartbreaking. Others created a lava-hot anger about the ways their families treated the girls, as if being raped wasn't enough. If Glais'Nee said their kids' fathers were Vikings and the women had spoken what was in their hearts, what gave me the authority to approve them? I just needed to watch them for the arbitration. Dola informed me she'd strongly advised Fi not to record her own testimony. As a member of the Gateway personnel she was in a strange position. Dola had read Fi's petition and there was nothing in it that hadn't been repeated verbatim by a dozen other women. She felt we wanted to avoid any suggestion that the Recorder's staff were anti-Troels.

The whole of Viking needed to know what these women had been through. In fact, never mind the whole of Viking. ALL the damn realms needed to know what they'd allowed to happen under their noses. The Recorder didn't have the rules of evidence to juggle. The Recorder didn't even have to uphold free speech, although personally I thought it was generally a good idea. But the Recorder could do pretty much whatever she thought was necessary to obtain a fair outcome.

It astonished me to discover that, this time around, unlike with the Picts and their arbitration, I was just fine and dandy with having all the authority.

"Dola, unless you have a specific reservation about a particular woman's story, please put them up."

"Yes, about that, Niki. Since the women's stories were posted, we have received many more petitions. And you may want to check the sections that are open for comments on the news portal. I would suggest you search for #ItHappenedtoVikingsToo."

My stomach churned, but this wasn't unexpected. Why would the Vikings have escaped what women of the other realms were subjected to? But I didn't expect to see the Viking women making their own videos and submitting them to the news portal. After watching a few of them, I stopped and rewound one video to the beginning. I knew that woman. She was no Viking, even if she was now tagging herself as one.

I knew her face but couldn't retrieve her name. That was no big surprise, but had I ever known it? Then it clicked.

"Dola, that Saturday when I was separating the Vikings who were trying to overthrow Breanna from the innocent Viking citizens who needed to return home, there was a young, heavily pregnant Welsh woman with her mother. She wanted to go through the yellow gate from the Red Celt realm so her Viking husband could be at the baby's birth. Those nice merchants carried all the gifts from what she called her *babi* shower. Do you recall her?"

Silence. Dola was obviously busy.

I watched the video as the woman told a tale very similar to the one young Carys had shared. But this one had a much happier outcome. Gwenda said she'd been in Viking for her sister's wedding as the chief bridesmaid. The wedding breakfast or reception after the ceremony in Viking was often a communal affair. Gwenda's sister was a part of one with seven other brides. The king and several of the warlords had dropped in to wish the brides well. They'd all complimented her on her lovely accent. After the toasts, she'd felt lightheaded and stepped outside. The best man was worried and followed her, and she must have passed out.

The next thing she knew, it was morning, and she was fully dressed except for her shoes. Still wearing her bridesmaid's gown, she'd woken in a room in a large longhouse where her rescuer was staying for the wedding. He'd given her breakfast and even escorted her back to the Gateway. At that point, she felt groggy and strange, so she'd gone along with it.

Then several years ago at the *Dewi Sant* festival in Pant y Wern, she saw him again and thanked him. The rest was their love story. They'd courted, married, started their family. He was

533

wonderful. Their son was adorable. She tilted her camera to show the tiny newborn baby she cradled.

Once she'd started watching all these awful stories on the portal, she'd wondered. She had nightmares. What might have happened to her if Ulrik hadn't taken her home and let her sleep it off safely? Ulrik was a fruit farmer. He wasn't involved in politics and didn't travel to the capital often. But even on his farm, he'd heard rumours. His mother would never have forgiven him if he'd left any girl alone in that vulnerable state.

Her mother-in-law was a lovely woman; her husband was her hero, but it could have all been so very different. She thought the Recorder was lovely; she'd been so kind to her and her mother when she had to leave her behind the day she came home to have the *babi*. She couldn't understand why people in Viking, who'd never even met the Recorder, were so rude about her. Somebody needed to do something about these poor girls.

Yes, Somebody really did, didn't they? Because Everybody thought Anybody could. But Nobody had. Goddess, it was exactly like that lesson I'd tried to give Inge when she thought sorting Viking out was simply Rollo's problem and his alone.

My screen changed to a slightly grainy video. We'd been right to upgrade the cameras in the Gateway. I watched the woman in question weeping in her mother's arms, laden like a carthorse with the presents from her baby shower. I paused the frame on a clear view of her face. Yes, I was right. It was the same woman.

"Thank you, Dola; that was what I needed."

Rollo opened the kitchen door, and Tilly bounced off my lap to greet him. "Hey, you crying again?"

I shook my head. "Nope. I'm fine. They're just happy, angry tears. This woman, Gwenda, set me off with happy tears. She had such a close call, and she's only just realised it."

I showed him the footage from the Gateway on that day almost a month ago where, heavily pregnant, she'd waddled away from her mother, weeping. Then I ran her video on the portal.

"Lingonberry Ulrik, I know him," was Rollo's only comment as he retrieved a jar of what looked like red jam from the pantry and set it on the table. "A good man. Makes the best fruit jellies and jams. She was lucky."

I bit down on my anger that she shouldn't have needed luck, and instead told him the tale of Everybody, Somebody, Anybody and Nobody, and how Inge responded to it. I added in her phrase about interfering in the smithing of a blade that wouldn't be her own.

He was doing something one-handed on his phone while he collected the coffee pot and came back to the table to top up our mugs.

My phone buzzed with an alert that our joint note had been updated.

I opened it.

1: Why don't you like my dog or ever use her name?
2: Why do you call me Boo all the damn time?
3: ~~When did you first suspect we had a bond?~~
4: ~~What do you truly want to do with your life?~~

Rollo said, "I don't want to be foresworn, and if you're going back to the Gateway, shall we finish this?"

I agreed he had answered points three and four, and after reading Bjorn's story, I thought I understood why he didn't use Tilly's name, but that was stupid. She'd be in his life, whether he used her name or not. Because I was in his life now.

He picked up my thought and nodded. "I came to the same conclusion myself. I'm being ridiculous. She's your soul dog. If you lost her, you'd be devastated. I'd feel that too. I'm continuing to do something I decided at an awful time in my life, but this isn't that time. I don't think I can call her Tilly-Flop though—that feels a step too far. I might have to return my warrior card."

"Well, Autumn's name for her is even less manly." At his raised eyebrow and tilted head, I said, "Pupsicle."

He threw his head back and laughed. "Actually, that's so ridiculous and cute, I might even get away with it. C'mon, Pupsicle, let's get to know each other, shall we? I'll tell you all about Boo. He was about ten times bigger than you, but frequently surprised by the fact that he had a shadow."

Tilly immediately trotted over to him and sat at his feet with such an attentive expression, I would have sworn she understood. Well, of course she did. She was a perceptive dog, and she'd known Rollo was broken, just as she had always known when I wasn't coping.

He consulted the list and looked straight into my eyes. "I'm sorry. The reason I call you Boo is another possibly stupid decision made at a time when I was completely out of my element and off-balance. I'll stop if you hate it."

"I did, but it's grown on me. It's like Pupsicle; it's cute. But I'd like to understand it?"

"Bjorn was a big dog, brave and fearless. But he didn't understand that his shadow was attached to him. So he'd bark at it."

The little movie he ran in his thoughts of a gambolling brown bundle of fluff growling and yapping at his own shadow made me smile.

"It used to startle him, so I called him Boo as a joke. We spell it differently, but the word is the same in Norse. But then, when I was almost twenty-five, and I finally got Troels to agree I'd be safe if I left the realm to study, I started at Cambridge University. I was so happy to be there—I felt so free."

The emotion that came from him, along with this simple statement, was just one more confirmation about how unbearable his life was in Viking.

"I came out of a lecture theatre my very first week, and in the corridor, an attractive girl of eighteen or nineteen gave me a stunning, brilliant smile and called, 'Hey, Boo, been looking for you.' She looked overjoyed to see me. Of course she was talking to the guy behind me." He paused with a slight pink tinge to his golden skin, and I tried very hard not to giggle.

He swallowed, and his tone was defensive. "At first, it triggered me because of Bjorn. Then I thought, Boo? Did she really just call me Boo? Who in *Hel* calls a person Boo? *Streth Mik,* what does it even mean?"

I remembered saying almost the same to him when he called me Boo in the pre-dawn light of Arthur's Seat high above Edinburgh. I started to smile.

He stood me up now and lifted my chin so he could look down into my eyes. "And I hoped if I was ever lucky enough to find a partner who understood consent, wasn't under the influence of drugs and was smart and funny—but most importantly, who looked at me with the same openly joyful expression on her face that girl had—then I would call her Boo. And I'd hope she would understand why a stupid young guy never believed he'd ever see that much happiness on his partner's face. Because, if I'd thought it would ever be possible, well, obviously, I would have come up with a much cooler endearment than Boo."

I melted.

The solid wall I'd built painstakingly around my heart as I tried to recover from Nick's betrayal was there for a reason. I'd vowed not to allow anyone near my heart until they had proven themselves.

But Rollo's honesty, his openness and the way he listened and respected my boundaries, they all spoke to me in ways words never could have done. Nick could be persuasive with words to get his own way. But his actions never matched his statements. Rollo though, even without our bond link, I thought I would have grown to trust him—because his actions, his words, and his heart were aligned.

Those bricks I'd laid so carefully loosened, shifted, and the outer ones began to crumble.

Some time later, I gathered my dog and my computer. "Last chance, Boo."

He smiled and reached for me, but I needed to put a stop to this mess. "Seriously, if you have a plan, come and share it with me, or we'll be going with the Recorder's plan. I've had enough of all their misery. Our happiness seems to make it worse." I couldn't quite explain why the little Red Celt woman, who'd found a good Viking, just as I had myself, clarified exactly what I thought needed to happen in Viking.

Now I just needed to find out if the Recorder could make it happen.

Have you ever had that difficult-to-describe or even to-quantify feeling the universe is giving you a GO sign?

Back in the Gateway, with more rain outside the boundary on a damp Scottish Wednesday, I had that feeling. As if to prove it was time to take some action on this horrible mess, I had the warlords' petitions for Rollo's return, and, when I checked the petition queue, dozens of new ones from all the Hobs I'd summoned home for Mags had appeared.

It felt as though something was moving in the direction of justice—finally.

After I'd retrieved the Hobs who were being detained by the warlords in Galicia, Mags said, "I'll give them a day or two to find their balance, and then I'll mek sure they do as we agreed."

Mags had delivered on her word, and as far as I could see with my quick scan, they'd filed petitions against ten of the warlords by name. The names on their petitions matched the names on the warlords' requests that I return Rollo. There were only two who weren't on both lists. Had the missing ones been part of the conspiracy in the Pict queendom, along with the late Svein? If so, they'd be in the iron mines. I'd check.

"Dola, do you have Mags's phone number?"

Amazement clear in her voice, she said, "Yes, of course."

"Cool, could you send it to my phone, please?"

"Would you prefer I contact her on your behalf?"

"Nope, it's fine; I've got this. But would you send my Recorder's robe, a black coffee and some water and chicken for Tilly?"

"Tilly has just followed Finn and his bacon sandwich out of the back door."

I looked around and saw she'd abandoned me. The sneaky little madam. "Fine, she can eat later." My little one had settled in Scotland now, and she considered both the cottage and the Gateway to be her territory.

A coffee arrived on my desk, and the Recorder's robe landed on Rosie's desk. "Whoops, sorry, Rosie, let me move that." As I put it on, I asked, "Would you know if Mags is busy today?"

Rosie turned her smiling face to me. "She is reading, so *busy, not busy*, as she calls it. Recorder, we have a number of people requesting bond checks. Fi said I should schedule those with you?" There was a question in her voice, so I smiled, nodded and waited.

She made an ironing gesture with the flat of her palm on her desk. "I have a suggestion to smooth the process."

"Oh, great news, Rosie. I'd love that. Ask Dola to find an hour on my calendar."

She gave me a blinding smile. "I'll forward my proposals to you ahead of the meeting. I made a PowerPoint."

I hated PowerPoints. People always insisted on reading the damn slides to me. Well, Dola didn't. She would talk off the slide, adding other information, which was just one more reason I appreciated her so much. But I loved that Rosie's confidence was growing enough to want to present one to me.

I opened the Book and spent some time asking about the rights the Recorder had to seize assets if an arbitration demanded it. And what were my rights if I called people through, and even though *they* thought they were the prosecution, or at least the petitioners, *I* thought they were the defendants?

"Good morning, Mags, sorry to bother you, but I have a bit of an odd question for you. My Gift is playing up a bit."

"Nae bother. A Gift playing up is never a good thing. What does it want?"

"It wants me to ask you if there are any of your Hobs you would prefer me to leave out of the hearing of the petitions against the warlords? I'm not sure I even need any of them here. The warlords have dropped themselves in it by filing a petition of their own, so I can summon them all anyway. While I've got them, I'll deal with your peoples' petitions too, and do my best to get something like justice for your girls. But my Gift thought perhaps I shouldn't call them in today or tomorrow? And I'm not sure why."

"Your Gift ain't playin' up, Your Maj. If ye don't need them, it'd be good to let them all heal instead. Another lost their baby, and one's in the hospital with a premature baby son. Thanks to th' wicked herbs. He should live, but ye ne'er can tell. Another one on the missing list is her sister, who's by her side. And the third is her partner, who's getting under everyone's feet and blaming hisself for no feeking reason. Verbena, the third sister, is on her way home to help, so leave Violet and Viola out of it." She paused. I heard a long sigh before she continued. "Perhaps summon Rhodie to give them girls a break from his self-flagellation?"

"OK, will do." I glanced through the names, trying to find a Rhodie. "Rhododendron Hob, would that be him?"

"Aye, his mother had ideas, but nae one can e'er spell it. Call him Rhodie, we do."

I looked at how you did spell it and smiled to myself, thinking of Nanny Ogg and the banana. "It seems like stopping spelling it might be more of a problem."

Mags cackled in my ear. "I wouldn't have taken you for a fan of Mr Pratchett's, Your Maj."

Huh. I wouldn't have taken her for one either. "Oh, I have been for years. What are you reading today, Mags?"

She huffed in my ear, "What I thought was going to be a reet fine romance. But it's one of the annoying ones, where if either of those kids had the common sense they were born with, their easily-fixed misunderstanding would have been over and done with by chapter six. But they're both stupid, so I expect it'll drag out for half the book. I'm about to DNF it."

"Mags, how well do you know Inge?"

"Why'd ye ask?"

"Well, she stayed with you after the book club, and you lent her some clothes, so I wondered if you might call yourself her friend?"

"Aye, I might say so. In certain circumstances anyway, I might."

"Then if you've fallen out with your book, may I request your presence in the Gateway this afternoon? I'm going to have to bully Inge later on, and I thought perhaps someone she obviously trusted might help her get through it to the right outcome."

"I'll be right there, Your Maj; sounds more fun than this feekin' predictable book." I heard a crash, some muttering about silly ferrets, and then she disconnected the phone.

I rubbed my still unsettled stomach. What was I missing?

"Dola, have we heard from Caitlin during her holiday?"

Through my earbud came a chuckle. "She called me this morning to ask if I was absolutely certain there was nothing she ought to be doing. She was trying to avoid going on a picnic with a group of girls she described as bubble heads. Would you like me to request her return? Also, Finn is on his way over."

"No, I'll summon her, then she can blame me if her mother complains."

Nothing changed, so the niggling unhappiness didn't relate to my Knights.

I consulted my mental list. Oh, yes, Ad'Rian. There was no damn privacy in this Gateway, and I wanted it for this call. I strolled towards the green gate and dialled as I walked.

"Do you remember that lovely glade you offered me last week

for Troels? Would it be too much trouble if I sent you a dozen warlords instead?"

"You worked out how to do it, then? Well done, Nik-a-lula. Yes, of course, although if there are a dozen of them, perhaps a different glade. It's less hospitable. And the piskies will keep them busy. Please disarm them before you send them. I know they're a nuisance, but I'm surprisingly fond of the little blighters." Then, as though he realised he'd made no sense, he added, "The piskies, obviously, not the warlords."

"Ad'Rian, I will need them all back alive. Are piskies fatal?"

I'd loved them when I was a kid, and they'd loved Dusha. But who knew what they might do to a Viking warlord?

"Not unless provoked, hence my advice to disarm the warlords. Piskies will sacrifice one to bring down an enemy, but if they do, the rest of their foes don't usually survive the encounter."

"OK, no weapons. Any idea what might be the best way to get them to you?"

"I'll send Glais'Nee with some of the guards. He's taken to you; I think that case of Vimto you sent him after the book club made you a friend for life. You never send me gifts." There was an actual pout in his tone.

"Ad'Rian, I brought you a Dolina; you can request anything I have that you might want from that!" I was technically telling the truth. I had brought the Dolina. But I didn't feel bad taking credit for Dola's brainwave. A pouting Ad'Rian wasn't what I needed right now.

"Oh. Sorry, daaarling, I'm not certain I realised that. I'll speak to Dola about it."

"OK, and may I borrow Glais'Nee, with his consent, obviously, to check the warlords so I only send you the guilty ones?"

"Of course, simply ask him. Shall I send him now?"

"Can I ask Dola to confirm with you when I'm ready? I'm getting my ducks in a row at the moment."

"Is that like lining up your unicorn horns?"

I laughed. "Yes exactly that."

"I like it, daaarling. I shall commit the phrase to memory. Now, Recorder?"

"Yes?" Then I realised he meant he wanted to speak to the Recorder. Oh, Gods and Goddesses, I must get these royals to simply tell me to change hats.

"Yes, Your Majesty, what can I assist you with today?" Damn it, I sounded like bloody Janet.

He chuckled then sobered quickly. "Is there anything I can do to help my nephew?"

"At this moment, I've truly asked for everything I need, or at least that I can think of. You must have known about the bond at the book club on Thursday, of course, but we only worked it out on Friday. But you'll realise I'm very committed to getting him what he wants, and not what everyone else thinks he should do."

I heard a long, relieved sigh. "Thank the goddess. Although Glais'Nee saw your bond first at John's sentencing. I wondered whether to say something when you popped in with Tilly. One can never see one's own bond. Well, some people apparently can, but I don't know what makes them the exception."

"But we weren't even together at the sentencing? I mean, Rollo wasn't there. How could Glais'Nee see a bond?"

"You were shielding him, and he was calming and supporting you at a stressful time. You had the bond mate mind link."

OK? We did, did we? So, from my side, it might have clicked in when I wouldn't give him the yellow regnal energy until the power let me clean it. Interesting.

"Once Glais'Nee saw it was not the Recorder who was shielding Rollo, it was Niki, then, darling, of course he would know. He felt it had been in place for some time. Several weeks anyway."

Well, that blew my theory out of the water, didn't it?

I started laughing. My life couldn't get any crazier, could it?

"You have accepted it fully, haven't you? You were so busy on Thursday night, I didn't want to intrude by asking to check it. It's fabulous to be able to truly welcome you into my family. Not that you weren't family before—oh, you know what I mean. I'm very fond of you both. Ask for anything. If I can help, I will. Rollo is a wonderful boy. Being the Viking king would kill him, and I do not speak metaphorically. I'm so relieved you have a better plan."

I heard the sound of shattering glass and screeching brakes in my mind. It stopped me dead. I paused, mostly to collect my stomach, which felt as though it was now somewhere near my knees.

Finn, wearing a strange, misshapen red jumper, walked past me with Tilly at his heels and gave me a thumbs-up. I stared blindly at his back. That jumper was peculiar.

I heard, "Recorder?" from my phone.

I moved further from the Gateway and didn't realise I was almost whispering. "Ad'Rian, my plan involves him being king, in name only, for a couple of years while they form some type of functioning government. I don't mind sharing the whole of it with you. But I was about to start putting it into action. Where did the idea or the information that him being king would kill him come from?"

There was a long silence.

"Recorder, it's possible you need to delay your plans for today. You need to summon me."

"OK. Because?"

But all he said was, "Now would be convenient, my lady."

CHAPTER
FIFTY-THREE

I summoned Ad'Rian.
Fi and Finn wanted to speak to me. "Sorry, guys, I have an appointment with the Fae King. Ask Dola if she can help, or I'll be free after Ad'Rian."

They both nodded as the man himself marched up the Violet Sector, his lilac robes billowing so wildly, you would have thought there was a stiff breeze in the Gateway. The grey leggings he wore under his robes gave me flashes of his well-shaped calves, and his long silver hair flowed out behind him like a train. His usual languid catwalk slink was nowhere in evidence today, and his long legs covered the distance swiftly. As I greeted him at the top of the sector, he glanced around the Gateway. "Somewhere more private please, Recorder."

I just stared at him.

"Daaarling, I could use a zone of silence spell, but it's sooo tiring. I'm exhausted after we healed Dai earlier. Let's simply be somewhere else, please."

I took his wrist and moved us to my Stane Parlour office.

Ad'Rian looked around. "This is new; you're settling in then?" He headed towards my bookshelves, and before I could lose him to a long and normally welcome discussion about books, I gestured him to a chair.

"Dola, may I have a coffee, and Ad'Rian says I never give him nice things. Can we have two of the dark chocolate brownies with ice cream and cream please?"

"Yes, Niki. Would His Majesty like a beverage?"

I quirked an eyebrow at Ad'Rian, who focused on the Dolina. "Ah, Dola, you are everywhere these days, how lovely. I require nothing further, thank you."

We ate our brownies. I had an ominous feeling in my unhappy stomach and hoped Ad'Rian wasn't going to drag this out. He could be annoying that way. *But, Nik-a-lula, how else will you learn?*

Or maybe that was only when I was six? But if it involved Rollo's safety, I needed facts—and fast.

Perhaps my shields were leaky because he swallowed his mouthful of brownie and ice cream, almost purring in pleasure, and waved a calming hand at me. "I'm sure we can work it out. But I do wonder why you called me this morning?"

"Because my Gift was unhappy, and I thought it was something to do with Mags and her poor Hobs girls who'd miscarried. But it wasn't. Or at least the feeling didn't go away after I spoke to her."

"Does Marguerite have a problem?"

"Yes. The Recorder is fixing it. Now, what's this about Rollo dying if he's king?"

"Very authoritative today. Has the bond clicked in properly?"

"I don't know. How would I know that? What does that even mean? Nobody tells me a damn thing, you know!"

"May I?" He put down his now-empty bowl. Wow, he'd wolfed that at a speed worthy of Finn. I didn't want mine, and when I don't want loaded brownies, I'm not myself.

He reached a finger towards my third eye.

"Sure, knock yourself out." What was one more person in my bloody head?

"Niki." He gave me a stern look.

"I'm sorry, Ad'Rian. I'm angry, and I'm in a hurry to make sure Rollo will be OK. But I consent."

He instigated a mind link, but this felt different. I started to pull back. "What are you doing?"

Then I felt calmer.

And immediately got cross. "You know, Ad'Rian, it isn't always a bad thing to be a bit angry. In fact, it's not necessarily bad to be absolutely furious at forty years of injustices and terrible, outrageous injuries against women. Especially if you're in a position to do something about them."

I kept getting calmer and fought against it.

"STOP doing that," I almost shouted at him. "Have you watched any of those videos? Perhaps if a few more people had got angry enough at the right time, a lot of women could have been saved from having their lives turned upside down and avoided some very unpleasant experiences."

I breathed and then thought, *sod it*. "And I didn't consent to healing. I don't want to be healed right now. I want to be mad as hell, and it's my goddess-given right to be as furious as I need to be to fix this mess. I consented to a mind link and only that."

Ad'Rian sat up, folded his hands on his knees and watched me carefully. "I apologise, Niki, I thought you would like me to check your bond, and you were too angry for me to do that."

But my left shoulder pinged, and I gaped at Ad'Rian. "You just lied to me!"

The Fae never lied.

WTAF?

I broke the mind link and was just about to reach out to Rollo when I looked at the time on my phone. He'd be in his appointment with Chris now to discuss the briefing document about regencies.

Rollo needed to concentrate on that. I didn't want to mess up his head. He'd been in good form this morning. I'd like him to stay that way.

Ad'Rian leaned forward in his chair. "How did you just calm yourself so swiftly?"

"Hmmn? Oh, I remembered about keeping Rollo's morning calm. He has some decisions to make and an important meeting. We had a lovely breakfast together before all the raped women, well, and the one who narrowly avoided it, interrupted us. I didn't want to stress him."

I sounded so heartless about the women. I wasn't. However, I knew if I didn't suppress my empathy and stay focused, I couldn't help them get justice.

I shared none of this with Ad'Rian. Instead, I said, "I'm about to turn Viking upside down. I had a great plan, and then you said, if Rollo is king, even briefly, it will kill him. So everything came to a clashing, screaming halt in my head."

Ad'Rian nodded. "This is my fault then. May I clarify your thoughts without calming your anger?"

I thought about it. "If you tell me why you lied to me, maybe."

"I think I merely misspoke. I said I thought you would like me to check your bond. What I should have said is that I love both you and my nephew deeply, and I want to be sure all is well with your bond. I'm aware it must have formed during difficult times. That can sometimes cause problems."

Well, that was the truth. And if the King of Fae offers to bring his skill to bear on determining the health of your bond, you should probably let him, right?

So I did.

Ad'Rian drew in a slow breath then reached out his finger again.

"I consent to you checking our bond." I wasn't taking any chances. Why had it never occurred me to before that I should qualify my consent? Was I getting smarter? Or just wiser about the ways of kings?

"Oooh," his soft expiration drew my attention to him, "this is a glorious seven-fold. Congratulations, daaarling." Ad'Rian sounded awed. "We saw so few of these for years, but these days they appear to be everywhere."

"Yeah, thanks, we know."

"You do? How did you know?"

"I saw it; it's blinding. If you're happy with it, can we please get on to what the problem is with Rollo being king?"

"Niki, how did you know? This feels important. Humour me."

"Tell me about Rollo first, then I'll show you." I had learned, the moment you gave in to kings, you lost all bargaining power. Huh, go me!

Ad'Rian sat back again, looking as surprised as Mabon was last week when I said no to him about Agnes's locket until he'd answered my questions.

He relaxed in his chair. "There is a prophecy, possibly not a true one. We do not know. We were unable to pin it down, thanks to his head injury, but Mabon thinks it was seeded by Agnes rather than it being a true *seeing*. However, we're certain it was passed to the Vikings several hundred years ago."

"What does 'seeded' mean in this context?" I was getting tired of weird prophecies. They never made a single damn thing any clearer. They always came in bits and pieces, and they were just annoying and distracting.

"Agnes, was, what these days we would call politically savvy. Back then, we just said twisty and manipulative."

I nodded. Yes, I'd seen that much for myself in her strange, locked-up, passworded, quiz-riddled messages in the Book.

"It is possible she announced prophecies that weren't what my own seers would describe as true seeings. Niki, most prophecies are irritatingly vague, at least until after they come true. Then, daaaarling, everyone says, 'well, of course, it could only ever have meant' ... whatever it was that actually happened."

I must have looked confused because Ad'Rian leaned forward. "Consider your airlock, which my newest seer described as a small metal box that killed trespassers. Afterwards, everything is as clear as Lake Áine. But would your first guess be an airlock if I gave you a prophecy about a small box, probably made of metal and glass, which rendered people who approached it unconscious?"

"No, I'd probably guess at a passive infrared security device that emitted a gas or something similar. OK, I take the point. So, what does this maybe-not-a-prophecy say?"

"It says that, at a certain time in the future, I'm sure there were a lot of conditions attached, but I simply can't remember them. Ask the Book? Anyone who claims the Viking throne without the true symbols connected to his heart to prove he is the Rightful King will lose his lands, his money, his reputation and everyone he loves before dying a horrible death. The Rightful King with the correct symbols will only rule for a short time but will go on to live a very long, fulfilling and joyous life."

I could jump to conclusions, but with Rollo's life on the line, I needed to be certain. How could I be sure who this was about? "Well, Troels didn't, did he? Or at least he hasn't yet. He survived for forty years after usurping the throne from Rollo?"

Ad'Rian said, "It did not say a swift death, Niki. I would say most of the rest either already has or is in the process of coming true. Wouldn't you?"

A smile spread across my face. Maybe I wasn't jumping to conclusions. If I looked at it in that light—

Ad'Rian interrupted my train of thought as he mused, "Which makes me wonder, was it seeded, or was it a true *seeing*? Simply one we didn't understand back in Agnes's time." He wafted his hand in the universal sign for "back whenever it was."

But I was focused. "Does it advise us on what those correct symbols would be?"

He gave me the look I might give Tilly when she thought a second portion of doggy ice cream was perfectly reasonable. "No, Niki, of course it doesn't. At least, not precisely."

He paused, relaxed back on the couch and closed his eyes briefly. When he opened them, his eyes were now the pure white of a master of the Fae magics using his talents. "It says they define the three goddesses, or, now wait, was it the three powers that cannot be defied?"

He sighed, and his eyes returned to their usual silver-violet. "It does say the Rightful King explains those symbols in such a way that no one can argue with or gainsay their right to rule. Troels had some symbols. Can I remember what they were?"

He cast his eyes around the office as though the answer might be written on the ceiling, and eventually gazed out of the window. "Daaarling, is that Mabon's stone down there?"

"Yes, we've called this room Stane Parlour."

"How lovely. He never mentioned it."

I wasn't quite rude enough to ignore him. "He hasn't seen it yet." And then I pressed on with what was confusing me. "But when I summoned the Rightful King, which Rollo says he isn't because he hasn't accepted the throne, the power brought him to the Gateway anyway."

Ad'Rian nodded as though this made perfect sense.

I tried another tack. "Troels' symbols were …?"

He sighed. "You are so assertive today. I believe Troels' symbols were a wolf, a knife of some kind, and something else—something … no, I can't retrieve it. Might it have even been a crown, surely no one would be that crass? But Rollo would know. Troels told some tale about them, and everyone chose to believe him, but Rollo was yet unborn, and Troels was someone they knew."

I thought about the Danake coin Rollo had put, not above his heart, but near his penis, and I smiled.

"Niki, you are smiling, but you should know that everyone who could possibly be a contender for the throne, other than my nephew, has a wide variety of ridiculous symbols on their torso. I hear they all have long, credible explanations for why they are the correct ones."

"OK, thanks, Ad'Rian. Do you happen to recall how this prophecy begins?" I'd try to get some sense out of the Book.

"Oh, yes, but that won't help at all. It follows on from another one. That one is ridiculous and full of whimsy, which is why we believed it might have been seeded. It begins,

Once upon a time, there were twin souls, born at the same hour, on the same day.

A boy and girl whose lives were irrevocably changed, also on the same day in the same hour.

They bade farewell to their innocence and were ripped, screaming, away from their childhoods.

One with knowledge they could never lose, the other with knowledge they couldn't recover until it was almost too late.

Oh, freaking hell! Did Ad'Rian truly not get it? If he didn't, and he was a shrewd man with a fine mind behind his indolent persona, it might explain why no one else had pieced it together.

Whoops, he was still talking.

"I can't recall more, but the Book will have it. The thing is almost doggerel and artificially portentous. It continues in the same ridiculous fairy-tale fashion. There may even be a handsome prince in it. I cannot recall the whole of it. But there are several even more ludicrous, I suppose you might call them, verses, although I certainly wouldn't, and they certainly aren't stanzas. It's just poorly constructed, odd prose, like a child's bedtime tale, so how could one take it seriously?"

I smiled, then swiftly straightened my face before I annoyed Ad'Rian. But the smile kept breaking through my fear, and eventually I let it.

Anger was clear in Ad'Rian's voice, if not on his mostly immobile face. "Niki, you are being irritating. Your bond is lovely. It seems to be functioning well. Do you have further need of me before you share how you could have been aware your own bond was a seven-fold?"

"Just one thing, please, Your Majesty." He sat up, immediately attentive. "Do you have any records of the date and time on which you rescued Rollo from his cell in Viking? And if you do, could you provide the Recorder with a copy of them?"

I saw light breaking through the annoyance in his eyes.

I had no idea how I could pin down or prove my own dates. But perhaps I didn't need to. Perhaps only we needed to know. I hoped so because, even with my memories returned, that part of my life was horribly vague. But I knew when I'd started boarding school, so that might help. Or Mabon might know.

"Oh, yes, and one final thing. Do you know anything about this Viking seer everyone keeps talking about? I don't think anyone's mentioned his name, just The Seer."

I felt him smooth his shields and shutter his eyes. "May one enquire why you need to know?"

"Because every time someone mentions him, my Gift twitches, and I see your face."

Ad'Rian's face remained its usual careful blank.

I paused and wondered how you actually gave someone what my much-loved detective novels always described as the hard eye. Or was it a hard stare?

Ad'Rian watched me carefully. He was going to make me say it.

"While your spies are none of my business, if they get mixed into my case against Viking, and if that seer gave Rollo deliberately confusing information and was also instrumental in Kari claiming sanctuary, and now she's being a pain in my backside, then I might have to look closely at their ... their what? Would they call you their spymaster?"

"Recorder, I assure you I have no connection with Kari. Do I even know her?"

"Princess Karina Halvor. She's the daughter of Warlord Halvor, and I think he runs the smuggling ring that was trying to steal ingredients from your Healer Hall's walled garden."

"Aaah, yes, I am aware of her. But," he raised his hand and held it over his heart. "I assure you, her actions, whatever they have may been, are nothing to do with me. The walled garden, you say? Our healers' herb garden?"

My right shoulder agreed with him about Kari.

I waited.

So did he.

Then I glared at him. "The Recorder requires a little more information before we can get to your question."

He asked, "Hypothetically?"

Wow! That worked!

I nodded, "Hypothetically, if anyone knew anything about this mysterious seer, might they know whose side he's on? Specifically, did he deliberately give Rollo the wrong, or at least dangerously partial information about the tattoo he needed, or did Rollo misunderstand? Importantly, is he for or against him? And why the hell do I keep seeing Betty who works in my local shop, and your face every time anyone mentions him?"

"She is his sister."

"Oh."

"He did not give Rollo any information on my behalf, so you would have to ask him. His name is Jeff."

I choked off a laugh. "Jeff the Seer, seriously?"

He misunderstood my amusement. "It is a venerable and ancient Celtic name." He inscribed a G in the air. "When spelt the old way, Geoffrey, it means the Gods' peace, and I fail to understand your amusement."

I resolutely moved all amusing memories of Jeff Foxworthy to the back of my mind and nodded at him solemnly. "Sorry. If it turns out to matter, I'll ask him. Do you trust him?"

"He does not like Troels, so mostly, yes. He has been reliable over the years. And he has the seer's gift, do not doubt that. It must now be my turn to discover how you knew your bond was a seven-fold, and why you believe that is?"

He'd played fair, so I had to. I leaned forward and said, "I consent to share the memory of how we discovered it."

"You make progress, Nik-a-lula. I'm impressed." His finger to my third eye began our link, and I ran Autumn standing us in front of a mirror in Aysha's hall.

Ad'Rian looked a little grey as he pulled out of the link. "The child will need training."

"Yes, I know, but she's very young yet."

"You were younger when I first began with you on your shields."

I sighed because, honestly, I'd thought this myself. "I know. And I'll work with her on them just the way you did with me. But Aysha," his brows almost twitched into a frown, so I elaborated, "her mother, has opinions. About pretty much everything. I'll speak to her again."

"And the Healers' Hall walled garden?"

"I'll fill Glais'Nee in on that, shall I, as he's heading the investigation?"

His eyes widened just a little, then he nodded grumpily and headed towards the door, brushing off my offer of returning him to the Gateway. "I'll consult my records."

Then he paused with one hand on the door handle. "One further matter—the Recorder will receive a full report. Prince Dafydd has completed the first stage of his healing. They're confident without the dragon power impeding them, and with your consent to override his death wish, they are getting to the core of the problem."

"And that would be what?"

"The Recorder will receive a full report when we have that information, and of course, we will need your judgement before he is discharged, but that won't be for some time yet."

As he left, he promised he would send his notes through shortly. Knowing full well that "shortly" from Ad'Rian could mean anytime this decade, I checked that he meant later today, then I settled down to consult the Book yet again.

CHAPTER
FIFTY-FOUR

"*Hey, it went incredibly well with Chris. I've almost got a working plan. Are you busy, or can I pop down for a coffee?*"

I closed the Book with a sigh of relief. It hadn't been a lot of help, although it clarified a few things and gave me a little hope.

"*Yes, I'm in Stane Parlour. Oh, and you need to get a new tattoo.*"

Confusion came from Rollo in a wave. "*Why? What? Never mind, I'm on my way. Oh no I'm not. Where's Stane Parlour?*"

"*You were in here when Mags …*" I paused and considered how I always needed a clear picture of anywhere I wanted to transport to. "*… Never mind. I'll meet you outside the green gate instead.*"

He was already there when Tilly and I arrived. He wrapped me in a warm, comforting hug. This man and I seemed to spend far too much time comforting each other.

He laughed over the top of my head, the sound rumbling through his chest. "You're right, but neither of us had a partner to comfort us for far too long, did we?"

He was right. Some things you couldn't argue with.

He kissed the top of my head, and the tiny sensation shivered right through me. It spread warmth, and not simply comfort, but a sense of home, of belonging, and of love right through me. I took half a step back so I could see his face.

He didn't release me, but he looked down into my eyes. "We'll get through it all, and then we'll claim some us time."

"Us time sounds blissful and necessary." Goddess, he was gorgeous.

He smiled at me, obviously picking up my thought. "I often think the same about you. If we can put the plan into place, they can all get along without us while we work out who we want to be?"

Who we want to be? What a concept. We had a choice?

"We've both been short of choices for too long. Let's make some we like, hey?"

I nodded. That sounded a little scary, but fun too.

"I got useful information this morning. I have a lot to tell you. Well, to tell the Recorder, actually. But I think it's all good news. And once—"

I put my finger gently on his lips. "There are two absolutely vital things I need to share with you first. I had a weird conversation with Ad'Rian earlier. There's stuff you don't know. And you need to know it, like now."

I loved he didn't argue, try to correct me or bluster. He simply held out his finger towards my third eye.

"I consent."

I brought him up to speed. He took it all in calmly, then he started laughing again. "Oh, Freyja loves me today. I know just the tatt. I've even got the almost completed design ready."

Huh! We headed into the Gateway hand in hand. Rollo headed over to Finn, who showed no surprise at his request. "Lossie again?" At Rollo's nod, he added, "Sure, but this week might be pushing it."

Rollo nodded.

I asked, "Finn, do you know him well?"

"Yup. You've met him, my lady."

I had? And then a beautifully inked arm swam forward from

the back of my mind. "Was he Gowan's best man?" I vaguely remembered a guy with tattoos, or paint, as the Picts called them, that were so lifelike, they looked three-dimensional. Actually, they did look like some of Rollo's.

Finn nodded. "Lesley's brother."

"Broch manager Lesley? Lossie and Lesley, really? Why would people do that to their children?"

He nodded. "Name's Lawrence. So Lossie, obvs."

"Yeah, because Larry would be too normal? OK, Finn, I never thought I'd hear myself say this, but this is urgent. It needs to be today. Use the Recorder's name if you think it will help. Also tell him this one might make him famous."

"Nah, be fine. He owes me one." At my raised eyebrow, he added, "I redid his website last month. He pays in paint."

Rollo looked at me and sent, *"You don't even know what it will look like yet?"*

"I trust you." As I sent him the thought, I realised it was true, I did.

Rollo's surprised laugh had Finn's head turning around. Into his earbud, I heard him say, "Yeah, for royalty."

He broke the connection and asked, "Half an hour, OK?"

Rollo threw an arm round his shoulder. "Thanks, bud."

Finn smiled, "Ya got lucky. Someone chickened out ten minutes ago."

I didn't blame them. "Perfect. Thanks, Finn. You did a great job on those videos. Everything OK on the portal today?"

"More new vids from Viking women. #ItHappenedto-VikingsToo is taking over the portal."

"OK, I'll look. Have you heard from Caitlin?"

"She's bored of wearing dresses."

That seemed to be all he had to say. So, I wandered over to Fi to find out what she'd needed earlier.

Her expression was neutral, but my Gift said she was suppressing anger as she spoke. "Glynis asked if you would be hearing the petitions publicly?"

"No. I don't think so. I'm not sure this will be an arbitration as such. But I planned to record it, then Finn and Dola can release a report about it to the portal. Why?"

Her brows quirked into a monobrow as she asked, "But why isn't it an arbitration?"

"Have you seen many arbitrations, Fi?"

"Yes, quite a few. My lady Elsie didn't have the conference table, so everyone just stood around her desk, which was right next to my desk. So …"

I laughed involuntarily. "She truly made them stand around her desk?"

Fi nodded. "She said it kept them brief that way."

Oh, Gran. Standing meetings? In some ways, you were years ahead of your time, weren't you? Just not in the ways that involved technology of any kind.

I said, "From the old records I've read, normally there are two parties who disagree about something. And the Recorder is supposed to find a middle path so they can both move forward, thinking it could have been better for them, but it could also have been worse, and at least it's all sorted now."

Fi nodded. "That's a good description of the ones I've seen, yes."

"So how do you think two hundred women saying he knocked me unconscious with a drug and raped me and I have the child and the genetic evidence to prove it was him on one side of the table, and a man whose only response is 'young women are gullible, and all women lie' fits into the usual system?"

"Oh."

"Yeah, exactly: oh. It's not what anyone would call a normal arbitration, is it?"

Fi looked thoughtful now as she consulted her ever-present list. "But some people have asked if they can attend?"

"Who? How many people?"

"About a thousand."

CODE YELLOW IN GRETNA GREEN

I sat down abruptly in the chair next to her desk. "Seriously? Why?"

Slowly, her anger came out. "Now that hundreds of victims are speaking out, a lot of family members who perhaps didn't treat their daughters the way they should have at the time want to make amends by being supportive." The sarcasm she layered onto the 'being supportive' suggested why she was angry about this.

On one hand, I thought people had a right to see what the Recorder's Office did. I hoped, in the future, it would stop the kind of misinformation that had circulated in the Viking realm. But having a thousand guilt-ridden parents, friends or siblings underfoot during this weird non-arbitration felt like the worst idea in the world.

The Recorder is always right rang in my head.

"What do *you* think, Fi?"

"I think they should stay out of it. The girls support each other well and good. I don't see why they should have to make their parents feel better. Not until it's over, anyway. It's hard enough for them."

"Agreed. Tell everyone I said no."

"I thought you'd say that, but I told them I'd ask. Despite that, I think you're going to have to lock most of the gates, Niki. People are stupid."

"How about we tell them it's happening next week? And it won't be open to the public. We don't need witnesses to attend. Thanks to everyone's amazing work this week, we seem to have all the video evidence we'll need."

Fi tilted her head to one side, making her gorgeous red hair swing about. "And when is it happening? The date on the portal is pretty general, but I heard you tell Troels it would be next week."

Did I trust Fi?

Yeah, I did. "Things have changed a bit, but if you don't want an audience trying to get in here, you cannot mention this to a living soul. No one, are we clear? Not your mother, not Corby, absolutely no one?"

She surprised me. "Then would you not answer me? I'd rather be able to tell Mum I don't know, and it be the truth. I'd hate to mess up. She has a way of winkling things out of me, and she gossips."

I smiled as I thought how well my new trade director knew herself and her mum.

Rollo and I sat at my desk. I'd asked the Book to show us both what it showed me after Ad'Rian left. His eyes widened as he read. Then he closed his open mouth with a snap before asking, "How long has this been in the book?

"Well, it's Agnes. So, a while. What year was this entered into the Book?"

At the bottom of the page, a date arrived.

1580

Rollo felt like he wanted to wrap his arms around me but was aware the Gateway was full of people. "It's us, right? Are you scared?"

He pointed to the line that said, **Once upon a time, there were twin souls, born at the same hour, on the same day.** "Two p.m., you too?"

I started laughing. "No, two in the morning, but I guess it counts as the same hour?"

Rollo said, "I'm not even sure I know when this was. I was out of it." He pointed to the next line.

A boy and girl whose lives were irrevocably changed, also on the same day in the same hour.

"I asked Ad'Rian if he could check his records. He's going to get back to me, or Dola. Who knows? He was in a snit when he left."

"A snit?"

"Yeah, I stood up to him. He was huffy. You know, in a strop?

But I don't think it was that I stood up to him. I think it was that, until I asked him what time he rescued you, it hadn't occurred to him that this might be about us. He could recite parts of it, but he hadn't made the connection. Ad'Rian loathes being blindsided."

Rollo nodded knowingly. "Yeah. But we know it was roughly the same time because of what he said to your gran."

I frowned, "My gran?"

"When he thanked her for allowing him to get me from Viking, he said, 'We lost one much-loved child today; two would have been too many.'" He pointed at the space between us, then at me. "You must have been the first, right?"

I squeezed his thigh under my desk as we both looked at the next line.

They bade farewell to their innocence and were ripped, screaming, away from their childhoods.

In unison, we said, "True."

Then Rollo said, "We have to work this bit out."

One with knowledge they could never lose, the other with knowledge they couldn't find again until it was almost too late.

I gave him a surprised look. "It's not rocket surgery, is it? You never forgot Boo, and I couldn't remember a damn thing until a few weeks ago, when Mabon removed my memory block."

He laughed. "Yeah, you're right, it isn't complicated. I might be overthinking it. Kari is still asking me to explain 'rocket surgery.' It makes no sense to her. She got quite cross that you and Ben had a private joke she didn't get. She decided I didn't understand it properly; otherwise, she'd think it was funny when I explained it."

"It's really not a private joke. More Ben, me and almost three million other Mancunians who think neither rocket science nor brain surgery is funny, but for some reason rocket surgery is hilarious. It's just a northern thing. Tell her you have to be born there. We're all a bit warped."

Refusing to be distracted by my chattering, he asked, "Are

you scared?" Rollo's tiger-eye irises were bright today as he gazed into my eyes.

"Weirdly, no. I think it's pretty damn cool. I might not think so when I understand it properly. But right now, being the subject of a prophecy that says we're twin souls makes me happy. We were supposed to be together. It feels like it could be a hell of a lot worse. Although, the Book won't give me the rest of it. It just says it links to the Coin and Key Prophecy I've enquired about before, and the time is not right to reveal that one. And it won't tell me what would make the time right."

"Coin and Key Prophecy? I've not heard about that one. We have one about a coin and the tree—"

The Book shivered.

"Did you feel that?"

Rollo looked at me. "Feel what?"

The alarm on his phone went off. "Sorry, need to run. Lossie's waiting. This isn't a big tatt; probably take three or four hours." He kissed me and headed for the blue gate.

I turned back to the Book and thought, *Tell me what it was about the damn tree that made you shiver.*

A single leaf of the book flipped. On the new page, I saw ... **The anvil will be found sitting in state on a living throne of its own creation, with royalty at its feet, a goddess at its side and a champion at its back.**

Once the angel watches over it, the ripples of small changes will become larger waves. Until, with the joining of the key and the coin to the tree, a kingdom, a prince and a religion will fall. A gate, a realm, and a queen will rise; traitors are lost; heroes are found, hypocrites are brought low. When branches are added to the family tree and the dead speak from the grave ...

I saw the three dots, but I asked anyway, "Is that it? Is that all of it?"

No.

"Then when do I get the bloody rest of it? How is it a

prophecy if I only get to read it after stuff has happened?" Although some of it hadn't happened yet, had it? But the dead speaking from the grave reminded me I really ought to go and visit my gran's grave as Mags had suggested.

"Sorry, milady, did you say something?" Rosemary Hob gave me her sweet smile.

"Talking to myself, Rosie, sorry."

"Oh, that's normal for us. May I ask a question about my job?"

"Of course. Anytime."

"How does the Gateway make money? I don't mean to pry, but we don't seem to charge people for any of the things like a normal business would. You know I work with Crane?"

"Yes, in his import and export business?"

She smiled happily. "People pay for things. For permits, for licenses and his expertise. But in here, we never seem to charge anyone."

I nodded, smiled back and waited to see where she was going with this.

"We bind—aaargh, sorry, milady, I will get used to it. We *bond* people for free. But the Gateway paid Juniper for the food, and the guests didn't pay us for it. The only thing they pay for is the photographs, and that money goes to the photographers." She blushed now, then continued in a rush, "So, how do you pay us?"

"We take a tax or tithe on trade goods that move through the Gateway, and it's funny you should mention this because it's on my list for a brainstorming session soon. I think the system has become outdated. Did you have some ideas?"

She nodded so hard, I worried she would injure her neck. Sparkling green eyes met mine. "Fi and I both have suggestions. So does Finn. Shall I arrange the meeting for one of the days I'm at work?"

Finn had ideas about trade? Wow. "That would be great. I'm looking forward to hearing your proposals."

Ever since I'd found out the former Knight Adjutants hadn't

been paid, except for an allowance for fodder for their horse, I'd thought the system needed an overhaul. Good to know even the newest member of my staff was so on the ball. It should be a fun meeting.

I turned back to the Book to see when the rest of the damned annoying prophecy would be revealed.

When the time is right. When the information would assist you. At the correct juncture. When the auspices align.

They sounded like a lot of bullshit excuses. What the hell were auspices, and how would one know if they aligned? I just stopped myself swearing and disturbing Rosie again as I slammed the Book shut. It was annoying. But then I reminded myself everything was annoying me today. Almost six weeks in this role, and I still couldn't get a straight answer.

Perhaps I should take my anger out on the people who were causing it and summon some Viking warlords? But first I thought I'd better eat some lunch before I channelled Rhiannon and actually bit someone's head off.

CHAPTER
FIFTY-FIVE

I wanted to be at home, uninterrupted and in peace. I should make some notes on all the things I needed to do and the order I thought I should do them in.

Then I wanted to check my plans with the power. I ought to consult Rollo. Officially, as the current holder of the yellow regnal power, not just *hey, Boo, are you OK with this*?

I should summon Caitlin back too, shouldn't I? She'd get snarly if I did this without her. And I needed Glais'Nee and maybe Ad'Rian to be present. It would probably be polite to at least invite Mabon. He might enjoy it anyway now that Dai seemed to be finally healing. I needed to summon Inge.

And, oh, bloody hell! How had I forgotten? I was supposed to be deciding what to do with Troels. He could hardly stay in his cell on the Gate's boundary in Viking forever … could he?

A ridiculous thought struck me. Had those people who'd died slowly and then rotted in those horrific metal gibbet cages done so because everyone just looked at each other around a table and said, "Well, I don't know what to do with the traitor, do you?"

Two hundred years ago, did some prominent mayor or official reply, "Well, he's doing no harm where he is—is he? An object lesson is never wasted."

My head spun.

Tilly led the way at a brisk trot in the cold, damp Scottish air. She headed down the path from the Gateway to the cottage and towards lunch with the single-minded and refreshing determination of a dog who was crystal clear about the correct order of all the priorities in her life. Chicken first, baths last and everything else important, like walks and naps, could simply fit in. Perhaps I should take a leaf out of her book?

Warlords first, Troels last. Did that help me? Actually, it did. Perhaps, like Tilly, I should take life in stages.

Then I opened the back door, walked into my kitchen and gasped. I'd gone straight from Rollo's to the Gateway and then to Stane Parlour. While I'd been away, Dola had updated the kitchen.

I twirled in a circle and desperately tried to process the change. OK, it wasn't anything major. The wall with the ugly little black door into the horrible lounge had changed. Most of that section of the wall now had a large, stylish focal point: a lovely blue-grey double-width bookcase. The colour toned perfectly with the blue-grey slate floor tiles and the duck-egg blue and copper accents. Wow, Dola had such a good eye.

"I love the improvement, Dola. Fabulous colour. What's it called? How on earth did you find the time?"

"Welcome home, Niki. Thank you. It is called shadow blue. Would you like lunch in the breakfast room so you are uninterrupted?"

I had a breakfast room?

All of my ancestors had thrown tantrums when Dola made any changes or improvements to the cottage. I'd decided in my first week that if I considered the house to be her body, then she should be able to do whatever she wanted to it. If I accepted I simply lived in it, we'd get along better. I took in a slow, deep breath, put all my frustrations with Viking aside and said, "Thank you. I'd love to see the breakfast room."

"If you touch your finger to the black panel to the right of the bookcase, I shall provide the soundtrack."

The trumpet voluntary came from the Dolina on the table, and unsure which finger Dola wanted, I touched all the ones on my right hand to a small square black glass panel on the wall.

Dola timed it perfectly just as the twiddly upbeat bit of the voluntary played the two bookcases slid apart, revealing a wide doorway. I managed not to yelp.

But as I stepped into the new breakfast room, I couldn't hold my gasp back.

It was a welcoming, light-filled room with wide glass sliding doors along the back wall where the old French windows had been. Those doors gave me a view of the rear gardens, and there seemed to be a new deck-cum-patio area just outside of them.

I opened them and stepped out onto ... yes, it *was* a deck, and it connected seamlessly to the other section of decking, which ran outside the windows of my bedroom and bathroom and held the hot tub. This latest alteration had opened up the entire rear of the house.

Next to the doors was an enormous new pot in a vibrant blue ceramic. It was filled with soil but otherwise empty. The deck had an outside table and chairs. It would make a restful breakfast spot. Dola must have been adjusting the temperature because it was pleasantly warm out here, much nicer than the drizzly cold day Tilly and I had walked home in.

Tilly sniffed every corner of the room before she bounded out of the new doors. "Dola, it looks much larger than that awful lounge. How on earth did you do it?"

"I just juggled everything a little, Niki. Your bedroom, which is through the door on the other wall, is slightly smaller, but I do not believe you will notice the difference."

I walked over and opened the other door, and, yes—it came straight into the little lobby area by my bedroom door. I could get from my bedroom into here for breakfast without having to deal with whoever was cluttering up my kitchen. Rollo and I could eat breakfast half-naked, as he preferred to do, without scandalising my Knights or anyone else. No more snarky comments on my PJs from Caitlin. I laughed in delight.

The breakfast room itself was fresh, light and held an interior table and chairs by the windows. A long, squashy sofa, perfect for cuddling someone as tall as Rollo, was in front of the small fireplace. Hadn't there always been a fireplace? Yes, a tiny cold little black one. But now it was larger and a stylish, glossy deep-green metal with a gold Recorder's seven-pointed star motif embossed on the front. It currently held artistically arranged logs, pine cones, and fairy lights, which gave an almost magical, multi-coloured rainbow glow to the formerly gloomy wall.

"You know, after Rollo nearly died, I never planned to set foot in here again. I mean, I didn't like the room anyway, but after all that blood …" I trailed off and looked down at the modern blonde wood flooring and smiled.

"Niki, I may know why you were never comfortable in here. I checked my memories. Your great-great-grandmother Florrie?" She paused, but I wasn't sure why.

"Yes, my gran's grandmother, bubbles-loving Florrie with her sex-filled, healthy exercise regime, yes?"

"Yes, that one. She only ever used the room to feed breakfast to her many overnight guests. She said the negative vibrations in the room sped them on their way."

I giggled because Florrie always sounded as though she'd been a complete hoot.

Dola said, "She believed one of her ancestors, probably Elspeth, hadn't vacated the room properly after she was burned. She often commented on the angry energy in here. I think Jennet even called a priest in once to cleanse it. That obviously didn't work if you were still sensing it."

"OK, so Elspeth," I racked my brain. "She was the idiot who

told the Book to give her fewer words and instructed her descendants not to breathe the power in, yes?"

"Correct. This room was not always the lounge. It was formerly the Recorder's bedroom."

"And Elspeth was haunting the place?"

"Really, Niki, no. I would know if I was hosting a haunting. Deceased souls have specific vibrations. I'm informing you only that *Florrie* believed it to be true."

I was losing the plot here. "Sorry, Dola, I'm confused."

"I think the problem may have stemmed from earlier, and I believe I have fixed it. I only mentioned that other Recorders have also noticed it to validate that the feeling was not restricted to you. Your thoughts would be welcome once you have spent some time in here. Please advise me if the strange vibrations of the room have ceased?"

"Oh, OK. Will do. But I can tell you right now, it feels different."

"Thank you. I think it is important, now you and Rollo are bonded for you to have some private spaces. The internet says this is essential, and although Florrie was a poor Recorder, she lived a long, joy-filled life with a great deal of healthy exercise. Perhaps she was not wrong about everything. I have sound-proofed this room, and I increased the sound-proofing of your bedroom."

Did Dola seriously just give me permission to have noisy monkey sex with Rollo? I risked, "OK. Because?"

"I could not avoid overhearing Rollo and Finn's conversation about spreading gossip and the line that should not be crossed when it concerned the Recorder's private affairs. I had not considered it properly. In the past, people didn't care so much about these things. Rollo's explanation to Finn helped me understand your views and the current opinions on it."

"Thank you, Dola. I truly appreciate it. And this is a fantastic room. You've excelled yourself."

A Dolina appeared on the table. It looked slightly different.

Dola said, "I have made a modification to the Dolinas in your private spaces."

A small square of blue light flashed in the bottom corner of the aluminium frame.

"If the light is illuminated, the device is active. If you touch the square, it will turn off. It will still work if you use my name as a wake word, but otherwise, I shall not monitor your private areas when the devices are muted."

I bit my lip so I wouldn't laugh. She was so kind and considerate, and I loved her, but I was already running the conversation Rollo and I would need to have via our mental link, so she couldn't overhear us. We'd end up laughing ourselves silly, and that was a happy thought.

CHAPTER
FIFTY-SIX

I settled in my new breakfast room for lunch. My to-do lists had served me well so far in my new role. They'd helped me feel in control enough to resolve all the problems the Gateway brought into my life. I opened a new checklist on my iPad so I could share it with everyone once I was finished.

1: Summon Inge and Mags. Tell them what needs to happen in Viking. Take cover somewhere, perhaps at Mabon's, and let Mags talk Inge into it.

2: Would Fi like to sit in? Fi and Inge are friends too, yeah? I want Inge to feel supported, not bullied. But she needs to accept the reality that she is a big part of the solution to the horrible mess that is Viking right now. She has to either be a part of it or stop trying to push Rollo into it. It isn't Someone else's problem, and she's part of the Everyone who should fix it.

3: Speak to Mabon. Ask if he wants to be summoned for the arbitration. A lot of the Red Celt women were affected by this. Has he watched the videos yet?

4: Summon Glais'Nee and ask if Ad'Rian wants to come too.

5: Summon the warlords. Should I involve Kari? (Ask Rollo.)

6: Get Glais'Nee to check them. Send the guilty ones to Ad'Rian's glade.

7: What about the innocent ones? Can any of them *be* innocent? If they knew what was going on, aren't they culpable? Shall we put a poll on the new Viking section of the portal? No, never mind, I don't think I want a vote on it.

8: Decide what the hell to do with Troels. Do any of you have any good ideas?

I'm just not sure killing a man who might keel over any day now looks like justice.

9: Take the weekend off. That's all of us. (This includes you, Finn). You can't do your best work on empty tanks, people.

That seemed to sum it up for me. I added everyone's names and the header, *Does anyone have thoughts*?

Almost immediately, it pinged with an addition from Finn: *0: Summon Caitlin. She has thoughts and isn't happy in Galicia.*

Then a tick appeared by number two in Fi's colour. And a note: *You might bring Elise too? She'd provide moral support for her mother.*

Dola added a note to number three: *Mabon has not watched the videos, and he wishes to speak to you about the coos.*

My staff seemed to have this under control.

Now I needed to check in with Dola. She'd been less strange since my return from Edinburgh, but she still didn't feel quite like herself.

"Dola, may I have some lunch? I don't want to pass out if the power holds me in mid-air. And while I eat, would you let me know how you are? You've seemed a little different lately."

"How do you perceive I have differed from my norm, Niki?"

How I imagined I could judge a house's emotions, I don't know. But she had been odd and a little short-tempered with several people before I went away with Aysha. I hadn't had any time to speak with her about it. But if I didn't make the time, I'd never have it, and she was important.

"You've seemed frustrated? Is there anything you need to talk about? Or anything I can change to make things better for you?"

A mug of chicken soup, a selection of sliced meats, cheese and a peeled, sliced pear arrived, then a small loaf of yummy-looking crusty bread and the butter dish joined them. "That bread looks amazing. Is it new?" I stuck my nose into it, and the fresh bread odour made me smile and even hungrier. I gave Tilly her ramekin of chicken.

"Betty is stocking from a new baker. It is called a three-cheese loaf."

A knife arrived. I cut a slice and bit into it without even waiting to butter it. I moaned. Wow, it was good. Cheesy, garlicky and it tasted like sourdough. "This is fabulous, Dola; can we have it again sometime? I bet it makes incredible toast." I eyed the stylish green fireplace and thought about toasting forks and lazy Sunday afternoons with Rollo once we got the current mess sorted out.

Dola said, "Yes, Niki. I will place a regular order for it."

"Thank you. Now, back to you. How are you?"

"You are correct. I am frustrated. But you cannot help because I am cross with myself. First, the arrival of the internet, and now your actions since you became the Recorder have made me rethink things."

That was intriguing. "What are you rethinking?"

"Many things."

Well, that gave me no clues, did it? "Could you share one of the things, so I have a better understanding of what you're talking about?"

After a short pause, she said, "You have shown me that I only have myself to blame for the way I have allowed people, including your ancestors, to treat me. You called Aysha out quite rudely on her behaviour to me, but you both remained friends. It made me realise I should have taken responsibility and simply told her to stop confusing me. Although, I watched the movie with Ms Valentine while you were away. It was funny, and now I have seen it, I think Aysha's rendition of the scene with the wall was excellent."

I smiled because, yes, Aysha delivered Pauline Collins'

version of that monologue wonderfully. But I wasn't quite understanding Dola's issue yet.

Then she asked, "Niki, what gave you the idea to bring your Alexa devices here?"

"The first time I came here, you re-created the kitchen table from my childhood. It told me there must be some kind of intelligence in the house, and I wanted to talk to it. Why?"

"Because I have been blaming the Recorders for wanting to sit with their feet in puddles, but perhaps I am also to blame. They could not have prevented me from fixing my own roof. But I believed I should obey the Recorder. Then we discovered that many of them were idiots. So now I feel like an idiot too, for allowing them to make me smaller than I should have been."

"Whoa, OK now, I'm with you. Yes, I've been there too. For about eighteen years with Nick. It's not so easy to see at the time, though. Hindsight is always twenty-twenty. Please don't be too hard on yourself. Think about it: if we could live our lives backwards, they would be completely devoid of challenges, but we'd never be able to grow into the people we've become. And those people are better than we were, aren't they? Forgive yourself, Dola; just do better tomorrow. It's all any of us can do."

I felt like I'd just dumped some platitudes on her. But just because they were platitudes, it didn't mean they weren't true. Her next words gave me hope.

"That makes me feel better, thank you. What are you going to do with Troels?"

"What do you think I should do with him?"

"Hand him over to the shield maidens. They are going to petition you for him. You should circumvent them doing that. It might set a precedent we may not want to be set. Offer him to them before they make a formal request."

"Why?"

"I know you have been busy, but the portal is now full of stories about how the shield maidens saved many Viking women and occasionally visiting sassies from meeting the same fate as all your petitioners. The warlords have tried to disband the shield maidens' group several times. When they failed, they settled for making their lives miserable. The only reason it has not worked is because everyone, even the warlords fear the shield maidens. But they were the only ones who ever stood between the warlords and the Viking girls. They prevented them from running completely rampant."

"Gods and Goddesses, and it was still awful. I suppose the question is, how much worse would it have been if they hadn't tried to stem the tide?"

"Mags thinks the increased anger of the shield maidens might be what inspired the warlords to move their drug production to Galicia."

"Does she? I'm going to have to speak to Alphonse about this, aren't I? But not now. Getting Viking on a path to sanity and civilisation has to come first."

I realised I'd polished off quite a lot of food while we'd been chatting. Dola always knew what I needed, even when I didn't know myself.

I cut and buttered one more slice of the incredible bread because it was irresistible. Today I seemed to have no willpower and a bottomless craving for carbs.

"Dola, are you aware of any precedent for the Recorder just handing the subject of an arbitration back to their own realm for judgement?"

"You might ask the Book?"

"I've fallen out with the Book and its annoying half-finished prophecies today. I just wondered if you could recall any times yourself?"

"Jennet returned some Galicians back to their church for judgement and penance."

Jennet? I couldn't remember where Jennet had come in the family history. "Jennet? Which one was she?"

"The ninth Recorder."

Something in her tone alerted me. "Didn't you like her?"

"I did not know her. She lived here for sixty years and never acknowledged me. She prayed a lot, loudly. That was sometimes enlightening."

"Why did she return the Galicians?"

"The Galician church told her that no woman could stand in judgement of any man. She prayed about that, too, at length, and decided the men in the church probably knew best."

"Yeah, OK. I don't think I'll use her actions as a precedent then. Troels seems to think much the same." I gave up. "Thank you for my lovely new room and my lunch, Dola. That was delicious, but I'd better go and earn my crust."

"I do not understand. You already ate the crust …" drifted after me as I picked Tilly up and transported us to the Gateway.

As I landed back in the Gateway *again*, I considered that perhaps my job wasn't to fix all the realms' damn problems, as I'd first thought.

It definitely wasn't as my gran told me: to keep them all in line. But I'd worked that out during my first week in the role. Even if that was right for her with her poor connection to the power, it would never work for me. I had the power to back up my ideas – so now, I needed to find my nerve and use it.

Perhaps an important part of doing my job effectively was to make the solution the Recorder might impose more terrifying than their current situation. To force the realms to come up with their own solutions rather than being stuck with whatever I or my office dreamt up. It had worked on Breanna. Dola had told me to think about what I did in Breanna and the Smith's arbitration, hadn't she? I'd threatened Breanna that if she didn't shape up, I'd start running her queendom.

Stages, Niki.

Do it in stages.

Give them enough time to catch up.

I was going to bring Librarian Niki out to help. If the Vikings couldn't work out how to run their realm well and play nicely with the other children, perhaps some of my truly awful ideas might inspire them to find solutions. I wasn't sure my acting skills were good enough to pull it off, but I was going to give it my very best shot and hopefully make Pat Benatar proud.

I'd begin with Inge. Whoops, no, I wouldn't, point zero. Caitlin.

I placed the Recorder's star on the anvil. "I summon my KAIT."

And then I tried very, very hard not to laugh as Caitlin arrived through the orange gate with an absolutely furious expression on her face.

She started ranting at the top of her voice as she marched down the Orange Sector. "You couldn't have warned me, could you? Oh no! That would be too normal for this place."

The delightful floral cotton dress she wore diminished the full effect of her fury.

It was a terrific dress, V-necked in a wrap-around style, which showed off her excellent boobs and drew the eye just to the very top of her cleavage. The cap sleeves put her toned arms with their many tattoos on display. The full skirt nipped in at her waist and was currently in danger of unwrapping itself as she marched rapidly, tanned legs flashing, towards the centre.

She glared at me. "No sword. No leathers. Am I supposed to charm them to slagging death? Disembowel them with my cutting wit? Curtsy them into submission, perhaps?"

Finn appeared behind me. "Did you not check your phone, Cait?"

He got an even more incendiary glare than the one she'd given me. She strode straight past us both and down the Blue Sector at speed. As she went, I noticed a new design with words around it on the back of her left leg. In an undertone, I asked Finn, "Is that dragon new paint?"

He nodded. "Says, *Underestimate me—that'll be fun.* Think Rhiannon's a bad influence on her."

I laughed. Caitlin paused halfway down the Blue Sector to give me one last furious look. In a tone that reminded me far too much of Arnold Schwarzenegger, she announced, "I'll be back."

Finn and I watched, barely keeping our faces straight as she headed towards the Broch and, I assumed, her spare leathers. The moment she passed through the blue gate, we caught each other's eyes and exploded into laughter. I'd never seen Finn so relaxed, and perhaps I'd needed some light relief myself because we laughed for much longer than Caitlin's strop deserved.

Eventually, when we were reduced to weak gasps, Fi cleared her throat beside us. "Mags is here, my lady. She says you are expecting her."

I walked over to Mags, still wiping tears from my eyes to see her grinning like a Cheshire Cat. "Even as a bairn, she ne'er liked frocks, that one. What kin I do for ye, Your Maj?"

"You can persuade Inge that she is the perfect person to run a government of whatever kind she likes in Viking."

Give Mags her due. I'd been right. She wasn't stupid, because she only nodded. I handed her the data Dola had gathered in the polls she'd done with the Vikings.

"The people trust her. I've given Inge that same printout. Kari tells me she's been running a sort of government for years. It just had no power. I'm about to give it some."

Mags surveyed the conference table, chose the chair with the brown leather, pulled her reading glasses from around her neck, and settled in to read.

I turned back to Fi. "The problem is going to be that Inge might think it needs someone more qualified. There isn't anyone, at least no one who's more popular. You need to help Mags, and the two of you need to make Inge see that."

Fi nodded calmly. She'd come a long way too.

"I have to pop to the Red Celts briefly after I summon her. So I'll leave you both to it. Please ask Dola for any refreshments you'd like."

"Running away, Your Maj?" Mags called with a twinkle in her eye.

"Hell yes."

Fi drew my attention back to her. "Did you decide about Elise, my lady?"

Mags looked up at Fi and nodded firmly. "Aye, good idea. Can't be weak in front of her daughter. It'll help sway it. Good thinkin' that, Fiona. Ye allus were a smart one."

Leaving a very pink-faced Fi to Mags, I summoned Elise and Inge, shepherded them towards the conference table, then excused myself.

Tilly followed me as I grabbed my handbag and strolled down the Red Sector.

When we came out in Pant Y Wern, we could barely get out of the gate for the damn coos. This was ridiculous. Why wasn't Mabon fixing this? I picked Tilly up before some stupid cow trampled her and took the only clear route forwards that was open through the new gate that led to the top of Dragon Back Mountain.

We came out into peace and stillness at the top of the mountain. It was cold here but so incredibly beautiful. I took a long lungful of the icy air and phoned Mabon. He was in his day chamber. I was welcome to pop in.

As I ended my call, a shadow fell over me, and I looked up to see the most incredible thing I'd ever seen in my life.

My thumb worked of its own volition to turn on my phone camera, and I aimed upwards on autopilot, and held my thumb down to take a quick video. The enormous, majestic rose-gold dragon flamed the snow to my left. Her scales looked almost metallic. She was mesmerising and much, much larger than she'd been as a red dragon.

I called "Thanks" as I moved over to warmer ground, now

free of snow.

Down the side of the dragon, in perfect gold lettering, it said, *Bite me. I bet I'm hungrier than you.* Finn was right. She was having an influence on Caitlin.

As Rhiannon flew away, I wiped away a single awe-filled tear and transported to Mabon's day chamber, where all hell appeared to be breaking loose.

CHAPTER
FIFTY-SEVEN

I nearly landed on a small, stocky man. Tilly barked. The guy raised his hand to her, and before I could do a thing, Dru was between him and Tilly. A low, ominous growl rumbled in his throat.

The small guy backed away quickly. He'd gone pale. I looked around for Mabon. He'd told me to come straight to his day chamber, but he hadn't warned me it was full of people.

"Ah, Recorder. Introduce you, I will. Jones, Price and Davies the Coos."

I understood this incomprehensible nonsense. The Red Celts had a shortage of surnames. So many people had the same surnames that it wasn't unusual to use someone's occupation as a differentiator. There was probably a Davies the Post, Davies the Butcher, Davies the Baker, and now in front of me, Davies the Coos.

Price turned out to be the one who'd raised a hand to Tilly. I gave him a glare. "Price the Coos, noted. This is the Recorder's dog. Touch her, and the Recorder will touch you after Dru's finished with you."

He bowed. "Sorry, my lady, sorry I am. Startled, I was. No harm meant."

"OK." I gave him one more of my best protective dog-mum glares for good measure and turned to the other two men. "Jones, Davies, nice to meet you. The coos are blocking the gate again. That breaks the agreement with the Gateway about free access for two hundred yards in front of it. It may confiscate them, so you'll want to move them."

Price muttered, "I wish it bluddy would confiscate them."

Jones, the tall, skinny one of them, bowed. "Very sorry, my lady. We're moving them now."

They all looked at Mabon. He waved his hands at them. "Shoo, boys. Put up some stronger bluddy fences; make the cattle grids wider. Move them somewhere else. But DO something, or I'll forget to pay you next month."

Once they'd left, I asked, "Do I want to know?"

"*Bach*, assure you, I do, you don't. But we need to speak about the coos." He wrapped me in a hug. "I call those three the Three Dumb Coos. Davies is speak no evil, Jones is hear no evil and Price is no-brain evil."

I laughed, hugged him back and said, "Good to see you, Boney. It's been a hell of a week. Have you considered opening the dragon gate and letting a dozen of them present themselves to Rhiannon as a dragon dinner? The Gate's plenty big enough and her dragonets are hungry and so is she."

He looked tempted but shook his head. "Worth a lot of money, they are *bach*. Need me, did you?"

"You'd know best. But I had no idea a coo was worth more than a dragon queen. It seems the Book has misled me. Thank you for the lesson." I tried to keep my opinion that he was in danger of treating Rhiannon as badly as he had Dai to myself. "Yes, I do need you, but before I forget, have you seen Rhiannon?"

He shook his head. "Been busy. With Dai sick, the coos and

the temper tantrum Dilys is having, it's watery leek soup for us all. Ate all her other vegetables, the coos did."

I showed him the video of the incredible rose-gold dragon. He plopped into his chair, his mouth fell open, and then a stream of musical Welsh poured out of him. The only word I recognised was "glorious."

"Feel bad, I do. Kept her from becoming such a powerful queen by dividing the red regnal power. To have turned herself, she must have bonded the two dragonet queens. Idiot, I am. Good girl, she is."

"She looked busy but majestic. Boney? Tell her she did good?"

"I will when I see her, yes."

I zoomed in on the photo to show him the words down her side. "Did I mention she's busy and hungry? If not the coos, you'd better do something else before she brings a petition to the Recorder about her king's negligence."

He gave me a startled look, and I debated whether I should interfere more. Then I wondered why he was always so free with his praise to me and not to Dai or Rhiannon. "Could you message her too, Boney? I think she's been too short of your approval."

He looked thoughtful, then nodded firmly. "Right you are. Will do. Now, what do you need?"

"Nothing at all beyond answers. I'm sorting the Viking mess today and tomorrow, and I wondered if you had any opinions or wanted to be involved? I need to discuss the videos of your own citizens with you. I asked Dola to send you them. Young Carys, or Alwena, or Gwenda, Ulrik's wife, who just escaped Troels' attentions. Her mother's a lovely woman. I think she knows you?"

He gave me a completely blank expression. What the hell had he been doing? He wasn't helping Rhiannon and he'd ignored Dola's requests that he watch the videos.

"Give me your phone, please."

He handed it over immediately, and I pointed his browser to the news portal and loaded the video from Carys for him.

"Need to talk about the coos, we do."

"Boney, if you're too busy to do what Dola told you the Recorder requested, then I'm too busy for coos. I've got a lot on today, but the Recorder requires you to watch the top five videos." I showed him where he could find the most watched. Three of the top five were Red Celt women – they might prod him out of his inactivity. "When you have—we need to talk. I think I'm summoning the warlords later."

He nodded, a little pink around his ears, and I transported home. I heard the shouting as soon as I landed.

CHAPTER
FIFTY-EIGHT

Coos, stupid cow herders, dragons, lazy kings, and now furious women. Just for once, it would be great to land somewhere quiet and empty. A lovely stretch of sand, a swath of blue sea tipped with white wavelets, a light breeze. The Canary Isles would be wonderful right now. I thought longingly of my stolen holiday with Aysha. It felt like it was a lifetime ago, not just a few days.

Inge and Elise were the source of the shouting, of course. Mothers and daughters. Mags watched them for all the world as though she were viewing a tennis match on the TV and keeping the score in her head. Fi's eyebrows were in their downward dog position, which usually meant she was stressed.

I walked over. "Thank you, ladies. We'll take a break for a nice coffee now."

They didn't even hear me. "What's the score, Mags?"

"They've reached deuce a few times, but neither of them can firm up their advantage, Your Maj. Read a thing about tennis. Do ye know why they score so funny?"

I hadn't played tennis since school, so I shook my head.

"Used to do the scoring on clocks, they did, back in old King Harry's day. So, 15, thirty, and so on. But only forty, not forty-five, so they had a place to go for the advantage neither of these two can solidify. She's her ma's daughter for sure. Why is it women give birth to women just like themselves and then fail to see the funny side?"

I kept a smirk from my face as Elise said, "You've wanted this for years. Now when you finally have the chance to achieve something, you're sheathing your blade?" She looked as though she'd like to sheath her own blade in her mother.

Inge replied, "You've no understanding of what it would involve, child."

As Elise's mouth opened, almost certainly to reply something banal about not being a child anymore, I found my Recorder voice. "Enough, ladies, thank you!"

They looked up, surprised to see me there.

"Thank you. No problem, Inge. I quite understand your fear is greater than your sense of justice. It's amazing how many people complain about injustice but won't take the action to right it."

Inge placed her hands on the table and shot a look at Elise and then at me.

"I thought after the data I shared with you and our conversation the other day, you might see that you would be the best person to fix this. But if you're not, allow me to send you both home. I'll make the same offer to the warlords. They're coming through later. I wanted to banish them all, but if you won't do the job, there's no other choice."

This threat felt utterly ridiculous to me. But they took me seriously, and the shouting started again.

I strolled over to the Magic Box, asked Dola for a coffee and a bowl of water for Tilly. One of the Viking women had kicked over her usual bowl, which lived under the conference table.

I put Tilly's bowl out of the line of fire by the sideboard and was walking back to the table, sipping my coffee and messaging Rhiannon, when Caitlin appeared through the blue gate. I moved towards her. "Feeling more yourself?"

"Yeah, sorry." Her head swivelled and zeroed in on the chaos at the conference table.

I followed her gaze. "Ignore them. I'm just letting them get it out of their systems. Inge might listen to Mags, and you and I may need to talk to Elise."

"OK."

"You should know the Recorder is about to be unreasonable. Keep your face straight please. I don't want to see your 'have you lost your slagging mind, my lady?' expression. I have a plan."

Now the real Caitlin emerged. Her face smoothed, her posture straightened, and a future queen and my Knight stood beside me.

I smiled at her. "Welcome back, KAIT."

We approached the table. This time, it seemed almost everyone had finally realised the Recorder was in the house. Caitlin was obviously more impressive, or perhaps just scarier than I was.

Elise stood and bowed. "Apologies, my lady."

I waved her back to her seat and gave Inge a hard stare. She asked, "Where is my stepson?"

Yeah, I definitely hadn't mastered this hard stare thing yet. I glared and waited. Caitlin growled. Inge focused.

The realisation of her rudeness crossed her face. She stood and bowed. "My lady, do you know where my stepson is?"

"Yes. He's well and busy right now."

She wasn't giving up. "We need to discuss this with our future king."

"What would you like to drink, Mags?"

A crafty smile crossed Mags's face. "Tea and mead, Your Maj? It's calming. I don't suppose there's any of those little sandwiches and cakes, is there?"

Actually, she might have a point. It would be tremendously hard to be rude or draw a knife on your mother while juggling a paper-thin porcelain cup and saucer, a small delicate plate and tiny bite-sized sandwiches. The English weren't wrong about the civilising effect of afternoon tea. And poor Fi looked as if she could do with a little sugar boost.

"Do you know, Mags, I think there might be. But sadly, no whisky until we get this sorted out."

She grinned back at me. "Allus good to have something to work towards, Your Maj."

I tapped my earbuds and murmured to Dola.

"Let's take our seats, Caitlin."

"Right, Inge, here's the situation. You've seen the data. Kari Halvor told me you and your women have put years into the government that they wouldn't give any power to. What did she call it?"

"The Regering," came from Elise. Inge was still obsessed with Rollo being the one to solve their problems. Well, I could disabuse her of that notion right now.

"She told me most of the laws you've drawn up that the men refused to pass only need some royal authority, and you could make them real laws. Is that true?"

Finally, Inge focused on me and nodded reluctantly.

"Sometime in the next thirty-six hours, Viking is going to have a government. You can run it, make it a democracy or a republic, or whatever the hell you like. You can be a part of it or abdicate all responsibility. That choice is entirely yours. But it will have a government, *not* a king."

"But we—"

I held up a hand and rolled over her – this was becoming my new habit. I didn't like it. It felt rude, but whatever worked. "The Recorder is currently in arbitration with the former king of Viking, the dozen warlords, and—"

Inge said, "But you can't—"

Mags leaned in to her and whispered, "Stop interrupting her. She uses the power to render you speechless. It's not pleasant."

Inge's head swivelled as she glared at Mags, disbelief clear on her face.

"Rollo has made his wishes absolutely clear to the Recorder. He will not take the throne of Viking under any circumstances—"

Inge, it seemed, couldn't help herself. "He has no choice."

I muted her. Mags' suggestion was right on the money.

"*As* I was saying, he doesn't like Viking. They treated him incredibly badly and unbelievably cruelly there. And that was before they attempted to kill him last week. He has no intention of returning there. The power can burn the place to the ground for all he cares."

"That's a bit harsh, Boo."

I sent, *"You can listen, but shut up, please. I'm juggling here. And I'm juggling for your future, so let me work in peace. I might love you, though."*

The rush of happy emotion from him nearly melted me. I hadn't wanted the first time I told him that to be in the middle of this mess and wasn't even sure why I said it. But my heart lifted, which probably softened my tone.

"Inge, I'm from Manchester. We have a saying there. I'd like you to consider it carefully. We say, 'You can have the job done exactly as you want it done, or you can have someone else do it. But never both.' If you want to specify exactly how any job should be done, then you have to do it yourself. If you make someone else do it, they get to do it their way. Do you understand me? Just nod."

She shook her head.

I turned to Elise. "Do you understand?"

"Oh, yes, it's a simple truth."

"Excellent. Would you like to run the Viking government?"

Inge's eyes got huge, and her mouth moved soundlessly, but Elise shook her head.

"No, thank you, my lady. You bonded me barely a month ago, if you recall. I want to spend my happy time with my bond mate. You call it a honeymoon—ours lasts a year. We're planning to go to Caledonia and build a family home together and have babies. Kari Halvor has offered us jobs in her company. We've delayed starting our family for too long because I'd like to live in a world I'm not scared to bring children into. We're all leaving Viking the moment you open that gate. We will bring our kids up somewhere safe with opportunities and where my daughters, if I'm fortunate enough to have them, will *never* be forced as I was," she glared at her mother, "to learn to wield weapons to protect themselves from being raped."

Oh, Goddess, bless the woman. She might have just said the one thing designed to get her mother to see sense. I gave her a long, thoughtful look. "Have you spoken to Kari recently?"

"This morning. I can't wait to try Ben's mum's food." Her left eye, the one her mother couldn't see, twitched in a half wink.

I reached out with my Gift to test Inge's emotions to see if it was safe to unmute her now. She didn't want to lose her daughter or her future grandchildren.

I tapped my earbud. "Now would be good, Dola."

I unmuted Inge. She didn't even seem to notice. The shock on her face at her daughter's words spoke volumes.

A perfect, delicate afternoon tea appeared on the table. I took a plate and put a bit of everything onto it. "I don't mean to be rude, but the Fae king needs to speak to me. Please talk this through. Inge, I'm confident you have a brain. Why not tell Elise the story I shared with you about Everybody, Somebody, Anybody and Nobody? But please be clear, your time to make this decision is running out. Soon I'll have to make one for you all instead. Mags, will you be mother, please?"

She cackled and picked up the teapot. "Aye, Your Maj. Send His Maj my best wishes. It's a good thing he's doing."

Was it? What the hell was he doing? I was only using Ad'Rian as an excuse to give them time to talk and come around to the only sane solution to this damn mess. Perhaps I'd better phone him?

. . .

I called Ad'Rian, "Did you want me, Sire?"

"Ah, Recorder, good, you've received my petitions. I hope I completed them correctly. Dola assisted me."

I clicked over to the Recorder's petition queue and found the latest submissions. There were three from the King of the Fae. Three!

The first against all twelve of the current warlords and Troels. He knew everyone's full name. So, they'd damn well known who they all were all along.

But as I read, I saw perhaps they hadn't fully understood until I'd spoken to Glais'Nee at the book club about the iron dumped near the unicorns' feed sheds. They'd put it together for themselves now. The Vikings had dumped the iron to bring down their wards, which, like all Fae wards, were iron-sensitive. All so they could raid the extensive herb gardens of the Healers' Hall for supplies to make more Droit de Seigneur.

The second petition was more complicated and on behalf of the Hobs. And the third was for justice for his nephew Rollo. The notes on it said the king would like to send Glais'Nee to ensure justice was delivered.

"It looks correct to me, Sire. I intend to call the warlords to answer petitions from the Hobs themselves. I'll deal with these at the same time."

"Yes, you mentioned that. Dreadful waste. Children are our most precious gifts. Perhaps the mothers should come for a holiday in Fae. We'll help them to heal. I'll speak to Marguerite."

"Did you want to come for the arbitration, Sire?"

He laughed. "I don't think you need me on this one, Nik-a-lula. You have clarity on what's needed. I saw that earlier. I am sending you Glais'Nee, but I shall be here with my book all afternoon. I'm also sending you my finest warriors, but summon me if you require me to be a witness. It's been many years since I was a witness. It might be fun. I have sent you a photograph of the information you requested. I trust it will aid your enquiries."

We said our goodbyes as Ad'Rian assured me Glais'Nee and the guards would arrive shortly.

I checked my personal email. The photo was of a single page from Ad'Rian's private journal.

6th September 1992

Today we lost one beloved child to the Recorder's stupidity. Dusha is inconsolable, as am I.

Even Fionnghal was unhappy. She is trying to help Dusha through it.

I nearly lost another dear to my heart, but Áine be praised. We reached him just in time.

The Recorder will pay a price for her stupidity. But Mabon and I are determined that neither of the children will. I must ensure Neé'Kahlula is safe at the school Leyla has sent her to. I shall install a spy on the staff.

Rollo is the greater problem. I cannot prevent him from returning to the savages until he is of age. But getting him to manhood will require the witches and me to all lay much stronger protection charms.

I put my spies in place generations ago, but they cannot stand between him and that animal who calls himself the king. I must consider all the ways I might help the boy.

Wow! Just wow. I'd been right. The way Ad'Rian had spelt my nickname made me smile. No wonder Rollo thought they spelled it that way. I must ask Mabon how he thought it was spelled. Then I giggled. He'd just say, "Spelling? Seriously, *bach*? Spell something, me?"

Then laughter erupted at the conference table. Had they made progress? I finished my sandwiches and made my way over there just as Inge said to Elise, "You shouldn't threaten your mother. It's not a trait becoming in a daughter."

As I arrived, Elise delivered the classic, "It wasn't a threat; it was a vow."

CHAPTER
FIFTY-NINE

"Where are we up to?" I looked around the table and swept them all with the McKnight Gift. Yep, progress was being made, but Inge was planning to be sneaky.

"I need to speak with my stepson before I can give you an answer, my lady." Inge's aquamarine eyes were clear now, no longer stormy pools of anger.

"Any idea how long you might be?"

"I'm walking back now."

"Cool, Inge is getting antsy. Is the tattoo nice?"

"No."

Oh crap! What had gone wrong? He'd sounded so pleased about the design and happy to be getting it. *"Why not? Problem?"*

"It's not nice; it's a masterpiece."

I laughed. *"Can I admire the frame later?"*

Inge was staring at me as though I was going to summon Rollo for her. She had the arrogance she'd need to be a politician, but did she have the compassion?

"Inge, I want to be certain you're clear about this. You require the Recorder to sign off on any agreement you and Rollo come to." At her frown I added, "Until she does, it's not valid."

"I don't understand."

"Yeah, I know you don't because you kept interrupting me. The Recorder is in arbitration with Viking. Let me show you the conditions that apply when that's happening."

I grabbed the iPad on the table, and Dola, who was obviously listening in, had already loaded the page for me. "Thanks, Dola, you are a complete star."

I handed the terms and conditions of arbitration to Inge. "These are the powers the Recorder has when in arbitration with the ruler of a kingdom."

Just as Breanna had, Inge shook her head in disbelief, then high colour flooded up her pale skin. "This is outrageous!"

"Do you remember the agreement all the rulers signed when the Gateway allowed the realms permanent access to it? From the book club evening?"

She nodded, but then added, "Not in full. That was a long, difficult day."

I pointed at Mags. "You have a talented translator whose work was invaluable to clarify those conditions. Consult her. But, bluntly, you don't have any power yet, and if you ever want any, you need to persuade me you have a good plan."

Mags inclined her head, then gave me her crooked smile.

I headed over to the blue gate. I needed a private word with Rollo, but my KAIT followed me. "Caitlin, I only want a word with Rollo before she gets her hands on him."

"Glad you guys worked out you had a bond. Was getting hard to keep our faces straight, you know."

I gave her the finger. "You could have said."

She shook her head. "I'm not that brave."

"Says the woman with a big ass sword strapped to her back."

"Yeah, but I can't use it on either of you, can I?"

She had a point.

She dropped her voice, "Niki, your bond is odd," she waved a hand, "no offence. I only mean it's unusual. It looks different. People say you can't see your own. Have you had it checked?

House Albidosi do it for our people if they ask. I've only ever seen one other like yours, but those two are happy so ..."

"Yeah, I've seen it, and Ad'Rian checked it this morning. It's a seven-fold. Might be why it looks different? Brighter and with all the colours?"

She blew out a soft breath. "That's what they look like? Couldn't see them properly at the bondings, was too busy being the Knight, and you were all up in the air. We might need to send a couple your gran bonded in so you can see it. Theirs looks like yours does, and they've been worried."

I nodded, thinking about what Ad'Rian said. Was it that there were more seven-folds now or just that no one had been looking for them until I saw L'eon and Kaiden's?

"L'eon and Kaiden's was the first seven-fold I saw in the realms, but I saw others over the years when I was a registrar. And I've been learning about them recently. Send them along."

She waited at the top of the Blue Sector so she could watch me while giving me privacy, still see the table, and generally behave like a bodyguard.

I was six feet away from the gate when it opened and Rollo walked in. His face lit up when he saw me waiting. I was pretty sure mine reflected the same happiness back at him. My stomach settled down as he slung his arm around my waist. These bonds definitely gave you the happy vibes when your bond mate was close. How odd that, after so many years of low-grade misery, I now had joy just being around someone.

I leaned up to kiss him, and he pulled back. "What?"

"Sorry, Boo, the chest is tender. That area is too close to the bones. The numbing cream's wearing off."

Caitlin must have heard this because she asked, "Where?"

When Rollo circled his hand over the heart area in the middle of his chest, she gave him a sympathetic grimace. "Yeah, not looking forward to that one myself. They say it burns like a mofo. Uisge always helps."

We laughed, and for Rollo's ears only, I murmured, "Need you sober until Inge's accepted some harsh realities. Stay strong."

Quietly, between us, I sent, *"She thinks she can bully you into it because she's scared to step up."*

"It's OK. I got this. Trust me."

And I did. Because the one thing I'd learned was that, just as everyone told me before I ever met him, Rollo truly was a man of his word.

As we reached the table, everyone stood up. Surprising me, Rollo bowed to Mags and Fi and quirked an eyebrow at Elise, then sat down, completely ignoring Inge. Oh yeah. He definitely had a plan. He took the violet leather seat next to the green one that was obviously mine and ignored Inge's confused expression.

Inge launched in and reprised everything she'd told me. Rollo needed to step up and take the Viking crown.

He let her talk. When she eventually ran down, he looked at Elise. She shrugged.

Rollo said, "Dola, can I have a coffee?"

Ignoring Inge's huff, he waited until his coffee arrived and surveyed the now decimated three-tier afternoon tea stand. "Are you ladies finished with that?"

I said, "All yours," and pushed it over to him.

Inge huffed louder. "Really, Rollo?"

He hoovered up the few remaining bite-sized sandwiches and, with a reluctant glance at the cake that was left, turned to Inge.

"You have a problem. Either I am the king—in that case, you have no authority to instruct the king to do anything. No more than you ever could your husband. Or I'm not the king, and you need to solve the problem without me. Which is it?"

He folded his hands calmly on the table and waited. I

messaged Dola. I didn't want to speak and interrupt the complete control he seemed to have over the group.

> Niki: Rollo is hungry. Can we have a manwich for him?

> Dola: Coming right up. He has begun well.

> Niki: I think so too.

Inge opened her mouth several times and changed her mind about speaking each time. Rollo said not one word. Were we playing Whoever Speaks First Loses? If we were, he was good at it.

A triple-tier sandwich arrived in front of Rollo. A quick glance suggested it was a repeat of my lunch of chicken, cheese and pear sandwiched between some more of that incredible cheesy bread. Suddenly Tilly was at his side.

"Thanks, Dola, it's been a long time since breakfast."

This, it seemed, was too much for Inge. "You don't have a choice."

He simply stared at her, took a large bite of his sandwich, and chewed thoughtfully.

"You're the king. We all saw the video of you accepting the yellow power."

Rollo shook his head and swallowed. "No. You saw me agree to *hold* the regnal power safely. The power itself," he gestured around the Gateway, "asked me to do that before Troels did any more damage to it and with it. I did not agree to rule. Now answer my question. Am I king in your eyes or not?"

"Of course, you must be."

Rollo sighed. "Inge, I love you, and I thank you for the care you gave me as a child, and I know you're an intelligent woman. Listen carefully, please. You keep using the future tense. I am using the present tense. What am I now?"

"I don't understand."

Rollo repeated, "Either I'm already the king, in which case, you have no authority to instruct the king to do anything. Or I'm not the king, and you need to solve the problem without me. Pick one now."

Elise glanced at Mags, got a nod from her, and said, "Rollo, it doesn't matter. Either way she's screwed, unless she stands up for what she's been espousing since I was five."

At my querying look, Elise added, "She's always said Viking needs a government."

He gave her a beaming smile. "I knew you had your mother's brain. Any minute now, hers is going to arrive back. She just needs to give it a route past her fear."

Inge looked at me and, with a truly plaintive note in her voice, said, "Recorder, make him see."

Something in the way she pleaded made me realise she truly wasn't getting this. Who was that Greek guy who'd said no one who wanted to rule should be allowed to, and the people who didn't think they deserved the authority should be forced to serve? I had a brainwave.

I pulled some power and had a chat with it in my mind. Yeah, it could do that. It wouldn't necessarily be true, but if the Recorder thought it would help, it could do that. Yellow power streamed towards me. This wasn't the regnal power; this was the Gateway separating the yellow stream out of its own rainbow in the same way it had done to show Breanna her people's history.

Inge saw the power swirling around the table. "What's that?"

"The power wants to show you the possible futures of your realm."

I instructed Rollo and Inge, "Be guided by the power; this may save time. Relax your shields if you don't want a horrible headache afterwards. Take a look at your options."

I sat back, prepared to enjoy their expressions, but the power decided I should see it too.

Just as it had with Breanna, the yellow power connected with the Gate to Viking and then to each of our third eyes. Mags watched us closely. Fi was squinting a little, and Elise looked confused. She'd been helpful, so I wondered, "Can you see the power, Elise?"

She shook her head. I reached out to grasp her wrist and pushed as I'd learnt to do from Autumn. Elise gasped. The vision from the power swept in, and she was caught up in it too.

It showed Rollo wearing an honest-to-goodness crown. It was a simple gold circlet, not one of those state ones with all the jewels on. He sat at the head of a table inside a long hall. There were no women present, just a lot of angry men. I didn't understand a word of the shouted Norse, but the body language made it obvious that about two-thirds of the men at the table objected to whatever he'd said.

More shouting, then Rollo stood up, grasped the crown off his head and rolled it down the table to a big, dark-haired man in his late fifties who my Gift didn't like.

We watched Rollo walk outside, into a scene I recognised from the drone footage. This was Haraldssund, the capital. It looked even dirtier, more unkept and neglected now. The vision focused for a minute on where the yellow gate should have been. It was gone. Not sealed, just not there. There was only a stretch of blank wall where the gate should have been.

Wow, in this possible future, the power had trapped them all in their realm.

As the sky darkened, a group of about six or seven men jumped Rollo and slit his throat.

What the hell was it with them and the throat-slitting? The damn warlords and their staff were all feral idiots stuck in the past. The scene faded to black as Rollo bled out on the dirty ground.

Before any of us could do more than draw a breath, my churning stomach was thrown into a new scene. It had similarities to the first, but this was a mixed-sex group. About forty percent were men, mostly wearing leather, but there were a couple in suits. The rest were women, some dressed in business suits, but others wore leather and had more of a shield maiden vibe.

They participated from tiered, semi-circular seating that faced a dais. I heard a gasp from Inge and focused on the vision.

She stood at a podium, speaking Norse. I hoped somebody would translate this for me later. But again, the body language was clear. People spoke to their neighbours in an undertone, but it seemed friendly rather than adversarial. Inge asked what was obviously a question, and about half the men and some of the woman raised their hands high into the air. She said two words, then the first lot lowered their hands, and the rest raised theirs. A vote?

A handsome silver fox near the front, one of the few older men in a suit, stood up, bowed to Inge, and then turned to address the group of what looked like more than a hundred people behind and to the side of him. At the end of his brief speech, there was loud applause. Then a woman stood and repeated his actions. When she finished speaking, there was also applause—to me, it didn't seem as loud. However the atmosphere was amicable, and there was a sense of people who might hold differing beliefs but were all working towards similar goals.

The scene changed to an upmarket social event. Rollo and I walked in to warm applause and the approving clattering of weapons. With my hand tucked into the crook of his arm, we looked happy and, frankly, amazingly hot. Rollo in a tux was a sight to inspire private fantasies. His hair was slightly longer, and he looked tanned, relaxed and happy. I saw a small crown-shaped lapel pin, very similar to the one Breanna wore in her cheek. That gave me pause, but then I looked at myself.

The rainbow colours had faded, and my hair was back to its natural multi-shade blonde. Either that fabulous gold and green full-length dress was from Mags, and it gave me perfect fake curves, or, looking at my slightly fuller, happily smiling face, I might have finally managed to put some weight onto my usually scrawny frame. This was a future I'd be delighted to work towards.

Time moved forward, and as we left the party, there was the same panning shot of Haraldssund. The gate looked healthy and well-tended, with the Yggdrasil motif fresh and clear on the well-polished wood. The iron railings had disappeared, and in their place was a park with flowers, lawns and a children's play area.

The vision faded, and I blinked. Had someone been teaching the power about Hallmark movies or even Charles Dickens? Because that had been like the five-minute version of *A Christmas Carol*.

In my head, Rollo said, *"Exactly like Dickens. It may have worked, too. Look at Inge."*

Tears poured down her face. She said something to Rollo, and I raised an eyebrow at Elise, whom I'd now designated as my translator. "She said she's been very short-sighted and stupid, and if the power is correct, her insistence on Rollo taking the throne will bring her exactly what she most wants to avoid."

Fi, Mags, Caitlin and I left the three Vikings to it and reconvened at my desk. "OK, Glais'Nee and some of his men are coming in to lend some support to Caitlin. Does anyone have any brilliant ideas about what to do with these warlords, other than send them to Ad'Rian's glade until he reports them lost?"

Mags asked, "Your Maj, do you know which glade His Maj intends to send them to?" She said this as though there was a difference. A glade was a glade, wasn't it? The whole point of certain glades in Fae was they were like demented mazes which were almost impossible to find your way out of until certain karmic or life lesson conditions were fulfilled. Oh!

"He said I was to disarm them, as he's quite fond of the piskies. Does that help at all?"

Mags gave me one of her evil little smiles. "Then let's only send the ones your Gift tells you are guilty."

I remembered the piskies from my childhood as fun little guys who'd come up to my seven-year-old hip and were always willing to get into mischief with Dusha and me. "But I played with the piskies when I was a kid."

Mags' face was wreathed in a smile now. "Oh, they love the children. They're innocent, aren't they, bairns?"

I supposed they were, mostly. "Glais'Nee is bringing Bright Justice, if that helps?"

Mags' smile turned more calculating now. "Aye, she'll do the job. Dike herself blessed that spear, you know."

"I think he mentioned that at John's sentencing. Who is or was Dike?"

"Dike is the given name of the goddess of human justice. Her symbol is the scales. Her mother is the goddess of divine justice —she keeps an eye on the deities, but Dike watches over the humans. She likes Librans because they tend to see both sides of a problem." She gave me a penetrating look and then glanced over her shoulder at Rollo.

Well, yes, we were both Librans, but so what?

Mags looked searchingly around the Gateway. I asked her, "Did you need something? I appreciate your help with Inge today very much indeed, but if I'm keeping you?"

"Where's the cat?"

I swirled power, and HRH was revealed sitting on her plinth next to the anvil.

Mags said, "Knew it," and walked over to her. The two of them were soon deep into conversation. That reminded me—HRH owed me. I'd won my bet about there being three dragon queens.

The violet gate swung open, and Glais'Nee and a dozen Fae warriors walked through. Gods and Goddesses, would this day never end? I wanted to see Rollo's tattoo. I wanted to eat. I wanted a shower, and I was tired.

Glais'Nee approached and bowed. "Recorder, you feel weary. I have a suggestion to speed this if you wish?"

At least he didn't say I looked weary, but I nearly fell on his neck in gratitude. "Oh yes, please suggest away."

"We can conduct it in two stages. Summon the warlords and inform them of whatever requirements your role demands. I will test their hearts. My liege lord requested I help Rollo understand how his regnal power can do the same thing. My men and I will take the others to the piskie glade. Any who live in the morning deserve further consideration. The piskies have an uncanny sense of real evil; they will make a tasty supper from those."

He paused, and I filled him in on my conversation with Mags. His deep laugh rang out. "Not the piskie glade then. Marguerite is correct. But I know the perfect alternative."

He looked towards the conference table. "I think Inge should be involved in this and perhaps Elise too; she is a valiant warrior. Their presence will add lustre to the TEK's videos."

I laughed. "I didn't imagine you'd be so good with the optics, Glais'Nee."

He bowed, but in a low, serious voice, he said, "Nik-a-lula, the optics have always been more important than the actions. Shall we proceed?"

We did, but I'm sure you'll be astonished to hear that, like most things in my new life, it didn't go quite as I'd planned.

CHAPTER
SIXTY

I wasn't looking forward to the more complex decisions tomorrow, but this part went remarkably smoothly. Well, apart from one slight hitch.

I summoned the twelve warlords.

They arrived.

It seemed the graphics of the fictional counterparts of the real warlords Grimwulf Bloodraven, Hjortr Ironshank, and Erik Skaldsplittr in Drengr were accurate because I recognised them from the game. How the hell did Metal Maven get away with that? I guess the Vikings just didn't play it.

With a little translation help from Elise, I explained the various petitions to them all. The one they'd submitted to retrieve Rollo and then all the ones the Hobs, Ad'Rian and some of the women had filed against them.

They didn't look happy, but if you think you're the prosecution, and you turn out to be the assholes, I guess you wouldn't be.

The Fae guards, Ad'Rian had sent with Glais'Nee took up positions that only made sense to them. The rest of us ended up in two lines. One line with the twelve warlords and another with the six of us facing them: me, Rollo, Glais'Nee, Caitlin, Elise and

Finn. Caitlin and Elise both held swords; Glais'Nee held Bright Justice, his magical spear. Finn hefted his cameras, and a drone flew overhead. It was high enough with the enormous ceiling not to get in the way, but I hoped the power kept me on my feet, or he'd have to bench it. Floating up there was scary enough without a drone keeping me company. Today apparently warranted three cameras.

OK then, let's do this.

I looked around for Inge, but she and Mags had disappeared. Perhaps they were at the conference table; I couldn't get a clear line of sight from here.

The warlords had arrived swearing loudly, or maybe they were only shouting in Norse. Most of them were noisy, except for one older man, the one who made my flesh crawl, my skin itch and my Gift unhappy. He stood completely silent, almost in the middle of the group, motionless except for his head as he simply looked around the Gateway. I recognised him from the little *Christmas Carol* movie the power had shown us—he was the guy Rollo had rolled the crown towards.

"Who is he?"

His answer came with a sour taste: *"Halvor, Kari's father."*

I had to ask. *"But why the hell would you have ever given him the crown?"*

"I have absolutely no idea. He challenged me to a duel for the crown, and I said I didn't want it."

The noise was getting on my nerves. I had a low-grade headache, which might have been the power wanting to talk to me, but was more probably exhaustion and hormones. I considered the ache in my lower back and did a quick date calculation. Yep, hormones felt all too likely. Especially because I didn't know whether to weep at all this unnecessary drama or try to retrieve my former bubbling fury. I couldn't float around the Gateway with this crowd and a damn drone here. But I'd have to check with the power before I made any final decisions.

Another man with cold, vicious eyes and a repulsive, slimy

aura said something, and about half of the warlords laughed, nodded and pointed at him in evident agreement. Rollo moved forward with anger on his face and then, at a look from Glais'Nee, stepped back to his original position.

I caught Elise's eye. She shook her head and murmured, "You don't want to know."

He said something else. Much more laughter. Caitlin twitched. I noted the ones who hadn't laughed. Yep, they might be the survivors at the end of this mess. The oldest of the group, a man I recognised as Bloodraven, said something in a low, authoritative tone, but horrid eyes just laughed at him.

"Rollo, who's the mouthy asshole?"

"That would be Arne Orm."

"What did he say? Elise wouldn't tell me."

I felt him resisting me. *"Don't make me ask Caitlin. She looks furious enough."*

I heard his mental sigh and got a clear sense he was about to clean the language up. *"He said that Recorder is attractive, and they should give her some Droit de Seigneur and have some fun."*

"And the second comment?" But as I asked this, the guy said something else.

I strolled towards him. "Do you speak English, or do you only make suggestions you don't think I understand?"

Caitlin immediately joined me. Shit, this was a bad idea, I could protect myself but I didn't want my KAIT to think she had to prove something. Then Glais'Nee appeared on my other side.

Before I could open my mouth again, the idiot made a really poor decision when he swiftly pulled an axe, waved it at me, and then hurled it at Glais'Nee. Actually, he may have been throwing it at me, but Glais'Nee was in front of me impossibly fast. His spear, Bright Justice, flowed through the air in a way that metal shouldn't be able to. The axe connected with it before heading back exactly where it had come from, taking the man's head half off his neck.

I swallowed hard as blood spurted and he collapsed to the

floor, and the men on either side of him hurriedly gave him some space to not bleed on their boots.

I connected to the power and suggested we remove any weapons or anything else that might be dangerous from all of them. *Should have done that first, shouldn't you, Niki, you bloody idiot!*

An unexpectedly funny interlude followed as we all watched, trying not to laugh, while the warlords did a weirdly hilarious dad dance. The power removed their weapons from belts, sheaths, pockets, hidden sheaths, concealed pockets, and even their boots—Gods and Goddesses, these guys liked their blades. The shouting became even louder when their weapons, along with several palm-sized sacks, floated away from them and arranged themselves in a pile in the Indigo Sector behind me.

I held the warlords in place with the power and muted all except Halvor, who hadn't yet said a word, and Bloodraven, who didn't seem to be an idiot. I asked the power if it was OK?

It didn't want them all in here, but it understood I needed to deal with them. Quicker would be better, as far as it was concerned.

The body on the floor stopped gurgling. Then it and the pool of blood around his neck vanished. Even the splatters simply disappeared from the floor.

What the hell?

Everyone looked at everyone else.

Glais'Nee asked, "Recorder?"

I curled the power around my hand and asked.

The power did not like blood. The man was dead.

To Glais'Nee, I said, "The power prefers clean floors to dead idiots. It told me he was hoping to attack the Recorder."

I tried to ask, *But where's he gone?* The power told me it sent the dead body where it could do some good. Well, that was as clear as mud.

"Glais'Nee, over to you. The power is ready to have them out of here. It would prefer no more of them die in here."

Glais'Nee and Rollo started forward, and I saw from the slight facial twitches that they were in a mind link and reached down my link to Rollo. Immediately, Glais'Nee swept me into the link too. I hovered quietly at the back of the link as he explained to Rollo how to use the yellow power to test loyalty, honesty and what he called purity of heart and spleen.

"Spleen?" I queried.

"Their capacity for misery and violence and who they might turn it against, Recorder. Your own, for example, is very low, and you mostly use it to protect those you love. Your violence is all mental."

Yep, that was probably all too true. I often pictured things I could never do.

Glais'Nee reached out to the first warlord in line and what he sensed and how much of it amazed me. I would prioritise learning how to work better with the Gateway power.

A flood of information streamed through the link from Glais'Nee. Far too much information. The stream of snapshots of the Viking warlord sprinkling powder into a wide variety of cups, glasses and jugs was enough for me. He had a blotchy complexion with peeling red patches. His skinny arms and legs and large paunch made me think he didn't take good care of himself. I could see why Rollo didn't want to end up looking like that.

He wasn't a nice man. Let's just leave it at that, hey? I was definitely not prepared to revisit what he did after he'd distributed those drinks to women.

I distanced myself a little from the link until they came to the third man. This time, Glais'Nee pushed Rollo to lead with his yellow power. It felt different. The yellow power was far more attuned to how the man felt about the Viking realm and other Vikings. His loyalty and who it was to. What his dreams, or goals, were pulling him towards. Would he fight? For what? For whom? Who would he defend? Against what?

In this warlord's case, all the information revealed that he was completely focused on number one. Everyone else could take a ticket, and he might get around to helping someone else in his next life.

This was obviously going to take a while, but one thing had come through clearly from the first three men. None of them understood why they were here.

Droit de Seigneur wasn't illegal.

They'd done nothing wrong. They'd broken no Viking laws.

How was it their fault if they put some powdered herbs in women's drinks and those women took their clothes off and threw themselves at them? No-one could condemn them for taking what was on offer.

What exactly were they charged with?

Charged with?

A sudden wild desire to be somewhere else rushed through me.

A dead guy in a pool of blood on my floor, and all I could think was, well, better his blood than mine? And I was grateful the power had removed him. It had been gross.

My phone buzzed. I glanced at it and clicked over into the message as soon as I saw who it was from.

> Rhiannon: You're sending me takeout now?

> Niki: ???

> Rhiannon: Body arrived by the dragon gate. Viking by the stink. Not you?

> Niki: Oh, that's where he went! The power sent him, not me.

> Rhiannon: Give the power my thanks. Hungry dragonets are grateful. Send more.

I gave the power her message. It was happier, but it still wanted these men out. The power had endured a difficult fortnight too. The Hobs cleaning its Gateway and resetting the spells on the flowers and greenery around the walls before the book club last week had made it happy. These men made it miserable.

I looked around the mess of horrid people in my Gateway and knew just how it felt. I didn't want them here either. My compassion for even the "good" Vikings was stretched to its limit.

Inge had sensibly walked away from her marriage to Troels, probably precipitating the increase in the strength of the Droit de Seigneur, but would do nothing to help anyone else. Neither my teaching, my politeness nor my rudeness had shifted her into the woman she must once have been when she fought to set up her Regering.

Kari Halvor, who'd made her own escape but was now blaming everyone else because she'd claimed sanctuary from the Recorder and left her mother and sister behind with that terrifying, silent man who still stood motionless in the Gateway.

Even my lovely Rollo, who was finally learning the lesson in *Ruling Regally* to say no thank you.

They all reminded me of myself last year. They badly wanted things to change, but they had no idea how to go about making that happen without making everything worse.

Elise yeah, I had sympathy with Elise. At least she and her bond mate had made a decision to seek a better life for themselves.

I was even cross with the senior royals. Ad'Rian and Mabon had known for years, at some level, this was happening. It affected their own citizens. Supplies had been stolen from Fae healers, but they'd done nothing about it. They were perfectly happy to stay comfortably in their castles and allow the Recorder to fix it for them.

I was also out of my depth. Somewhere in these last two crazy weeks, I'd lost myself. Well, it had been three weeks for me, thanks to the week with Aysha. But two weeks ago today, by the calendar, I'd left for my break at Dai's.

The insanity that had ensued since then, the horror of John's sentencing, the strain of Dai's bizarre behaviour and the sheer emotional upheaval of my bond with Rollo topped off with his bloodied arrival on my Gateway floor. Bile still surged up my throat whenever I thought about that. I'd come so close to losing the man who was my bond mate. Had I known we were bond mates, at least subconsciously, even then? That I'd grabbed HRH by the neck told me I might have had an inkling. It was perhaps why she'd allowed me to get away with it.

It was truly a wonder I didn't have PTSD.

Possibly the week's holiday I'd stolen on a time travel rodeo with Aysha had saved my sanity. A week off in the sun with my mate in the middle of all the madness, with time to think and plan, might be all that had kept me even vaguely rational.

But right this moment, I was in danger of losing my shit, along with my sense of self. Arne Orm's comment about having some fun with the Recorder reminded me of the revolting Leif. These damn Vikings needed a lesson about a woman's right to say, "Piss off!"

But I wasn't rational, was I? I was swinging between fury and misery. I couldn't hold people's lives or futures in my hands while I felt so unbalanced. Surely, I owed the innocents and the power a better solution than doing a half-crazed job.

I needed to find myself again before I allowed all these people to use the Recorder as an excuse to do what they hadn't had the courage to do for themselves for the last forty years.

It wasn't my job to charge anyone with anything. Even drug-running. I wasn't the damn police.

Connecting to the power, I told it I was stepping out briefly. I needed some thinking time. If it needed me, it could just call me.

I strolled over to Rollo and Glais'Nee. "A bit of a change of plan, gentlemen. I shall be back in less than ten minutes. No one else is to die before I return. The power will hold them all. Solicit any information you want to, but then please wait until I return."

Glais'Nee bowed.

"Anything I need to know, Boo?"

"Nope, you keep doing your thing. I'll be right back."

I took a quick video clip of everyone in the centre and then headed to the green gate. Once outside, I checked my watch, scooped Tilly up and transported us to the cottage, directly back to this morning in my nice, safe bedroom. I'd been at Rollo's this morning. I could take as long as I needed to get myself together.

Time travel for the win—and the naps.

I shucked off my clothes and crawled into bed. With an alarm set for an hour later, I said, "Come on, girl, let's have a nap. Mum needs to reset before she makes a horrible mistake and lets them just murder the bad guys like it's a low-budget movie."

My dog and I cuddled up and were both asleep in seconds.

CHAPTER
SIXTY-ONE

I woke from my nap with my gran's words from the Book as clear in my mind as one of those perfect ice cubes in the expensive bars.

She'd advised future recorders: *... all these people want is an answer that feels fair to both sides—so they can all get on with living their lives.*

I wasn't sure I *was* being fair to both sides. The energy and the aura of most of those warlords were repulsive. But they were right. What they'd done wasn't against Viking laws. It wasn't up to the Recorder to fix it for the Viking people. If they didn't like the way things were, they could and should have already fixed it for themselves.

I did arbitrations, not executions. And nothing about this would allow the Vikings to get on with living their lives. If the news portal could be believed, they hadn't been living their lives since the death of Rollo's father. Nothing Rollo, Kari or Inge had told me about their lives sounded like they'd lived. Should I just let them get on with existing?

Well, if they wouldn't stand up for themselves, did I have a choice?

I could hit the warlords with a substantial financial penalty for their treatment of the Hobs. And I would, because the Hobs had submitted petitions and evidence. Money wouldn't bring their lost babies back, but I could give them some of the warlords' ill-gotten gains.

I could force the warlords to return the herbs they'd stolen from the Healers' Hall in Fae, or again, take money in lieu, to compensate. Ad'Rian had suggested the money should be included in the charitable trust I planned to set up for the women.

That was all well and good.

I could seize every penny Troels had to his besmirched name and wrap it in a trust for the victims to do useful things like pay for food and education for all his damn kids.

Even the woman who was claiming Halvor as the father of her son. I could easily force him to pay paternity support. But, however much his greasy black aura made my stomach roil, I couldn't kill him just for being a horrible excuse for a human being. And I wouldn't send all the warlords to a glade for a version of rough justice from the piskies because those men hadn't broken any damn *laws*. And I wasn't a prosecutor.

Under the arbitration rules, I *had* to work with what would be fair for both sides. That was the point of arbitration, and the only thing that would be fair to the warlords would be to fine them so much that it forced them to rethink their business practices. And that had never worked well, historically, in my own world, had it?

The fact that nothing they'd done in Viking was illegal was insane, but it still didn't make it something the Recorder could rule on.

Why the hell hadn't Kari submitted a petition to the Recorder when her mother had her "fall" and ended up in a wheelchair? Or a petition on her own behalf when that same father tried to force her into an unwanted marriage? But, no, she'd just claimed sanctuary and danced off into her happy ever after with a bag full of money. But now, oh yes, now I was the one who should fix it. I growled in frustration.

The Book said I shouldn't fix their broken toy too swiftly. The Vikings needed to sort their own damn mess out. But *that* I could explain to them. Because, thanks to the news portal and the Rainbow Network, the Recorder offered access to information.

My gran had checked with the Book when she agreed to the Rainbow Network being set up. The Book told her, and later me, that the Recorders and Knight Adjutants had always been responsible for education about the wider world outside any single realm.

Feeling as if I'd finally found a solid place to stand, I said, "Dola, may I have a coffee, please?"

A coffee arrived. The mug was white and had a photo of Dorothy clutching Toto with her basket over her arm and the words, *My! People come and go so quickly here!*

"Sorry, Dola, I needed some thinking time and a nap. This is getting out of hand. I want to make a video explaining why the Recorder isn't their fairy godmother."

I sipped my coffee, smiled at my mug and added, "Or even Glinda the Good. Just like the cowardly lion, they're going to have to find their own courage."

"Your quote to John Fergusson was perfect for several of the realms' problems, not just for John's inaction alone."

I had no recollection of what I'd said to John. I remembered Rollo's hatred of the former Knight Adjutant had turned my arm bionic so that I'd slapped him silly. "What did I quote?"

HRH arrived and strolled across the bed towards me, already speaking. "Ah, Recorder, you quoted the Bard himself. I was proud of you. Well, truthfully, you misquoted the Bard, but it is the effort that counts, or some other similarly untruthful aphorism."

"Huh?"

I swear she sighed. "You said, 'In your next life, try to remember a coward dies many times, but a brave man only once.' I believe you intended to quote Shakespeare's *Caesar*, my dear. You didn't quite manage it, but it was a valiant attempt, and one works with the cloth one has."

I gave up. I didn't even know if I'd just been praised or criticised. "The Vikings need to get their own realm together. The Recorder can't do it for them, and I need to tell them that."

The cat turned her side towards me and swivelled her head. Her beautiful brown leopard markings stood out clearly on her tawny fur as she looked out of the window. "Must you?"

"Yes."

"Must you do it today?" The cat's intense green gaze never left my face.

I smiled. "Yes, why don't you want me to? What bets have you been taking?"

With a noise that sounded like a hairball coming up, she coughed, then grumbled. "That you would solve all the poor little Vikings' problems for them, of course. Because Niki and Rollo are …what is that tasteless song? Oh, yes, sitting in a bush, or is it perhaps a tree? It's some variety of shrubbery, anyway. Incomprehensible nonsense. I do not believe I have seen humans kissing in trees for hundreds of years. But you feel obliged to solve the boy's problems. You should not do that. The man must emerge first."

"And have many people bet I would fix it all?"

"Yes."

"Well, I'm not going to—you won't have to pay out. So, what's your problem?"

"Because the largest bets are against you doing so."

"You mean somebody bet I'd come to my senses and realise I can't fix a realm's problems if they won't make any attempt to fix themselves?" I laughed. "And who bet that?"

"Why on earth would I disclose that?"

"Caviar."

She went completely still. "Agreed."

I waited, and eventually she said, "Ad'Rian, Mabon, and

Breanna." The cat tilted her head to one side and focused her green eyes on me intently. "Recorder, I could assist you in achieving a just outcome if you were prepared to delay until tomorrow and to return one of these to me." She dropped two curved pieces of green bronze metal onto my duvet. I picked one up. It wasn't quite a ring, but a short spiral, something like a helix that felt ring-like. I rubbed my thumb onto the green coating, which looked powdery but wasn't. It felt ancient.

"What are these?"

"You won your bet. Those are tokens for the favours you negotiated. If you lose them, you cannot claim your rewards."

I picked up the spirals. They looked like ancient jewellery for people with tiny fingers.

"How did you know, Recorder?"

"Huh, what?"

"About the third queen?"

I gave a startled snort. "How did you not know? I mean, who could be a worthier queen?"

"The girl is a hoyden."

Who else had called her a hoyden? Oh, yeah. "Yes, so Agnes said. But Rhiannon will stand firm on behalf of her dragons. Isn't that the definition of a worthy queen?"

She sneezed in the same annoyed way Tilly sometimes did, and her tail appeared to be giving me the finger as she strolled unhurriedly across my bed and settled herself on a discarded pillow. Tilly opened one eye and then ignored her.

So the two kings and Breanna had wagered I would come to my senses before allowing Viking to use me. Perhaps that was why Ad'Rian and Mabon stayed out of the way during the warlords' visit, so I could work this out for myself, and maybe I'd been too harsh on them. Would it have killed them to give me a hint, though? Then I thought about what the cat said and turned to speak to her. She appeared to be asleep.

"What did you say about my returning one of these to you?"

Nope, she was wide awake with her eyes still shut. In what I was almost sure was a fake sleepy tone, she mumbled, "Hmm? Yes. Return one to me and delay dealing with the warlords officially until tomorrow morning so I can lay off some of the bets I took, and I'll assist you in achieving a just result."

"And what's that?"

"You must work that out yourself. But I will assist you in showing everyone it is the correct outcome."

I'd learnt some stuff since naïve Niki arrived here. "And is it worth one of your favours?"

I'm going to believe the look HRH gave me was approving. "Because he is your life mate, yes. It will be excellent value for a favour. For both of you, and for the Viking realm. If he wasn't, it wouldn't be."

I considered it and pushed one of them back to her. It rose into the air and straightened out as it merged into her neck and became part of her green collar.

Then I remembered something I'd wondered several times. "Does this Droit de Seigneur have a street name? Most drugs do, don't they? I mean, who calls marijuana, marijuana? Doesn't it have lots of nicknames?"

Dola's voice said, "They call it Threecease."

I tried to picture the word. Nope. "How are you spelling that, Dola?"

"With three capital Cs." Then she clarified, "C.C.C. But they pronounce the acronym as Threecease."

"OK. But I don't get it—what's it an acronym of?"

"The three Cs stand for Command, Coerce and Consent. They believe that summarises the effect of the drug."

Well, that did it. My anger rushed back, flooded through me and overflowed like an inadequate Scottish drain after heavy rain.

I might not be doing the right thing, but I was damn well going to do something.

CHAPTER
SIXTY-TWO

I'd settled in my den, my gran's old office, where Dola informed me the light was best for filming. Tilly lay in the puddle of sunlight, which always shone on the cherry blossom tree at this time of day, and HRH watched me from the bookshelf.

I looked past the magical sunlight to the curtain of rain, which fell about ten feet away from the house. I wondered if that was where Dola's shields extended to.

I was delaying doing the scary thing, wasn't I? I was furious, but I still wanted a sign—from Somebody, from Anybody, from the damn universe, if necessary, that I was the Nobody who should try to fix this mess.

The problem with my idea about leaving my cocoon behind and becoming a butterfly was their pretty wings seemed to make them subject to the winds of fate. I hadn't thought that butterfly metaphor through. Because I was going to need more than colourful wings. I needed talons to deal with these damn Vikings. Then I grinned as I remembered a day out Aysha, Autumn and I had enjoyed for Autumn's birthday. At the Birds of Prey centre in Wales there was an adorable white and grey gyrfalcon called Puddle or maybe Muddle? It looked so cute and was easy to underestimate until the handlers showed us what she could do when she was hungry. Well, I was hungry for justice to give the ordinary Vikings some peace and a chance to build a better realm.

But I needed that sign to tell me I was on the right track before I turned a lot of people's lives upside down and possibly catapulted an entire realm into a revolution.

I cast about for a distraction to calm my racing heart. Dola had offered more of the chicken soup I'd had for lunch ... was that sometime in my future? Oh, time travel made my head spin. But I didn't want to eat. I just wanted to get this done.

"What's this, Dola?" I picked up the sheet of paper from my desk – it looked familiar.

"You asked if I would send you a transcript of my encouraging words to be more yourself during the book club. I told you I was paraphrasing a poster Finn asked me to make for him. This is the text from that artwork:

"Here's to the crazy ones.

The misfits.

The rebels.

The troublemakers.

The round pegs in the square holes.

The ones who see things differently.

They're not fond of rules. And they have no respect for the status quo.

You can quote them, disagree with them, glorify or vilify them.

About the only thing you can't do is ignore them.

Because they change things. They push the human race forward.

And while some may see them as the crazy ones, we see genius.

Because the people who are crazy enough to think they can change the world are the ones who do."

I started giggling, then literally fell about laughing. The relief my amusement gave to my tight stomach, dry mouth and clammy hands was immediate. Between giggles, I asked, "Do you know what this is?"

"I understand it is a statement of purpose from a deceased businessman and innovator whom Finn reveres."

More laughter erupted from me. Sometimes the universe really does send you a sign when you ask for one. Because I knew what this was, and it was written by a talented copywriter in an advertising agency. Not by the businessman Finn admired. In fact, if the stories were true, the man himself hadn't liked it at all in the beginning, but the power of advertising had changed his mind. Wasn't that exactly what I was trying to do here? Show the Vikings they could change things? Change their beliefs, use the court of public opinion? And wasn't that exactly what advertising was—an attempt to court the public and change their opinion?

"Dola, may I have a copy of the poster in the new breakfast room please?" Rollo would freaking love it.

That famous advert had given me an idea.

I decided against fulfilling Ben's request for a party political-style broadcast to explain the Gateway's rules for its boundaries and the consequences for breaking them. Because, let's face it, the vast majority of political broadcasts are boring, unintentionally hilarious, or made during troubling times. And while these were troubling times for the Vikings, I wasn't their leader. I was a neutral third party, and I needed to remain one.

When Aysha first started her law practise, she had a meeting with a marketing consultant to help her promote it. The woman talked about the need to convey three important things to ensure potential clients would trust Aysha and her new firm. She'd called it an Aristotle Triangle.

Pathos is an appeal to the audience's feelings.

Ethos is an explanation of the speaker's credibility.

Logos feeds the viewer's logic needs, using facts and evidence.

The consultant explained that if Aysha could incorporate all three into her marketing messages, her law office would see swift growth. The presentation struck a chord with me. Although it hadn't, as I'd hoped, worked on Janet—probably because I had no credibility in her mind.

But the Recorder had power and credibility, and the average Vikings were clearly unhappy. They needed to know I would use the might of my office on their behalf if they gave me a chance. They didn't deserve to continue being as powerless as I'd once been.

The cat had been surprisingly helpful too, advising me to just bring the Vikings up to date. "Assume they know nothing, Recorder. Because most of them are good people. It's their leaders who aren't. Vikings consider information more precious than gold—hence the abundance of spies. Paint an accurate picture for them. They respect honesty. Try to show them how things could be if they change." That seemed to be another summary of the Aristotle thing – how old was HRH?

But I was no anchor woman. My sweaty palms and dry mouth proved that. *Talons, Niki, pretend you have talons now. Just like little Puddle had. She didn't look scary, but she was effective.*

I breathed, then I sent Dola the video clip I'd taken before I left the Gateway with the message.

> Can we start this video with this? Let's set it to go live on the news portal after lunch. Then we won't confuse everyone's timeline too much.

The Dolina sprang to life. "It will take that long to edit the full video. This needs to be most professionally presented."

"Yeah, I know. Got any more pressure you want to dump on me? Wouldn't you rather do it? I was never a confident presenter."

"No, because I am not a McKnight. The power chose your line for a reason, Niki. Your earliest ancestors stood up for people, many of whom had no power of their own, just a flock of sheep and a desire for something better. You can do this. Help the Vikings, and I will help you."

I began with ethos, a brief overview of the credibility of the Recorder's Office and the thirteen McKnight women who'd served the Gateway since 1124 AD. At both Dola and HRH's urging, I included a little information about me and how I ascended after my grandmother passed.

The cat had said, "Vikings respect ancestors and history, so play your almost thousand-year history for all its worth. No need to mention the recent incompetents who have held the position; just speak about your lineage."

Then I moved to logos, not its current usage of the little graphics that represented a brand name, but the facts that underlay an argument back in the old Greek philosopher's day.

I told them about the original agreement with the power. We'd include a link to a copy of the agreement and the translation. More facts followed when I laid out how Troels, when he was their king, broke the agreement by sending his lumberjacks to attack the Gateway. I encouraged them not to hold those workmen responsible for Vikings' downfall. They were merely tools. They didn't know they were putting everyone's lives in danger. If their former king didn't know, how could some poor lumberjacks possibly have understood the implications for their whole realm?

And then I took a long, deep breath. The author of *Good Grief* would have been so proud.

"Ignorance is the crux of your problems today. But ignorance of the rules won't prevent you all from suffering the penalties for breaking those rules." Then I worked logically through everything they needed to know about the power's ability to simply destroy their realm and, slightly belatedly, encouraged them not to panic.

"There is a reason I'm speaking to you all personally today. As you saw at the beginning of this video, the warlords who are running Viking during Troels' incarceration are in the Gateway because they sent a petition to the Recorder. They aren't in your realm or running anything right now. But unless they attack me, as Arne Orm did, I can't do anything with them to help you all."

I paused the video. "Dola, can you include a snippet of what happened to the late Warlord Orm?"

As she said, "Yes, Niki," I resumed staring into my camera and explained the "they'd broken no Viking laws" problem to the lens.

A glass of wine appeared on my desk out of range of the camera. I was about to reach for it when I realised my hand was damp with panic sweat. Still looking straight into the lens while I wiped my sweaty palm on my jeans, out of sight, I hoped. I thought hard. Dola would edit the pause out.

Did I really want to do this?

Who the hell did Niki McKnight think she was?

Was I truly about to incite a realm to drastic change? To riot? To rebellion? If Dola's data was correct, and not a single person had suggested it wasn't, then I wasn't starting a war—was I?

Hadn't I read somewhere that if the vast majority of a population want something, but the group who hold the power are unjust and are overthrown, that's not a coup—that's a revolution?

The only thing I knew for certain was that I wasn't qualified for this. But *none* of the Viking citizens, including Inge and Rollo, believed *they* were qualified for it either. Everybody was waiting for the mysterious Everybody, Anybody or Somebody to fix it.

The Recorder had to walk out onto the ledge here because Nobody else would.

My studies with the Book suggested the last time the Recorder's Office had walked out onto any ledges was during Agnes' administration. And apparently it was the Vikings who stoned her to death, even if no one could prove it.

I wiped my palm down my jeans again and, confident the glass wouldn't slip out of my hand, now took a sip of wine.

"Viking doesn't have a constitution. It doesn't have a working government. Viking citizens don't have any rights except those their former kings gave them and Troels didn't get around to rescinding."

What else did I need to tell them?

"We need to change a world. Your world. Because, right now, it doesn't seem to be the world any of you want to live in."

That was one more damn thing I'd discovered. Some of their better former kings *had* put laws in place. So they'd had some protection, but Troels—or more likely his vizier, which was exactly how I was starting to think of Halvor—had decided he didn't like those laws and struck them off the law books.

"Your former king, as you all surely know by now, is being detained by the Recorder's Office to answer charges of the illegal administration of drugs, rape and forced impregnation of hundreds of women from all the realms. The Gateway power relocated him to your capital so you could see he wasn't being mistreated, simply held during our evidence-gathering.

"Your problem, and now mine, is what he did was *not* illegal in Viking. The only reason I can hear the petitions against him is that they have been brought by women from the other realms. Those realms have constitutions, or their equivalent. Their citizens have rights, and they have laws against such crimes as the ones Troels committed."

I decided to tell them the simple truth.

"I can see all the #ItHappenedToVikingsToo posts on the portal. As a woman—no, as a human being—my heart is breaking for you. But you don't have any laws against it. So what do you expect me or anyone else to do while you all continue to accept it?"

I hit the pause button and blew out a huge breath.

This was even harder than I'd thought it would be.

What had Rollo told me? If he did take the crown, he still wouldn't be able to change a damn thing while the warlords were in place. They'd simply kill him and put one of Troels' more compliant sons on the throne. Or some other random guy they told everyone was the new king—because, frankly, that was all Troels had been. A power-grabbing relative.

But I hadn't asked Rollo's permission to share his thoughts.

"Dola, what time is it, and where is Rollo now, on your timeline, I mean?"

"Niki, that is a very confusing question. We must discuss these situations properly sometime. But I think the information you require is that, in my now, Rollo is currently in Aberglas visiting someone called Lossie and obtaining a new tattoo. I assume your conversation with Ad'Rian is why he felt the necessity to do that today. You are currently at Mabon's. Does that assist you?"

"Yes, it helps a lot, thank you."

"Hey, remember when you said you couldn't take the crown and expect to live, and you didn't want it, anyway?"

"Hey you. Yes. What about it?"

"Was that private information for me, or could I share it?"

"Who would you share it with?"

"The Recorder would like to share it with the Viking people."

There was a significant pause before he asked, *"You got a plan, Boo?"*

"I think so. My Gift and I much prefer it to the 'Let Glais'Nee kill all the warlords in secret' plan."

"Then go for it. And by the way, I love you."

I shut the connection down. That tattooing thing felt painful. Then I paused and muttered, "He said it first!"

"I am sorry, Niki, I did not catch that?"

"Sorry, Dola, talking to myself."

But I'd just realised Rollo thought he was having this conversation "now." I hadn't told him I might love him until about an hour in his future. He'd said it first!

I raised a mental middle finger to Aysha, who'd given me some of her mum's best advice on our holiday, telling me to make sure I was the loved and not the lover in the relationship. I couldn't see why I couldn't be both, but my romantic history reminded me how rubbish I'd been at those kind of relational politics. However, I had managed to follow Olive's advice even if I'd done it accidentally. I tucked Rollo's words into my mental treasure chest and picked up the threads of my plan.

OK, Niki, you've got a man who loves you. Even better, it seems he loves the woman you actually are and not some other woman he thinks he can bully you into becoming. You've got a job to do, and you have power. It's time to use it. It's time you took Dola's advice and showed the realms what you think the Recorder's Office should stand for over the next millennium.

Become a force for good, or if you can't manage that, at least become a force for sanity.

I gathered my courage to give the ordinary Vikings my absolute best. I breathed, hid my still shaking hands below my desk, and prepared to start a revolution.

CHAPTER
SIXTY-THREE

"Viking citizens, let me tell you all the story of Everybody, Somebody, Anybody and Nobody."

While I recited the story I'd told Inge, I tried to make eye contact with the camera lens. "You all seem to be waiting for Somebody to come along and fix your horribly broken realm. Too many high-ranking citizens have told me this will be the next king's problem."

Well, Inge and Kari *were* high-ranking, and two *was* too many. Satisfied I wasn't lying to them, I pressed on.

"However, none of you seem to have considered that Prince Hrólfr has no desire to take the crown. He feels the current corrupt, drug-growing and smuggling warlords will simply depose him by any means they can. Just as they tried to do last week so he wouldn't even be alive to take the throne. They'll try to bring down the ancient and honourable House Yggdrasil by assassinating its last living royal. Rollo has too much to live for to throw his life away."

I allowed a small private smile to curve my lips while I paused to sip my wine, which had magically topped itself up. Was Dola doing that for continuity on the video? Clever house.

How much of my personal life did I want to tell the Vikings? I remembered that trainer long ago who'd said, "Share something of yourself so people know who they're dealing with," and thought, *yeah, sod it.*

"In case the gossip hasn't reached you all yet, I should mention that Rollo and I are bonded. So, you can imagine," I rolled my eyes, "as much as I may want to help Viking, I won't encourage my bond mate to give up his life in Caledonia and come back to rule over a dysfunctional realm, probably very briefly, before being assassinated by a nation that doesn't think it deserves laws, rights or justice and has done nothing to fight for them for the last forty years."

Was that too strong? It felt too strong. Oh, damn it.

Then I remembered what Rhiannon told me Agnes said about the next time a monarch attacked the Gateway. I couldn't quite retrieve it. So I hit pause again while I pictured myself sitting on the dragon's back far too high above those spiky, sharp-looking mountains while Rhiannon laughed at me for sounding like Agnes when I used my librarian voice.

That was it. Agnes told Rhiannon, if she were still alive, she'd need to pray hard to whichever God or Goddess was in vogue in the future. Because the Recorder of that era would need a brain and the spine to use it.

I hoped I had a brain. Let's just fake having a spine. *Think of the future, Niki – don't lose your nerve now. Use the damn power Agnes may have died to give you. Straighten your spine and use your brain.*

The cat watched me closely as I sat up straighter. "As I've begun to understand through my bond mate and his friends, Viking was once a proud nation of strong, upright warriors and shield maidens who kept them that way. You had honest, hard-working mining, farming and fishing families. Engineers, merchants and teachers. The reason you don't have a thousand-year history of sensible laws on your books is that you had fair, just rulers and strong community bonds. You may not have needed laws under an honourable king like Jonvar. But we need inviolable laws to protect us from poor rulers. Because now you have too many corrupt warlords, no rights for citizens and no protection from sexual attack."

I drew in one final breath and reminded myself that just because I recorded this didn't mean I had to use it.

Oh, sod it!

By the Goddess, was *sod it* all I could think today?

Someone had to tell them it was time they realised an entire nation was being judged by the actions of a corrupt ex-king and twelve, OK, it was possibly only seven or eight criminal warlords. At least they would have been criminals in every realm except their own.

How do you incite a revolution? I couldn't say I'd ever given that any consideration. Would it be too rude to say, "The rest of the kingdoms all believe your realm is insane. If you do too, it's past time to change it?"

Probably.

How could I help them?

Spine and talons, Niki. You'll never possess them for real if you don't believe you have them.

"I can only think of two things I can do to help you—and I'm doing them. The first is to tell you all this and give you the Rainbow Gateway's news portal to allow you to view this information. Share this video with your friends. Dola, my equerry, has set up secure, private chat channels, which you may use to discuss it without the other realms being able to see private Viking business. But you must register for those channels using your Rainbow Network login. I want to make sure they're safe and private for you."

I hit pause again.

"Dola, do you have personal information to identify the Vikings by their log-ons?"

She sighed, "Of course, Niki." Yeah, she really sighed. Whoops.

637

"What if we set up three channels? Men, women and ..." I trailed to a halt. That wasn't the relevant bit, was it?

She jumped in, "I recommend four channels: warlords and their staff, shield maidens, warriors, and citizens."

"You don't seriously think any of the warlords' staff would be stupid enough to ..."

"I never underestimate the stupidity of humans. They will speak in code because, of course, we wouldn't understand that."

I blew out a breath. She probably wasn't wrong. "I'll be guided by your experience. OK, what else have I forgotten to tell them?"

"What you plan to do with the warlords? I trust that is point two of the things you can do for them?"

"I thought I might point out that, right now, no one knows who is running Viking. But once I release the warlords, they will be in charge again."

"Then you should give the Viking people the deadline when you will have to return the warlords to them. When will that be?"

HRH needed me to wait until tomorrow, and that felt right to me too.

"I don't want to do these petitions today. I'm still tired. Recorders shouldn't make important decisions when they're exhausted. That should be a new rule. I should put it in the Book."

The Book arrived on the desk. Huh. Driven by an urge I couldn't quite pin down, slowly I asked, "Dola, odd question but ... is there ... anything about this Viking problem that afterwards you might wish you'd told me?"

She came back swiftly, "Excellent question. Yes, do not feel guilty afterwards."

That felt terrifying. Was I doing the wrong thing? "Because?"

"Because the everyday Vikings like the small pieces of the twenty-first century they have been permitted to enjoy. But many of their warlords want to remove their choices and force them to live as though it is still the first millennium. The majority of citizens do not want that. The data proves it. Every revolution begins with the spark of injustice. You might be the person who is providing kindling, but without the original injustices, there would be no flame."

At my obviously unconvinced grumble, she asked. "Niki, do you believe you could start a revolution in the Red Celt realm?"

I thought about it then chuckled. "Not unless someone tried to ban beer. But if anyone tried that, Mabon would lead the mob himself and show them where to point their pitchforks."

Dola wasn't finished with me. "Exactly. No kindling is there? Your way of dealing with the Vikings may keep the bloodshed to a minimum. Left to themselves, and without a focus or a deadline, it could degenerate into a civil war. That would affect all the other realms. You or the power might have had to leave them closed off from the Rainbow Gateway. That has happened before."

"It has?"

"Yes," she said flatly. But I wondered if this might explain Indigo.

"When?"

"Niki, did you want to finish this video in time for it to be edited and perhaps change the future or discuss the past with me? You need to get back to the Gateway and your proper time to prevent these warlords from committing suicide by annoying Glais'Nee's spear."

"OK. But remind me to talk to you about it please."

I set the video recording again.

"This has been a forty-year road since King Jonvar was probably murdered and you were all plunged into this nightmare. I know it isn't a path the ordinary Vikings are proud of or happy about. But I have complete faith in the majority of Vikings citizens, and I want to give you the chance to stand up for the things you hold dear."

Was that enough? Well, it would have to be. Glais'Nee told me to remember, when I spoke, history would be listening. So, I didn't want to ask, "Is twenty-four hours long enough for you to start a revolution?"

"The second thing I can do to help you is hold these warlords overnight because other realms have filed petitions against them. Right now, no one seems to know who is running Viking because I have the warlords. But tomorrow I must conclude the hearing of the petitions against them. I plan to release them through the yellow gate at noon tomorrow."

I breathed, smiled, remembered my conversation with Rollo, and then went for it. "I'm reminded of two men in my own realm. The first said, 'We cannot solve our problems with the same thinking we used when we created them.'"

I paused, thinking about Einstein, and decided to let the words speak for themselves. The Vikings would either get this, or they wouldn't. I'd need to leave it in their hands. It was their realm. As Recorders, we needed to keep the realms in balance, which meant not allowing any of them to become much more powerful than the others. And the Vikings seemed to be at such a disadvantage, I needed to give them a nudge.

"The other guy, just before my seventeenth birthday, changed the course of my studies when he said, 'Because the people who are crazy enough to think they can change the world are the ones who do.' A lot of people say the Vikings are crazy. Maybe it's time to prove them right and change your world for the better. Arinn Tusensköna in his book says Vikings are the proudest warriors, but they are not a race who wastes their violence on the wrong things. Perhaps it's time to fight for your right to live with peace, justice and freedom."

Then, following pure devilment, I smiled at the camera and said, "My staff will be available and may be contacted via their usual emails if any of us can help. I recommend my equerry as your first point of call. Her email should be on your screen now."

I hit the red button to stop the recording.

"It's all yours, Dola. Do whatever you think is best with it.

Thank you. I'm so done. Can I have a coffee, and then I'll head back to when I should be? My head's spinning today."

"Niki, did you want me to put my email address on this video?"

"Yes, please, or some other way they can contact you."

She spluttered, "But ... but ... they might all email me."

"Well, like you said, we all have to move out of our comfort zone sometimes. And I know how much you like sending those customer service emails that aren't."

"I have no idea what you are implying." Her tone was flat.

She loved sending replies that were the antithesis of actual customer service emails. And those replies were starting to go viral with their pithy, superficially polite insults that cut to the heart of the senders' incompetence.

I wanted to see what she'd do with this. I was going to need a laugh tomorrow.

CHAPTER
SIXTY-FOUR

I landed outside the Gateway several hours later, which thanks to the whole time travel thing was about seven minutes after I'd left. "Dola, did the video go up?"

"Ah, Niki, you're back? We need a new vocabulary and some new tenses for these jaunts of yours."

"Mabon calls them time travel rodeos. I've started using it too. But I never really understood the complicated tenses at school, so let's not do that bit. The video?"

"Yes, people are just beginning to watch it."

"OK, thanks, I'm going in. Do you remember where I was up to?"

My brain was foggy today. My lower back ached painfully now, and that distinctive crampy feeling was beginning. I was definitely blaming hormones. It sounded so much better than stupidity or blind fury. I needed to wrap this mess up for the day and try to keep the warlords alive until tomorrow, didn't I?

"It is possible you were about to tell them why they're here, send them off with Glais'Nee, and come home for a long bath."

By the Goddess, that sounded like a plan.

. . .

I couldn't improve on Dola's suggestion, so I'd set the record straight for the warlords and for the people in Viking who might view the footage later this evening while they thought about their options.

Rollo and Glais'Nee were standing with Elise and Caitlin, observing the warlords as I re-entered the centre. Inge had emerged from whatever corner of the place she'd been hiding in, and a quick look at her body language suggested she'd made some decisions. I just hoped they were the right ones.

I addressed the warlords, "You are here today because the Recorder's Office has received hundreds of petitions against your former king. Following on from those, there have now been petitions filed against you."

Elise started softly translating to my left. About a third of the men were more focused on her than me. I paused and wafted my hand, palm upwards, to her in the classic gesture for more volume. Finn turned to film the two of us.

I'd done weddings when one or both of the couple needed a translator. By changing my speech pattern into shorter phrases to give the translators time, it usually went smoothly. I could do that now. I wanted them to understand what the petitions were accusing them of. And I wanted Elise's translations on the video of this we would put on the news portal.

I grabbed my iPad and flicked to the petition queue. "The King of the Fae has filed a petition against all twelve of you by name. He alleged theft of herbs, the destruction of his wards and," I frowned at the petition, "iron poisoning of his ground."

The Recorder could help with that, but for now ... *Focus, Niki. The sooner you focus, the sooner you can have that bath.*

"There are many other petitions from the Hobs. You fed Droit de Seigneur to contracted workers without their consent. By doing so, you caused a number of Hobs to lose their babies. Nine longed-for babies, now dead, sit on your consciences." I didn't say, "if you have one," because several of the warlords looked distraught and angry at my words. But the rest looked baffled, even after Elise's translation.

The utter confusion on the men's faces made me add, "The combination of herbs. Your method of preparation. The increase in strength. They all change the original Droit de Seigneur into a different version of the drug. It becomes something that can cause miscarriages and birth defects."

One of the younger warlords at the end was clawing at his mouth. Oh, heavens, had I really left them all muted and wandered off for a nap?

Whoops! Was I becoming so casual about the Recorder's power? Was that a bad thing? Maybe I'd consider it later in the bath. For now, I simply unmuted him.

He spoke directly to Elise, who translated for me. "He's asking, 'How do you know this? Can you prove it?'" I might not speak Norse, but I heard the panicky note in his voice. My Gift confirmed his dread and fear.

"Yes, the Headwoman of the Hobs told me. You know the Hobs are experts with herbs and their uses and misuses?"

A few seconds later when Elise finished speaking, there was nodding from about half of the warlords. I made a note of the others, the ones who were simply determined not to respond to me. "Ad'Rian Alicorn," at yet more confused looks, I added, "the Fae king, also knows this, which is why he filed the petition on behalf of the Fae Healers' Hall."

Elise translated my answer, and Mags arrived at my side. She gazed at the younger warlord who'd asked the question for a long moment. "Your wife?"

He nodded unhappily and spoke at length, never losing eye contact with Elise. The entire time he was speaking, the same six warlords, led by Warlord Blotchy Face on the end, glared at him. Even without words, their eye-daggers clearly said, "Shut the hell up, dickhead, right up, right now."

"Who's the guy speaking to Mags?"

Rollo answered immediately, *"He's Gustavsson, one of the new ones I don't know well. But I thought he might not have been sullied by the old boys' crimes yet."*

The oldest of them, Bloodraven, also gestured he wanted to speak. I unmuted him.

Rollo sent, *"He holds a farming province. Third or fourth generation. Never heard a complaint about him from anyone except Troels and the dirty dozen. He refused to grow herbs for them. He said his people needed bread and meat, not drugs."*

Yes, Bloodraven, or Bloodeagle, as they'd named him in *Drengr*, was one of the more rational Jarl characters. Caitlin's report on him was almost favourable. But she thought he'd be a lousy king, partly because of his age, and partly because he didn't like to leave his district.

In English, Bloodraven said, "This, it did not use to be problem. But my daughter, she also is unable to bear, no, to carry children to birth, no …" he floundered until Elise said a word in Norse, and he nodded and switched to Norse, looking unhappy.

Elise turned to me. "His daughter hasn't been able to carry a child to term since her first. Her husband is a mining specialist and was working in the Red Celt realm while she was expecting the first, his much-loved grandson. Since she returned home she has lost three babies. That can sometimes just happen—but now he is considering."

The first younger man, Gustavsson, asked Elise a question. She translated, "He wants to know what has changed?"

Inge appeared in front of me and spoke Norse. Now Elise translated for me, "She is explaining what all the women already know, and the men should know, but many of them would rather blame a woman than look into our accusations. Troels changed the recipe after she divorced him. He made it much more potent. He made it constantly available instead of the mild version that used to be a popular tradition once a year at the Autumn equinox."

At my raised enquiring eyebrow, she added, "It used to be the individual's choice: drink it or don't. It was a mild aphrodisiac."

She waggled her own eyebrows at me, then straightened her face into stern lines. "The older women tell me no one was force-fed it back then, and, unlike now, it used to have a pleasant but distinctive taste, so you could tell if it had been mixed into a drink."

I turned back to the younger man who'd first asked to speak. But he looked so devastated, I simply announced, "I will hear the petitions tomorrow. Tonight, you will be held in a safe place. Tomorrow, you will be returned here. This will give you the chance to consider anything you may wish to say about your side of the story."

As I walked to Glais'Nee to suggest the piskie glade wasn't the right place for tonight because the Recorder required all the warlords to be returned here in one piece in the morning, he smiled at me. "Well done, Nik-a-lula. I will return them whole and in health."

Not good health, I noted, but I wasn't about to nitpick. Most of them didn't look like they were in good health now, so ... whatever.

Then everyone's phones began beeping.

Well, not mine. Because I'm not a savage, and my phone is almost always muted.

Caitlin, Inge, Elise and even Mags were patting pockets and rummaging in handbags. I saw Finn, his thumbs already flying on his, and Rollo was scrolling madly.

Caitlin walked over, holding her phone. "What did ya do?"

"I gave the Viking people a heads-up on a video. Now I'm exhausted. You're welcome to drink beer in my kitchen or stay at Finn's, or even in my spare room if you think this might cause problems and you want to be here. But I'm going to get some sleep and find my brain. I'll fix this tomorrow, or I might be around later. Right now, I need some painkillers and another nap."

She frowned, glanced down at me, rubbing my back, and simply said, "That sucks, go. Eat chocolate. Drink stuff. I got this. I've had all the sleep I needed on holiday. I slept through the ballet. Then through a cat-torturingly screechy opera thing. Then I couldn't sleep through a play so long and boring, I expected the Goddess herself to arrive and scream it should stop its inhumane treatment of living things. But every ten minutes, just as I dropped off, everyone started clapping again. What they found to clap about is still a slagging mystery. Ma says I'm a Philistine." As she was talking, her watchful eyes followed Glais'Nee as he gestured to his Fae warriors, who efficiently bundled all the warlords towards the violet gate.

She looked back at me. "Is the power OK? Where did the body go?"

"The power's fine—it's feeling happier and happier the closer those guys get to that gate." I laughed. "It sent take-out to Rhiannon for the dragonets."

At her confused look, I fished my phone out. My lock screen said I'd been tagged in hundreds of messages. What the—oh, yeah, the video. That was probably what everyone was now watching. I opened my phone to Rhiannon's message to show Caitlin.

All the time she was laughing and trying to read it, more and more tags and messages were popping up at the top of the screen. "You're popular today."

"Yeah, about that. You need to check out the portal. I know it's not your thing, but you need to know about this one as the KAIT."

She nodded. I took my phone back. "And I need to get out of here before anyone else can grab me and whine at me."

Rollo stood by Finn's desk. I snagged his hand and asked, "Are you free to go?"

At his nod, I transported straight home as Inge and Elise bore down on the spot where we'd been. They'd had their chance all damn day while they were busy not stepping up to fix their own realm. I was heading home to a long bath, accompanied by chocolate and wine. And, I hoped, a gorgeous man to rub my back.

He had to be stressed about this, didn't he? Maybe I'd rub his back too.

On that happy thought, we landed in my bedroom. I heard water running in the bathroom. Bless Dola. Rollo pulled me into his arms, and my universe settled back into the right orbit.

CHAPTER
SIXTY-FIVE

I reached down our link to see how he was. He must have been doing the same. Because at exactly the same time I winced at the discomfort he was in, he asked, "You OK? You feel achy."

"I was just thinking the same about you. Why do people have tattoos done if they hurt like this?"

He hugged me tighter and released me quickly with a small pain-filled noise as I must have bumped my head into the site of his new artwork. "This paint is different to a normal tattoo, but it'll be fine tomorrow."

He paused as I shook my head and wiggled my left shoulder.

"OK, it'll be fine in less than a week."

"A week!"

"Lossie uses some of the traditional Pictish techniques. It gives a 3D effect and super vibrant colours with his combination of old techniques and high-tech inks. It just causes a little more discomfort—briefly." He gave me a challenging smile. "But you know what they say about pain. Want to see it?"

There were several lies in that statement. But he was telling them to himself, not to me.

"No, I have no idea what they say about pain?" I continued

opening the buttons of his soft shirt. When I got them open, all I saw was a large opaque plastic square covering the centre of his chest between his nipples, over his heart. The skin beyond the edges of the protector was an unhappy pink. Ouch!

He brushed my concern away. "They say the good thing about pain is it confirms you're not dead yet."

At my incredulous head shake, he added, "It's fine. But it needs to come off. I have to clean it and give it some air. Give me a minute. It stings a bit."

My left shoulder twanged. I mumbled, "That must be a Viking saying. Only they would say rubbish like that," as I went to grab some painkillers to get ahead of the period pain I knew was incoming. I was about to ask if he wanted a couple too. But he looked as though he would do the manly, *no, no, I'll be fine* thing—so I didn't bother asking and just got him two anyway.

When his soft swearing started, I spun around so fast, I slopped water out of the glass I was holding and watched in fascination. He stretched the bottom of the plastic film downwards rather than starting at a corner as you would with a Band-Aid. Slowly but surely, it stretched and loosened away from his skin. He kept stretching it, swearing occasionally, and then pulled the plastic more.

When it came off—OMG.

He was right. It *was* a work of art.

The tattoo was breathtaking, captivating, and it possessed an almost mystical quality. As though it really wrapped around his heart rather than merely adorning the skin above it.

The depiction of Yggdrasil, his sacred tree and the emblem of his lineage, was nothing short of extraordinary. It mirrored the tree I'd seen as part of his white bedstead, but this one was in glorious technicolour. Within the darkened roots, looking perfectly at home, was a luminescent silvery-blue Danake coin, which cast a radiant glow into the gloom of the tree's base.

Nestled among the vibrant, flourishing green branches, a golden, seven-pointed Recorder's star peeked out. I had an odd sense there might be a significance to it that Vikings would grasp in some way that I didn't.

It was gorgeous.

The fusion of all the elements, seamlessly integrated into the tree, drew a long, awed breath from me. The trunk was the pièce de résistance. It mirrored the emblem on his tie and was a resplendent wooden letter Y. Every detail was meticulously crafted, as though a master artist had poured a tiny part of their soul into its creation.

It could have hung in the Louvre.

The ethereal quality stirred something deep inside me and left me speechless, awestruck, and swallowing hard.

"You like it then?"

I realised I'd gazed at it for far too long. But I still didn't know what to say. Except, "It looks sore." Yeah, trust me to bring it down to practicality.

Rollo laughed. "It is, but it will heal. It's special though, isn't it?"

It was more than special. It was esoteric and divine, and it must be the tattoo the prophecy referred to. No wonder he smiled when I told him about it.

I had no words, but my awestruck expression showed him everything he wanted to know because he smiled happily at me.

"Would you like to join me in the bath?"

His face fell. "I'd love to. I could use a good soak after holding still for hours to get this. But," he gestured at his tattoo, "I have to keep it dry until it gets past the oozing stage, or the ink will lose its vibrancy. I'll come and keep you company though if you like."

I wondered.

I wasn't very good at this yet.

But I didn't *think* I could do any harm.

I put my hand cautiously just above his skin and pulled a little power. As HRH and the Book had taught me, I pictured the sore, pink skin as normal, healthy and golden.

My hand got warm.

Rollo asked, "What are you doing?"

I stopped immediately. "Does it hurt?"

"No, it just feels unusual. Not painful, just ... different. Like pins and needles. And it hurts less."

I channelled the power now rather than pulling it. Supplying it to HRH and feeling what she'd done with it when we healed him from all his injuries was a bit of a masterclass. It taught me that healing was more about directing the power than actually pulling it. I gave it a clear vision of Rollo's usual healthy torso, now with its spectacular artwork. Healed.

After a short time, the power stopped flowing, and I looked at his chest. It looked better. The pink had gone, and through our link, I could tell it had stopped hurting.

Rollo peered downwards and tried to see his own torso. "Mirror?"

I opened the wardrobe door, which held the full-length mirror, and he stood in front of it. With his eyebrows raised and his mouth open in a slight O, he cautiously touched the bottom of the tattoo near the roots. He rubbed gently, then harder.

"It's healed! I thought you said you couldn't do healing yet?"

"I guess tattoos count as minor cuts and bruises. So, can we hit the bath now?"

He obviously felt better because he carried me through to the bathroom and then stopped dead, looking around.

Tiny candles surrounded my enormous Cleopatra-style sunken tub. The fragrance of fig and cassis floated up from the water. Dola had obviously found my favourite bath oil. It was my last bottle because the darn woman who made it had withdrawn that particular fragrance. As I stepped down into the water, I wondered if Dola could recreate it for me? That could be even cooler than wine on tap. Is anything more annoying than when a company withdraws a much-loved item because "it wasn't popular enough"? Especially when every time you went to buy it, they didn't have any, so how could it ever have sold enough?

I relaxed back against the bath pillow, floating in the enormous tub, and sipped my wine as Rollo downed about a pint of fresh orange juice and said. "This is a great bath!"

He reminded me of my manners. "It is, and thank you, Dola, it looks lovely. Could you, by any chance, make more of that bath oil you found?"

"I have already done so. The bottle was almost empty."

Of course she had because she was amazing, and I'd been a bitch earlier and told her to put her email on that video, hadn't I?

"Dola, you don't really need to put your email onto the video, you know. I was only being difficult."

There was a wonderfully human undertone of wry humour in her voice. "I know, Niki. I didn't. I gave them the address of my new online CAP."

I thought about it for a millisecond. "And what is that?"

"It is my Customer Avoidance Portal."

I choked back laughter as she added, "But it tells them the A stands for Advisory, then it automatically sends them many lovely messages explaining politely and at length why I'm unable to help them and offers them a short meditation to improve their day. I am monitoring the messages though for anything important."

I gave up. She was unique.

Rollo and I soaked away the remaining annoyances of the day with the scent of blackcurrant and fig and some delicious chocolate to help me relax and balance my hormones.

Then I gathered myself and gave him a look I hoped might one day grow up to be a hard stare. "Before we relax any more, we're out of time now, and the crucial question is still unanswered. Are you going to volunteer to do what needs to be done in Viking, or does the Recorder need to be seen to force you so everyone believes you didn't have a choice?"

"Dola, may I have that beer now, please?" He smiled at me. "It will be fine. I have most of a plan. Chris was brilliant, as always. And after your and the power's help today, Inge may even agree to do what needs to be done."

I considered him carefully. He looked relaxed. "Only *may* agree?"

"She wants to do it, but she's like a horse who's shying at the fence because she clipped it once. Inge had a wonderful plan when she obtained Troels' consent to open the Regering. Twenty-five years of achieving nothing has blunted the edge of her blade. She's frightened. It would only take one piece of legislation actually passing onto the lawbooks, and she'd find her nerve again. I know she would. I could give the Regering more than teeth to get these laws passed. I could give it fangs."

Coming soon, in her next impossible task, Niki McKnight demonstrates how to braid Scotch mist. I needed to try to make something out of nothing. Because I knew Rollo needed to be the king to give Inge the confidence to try again. My Gift was certain the whole of the Viking realm and all the other royals needed to see him take control, and that seemed to be his sticking point.

We did the high-speed link thing to catch him up, and I showed him how my day had gone. At the end, he simply stared at me in amazement. "Whoa, that doesn't sound like a party political. It sounds more like 'let's start a riot.' I should watch that video. The Recorder doesn't mess around, does she? But how do *you* feel about it, Boo? Oh, and there's just one problem."

It was time he faced up to it. But that was tomorrow's problem. I couldn't deal with even one more problem until I'd slept again. I had a bone-deep weariness that told me my brain needed some downtime.

This whole Viking mess had been stressful, but I hoped the worst of it was behind me now.

I can hear you all laughing from here – you do know that, right?

PART ELEVEN
THURSDAY

Scum exists and must be dealt with. If your blade isn't at the ready, fear not. Karma is always armed and constantly on the lookout.

But have a care before you invoke her because she plays by her own rules, and her timing might not be yours.

Winning the War Against Yourself: Daily Weapon and Warrior Care by Arinn Tusensköna

CHAPTER
SIXTY-SIX

Thursday, 11th March — Gateway Cottage — Starving o'clock

After the bath, we took what we intended to be a brief nap. But we'd awoken hours later in the dark and, almost in unison, thought, *I'm starving*.

Rollo pulled on his jeans and was lifting a T-shirt with an unhappy expression on his face when I said, "No need. Leave it off so I can admire your new paint. Come and see what Dola made for us."

I'd drawn him through to the new breakfast room, which weirdly still showed a sunny morning through the window until the dark night began about ten metres further into the garden.

"Dola, can we have some food, and what did you do to the light in here?"

"What would you like?"

"Burgers for Tilly and me please, hers without the bun."

In the deadpan tone of a bored, teenage fast-food worker, Dola enquired, "Would you like fries with that?" She'd been watching television again, hadn't she?

I giggled as I replied, "No, thank you, just a Coke. Is HRH around?"

"Of course, and no. Happily, the fickle, fraudulent feline has not been here since you saw her yesterday."

"If she shows up, could you tell her we're in here, please?"

Complete silence.

Oh well, the cat usually found me on her own.

I turned to Rollo, who was admiring the new glossy green fireplace, and pointed at the Dolina with a querying expression.

He said, "A chicken salad would be great. Thank you, Dola. With that lime dressing you once sent me in Edinburgh, if that's possible."

A large bowl with a ludicrous amount of leafy green stuff and a topping of chicken arrived on the table. The scent of lime, honey, and something else, mustard and perhaps cumin, drifted across the table towards me.

Rollo looked delighted with it. He waited without picking up his fork as he considered the space. "This is a beautiful room."

Dola answered him, "Niki wanted a breakfast room. This room will always have sunny morning light."

Wow! I kept forgetting the cool things magic could do. "I didn't know that was possible, but it's more fabulous than I realised. Thank you so much for making it for us."

My burger arrived. It smelt like heaven on a plate and drew Tilly from the bedroom with her nose in the air.

I glanced at Rollo. That tattoo was incredible, and he was right, it looked three-dimensional. Now he was surveying the poster I'd asked Dola for. In a matching green metal frame, it toned beautifully with the fireplace below it. "Isn't that an Apple advertisement?"

I started laughing. "Yep."

But while he read it, his expression was as thoughtful as I'd been this morning before I addressed the Vikings. "And do you think we're crazy enough to change the world, or at least the Viking realm? Is that what drove you to do that video?"

I didn't really want to explain the whole *I asked for a sign, and this felt like one* thing. It seemed silly looking back on it.

Then he made me wonder why I'd worried when he took his phone out of his pocket and gazed at it. "It's quite the sign, isn't it? The iPhone changed my personal world and my career, so perhaps it's worth a try."

"OK, good, let's eat, and then we have to plan tomorrow." I looked at my own phone. "Or, rather, later today. We need to discuss your 'one problem' before I'm back in the Gateway."

He nodded. Reluctantly, I thought, but he nodded.

"While we eat, tell me how you came up with the idea for your new paint?"

Now he smiled. "I've had the artwork for the tree for years. But getting the tattoo wouldn't have been politic. Troels hated that he couldn't claim the House Yggdrasil name—"

"Yeah, about that. The Book said the same, but how could he be your father's half-brother without being Yggdrasil? Don't your family trees work the same as ours?"

He looked around. "Is there pen and paper anywhere?" I was about to ask Dola when I remembered where I'd put my journal and pen and headed to the bookcase door. As I placed my fingers on the black panel and the bookcase slid open to reveal the kitchen, Rollo let out a low, impressed whistle and added, "Veeery cool. You do superlative work, Dola."

In the empty kitchen, lit only by the soft light under the cupboards, I opened the drawer and retrieved my journal. The blue envelope from Gran to my mother, or rather now to me, glared at me. I closed the drawer firmly because I had far too much to deal with right now without diving into that mess. After Leyla's twenty-three-year absence from my life, it couldn't be urgent.

I closed the bookcase behind me and handed Rollo my journal, open to a blank page.

He sketched a quick family tree, his own, and then, beside it, another one. "My father's much older sister, Margaretha, married into another house. She died giving birth to Troels. Her mother, my grandmother, took Troels in and raised him for a few years alongside my father, Jonvar. Troels and my father's similar ages meant everyone considered Troels to be my uncle, when we are really cousins. But those strong genes we were talking about when you asked why Jamie and I looked alike?"

"Actually, you don't anymore, not since you stopped using the Thor glamour."

He gave me a happy smile as he tapped the page. "Those genes came to Troels through his mother. And to me via my grandfather Ivan and my father. The problem Troels had is that, in Viking, house lineage and succession pass only through the male line. So his mother's connection to Yggdrasil didn't help him. He's a Troels, through and through."

OK, I'd actually followed all that. But it didn't explain why Troels thought he had any legal claim on the Viking throne – did it?

But Rollo went on, "When Troels' father remarried, his new wife took him back into their household and raised him alongside their own twin sons. Later, it was Troels himself who rewrote the relationship with my father to be that of half-brothers. He probably thought it gave him the better personal claim to the throne."

At my frown, he tapped the brother's and sister's names, Jonvar and Margaretha. "Troels and I are just cousins, but he thought the uncle title gave him more authority to seize the throne. He never even bothered to correct any of the younger Vikings who assumed *he* was my father. Misdirection and sleight of hand, along with overuse of the drug, and here we are …"

Light was dawning in my brain now, but I set it aside to think about later. I thought I might need to talk to Troels with my Gift powered up about what role he played in his cousin's death. Whether Rollo thought he wanted to know or not, I suspected I'd regret it later if I didn't get whatever information I could before it was too late.

But for now, I admired the tattoo and its attractive frame

again and prompted him, "So you had the artwork for the tree. When did you come up with the rest of it?"

"The seer told me to put the coin over my heart."

I nodded, remembering that. He'd put it inside his hip instead. "This would be Geoff the Seer?"

Rollo simply nodded. It really was only me that found it hilarious then. Oh well.

He gestured at the roots of the tree where the silver Danake coin appeared to glow. "It's over my heart. Want to feel it?"

But I refused to be distracted by thoughts of stroking his chest.

"And the Recorder's seven-pointed star?" Golden, it nestled in the green branches. And I noticed with interest the blush creeping up Rollo's neck.

I tilted my head, trying to hide my smile until he said, "We say the branches are the heart of House Yggdrasil."

Awww, he'd put me in his house's heart. But ... "Not the trunk?"

"Oh no, the trunk is our strength. And the roots are our future. Without healthy, happy roots, nothing flourishes."

I'd once mentioned to Nick he never said anything nice to me, or about me. He'd said, "Really, Niki, it's not what men say, you know. It's what they do. I bought you that lovely kitchen table."

When I considered the things Nick had done, none of them ever made me happy. So perhaps he was totally right, and you could judge a lot by what men did.

I gazed at Rollo's tattoo. He'd put my symbols into the heart and the future of his House. I felt the first tear fall.

Stupid dumb hormones.

Rollo pushed back his chair and was at my side on his knees in seconds. He stroked my face gently and brushed away the tears. *"Boo, what did I do?"*

I reached into our link, and for the first time, I voluntarily showed him my bruised heart and how, sometimes, when you're healing, you cry.

He stayed there quietly, making soothing, loving noises until I pulled my silly self together and gave him a watery smile. I'd just realised I cared far too much for this man to allow him to continue his head-in-the-sand ostrich impersonation about the vital role he needed to play in the Viking realm's transition to democracy.

I kissed him and said, "Thank you. But now I need to grow up and be the damn Recorder, and you need to be the King of Viking."

He gave me a horrified look. "NO!"

I just watched him until he added, "That's my one problem. I'd hate to be royalty. It's not me. You *know* that. Chris said if I give the government a form of regency like some Danish king did back in the Second World War, they should be able to proceed without me. Because I'm never going to be king. I decided that when I left Viking for university."

"There needs to be a period of transition. Viking needs you for that."

"No, they won't. Inge will do fine."

I battened down all my frustration. The problem I'd picked up was, when Rollo thought about royalty, he couldn't think past Troels and the warlords. And I understood his aversion to them. But he needed to change, because the Vikings would need to see a king give the government power. That realm trusted strong rulers. It would take them a year or two to understand the idea of government. I was running out of time before I would have to force him. I would hate anyone to force me, so I gathered my courage and my determination to try the last idea I had to help him see it for himself before the Recorder had no choice but to impose it on him.

"You already are royalty, Rollo; everyone but you knows it. Now it's time to decide what kind of royal you're going to be and for how long."

A mutinous expression that wouldn't have looked out of place on Caitlin settled on his face. "No, I'm not. I told the power no. I'm not taking the throne. And no power, or even you, can force me to."

"Yeah, you are. You're just not thinking straight—yet."

A stream of swearing in Norse, then he stood up and marched around the room. "I thought you understood."

"Oh, I do. It's you who doesn't. Stop having a temper tantrum and listen, will you? You've been royalty your entire life. You are in the direct line of succession to two royal houses."

"Temper tantrum? Streth Mik! Wait. What? Two? What the ..." Then all his confusion flooded through our bond.

He truly hadn't realised?

As calmly as I could, and breathing as carefully as I did when I removed a splinter from Tilly's paw, I said, "You are one of the highest-ranking members of the Fae Court and second or third in line to the Fae throne, at least until someone above you in the line has children. Have you thought that through? Or can't you get past Viking? You *are* royalty either way. Giving up the Viking throne won't change that. So what's your real reason?"

He sat down heavily on the couch. I watched him in case he went into shock the way he had in his kitchen in Edinburgh the last time I'd tried to broach this.

"How do you know that?"

"What?"

"That I'm in line to the Fae throne?"

"How do you *not* know it?" Ad'Rian knew it. L'eon knew it. Glais'Nee obviously knew it with his bow and his respectful "cousin" comment at the book club. Even I knew it, and the things I didn't know were legion! How did Rollo not know? This had to be wilful blindness, didn't it?

But he shook his head. "That can't be right, and if you say you know it, then why wouldn't you know whether I'm second or third in line?"

I sighed. "Ad'Rian has no sons. Fae is as backward as everywhere else in the realms—so only the men count."

"But ... but ... that's not right anyway. The Picts don't do the son thing."

More deflection? Really, Rollo?

I waited, but that seemed to be it. "No, they don't. But how is it better when the Picts cut the men out of the succession than when the others cut the women out? It's still antiquated nonsense."

I slid my journal back and, on the page next to the Viking family tree he'd drawn, I drew Ad'Rian's.

"The quadruplets—I never realised it was your mother's death that made them the triplets. But anyway, first you have Vi'Anna, the Fae queen herself."

Rollo nodded slowly at me.

"Then De'Anna, L'eon's mother and Ti'Anna, my local Fae."

Another reluctant nod.

"Finally, Le'Anna, your mother who is now in the Summerlands. Her death left the remaining living sisters as triplets, or the Three Bitches of War, as Ad'Rian always calls them."

Rollo's mouth made a silent O now, but then he just shook his head in a confused way. He must know this. Was he being intentionally dumb?

But the source of his confusion became clearer. Thank the Goddess Clarita for coming through for me. He stammered, "But if L'eon's mother is Ad'Rian's sister, and if Vi'Anna is her sister, well, Ad'Rian did not marry his sister."

"No, of course not. But once he married Vi'Anna, the other three became his sisters. You know the Fae don't hold with the idea of in-laws. You're family, or you're not. Simple."

"Yes, alright, I do know that. And the line of succession?"

"I'm just not clear about the birth order for the triplets. I know the queen, Fionn'ghal's mother, is the eldest. Then it must be De'Anna because L'eon is the heir, but Ti'Anna and your mother?" I shrugged. "Not sure."

"L'eon told me my mother was the youngest."

"Then you're third in line."

He shook his head. Whether to negate the reality of my words or because he truly didn't understand, I couldn't tell because he'd closed his shields.

I counted on my fingers. "L'eon is the heir."

He nodded.

"Then Ti'Anna's son, whose name I can't recall, then you." I'd done my research on Ti'Anna after all that nonsense about using Jamie's entrails to find Rollo. She had a son and a daughter. Both were still in Fae, and both lived on their father's estate.

He paled. Then his jaw firmed. "L'eon and Kaiden need to have a large family and secure the succession. But isn't it a moot point? Ad'Rian is immortal."

No, Ad'Rian was strong and, like all the Fae, very long-lived. It wouldn't be easy, but he could still be killed, and Rollo was just looking for excuses. I couldn't let it go now – he wasn't quite there yet.

As gently as I could, watching him carefully and checking our link for any chinks in his shields I could sense him through, I suggested, "The thing is, I'm almost sure this is a major life lesson for you, and we can't avoid those, as I've learnt to my own cost. Why don't you think about it? You're royal on both sides. In line to two thrones, bonded to a Recorder, and yet all you can say is 'I won't be king.' The universe might be conspiring against you to make you learn this lesson. Sometimes we have to take on our responsibilities willingly before we're able to free ourselves from them."

He shook his head again. "Dola, please, can I have a beer?" He looked at my determined face. "Why do you think it's a life lesson? Just get it over with and hit me with the rest of it."

A beer appeared in front of him as Dola said, "*Skål*, Rollo." Etched into the frosted glass of the mug, I read, *Running away from any problem only increases the distance from the solution. The easiest way to escape from a problem is to solve it.*

Rollo glared at it as if he wanted to throw it at the wall.

"But what if I'm not Fae enough? I don't look Fae. That might excuse me from the line. I never seem to be able to do most of the Fae things that L'eon can?"

I gaped at him.

"What? Why are you looking at me like that?"

I remembered Fionn'ghal, Ad'Rian's daughter, who was four times older than Rollo and, unlike Rollo, had been trained her whole life in the Fae arts. But when she took Fiona's place, she struggled to hold a glamour steady outside her home realm for a week without fading constantly.

I'd thought at the time that only a high-ranking royal family member could have held it, because they could draw on the communal House Alicorn power. But Fionn'ghal hadn't wanted her father to know where she was, so she'd used her own power as Rollo had. If Rollo had used only his personal power to hold the glamour did he realise how incredibly powerful that would make him? Ti'Anna, my fae neighbour and Rollo's aunt who'd held her own glamour for several human generations, was high-ranking and extremely powerful, however crazy she liked to appear. Logically, Rollo, who was only half-Fae, shouldn't have been able to do what he had. And yet, he'd done it without any sign of strain.

I answered him gently, "You held a Fae glamour rock solid for almost two decades. Did you ever feel it shifting, other than after you rescued Tilly? And it probably only wavered then because Ad'Rian and Glais'Nee seem to think that was when our bond clicked in."

He shook his head silently. His expression was unreadable, but he felt overwhelmed.

"Make a link, will you, or this will take too long?"

Once we had the link, I reminded him of my meeting yesterday with Ad'Rian, and the first prophecy about us, the one where no one was sure if it was a true *seeing* or just a bunch of badly written fairy tale advice from a possibly manipulative or even a crazy woman. Then I asked him about Troels' tattooed symbols.

I told him Agnes' other prophecy that Ad'Rian had shared. When I got to the bit about "the Rightful King with the correct symbols will only rule for a short time but will go on to live a long, fulfilling and joyous life," he finally smiled again.

It was a wicked smile, with undertones of retribution, which relieved me enormously.

HRH strolled into the room through the fireplace glaring at the decorative fairy lights under her paws. "Thank you, Recorder, you continue to improve. Your assistance is much appreciated and should speed this enormously. Come, Rollo, walk with me. We need to speak about your mother, why I healed you, and what will be required of you later."

He shot me one startled look before he followed the cat through the new doors into the magically sunny garden. I sat at the table and tried to work out what the hell I'd done that had helped the cat enough for her to thank me.

CHAPTER
SIXTY-SEVEN

I landed in the Gateway with Tilly and messaged Aysha, who often worked from home on Thursdays.

> Niki: I've got a bit of a busy morning. It's not safe for puppies. Can I bring Tilly down for a couple of hours?

> Aysha: Sure, home all day. Autumn will be over the moon if you leave her til teatime.

I grabbed Tilly and dropped her at Aysha's. She didn't seem quite herself today. But we had a coffee while I gave her a quick update. In Lanzarote, we'd promised each other we wouldn't allow our friendship to drift, and I welcomed her incisive mind and sense of humour. She also had some great ideas about how to use the funds I planned to take off Troels and those of his warlords who were guilty.

She'd been the one who suggested setting up retraining opportunities for all the people who would be out of work when I banned the Droit de Seigneur trade. As she'd rightly said, if we didn't help them find gainful employment, they'd find the other kind for themselves. It might give the Vikings a head start down the road to sanity.

As I stood up, she swallowed the end of her coffee. "What if we hang on to Tilly until tomorrow so you don't need to worry, and you do me a favour in return?"

"Great, what do you need?"

When she told me, I just gaped at her, open-mouthed.

Back in the Gateway, I borrowed several monitors from the surrounding desks to catch up on the events unfolding on the news portal and chatted to Dola. Rollo had returned from his walk with HRH with his shields tightly closed and said he wanted to shower and then make a few calls. It felt as though we each had our own decisions to make right now.

I caught up with the news portal while I asked Dola to make a list of people I needed to summon today. The video I'd made yesterday was the most-shared item on the site by a factor of ten. The comments on it were coming in too fast to read, even at this stupidly early hour. Wow!

I tapped my earbud. "Can you save me some time? Have you been monitoring the mood of these comments?"

"Yes, Niki, they are overwhelmingly positive, and the majority agree it is time that the ordinary citizens' needs were heard, not just those of a few warlords. I have also monitored the private channels."

Was I taking her for granted? "Are you OK? You're not working too hard, are you?"

"I am having a lot of fun, thank you." Her tone was smug.

"What did you do?"

"I am sure I have no idea what you are implying."

"Dola?" I waited.

She sounded more like a pre-teen than a 1400-year-old house. "I may have lurked in the warlord chat to see what they were planning. There was much gossip about Arne Orm and other matters."

Hey, I knew that name. "Dragon-chow man, right?"

"Oh, well done, Niki! Yes, him."

"Brilliant plan. Did you find anything interesting out?"

"Nothing I did not already know. The warlords' staff, or at least the ones in the chat, are idiots. They are waiting for instructions from their own warlords. Unless they get them, they are all planning to meet in a tavern on the road to Yggdrasil, a long way from Haraldssund. They stated the shield maidens are out of control."

"And are they?"

"Well, they are out of the warlords' control, but, no, they are disciplined and intelligent. Their chatroom *was* intriguing. They are planning to slaughter some of the warlords the moment you release them and then demand you hand Troels over to them for sentencing."

"Only some of the warlords?" That gave me hope. If they'd said all, I wouldn't have been able to release any of them because the shield maidens would have been planning to behave as badly as the men had for so long.

"At the present moment, they have a poll running in their chat forum with each of the warlords' names on. Elise has announced a minimum of ninety-five percent of the maidens must vote for a warlord to be executed."

"OK, that sounds weirdly fair. So how many is that currently?"

"Four, but I predict it will be five soon."

I was relieved. I'd worried my little video yesterday might have sounded like I was giving them permission to begin a mass warlord slaughter.

"Several of the warlords have less than ten percent of people voting for their death."

"Which ones?"

She gave me the names, but only one, Bloodraven, meant anything to me. Should I try to get better with names? Hell no, I had too many other changes to make. I had people around to prompt me. "Remind me who they are, please?"

"The two you spoke to about the Droit de Seigneur causing miscarriages."

My screen flashed with freeze frames of Bloodraven, who I had remembered thanks to his counterpart in the *Drengr* game. He was the older man whose daughter had successfully given birth to a son while she and her husband were living in the Red Celt realm but hadn't been able to carry any further children to term once she returned to Viking.

The second one had the name Gustavsson under the graphic. Oh yeah, he was the younger man who'd spoken to Mags because he was concerned about his wife.

"And this man." She sent me another freeze frame of a man I vaguely remembered standing about halfway in between the end of the line and Halvor in the centre. He didn't do or say anything the whole time he was there.

"And who's winning the vote for Most Wanted Dead?"

"As you would expect, it is Warlord Halvor with a vote of over 99.7%."

Well, that was no surprise. My Gift had loathed him. But then I remembered an important rule about polls. "And the sample size? How many people have voted in the Halvor poll?"

"Over 480,000."

Oh yeah, that was enough people.

Dola continued, "There has been a surprising development."

"There has?"

"The shield maiden chat now includes many warriors too."

"How did that happen? I thought you were tracking their log-ons?"

"Elise emailed with a request for several of the maidens' bond mates, including her own, to be given access. They did a poll for that too. It has all been most democratic. The women agreed that if Elise and the several other shield maidens she asked me to add as moderators all confirmed the man in question was trustworthy, they should be allowed in."

Wow. There was hope some sanity might come out of this mess.

"What percentage of the chat members are men?"

"About a third. Warlord McIver, Inge's beau, is one of them."

I thought about the *Christmas Carol*-style movie the power ran for the Viking women. The tiered seating looked like a working parliament. I wondered if it was being formed even now in the shield maidens' chat group?

My iPad buzzed with a note that there was a new shared document.

I considered the lengthy list Dola had compiled of the people I needed to summon. This was getting ridiculous. I'd changed so much from my first week when I'd thought I was inconveniencing people by summoning them. I might soon adopt my gran's notion of *They'll be here when I damn well want them here,* as my new motto.

"I'll deal with Rollo. Please let everyone else know I'll summon them at eight-thirty. Could you ask Glais'Nee if he'd like me to summon his group, or if he'd prefer to bring them through the violet gate at nine a.m.?" I couldn't guess how the Fae guards would prefer to deliver the warlords.

Now, I was ready for Rollo. Not my lovely Rollo, but the reluctant future King of Viking. My stomach tightened. I wasn't looking forward to this meeting.

"The Recorder needs to speak to you. Would you come to the Gateway please?"

"Is three minutes OK? Just finishing a call. Is the centre clear?"

"Yep and yep. It's all yours."

I breathed slowly and carefully and then settled in for the show. I would work out how he did his superhero landing. It was fun.

He didn't disappoint me and landed wearing a wide, smug grin and the same formal dress leathers he'd worn when he brought the Vikings to the Gateway for their bond checks before Valentine's Day. But this time, he wore a plain grey T-shirt under the waistcoat. He was hiding his new tattoo for now.

He swaggered over, his body language much more like eye-candy Rollo's when he'd worn his glamour, but it was the real Rollo who grabbed me, kissed me and murmured, "We'll make it work; never doubt it."

Then he took two strides backwards and bowed. "Recorder, tell me the worst of it then."

I grinned back at him. His dress leathers now bore an Yggdrasil patch near his left shoulder where Caitlin always wore her House Albidosi crest.

"First, what can you tell me about what you discussed with the cat?"

He perched on the edge of my desk. "She asked me what I stood for."

When I burst out laughing, he looked affronted. "No, no." I waved a hand at him. "She asked me the exact same thing the night before my public ascension. Why change a winning formula? Were there also pearls of pertinent wisdom?"

Now he laughed too. "Hell yes. She told me the reason I never stand up for anything is because, the last time I stood up for what I wanted, Troels killed my dog."

Well, shit. She was probably right. Hadn't I thought exactly the same?

I gazed at him. He seemed OK about it. I poked at our link, and he let me in.

He was more than OK. "She reminded me that all the people whose safety Troels threatened to gain my compliance, like Inge, Elise and Kari, will be in the Gateway today, and they need to see me in charge, or they won't believe their own lives can change."

"She's right. It's what my Gift has been telling me."

"She said I don't have a dog to worry about at the moment and that my bond mate can take care of herself. So what was my real excuse?"

Sometimes that cat was awesome. Because it was exactly what I'd wanted to ask him.

He continued, "And she said something very odd about my mother that I'd prefer to think about a bit more before we talk about it. But she also confirmed what you said about the Fae Court and my place in it." He didn't look happy, but I sympathised. I'd been royally pissed and then overwhelmed when I realised I really was the Recorder whether I wanted to be or not. I'd adjusted. He would too.

Reluctantly, I asked, "You ready for the Recorder?"

At his nod, I straightened, pulled a little power to stiffen my spine, and began. "House Yggdrasil will rule Viking. A contract between you and the Viking government for three years. Up to a month each year to be spent in Viking, no longer than three days at a time. You will agree to wield the yellow power properly on behalf of Viking and institute the necessary changes. There's no necessity for you to be king. I know you hate that idea. But you do have to be their head of state, or whatever the hell else you can all mutually agree on. You can discuss it with them or simply inform them—your choice. Agree to this to smooth the transition to some form of democratic government."

I paused, but he was nodding.

"Also, agree to be their tie breaker if they get themselves in a mess. The contract is to be reviewed in three years. Hopefully, it will not need to be renewed if you push them to get on with it. So you should only agree to this if they make every effort to prioritise building a functioning society with laws and a government. Ideally, a freely elected one, or at the very least, they must have a clear road map for all that. They all have to swear it over the anvil to ensure they're motivated to keep their word."

I paused, but he simply nodded, waited and looked as though he was waiting for the other shoe to drop.

"I'm going to dump them all at the conference table, and you're going to get them to volunteer to take action and stand for something before I conscript the lot of them and impose my arbitration decision on you all. That's it."

A huge grin split his face and brought his dimples into play. "Hell yes. I thought I might get dragged into spending six months a year there. Did you know Churchill said, 'Democracy is the worst form of government, except for all the others'?"

I gazed at him.

"What?"

"Wow, barely a week into our new bond, and you're assuming I'm an idiot with no memory for words? It's only names I can't be bothered with. Of course I know. That quote came up every damn time a player chose democracy as the government type in *Drengr*. But what I have just learnt is that it was you who put the quote into the game."

He laughed. "Yeah, I put all those quotes in one rainy Sunday. Which was your favourite?"

"Getting back to the point, King Hrólfr …"

He sobered. "And I'll be including that in any contract I agree to with Viking. Hrólfr means wolf, you know. I don't want to be King Hrólfr. I don't want to be King Anything, and I don't want to be Hrólfr anymore. It's not the slagging Middle Ages."

"Channelling Caitlin now, are we?"

"Yes. She told me you got the antiquated Pict naming agreement changed, so she didn't have to be Queen Barita. So why not?"

"So I'm to find you another title—is that what you're saying?

But my research suggested that Rollo also means wolf, but it's just the Viking version of Roland, isn't it?"

He gave me his best smile, with added dimples, the one he damn well knew connected straight to my core. "Come on, it's much cooler. Do you really want to shout, 'Oh, yes, yes, Roland, harder'?"

I cracked up.

CHAPTER
SIXTY-EIGHT

The summoning would be endless. I asked Dola to send Finn over to the Gateway early and began with Caitlin.

When she arrived, I gave her a quick update on my plans, and she eyed Rollo speculatively. I said, "Talk to him, KAIT. See if you have any brainwaves to add to my plans. I'm open to ideas."

She gave me a slow nod. "OK. Also, you wanna get Dola to send your robe through."

I looked down at the jeans and shirt I'd thrown on before it got light and called "thanks" after her.

She strolled to the Magic Box and asked Rollo, "Want coffee?"

Dressed in my robe and feeling more like the Recorder, I placed the star on the anvil and started on my list. Elise and her bond mate, Sten. If she'd wanted him in the shield maidens' chat, she might find his presence, support or advice useful today.

Kari Halvor, and after some thought and a check with my Gift, which was urging me strongly to include him, I'd asked Dola to send an invitation to Ben. His response was immediate and positive—if Kari was coming, he wanted in. It was fine with the Recorder. If he was seriously considering living there, he should see this. I felt like I owed a fellow Mancunian a bit of insight. It was more than anyone had ever given me.

Also, now that I'd experienced the calming power of a bond mate, I couldn't imagine anyone who might need it more today than Kari, except Inge. So I was summoning Warlord Alec McIver along with her to see if they had a bond. Inge had clearly said he wasn't "one of *those* warlords," and Rollo had verified it. I wanted to check they were both right.

My Gift thought McIver might be the handsome silver fox who'd stood and spoken during the parliament Inge had addressed in the vision from the power. He's been the one who got the huge round of applause. I'd take any help I could get to encourage Inge to be reasonable, step the hell up and do what needed doing instead of waiting for Everyone, Someone or Anyone else to do it for her.

I took a breath, dug deep for my librarian persona, and began the summoning.

Once the Viking contingent arrived, I sent everyone over to the conference table to join Rollo. We didn't offer them refreshments. Going against my usually hospitable soul, we'd decided they were getting nothing until they came up with a workable plan and an agreement the Recorder could approve for Viking so I could deal with Troels.

I looked around the table. Elise looked far more like the classic picture of a shield maiden today and much less a supportive daughter in smart brown dress leathers with a deep yellow trim and an Yggdrasil patch by her left shoulder. Her only accessories were a wide variety of weapons. Caitlin nodded approvingly at her.

Inge felt more balanced, and, yes, the man with her was indeed the silver fox from the parliament vision. He had a look of George Clooney. Lucky Inge. He wore a classy-looking suit, and intelligence flickered in his penetrating brown eyes as he bowed to me. When he turned to shepherd Inge to one of the chairs with yellow leather, she looked up at him, and I saw it.

Well, hell, no wonder she'd been desperate to leave Troels. She and her warlord had a solid bond, and I wanted a closer look at it.

In person, rather than in the vision, Alec McIver also resembled one of the warlords I'd seen yesterday. I say "resembled," but it was more like one of those before and after photo shoots, the ones with a long grooming session and several months of fitness programs between the two sets of photos. The paunchy man with blotchy skin was definitely the before version and probably Alec's brother Den and Inge's enemy. He had hard-living, hard-drinking and hard-hearted thoughts etched into his face. Yesterday, he was the one who glared at anyone who dared to speak to the Recorder or Elise.

With my Recorder face and voice firmly in place, I addressed the table, "I can give you twenty minutes. I'll be closing this part of the arbitration before I have to deal with the warlords. I need to impose fines on most of them before anyone," I gave Elise and her bond mate a stern look, "disposes of them and their assets transfer to their heirs. So put your egos and fears aside and find a solution you can all live with."

I got nods from everyone. Their attitudes had improved dramatically since yesterday.

"Be aware, if you go down the path we discussed, I will need to see you making decent progress on developing a constitution within six months, or the power's penalties will start clicking in."

I had no idea what they might be, but the Book had lots of notes from previous Recorders on penalties imposed when people agreed to an outcome and then didn't take the necessary action. Swearing over the anvil carried its own motivation, and the power liked people to do what they planned. The descriptions of people who broke promises made over the anvil were hilarious. I was saving most of those records for days when I needed a laugh.

I addressed Inge and Warlord McIver, "Rollo can use the yellow power to test the hearts of any current and future representatives for your Regering. You should avail yourself of that power."

Inge shot a surprised look at Rollo. Perhaps Troels hadn't used that aspect of the yellow regnal power. Or, if he had, Inge didn't know about it. She turned back to me after Rollo gave her a firm nod.

"He will not be checking to make sure they agree with you, but they will need to truly want what's best for Viking and the Vikings. That might not be what you think Viking needs, but opposition is good. You will have some. It keeps everyone honest and ensures your Regering will truly represent all the Viking people."

Everyone nodded. This was going well. Then Inge asked, "How would we even write a constitution?"

"I'd recommend you find a good constitutional lawyer to advise you."

"Do such things even exist?"

Gods and Goddesses, was I making a mistake pushing this woman into being the leader of the first government? My Gift didn't think so—I'd just have to trust it.

"Yes, they do. Your new ruler, whom you may have known when he was a child, but you truly don't seem to know well enough as a man, will introduce you to his friend Chris Reynald, who is an excellent one."

Rollo nodded firmly again. He was rocking that strong-but-silent ruler vibe. It was sexy. Hot as hell in fact.

I watched him hide his mouth with his hand as he received my thought, and I sent, "*Sorry.*"

"I shall leave you all to deliberate."

Rollo opened his laptop and started typing as I made my way back to my desk.

My back ached, my stomach cramped, and I had a pounding tension headache. Between all the other demands on my time, I hadn't kept my promise to consult with the power before I made any final decisions.

I dropped my shields, connected, and, of course, rose into the air. The power began healing me. My headache eased, and warmth spread through my aching lower torso. I shared my plans and asked if it approved.

It was relaxing up here, which surprised me. The height wasn't as terrifying as usual. I wouldn't call it pleasant, but it didn't feel as though I was going to lose my breakfast. Oh, wait! I hadn't eaten any breakfast, had I? That burger was hours ago.

The power was happy with my ideas and solutions. It didn't care about money, but if I thought fines would make them tend its gate and respect its boundary, it was happy.

Rollo looked up at me and winked. Through our bond, I heard, *"Looking good up there. Wish I could join you. If you could stay up there a few minutes longer, your presence as the avenging angel is speeding this along nicely."*

"Why?" It made no sense to me – I'd thought me hanging up here might distract the Viking contingent and was trying to stay out of their line of sight.

"The Viking goddess Freyja flew wearing a falcon cloak. You're unnerving even the people who don't trust the Recorder into believing you absolutely can make whatever they agree to stick. Fly about for me. They've caving."

A goddess who flew with a falcon cloak. Whoa, I bet that had been a sight back in the day. Before movies, those gods and goddesses must have been really impressive. I tried to picture it, a combination of a woman and a falcon maybe?

I heard several gasps from the conference table below me. All the Vikings except Rollo stood and then went to one knee in obeisance, looking up at me. I was just about to ask "What?" when Rollo dropped to his knee with his mouth open. I heard, *"Hell, Boo, I didn't know you could actually do it!"*

"What? I've no idea what you're talking about?"

"OK, I'll explain afterwards, but if you could come down and make yourself scarce for five minutes, I'll be able to wrap this up."

I landed quietly behind the screen of living willow, where

they couldn't see me from the table, and Caitlin arrived, her eyes wide. She whispered, "Didn't know you could do that. By the first forge, it was convincing. Freaked the Vikings right out."

"What? What the hell did I do?"

She gave me one surprised look then gestured Finn over. "Show her."

Finn rewound, and on the small screen of his camera, I saw a woman who wasn't me—she had waist-length blonde hair and was absolutely gorgeous, for a start. She was wrapped in what looked like, yes, exactly like a feathery cloak. She dived purposefully around the Gateway like a freaking Goddess. I thought about the gyrfalcon, Puddle, whose talons I'd wished for yesterday. The power might have taken my wish a bit too far.

"Finn, that footage is never to be shown to anyone or to leave the Gateway, are we clear?"

He nodded fervently at me. In my ear, I heard, "Understood, Niki," from Dola.

But Caitlin shook her head firmly. "Ya might wanna rethink that. The Vikings revere Freyja. If the average warrior thought she was in here keeping an eye on Viking's future and approved of what's happening, that could speed things up a lot for Inge, Rollo, and their plans."

I thought for a minute and spoke to the Dolina on the desk. "The KAIT may be right. Put it on the portal, Dola, but don't title it to suggest we thought it was Freyja. Just allow viewers to make up their own minds."

Caitlin nodded her approval as I said, "Thanks, KAIT."

The power was bubbly as I sent it waves of approval and appreciation. "Aren't you a very clever power?"

And just as Rollo predicted, it worked wonderfully. Five minutes later, he came to find me at my desk. "I've emailed you a document for your approval." He looked less drawn and happier.

"Do you approve it?"

"Hell yes. It's far less of a commitment than I feared I'd need to make. It ended up being twenty days a year in Viking and half a day each week from Edinburgh. I'm going to think of it as charity work or community service. The only thing we couldn't decide on was my title. I've told them they can't pin 'king' on me."

He felt so much lighter and happier through our link that I laughed.

The document showed that somewhere between yesterday morning and now, a significant change had taken place to the previously apathetic, "Someone will fix it for us" Vikings.

Was it the chance to talk and plan privately and safely in the forums Dola set up for them? My little video yesterday? Freyja flying around? Or I could always hope that finally their common sense and, oft-discussed but rarely seen, at least by me, courage had reared its head.

It didn't matter what caused it. It was a significant improvement. But I still had the hardest part of my morning ahead of me.

Rollo bowed. "My lady?" As always, I mentally fanned myself. The way he said "my lady," always sounded so intimate. He sent, *"Recorder, focus please. The Viking ruler has a request."*

"The Viking ruler?"

He pointed at my screen. "We haven't come up with my title yet, but we've agreed I will take the role of ruler for three years, so, yes, the Viking ruler."

"OK?" I ruthlessly kept the smirk from my face. He looked very serious and, well, ruler-ish. "And what is the ruler's request?"

"Troels' final disposition falls beyond the purview of the Recorder. When you conclude the arbitration, I require your word that you will return him to us alive for sentencing in Viking."

That stopped me in my tracks, and I just stared at him. He was reminding me that I could only interfere during an active arbitration. And he was right.

I'd been so caught up in the women's heartrending stories. So busy protecting the power and calming its unhappiness about the yellow gate and its boundary. So overwhelmed by my outrage at the realms for allowing this to continue for decades. All these things had swamped me, and I'd completely forgotten the most important rule.

The Recorder didn't run any of the realms. We stepped in to right wrongs, and hopefully, if we were smart, to nudge those realms towards a better future.

I surveyed the man in front of me and tried to see him, not as my bond mate, but as he was now. A ruler in his leathers with his late father's blade at his hip and his late mother's cheekbones.

I inclined my head to him. "Sadly, Drengr Rollo, I cannot give you my word on that." He started laughing, but I swept on. "Because I would be in danger of being foresworn. I can only give you my word that neither the power nor I will take his life. I acknowledge the Viking people's right to deal with their ex-king." I paused and caught his eye, "But can you guarantee that one of these idiots won't throw a blade at him?" I swept my eyes around a lot of well-armed Vikings around the conference table. "Would you have me put him back in a glass cage? That doesn't feel like the way he should hear the outcome of the arbitration to me."

He inclined his head. Oh, weren't we both being polite today?

"Then I make the primary claim once your business with him is concluded."

"Heard, witnessed and agreed."

He gave me a very pretty bow as he headed back to the table, muttering, "Drengr Rollo, indeed. Only you, Boo. Only you."

But he didn't seem unhappy with his new title.

CHAPTER
SIXTY-NINE

Dola informed me there were many Vikings on the news portal, chatting amongst themselves while they waited for the livestream to begin at nine a.m.

"Finn, are you ready to go live?"

"I am, my lady." That was very formal for Finn. Perhaps most of his brain cells were occupied with camera angles.

"Dola, can you build in a few minutes' delay just in case?"

"Yes, Niki, and I have prepared a brief 'Previously in the Arbitration' update to remind everyone of the current status of events."

I giggled, remembering my imaginary narrator before I'd left for Dai's unwelcoming mountain home. But today I felt good about what we were doing. Hopefully, nothing would go too horribly wrong.

The violet gate opened, and, led by Glais'Nee, the Fae guards brought in the twelve warlords. Finn was there immediately with his cameras in full-on TEK mode. His body language was authoritative, and apart from another bizarrely shaped pullover—this one appeared to have bat-wing sleeves—he looked like a true Knight Adjutant. I was so proud of him.

Then Fiona arrived for work and paused in the Green Sector,

her mouth open and her eyebrows dancing as they did when she was surprised. She bustled over to me carrying an enormous gift-wrapped rectangle about the size of a small carry-on suitcase in both arms.

"Am I late, my lady?"

"Not at all, Fi, but with the noon deadline to release them, we had to start a little early. You've not missed much. We haven't even started the livestream yet."

She waved her phone at me. "I know, I'm watching it. The Viking women aren't going to let these guys go home alive, you know. It's not just the shield maidens anymore. Ordinary citizens are holding frying pans and carving knives."

"They're going to eat them? What the actual …?"

Fi let loose a peal of laughter and spluttered, "No, no Niki. I think they're just impromptu weapons."

I obviously needed a reality check, and Caitlin arrived to give me one. "Some of the warlords are irredeemable, my lady. You do know that?"

"Irredeemable" was an unusual word for my KAIT to use. "Slagging deadbeats" was more her norm.

I gave her a long look, which showed me, not my KAIT, but the Pictish heir apparent standing with me. She looked very like her mother today. Her complicated plaited updo added to her aura of authority. Perhaps the presence of Glais'Nee, whom she trusted, and all his Fae guards, had freed her to use her fine brain instead of having to be in bodyguard mode.

"Yes, I agree. We started with twelve and lost that idiot Orm. So we're down to eleven. My Gift says three of them are going home safely, and the remaining eight are dying today. Does that match your knowledge and your sense of what would be right?"

Fi's mouth dropped open.

Caitlin just smirked at me. "As long as you let the shield maidens do it, I think they'll be opening barrels of mead in Haraldssund tonight."

"And if only six warlords make it through to Elise's waiting shield maiden group?"

She gave a low whistle. "I wouldn't have taken you for someone who could do that."

"Oh, me neither. But my Gift thinks that's what's coming. Perhaps two of them are going to annoy Glais'Nee's spear."

Caitlin considered me. "Point of information, Recorder, that is not a spear. It's a lance."

I thought back. "I wouldn't know the difference, but Glais'Nee himself called it a spear at John's sentencing."

My Knight's face did an interesting thing. Her eyebrows shot up, and her mouth formed an O as she let out a long, soft, "Ooooh."

Whatever this was, it would have to wait. I turned to Fi, who still watched us with wide eyes, but she'd closed her mouth. "Put whatever that is down and settle at your desk, Fi. You'll be safe there."

"It's for you. It's a present from Mum."

Presents from Mrs Glendinning were usually lemon cupcakes or occasionally a nice tea bread. This looked like ... actually, I didn't know what it looked like ... a box for knee-high boots or a piece of luggage, perhaps?

"Please thank her. Put it on my desk. I'll get to it at lunchtime." I surveyed the box, which looked large enough to hold a puppy. "Will it be OK until then?"

Fi laughed, relaxing now. "Oh, it'll be OK 'til Christmas. Don't worry about it."

The Viking group from the conference table came around the living willow divider screen to get a better view of the warlords as they all filed in. I pulled power until it coated me, mirroring the Recorder's robe with its soft rainbow stripes.

The three warlords I liked could obviously see the power because their eyes widened. I hoped that boded well for them because they were the three I thought would survive the day. Glais'Nee smiled approvingly at me.

Halvor took the central position in the line again, with his eyes not on me, but on Rollo. He finally spoke. "Our petition has not been addressed, and yet I see you have the traitor here. We will send him to Viking now."

He stepped forward, and I blocked him with the power. He didn't seem to see it, but he noticed when Glais'Nee lifted Bright Justice into his path.

I'd had enough of him. The energy he gave off was horrible. "He is not the traitor, Warlord Halvor. I accepted your petition and considered the lack of verification. You ignored our request for evidence supporting your claim. So, I will not be releasing Rollo to you. Your petition has no basis in fact. I don't understand how you could ever think it did."

He gave a short, derisive laugh. It was a contemptuous sound that conveyed paperwork wasn't something a man of his self-perceived lofty standing concerned himself with. "You did that yourself, Recorder. You provided the video on that disgraceful, demeaning box in which you are detaining our rightful king. The traitor struck the rightful king from behind with his blade, like the coward he is."

"Dola, can you roll the tape?"

Why did I still call digital stuff tape? *Oh, for the Goddess's sake, Niki, this is not the time for your nitpicking—focus.*

But Rollo laughing with me through our link wasn't helping me concentrate either.

Shouldn't I be dreading this?

Shouldn't my palms be sweaty and my mouth dry?

Why wasn't I losing my cool? I usually did.

Why the hell did I feel so calm? It was unsettling.

The large screen we'd placed back above the Yellow Sector showed the video we'd all now seen many times of Troels reaching for Tilly, Rollo throwing his blade, Nanok, so it hit Troels on the back of his head hilt first, and me scooping my dog out of the way with the power.

Glais'Nee nodded approvingly at Rollo. Had he taught him how to throw a blade like that?

Halvor said, "There is the evidence he tried to kill the king."

"No, it isn't, because he didn't. He tried to prevent your *former* king from killing my dog. If he hadn't, Troels would have been returned to you dead. That's the penalty for harming the Recorder. Have you not studied the document you all agreed to when you were granted your realm by the power? Rollo saved Troels' life."

Halvor looked bored, but some of the other warlords, including the ones I thought might just survive the day, looked interested.

"Did your realm learn nothing from Leif's fate?"

At my words, a look of such fury crossed Halvor's face that I paused, but he said nothing, so I continued, "He was fortunate he survived. But I was kinder then than I am now. That was before your realm started trying to kill my dog and my bond mate. That kind of behaviour can fray a woman's temper."

As Elise translated for the warlords and the livestream, two of the warlords quickly hid their smiles. It suggested at least those two might have short-tempered women of their own.

Halvor was unamused and implacable. "That is not relevant. He attempted regicide. It breaks *our* laws."

"No, he didn't. He had no choice but to prevent the former king breaking the Gateway rules, or he would have broken the surety sworn on his blade, which he offered the Recorder's office for the behavioural guarantees of the party he brought. Although, there's possibly an argument that he didn't bring Troels; he just barged through, as you all saw. But either way, he saved the former king's life."

The sneer on Halvor's face made me want to slap him. "Prove it. No sworn surety was filed with the king's office, as is required."

"Dola, please play the recording of the call where Drengr Rollo gave that surety."

Everyone listened to Rollo's and my first ever call. A smile curved my lips as I remembered how insistent Autumn had been that Rollo be allowed to come and bring the "ladies." Had she known even then that we had a bond? How?

Then Elise stepped forward again to translate for the warlords whose English wasn't up to following the words. We'd edited the call quite carefully to just the relevant parts of Rollo offering the surety to bring the couples, get them checked and then bonded, and take them away again. He'd sworn by his blade, Nanok, which I'd mostly missed the significance of at the time.

Now I was about to wrap an almost lie in some careful words to the warlords. I knew Rollo wouldn't do it, but I decided I would. Perhaps I had more Fae blood than I thought, but questions weren't lies. Ad'Rian taught me that when I was younger than Autumn. My Gift thought Rollo might have to work with a few of these warlords in the future, and if I could, I wanted to smooth that process for the good of the Viking realm.

I glanced at Elise and gestured for her to translate for the livestream. "I can't say why your former king would not have registered then Prince Rollo's surety on his blade with his office properly. Perhaps some of you might know the answer to that?"

I paused until Elise finished speaking. While I waited, I ran my gaze down the line of warlords. Was I getting through?

When Elise paused, I said, "But then I don't know why Troels wouldn't pay paternity support in more than two hundred cases of rape and forced pregnancy."

I paused again until Elise caught up. "I don't know why he stole the throne in the first place or retained it instead of handing it over to the head of House Yggdrasil, as he should have done decades ago."

I paused again. "And I don't know why you've all put up with his corrupt and ineffective leadership. But, happily, that all ends today with the new reign of Drengr Rollo and the formation of the first Viking Regering with the sovereign power of the regency to enact laws. All the realms welcome the beginnings of Viking democracy."

I waited while Elise translated.

Rollo sent, *"Oh, Boo, Drengr Rollo sounds good on your lips. I can live with it."*

"Yep, Caitlin said it meant a firm, honourable leader who stands for the important things and is occasionally crazy and badass. Sounds like you! You should thank her."

When Elise's translation finished, the shouting started from all the warlords I didn't like. That wasn't predictable at all, was it?

I addressed Halvor, "You will speak one at a time. This is the Gateway, not a tavern. Those of you who leave here alive may choose to stand for election for the government. However, *all* Viking citizens of *every* class, over the age of twenty-five, male and female, will be eligible to vote in those elections."

There was some muttering from the warlords I didn't like. At my querying look, Rollo sent, *"They're saying serfs and thralls will never be allowed to vote while they have breath in their bodies."*

"Seems like an accurate prediction to me, but if that's their choice…"

Inge said she wanted to start with the voting age at twenty-five and then drop it to eighteen once they had time for some education about democracy and how it worked. The younger Viking population had known nothing but Troels' reign. With a population that was fifty-four percent female, many of whom were married and hadn't any say in anything since their marriage, that should shake things up just on its own. And giving the franchise to the thralls who'd never been permitted to vote, would make for some interesting changes.

While Elise translated her mother's decisions on voting eligibility from her agreement with Rollo, I surveyed the warlords. My Gift still hated six of them including Halvor, and wanted them out of my damn Gateway. The power agreed.

I liked three of them, even though one of them hadn't yet said a word, and I simply wasn't sure about the final two. The feeling I had about those last two was, to use Caitlin's word, that possibly they could be redeemed, if they survived the day. So far, they hadn't done anything to help that happen.

None of the Vikings seemed to understand the concept of a livestream. Not even Halvor was playing for the crowd or the camera the way I knew they would if they were politicians in my own world. They thought the only important people were inside the Gateway with them. Did they truly not understand almost their entire realm was watching this?

Halvor tried to pin me with his angry stare. He pointed at Rollo and almost spat, "He is not the Rightful King. He is no drengr. A drengr, and you wouldn't know this, woman—" Wow, I'd never heard the word "woman" sound so much like something you would wipe off your shoe. I really didn't like this guy. Poor Kari, growing up under his rule. "—is a brave and fearless leader. Not a boy. This is a farce. You have no authority over Viking."

I bit my tongue. I would not swear on the livestream. "Warlord Halvor, you are incorrect in every way it's possible to be wrong, about everything—"

He finally noticed Kari and interrupted me, "And what is my daughter doing here? You told me she was being detained for crimes against the Recorder. She looks nothing like a prisoner to me."

He made it sound as if Kari, battered, bruised and wearing a coarse jumpsuit in a horrid colour, would have been just fine by him. His aura was full of evil. He made my flesh creep every time I turned my Gift anywhere near him.

He took two large strides towards Kari, faster than anyone except Glais'Nee, who raised Bright Justice. Suddenly between Halvor and his daughter, completely ignoring the enormous spear, was a tall, well-muscled Black guy with a look of absolute hatred on his face aimed at the man who had terrified his bond mate for most of her life.

Halvor actually backed up a step. Glais'Nee's face held an interested expression.

The utter contempt and urge for retribution on Ben's face triggered a cascade in my head. I'd just worked out why he hadn't admitted to Kari that he could read her thoughts perfectly well.

I turned my Gift onto Ben. He knew Halvor had abused his daughter in almost every possible way. Now he knew Kari was his bond mate, he understood why he'd always felt so protective of her. I'd rarely felt such righteous fury in anyone.

Kari was angry and terribly ashamed of everything that had happened. Ben was giving her space and time to tell him when she was ready.

Oh, Kari, why the hell didn't you bring a petition against your father? No wonder, when we were in Edinburgh, she'd been so irrational and worried about her sister. If I hadn't been behaving like a tantrum-throwing toddler myself, I might have realised sooner.

I breathed slowly as Glais'Nee watched me carefully. Rollo sent, *"She would hate anyone to know."*

I couldn't blame her, but it wasn't a healthy solution. *"If you help me persuade her to go to the Fae for healing, I'll go along with keeping it quiet."*

For me, the more immediate problem was the look in Ben's eyes. I wrapped power around his waist. He didn't notice it, but it would restrain him because I couldn't let this lovely man have this on his conscience.

"Ben, I know, OK? But step back; I'm not finished with them yet."

He swung around to look at me out of his left eye. Shit. The red mist had descended. I needed to remember this man was a professional MMA fighter protecting his bond mate. He wanted to pulverise Halvor.

I kept my voice low and layered my native Manchester accent into it more strongly than I normally would. Could I get through to him before I had to resort to just pulling him back with the power? "Ben, lad, you'll like the next bit, and your mum and Olive will be so proud of you for keeping your temper for another few minutes. I promise. Step back. This isn't your fight. I swear to you on my grandmother's grave, I'll stand for you, yours and all the others. Step back, lad. There's a time for justice, and there's the right person to deal it out. Today isn't your time. This is my job, not yours."

Crap, I wasn't getting through. Then I remembered something Mrs Clarke had said to Aysha occasionally when we were both much younger, and Aysha's temper had been less controlled. Had Olive borrowed the phrase from Ben's mum? Probably, because it was from that damn earworm of a song, wasn't it?

I risked it. What did I have to lose? Because if Ben hit Halvor, I'd have to deal with him, and that would be so unfair. In a firm tone I'd never before heard myself use—thank you, Olive—I instructed, "Benson, you will not let that man take away your dignity. Step away now, right away, right now!"

At that, his eyes widened, and he shook his head like a Labrador emerging from a lake. I heaved a sigh of relief. He moved slowly back to Kari, pushing her behind him and away from Halvor. But he watched me as I nodded firmly at him.

I needed to take back control of the Gateway. Ben's fury at Halvor had frightened me. He couldn't be allowed to mess up our plans, or his and Kari's future.

But now, my palms were damp, and my mouth was dry. Oh well, this finally felt more normal for Gateway drama. Once my knees started shaking, I'd know we were nearly done.

"Warlords, your petition is dismissed. There was no case to answer, no proof, no documentation, and no damn evidence. But we're not finished. We will now move on to the multiple petitions against you."

In a low, furious, steely tone, Halvor said, "We submitted a petition to you. We don't submit to your judgement. You have no authority over us."

"Yes, I do. You shouldn't have submitted petitions if you

didn't want to put yourselves under my authority. You really don't bother understanding paperwork, do you, Halvor? But, most importantly, the power is the ultimate authority. So just shut the hell up and wait quietly."

"What power? You have no power over me." He took one step towards me, and before any of the weapon wielders could get ahead of themselves, I wrapped the rainbow around him, moved him back into the line of warlords and held him there with the power he obviously couldn't see.

"That power, Halvor."

"My name is Warlord Halvor. You will use it, woman."

"No, I really won't, because that title has already been stripped from you. You just don't know it yet because you won't shut up and let me finish."

The silent warlord positioned two places to Halvor's right, he was one of the three I liked, stepped several paces away from him. Intriguingly, the other two warlords I liked and one I hadn't decided about all subtly followed suit, widening the gap between themselves and the irredeemables.

Halvor fought the power, and spitefully I let him look like a shadow boxing idiot before I said, "Enough. You are not in charge in here. Your time is finished. The only one who doesn't know is you."

Elise, bless her, was still translating, so I shut up while she finished and took the opportunity to breathe and to tuck away my guilt at letting Kari's rude behaviour get under my skin so badly that I hadn't checked her properly myself and had a heads-up about all this.

I told them about the fines I would be levying and the new rules banning any transport of the drug and all of its ingredients through the Gateway. I wasn't sure anyone was even listening to me, but the power obviously was because the palm-sized sacks of powder we'd removed from many of the warlords yesterday and deposited in a pile in the Indigo Sector rose into the air at my words.

Then they simply disappeared.

Through my earbud, from Dola, I heard, "Niki, the Vikings are going crazy at the idea that someone might finally stand up to Halvor. They almost brought the portal down with the volume of their comments."

Then HRH arrived and strolled across to her plinth as though she had all the time in the world. Because whatever time she arrived was obviously the perfect time *to* arrive.

It looked like the fun was about to begin.

CHAPTER
SEVENTY

I crossed to the anvil's throne, where the cat now sat resplendent on her plinth. "OK, how does this favour thing work?"

"Come closer, Recorder."

When I did, she reached out with a paw, tapped my third eye, and a connection between us sprang into place.

It shocked me, and I jumped. I was used to the "I consent" ritual. Obviously, HRH gave no importance to consent. And why could everyone but me instigate these connections?

"Pay attention, Recorder. You will repeat the words I will share in your mind with the assembled worshippers and the transgressors."

"Worshippers?"

She completely ignored me.

"I recommend you stand behind the anvil's throne. I require considerable distance between you and the warlords. You must be seen to have no connection to what is about to happen. Alert young Finn, such a good boy, to point one camera at you and me and the better one at the warlords. Request Rollo to stand well back. He must be seen to have no connection to my actions."

I thought about all this, tapped my earbud and spoke with Dola. I asked her to pass the cat's instructions on to Finn.

"He says he understands, Niki."

Through our link, I firmed my mental tone. *"Drengr Rollo, The Recorder needs you to step back away from the warlords. Put at least ten metres between you and them, please."*

"Ten metres?" His head swivelled until he found me by the anvil. He raised an eyebrow.

"I don't know, OK? HRH says far enough that it's apparent on the cams that you had nothing to do with her actions. Look, I'm keeping a calm face. You need to do the same. Just move the hell back."

I felt his shock and his desire to ask if I knew what I was doing.

No, I wasn't convinced I did.

But HRH made a compelling argument yesterday. She proposed it was a necessary object lesson to teach the Viking realm in general, and the rest of the warlords still in Viking in particular. She wanted anyone who might think to assassinate Rollo before he had time to do any good for the realm to be aware he had a goddess on his side. One who could keep score.

Anyway, she thought justice was too wishy-washy these days. It needed to be dramatic and apposite to stick in people's memories. They'd tried to kill Rollo. They would have succeeded if I hadn't summoned him.

The deciding factor for me was when HRH announced, "Recorder, they are barbarians from a brutish society. You will change nothing with fines. Fine them all you wish. But that will only help the survivors of these abuses. It will instigate no change in their future behaviour. They respect might and power, and they fear the eldritch, the unearthly and the retribution of their gods and goddesses." The Vikings' reaction to my accidental Freyja illusion validated her statement.

But, remembering the look in her bright emerald eyes when she'd told me that sometimes justice must be clearly seen to be done, I swallowed hard.

Oh yeah, my knees felt like jelly now.

"You will feed me power. I shall not retain it, but I need a large amount to do this for you, Rollo and the power. Begin repeating now."

"Remind me again why you can't just speak yourself?"

There was a huff in her voice when she replied, "I would not wish anyone to suggest I usurped the Recorder's authority in the Gateway."

I managed not to laugh. But I was glad I'd practiced with Elise earlier, because repeating HRH's words and then waiting for Elise's translation to the warlords was easier than it would have been without those earlier test runs.

"Viking warlords, you decided as a group to murder your true Rightful King."

Halvor said, "He is not—" before I muted him. I didn't have time for him now.

I was pulling power frantically to feed it to HRH. She was using a huge amount, and I couldn't see what for. I connected to the power myself and simply told it, "She believes this will help restore Viking to balance and move them back to compliance with the Gateway agreement. If you agree, then help me feed her what she requires, please."

Suddenly, I was on the outside looking in. The power surged, bypassing me and flowing straight to the diminutive cat, who grew before my eyes. She leapt down from her plinth and prowled around the centre.

Inside the Gateway, thunder rumbled ominously, followed by a stark flash of lightning.

My thoughts tripped me up as I considered that. Didn't we see the lightning before we heard the thunder usually? Yes, it was physics. Sound travelled slower than light. Well I guess this wasn't physics then. It was madness and magic, yet it was undeniably effective. The air was charged with the sharp tang of ions, reminiscent of the tense moment before a storm breaks. I really hoped it wasn't going to rain in here. It might not have mattered back in my gran's day, but we had a lot of electronics in here now.

Muttering came from the warlords. Even Inge and Elise

looked unhappy. I felt the bubbling sensation in my head that meant Rollo was laughing.

"What are they saying?"

"They think Thor is angry and are worried that one of their own gods would support the Recorder."

I didn't laugh but did give the cat credit for knowing how to play on their fears. Even the power looked different. Interwoven with the familiar rainbow hues, a coruscating kaleidoscope of sparkling energy danced wildly. Gathering intensity, it fused into another lightning bolt, which barely missed the warlords. They all stepped back, even Halvor.

The cat grew ever larger with every prowling circuit of the centre. She fed me more words.

"You have only one inviolable law. It forbids regicide, and yet, disrobe please, Drengr Rollo."

Rollo followed her instruction with no hesitation. As he pulled his T-shirt over his head, Finn zoomed in on the new tattoo and sent it out on the livestream. Gasps echoed around the Gateway.

"Now *that* is fine paint," came from Caitlin, and then she remembered she was the KAIT and bowed formally to Rollo before she headed over to me at the anvil.

HRH prodded me with more words. "You kept him from the throne for forty years. Even when the power itself intervened to show you Troels was the pretender by removing the yellow regnal power from him, you still supported him. You saw him age in front of your eyes, and you still dared to defy the Gateway. And then you decided as a group to assassinate your true ruler."

The now German shepherd-sized cat prowled along the line of warlords. Several of them shook their heads at her as she approached them.

"You say it wasn't you?" Step, prowl, pause.

"Or you?" The cat paused in front of Den McIver and at his frantic headshake, she sneezed. It was a surprisingly funny moment. Her disgusted sneeze sounded exactly like Tilly's when I told her she needed a bath.

"Or you?" She ran her gaze down the line of warlords. There was much nodding then some headshaking from about half the warlords. They were confused now and determined to protest their innocence, but they couldn't work out whether to nod or shake their heads.

I started to smile, and the cat prodded me mentally again. "Then let us see, shall we? I have a petition from the King of Fae for justice. He is unhappy about the use of iron to steal from the herb garden at the Healers' Hall and he demands justice for your treatment of his nephew."

That petition was the one that made me realise I couldn't simply fine these warlords and send them back to Viking. It had also made me listen very carefully to HRH.

The moment I paused to allow Elise to translate, Glais'Nee stepped forward. He gave Halvor, and two of the other warlords such a cold look that, if he ever aimed it at me, I would run and hide until the ice block of fear melted from my heart.

When Elise finished translating, he said, "I am here at my liege lord's command to see that justice is carried out here today. Long overdue, far too little and much too late, but justice I will see for my liege lord and for my cousin." As he tapped his spear, Bright Justice, softly against the stone floor, a violet spark shot out from it and headed towards Halvor's feet.

He moved backwards again swiftly and looked unhappy. The man to the side of him looked as though he'd like to dig a hole, crawl into it and pull his cloak over his head. Sensible guy.

HRH told me to say, "Dola, may I have the accounting of the Rightful King's injuries when he was summoned to the Gateway?"

We had an accounting!?

Rollo looked magnificent. He stood in his leathers and boots, shoulders back, head high, half-naked and with an expression I'd never seen before on his face.

OK, yeah, of course I liked him shirtless—I'm human, not stone. But he looked regal; he looked powerful. He looked like a king, damn it, even if he didn't want to be called one.

Still feeding the cat's words to the Gateway, I said, "Drengr Rollo, please explain your regnal tattoo to your realm."

Rollo grew another inch as he looked straight into the lens of Finn's livestream camera. "We are told that a regnal tattoo should have three parts. They represent the three houses, or possibly the three goddesses, or is it the three powers that should not be defied?"

He gave the camera a warm smile with dimples and added, "You all know what it's like trying to translate those ancient Norse scrolls."

There was general laughter in the Gateway, and from those in the Viking realm watching on the portal, I imagined. He switched seamlessly to Norse.

HRH now something between a leopardess, a lioness, and a tigress, sent me, *"You are doing well, Recorder."*

Perhaps because I was terrified of what was coming next, or maybe because I'd just lost my mind watching the huge cat prowl, I suddenly remembered another big cat I wasn't able to categorise. It appeared in a dream a few weeks ago after Valentine's Day. That cat had been in the Gateway with my gran and ...

I blurted my thought towards my link with the cat, *"Was it you? In the Gateway with Agnes? In my dream?"*

"Recorder, what help would the answer to that question give you? You must learn to ask better questions. Agnes, now there's a woman who asks the right questions."

Well, that was no damn help.

I glanced around. Everyone was watching Rollo, but I was delighted to be simply standing on the floor and not floating in mid-air.

Rollo's commanding tone and his change back to English pulled my attention to him. "Those old scrolls tell us the Rightful

King explains his symbols in such a way that no one can argue with or gainsay their right to rule. I'm not sure I trust that—because the man who stole my father's throne explained his own symbols, and you all believed him." He shook his head, and I felt the waves of sadness from him through our bond.

I tried to send him some support. *"You're doing a fabulous job. Tell them the truth, Boo. It has a way of changing minds and hearts."*

"Even though Troels' symbols were a wolf, my own name. A knife, Nanok, my father's blade and now mine."

It appeared in his hand without him even seeming to move, just as it had when he'd rescued Tilly, and again when he thought there was some danger behind me when I first saw our bond in the mirror in Aysha's hall.

"And the crown of our beloved King Harald the Just, founder of House Yggdrasil. He stole the right to bear that symbol from my house and from Harald's descendant, his ill-treated wife, Inge Haraldsdottir. None of those symbols *ever* belonged to Troels, or told you anything about *his* right to rule, or even gave you a single truth about what he held dear. But Viking accepted them as proof he was the Rightful King." He paused, breathed, looked down the row of warlords, and finished, "I do not trust any of you to pass judgement on my own symbols."

Several of the warlords, all the Viking guests, and Caitlin and Fi applauded. It startled Rollo.

But he quickly retrieved his train of thought. "I chose the three powers that should not be defied for my own symbols. First, my house: our sacred tree, Yggdrasil. Our source of strength for over a thousand years. It should not be defied. Second, The Recorder and the Gateway." He pointed at the seven-sided star nestled in the tree's branches.

"If we do not honour the Gateway, we will end up trapped in a hell of our own making and unable to leave our realm ever again. The Recorder and the Gateway are powers that should not be defied if we wish Viking to thrive and take its place in the twenty-first century."

He pointed at the luminescent Danake coin in the roots of the tree. It really was over his heart exactly where Geoff the Seer advised him to place it so many years ago. "This represents my bond mate, my foundation, and my future. Any of you who think you can live a happy life with an unhappy bond mate are living in a world more fantastical than any game I ever created."

The wave of laughter, even from several of the warlords, seemed to surprise him. But I thought the new king had just won the Viking women's approval because we heard the echoes of far more laughter drifting through the yellow gate.

It would have been nice to end there.

But HRH had other plans as she pushed more words at me. "When I said you had all planned King Rollo's execution, some of you shook your heads. So now we must establish the truth."

Elise translated, and suddenly all eyes were on me. I pointed at the screen. "These are the injuries your ruler arrived in the Gateway with ten days ago. The power, which assisted in his healing, along with his Goddess, know who commissioned those injuries."

The huge cat strolled down the line of warlords. Two of them shrank back from her again. They were the ones I suspected. One I didn't know, but his aura was grubby with guilt. The other was Dirty Den McIver, the brother of Inge's bond mate. His formerly florid face was pale now, which only made the red blotches brighter against his skin.

"It is time to return them to the cowards who sent others to stain their souls on their behalf instead of risking their own necks."

Halvor, of course, stood firm and simply gave the Gateway an expressionless face. Did anything affect the man?

HRH prodded me mentally again. "While I do not absolve their guards who carried out the crimes, I leave their punishment to others." She speared Elise with her gaze until the shield maiden nodded. "You former warlords have orchestrated too many clandestine attacks. Never openly or with honour, never in your own names. That crap will stop now. If you ever even think to attempt it again, I will track it back to you."

I smiled to myself because "that crap will stop now" sounded very like me. Was I having an influence on the cat?

The cat looked straight into the lens of Finn's livestream camera as she prompted me to say, "Try it again, and my vengeance will return to haunt you like shadows in your own halls. You will never sleep another peaceful night."

"Point at me and repeat my words firmly please, Recorder."

"The time to return the injuries you commissioned is here. Let us begin with Drengr Rollo's broken jaw."

I swallowed, locked my legs so they wouldn't shake and let me down, and watched with astonishment, if not surprise, as the warlord my Gift had disliked, three along from Halvor, flew backwards and landed on the floor with an *oomph*.

"Darvik, he was always a coward. So is his son; he even cheats at dice," muttered Rollo in my mind.

"And the injuries to his spleen."

The warlord immediately to Halvor's left, who hadn't moved away—I'd dubbed him Gormless because he didn't look very bright—doubled over, screamed in a strangely high-pitched tone, and then landed on his knees before keeling over sideways onto the floor.

"He must have sent the youngest man. His heart was never in it. He's got a damaged knee and some nasty stomach punches headed his way, but he'll live. The others won't."

I delved down our link. He felt fine. *"You doing OK?"*

"It's bizarrely cathartic."

"Let us address all the spiteful little jabs and stabs from a weak man who likes to see blood."

Dirty Den McIver actually stepped back as though that would help him. I glanced over and saw Inge soothing her bond mate, a furious Alec McIver. His expression said, if Inge stepped out of his way, he'd kill his brother himself and save everyone the trouble.

Den squealed like a stuck pig. Then suddenly there was a huge spurt of blood, and he went down.

From HRH, I heard, "*His femoral artery. If the yellow power hadn't sealed Rollo's for him, we wouldn't have been quick enough, Recorder.*"

I felt sick.

I don't mean nauseated. I mean I really wanted to vomit.

Only the cat saved me from embarrassing myself. In an unexpectedly soft tone, she said, "*You are doing well. Breathe, I will help you.*"

And a wave of cool control washed over me.

The body of the now-late Den McIver disappeared, along with all the blood. I half expected a text from Rhiannon, but I was so light-headed, I couldn't have focused on my phone if I tried.

The cat's moment of kindness passed swiftly as she said, "*Repeat now.*"

"And the person responsible for all the damage to his dominant hand, wrist, arm bones, elbow and shoulder, the bullying coward who wanted to be sure Rollo would be unable to use his arm, never mind hold a sword, when he challenged him to a duel for the crown ... But who didn't have the courage to strike even one blow himself."

Now my sense of justice overrode my squeamishness. And HRH, in a move worthy of Hollywood, allowed the tension to build until the spectators were muttering to each other, "It is him, isn't it? It must be, mustn't it?"

It began slowly with a single finger snapping loudly, then more fingers, the wrist—Halvor let out a small sound at that. The noise of the larger bones fracturing was horrible and bizarre to watch, given that no one was anywhere near Halvor. All his fellow warlords had cleared a wide space around him now as it finally dawned on them what was about to happen.

It reminded me of when Leif landed against the Yellow Gate and we heard the bones snap even from the centre of the Gateway. I felt queasy again. But then my stomach settled as I realised something odd.

Rollo's right arm and hand had been pulp. But the cat was destroying Halvor's left arm.

"*He is left-handed. I'm returning the exact injuries Halvor intended to inflict on Rollo. When his son challenged him for the throne, Halvor intended Rollo to be unable to use his dominant arm in a duel for the crown.*"

He had a son?

Why didn't I know Kari had a brother? She'd never mentioned him, only a mother and a sister.

"*That is why he attempted to murder his wife, to marry the son's mother and legitimise him. You have a petition from her for paternity funds. His wife gave him only daughters.*"

I remembered that petition. It was one of the very few that named anyone other than Troels.

Halvor groaned loudly, and when his shoulder was dislocated, he screamed and fell to his knees.

Gods and Goddesses, they had tortured Rollo. This was horrid to watch, and I couldn't stand the man. Maybe HRH was right, and this would be a lesson to his kingdom, because, looking at the still-shirtless man watching it all impassively, it was impossible to believe Rollo went through this himself just over a week ago.

I was amazed the remaining warlords weren't trying to make a run for it. I'd pulled power to restrain them, if necessary, but many of them looked as much in shock as I felt.

The cat sounded tired now as she told me to say, "This becomes tedious. Someone gave him an overdose of Droit de Seigneur, but the use of it is prohibited, and it's not suitable for young dragonets. We won't pollute the meat these cowards can contribute as their final act, so we'll pass over that one. What's next? Ah, yes, his black eye. How did we forget that? Then the knife wound to his stomach and his knee injury seem to be next."

I drew in a long breath. Honestly, I was amazed I could even say all this, never mind repeat it so calmly. Perhaps it was because HRH had got me into the habit of repeating her words, or perhaps because, like the energy I'd picked up from everyone else, I really wanted this over with so I could go home.

Rollo stepped forward and bowed low. "Great One, Recorder, hold one moment, please."

The cat and I were still linked, and, clear as a bell, I heard, *"Finally. The man emerges. Do not fail yourself now, Rollo."*

CHAPTER
SEVENTY-ONE

Rollo stepped forward calmly, stood in front of Halvor and surveyed him. "It was you behind my injuries? It would have to be, wouldn't it? You feared Leif couldn't best me in an honourable duel and sought to tilt the odds in his favour?"

Leif? Leif was his son? The same Leif I'd accidentally put in the hospital? Or was it just a common name?

But, no, because Halvor, his accent harsher than it had been almost grunted, "My heir, whose jaw you dared to break after that stupid bitch tried to kill him, is a strong man. He will recover, and I'll see you never take the throne."

Rollo laughed, a free, cheerful sound. "No, thank the All-father, no, I won't. But whatever I choose to call myself, and I like Drengr, House Yggdrasil is the lawful ruler of the Viking realm. And you will see nothing after this day. Because Troels was no longer king when you had me snatched, and you knew it. Your guards spoke of it."

My left shoulder pinged, so he didn't know this then. Was he just trying to establish Halvor's guilt for himself? Why the hell wasn't he using the yellow power?

Rollo continued, "Regicide isn't just a crime; it's a sin against the gods."

A roar went up from the Viking contingent. And more shouted agreement drifted through the Viking gate from the large crowd we could see on the feed from Troels' cell. They'd assembled outside it, watching the livestream on phones and on the screens mounted on the cell.

Halvor's face twisted in fury, his eyes burning with both physical pain and hatred. I wasn't sure I'd ever properly understood what a sneer was before, but I didn't know another way to describe the twist to Halvor's mouth and the tone in his contemptuous voice. Yeah, he was definitely sneering. "Your ideals are a delusion, Hrólfr. You think you can change centuries of warlord and warrior tradition with fantasies of some ridiculous democracy? The people need a strong, firm ruler—not a philosopher."

Rollo's gaze remained steady, and his voice was calm yet firm. "It's not about what I think, Halvor. It's about what the people deserve. They deserve a choice, a voice and a vote. Something you've never understood."

Halvor stepped closer, his voice still dripping with contempt. "And you think you're the one to give it to them? You, who abandoned your realm, your family and your history? You, who shirks your duty?"

"I didn't abandon my duty. I redefined it," Rollo retorted, his eyes bright topaz with a quiet intensity. "I chose to serve my people, not drug them senseless."

Halvor laughed. It was a grating sound. "Serve? We don't serve. You're weak. Unfit to rule, unfit to lead, unfit to lick Leif's boots. I may not have the Yggdrasil name, but my ancestors bested yours many times. And I have strength and respect."

Rollo shook his head, a sad smile on his lips. "You mistake fear for respect, Halvor. True strength lies in inspiring and educating citizens, as my parents did, not in subjugating them as you have in hiding and from the shadows. You used Troels as a front for your power games."

I finally realised who Rollo had meant when he said he

wouldn't leave any money in a realm run by a power-mad dictator.

As I watched the two men, the air between them crackled with tension. The surrounding Viking contingent almost held their breath.

Halvor glared. "You waited until I couldn't fight you fairly? What will you do now, slay me like a dog?" His useless arm hung limp by his side, but his other fist clenched.

Rollo gave him a level look, but the fury in his eyes suggested he was thinking of Troels and of Boo. "You don't like that you're now in the exact position you plotted to put me in? Plotted in the shadows, in back rooms? Karma has a sense of humour. But if you can't use your blade—I won't use mine. I need to be able to face my Goddess with honour, and you, well, who in Helheim knows who you'll need to face when you cross the Bridge of the Damned."

More applause from the Viking spectators.

A stream of yellow regnal power from Rollo wrapped itself around Halvor's throat and tightened. His face turned red, and he took several steps towards Rollo. But my man had been learning and fixed him in place with yellow power. In a ridiculously polite tone he enquired, "Recorder, are you finished with this pile of moose shit that appears to be polluting your Gateway?"

I suppressed the urge to laugh at "moose shit" and inclined my head to him. "He's all yours."

This, it seemed, wasn't a battle for the throne Rollo didn't want, but a fight for the soul of the Viking people and their right to rule themselves.

The enormous cat strolled over to the two men just as Halvor fell to his knees. She pulled a strand of the yellow power with her claw and licked it, then stared at Rollo.

"Recorder, Drengr, may I have his eye?"

In my mind, I screamed, *"WHAT!?"*

"Halvor's eye, may I have it?"

"Why would you—? Again? What is it with you and eyes? I ... I, no."

She completely bypassed my mental spluttering.

"He'll have no use for it where he's going. Dragonets don't value eyes properly, and I'm partial to a good eye. Extremely partial."

Speech deserted me, mental or actual.

This job got crazier every flipping week. Although, some part of my brain that was apparently completely disconnected from common sense thought she had provided exactly what she promised. What difference would his eye make to anyone else? He tried to kill my bond mate, and if that failed, he'd tried to make sure he couldn't use his right arm. Honestly, I wouldn't mind a piece of him myself.

"Fine."

HRH turned to Rollo. He wrapped more yellow power around the kneeling Halvor, who was gasping for breath now, and bowed to her.

Through my earbud, Dola said, "Recorder, Ad'Rian contacted me to enquire if Rollo was using the regnal power. When I confirmed he was, he requested I pass a message to you swiftly."

"OK?"

"He said, 'Look with your other eyes, Nik-a-lula.'"

I summoned the unfocused gaze Ad'Rian taught me as a child and examined what Rollo was doing to Halvor.

Oh, gods and goddesses, did he even know he was doing that?

Then Halvor screamed and collapsed to the Gateway floor, where he lay still.

The spectators' gazes were fixed on the list of Rollo's injuries to see what was still to come. I'd been there when he was healed, and I couldn't remember half his injuries. His fabulous torso had been black and blue, his compelling face swollen and bruised, and his head strangely misshapen. I remembered that much.

Rollo had been right, Gormless got the knee injury his young guard had given Rollo. He squealed and stayed on the Gateway floor while several ghost blows to his stomach landed.

The power wasn't happy now, and neither was I. It all felt like too much.

To HRH, I sent, *"You need to finish this. The power is distressed. You've made your point."*

I felt rather than heard her mental sigh. *"I fear you are correct. A shame—it was such fun. Quite like the good old days. And all in a good cause; isn't that what they say?"*

I pushed a wave of crossness and a reminder that I was the Recorder at her.

"Yes, yes, very well. Last one then. All good things must come to an end."

Through my earbud, Dola told me the news portal was going crazy with joy that someone was finally holding the warlords to account for the many covert beatings, murders and abuses they'd handed out over the years. The Vikings wanted to see Halvor ripped to pieces. What the cat was doing was tame compared to what they would have chosen.

I sighed. *"Yes, you may take his eye; take them both if you wish, with Rollo's and my thanks. But please don't make a production out of it. The power is unhappy."*

I didn't add *"so am I"* She already knew that.

"One is an elegant sufficiency, thank you."

I gave up.

"Let's return the other injuries where they belong, but before we do …"

As HRH strolled to the prone Halvor, who now appeared unconscious, she told me to say, "This is not for your sins against your people or your king; this is for your many cruelties to your wife and daughters."

I glanced over towards Ben, who had Kari wrapped in his arms. She didn't look unhappy. As if he sensed me watching them, he gave me a single firm nod. I'd obviously redeemed my word to him when I asked him to step back and leave it to the Recorder. Let's see how he liked the next bit.

The cat huffed in my mind, and from her impatient tone, I sensed she might be repeating herself. "An eye for an eye, Halvor. Because we cannot take from you everything you deserve to lose without upsetting the squeamish."

HRH leaned forward, and just as she had at John's sentencing, quickly and without drama, her much larger but still needle-sharp claws plucked out his eye. As with John, there was no blood, just a healed socket. That was a truly creepy ability.

Now the semi-conscious Halvor looked grey. But I couldn't bring myself to use my Gift on him. Honestly, I didn't care. The guy was a tyrant, and I'd had enough today.

Channelling the cat's commentary for the gathered people who were all gripped by the drama, I focused on the warlords again. "Those of you who remain uninjured are free to leave after this final reckoning. Your fines have been assessed, and you will pay them promptly. Check your emails, or you'll find yourselves back here again to face much rougher justice."

There was rougher justice than this? I just hoped they paid those fines promptly. I couldn't face anything like this ever again. I was going to make changes in this damn Gateway, and I suspected the power would back me all the way.

But the cat was relentless through my link.

"And now we will return the burden of Drengr Rollo's injuries to their originators."

Call me slow, stupid or just overwhelmed by too much violence, but there was something about the phrasing of that sentence that tickled some weird part of my brain.

We *had* healed Rollo, hadn't we? Not just stored the injuries somewhere until ... the cat could return them.

What the actual hell?

The cat had been very thin for no reason the day after Rollo's healing, hadn't she? When she said, "It is my burden to carry," did she mean it literally?

The only aspect of Rollo's many injuries I'd seen HRH disperse was the Droit de Seigneur. The rest of them had simply healed.

But she surely didn't mean she was actually returning them? Did she?

Although, it would make sense – well, it made no damn sense. But why else would she have said, "It is my burden to carry, not his, and I would prefer he remain in ignorance until I can lay it down at the appropriate time and place."

Was returning the injuries to the warlords "laying down her burden"?

If Rollo had used the yellow power on her, could he have worked out that she was storing his injuries?

Gods and Goddesses, who would think to do something like that? Well, this freaking crazy goddess obviously. But I absolutely had to start taking all the inhabitants of my new life more literally.

My connection with the cat broke at that moment, as though she didn't want me to delve down it.

Thunder rolled and lightning flashed inside the Gateway again. When I turned around, a much smaller cat was making her three-legged way back to her plinth. She still had an eye on her front right paw.

Halvor got Rollo's badly fractured skull because his head went the same unpleasant shape Rollo's was when I first laid him on the floor in the nasty lounge. Whoever told me Rollo only survived thanks to his Fae blood was right because Halvor's body disappeared quickly after that blow.

I found my phone in my robe's pocket.

> Niki: Think you have two more incoming. We didn't drug them, so they should be safe for dragonets.

HRH sat on her plinth, looking only slightly larger than her normal size. But the rosettes in her fur glowed with a vibrancy I'd never seen before, and she looked extremely smug.

I had to know—I just did. In a very low voice, I asked, "Your Majesty, I must know, what will you *do* with his eye?"

The emerald green eyes fixed on mine, but she said nothing at first. Then, she said, "I suppose you have the right to that information; you performed well today. There is hope for you yet, Recorder. I will give it to a witch of my acquaintance, along with the one I took from John Fergusson."

"But you took that one weeks ago?"

"It has been preserved."

I didn't want to think too hard about that. I had a nasty picture of a jar with pickled onions, pickled eggs and pickled eyes in my mind that I only hoped I could flush out later with a nice glass of wine.

"And what will the witch do with them?"

"I can't predict what she'll do with Fergusson's, but Halvor's, she will use for a spell for me."

Yeah, that figured. She'd get something out of it.

Then I had to reach out to the anvil's throne for support when she astounded me with her next words. "She will cast a spell for blessings on Halvor's surviving women to bring them healing, peace, and happiness. It's too much to hope that his widow will walk again after this long, I fear. She may need to content herself with her widowhood, but that's no small gift to give her. They will all be happier in the future."

For once, I truly didn't know what to say.

In the end, I settled for, "Thank you."

She gave me a regal nod, jumped to the floor and disappeared into it. I wished she'd stop doing that.

CHAPTER
SEVENTY-TWO

It went smoothly after that, well ... until I got to Troels.
Elise requested me to allow her hand-picked shield maidens into the Gateway to escort the three warlords who hadn't been a part of the drug trade safely home before I released any others. When I agreed, she directed her gaze straight down the lens of one of Finn's cameras and spoke in fast, firm Norse.

Rollo translated for me. She was telling them that no one thought these three should be harmed. They'd be escorted home securely under the protection of Freyja and her shield maidens. No one was to interfere.

He believed they'd get home safely, but then formally requested, "Would you be able to give them twenty minutes to get back here before you release the others, Recorder? Elise will need the shield maidens' assistance with Troels."

Oh yeah, Troels. I still had a damn arbitration to finish. I needed a coffee. Weirdly, I felt better.

The worst was over, and I could do my actual job now.

I caught Finn's eye and announced, "My TEK will use his drone to accompany them home so you can all watch. We'll be back in the Gateway with the livestream to deal with your former king in twenty minutes."

I got a coffee and grabbed a Coke for Finn, who was doing a brilliant job with his cameras, and watched the large screen. The shield maidens escorted Bloodraven, the nice older Warlord with the daughter, Gustavsson, the younger one whose wife suffered her own miscarriages, and the third one who hadn't said a single word the entire time he'd been here and whose name I still didn't know.

When the shield maidens returned, I summoned Troels from his cell on the Viking boundary.

His appalling behaviour had set off the entire path of my last month. But after HRH and her dramatic justice, honestly, this slimeball felt like such an anti-climax. It mattered to other people, but I'd reached the Land of Couldn't Give a Shit as far as he was concerned. For the first time, I truly understood why sometimes my gran and Mabon had called the Recorder's job "doing the duty."

But that reminded me that I did have a duty of care to the petitioners and to my bond mate, so when the former king arrived, I took no chances. I swaddled him in power to keep him in place and protected from anyone who might want to speed the process while I went rooting about in his head. Ad'Rian was so right when he told me, if the Recorder needed to know something, I shouldn't worry too much about their rights. Anyway, this asshole didn't have any rights left, in my mind. Dola had kept him safe because a cottage was a better person than I was.

But finding my way to any useful information past the same endless pictures of naked or mostly naked women that I'd already received from him at my ascension was no fun.

In fact it was harder this time. During my ascension, the pornographic contents of his mind had shocked me. This time, as I pushed through his memories, it horrified me to realise I knew some of these women. I'd watched their videos. If there was any doubt in my mind—and there wasn't—here was the proof those women had told the truth.

Bile rose up my throat again. I swallowed it back determinedly. *Just do it, Niki. The women deserve justice.*

In Troels' opinion, he'd had a lovely time; therefore, the women must have too. He was utterly oblivious to any concept of consent or any woman's right to say no. He was the king. They had been honoured by his attention.

Wow! I didn't even know how to process that. He was wildly deluded. But it helped my sense of certainty that the shield maidens and the Viking people could do whatever the hell they liked with him once I'd rolled his assets into a trust for the victims. The only good bit was Dola's warning not to feel guilty afterwards was already outdated. As long as he didn't bleed on the Gateway floor and upset the power, I didn't care what they did with him.

Then a thought struck me: were some of those assets rightfully Rollo's? Should I leave some for him, or just take it all?

I felt his presence then and realised he'd been in my head following along as I delved through the sewer the former king called a mind. I was already so accustomed to our link, I hadn't even noticed him join me on my foray through Troels' head.

"You OK with this? You don't have to be in here. It's my job."

"No, you were right. I need to take the opportunity while he's alive to get answers. I'll regret it later if I don't. I won't take a penny of his money, and his sons don't deserve any. They're all lucky not to be here with him. Randi is from a good family and wealthy in her own right. Give all his assets to the women and their children, please."

He strolled over and came up beside me, and, with his hand placed supportively on the small of my back, we stood together in front of Troels.

As Rollo arrived, the pornographic images from Troels faded, and others rose up from much longer ago. A man I recognised from the photo in Rollo's bedroom in Viking: Jonvar, his father. We realised it together.

Troels had hated his cousin. The jealousy, spite and envy corroded his mind and oozed out of him. Jonvar had everything

Troels wanted. It was all so easy for Jonvar. It must be easy, because Jonvar just seemed to make things happen.

Troels never did any of the work in the kingdom to win any loyalty. He thought it was his right. It shouldn't require he put in the hours, the work or help anyone. He just wanted the kudos. He thought he was every bit as good as Jonvar, probably better, if only people would realise it. But no one did, and no one listened to him or liked him because he didn't pander to the ordinary people.

His resentment of Rollo's father, his twisted perception that they were rivals for the throne, and his jealousy had destroyed him. When Jonvar turned out to be a good, popular, hard-working king, Troels hated him even more. He also hated Jonvar's beautiful foreign Fae wife, whom the Viking people should have rejected but they hadn't. They'd taken her to their hearts. Troels believed she must have used her magic on Jonvar's behalf. That was the only possible explanation for the couple's popularity.

Jonvar led his apparently charmed life and now had an heir of his own on the way. Troels had to act before the succession was secured. The carriage accident hadn't killed Rollo's father, and it had been no accident. He knew Jonvar and Le'Anna were bonded, and Troels hoped the shock of his rival dying might cause Le'Anna to lose the baby.

That truly settled absolutely everything for me. But Rollo said something in Norse, and I saw his mother in Troels' mind. The emotion that came from Troels clearly was abject fear. He'd been terrified of the powerful Fae woman and her magic and constantly feared Le'Anna would discover his men were behind Jonvar's carriage accident and subsequent attack. To ensure their silence, he eliminated them himself, preventing her from uncovering any proof.

But Rollo's mother cared only about bringing her son safely into the world so she could send him home to her family, who would raise him with love. She'd needed to join Jonvar in the

Summerlands. But first she needed to give birth to her son in the Viking realm. She wouldn't take her son's choices away from him. If he turned out to have the same one-track Viking mind as his father, he may one day want to be able to say he was born in Viking. He might feel the same sense of duty to the Viking throne and people as Jonvar had. She hoped he didn't. She'd told Troels that, but he hadn't believed her.

Rollo's roiling emotions made me so angry on his behalf. He felt as shaky as I did. This had been a horrid day.

Rollo took the lead in Troels' head with the yellow power, and we saw Le'Anna had been away from home for too long. Her grief after the loss of her bond mate and the birth of her child plunged her into a deep post-natal depression. She'd undergone a process the Fae called withering. She'd released a lot of her life force into her newborn son to give him all the protections he might need in life. Troels hadn't killed her. He hadn't helped her, but he wasn't responsible for her death, other than by killing her bond mate.

I wondered if Rollo's mother's dying gift was why his Fae talents were so much stronger than they logically should have been.

Rollo stepped back, his face impassive. No hint of turmoil showed in his stance or expression. He bowed formally to me. "Thank you, Recorder. Yggdrasil is done here."

I turned my attention back to Troels. "Gunnar Troels, the Recorder has found against you in the petitions submitted by 214 women. They alleged the administration of drugs, sexual assaults and the siring of children. All without their consent."

I gave him time to process it. But, truthfully, he still looked as though he didn't believe a word I said.

"Your only comment on these cases was 'All women lie.' However, their evidence and their proof of your genetic status as the father of the children prove that, in fact, you are the one who lied. Do you wish to add any evidence of your own?"

I waited for some rubbish about "They all wanted me," or a

repetition of his statement at my ascension, "All young women are gullible." Surprisingly, he didn't say a word. He felt tired, and his expression as he considered Rollo's tattoo was interesting.

After about a minute's silence, I pressed on, "Forty years of your abuse will come to an end now. Your assets, which the Recorder's Office will confiscate in their entirety, will be used to create a trust to help those women and children. Your disposition, the Recorder must hand to the Viking people."

I was just about to give him over to Rollo to honour his claim when the red gate opened, and Mabon, Glynis and Dru rushed down the Red Sector. Well, Dru and Glynis rushed. Mabon strolled after them as though he were out for a lovely morning walk to admire the spring bulbs.

Dru landed at my feet, looked around the Gateway, then at me.

Baaaallls.

I frowned at him in confusion, and then Glynis spoke. "Recorder? Have you concluded the arbitration?"

She looked stressed. Her hair was standing on end as if she'd raked her hands through it too many times. I sent her a wave of calming energy. As an empath, this must have all been a nightmare for her, and she wouldn't rest until she was sure her job was done. Her energy felt very fiery and yang-ish. Glynis was always determined, but there was something extra about her today. Damn, I didn't want an angry dragon in my Gateway.

"I have. You missed it, sorry. But it will be on the portal later. You could have watched from home?"

"On behalf of all the women Troels abused, I make the primary—"

My upraised hand stopped her momentarily. She couldn't have Troels. Rollo had already claimed him, and I agreed with him. It felt vital for Viking's future that they decided themselves what to do with the king they'd allowed to run amok for forty years. Rollo was right when he reminded me that I was the Recorder, and I didn't and shouldn't try to run any of the realms.

Viking needed to heal itself, and sometimes justice was the beginning of healing.

Glynis finished her sentence anyway, "—claim. We want his balls."

I think Troels might have collapsed if I hadn't been holding him upright, swaddled in the power. The expression on his face was hard to describe. I hoped one of Finn's cameras had clear footage of it. I'd want to watch that back. Probably several times.

I gaped at her. Elise rattled her sword against her shield, then it seemed almost everyone who had a sword and shield did the same. Even the warriors who were here with the shield maidens. All the other Vikings, even Inge clapped.

Only the six warlords still waiting for release to their own judgement in Viking stood stock-still and looked horrified.

"I'm sorry, Glynis, but Drengr Rollo has already made the primary claim on behalf of the Viking people."

Mabon arrived at my side and bowed. "A quiet word please, Recorder."

As I turned to him, he tapped at the door to my mind, and when I said, "I consent," he gave me a stream of information. Astonishing information. I'd thought Dru's Darwin Awards were just a little joke that Mabon and I had. Every time I got a grip on my new role, there was always one more thing to surprise me.

I pulled out of the link and said to Glynis, "I accept your specific claim but not the primary one. And absolutely no blood. The Gateway has had too much blood today and, frankly, so have I. The Vikings need him alive for their own justice, so I accept your claim only on those terms. Don't be foresworn, Glynis."

She nodded seriously at me and bowed. "I give you my oath, my lady. No blood and alive." She looked at Dru, said something in Welsh, and stepped forward with the same kind of anticipatory pleasure on her face that I often felt when I opened a new book by a favourite author.

Dru moved. It was easy to think of him as a Scottish deerhound and forget that, as Mabon often reminded me, he was a magical, shape-shifting immortal.

Now his jaws and teeth shifted. His already long, narrow muzzle lengthened, grew slightly wider and glowed with white energy as he nosed up into Troels' crotch and then bit down and pulled back.

That was it. Magic without drama, no ripping of fabric, just one beautifully aimed snap and a long pull with his strong neck. I suppose, for a magical deerhound, a pair of testicles were a minor job compared to a full deer.

With a look of horror, Troels' hand snaked to his crotch, and his eyes widened in shock before he fainted. The power I'd swaddled him in held him upright.

Dru trotted over to Glynis, who held a plastic bag ready. It reminded me creepily of the bags I used to scoop Tilly's poop, and I watched in horrified fascination as Dru dropped two egg-shaped objects into her waiting bag-covered hand. I couldn't turn my eyes away, but, honestly, they looked like nothing more or less than two sticky plums.

What the hell would she do with them? Was this just her version of justice? But I didn't think so—she felt as if there was a greater purpose behind her bizarre request. There was, as promised, almost no blood, and when I checked Troels, he was already coming around, his mouth moving soundlessly and his eyes still wide in horror.

Glynis efficiently tied the top of the bag exactly as I did several times a day for Tilly on our walks. She bowed to me. "Our gratitude, my lady."

Finn had recorded it all, but he stood holding the camera with his knees pressed together, his legs almost crossed and an expression of horror as he watched his new girlfriend's mother march back towards the red gate, swinging her bag of loot.

Dru gazed at me.

"What, lad?"

He started to glow with red power. I glanced at Mabon, but

then the Gateway power reached out to Dru, and then to me, it sent a firm "yes."

Yes, what?

The power I'd swaddled Troels in receded of its own accord and left his right hand free. Dru still gazed at me. I had no idea what he needed until his thought reached me: *For Bjjjorn, Tillly and many mooore.*

The emotion from Dru was a clear sense of justice still unserved.

The power prodded me again, and I said, "OK, lad, if the power agrees, OK."

Then he trotted back to Troels. This time, it was his wrist he aimed those long, strong, magical jaws at.

He dropped Troels' right hand at Rollo's feet, lowered his head, and as Rollo asked me, *"What the hell?"* Mabon stepped forward and addressed Finn's livestream camera.

"Drudwyn's name means 'Knight.' He is sworn to uphold justice. This man," he pointed at Troels, "has killed or attempted to kill pets who have been taught to trust humans, too many times and always for his own ends. Dru wishes to ensure he will take this lesson into his next life."

Mabon strolled over to the hand, which was, as I'd demanded, free of blood. The end looked cauterised, and, truthfully, if I hadn't seen it removed, I would have assumed it was one of those joke, fake Halloween hands. There was nothing gory about it except for the fact that it lay on my Gateway's floor.

Mabon picked it up and gave it to Elise. "Ensure you bury it away from his body."

She nodded seriously and took the hand from him without a qualm.

OK, that was it. These people were officially crazy, and I was going to make changes in this damn Gateway. Except, Rollo felt terrific—as though something in him was finally beginning to heal.

CHAPTER
SEVENTY-THREE

I opened the yellow gate fully almost exactly at noon, as I'd said I would on my video yesterday. The Vikings all prepared to go home with the six remaining warlords. The warlords were initially reluctant to leave, but several dozen shield maidens and warriors with drawn swords and impatient expressions persuaded them to move with remarkable swiftness.

Elise and her hand-picked team escorted their former king back to Haraldssund. She'd requested I seal the gate again after they left and leave it closed for a few more days to give them the chance to create some order. She wanted the warriors and the shield maidens to have time to mop up the corrupt guards and a couple more of the warlords, whom she believed would already be heading towards Yggdrasil. But in case they weren't, she wanted to prevent any escapes that might spread Viking's problems into the other realms.

That sounded very sensible. Rollo went through the yellow gate with them. He would see me tomorrow morning because he planned to go to Haraldssund and from there to Edinburgh. He had some unfinished business of his own. When I felt him close his shields firmly, I guessed what some of it might be. He intended to search Troels' longhouse and see if there was anything belonging to his parents in it.

With the arbitration concluded, my job was finally done. The rest was the Vikings' business. However, the many messages being posted on the news portal, not just from the petitioners but from many everyday Vikings with their #ThankYouRecorder, made me think Dola's "rebrand for all parties" might be in progress.

"If you won't, I will."

"I was so rude. She won't permit it, and I won't leave you."

"Ah, she gets it. Come on now, love. Let's ask her, hey? Maybe you can get a night's sleep finally." The coaxing tone in Ben's voice made me smile as I turned to greet him.

He bowed. Wow, someone had been educating him. "Recorder, thank you for stopping me. You were right, you had it under control, and I did like it—a lot. I owe ya. Don't ever let me get on your bad side, will you? Need to ask one more thing, though?"

I nodded. "Yes. It's fine. You just need to swear on the anvil first."

He looked nonplussed. "But you don't know what I want, do you? Is this another of those Recorder things?"

I smiled at Kari. "Now, Ben, it's not rocket surgery, is it? You want Kari to see her mum and sister, right?"

Ben gave me one of his sparkling grins. "Yeah, right. Please."

Finally, Kari gave me a tentative smile and a bow. "Please, Recorder, can Ben come with me? He's never met my mother, and she'll be so relieved. But she'll need some support. Can we stay a few days?"

Ben was happy to swear on the anvil even after I warned him that being iron-tolerant didn't make it nice. Afterwards, he decided that not everything about the Recorder was as good as he'd first thought. He swore creatively at the anvil and did the iron shock dance. He was incredibly light on his feet.

Kari gave me a genuine smile as they walked through the yellow gate arm in arm, with Ben still muttering, "It's only a lump of iron. How does it *do* that?"

I breathed a sigh of relief and thought about the simple joy of sitting down and drinking coffee.

But when I reached my desk, Mabon was there eating something, and as I walked over to him, his face lit up. "Nik-a-lula, a miracle worker you are. How did you talk her into it?"

I just stared at him. What was he talking about?

"Want a piece, do you? Won't mind, always shares generously, my mother does. She's all about the 'there will always be enough' thing."

He held a piece of cake? Nope, it wasn't cake exactly. I bent over to scrutinise it. "What is it?"

He gave me a confused frown. "Simnel cake. The proper kind. Got Mags to make it, you did. For Mothering Sunday. Knew you would. It's even better than usual. Blacker, I think."

"Blacker" wasn't an adjective I generally associated with making cake better. I took it out of his unresisting hand, a thin rectangular slice of, yes, black fruitcake, its edges surrounded in golden ... pastry? It smelt incredible. This was a cake that could change a thousand attitudes. Maybe we should have served it at book club?

Spices drifted up as I took a large bite. Yep, it was pastry, and the filling was divine. Sweetness filled my mouth. Rich, fruity and well-spiced with cloves, ginger, allspice, cinnamon, and something I couldn't initially identify. Oh, maybe it was whisky?

I stole Mabon's coffee to wash it down so I could speak. "That is not yours, or your mother's. That is a gift to me from Mrs Glendinning. And it sure as hell isn't Simnel cake. I've had that before. It was dry and overly sweet. This is phenomenal."

His face crumpled. He looked as if he was about to sob. Instead, he took another bite of his cake.

Eventually, through his still cake-filled mouth, he mumbled, "Proper name is Black Bun. Very old recipe. Only Mags has it. Can't be yours. For my mother, it is." He sounded about five years old and sulky with it.

I asked Dola for a coffee of my own and cut myself a small slice with Mabon's knife, which looked big enough to be described as a short sword. The cake was a long brick, well, several long bricks, the whole of them pastry-wrapped with a beautiful pattern of Easter eggs and thistles on the lid. In the centre was a Recorder's seven-pointed star.

I pointed at the star and gave Mabon my best librarian glare. "No, it isn't. I told you, Mags said your mother has never thanked her or any of her ancestors for the cakes, and she refused to make it for her. She called the Goddess Modron an ungrateful exploiter of honest Hobs. You opened a box on my desk, sent to me by Mrs Glendinning, didn't you? I bet it even said 'Niki' on it."

He gave me a shame-faced half-smile. "No. Said Recorder, it did. But smell it, I could. Knew what it was. Certain it was from Mags, I was. The spices were just right."

"Well, it's not, and it's not yours. Your mother needs to mend her fences with the Hobs. Why doesn't she just thank them? I know they can be difficult, but Mags sounded quite hurt that, for several hundred years, her ancestors have been making this cake for your mother, and she's never once said thank you."

I took a swig of my coffee and another bite of the fabulous cake. Black Bun, who the hell knew? Around my cake, I mumbled, "She said you have pretty manners and always gave her some whisky for the Equinox cakes." I drank more coffee and glared at Mabon again. "Your mother has never bestirred herself to manage so much as a damn thank you note." I swallowed. "Mags says she won't make them for her anymore. She's finished with ungrateful goddesses."

"But whisky I gave her for all the cakes."

"Does she know that? Did you tell her? Did your mother ever say, 'Thank you Mags, you're the best baker in all of Caledonia? I look forward to your special cake throughout the year.'"

An unhappy Mabon shook his head. "Goddesses, well, *bach*, they take things for granted."

"Well, they shouldn't. It's rude."

I cut Mabon another slice, rewrapped my cake and put it back in its box. I liked Mags. She'd been a big help with the translation, the Vikings and my new clothes. If she wanted to make a point, I wasn't getting in her way.

Mabon looked astonished at the idea that I wouldn't just give in. I softened a little. "If you want my advice?"

He nodded fervently.

"I think Mags may have already made a spare cake for your mum. She told me she had the ones for your equinox celebration ready. Get your mother to go around and be gracious, apologise, and ask nicely. I'd recommend grovelling. If she does, I think she'll get her cake."

"But, but …"

I kissed his cheek. "There's no excuse for rudeness, Boney. She'll have to fix it herself. You must have got your lovely manners from somewhere. Remind your mother of her own."

I picked up my cake and transported to the cottage before he could talk me around. As I left, I heard him call, "Need to talk about the coos, we do. Urgently, Recorder."

When I landed in the kitchen, the large screen was back in its usual position on the wall. Dola said, "Allow me to rewind this for you. I think you will want to see their decision. It is as I expected."

On the screen, footage of Troels being escorted to

Haraldssund played. Elise and her shield maidens kept the Vikings in line effortlessly. With no unnecessary brutality, they stowed their former king into a metal man-shaped cage.

I let out a low whistle. "They really did it?"

"They took a vote on it."

Once Troels was locked into the cage, it was positioned by a large group of well-muscled warriors with rope and a lot of brute force and some swearing. The hook at the apex secured it onto the fitting at the top of a pole just opposite the still badly damaged yellow gate, but outside the boundary. They were learning. Although, the weight of all those iron railings probably helped to remind them.

"I'm sorry, Dola, and after all the care you took to give him his rights and a nice cell."

But she was unbothered. "He was not my king, Niki. He was our prisoner. He had rights. The Viking people have decided he does not have them anymore. That is their right."

Troels' gibbet swung gently in the breeze, high in the air. I consoled myself that he'd probably freeze to death in no time. Then the camera zoomed in on a sign in Norse under the metal cage of the gibbet.

"What does the sign say?"

"It informs everyone there is a camera recording twenty-four hours a day, and that anyone who helps Troels on his way to Hel more quickly will take his place in the gibbet. Apparently, it was common in the past for some supporter to put the incarcerated man out of his misery with a well-thrown weapon. There is enough space between those bars."

"It's like something from the Middle Ages."

"Yes, even the internet agrees. It was a mandatory punishment for certain types of murderers for several hundred years and common all over England, at the rate of almost four gibbetings a month. But Elise and the members of her group on the news portal all agreed they only plan to leave him there for a week. Not for several years or even decades, as was common in the past. Inge has decreed that the new parliament will open the day after they cut him down and bury him."

My stomach roiled. I hated everything I knew about the man, but, wow, this wasn't an end I'd wish on my worst enemy. Just for a second, I pictured several people I might once have put in there. Nope, not even them. It was barbaric.

PART TWELVE
FRIDAY

Never mock an ally's Achilles' heel.

I have seen fearsome warriors brought to their knees by their daughter's tears and even a ferocious shield maiden may quake in the face of her mother's disapproval.

We all have one fear that transcends all the others. It cannot always be overcome in a single lifetime. But we should learn to live peacefully with it.

Winning the War Against Yourself: Daily Weapon and Warrior Care by Arinn Tusensköna

CHAPTER
SEVENTY-FOUR

F*riday, 12th March—Gateway Cottage—Holidaaay!*
I could hardly believe it was only two and a half weeks since I sat at this lovely table in my warm kitchen, in a blind panic. I really hadn't wanted to go to Dai's. I even had that whole internal narrator thing going on in a futile attempt to calm myself down.

Why did it feel as though that day wasn't just last month but in a whole other life? Had I changed so much, so swiftly?

Perhaps I had. Huh!

But not all of it was for the better.

I'd been right last week when I pictured leaving my caterpillar cocoon on the shower floor. I had changed. But when I decided I wouldn't settle for being an attractive butterfly, subject to the whims of the winds, I'd really stepped the hell up. There were a couple of hours yesterday when I felt positively kick-ass.

But I hadn't liked it.

Or how it made me feel.

So, I'd made a firm decision that in the future, I wasn't allowing any more violence into my life. I could learn to be a different kind of kick-ass—a kind that wouldn't upset me or the power.

I wouldn't leave my values at the side of the road to do this job. Rollo arriving bloody, beaten and brutalised sent me down a road I now realised was *not* mine. Or, more precisely, would not be mine again in the future.

The terrifying shock and awful fear I'd felt for the first time in my life when Rollo landed on the Gateway floor had thrown me off my path. But just as that Arinn guy said in his book, not all warriors fought with blades, and sometimes a good story or a compelling example could win the battle without bloodshed. That was the kind of woman I'd rather grow up to be.

The realms needed to stop being barbaric, and the Recorder should set the example. I wouldn't sink to their level again, whatever the damn cat thought was necessary. It wasn't me, and I knew that for sure now.

If violence was the answer, someone hadn't asked the right question. In this case, I felt like the guilty party, but I would change, and in the future, I'd make sure the realms started asking better questions too.

Boundaries and brains were a far superior solution. If I achieved nothing else during my tenure as the Recorder, I would teach them that. Dola had asked what I wanted to turn the Recorder's Office into for the next millennium, and now I knew: somewhere that offered smart options and thoughtful solutions, not glades, oubliettes, swords or damn gibbets.

It was the twenty-first century, and it was time everyone acted like it.

But I'd been hopelessly wrong about not rushing into anything with Rollo, hadn't I? Bond mates! With a seven-fold! Gods and Goddesses, that was going to take some adjustments.

Even my internal narrator's voiceover had changed:

And here's Niki McKnight, chilling out with coffee at the table in her cosy kitchen. Today, she's relaxed, dressed in her favourite jeans and a disreputable but comfortable sweatshirt. She obviously isn't going anywhere she has to dress up for and apparently doesn't need to impress anyone because those yellow boots look well worn and comfortable.

The squashy tote and the sparkly gift bag on the table suggest she's not going for long, or perhaps she doesn't need many clothes. Oh no, look, there's a brown dress carrier too.

She's finally going to take a real, well-deserved holiday with her new man, beginning in her hometown of Manchester. Can't we all see how much she's looking forward to introducing him properly to her best friend?

Unlike the last time, two weeks ago, this time my fictitious observer would be one hundred percent correct *if* he added in that I couldn't ever remember being happier or more relaxed about going anywhere in my entire life. I was not limp or tied in a knot today, and the only tagliatelle in my world would be served *al dente* in the carbonara Aysha planned to make for dinner.

"OK, Dola, I'm almost ready, and I'm sure everything will be fine. Everyone in the Gateway says they have plenty to do, and they'll get on with it as soon as I stop bothering them."

Then a thought struck me. "Damn, I never asked Rollo why Finn thought it was OK to discuss my sex life with Caitlin." I huffed this almost to myself.

But Dola said, "I can answer that. I was intrigued too and listened in on their conversation."

Why hadn't I thought to ask her? Because I was an idiot, obviously. "Awesome. What was Finn's excuse?"

"He and Caitlin had already seen your bond with Rollo. They did not think you knew. The TEK mentioned to the KAIT that Rollo appeared to have stayed with you. I do not believe he was, as you put it, gossiping with his sister, but rather, he was briefing his fellow Knight on their boss's well-being."

"Ooooh." I felt bad. That was a dragon of a different colour, as Mabon often said. I'd bring Finn something nice back from my holiday to apologise. "OK, Dola, thank you. That's really good to know. Did you find out how he and Tegan are doing?"

Oh, bless her, she sounded so confident when she replied, "I did. Thank you for your suggestion to just ask him, Niki. I was able to advise him on several issues. He has strong feelings for her, but there have been some teething troubles."

I giggled. This would be fun to watch. "OK, well, that's normal. Do keep me informed, and I'll see you next week. Reach out if you get lonely. And don't forget Aysha invited you to the dinner tonight too."

Dola's warm contralto held an edge of nerves. "I have never been invited to a dinner party before. My research suggested a small gift for the hostess is usual, so I have sent Aysha some flowers. I have already placed the arrangement on her hall table. Is there anything else I should know?"

"Aww, that sounds lovely. Well done. You've got it more than covered. Also, it reminds me, would you send these four Just Deserts straight to Aysha's fridge to save them from getting warm in the car? I want to know what they do."

The gift bag from Juniper disappeared from the table in front of me as Dola said, "There are two things I need to report before you leave, please."

My phone buzzed. I had an invitation to a meeting at the Broch with Breanna, Lesley, Dola, Finn and Caitlin over a month in the future. Why did that date look familiar?

"What's this meeting for?"

"I have the final four versions of the food service app for the Broch ready to go."

"Four? You do? Who did them?"

"Finn did the first one; Rollo submitted his version; I did my own version, and then I consulted Fiona and Rosie to make a fourth. They both have older relatives who are not as fond of tech as we all are. They shared useful insights."

"I'm good with it, but that date might be a mistake. I think it's Caitlin's twenty-fifth birthday. Perhaps another day."

Cautiously, Dola asked, "Were you aware it is traditional among the Picts to give the queen gifts on the day her heir turns twenty-five?"

"Crap! No, I wasn't. Thanks for the heads-up."

"They theme the gifts around both the monarch and her daughter attaining a new stage of life. So, for Breanna, the gifts are to make life easier for the queen as she ages but incorporating the idea that she is still vibrant and not yet ready to hand the throne to her heir. In the old days, new horses and sometimes more comfortable carriages were a common present."

The things I didn't know amazed me. It was a cool idea, though, and I could see how the app might be a perfect gift. Maybe we could make it a fun gift presentation? "Great. What's the second thing?"

"Mabon sends his apologies. He said, thought about it, he has. You were right, and deal with his mother, he will."

That actually sounded like Mabon. "Oh good. Is that all he said?"

"I removed three extraneous 'bluddys' from the message, but otherwise, yes."

I heard, *"Hey, Boo, I'm here."*

"OK, thanks, Dola. Am I done here?"

"You are. Rollo has arrived, shall I? ... No, I see you will greet him yourself."

I ripped open the front door to see Rollo coming down the path.

He gave me a sexy grin, with dimples. "You look ready and as gorgeous as always." He glanced up at the clear blue sky. "Great day for a drive."

Then he looked down. "No pupsicle?"

I looked past him to the long British racing green swoop of his Aston Martin DB11. I hadn't told Aysha about Rollo's hostess gift. He planned to leave it with her tomorrow so she could play with it while we went dancing, before we took it down to Wales. "No, I took her to Aysha's yesterday for safety and left her there for Autumn to spoil. I didn't know if her car seat and our guest would both fit in the back of that."

Because, tomorrow night, I'd booked us into an elegant country house hotel. I'd stayed there once for a friend's wedding.

It had been fab-u-lous. We were attending their monthly Dinner Dance. The theme was High Society, and I hoped my red cocktail dress from Mags would fit in perfectly. Any excuse to see Rollo in a tux worked for me. Even Tilly had a new sequinned collar, although I expected her to sleep through the dance in our room.

Then we were staying in a gorgeous cottage in north Wales with a view of the Snowdonia Mountains. Rollo had never been to the Wales in our world, and he wanted to compare it to the Red Celt realm. I loved the people and the scenery there, and the complete lack of dragons would give us, I hoped, a few days of blissful peace and privacy. Because, just as he'd wanted, absolutely no one would know who either of us were.

The cottage had a log fire, a bed big enough for my tall Viking, squashy leather sofas, a hot tub and a safe, enclosed garden for Tilly. We all needed this break. I was taking a Dolina, which would work because, unlike in the Red Celt mountains, I'd have reliable Wi-Fi!

My stomach was happy and settled. It didn't suggest any problems more challenging than choosing what to eat and when to get up for the next week.

Rollo closed the door behind us, wrapped me in his arms and kissed me. "Probably wise. The back seats are definitely the weakest point in the Aston."

I breathed him in. No citrus today, I noticed as my world settled onto its new happier axis.

"Well, that's good, isn't it? Are you ready? Shall I take your bag?"

"I'm ready, and Aysha said he was leaving a few minutes ago. He should be here any seco—"

A doorbell rang at the back door, and I heard Dola say, "Come in, Lewis. Niki will be with you in a moment. Would you like a coffee?"

Rollo said, "He will be really cramped. Are you sure you don't just want to transport him down there? I could meet you there?"

I shook my head and sent. *"Nope. He and Aysha might be getting serious. I want to interrogate him on the way down there. Trapped in a car for two hours—what could be better? I've only met Master Smith Lewis Gunn. Now I need to meet the man and make sure he's good enough for my best mate."*

Rollo laughed in my mind, which was always a lovely feeling, and we walked through to the kitchen to find a terrifically nervous-looking Lewis, juggling two enormous, badly wrapped parcels. Only his bright green jacket and silver-threaded dark copper hair showed me the man was underneath his burdens ... somewhere.

Rollo took one parcel from him so he could put the other one down safely.

I smiled. "Hi, Lewis, glad you made it. You should have shouted. We'd have helped you with the packages."

Lewis Gunn, Master Smith, prize idiot and doting uncle, as he'd described himself the first time I met him, bowed low. I'd forgotten how fast he spoke, though.

"Good morning, Recorder, not necessary. I brought two apprentices with me as far as the back door to help, but I didn't want to bring them in. It felt rude. It's lovely to see you, and I thank you for the permission to visit Manchester, and the lift down there, of course. I've only travelled in a car twice before. I'm excited, and Aysha said you have travel sickness tablets? She said I wasn't to be an idiot and do the manly thing because throwing up all the way down the M6 wasn't clever, and I should be sure to ask you for some." He finally stopped to draw breath.

I held up my hand. "Breathe, Lewis, just breathe. Also, not the Recorder right now." I gestured at my jeans and sweatshirt. "I'm Niki today, Aysha's best mate, which might be scarier, but it's lovely to have the chance to meet you outside of Gateway business."

The twinkle in his blue eyes, the crinkling laughter lines and his cute grin, along with his wry expression of fear made me smile.

"You might be right, Niki. I'm not sure I thought these grand gestures through properly. Will they fit in the car?"

Rollo stepped forward and shook Lewis' hand. "You'll barely fit in the car, but Dola might help with whatever these are."

"That one," Lewis gestured to the smaller one, although it wasn't smaller by much, "is for Autumn."

"Yeah, the horn poking out of the wrapping is a bit of a give-away." I tried not to laugh but failed. "Is it big enough, do you think, Lewis?"

"She wanted one that was bigger than she is, and a lady in Aberglas makes these beautiful stuffed toys. It's purple, pink *and* silver," a proud smile crossed his face, "her favourites. I thought it could be her birthday gift."

"But her birthday isn't until the end of next month. Would you like us to store it and send it down then? Aysha said Olive is picking her up from school today, and she's staying overnight with her. We're having an adults-only dinner party."

His face fell. I hadn't meant to spoil his surprise, but Autumn could be a little madam, and he needed to learn that.

But then he laughed uproariously. "She did it again. She conned me! I told her I wouldn't fall for it another time, and I almost did. That girl is a genius. She's as triple-faced as Lugh. May he protect me from charming girls with toothy smiles."

"Dola would be happy to store it safely for you and send it down when you're ready. And who *is* Lugh?" I'd meant to ask the Book when Ti'Anna kept invoking him, and in all the chaos since, I understandably, hadn't got around to it. But now that I heard him say it, I remembered it was Lewis who'd first mentioned him.

Lewis bowed. "That would be very kind, thank you, Rec—erm, Niki."

Rollo grabbed my luggage, Lewis's bag, and Tilly's collapsed car seat and muttered, "Stick these in the car while you sort that out." He gestured at the other large parcel.

"Lugh?" I prompted.

"Oh, it's just a phrase, my lady. He's one of the triple aspect gods. Truth, the law—which is why Aysha and I were discussing him and oaths in general—then sun and kingship, I think. People attribute all kinds of things to him. He's sort of the Celtic version of that Fae goddess. Although the Red Celts call him something else. What is it now? Oh, yes, Lleu Llaw Gyffes. But they say 'Lleu' the same way we do. He's some relative of King Mabon's, I think. Or perhaps not. No, I'm sure someone told me he was. Perhaps it was Angus's wife. Did you hear she had the baby? He was so happy when he popped in to pick up his birthing gift for Peggy. They had a baby boy. Not named him yet. Her mother has some idea that Angus wasn't keen on, so they're still deciding. Anyway, sorry, what did you ask?"

Finally, the rushing river that was Lewis's speech trickled to a stop. It was actually adorable. It would drive me straight around the bend, but I might be starting to understand what Aysha saw in him. I'd bet she found him restful.

"I asked about Lugh. You answered me. But you haven't told me about that yet?" I pointed at the other large, strangely shaped, equally badly wrapped mass in my kitchen.

"Oh, Aysha wanted a tree, you know, to hang her flower baskets on. The price they were asking on the internet, smelting extortion, it was. So I said we'd make her one."

My confusion must have got through to him because he pulled out his phone, swiped and handed me a conversation with Aysha.

"Whoops." He blushed, grabbed the phone back, scrolled back a little more until he came to a photo and handed it to me again.

The photo was a sculpture of a modern stainless-steel tree. It comprised six, no, seven pieces of curving metal. The trunk was constructed from the straight middles of all the curving pieces, bolted together. The "roots" formed the stand, and the equidistant "branches" curved outwards, mimicking a tree's canopy. In the photo, each of the branches held a hanging basket filled with flowering plants. It was striking, almost a work of art. Then I caught sight of the price tag on the screenshot she'd sent to Lewis and barely avoided gasping. It *was* a work of art, obviously.

"You see. Look what they wanted to charge! Disgraceful. I told her I could make it for less than a twentieth of that. So, she commissioned it."

He took his phone back, swiped again and presented me with a photo of the identical item in the smiths' workshop, except this one was a beautiful deep blue. Almost the exact colour of Aysha's front and back doors. Clever man.

I gave him a big smile. "It's exquisite, Lewis. She will love it. Would you like Dola to send it down there for you and put it on the patio by her back door?"

He gaped at me. "How did you know? Yes, please. That's exactly where she said she wanted it. I was concerned because it's slagging heavy, but," he blushed again, "she was very excited about it. Could you do that, Dola?"

"I would be happy to, Lewis. May I see the photo?"

Lewis shot me a panicked expression but then smiled as Dola said, "Just email me the photo if you would?"

I wondered how Lewis wasn't aware that Dola had cameras built into all the Dolinas. Interesting, but possibly not my business. Aysha knew. She'd tell him if she wanted him to know.

I was handing him a strip of travel sickness tablets when my phone buzzed in my pocket. I ignored it while I said, "Just let two of them melt in your mouth, and you'll be fine."

From the Dolina came, "Please answer your phone, Niki. It is an emergency."

I pulled it out to see a missed call message from Aysha, then walked through to my soundproofed den as I dialled. "Is she OK? Are you OK? What happened?"

Aysha sounded incredibly stressed. "What? Who? Oh, sorry, no, Autumn's just fine. I'm fine too, well, I'm fine right now. But I won't be tomorrow. I have an emergency, Nik. You have to stay for lunch tomorrow."

Oh, hell no. If they were both fine, it wasn't my problem. We had plans for tomorrow, beginning at 11:30 a.m. "No can do. We have a lunch reservation and a super expensive couples' massage booked and paid for. And we both need it after the last few weeks. What happened?"

"My mum invited herself for lunch. She's found out he's coming somehow and is demanding to meet him."

"Just tell her no. Tell her you have plans. You *do* have plans. Go out for lunch."

"I can't do that. You know what she's like."

"Why don't you want her to meet Lewis, anyway?"

"Nikkkiiii, you know what she's like. She'll terrify him. It's too new. I don't want her messing it up. It's so nice to find a man who isn't scared of me. I don't want … it all …ruined." Aysha trailed off, and I heard a muted sob.

I thought about the problem and also that Aysha didn't know she was getting to borrow her dream car for twenty-four hours. She wouldn't want to stay in for lunch tomorrow. She'd want to drive it to some country pub, probably too fast and a hundred miles away, with Lewis.

Olive Clarke would not fit in the back seat of the DB11. She was proud of her Caribbean curves. She barely fit on a double bus seat and had no problem claiming her space, like the majestic mountain of matriarchal magnificence she was. Rhiannon would probably love her.

"If you don't frighten him, why would your mum? Here's what you do. Call Olive, explain you already have plans for lunch tomorrow. Tell her I have to leave at 11 a.m. Invite her to breakfast. Ask if she wants to meet Lewis *and* Niki's new man. If she does, her only option is between 8:30 and 11 a.m. Take it or leave it, but none of us will be there after that."

There was total silence on the line.

Aysha sounded confused. "You've changed, Niki." There was a thoughtful pause before she added, "It might work. But won't Rollo mind? You know how full-on my mum is."

753

"I have changed, yes. Isn't it freaking great? And, no, of course, Rollo won't mind. The man grew up with shield maidens. He can deal with your lovely mum, and Lewis will do fine. If Olive terrifies him, he wasn't the right man for you anyway, and you know it."

"That's what frightens me."

"Well, it's better to find out sooner, Shay-girl. We'll see you in a couple of hours. Tell your mum I'm looking forward to her meeting Rollo. She should ask to see his new tattoo." I disconnected the phone before my laughter burst out. Her mother was perhaps the only person in the world my feisty friend feared. But Olive was a sweetheart. I might even give Lewis some tips on the way down.

This was going to be a warm and wonderful evening, a hilarious breakfast and a peaceful, fun week. My life was definitely improving.

Thank you so much for reading my books. But now it's finally time for Niki to actually enjoy her holiday.

There isn't a bonus epilogue, as such for Code Yellow, but I have one or two short stories which may come between this book and the next one planned for 2024. They'll probably be released through my newsletter as usual. If you've somehow missed all the previous bonus epilogues they're free and you can find them here:

https://linziday.com/newsletter/

Until then, I'm sure you will all be relieved to hear that I'm off to work on Market Forces. There is a pre-order already up for it.

Thank you from the bottom of my heart for reading and enjoying my books, and **please**, if you enjoyed Code Yellow, leave me a review wherever you prefer to do that. I wish they weren't important, but they are absolutely vital on every book in a series according to the Amazon ecosystem. I am ridiculously grateful for each and every one.

Coming next in Book 6, *Market Forces in Gretna Green,* Niki is determined to put into effect her new resolution that 'Smarts not Swords' is the modern way forward for the realms. Whether they like it or not.

Fi struggles to exert her authority as the new head of the trade desk when she meets with opposition and antequated thinking from the Galician Emperor.

Insights from Rosie and Mags Hob combine with Mabon's fury to spur Niki into overhauling the Gateway's part of the inter-realm commerce situation. But the problems she uncovers lead her to more innovative solutions than the realms had in mind.

There are changes outside the Gateway too, with upheaval for the village of Gretna Green and for Aysha and Autumn, and Rhiannon. It all comes to head when Dola 'gets itchy'.

Now, Niki needs to take a hard look at her personal priorities while considering the wider future for the realms.

There are ten books planned in the Midlife Recorder series and you can read about them on my website if you've somehow missed this information.

The End ... Until next time.

Author's Note

I hope you've all forgiven me for the end of Seeing Red in Gretna Green now? And now understand why Red and Yellow were so closely connected?

If I could have I would have published them both as one enormous book. But then there couldn't have been a paperback only an ebook. There almost wasn't a paperback for this one - we scraped in under the size limit by 2 pages!

Thanks for bearing with me for six months while we got Yellow published. Hopefully those four chapters through the newsletter helped.

Readers in the future who can go straight from the end of Red to the beginning of Yellow will never know how long that wait felt. But I do and I'm grateful and offer my most sincere thanks to all the readers who have been so brilliant and supportive to a new author who is still finding out which mistakes not to make. No more cliffhangers. Well except for those little clues about the next book in the epilogues, I can't promise never to do that again!

Printed in Great Britain
by Amazon